More praise for *Saints and Villains*

"*Saints and Villains* is a comman̴̶ng novel about a figure who uniquely represents the case for moral̴̶ a world where morality itself has been nearly erased. With a ̴̶nding of historical fiction—its parameters and rare obligation̴̶ has called up a parallel universe, drawing us into the mind̴̶ of Dietrich Bonhoeffer, whose story is surely one of the mo̴̶ emerge from World War Two. This capacious, unsettling n̴̶ attract a wide and grateful audience."

—Jay Parini

"A powerful and disturbing novel, searing in its impact, which combines fact and fiction in capturing the spirit of a good man caught in the conflicts of ethics, morality, theology, and loyalty to his country."
—*The Chattanooga Times*

"[A] panoramic story . . . This novelized version of the pastor's life by Giardina manages the extremely difficult task of giving a known story genuine tension and spiritual resonance."
—*Publishers Weekly* (starred review)

"[Giardina] illuminates the web of moral decisions within which we all exist. A compelling, frightening, yet beautiful novel, written with passion, understanding, and eloquence."

—*Booklist*

"An astonishing historical novel that evokes the danger and heroism of the Nazi resistance through a fictional re-creation of the life of Dietrich Bonhoeffer."

—*Fodder* (St. Paul, MN)

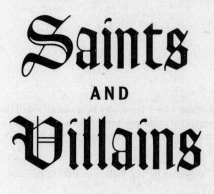

Saints
AND
Villains

A NOVEL

DENISE GIARDINA

Fawcett Books
The Ballantine Publishing Group • New York

A Fawcett Book
Published by The Ballantine Publishing Group

Copyright © 1998 by Denise Giardina
Reader's Guide copyright © 1999 by The Ballantine Publishing Group, a division of Random House, Inc.

All rights reserved under International and Pan-American Copyright Conventions. Published in the United States by Ballantine Books, a division of Random House, Inc., New York, and distributed in Canada by Random House of Canada Limited, Toronto.

Fawcett and colophon are registered trademarks of Random House, Inc.

http://www.randomhouse.com/BB/

Library of Congress Catalog Card Number: 98-96914

ISBN 0-449-00427-9

This edition published by arrangement with W. W. Norton & Company, Inc.

Cover design by Jennifer Blanc
Cover photo courtesy of Corbis

Manufactured in the United States of America

First Fawcett Books Edition: February 1999

10 9 8 7 6 5

For Arla,
Colleen, David,
Sky, and Tim

A portion of the "Gratias" section appeared previously in *The Carolina Quarterly* as "Dietrich Bonhoeffer in West Virginia, 1931."

Bonhoeffer's Reformation Day sermon is based on a text in *The Life and Death of Dietrich Bonhoeffer* by Mary Bosanquet (New York: Harper & Row, 1968). She in turn is quoting from Dietrich Bonhoeffer, *Gesammelte Schriften*, translated by Eberhard Bethge, 1st ed., 4 vols., vol. 4, pp. 93f.

The lines from Georg Kaiser's "From Morn to Midnight" (1912) were translated from the German by Ashley Dukes and appear in *Masters of Modern Drama*, edited by Haskell M. Block and Robert G. Shedd (New York: Random House, 1962).

Bonhoeffer's "Peace Sermon" is a translation by John Bowden found in *Dietrich Bonhoeffer: A Life in Pictures* (Philadelphia: Fortress Press, 1986).

Quotations from *The Cost of Discipleship (Nachfolge)* are from the translation of R. H. Fuller (New York: Macmillan, 1949).

Some of the quotations from Bonhoeffer's *Ethics (Ethik)* are from the translation of Neville Horton Smith (New York: Macmillan, 1949).

Leaflets of the White Rose resistance were translated from the German by Arthur R. Schultz in *The White Rose: Munich 1942–1943* by Inge Scholl (Middletown, Conn.: Wesleyan University Press, 1970, 1983).

"I'll Be Seeing You," Music by Sammy Fain, lyrics by Irving Kahal, 1938.

The Four Horsemen, woodcut by Albrecht Dürer, from *Albrecht Dürer: Master Printmaker* (Boston: Museum of Fine Arts, 1971). Distributed by New York Graphic Society, Conn.

Today there are once more saints and villains. Instead of the uniform grayness of the rainy day, we have the black storm cloud and brilliant lightning flash. Outlines stand out with exaggerated sharpness. Shakespeare's characters walk among us. The villain and the saint emerge from primeval depths and by their appearance they tear open the infernal or the divine abyss from which they come and enable us to see for a moment into mysteries of which we had never dreamed.

—DIETRICH BONHOEFFER, *Ethics*

W. A. Mozart: Große Meße c-moll KV 427

PROGRAM NOTES

Mozart intended his Mass in C Minor as a thanksgiving offering after his father, Leopold, grudgingly acknowledged the composer's marriage to Constanze Weber. The Mass was unfinished when Wolfgang and Constanze traveled from Vienna to Salzburg for a long-postponed meeting with Papa. This visit ended with a performance of the partial work at the Collegiate Church of St. Peter. Constanze was the principal soloist, and many in attendance were scandalized by her arias, which had been composed in a style considered more suitable to the flamboyance and eroticism of an opera than to a sacred work. Wolfgang and Constanze left for Vienna the next day. The Mass remained incomplete, and would never again be performed in Mozart's lifetime.

Mozart's original manuscript came into the possession of music publisher Johann Anton André, who issued it in 1840, noting the Credo was incomplete and the Agnus Dei absent entirely. The original manuscript then went to the Prussian State Library in Berlin, where it was noticed, years later, that the Sanctus and Benedictus were missing.

Using the original manuscript and André's notes, the Mass in C Minor was edited and reconstructed in 1882 by Philipp Spitta, and again in 1901 by Alois Schmitt, when it was performed for only the second time, in Dresden. A subsequent reconstruction was completed in 1918.

The original manuscript, still minus its closing Sanctus and Benedictus, disappeared from the Prussian State Library during the Second World War.

Kyrie eleison
Christe eleison
Kyrie eleison

Lord have mercy
Christ have mercy
Lord have mercy

Sabine

WHEN HE WAS SMALL, he was often mistaken for a girl. It was still the fashion in many well-to-do families to dress little boys in gowns of lace and taffeta, and Paula Bonhoeffer considered a skirt a convenience to Fräulein Horn, who must change the diapers. Dietrich's featherylight blond hair, worn long and curling in corkscrews at the ends to frame his round face, added to the effect. And since three of the four youngest children were girls, strangers who admired Christel, Sabine, and Baby Suse in her pram included the fourth Bonhoeffer "daughter" in their praise as well.

"Astonishing," people would say when the children went with Fräulein Horn for a stroll in the Tiergarten, "that two little girls with such different coloring should be twins"—this because Sabine had dark brown hair and black eyes, while Dietrich was fair.

Fräulein Horn would nod as she pushed the pram and say, "After all, they aren't identical twins. This one in fact"—pointing to the blond head—"is a little boy."

"You don't say."

At three he wore lederhosen and his hair was trimmed to the bottom of his ears, so he was no longer sometimes a she. But with his large eyes and pale skin he was still a beautiful child. Now people said, "With that hair, this one should have been a girl."

To make up for it, he tried to act as he thought boys should act. He took charge of Sabine and Baby Suse, not in a bullying way, but in the role of teacher and defender, directing their play and watching out for dangers beneath the bed and beyond the garden wall. He did not know that Sabine felt the same. When the twins sat for their portrait at age seven, it was Sabine's hand that rested protectively on Dietrich's shoulder.

They lived then in the Brückenallee, near the zoo. Sometimes at night the children could hear the animals in their cages, the trumpeting elephants, the grumbling lions, the sharp cries of monkeys and plumed birds. During the Great War, the cries grew more desperate, then weaker. Sometimes they were screams of agony. The oldest brother, Karl-Friedrich, said poor people from Wedding and Prenzlauer Berg would slip inside at night and slaughter the animals, strip the carcasses to the bone, and carry away the exotic meat in bloody sacks. At night, high in their third-floor room, Dietrich spoke with God about the animals, while Sabine remained anchored in the world, watchful. He thought he heard God answer, but still the animals died.

Karl Bonhoeffer was Germany's leading psychiatrist and a great opponent of Sigmund Freud and psychoanalysis. His wife, Paula, was the daughter of Prussian aristocracy. So it was fitting they should possess a large household. There was Fräulein Horn, the governess. A butler, Schmidt, and two housemaids, Elli and Maria. The cook, Anna. The chauffeur, Keppel. But during the Great War, even the Bonhoeffers' bread was more sawdust than flour.

The house in the Brückenallee was near the Bellevue station, and convoys of lorries passed by each day on their way to meet trains bearing the remains of soldiers killed in France. Before long the lorries carried familiar dead, first the relatives of schoolmates, then a Bonhoeffer cousin from Schwäbisch-Hall, then von Hase and von Kalckreuth cousins. Paula Bonhoeffer lost several Prussian nephews. She could not bear the rows of coffins at the Bellevue station, was frantic to keep her children from seeing them, as though they might be cursed by the sight. So her husband moved the family to Wangenheimstraße 14 in the Grunewald quarter. It was a large house with a garden, so the family could grow its own produce, and every evening when lessons were done, the children of parents who had never known menial labor put on their gardening smocks and took up their hoes.

Then the two oldest boys, Karl-Friedrich and Walter, were conscripted. Dr. Karl Bonhoeffer could have called upon his extensive connections and obtained safe commissions for them; he was pleased though apprehensive when they rejected such special treatment and requested frontline duties. Dietrich, who was eleven, noted his father's pride and wished he were old enough to join his brothers. He secretly followed the progress of the Kaiser's troops on a map in his desk drawer, blue-flagged pins for the hated Allies, red pins for the Fatherland.

The secrecy was necessary because of his mother. In 1914, Christel had come skipping down the Brückenallee sidewalk calling, "Hurrah, there's to be a war!" Paula Bonhoeffer had slapped her daughter's face. When Karl-Friedrich and Walter left for the front, the family and servants walked in a small parade, carrying hampers of food, to the Halensee station to see them off. The parents kissed each of the young men in farewell. More than anything this marked the solemnity of the occasion, for in the Bonhoeffer family kisses were bestowed only on birthdays and at Christmas. Dietrich thought the day a glorious one until the train pulled out of the station and his distraught mother ran the length of the platform calling out the names of her sons.

That night Dietrich paid for his war lust, like a glutton who suffers stomach pains after an evening of indulgence. He and Sabine shared a room overlooking the garden. The plain oak beds stood side by side with a table between. A cross hung on the far wall—their mother's doing. It was also Paula who led mealtime and evening prayers, while her husband sat by with a bemused but tolerant expression. Karl Bonhoeffer was an agnostic but believed religious observance to be useful and character-building for women and children. The older boys soon followed his lead and openly expressed their doubts about their mother's faith, but the twins enjoyed the prayers and the hymns their mother sang as she tucked them into bed at night. They liked to lie on their backs and stare at the cross, iridescent in the moonlight, its surface shimmering as though it were underwater.

On the night his brothers went away to war, Dietrich said, "Mama told us good people go to heaven when they die. But what if they don't like heaven? Or what if they don't go anywhere?"

Sabine turned away from the cross and shut her eyes. "Don't think about it."

"It's for eternity," he said. "Think what that means, Sabine. You can say the word over and over and over and over and still not be at the end of anything."

He flopped onto his stomach, wrestled the bedclothes a moment, then turned over onto his back again.

"Say it," he said. "Say 'eternity.'"

"Eternity," Sabine replied.

He began a chant. *"Eternity eternity eternity eternity eternity . . ."*

"Stop!" Sabine commanded.

He fell silent. She heard him breathing loudly. Then he whispered in a terror-stricken voice, "Sabine! I'm afraid I'm going to die!"

She sat up. "What?"

"I'm afraid I'm going to die, right this minute. I have to think about every breath. Talk to me, Sabine."

"Shall I read to you?"

He lay back on his pillow, breathing heavily. "Yes, please."

She turned on the light between their beds and found a copy of fairy stories left on the table by Fräulein Horn. She began to read the story of the Wild Swans. By the time the princess sat spinning shirts from nettles, he was asleep.

They fell into a ritual then. Sabine must read to Dietrich, or tell him good night until he fell asleep. As long as he heard her voice, he couldn't die. Night after night she fought to stay awake so she could keep her brother alive.

"Good night."

"Good night."

"Goodnight."

"Goodnight."

Goodnight.

Goodnight.

Goodnight.

Goodnight.

Goo-night.

Goo—

Most nights, he was still awake when she nodded off.

Then Walter was wounded. In his last letter home, he wrote,

Dear Family, I've had my second operation. It was disagreeable, because the fragments of shrapnel were quite deep. I have been given two camphor injections. Perhaps that will suffice. I refuse to contemplate the pain. Instead, I think of you, my family, with every ounce of strength that remains.

Karl Bonhoeffer read the letter aloud to the family gathered in the parlor, Paula seated with her hands in her lap and the children gathered around her. Then he removed his eyeglasses and looked at each of them in turn. "You see," he said, "how Walter writes? He does not seek to deny the pain of his circumstances, yet he is modest. He does not complain. This is how a Bonhoeffer conducts himself. Your brother is a great credit to our family and to Germany."

When word came of Walter's death soon after, Karl Bonhoeffer called the family together once more to read the official telegram. The children began to sob, and Paula, who was receiving the news at the same time as the others, gave a small cry and stood with a stricken look on her face. Her husband raised his hand and said, "For the sake of the children, my dear, we must show strength and forbearance." His wife looked at him and walked out of the house. The next-door neighbors, the von Harnacks, found her sitting in their drawing room, rocking back and forth, mute. They put her to bed for several weeks, and when she finally returned to her own house, she still could not speak. This continued for several months, until one morning she said, as though nothing had happened, "I think I should like a cup of tea." Her husband took off his glasses and laid them on the breakfast table, kissed her on the forehead, and poured the tea. When the children came downstairs with Fräulein Horn, he said, with a severe glance that warned off an emotional response, "Your mother is feeling better and has asked for tea." Dietrich, who had prayed daily to hear her voice once more, watched her closely while she drank, his hands beneath the table to conceal their trembling.

After Walter's death, Dietrich was given his room and Baby Suse moved in with Sabine, because Karl Bonhoeffer made all family decisions during his wife's illness, and he judged it to be time. The twins had never before stayed apart. Because their mother was not there to tuck them in and help them with their prayers, Dietrich decided he would himself lead their devotions. He would knock on the wall above his bed, and Sabine would knock back. Two knocks meant *I'll be asleep soon*. Three knocks meant *Think of God*.

On warm nights they could open their windows, lean out, and talk to each other, their heads dark ovals against the faint light of the moon. When they were done, they reached out, arms white in the moonlight. They couldn't touch.

He thought he was being punished for Walter's death.

For most of his childhood, it was assumed that music would be Dietrich's vocation. This was what his father foresaw, and so it was accepted. Karl-Friedrich would be the scientist, Walter would have been the lawyer, the girls were talented but would marry and raise families. As for Dietrich, he might have chosen law as well, or medicine, but he seemed to have an aptitude for neither. As he grew older his teachers praised his ability in philosophy, but this made little impression on his practical father. He was an excellent tennis player, and excelled in track, but these were not important at home. Dietrich was dreamy, and a loner. Though he was well liked at school, he had no close friends. The artist's temperament, Karl told his wife. It was the same with Mozart, who also showed great promise at a young age. For at ten Dietrich had mastered Mozart's piano sonatas, and soon after began composing his own work. At the family's frequent musical evenings—for everyone played an instrument—Karl Bonhoeffer often spoke of the Berlin Conservatory and a career as a concert pianist for his youngest son.

When Dietrich was fourteen, he was taken to the conservatory to play for the famed pianist Leonid Kreuzer. He played a Schubert *Lied*, his back ramrod-straight, while his parents sat, formally dressed, in the back of an empty auditorium. When he was done, Kreuzer, in the front row, nodded his head. A woman who had been seated beside him rose, went to the stage, and stood with her hands clasped at her waist.

"Now the Mozart," Kreuzer said.

Dietrich had chosen an arrangement of the Kyrie from the Mass in C

Minor to demonstrate his skill as an accompanist. He played and the
woman answered in a throaty soprano. Paula dabbed at her eyes with a
handkerchief.

Later Kreuzer met them in a small room down the hall, where they were
served Linzer torte on a silver tray and coffee in white china cups. Dietrich
was too nervous to eat. They sat in a circle. Kreuzer leaned forward, raked
back long gray curls with his hand.

"There is talent. *Ja*. Competency. But interpretation—" he made a slicing motion with his hand—"missing. The Kyrie is about *passion*, the
intense passion of a tormented soul lusting for God. I heard no lust in this
performance. Reverence, *ja*, but no apprehension of what Mozart was trying to do in this piece." He looked at Karl Bonhoeffer instead of Dietrich.
"Competency, as I say. This boy is quite likely to be admitted to the conservatory. He might teach. Or play with a provincial orchestra." He
shrugged. "Stuttgart or Leipzig, that sort of thing. But a major soloist? No,
never. What is missing, training cannot provide. I can't see him with the
baton, either. His is not the gift of interpretation."

On the ride home they were silent. Nothing would be said, one way or
the other, in front of the chauffeur. Dietrich could not look at his parents,
so he stared out the window at the monotonous blocks of Wilmersdorf flats.
At home, Father called the family to his study.

"Dietrich played well. Mother and I were very proud. But it is Kreuzer's
opinion he would never be in the first rank of pianists."

Dietrich's fingernails scrabbled an arpeggio on the rough fabric of his
chair. He could sense that Sabine was trying to catch his eye but he avoided
looking at her. His father spoke quite gently. "Would you still wish to study
music, Dietrich?"

"No, Father."

He didn't cry. It would be unthinkable in front of the family, and when
he was finally able to escape to the garden, the moment had passed, leaving behind a dull ache in his midsection. He huddled on a bench behind a
stand of japonica. Sabine found him at last, and they sat side by side without touching. That evening they played music as usual, and everyone made
a great pet of Dietrich. When Sabine and Baby Suse turned out their light
and climbed into bed, he knocked three times on the wall.

Several months later, Dietrich announced at the dinner table that he
would study theology when he went to university. Everyone stopped eating
and stared, while he kept calmly cutting his schnitzel. "I've been thinking
it over ever since I decided not to study music. Herr Heininger at the
Gymnasium is a pastor's son, and he says I've a gift for it. And what could
be a larger subject, after all, than God?"

Karl-Friedrich, who had returned from the war and declared himself a Socialist (much to his parents' consternation), was the first to recover. "You don't even go to church," he said.

"No," Dietrich agreed. "It isn't necessary. Theology is an intellectual discipline, like philosophy, only more specific and therefore more rigorous."

Karl-Friedrich laughed. "Of all the nonsense! Theology? I can't imagine anything more fuzzy-minded, or irrelevant!"

"Karl-Friedrich!" Mother said sharply.

"Sorry, Mother. But you don't go to church either."

"Still I pray every night," she said. "And I read scripture. Certainly you've been taught it is rude to mock religion. Has he not, Father?"

"He has," Dr. Bonhoeffer agreed. "I myself participate in Mother's devotions out of respect for her, though I admit to knowing little of such matters myself."

"Or caring little," Karl-Friedrich whispered beneath his breath so that only Sabine heard.

"If theology seems irrelevant," Dietrich said to a parsley potato stuck on the end of his fork, "then it is because it has been improperly presented. I shall change that."

Then everyone laughed, except Sabine. And Karl Bonhoeffer. After considering his son for a time he said, "I'd hate to see you waste your years at university. There was a time when theology and philosophy and science were one. But that hasn't been true for centuries. The best minds of our time concern themselves with the latter two disciplines, because there lie the most possibilities for the improvement of humanity."

"There's von Harnack," Dietrich said.

Adolf von Harnack was the leading Protestant theologian in Germany, and the next-door neighbor of the Bonhoeffers, an elderly man pitied by the other intellectuals in the Grunewald because his field was archaic and his nephews were rumored to be Bolsheviks.

"That's it," Karl-Friedrich said. "Old von Harnack's got hold of you."

"I haven't spoken to him," Dietrich said. "I didn't tell anyone until today, when Herr Heininger asked us in class to declare a field of study." He looked around the table. "I said 'theology.' It just came out suddenly, but I realized I'd been considering it quite a while."

Sabine nudged his leg beneath the table and smiled at him. He smiled back.

"What did your classmates say?" Christel asked.

"They looked at me as if I'd said I was going to take up big game hunting."

"At least with big game hunting you'd have a chance at some solid results," said Karl-Friedrich. "A theologian is about as useful as a maker of paper airplanes."

"Dietrich," said his father, "you suffered a very great disappointment when a musical career no longer seemed likely, and I'm sure you're not yet over the hurt. Still you will need to make a decision soon, and I urge you not to be rash."

"But why shouldn't Dietrich study theology?" Paula Bonhoeffer asked. "After all, my side of the family includes a number of distinguished clergymen."

"Great men in their day," agreed Karl Bonhoeffer, "but it was a different time, a less sophisticated time."

"When we were small," Sabine said, "Dietrich used to speak of God to me nearly every night when we went to bed. And we used to talk about eternity before we fell asleep."

"Eternity!" said Karl-Friedrich. "Now there's a sleep-inducing subject for you."

"Karl-Friedrich, that is quite enough!" his mother admonished.

But Dietrich was looking at his father as though no one else had spoken.

"It's what I want," he said. "And I don't care about the disappointment of not studying music. That sort of life would have been too easy. Not this. This will be the hardest thing in the world."

He asked to be excused and went to his room.

Dietrich and Sabine celebrated the passage of their school-leaving examinations with a hiking trip through the Thüringer Wald. They began at Meiningen on a spring day so warm their blouses were damp beneath their backpacks, and for sheer joy they clopped through mud puddles in their heavy boots. But though they spent their vacations at the Bonhoeffer summer home in the Harz, they were children of the city, unused to the vagaries of nature. On the Inselberg they climbed into a blowing snowstorm and lost their way. Their light jackets were not much use against the cold, and they stopped often so Dietrich could kneel in the drifts and knock crusts of ice from the skirt of Sabine's dress. Then they floundered on, arms around each other's waist, free hands clutching walking sticks that propelled them along, a single creature, like some huge ungainly snowbird.

With no clear path, and night coming on, they thought it best to simply go down. This way took them through stands of dark green fir that forced them time and again to alter their course. Night fell. They sang, Dietrich booming out *Horch, was kommt von draußen Rein?* in his fine voice, Sabine *Heula hie, heula ho!* Their feet were numb and each step jarred them to the teeth, and they were happy, and pressed on, Hansel and Gretel in search of a hearth.

At last they slid down an icy funnel and landed in a heap at the edge of an open meadow. Through the white curtain of snow a warm light glowed in a cottage window. They sat in a drift and knocked snow each from the other, pointing at the light and whispering.

At the door, Sabine stepped forward first and knocked, then Dietrich pulled her back to the shelter of his arm. They waited, faces turned to the single ice-glazed window. The door opened. A table, and the faces that hovered around it, seemed a great distance away. The large man who had opened the door leaned forward and blocked their view.

"*Ja?*" the man said.

"Pardon," said Dietrich, "we have lost our way in the snow. May we find shelter here? A bit of food, perhaps?"

He stepped away from the door and ushered them inside. The faces still watched them, then moved off, accompanied by a strange and comforting clatter of clogs on the stone floor. The man led them to a bench. Wooden bowls and spoons appeared, then ladles of potato soup. The soup was luke-warm, with thick, milky bits as though the bottom of a pot had been care-fully scraped to find enough for them. Wedges of goat cheese and heels of black loaves daubed with pork fat were laid beside their numb hands.

They ate slowly while the faces retreated to the hearth and began mur-muring. There were as many as in the Bonhoeffer family, but they seemed more worn and brown around the edges. At first Dietrich's eyes felt frozen but then seemed to melt and it was easier to look about. Every wall of the cottage was covered with implements, pruning hooks, blunderbusses, wash-boards, clocks, crucifixes, salt shakers, bric-a-brac shelves, jars of flour and beans and preserves, mattocks.

Sabine leaned against him and whispered, "It's like living inside a drawer." He nodded and smiled.

When they had done eating, the old woman of the family approached, pulling her shawl about her shoulders.

"Come, children," she said, "and sit by the fire. The young ones want stories."

She placed warm cups in their hands, and they sipped rich homemade beer.

"A story," the youngest girl said. "A story."

Sabine was struck dumb. But Dietrich pulled his knees to his chin and looked into the fire. "Shall I tell of the Wild Swans?" he said.

"*Ja, ja,*" the children chorused.

He began, "Once upon a time, a king hunted in a dark forest."

Of course they knew it, as well as he did. And still Dietrich held them. He told of the widowed king who lost his way in the Thüringer Wald and was tricked into marrying the daughter of a witch.

"Once the wedding was performed," Dietrich said, "the king's eyes were opened and he saw what he had done. He feared at once for his children, six boys and a girl, and sent them away to live in this very forest, at the foot of the Inselberg. But the wicked stepmother found them out. She wove six blouses of white silk, enchanted blouses with the power to transform. Seeking out the young princes, she threw the blouses over them, and each in turn was changed into a white swan, and flew away. Only the witch did not know of the girl child, who hid and then ran away deep into the forest.

"One night, as the girl huddled hungry and frightened beneath a giant spruce, the six swans found her. In their beaks they carried blankets and baskets of food, which they laid about her. For a moment they were changed back to their human forms. And they told—"

"Pardon!" A small girl tugged at Dietrich's arm. "How were they changed back? Why did the witch allow it?"

Dietrich thought a moment. "Perhaps the witch didn't allow it," he said. "Perhaps it was their care for their sister which broke the spell ever so briefly."

"Of course," said the old woman. "Go on with your tale, go on."

"The brothers asked their sister to weave them shirts of thistle and thorns," Dietrich continued. "Only in this way would the spell be broken for good. And she must not speak to a soul until the task was completed.

"The girl set about her work. Think how painful it would have been to weave thistles and thorns, day in and day out."

"Her fingers would bleed," a boy said.

"They would not stop bleeding," Dietrich agreed.

"Like the hands of our Lord," the old woman said from her corner.

Dietrich looked startled but went on with the story, told how a handsome prince married the girl, who remained mute, and how many began to accuse her of witchcraft because of her silence. At last her enemies prevailed and she was to be burned at the stake, but even as the pyre was built, the swans swooped from the clouded sky to the prisoner's balcony. One by one the girl threw the blouses over the swans, who became her brothers once more. At last she could speak in her defense, and so was saved. Only one blouse was not finished, so the youngest brother kept the wing of a swan for the rest of his days.

They heard Dietrich out in silence, the youngest with her thumb firmly in her mouth.

"Well told," the man said at last. The woman nodded, and set down her darning to refill their cups.

"Where from?" the man asked.

"Berlin," they answered.

"Ah. Ah. Are there any stories worth telling about Berlin?"

"Nein." The woman paused in her pouring. "They will not have good stories about Berlin. Too many Jews there."

Dietrich sat up. "Why do you say that? Do you know any Jews?"

She crossed herself. "God forbid!"

Sabine caught Dietrich's arm and forced him to look at her, shook her head. "Leave it," she whispered.

"But it's wrong," he whispered back.

"Of course it's wrong. But they have taken us in and shared their food with us. And they have precious little for themselves. They're worn out—look at them—and so are we just now. You won't convince them. It isn't worth a row."

He leaned back against the leg of a table and shut his eyes. The children watched him carefully.

"Tell another story," the boy asked.

"Whsst," the man said. "'Tis past time for bed. Mother, see to the guests."

The old woman gave them a package of bread and butter for the morning, and refused their offer of pay. Then a thin boy of around fourteen carried a lantern before them to the barn and up a ladder to the loft. With apologies, he explained, "We've no more room in the house. But I sleep up here always and it is quite warm in the hay."

He helped them spread their blankets, then retreated to a far corner and was soon snoring. They wrapped themselves tight and burrowed deep, Dietrich with his back to Sabine. She knew he didn't sleep.

"What?" she asked after a time. "Is it because I asked you to be silent?"

"I don't blame you," he said. "But one never makes up for something like that."

"It's how human beings get on sometimes," Sabine said. "Who has the strength to always be right?"

At dawn the family went out for their day's work in the field. Though the ground was frozen, it was April, and they must begin to break up the soil. Through a crack between the boards, Dietrich and Sabine watched them go, clogs punching holes in crusts of ice, like gunshots, as they made their way clutching shovels and mattocks, and disappeared around the glazed curve of the meadow.

Doppelgänger

THE BOY ALOIS BAUER IS BEATEN by his drunken father, an unemployed mason in a Bavarian village. Alois covers his head with his arms, to no avail. The blows split his lower lip and raise welts on his arms and back beneath his thin blouse. The family dog, a short-haired mutt, half-leaps at the man, more inclined to plead than attack. The man turns on the dog and kicks it until a line of green urine spreads where it drags its hindquarters across the red-tiled floor.

The boy prays over and over, Please God make him stop please God make him stop.

The dog flees to the boy's bed, where both huddle together and whimper, too sore to move. At last the dog turns, slowly and painfully, rests its warm weight against the boy's chest, and licks his face. "Good dog," the boy moans. "Good dog."

He does not know the dog's kidneys have been irreparably injured.

Coming of Age

THE BONHOEFFER CHILDREN seemed to marry all at once, as easily and naturally as they excelled in everything. The new husbands and wives came from the same Grunewald social set. Karl-Friedrich chose Grete von Dohnanyi, a childhood friend, while Christel wed Grete's brother, Hans von Dohnanyi.

The Dohnanyi father was a noted Hungarian composer and pianist who had deserted his wife and young children for another woman and returned to Budapest. Hans's mother, accustomed to a large house with servants in the Knausstraße, moved the children into a seedily genteel Charlottenburg apartment and offered piano lessons. Her bitterness and longing were turned upon her son, who loved her and could not please her. When he was not tutoring children in order to pay for his schooling, he sat silently while she played Schubert and sipped brandy and paused now and again to berate her absent husband. Hans had not a musical bone in his body, to his mother's chagrin. He studied law and took a post in the Foreign Office; she reproached him for choosing work that kept him at his desk late at night instead of in her company, not realizing he was glad to escape.

Despite the need to flee one such engulfing attachment or perhaps in order to justify it, Hans von Dohnanyi fell in love with all the Bonhoeffers, not just Christel but father mother brothers sisters aunts uncles cousins in great busy swarms, ranks of ancestors embalmed in countless dusty oils on the flower-papered walls. Small wonder too he doubted if he belonged in such abundant company.

Dietrich, sweet and cheerful and not quite like the rest of the family, made Hans feel less an outsider. Dietrich had gone off to Tübingen, where all male Bonhoeffers took their university degrees. He joined the Hedgehog fraternity (composed of beer-swilling, sword-wielding nincompoops), which all male Bonhoeffers except his brothers had joined. Karl-Friedrich called fraternities absurd, but Dietrich wanted to please his father. He was miser-

able without the family, and returned to Berlin for good at the end of the
first year.

Karl-Friedrich, who had already been noticed for his research on split-
ting atoms, rolled his eyes and groaned whenever Dietrich brought up his
studies, so he learned not to speak of what he was doing unless Dohnanyi
was present. Hans, holding Christel's hand tight against his leg beneath the
table, always asked. Then he would sit with his elbow propped on the white
tablecloth and chin resting upon his left hand while Dietrich, swept away
by pent-up excitement, waved his knife and fork and rambled on about
Heilgeschichte and exegesis and hypostasis until Karl-Friedrich would
moan, "Can't you simply tell us how many angels can dance on a pinhead
and be done with it?" Karl and Karl-Friedrich would excuse themselves and
head to the study for a cigar. Dohnanyi and Christel, pleased for an excuse
to linger, nearly alone as it were, urged, "Go on."

Hans and Christel were married in 1926. Then it was the turn of Dietrich and Sabine. They, of course, would be different. Dietrich had found
no one, had not even tried, and Sabine married a Jew.

She feared her family might object, and so she announced her intentions with the added threat that, if denied marriage, she would bear Gerhard Leibholz's child out of wedlock. Father and Mother Bonhoeffer turned
pale and assured her such extremes would not be necessary. They gave their
blessing. It was the most sparsely attended of the weddings, since many of
the relatives who'd turned out before, if for no other reason than to sample
the food prepared by the Bonhoeffers' excellent cook, declined to attend.
Chief among the absentees was Mother Bonhoeffer's brother-in-law, General Rüdiger Graf von der Goltz. Uncle Rudi was famed for the length and
curl of his mustaches and for putting down a left-wing revolt in the Baltic
region with what he liked to call "decisiveness" (Karl-Friedrich called it
butchery). He was also known to speak with grudging approval of the
ridiculous Adolf Hitler. He cabled that he could not countenance his niece
marrying an Israelite. Furthermore, the Jew Leibholz's father was a Wilmersdorf councilman friendly with the Socialists. Uncle Rudi would most
certainly not attend. He was not missed.

Sabine's young man, as Mother called him, was tall and ungainly, with
a plain, kindly face and a head that seemed too large for his body. He was
also one of the most brilliant young legal minds in Germany, according to
Hans, who told this to Sabine as she and Baby Suse (now eighteen and very
pretty) stood arm in arm in their white dresses and waited for the dancing
to begin. The ballroom of the Grunewald house had been freshly painted
a pale green, the gilt mirrors and candelabra and parquet floor polished,
the glass chandeliers taken apart and cleaned piece by piece, the tables
decked with white lilies. Gerhard, the bridegroom, was trapped in a corner

surrounded by his new brothers and cousins, who teased him about the difficulties of living with Sabine. Dietrich was not among them. He stood at the door handing out nosegays of white rosebuds and baby's breath contrived by the parlormaids earlier that morning. His blond hair was carefully combed, and a starched collar forced him to lift his chin in a Prussian manner. He offered a nosegay to an uncle von Kalckreuth who was so caught up in conversation with a von Kleist cousin bemoaning the new Socialist government—"They bumbled into power and they've no more notion what to do than does a goose. It's time for men of breeding to take charge of the country"—that he waved away the nosegay without noticing what it was or who offered it.

"What of Dietrich?" Hans nodded toward his brother-in-law. "Will he ever marry?"

"Of course he will!" Suse said. "Why wouldn't he?"

"He seems such a *naïf*, that's all. It's as though he lives inside his head and nowhere else. He won't last this evening, you know, not even for Sabine. He'll be overwhelmed by the crowd and go off to his room for peace and quiet."

"Our Dietrich is a bit of a lamb," said Suse, who had bobbed her hair and shortened her skirts and learned to smoke Turkish hashish, though she hadn't told the family, "but he just needs someone who can draw him out."

"Why don't you take him in hand?"

"Perhaps I shall. I'll invite him to a party."

"Oh, Suse," said Sabine, "he'd be miserable. He's not a thing in common with your friends."

"You don't know. I'll trundle him along to Max's flat next weekend. All sorts of odd birds show up at Max's parties."

At dinner Sabine and Gerhard sat side by side on chairs draped with gold cloth. The bridesmaids, Christel and Suse among them, recited poetry to the new couple. Then Suse sang "Ringel-Reihe-Rosenkranz, ich tanz mit meiner Frau" to Dietrich's piano accompaniment and much applause from the audience. The dancing began. Gerhard came to claim the first dance with Sabine. Later she sought out her twin and led him by the hand to join in a waltz.

"Gerhard is so sweet," Sabine whispered in his ear, "but clumsy. And you, Dietrich, are the best dancer in the family."

He smiled at the compliment, but he was near tears. She squeezed his hand.

"You'll be fine," she said. "It's not as though Göttingen were a world away."

"I know. But everything will change. Not that I'm displeased. It's as it should be."

Dietrich danced with Suse, with Christel, with his mother. Then he disappeared into his room and only came out to say farewell after the newly-
weds changed to traveling clothes for the honeymoon trip to Lugano. He
went the next week to a party with Suse, where everyone sat cross-legged
on the floor and smoked hashish from pipes while Lotte Lenya moaned
from the phonograph. They argued about Brecht and Klee and the latest
films, waving their arms and talking all at once. Dietrich shrank into a cob-
webbed corner. At ten o'clock he kissed Suse on the cheek and escaped into
the crisp night air of Berlin. The hashish had left him quite light-headed.
He pretended every shadow that met him beneath the smoky streetlamps
was Sabine, run away from her husband and searching for her own true self.
Once, on an empty sidewalk, he even swept up such a shadow in his arms
and swung it around with a neat two-step, then stopped sheepishly and continued on his way home.

Gloria in excelsis deo
et in terra pax hominibus
bonae voluntatis.
Laudamus te,
benedicimus te,
adoramus te,
glorificamus te

Glory to God in the highest
And on earth peace to men of good will...
We praise thee
We bless thee
We adore thee
We glorify thee

New York

1930–31

UNION THEOLOGICAL SEMINARY was a world unto itself, an enclosed ivy-covered stone rectangle with a green courtyard in the center that purposely mimicked a college at Oxford or Cambridge. Nooks and crannies abounded and narrow staircases twisted inside corner towers. A stone's throw to the north was Harlem.

On the first day of the new term the seminary hosted a reception for new students in the refectory. Young men in suits and ties wandered uncertainly between the refreshment tables. Professor Reinhold Niebuhr marveled at how the setting—dark oak paneling and clusters of chandeliers—lent the well-scrubbed faces of the young men an air of angelic seriousness. They were by and large sons of the American middle class who would fit into one of two categories the faculty had jokingly devised. The Moles, a majority, would be uncomfortable with the neighborhood that surrounded the seminary and would retreat within Union's stone walls, would make book-lined caves of their rooms and, when they wanted to take the air, wander the cloisters with pipes in hand. Even many of those who were drawn by Union's growing activist reputation would find Depression New York to be a cultural trauma and seek a quiet haven away from it when they could. But for the Alley Cats, the minority closest to Niebuhr's heart, the seminary was itself a smothering source of cultural dislocation and the world outside its doors, where people scrabbled about in search of food, sex, art, and illicit liquor, was irresistible. The faculty were themselves drawn to one group or the other. The Alley Cats, Niebuhr thought, would make the best ministers, or at least the most honest.

Then there were the rare ones who belonged in neither place. Niebuhr had been charged by President Coffin with looking out for the two new exchange students and introducing them to their American peers. But Niebuhr thought they seemed more interested in sizing up each other. One was a slender man in an ill-fitting suit with a high mop of curly brown hair, a large nose, and stooped shoulders. The other, in expensively tailored pinstripes, was sturdy, with a round face, tight lips, and a shock of thin blond hair that promised to have disappeared in a few years' time.

"Who are they?" Niebuhr had asked Coffin before the students were formally introduced.

"Jean Lasserre is pastor of a working-class mission in the northeast of France," Coffin said, "and Dietrich Bonhoeffer recently received his doctorate from Berlin University."

"Let me guess which is which," Niebuhr said dryly.

The Frenchman and the German, standing near the door looking extremely nervous, were watching the room but stealing glances at each other and not saying a word.

"Get over there," Coffin said, "before they start another war."

But before Niebuhr could move, Harry Ward, Professor of Ethics, had descended upon the foreigners and was exclaiming, "You must be Lasserre, ah, yes, yes, yes, I admired your paper on the war immensely!" The Frenchman beamed and the German turned a brilliant pink.

"That's the kind of white man who wears his blood vessels close to the surface," said a voice behind Niebuhr.

Niebuhr turned to find that two seniors, Fred Bishop and Myles Horton, had joined him. They were among Niebuhr's favorites, quintessential Alley Cats. Niebuhr could recall an earlier reception when they had eyed each other as warily as did Bonhoeffer and Lasserre. Bishop, a dark-skinned Negro, had leaned nonchalantly against an oak-paneled wall and jiggled a cup of punch in his hand. Only the quick movement of his eyes had betrayed his nervousness.

He had spoken as soon as Niebuhr approached, before the older man could introduce himself. "I hear in the old days before Prohibition they used to serve sherry at this reception. Not that I miss that. I had sherry once. Far as I'm concerned, it tastes like concentrated cat piss."

And sipped his punch, never taking his eyes off Niebuhr, who stuck out his hand.

"Reinhold Niebuhr. Professor of Applied Christianity."

"Applied Christianity?" The Negro had raised his eyebrows. "Sounds like How to Put On a Bandage." Only then did he take Niebuhr's hand. "Albert Frederick Bishop," he said, "from Birmingham, Alabama. They call me Fred."

Just then another student had wandered past, a short wiry young man with slicked-back hair, wearing boots and a pair of pants an inch too short, staring up at the portraits of past presidents in black robes which lined the refectory walls and oblivious to the glances from other students that followed him.

Fred Bishop said, "If that isn't the crackerest-looking thing I've seen since I left Alabama. Looks like one of those hillbillies who still the liquor they sell in those speaks on Lenox Avenue."

"What do you know about Lenox Avenue speakeasies?"

"I got here night before last," Fred said. "I've looked around."

Niebuhr was amused. "Then why don't you go over and introduce yourself? Maybe he's from your neck of the woods and could use the help of a sophisticated fellow like yourself."

Fred's face tightened, but he said, "Sure," and wandered over to the student in boots. They shook hands.

"Fred Bishop."

"Myles Horton," the other said in a nasal Appalachian twang. "Glad to meet you. Where you from?"

"Birmingham. You?"

"Tennessee."

"I guessed something like that. You look like hills. Chattanooga maybe?"

Myles said, "My people were too far up a hollow to see the butt end of Chattanooga."

They had been angling nervously, like cats longing to sniff each other. Fred suddenly laughed and said, "Well now, ain't we the lucky ones? Poor little Negro boy and hillbilly boy been let in this here nice school by all these good Yankees?"

Myles smiled and said, "Well, they can go home and feel fine about being kind to us."

They had forgotten about Niebuhr. At reception's end they were still talking, huddled over their empty plates at a table in the corner. And they became fast friends.

That had been two years earlier. Now Niebuhr asked, "How's the South?"

Myles Horton said, "Going to hell, Reinie. They're eating dirt in Tennessee."

"Same in Alabama," Fred agreed.

Niebuhr asked, "How's your father, Fred?"

"*He's* doing just fine. Every poor old lady in the church brings him half her garden."

"Prerogatives of the clergy," said Niebuhr.

"Not for me," Fred said. "I don't like living off the labor of little old ladies. But my father still thinks I'm coming back after graduation. Assistant pastor at Sixteenth Street Baptist."

Myles said, "Me and Fred got it figured out. We're heading south to the hills and do some hell-raising."

"*You're* heading to the hills," Fred said. "You can raise hell up any holler you want to. I'm going to Atlanta, back to Morehouse soon as a position opens up. Just got to bide my time."

"I don't know," Myles said. "Waiting for some old guy to retire or keel over, that don't put the cornbread on the table."

Fred shrugged. "Maybe I'll stay at Abyssinian until then."

"Sure," said Niebuhr, who was looking over Fred's shoulder, trying to keep an eye on the foreign students. "Dr. Powell will take you ahead of his own son any day."

Dr. Powell was Adam Clayton Powell, pastor of the Abyssinian Baptist Church in Harlem, and his son Adam Junior was an entering student at Union Seminary. Fred had been serving his parish internship at Abyssinian Baptist.

"Where is Powell?" Niebuhr asked. "I'd like to meet him."

"He won't show for this reception," Fred said. "Adam Junior's been to Europe and Africa and he's already running the biggest soup kitchen and job bank in Harlem right out of his daddy's church. Not to mention what else he knows. It would be like hanging out with babies."

Myles said, "I'm getting bored myself. You fellows want to come to my room? I got something there from back home."

Fred nudged Niebuhr. "Come on up. This is the stuff for real. Nothing bad in it, not iodine or soap or formaldehyde. Pure corn stilled by a man who takes pride in his work."

"Thanks," Niebuhr said, "but I've got some responsibilities here. Matter of fact, you boys could help me out."

"Uh-oh." Fred followed Niebuhr's glance to where the foreign students still stood alone and farther from each other than before. "Them?"

"Them," Niebuhr agreed.

"Aw, man."

"It wasn't so long ago you were new," Niebuhr reminded him. "Remember how lonely you were, and you weren't even from a foreign country."

"Well," Myles said. "Alabama."

"Where are they from?" Fred asked.

Niebuhr pointed. "That one's from Germany."

"Oh, yeah, the red-faced fellow," Myles said.

Fred said, "Like I want to spend my senior year entertaining Kaiser Wilhelm instead of enjoying the last I'll see of Harlem."

"Come on, guys," Niebuhr coaxed. "Show a little compassion."

Fred said, "I'm not ordained yet, Reinie. I got one more year before I have to show compassion."

They did allow themselves to be led over to the exchange students and dutifully introduced, Bishop and Horton to Bonhoeffer and Lasserre. But they slipped away as soon as was politely possible and made for Myles's supply of bootleg whiskey.

Dietrich was constantly bumping into people. The corridors and rooms of the students in Hastings wing were as narrow and cramped as the servants' quarters at home in the Wangenheimstraße. And twice as noisy, Dietrich thought. He could not imagine his parents' servants carrying on in the manner of the American students, dashing down the hall at full speed when late for class, calling to one another in loud voices, entering any room with an open door and flinging themselves across the bed while laughing at some amusing story. At first Dietrich didn't go out much and kept his door closed. But after a few days loneliness forced him to try to imitate the others. He left his door standing open, feeling as awkward and foolish as if he were walking down Unter den Linden in his underwear, and sat at his desk pretending to study and trying not to notice who walked by. He heard the footsteps of passersby slow down and now and then caught someone staring curiously in at him. But something in his manner caused each one to mumble an incoherent apology and go on down the hall.

He was also embarrassed by the communal bathing arrangements. A bathroom at the end of the hall held showers, toilets, and urinals. There were pegs along the wall for hanging towels and clothing and no place to undress in privacy, though the showers had damp canvas curtains. One morning Dietrich left his room wearing an embroidered dressing gown with velvet collar and carrying a soap dish. Fred Bishop, still damp from the shower and wearing only a towel, was walking down the hall. Dietrich pulled the door to his room shut behind him. Fred looked offended and moved to the far wall to let Dietrich pass. Dietrich tried to be friendly, to show he had not meant to imply distrust of the other, nodded his head, and, forgetting to speak English in his nervousness, said, "*Guten morgen.*"

"Morning," Fred answered.

"I must remember to use my English," Dietrich said. "It isn't yet very good."

Fred said, "Oh. Well. You're doing all right. Lot better than I'd do in German."

"*Dank*— Thank you." Dietrich looked away, then back. "So. On to clean."

"Good. Clean."

Suddenly the coming year stretched before Dietrich like a barren, solitary eternity where he would never hear a kind word from someone who knew and understood him. He felt close to tears, and to cover it, he moved on down the hall. He was surprised to hear Fred call after him, "Stop by my room sometime. Listen to the Victrola. Five oh two."

Dietrich stopped. "*Ja*," he said. "Thank you. Five oh two."

Fred Bishop had just begun to tackle Kierkegaard when there came a knock at his door and there stood the German holding a promisingly dark bottle and two tiny glasses.

"Is this a good time?" Dietrich asked. "Do you now study?"

"I'm always ready for a break," Fred said. He couldn't imagine Dietrich sprawling on the bed, so he offered him the armchair. Dietrich placed the glasses on the desk and opened the bottle of schnapps.

Fred whistled. "Jesus, where'd you get that?" He went to the door and shut it.

"My brother Karl-Friedrich sends it in the mail. He cuts a hole in a cheese and puts it inside."

Fred shook his head admiringly. "Man, I wouldn't have thought you'd be the sneaky type."

Dietrich wasn't sure whether or not to be insulted, so he blushed. "Well, Karl-Friedrich has lectured once in America and knows I will want this. I much prefer a good wine, but this bottle is small and does not easily break. It is a great foolishness, isn't it? This Prohibition?"

"Your first lesson about America," Fred said. "We got a sizable portion of the population that thinks human beings should be deprived of sight, touch, sound, and taste. No contamination, go straight to heaven that way."

They sipped the schnapps, which tasted like wild cherries.

"You said you have music?" Dietrich asked shyly. He could not begin to say how much he missed his family's musical evenings.

"You bet. Don't know if it's your cup of tea, though." Fred pulled out a box which held his albums, laid out his favorites on the bed. "Some of these are older. Willie the Lion Smith. Stride piano on the Okeh label. These here are all on Black Swan." He held up one after the other as though displaying the contents of a treasure chest. "Chick Webb. Benny Carter. Fess Williams. Swing."

"*Was ist* swing?"

"Tell me what you listen to and I'll try to compare it."

"I enjoy Bach, of course. Some of Mozart. Schumann. Brahms."

Fred sighed. "We got a problem here."

"Oh. I'm sorry."

"Nothing to be sorry about, just I don't know if you'll like this. It's stuff you dance to."

Dietrich nodded his head, confused. Fred filled his glass again and said, "I'll put on some Benny Carter. Just shut your eyes and relax. And keep drinking that stuff."

"*Ja*," Dietrich said.

He shut his eyes and leaned back in his chair with such a look of concentration on his face Fred had to stifle a laugh. He switched on the Victrola and lifted the elongated arm carefully, ran the tip of his finger over the needle. "This Victrola is my most prized possession," he said as though crooning to a child. "I dust it every day. Dust the little dog on the label." He wiped the album before laying it on the turntable, set the needle on "Liza." Soon he was moving around the room, alcohol pushing the music into his fingers and toes. Dietrich was still reared back, clutching the arms of the chair.

"Let go the chair," Fred said.

Dietrich opened his eyes, startled, then let go of the chair like a man pushing himself out onto a precarious ledge. Fred was dancing back and forth to the beat, and Dietrich watched transfixed while the room filled with the rhythmic wail of a saxophone.

"Move your legs!" Fred commanded.

Dietrich started to jiggle his legs. He smiled.

"Stand up!" Fred cranked up the volume. The sax was howling. He whirled around, elbows up. "Move!" he yelled.

And Dietrich moved.

("Damn, he did," Fred told Myles later. "Got that body like a little truck and moved it around that room.")

Fred's hands were above his head and he was wishing Dietrich were Mavis Pruitt from Sugar Hill, who eyed him from her Abyssinian pew when he preached but wouldn't give him the time of day because she knew he would leave Harlem, and she *was* Harlem. Dietrich was outside himself as well somewhere in Berlin with someone whose face could not be seen. The trumpets had taken over, and they didn't even hear the pounding on the door until the music stopped.

Fred flung open the door to face a student named Krause.

"Some people are studying, Bishop," Krause said.

"It's the first week, Krause. You're a senior. Nothing to prove."

"I have seventy-five pages of Calvin to read for Baillie tomorrow." Then he noticed Dietrich and almost stammered, "Bonhoeffer. I wouldn't have thought—" He looked back accusingly at Fred.

"I like to dance," said Dietrich, a little tipsy. "I am the best dancer of my family."

"We'll keep it down," Fred said and shut the door in Krause's face, muttering, "Like I'm corrupting the Teutonic race."

Dietrich raised his head. *"Was?"*

"Nothing," Fred said. He replenished their glasses. "Pretty good dancing for the first time. Like that music?"

"Oh yes!"

"But a recording is nothing, scratchy, drums don't come through. You should hear it in person."

"Where? Do you know places?"

"Do I know places." Fred smiled. And because of the schnapps he added generously, "Bonhoeffer, how would you like to go to the Savoy?"

"It sounds very good." Dietrich raised his glass. "And please. Call me Dietrich."

In addition to his formal ways, Dietrich became an object of gossip because he never attended chapel. When Fred asked him about it, he shrugged and said he didn't see much reason for it, had never been a regular churchgoer. Fred looked surprised.

"Why go into the ministry, then?"

"Not the ministry," Dietrich said. "Theology. Very intellectual, very rigorous, very disciplined."

Which might explain, Fred speculated to Myles Horton, the German's behavior in class. For a couple of weeks Dietrich had been quiet, listening, not saying a word. "Biting his tongue, apparently," Fred said.

For Dietrich's silence, brought on by his shock at the informality and irreverence of American classroom discussion, came to an abrupt end in an ethics seminar. Niebuhr was lecturing on Erasmus and Luther.

"In *De libero arbitrio*, or 'The Freedom of the Will,' Erasmus makes the case for the freedom of the individual to choose the good. The individual, therefore, has an ethical responsibility to act morally, and to challenge any ruler who fails to act justly. So, for example, Erasmus might say when a rational man sees government troops breaking the skulls of striking coal miners in Kentucky, a rational man would exercise his free will to protest, even intervene."

Myles Horton, who had spent his summers with coal miners in Harlan County, was happily scribbling away. Niebuhr paced and rubbed his bald forehead, pushing back hair that wasn't there.

"Erasmus," he continued, "was the great humanist of his age. He anticipated the Enlightenment thinkers as a champion of reason and human freedom. Some would say a bit naively. Luther, for one, disagreed strongly with Erasmus. He responded with *De servo arbitrio*, 'The *Bondage* of the Will.'"

"Typical German," Myles said, just loud enough to be heard. He had completely forgotten Dietrich's presence. Fred, who was sitting behind Dietrich, saw the German's ears and neck turn a bright red. Niebuhr noticed as well and glanced at Dietrich uneasily but kept on with the lecture.

"For Luther, man is a sinful, irrational creature with no will of his own to act morally. Only the grace of God allows some to choose the good. Others receive no such grace and choose evil. God hardens such men. Now why, one might ask Luther, are only some given God's grace, and not all? Is this fair? Can such a God be called just? According to Luther, these questions are not to be asked. If God hides His reasons from us, it is no concern of ours. God is so far above us as to be inscrutable. And so we must not question why God hardens the man who does evil."

There were whispers in the back near Myles's desk, then titters. Niebuhr pretended he didn't hear. "Of course, I am not Martin Luther," he continued. "I do ask questions. Why would God harden one man and not another?" The titters were growing. Myles had his hand over his mouth and was looking at the ceiling. "Luther would say that God hardens a man for the salvation of other men."

"And the women love it too," said Myles.

Everybody hooted, even Niebuhr.

Dietrich slammed his notebook shut. "What sort of theology is this?" he cried.

The class fell silent. Then Myles said, "God can take a joke, Bonhoeffer, even if you can't."

Dietrich turned. "It is not just jokes. It is your theology. Or lack of it. There is no critical thinking here. I cannot take notes in these classes. There is nothing to write down, only this fellow's feelings and that fellow's opinion. Too much about the working class and politics. Not enough exegesis, not enough dogmatics."

"Hear, hear," said Krause.

Niebuhr, angry himself now, folded his arms across his chest. "By all means, then, let us hear what one of the leading intellects in Germany has to contribute to this discussion."

"If you are asking whether I am a liberal, a rationalist, a Calvinist, or a Barthian—"

"At this moment I don't care which you are," Niebuhr interrupted. "What does any of it have to do with human experience? What does it have to do with you?" When Dietrich looked puzzled, he added in what he meant as a joking tone, "You know, Bonhoeffer, I recommend a strong dose of the prophets. Can you find them in the Bible?"

Dietrich turned red again. "When you speak to me as if I have no familiarity with the scriptures, you insult me and you insult German theology. Not to mention the intellect. This is what I observe in America, to reject the intellect."

Fred said, "I know a woman in Harlem name of Ruth Jones. Her oldest son is serving ten years in jail, arrested on the picket line at a slaughterhouse for cussing a white policeman. Her youngest son had a tumor in his brain. Doctors cut it out. Said he was cured. Two months later a taxicab jumped the curb and ran right over him. What can Ruth Jones know about God?"

"He's got a mean sense of humor," said Myles.

Dietrich was staring at Fred.

Fred continued, "From what she knows, there's no sense to any of it, and tell you what, that's as much as you know too. So don't go to Ruth Jones with that intellect stuff. Know what she'll say? Woman will ask you if you love Jesus. Intellect! Take your intellect and argue her any kind of theology you want to. She won't pay you any mind. Mourns her sons. Loves Jesus. Won't let go of any of it."

Dietrich said, "Then why do any of you study theology? Why are you here?"

"I'm not saying don't study theology," Fred said. "I'm saying don't take yourself and your head so damn seriously. Man, spout all the theology you want, you can't scratch the surface of God Almighty."

He expected a response, but Dietrich had gone silent and distant. He relaxed as though the anger were visibly draining from him.

"Bonhoeffer, how well do you preach?" Niebuhr asked suddenly.

Dietrich looked around. "I have preached on a number of occasions," he said self-consciously. He ducked his head. "I have been told my sermons are very boring. Even my father says so."

Niebuhr turned abruptly to hide a smile and began erasing the chalkboard. "You know, Bonhoeffer," he said, back to the class, "you really should work with Fred this year at Abyssinian Baptist."

Behind Dietrich, Fred almost came out of his seat, shaking his head at Niebuhr as hard as he could. Niebuhr wouldn't turn around and look at him.

"You really should," Niebuhr repeated. "I think I'll mention it to Dr. Powell."

Fred decided the only way to get out of taking Dietrich to Abyssinian was if Dr. Powell said no. And the best way to get him to say no, since he wouldn't have any good reason to, was for Adam Junior to drop a hint. But Fred hadn't seen Adam Junior since school started, so he checked the registrar's office. He was told that Adam Clayton Powell, Jr., was scheduled for Church

History with Moffat at eleven o'clock, so he waited outside the classroom. The door was open, because it was still hot in the city; Moffat was lecturing away about the Desert Fathers who wore animal skins and fasted and lived their whole lives praying on top of twenty-foot-tall poles. Adam Junior was not in the classroom. But Rita, one of Abyssinian's church secretaries, was in the last row, wearing a neat white blouse and black hat and scribbling away in shorthand with an amused look on her face.

She emerged when the lecture was over, adjusting her hat. Fred said, "Rita, what you doing here? Where's Adam Junior?"

"He's too busy for this," she said. "Eleven o'clock the soup kitchen is just starting lunch and he's got a line a mile long asking about jobs. Why they have these classes so close to lunch?"

"And Moffat said you could do this?"

She leaned close to Fred and lowered her voice. "He hasn't said it. Fact is, he looks a hole through me every time I come in the door. Said this morning he was complaining to the president, see about getting young Mr. Powell kicked out if he doesn't start coming to class."

Which was almost what happened. Except Adam Junior quit before the seminary had a chance to expel him. Fred didn't see him or Dr. Powell until the next Sunday at church, and that was too late. The decisions had been made. Adam Junior would drop out of Union and Abyssinian would ordain him anyway. In the meantime Niebuhr had talked to Dr. Powell, who said he'd be happy to add the German exchange student Bonhoeffer as a second intern. Exciting for the congregation to have somebody from a foreign country, and a good learning experience for the young man. Working with Fred Bishop, of course, doing whatever Fred set him to do. So that was that.

Myles was visiting in Fred's room that night when Dietrich came by.

"So," Dietrich said, standing in the doorway, "we shall work together. Splendid, splendid."

Fred invited him in, tried to act as though he were happy about the new arrangement. Dietrich asked Myles, "At which church do you work? Is it Harlem also?"

"I do my fieldwork with a labor organizer in Brooklyn."

Fred said, "Myles isn't getting ordained. He belongs to the church of Norman Thomas."

"Who is Norman Thomas?"

"Union Seminary graduate," said Myles. "Also happens to be the Socialist candidate for president."

"And what has this to do with theology? Ah well, the Socialists. My brother Karl-Friedrich thought himself a Socialist for a time, but it was what my father calls youthful idealism. Nothing more." Dietrich waved his hand.

Myles glanced at Fred and rolled his eyes, got up to leave.

"Don't go," Fred said quickly.

Myles said, "You and Bonhoeffer have to make your plans."

"In fact," said Dietrich, "I cannot stay to talk. I must return to my room and write a paper. But I have an idea. I am a bit homesick, you see. Dr. Niebuhr tells me there is a German neighborhood on the Upper East Side, Yorkville. Many German restaurants. Let me take you there, Fred. You will be my guest."

Myles said, "Something you don't understand, Bonhoeffer. Fred can't—" But Fred waved for him to be quiet.

"Okay," he said. "Tomorrow night?"

"Splendid, splendid!" Dietrich said again, slow and loud, as though this were a new word he'd learned and liked a lot. He shook hands all around and left.

Myles sat back down. "No way," he said. "Especially not in Yorkville."

"I know. I want to see how he acts. May be a good excuse to get out of working with this sucker."

Fred had never been in Yorkville, which had a reputation, left over from the war, of being an unsavory place stocked with spies, black marketeers, and white slavers in search of pure Anglo-Saxon girls to ship back to Germany. But that wasn't why Fred felt so uncomfortable as they walked down East 86th. Too many people stared at them, which Dietrich didn't notice but Fred had to. They stopped beneath a sign.

Deutsches' Restaurant Platzl
Dining   Dancing

"Dancing," said Dietrich. He smiled at Fred. "You want dancing?"

Fred knew he wouldn't be doing any dancing there, but he didn't say anything except "Sure" and followed Dietrich up the steps. Inside the light was dim. There were tables with white cloths and oom-pah-pah music coming from the next room. Dietrich headed toward an empty table, and again Fred followed, aware that every eye in the room was on them. Dietrich sat down. He was ecstatic.

"Smell!" he cried. "It is like my mother's kitchen!"

They unfolded their napkins. Then Fred looked away and stared at the wall because a waiter was bearing down on them with an angry expression. He stopped beside the table.

"Of course you do not have wine?" Dietrich said, still oblivious. "You do not have any hidden in a cellar, I suppose?"

"Sir," the waiter said. "Of course it is impossible to serve you. You must leave at once."

"*Was?*" Dietrich exclaimed. "Because I ask for wine? My apologies. I know it is *verboten*, but I also have learned some places—" He fluttered his hand. "Is it so bad to ask?"

"Sir!" The man gestured at Fred. "We do not serve Negroes. You must go."

Dietrich's mouth was open, and his eyeglasses glinted in the candlelight. "Negroes? What are you saying? My friend? You will not serve—" He looked at Fred in disbelief. Fred stood, tossed his napkin on the table, and put on his hat.

Dietrich held on to the table and looked around as though he expected the other diners to take his side. "*Dies ist eine Beleidigung!*"

"English, please," said the waiter impatiently. "I don't know German except for the food."

Dietrich stood up so fast he knocked over his chair. He waved his arms. "An outrage! An outrage! Do you understand *that?*"

Fred said, "I'm going. You can stay if you want, and they'll serve you." He left.

Dietrich followed. At the door he stopped and turned. "We don't vant your *lousy* food!" he yelled, jerked on his jacket lapels, and marched out.

On the sidewalk again, Fred burst out laughing. "Where'd you learn the word 'lousy'?" he asked.

"How can you laugh?" Dietrich asked, astonished.

"Beats crying."

Dietrich shook his head. "I am ashamed for Germans."

"It's not Germans. It happens everywhere in America. Even in Greenwich Village, where all the radicals live. And in the South, forget it. I walk in a white place like we did tonight, they'd take me out back and lynch me."

"Lynch?"

"Hang. Hang me."

"*Mein Gott!*"

They walked awhile in silence.

"You knew this would happen," Dietrich said.

Fred shrugged.

"Why did you come?"

"Wanted to see what you'd do," Fred admitted. "Wasn't nice of me, was it? Sorry."

"No," Dietrich said. "Do not apologize. It was good for me to see this. I could not have thought. Imagine, in Germany, if a restaurant refused to serve Jews, for example. Such an outcry!"

At the subway Dietrich turned and put his hand on Fred's arm. "Take me someplace where no one is turned away. Surely there is such a place."

"Okay," Fred said. "We take the 4 train to Harlem and I'll find you some ribs and collards. And hooch."

"Hooch?"

"Don't ask."

They ate at Craig's, a writers' hangout, because Fred thought Dietrich might be more comfortable there. There was decent gin, made in a bathtub but without the medicine cabinet thrown in. The music was soft smoky jazz, good for talking instead of dancing.

"You must love Harlem," Dietrich said, looking around. "Here you will be yourself."

"Yes. I love Harlem. I could stay here too easy."

"Why not stay?"

"Too safe. There is such a thing as a call, isn't there? You believe in that?"

"A call?" Dietrich said. "You mean from God?"

"From God."

"This call," Dietrich said, "will take you—South?"

"You guessed it. Not to Alabama, though. Not too close to my father. I'm not Adam Junior."

"Who is Adam Junior?"

"You'll meet him soon enough. His father is the pastor at Abyssinian Baptist. Adam Junior was supposed to be a doctor. What he wanted. But changed his mind because his daddy's making him heir to the throne. Easier way to go, I suppose. Maybe not. Any way you try to help the Negro in America isn't easy. I shouldn't talk about Adam Junior. Hell of a nice guy, actually. Wild, though. He'll have trouble after he's ordained."

"Wild?"

"Loves to drink. Loves to party. Loves the women. Wild." Fred shook his glass. "'Course, by Alabama standards, by the Rev. James Johnson Bishop's standards, I'm wild too. Like my bathtub gin and my Southern corn likker. Like the ladies, even though I don't chase as many as Adam Junior. Hell, seminary corrupted me. I never cussed, drank, or chased skirts until I came to seminary. Tell that to the little old ladies back home."

Dietrich took a gold-plated cigarette case from inside his jacket, opened it and lit two, gave one to Fred. "Add tobacco to your sins," he said.

"How about you?" Fred asked.

"How about?"

"Let me guess. You probably cuss, but it's in German so it wouldn't mean a thing to me. I know you smoke and drink."

Dietrich waved his hand so blue smoke swirled around his face. "Everyone drinks in Germany. I was given wine when I was very young."

He was watching the vocalist, a tall woman with coffee skin and a large behind, breathing into the microphone *Oh Daddy*.

Fred said, "What about women?"

The darkness hid Dietrich's blush. He was slow in answering.

"I have never—" He searched for a word, whether an English one or a modest one, Fred wasn't sure. "Never been with a woman. I have never even had a girlfriend. I have my passions, it is true, but I am a difficult man. I know this. No woman would how do you say put up with me, I am thinking." He dragged deep on his cigarette, "Women, they are a bit fearful. No, that is not the word. Frightening. Except for my sisters, but that, of course is quite another thing." He stubbed out his cigarette and dug for another. "And you. Is there someone for you?"

"No one that would have me," Fred said. "Better to settle into a church, look for someone there. Takes a special woman to be a pastor's wife, you know. If I get messed up with the wrong woman I'll end up with no church to take me except Sixteenth Street Baptist in Birmingham, Alabama. And I couldn't stand working with my father."

On Dietrich's first Sunday at Abyssinian Baptist, Adam Junior was preaching. The round blueglass sanctuary window glowed and throbbed as though the church were not on 138th Street but at the bottom of an ocean. The choir sang *Savior, savior, hear my humble cry, while on others thou art toiling do not pass me by,* slow as though their hearts were breaking, and Fred sat in his black robe beside Dr. Powell, whose light-skinned son who passed for white to get in the Cotton Club climbed the pulpit and prayed. Fred surveyed the congregation, where Dietrich sat, pale among the beige chestnut chocolate hazel mahogany tan faces.

Adam Junior said, "My text today is from the prophet Daniel, the third chapter. Three young men are cast into a fiery furnace because they refuse to worship a golden idol. They are foreigners, strangers in a strange land. Their names are Shadrach, Meshach, and Abednego, or as some say, A Bad Negro."

Laughter.

Dietrich was smiling, his English good enough to catch at least part of the joke. Earlier, during the choir's anthem, he had been wiping his eyes.

After the service, as Fred pulled off his black robe in the vestibule, Adam Junior tapped him on the shoulder, nodded toward the sanctuary, and said, "Damn, Fred, if that isn't the whitest thing you could carry into Harlem."

My dearest Sabine, he wrote, *I am much happier than before. There is still little to interest me in my classes. Good-fellowship is more valued here than is*

*serious inquiry. And the informality is disconcerting. The eminent Reinhold
Niebuhr, for example, is called "Reinie" by the students. I cannot think that this
is beneficial.*

*But I now have a friend, an American Negro called Fred Bishop. You know
I have been very much alone. It is not so hard now.*

*I attend Fred's Baptist church in Harlem each Sunday, where I have been put
in charge of the Ladies' Bible Study Circle on Wednesdays and a boys' Sunday
School class. I also visit people too elderly or sick to leave their homes and read
the Bible with them.*

*I continue to be shocked at the treatment of the Negroes in this country. You
know very well the problems faced by Jews in Germany, you feel them now in
your own body. Believe me when I say Karl-Friedrich was correct; they do not
begin to compare with the ways Negroes are mistreated, the great variety of injus-
tices, and the hatred white Americans bear them, or at best the condescending
pity which must be as hard to bear. This scandal is not a vestige of the past, but
continues. Where it shall end, who can say.*

*My depression still plagues me, especially here in the dormitory where one is
expected to join in as a matter of course and always be jolly. I retreat to my room.
Sometimes I pretend I am not in, and ignore the knocking at my door.*

As for other matters . . .

Like all his letters, this one did not tell Sabine nearly enough. Dietrich had
always been more comfortable writing about ideas, and filled pages with
summaries of the lectures he heard, along with his continued displeasure at
the intrusion of politics into theological debate (a complaint he made less
and less, she noted, as the year went on). But he told her little of the
impressions New York made upon him. She was never to learn of the endless blocks of buildings, their brick flanks scored in the late daylight by the
shadow grids of fire escapes. Vendors in stained aprons hawking baked
sweet potatoes, brownroasted ears of yellow corn, grilled frankfurters and
sauerkraut. Clotheslines spanning back alleys like supporting cables, ava-
lanches of neon light, the sharp burn of illicit whiskey, skyscrapers that
forced Dietrich's neck back and mouth open.

The difference between German sirens and American sirens. German
sirens up and down, regular, crisis expected to be under control. American
sirens a chaotic wailing as though the emergency vehicles were themselves
in distress.

Sabine had written, *Dearest brother, our people are more than flirting with
fascism. On every side one hears expressions of the purest hatred directed toward
the government, toward Jews, toward emancipated women, toward artists and
writers. If this state of affairs continues, everything will be up with the likes of us.*

Dietrich's father had written, *Do not believe any alarmist news from Germany. Of course your sister is upset. The Nazis make noise, and regularly brawl with Communists in the streets. (Not in our neighborhood.) There is some harassment of the Jews as well. But the German people will never vote for Hitler. Only a putsch could bring him to power, but a putsch requires secrecy, and a popularity Hitler does not enjoy. Never fear, we are keeping a close eye on our little Austrian. Sleep well, my son.*

Dietrich did not know what to believe.

As for other matters, he wrote, *there is a Frenchman here, Jean Lasserre.* . . .

At dinner, on the first cold evening of the autumn, Dietrich joined a table that included Myles, Fred, and Krause. And Lasserre, he realized after it was too late to find another place without giving offense. He had so far avoided the Frenchman. The war was not so far in the past as to be easily forgotten. It was not that he hated the French. But they had beaten Germany with the aid of other countries, which was not fair, and had required the Fatherland to acknowledge guilt for a war that was as much their own making. Then there was Walter's death. Dietrich sat down, unfolded his napkin, and nodded at the others. He had nothing to say.

Platters and bowls circulated around the table. Roast beef cooked to dryness, parsley potatoes, creamed corn, hot rolls. Dietrich ignored the corn, which he had never seen before arriving in America and had quickly come to despise, and instead ladled extra potatoes onto his plate.

"So, Bonhoeffer," said Krause, "if it's clear tomorrow, how about a game of tennis? Good way to get the blood moving in this weather."

"Thank you but no," said Dietrich. "I watched you last Saturday and you do not play well enough for either of us to enjoy it."

Myles glanced at Fred across the table, then looked away to keep from bursting into laughter. Fred bit his lips and pretended to carefully butter a roll.

"Oh," said Krause. He looked miffed but was still in awe of Dietrich. He turned to the Frenchman. "How about you, Lasserre? You play tennis?"

Lasserre smiled. "I'm afraid no. I live in a place that does not play this game."

Myles said, "Yeah? Where's that?"

"Bruay, in Artois province. It is a coal-mining region."

"Coal mining!" Myles leaned forward with his elbows on the table. "You going back when you finish here?"

"*Mais oui.* I have always intended it."

"What are you doing there?"

"I live with one of the mining families and I try, quite simply, to share in the life of the community. My church pays me a small stipend, but I give away all but a few francs each month. Sometimes I go in the pit and work beside the men, help them load their coal."

Krause looked skeptical. "Why would a man with your education want to do menial labor?"

"I would like," Lasserre said, "to be a saint." He smiled and began to cut his meat into small pieces.

Everyone stopped eating and stared. Lasserre ignored them and reached for the pepper. Finally Dietrich said, "A little vain, I should think."

"It is not so vain as bragging about tennis," said Lasserre. He went on eating.

Dietrich stood suddenly and picked up his plate, said, "Pardon me," and moved to an empty table.

Fred followed, sat down beside him.

Dietrich said, "I meant nothing disrespectful by my words to Krause. I thought only to spare him. As for Lasserre, it was an outrageous statement he made. Besides, he mocks me because I am German."

"Aw, man, don't take things so damn serious. Have a sense of humor."

"I do have a sense of humor. But one cannot be humorous where one cannot be oneself."

He began to eat, not tasting a thing he put in his mouth. Fred watched him a moment, then returned to his table.

"Touchy," said Myles.

"Yeah," Fred said. "And I sure ain't taking him to raise."

The moon was full. Dietrich walked to the Hudson and sat on a bench. In the distance, the George Washington Bridge was draped from shore to shore like a strand of tatty black lace. He stared west toward the vast American continent, could feel it pulling at him. Behind him was the impenetrable city, a curtain of light-spangled darkness and noise. Home-sickness swept over him so strongly he felt ill, and he wept silently, now and again dabbing at tears with his knuckle.

After a time, a man in overcoat and hat sat beside him. Lasserre. He lit a cigarette and handed it to Dietrich, lit another for himself, leaned forward.

"I'll go if you want to be alone," he said.

"No," said Dietrich. "Stay, please."

They sat smoking while a tarpaulin-covered barge sliced the water's surface.

"Of course I must apologize," Dietrich said at last. "I am behaving very badly here. I am not always like this, please believe."

Lasserre waved his hand, kept looking across the river.

"There is a very big land beyond this city," he said.

"Yes," said Dietrich. "One can feel it bearing down. It is a bit frightening."

"Do you ever speak with Krause? He will tell you America is the greatest nation in the world."

Dietrich smiled.

"You, of course," said Lasserre, "love Deutschland."

"*Ja*," said Dietrich. "Very much."

"*Et moi? Pour moi, c'est la France.* At least, it is supposed to be."

"And isn't it?"

Lasserre shook his head. "I have a better country, *mon ami*. And all the nations are as dust in comparison. As dust."

"But your homeland!"

"One thing you must understand about me, Bonhoeffer, and if you grasp it, perhaps we may get along. I am no nationalist. I love France. And sometimes despise it. As I love and despise Germany, and love and despise America. I am a citizen of the Kingdom of God, Bonhoeffer. And one cannot be such a citizen and also a nationalist. *C'est impossible!*"

"But surely we are not required to renounce our—"

"Read the Sermon on the Mount. How can I promote the glory of France before the glory of God? My brothers and sisters are in every country. And how can I love my enemy if I am willing to take up arms and kill him? If I kill a human being, I kill Christ as well."

"I lost a brother in this war," Dietrich said.

"I did not kill him," said Lasserre. "Nor would I even if he leveled a rifle at me. Better to die myself."

"You are a pacifist, then?"

"Yes. That is it. And you, of course, are not."

"No. I doubt I am strong enough for that."

"Then at least," said Lasserre, "we are clear who we are. And whatever we are, Bonhoeffer, we are not enemies."

"No," Dietrich agreed.

"*Bon.*"

Dietrich smiled. "*Gut. Sehr gut.*" He reached inside his coat and took out a pack of cigarettes, handed it to Lasserre. "You were not joking about being a saint."

"No," Lasserre said. "Though I did not mean it to sound so arrogant as perhaps it did. I only meant this is my ideal."

Dietrich shook his head. "I would be content," he said, "if I could have faith."

"You do not have faith now?"

"I have theology. But very little of the sort of faith I witness among my Harlem churchgoers. They seem to feel the presence of God, and I feel nothing. I only think."

They didn't return to the seminary until after midnight, swinging their arms as they mounted the hump of Manhattan to Claremont Avenue. By the time they reached the heavy doors beside the chapel, Dietrich had made up his mind. He turned to Lasserre.

"You know this new film? *All Quiet on the Western Front?* The Remarque novel—"

"Of course, of course. Who does not know of it? In fact, I read the book last year."

"Perhaps we should see it together. Would you be my guest?"

"I should like that," said Lasserre.

They made an afternoon of it on Saturday, riding the bus to Times Square because they were in no hurry and enjoyed looking out the windows instead of speeding through darkened subway tunnels. They lunched in the cavernous dining room of the Algonquin at Dietrich's expense and then strolled to the Mayfair for the late matinee, standing in line beneath the marquee of orange lights, pale on this bright afternoon. Inside, Lasserre bought buttered popcorn and Dietrich, appalled at this even more bizarre form of corn, chose a bar of chocolate. They settled into velvet seats near the front of the packed theater. Lasserre looked around.

"Very popular film," he said.

"Yes," said Dietrich. "A good thing, I hope."

They munched as the lights dimmed. In the film a patriotic schoolmaster incited boys in their jackets and ties to stand on their chairs and howl for blood. Dietrich was enthralled by the images of a German schoolroom so like his own. He did not recall such dramatics, but the warlike sentiments (directed toward the insufferable French) were familiar enough to cause him discomfort. The American accents of the supposedly German soldiers, and their easy American swaggers, disconcerted him even more. The audience laughed as the recruits played tricks on their sergeant, rustled and murmured anxiously as battle approached, grew fearfully quiet.

The French attacked, running in crouched swarms across a no-man's-land strafed by white flashes of machine-gun fire. Men in the front lines were mown down. As more French soldiers fell before the young German heroes, a murmur of approval rolled from the back of the theater. A group of boys in the front row laughed and waved their arms at the flickering white screen.

A French soldier ran toward the audience, gun slung across his back, climbed barbed wire. BOOM! Bloody stumps of hands clung to the wire.

The audience moaned a long thrilling *Oooooo* and applauded.

Dietrich grabbed Lasserre's sleeve. "I cannot bear this. I must leave."

Lasserre nodded. They stood, ignoring the complaints of those behind them, and made their way to the back of the theater. The French had reached the German trenches and men wrestled, thrust bayonets into anonymous bellies. A Frenchman slipped and fell in the mud as he tried to run. The audience laughed.

Outside, Dietrich straightened his tie. He could not speak. Lasserre leaned against a wall warmed by the autumn sun.

"The Americans," he said. "They are so innocent, and so terrible."

My dearest brother, wrote Sabine, *the street fighting grows worse. Contrary to what some might say, it is the Right which provokes most of it, and the Socialists and Communists who fight back, often in defense of their neighborhoods. Nor are the Nazis an uneducated rabble, as Father likes to call them. The coal and steel magnates are reported to be negotiating with Hitler, bankrolling him, Gerhard says. The Nazis' strength grows in the universities as well. It is a terrible time for Gerhard at Göttingen; many of his colleagues at the university wear swastikas on their lapels and have stopped speaking to him. Each night students neglect their studies to don red-and-black armbands and venture into the working-class districts, searching for heads to break. Students, Dietrich! They also set fire to buildings. In one tenement a Jewish woman and her children burned to death, and two Communists were killed when their meeting hall was surrounded last week. When we go to Berlin for a visit, neighbors nod their heads and say, "Yes, yes, but it is good someone is firm with this government or next thing you know they will be expropriating our property. Regrettable the Nazis are so boisterous, but many of them are young, after all." You know the sort of thing.*

A new film has opened, based on the Remarque novel. Do you know it? Wherever it plays a gang of Nazis whistles and stomps and throws smoke bombs until the showing must be canceled. In Munich they even set fire to a screen. One would like to form some opinion about the film, but few theaters will show it now, and under the circumstances it seems best to stay away.

In January, Dietrich and his friends heard Paul Robeson at Carnegie Hall. Robeson was fresh from his London triumph in *Othello* and tickets were hard to come by, but Adam Junior managed it. Robeson stood in a circle of light, alone except for his piano accompanist, yet it seemed to Dietrich the man was an entire orchestra. He sang an impassioned version of "Go Down Moses," switched smoothly to German *Lieder*—"*Gute Ruhe*"— and then swung into a rousing "John Henry." He sang "Old Man River," which the mostly white audience seemed especially to appreciate, although Adam Junior and Fred grimaced at each other when he began it. Dietrich, lost in the music, didn't notice.

Afterward they went back to Pod's and Jerry's on West 133rd for a late supper.

"Wonder if Robeson will come in here," said Fred. "Even he can't get served south of 125th."

"One place in Greenwich Village he can go," Adam Junior corrected. He called for a round of drinks, then raised his glass.

"To Fred," he said.

Fred grimaced.

"Look at him," said Adam Junior. "The man should be happy. Proud. Landed a damn good job for just out of school, not to mention hard times like these."

"What's this?" said Myles. "You haven't told me."

"I'm still thinking on it myself," said Fred.

"You turn this down," said Adam Junior, "my daddy will be seriously put out. Stuck his neck out for you, brother."

"I didn't ask him to!" Fred said sharply. He drank his gin and tonic quickly and called for another, watched the piano player, tapped his foot nervously. "Sorry. I don't like quick decisions."

Adam Junior said, "The man has a call to a church, just waiting for when he gets that degree. Not an assistant, either. Temporary pastor of First Baptist Church in Charleston, West Virginia. One year trial, permanent after that. Biggest Negro church in the state."

"How the hell you get that?" Myles asked.

Fred gritted his teeth. "Dr. Powell grew up near Charleston—"

"—in the boom town of Pratt, West Virginia, named after our own illustrious Pratts of New York," Adam Junior broke in, because he knew it irritated Fred.

"—he grew up with some of the deacons at First Baptist—"

"—who moved into Charleston and became very big noises in the Negro community—"

"—and he spoke up for me." Fred watched the girl singer, who looked no more than fourteen.

"Last fellow they had wasn't so popular," said Adam Junior, "but that's okay. Makes Fred look better. And pastor before that was Mordecai Johnson, now president of Howard University. No way Charleston, West Virginia, is Atlanta, but this is still a church that gets noticed." He put his hand on Fred's shoulder. "Could be this man's ticket to anywhere."

"Nowhere that Mavis will go." Fred gulped his drink.

Myles said, "Mavis wouldn't go up Lenox Avenue with you, buddy. You got to forget that."

Adam Junior nodded. "Listen to him," he said. "Mavis likes *café au lait* and cash. Neither of which spells Fred Bishop."

"Spells Adam Clayton Powell," Fred said. Said it bitterly.

Adam Junior shrugged and lit a cigar. "If I was interested," he said.

Dietrich and Lasserre only half listened. The conversation meant little to them. Lasserre had his place waiting in Bruay, and a fiancée. Dietrich possessed his name and his scholarly credentials. He could choose any university in Europe, but he would go home to Berlin, and gladly.

Myles was saying, "West Virginia. You won't be that far from me."

"Like I want to hang out with you the rest of my life," said Fred.

Myles squinted at him. "If I hadn't known you for three years—" he said.

"Damn it!" Fred's fist crashed onto the table, spilling the drinks. "Don't put this on me!"

Dietrich and Lasserre started, glanced at each other.

"You can't stand success," said Adam Junior. "You'd be happier out on the streets, riding the rails. Piss your daddy so it would please you, wouldn't it?"

"Don't be stupid. And don't bring my father into this."

"Scares you to death, doesn't he?"

"You can't talk, man. You jumped when Dr. Powell said jump. Gave up every dream you ever had."

"Dreams are cheap, living's expensive." Adam Junior leaned over the table. "And tell you something. Not so scared of my daddy I stay away from Pod's and Jerry's. Not so scared I won't go to the Savoy tonight. What about you?"

Fred stubbed out his cigarette, killed his drink.

"Hell," he said. "Let's go."

Lasserre declared himself too tired, and returned to the seminary. The others piled into a taxi, which careered up Lenox as though already anticipating the next fare. Everyone was pleasantly tipsy, so the passing lights and crowds were a moving carnival—long tubes of purple and green and red, flashes of dark faces waving arms white smiles. At 140th they climbed out and waited while Adam Junior pumped the cabby's hand and dropped a sizable tip along with his name. While they waited, the Savoy's blinking marquee dared them to enter the

!!!!! BATTLE OF RHYTHM !!!!!
FESS WILLIAMS
AND HIS ROYAL FLUSH ORCHESTRA
— vs —
CHICK WEBB
AND HIS ORCHESTRA
Stomp Music

They swaggered. Even Dietrich, breath white in the cold air and blood warmed by the gin and the muffled throb of the bands inside the hall. They paid their six bits and broke through a wall of cold into pulsing warmth. Crossed thick carpet beneath tiered chandeliers, passed couples lounging on settees drinks in hand, passed the marble and polished brass battlements of the soda fountain. The dance floor loomed, red and green and blue lights slashing across the polished maple, legs of the dancers disjointed and jittery. The bands faced off at either end, Royal Flush in full swing, trombones poking the ceiling, while Chick Webb's band rested, wiped their faces with handkerchiefs, whispered among themselves, nodded their heads.

To Dietrich the air seemed bright with metal, showy as the trumpets and saxophones, sharp sound that pricked every part of him. He felt jumpy and his fingertips tingled.

Adam Junior headed for the Cats Corner close by the band where the best dancers gathered. Fred started to follow, then remembered he had guests. He stopped and gave Myles a pleading look, then said to Dietrich, "You want to hang with Myles here? He never dances anyway."

Dietrich was disappointed. "You do not dance?" he asked Myles.

"Naw," said Myles. "Fall over my own feet."

"I never saw a hillbilly could dance," said Fred, "except for that up-and-down thing you do."

"Buck dancing," said Myles.

"Whatever. They don't do it here, that's for sure." He kept looking around for Mavis. Last thing he needed tonight was to see her on the arm of some conk-haired bastard flashing a bankroll.

"'Course you know," Myles was saying, peering hard at Fred, "this is a place to have fun, not fret about your talent." Stepped closer and spoke softly. "The man wants to dance."

"Got my eye on Gloria Hill," said Fred, patting Myles on the shoulder, "and she isn't free that often. Maybe later. I'll think of something."

"Sure," said Myles.

Couples were grabbing each other by the arms, kicking their legs out, slinging each other back and forth so hard if one let go the other would be thrown into space. Dietrich and Myles leaned against the wall, hands in their pockets, watching.

"I would very much like to try that," said Dietrich. "Fred has promised to bring me here all year now and I have been looking forward, yet this is the first time."

"Ask someone to dance," said Myles.

"It must be someone who will teach me."

Dietrich looked around. Three girls, arm in arm, watched the dancers and giggled.

"One of those?" he asked.

"Why not?" said Myles. "I reckon they'd like to be out there too."

"They are very young."

"What's the difference? It's just a dance."

They didn't notice him until he was bearing down on them. Then they looked him up and down in two seconds, tweed jacket, thinning hair, round wire glasses that should have been a monocle, broad tight lips. Asking in his strong German accent, "Vould either of you vant to dance? But you must show me first how to do it."

They drew closer together. The one in the middle grabbed her friends' arms. "You see that Dracula movie? Listen to this cat. It's Bela Lugosi!"

They dissolved into giggles behind their hands and moved away, supporting one another as though they might fall over if they let go.

Hurt, he shrank back toward Myles, who pretended he hadn't heard. The Royal Flush stepped down for their break, and Chick Webb's bunch took out their instruments, pulled off mouthpieces, blew into them, wiped them with white cloths, and pushed them back on with the palms of their hands.

Myles tried to make small talk. "Ever smell a used clarinet reed? Stinks to high heaven. Wonder how they can stand it." Dietrich said his brother Karl-Friedrich's wife was quite accomplished on the oboe. He studied his fingernails, fighting off the familiar melancholy.

Myles said, "Wait here just a minute," and went in search of Fred and Adam Junior, who, flushed and relaxed from dancing, were returning from the back-room bar. Myles blocked their way.

"The man still wants to dance," he said. He nodded over at Dietrich, slumped against the far wall. "And he's got his feelings hurt, turned down by some kids."

Adam Junior lit a cigar. "Tell you what, Fred. I bet you five dollars you can't find a woman who'll dance with Bonhoeffer."

Fred had been thinking. "Naw," he said. "I already got an idea. Yolanda Pinkard is here."

They all noticed Yolanda then, sitting with a girlfriend at a corner table nursing her drink. Yolanda, who had a crush on Fred, was four foot ten, packed solid, and homely, so she was seldom asked to dance. Which was a shame, because she could move and was lots of fun. With a different body, Yolanda would have cut a rug in Cats Corner every night.

Fred, close to thoroughly drunk, pointed his newly replenished glass of gin toward Yolanda. "Woman," he drawled, "will dance with the man if I ask her to. Will look after Bonhoeffer the rest of the night if I ask her to. No question. Can't take your money under those conditions, wouldn't be fair."

But Adam Junior, also feeling very fine, was in a wagering mood. He dug into his pocket and took out his wallet, fluttered three limp greengray bills.

"Okay then. Thirty dollars says she can't get him to Cats Corner."

"Come on!" Myles scoffed. "That's way too much to just be throwing around."

Adam Junior waved his arm. "Just offering. Don't have to take it."

"You'll lose it, Fred," said Myles, "and you don't have it."

"I got it," Fred said. "Got it in my hip pocket. My daddy sent it to me. Said I should buy a good summer suit for my first Sunday at my new church."

"Well, if you want to get rid of it, go outside and give it to some poor sonofabitch on the street—"

"Hey! I already got one daddy. Okay?"

Myles raised his hands. "Okay," he said. "Forget I said anything."

Fred looked over at Dietrich, who was watching them, pointed a finger at the dance floor, turned his palms up in a question. Dietrich stood away from the wall and nodded eagerly.

Fred held up one hand, palm out. He said to Adam Junior in an affected German accent, "*I varn you—he is the best dancer of his family!*"—Then he went to talk to Yolanda Pinkard. She played tough at first, looked Dietrich over from a distance and nearly choked on her drink.

"You kidding! White boy with a poker up his ass?"

"Take him off in the corner," said Fred. "Practice a little."

"Aw, Freddie! Why can't I dance with you?"

"Half the money I win is yours, and you don't put up anything."

"So what! You ain't winning no money."

He leaned close. "He's never done this before. But I've seen the man move. Show him the steps, Yolanda."

She sighed and looked at her girlfriend, who shrugged and sucked her cigarette.

"Oh. Awlllll right."

She flounced over, took Dietrich by the hand, and led him to the lobby, past the bouncers, large, soft-spoken, and gentle in their tuxedos, past hostesses in long pastel gowns carrying trays of swaying amber drinks. Behind them Chick Webb's band burst into full flower. Dietrich looked back eagerly.

"Come on, honey," Yolanda said impatiently. "Fred says I got to show you some things."

"Oh yes. I want very much to learn this *swing*."

Yolanda rolled her eyes and stuck out her hand.

They forgot Dietrich. Drank some more and danced some more. Ordered a platter of boiled shrimp and cocktail sauce studded with horseradish.

Gloria Hill rested her hand on Fred's arm. The Royal Flush was back onstage, drummer leaning close over his traps, barely moving and yet thundering. Adam Junior noticed a crowd gathered near the bandstand.

"What's that?" he said.

The drummer was solo now, back and forth, side to side. Above the drums a woman's voice—*one two three four now get ready* GO.

Myles caught a glimpse as more people moved toward the bandstand. "Oh Lord," he said. "You won't believe."

They pushed their way through the clapping laughing crowd just in time to see Dietrich throw Yolanda over his shoulder. She landed square, big legs apart knees bent arms out. A necessary hesitation, then they crouched and shimmied and were in each other's arms again, Dietrich slinging her this way and that, kicking his legs straight, not graceful or fluid but vigorous. Intense, a vertical furrow between his eyebrows, cheeks pooched out. Counting. Saw the others as he flipped around, arm extended, and broke for a moment into a radiant smile, then concentrating again, mouth moving. They cheered when he threw Yolanda again and pulled her back, bulk to bulk.

"Jesus H. Christ," said Adam Junior. He dug in his pocket.

And Fred for some reason he was too drunk to figure out wanted to rush the dance floor and gather Dietrich into a great hug. The song ended and Dietrich slid Yolanda between his legs, lost hold of her with his sweaty hands as he tried to pull her back. She went skittering on her back across the polished maple floor, skirt up to her waist and a big smile on her face.

Gratias agimus tibi
propter magnam
gloriam tuam

We give thee thanks
We praise thee for thy glory

The White Tunnel
1931

SABINE. IT IS PROBABLY NO GOOD *sending this letter, as I am on board the* Bremen, *and may arrive home before the post. But I must get my thoughts on paper. We are off the coast of Newfoundland, near the place, I am told, where the Titanic sank. I fancy I can see lights beneath the dark water, hear the screams and alarms. Hear even the flight of souls. It gives one pause, especially when making even the most likely assumptions about safe passage.*

My thoughts turn in such a direction because of what I have experienced this past year, and especially the last month, in the America I am leaving. When I came aboard ship my professor Reinhold Niebuhr was on the dock to see me off. He told me I was a greatly changed man from the one he first met, and joked with me in his forthright way about my "conversion" to his point of view with regard to theology and society. But it is much more than that, Sabine, much more, though a conversion to be sure.

I am lying on my bunk with the porthole open to the warm sea air. Though you are so far away, I feel you close at this moment, as though we were back in our beds in the Wangenheimstraße, trying to guess each other's thoughts through the wall that divided our rooms and then hanging out our windows above the garden, whispering back and forth to see if we'd got it right.

I did write last month to tell you of my plans for the end of the school term, how I would travel to Mexico and back to New York through the American South with my fellow exchange student Jean Lasserre. You would have laughed to see me in a rattletrap Oldsmobile that must be fed a can of oil every hundred miles, in the company of a French pacifist who wants to be a saint. In addition, I was reading Dostoevsky. All this together was a bit surreal.

The flatness of the Deep South affected me strangely. The landscape is much like our mother's ancestral Prussia, and so seemed familiar. But in June Prussia would still know cool nights and damp, breezy days. In the American South, the heat rose in waves to distort the distant horizon like some troubled dream. Breathing was quite difficult. The Fatherland seemed very far away, and very comfortable.

Although I have read a week-old copy of the Börsen Zeitung *on board ship,
Sabine . . .*

On their way back from Mexico, Dietrich and Lasserre met Myles Horton outside Knoxville. Lasserre was to go on to the Kentucky coalfields,
where Myles had gone to work after graduation, and Dietrich would drive
on alone to Fred's new home in West Virginia. For their last night together
they pitched tents in the foothills of the Smoky Mountains. Fireflies—
"lightning bugs," Myles called them—were so plentiful they lit the night
air like the stars on a Van Gogh canvas. The air was cool and smelled of
fresh water and honeysuckle. They ate bacon, potatoes, and onions for
their supper, and a corn pone Myles baked in the hot coals. Then they
stretched full-length on the ground to smoke and watch the stars. Myles
was unusually quiet, and his face was drawn and pale.

"Tell Myles about Louisiana," Dietrich said to Lasserre.

"*Mon dieu!* Louisiana!" Lasserre sat up. "We stopped outside Shreveport
to spend the night. We had just set up our tent when a police car arrived.
A very large officer asked us our business and we explained we were touring the countryside. He informed us we were in fact Communist agitators
and should—how did he say—move our Red asses back North or pay the
price. His hand rested on the butt of his pistol the entire time. Tell me,
what had we done?"

Myles said, "Between your accents and your New York license plate, I
reckon that was sufficient. There's a big push to organize the woodcutters
and sawmills down there. They'd be checking anybody from outside. I'd say
you were lucky."

"It is crazy," said Lasserre.

"And these Scottsboro Boys," Dietrich added. "It seems Southern white
people will enjoy hanging them. And yet the churches preach against alcohol and bad language."

"Don't pull any European superiority on me," Myles said. "You burned
some folks in your time."

They fell silent, pondering the anger in his voice. Then Dietrich said,
"We stayed with Fred's father in Birmingham. He reminded me of my own
father. A man who knows he is a leader in his community. He's proud of
Fred, although it wasn't easy for him to show it."

Myles said nothing.

"What's wrong?" Dietrich asked.

Myles pulled his cloth cap over his eyes. He said, "Got a puzzler for you
boys. Especially you, Lasserre, since you're a pacifist. Pretend like it's ethics
seminar."

"All right," Lasserre said.

"Here it is. Take a coal town, like where you live in France. The miners are on strike and the president of the local union is your buddy. He's well liked in the community, and he gets called on a lot to speak out about what's going on.

"Now, the company has hired gunmen, and they're heard claiming they'll kill this union man. So he moves out of his house to try to keep his family out of it. People guard him, but nobody can be protected twenty-four hours a day. Not forever. And he won't back down, won't hide. Says he has to stay involved with the strike. So you know it's just a matter of time.

"You also know who these gunmen are. They walk around with their pistols in their belts like old-time cowboys. Everyone knows where they stay. So do you ambush them? Kill them first so they won't kill your buddy?"

"Violence is never the answer," Lasserre said.

Myles sat up suddenly, plucked a smoldering stick from the fire, and flung it, a fiery wheel, into the night. "Damn it, Jean, that's just what I thought you'd say! Think about it for two seconds first, why don't you!"

"Do you imagine I don't agonize over such questions?" Lasserre said, sounding hurt.

Myles leaned forward until his forehead rested on his knees. He said, "I've been back in the coal fields a month. First week back I went to Tennessee to visit the place I worked last summer. They'd just found out the thugs were gunning for Barney. Everyone was asking me what I thought they should do. 'You been studying on what's right and wrong,' they said, like seminary prepares you for this. 'You say it's okay,' they said, 'we'll shoot the sonsofbitches tomorrow morning.' I thought about it all night. Tried to figure what would Reinie say. What you would say. Next morning I told them if they shot these three, there'd just be three new ones come in. And they'd take it on theirselves to shoot a few more miners, and hang people for murder besides. I said you don't just walk up and shoot a man because you think he might do something first. And I said they might be bluffing, trying to scare Barney. And Barney, who'd been real quiet, said, 'Myles is right. We can't kill 'em in cold blood.'"

Myles lay back down and turned on his side.

"And?" Dietrich asked.

"And. Two days ago they shot Barney in the back while he was walking down the street."

"Mon dieu," Lasserre whispered.

"Yeah," Myles said. "I traded three gun thugs for Barney. Three human beings for one, so if arithmetic's all that counts, I did right. Although I suppose I should figure Barney's wife and kids in there somewhere. You still want to come with me, Jean? You could always go with Dietrich there to visit Fred instead. Good old Fred. I can just see him now, sitting in his new office planning Bible studies for the Ladies' Sewing Circle. But at least Fred hasn't got anybody killed."

"What could you have done?" Dietrich asked. "Could you have been the one to shoot those guards?"

"No," Myles said. "Not then."

"Then how advise someone else to do it? You mustn't punish yourself. You did what any of us would have done."

The next morning Lasserre left with Myles, hitchhiking north, wearing the look of a man soon to confront a challenge to all he holds sacred. Dietrich drove on alone toward West Virginia and Fred, reproaching himself for his very safe life and yet glad he was not going with them.

Charleston's situation between emerald-green hills and broad river reminded Dietrich of towns he had known in German river valleys, on the Neckar or Rhine. It was a working river with towboats and barges loaded with coal and sternwheelers stroking the water, taking their time. The streets of the town were narrow but lined with handsome buildings of brick and stone. Dietrich's only unfavorable initial impression was the stink that blew in from the chemical plant downriver.

Fred took Dietrich to dinner at the Ferguson, a "colored" hotel one block from his new parsonage. They sat at a round table with a white cloth and pink flower vase and stuffed themselves with roast beef and blackberry cobbler.

"Wish I could take you in the back to the Alhambra Club," Fred said, "and sip mountain-grown whiskey, but if someone from the church heard I was there, that would be it. Count Basie played back there two weeks ago and I was afraid to go to that too."

"You must miss Harlem," Dietrich said, "and the freedom you had there."

"Oh yeah. And I miss Mavis—or at least, the dream of Mavis. Or the notion I've had for years of going off someplace where nobody knows me and I can be totally free. Which I thought would happen when I got away from my father, but I know now it's impossible when you are the minister of a church. I don't care what kind of dictatorship you live under, you got more freedom than a preacher."

"Didn't you expect that? You grew up a preacher's son."

"Yeah, but it's different to expect it and to be in the middle of it. And there's more than just the expectations. I recall that first dinner we had together at Craig's. Telling you I had a call. Told that to the deacons here at First Baptist too, when I came for my interview. Every time I say it now, I know it's a load of crap. A call can be what any poor fool thinks God or the Devil is telling him to do. Voices inside your head. How do you tell who's holy and who's possessed by demons and who's just plain crazy?"

"I don't know," Dietrich said. "I've never felt such a call. When I decided to study theology, it was because that's what I wanted."

Fred was shaking his head. "Knew it was wrong," he said, "moment they ordained me. First time somebody called me Reverend. Knew it was wrong. Must be like when people getting married say 'I do' and know right then they should walk away instead."

"Perhaps," said Dietrich, holding his cigarette between two fingers, "everyone feels like walking away at such times."

"Not like this. I want to run."

"How long have you been here?" Dietrich said. "Just five weeks. It needs time."

Fred nodded. "Maybe. But all I can think is, I have not been me since I came here and was ordained. Not me at all. An actor, somebody answering to the name of the Rev. Albert Frederick Bishop, but not me."

Dietrich listened, his big face puckered with concern. "Have you made friends?" he asked.

"A few. Can't really be friends with anyone in the congregation. Can't get too close, you know? I mean, I'm already under their magnifying glass."

"Who are these friends?"

"Well, only one, actually. A doctor, older guy who never even comes to church. Got an office around the corner. Quiet man, but the things he's seen, mmm." Fred told Dietrich about Dr. Booker, a Socialist who had worked for years in the southern part of the state, where he had been in some big coal strikes. "Lot like where Myles is. I wish old Myles was here to meet Doc Booker. He'd love the old sonofabitch." Then he grew solemn. "Actually, there's a story attached to this, a kind of scary one. I've been wanting to tell it to you."

Dietrich folded his napkin neatly and said, "Let's go back to your house and I shall unpack my suitcase while you tell me more. I have a present for you from Mexico."

They strolled through a darkblue June evening cooled by breezes from the nearby hollows, past "the church," as Fred called it—he couldn't yet say "my church"—a miniature stone cathedral across Washington Street. The parsonage was a block away up Shrewsbury. Fred pointed out Doc Booker's office above the M&S Pharmacy. The shades were drawn at the upstairs windows and no lights showed.

The parsonage was a large wood-frame house with room enough for a man with a wife and several children. Fred rattled around in it, had only collected enough furnishings for the parlor and one bedroom. The church women who took turns cleaning for him would tsk-tsk about the empty rooms and bare walls, hint that the new pastor was in desperate need of a wife, and of course each of them had a daughter, sister, niece. . . .

Fred had brought in a second bed and spare sheets when he learned Dietrich was coming. The guestroom didn't have another piece of furniture, so Dietrich knelt and opened his suitcase on the floor. Even though he'd been traveling for weeks, all his clothes were pressed and folded as neatly as if they were new, and Fred couldn't help but think that Dietrich was the one who would make a good wife.

He took a carton from the bottom of his suitcase, opened it, and handed Fred a large bottle of mescal with a fat white worm in the bottom.

"Jesus Christ," Fred said. "How'd you get that through customs?"

Dietrich smiled. "I pretended very great ignorance of American language and American Prohibition. And then I bribed the guard."

"Hey, those suckers are mean down in Texas. They could have locked you away."

Dietrich's smile widened. "It was a very large bribe, and I had a bottle for him too."

"I better appreciate this, what you're telling me."

He shrugged, said, "It's for me as well. Get some glasses."

When Fred was downstairs washing two of the three glasses he owned, there was a knock at the door. He opened it to Doc Booker. Fred stood aside and motioned for him to enter, but Doc waved him off.

"I won't come in," he said. "I know you've got company."

"How do you know I've got company?"

"Everybody in the neighborhood knows there's a white man staying at the parsonage."

"You been gone," Fred said testily. "How do you know?"

"Been back an hour," the old man said. "One of the first things I heard."

Fred cursed under his breath.

"Get used to it," said Doc. "Like I told you before. You may have only been here a little while, but right now you're one of the most influential men in this community. That's why we got to talk."

"Did Earl Harvey come back with you? Was he telling the truth?"

"Earl's back, all right. And let's just say he ain't so crazy as some folks think. I'll tell you about it after your company's gone home."

"He's staying all week," Fred said. "You want to wait that long?"

Dr. Booker thought a minute. "No. This won't keep that long. You mind?"

"No. Actually, this is a friend from the seminary. German guy. I'd be glad for him to hear what you got to say. I wouldn't mind some advice."

"All right," Doc said. "But it's late. I'll let you be tonight. I promised Earl a cheeseburger and fries tomorrow. We'll meet you at the M&S at noon."

"Right," Fred said. He shut the door and went back to the kitchen thinking how badly he needed a drink.

They sat up late sipping mescal and lemon slices out of tall iced tea glasses because there was no way to keep shot glasses around a parsonage.

Fred said, "This is how I met Doc Booker. I'd been here three weeks. Preached my sermons, spent the rest of my time visiting people at home. I used to enjoy that in Harlem, but not here."

"Why?" asked Dietrich.

"Because I'm not visiting out of concern for them. I'm presenting myself for inspection like a side of beef. Over and over. I come back here after a visit, stuffed full of somebody's fried chicken or ham, and I throw up. Stomach churns now every time I walk across a strange threshold.

"Anyway. Doc Booker found me at the church one day. I'll show you the office tomorrow. It's nice, big desk, dark oak bookcases. Window looks out on a little garden with a birdbath at the side of the church. Flowers. Blue jays and robins hang around. I look out the window a lot.

"I saw Doc out the window first. Dark man with hair like a curly white helmet. Old gray suit too hot for this weather, red tie. He was fanning himself with his hat and looking up at the window like he could see me, but I sensed he couldn't. I stepped back from the window.

"He came on up, heavy on the stairs, slow and steady like there was no way to keep him out. Stood in the door, hat in hand, looking me over.

"'I heard you were young,' he said.

"I said, 'That right?'

"'You went to a white school,' he said. 'Reckon that impressed them. Otherwise . . .'

"I knew a polite young minister should be making over this guy, shaking hands, inviting him to church. But something held me back. Riled, I guess, at the way he challenged me, like he was seeing if I measured up to something.

"I said, 'How come you know so much?'

"'Evenings, I sit under an awning on Shrewsbury Street and play checkers,' he said. 'Not to mention looking after sick people in the neighborhood. Not much goes on I don't know.'

"He stepped closer then and stuck out his hand.

"'Dr. Toussaint Booker. Folks call me Doc. And you're the Rev. Albert Bishop.'

"Instead of answering I said, 'I haven't seen you around. You don't go to First Baptist?'

"'Don't go anywhere,' he said. 'Used to be very religious in the coal camps until I saw what I saw. Now I'm an atheist.'

"'Good,' I said.

"He raised his eyebrows.

"'I'm glad to find one person in this town who'll call me Fred instead of Reverend or Preacher,' I said.

"He laughed. 'Don't worry,' he said, 'you'll find plenty of white people here call you by your first name. Call you boy too, if you want that.'

"'You know what I mean,' I said.

"'I know,' he said.

"Long story short, I liked him, in a way. I think he liked me. In a way. Went to lunch with him, walked on over to his house and noticed how everybody we passed spoke to him. We sat on his porch with a pitcher of iced tea. Then he told me what he wanted and I wished I'd never set eyes on him.

"I'll try to explain it quick as I can. There's a chemical plant outside town. You'll smell it—it stinks in the mornings. Same company has a plant upriver, ferro-alloys they call what it makes. Kind of a mill with the big blast furnaces and vats of molten metal, and eats a lot of electricity. And this big river out here, it comes from up in the mountains. Drops so many feet in just a few miles, fast strong river with lots of rapids. Haven't seen that part myself, but Doc told me all this. At one point about thirty miles from here, just before it levels out and slows down, the river makes a big loop. So the company has this idea to drill a tunnel straight through the mountain. Greatest engineering feat in the world, they're calling it. When they're done, river will change course, rush through that tunnel, and make electricity. However they do it. I try not to think about stuff like that, makes me dizzy.

"Anyway, they're drilling the tunnel now, been at it a year. Mostly black men working inside, but they got some white men from the hills around there too. Pulling people off the breadlines in Charlotte and Winston-Salem and Durham and putting them on trains bound for Hawks Nest. And keep looking for more, because word Doc's been getting, they're dying like flies up there."

Dietrich had gone very still.

"How are they dying?" he asked.

"Don't know. Even Doc didn't know for sure, last we talked. All he knew was fellow name of Earl Harvey who rides the rails a lot has been up there and says so. This Earl has a reputation for being kind of crazy. Only saw him once myself, but I can vouch he's strange. Called Doc on somebody's telephone, said there are skeletons walking at Hawks Nest. Dead men walking at Hawks Nest. And said they need a doctor. Then there was yelling in the background and somebody cut him off." Fred poured himself another shot of mescal. "So Doc went up to check it out and see if Earl was okay. Now they're both in town and Doc wants me to meet them tomorrow."

"And you're frightened."

"Hell, yes. The man wants to drag me into this. Whatever it is. Wouldn't you be scared?"

"Yes," Dietrich said.

Fred tossed down the shot from the far end of the tea glass. "Walking skeletons, shit. Not even like Reinie's seminar in ethics, is it?"

"No," Dietrich said, as though concentrating very hard. "Nothing like it." Then, "What does this doctor want from you?"

"I think he wants me to go up there with him, then come back and tell people what we find out."

Dietrich nodded.

"Will you go with me?"

He looked toward the window, but Fred had drawn the shades so no one outside could see them drinking.

"*Ja*," he said.

After breakfast, Fred took Dietrich to the church. He read some James Weldon Johnson while Fred worked on his sermon for Sunday, then they went to lunch. Earl Harvey and Doc waited at the corner of Washington Street, surrounded by a small group of white men in shirtsleeves and ties. Earl was considered a local curiosity because in addition to being strange he was a mathematical genius. The white men called him Lightning, because he could think so fast, and were always trying to get him to perform. Like the trained horses that count by scraping their hooves in the dirt, Fred explained bitterly to Dietrich. When they drew closer they heard a white man saying, "Come on, Lightning. Bob here is from Cincinnati and he's never seen you before. Tell him how many bricks are in this side of the Ferguson."

Doc Booker had Earl by the sleeve as though he was trying to get away from the white men, but Earl struck a pose for Bob, who had a bald head and red hair that stuck out above each ear. Earl squinted at the brick wall of the hotel. He was a natural squinter, with a narrow face, a nose that seemed always wrinkled as though he was sniffing something unpleasant, and a deep vertical furrow between his wide-set eyes. He swung around and fixed an eye on Bob, who took a step back.

"One hundred seventy-two thousand, four hundred fifty-eight!" he snapped. "Would be two hundred sixty-four thousand one hundred fifty-two if it wasn't for the windows."

Bob looked at the hotel, then back at Earl. Mopped beads of sweat from his forehead with his handkerchief, because it was a hot day. Then a suspicious look crossed his face. "How I know you didn't just make that up?" he demanded.

Earl glared at him. "Count it yourself!"

Bob flushed pink, the local white men hooted, and Earl bobbed his head. His head was always bobbing up and down, especially when he directed traffic, which he did whenever he got a chance, standing in the middle of the intersection at Washington and Brooks waving his arms and swiveling his hips until the police ran him off.

Doc saw Fred and Dietrich. He said, "Excuse us, we got business to tend to."

"Aw," a fat white man said, "come on, Lightning! Do us some figures."

"Don't call me Lightning!" Earl yelled, head still bobbing. "Name is Earl! Earl! I ain't crazy, don't call me no crazy name!"

The white men laughed. Earl let Doc lead him down the street. A white man yelled out, "Cube root of one million, seven hundred and seventy-one thousand, five hundred and sixty-one."

"One hundred twenty-one!" Earl yelled back. Doc gained a firm grip on him and pulled him along. Earl had a long, swooping gait that was close to a limp.

Fred and Dietrich caught up to them outside the M&S and Fred whispered to Doc, "Was he right?"

"Earl," Doc said, "were you ragging that man?"

"I made up the bricks," said Earl. "I can do bricks, but I get tired of bricks. All they ask is bricks."

Dietrich asked, "What of the cube root?"

Earl just looked through Dietrich as though he weren't there. He said, "Doc, I'm hungry."

"Go on in, Earl," said Doc. Earl pushed open the screen door and was sprawled in a booth and playing with the salt shaker before the others could move. Doc shook his head and said, "Earl never misses a cube or square root. I know because I've tested him. Yet the man can't count out change. Can't read or write either."

"What I want to know," Fred said, "is can he tell the difference between a walking dead man and a figment of his imagination?"

Doc looked around cautiously. "Come on sit down," he said. "We'll eat first."

Several days later, Dietrich lurked among warehouses with Fred, Doc Booker, and Earl Harvey, all of them dressed like hoboes, waiting to hop a train. They passed through banks of fog, for the cool night air after a hot day caused the river to sizzle and steam like a teakettle. As the locomotive trundled toward the crossing, striped bars descended in the glow of pulsing light that smeared the wet pavement a smoky red. The train was moving slowly. After a string of maroon passenger cars, a lantern dangled from a hand that hung from the caboose window. They clambered on board, hanging from the gritty railing until they could haul themselves onto the narrow platform.

A man in a uniform with the insignia of the New York Central Railway opened the door to them. The train was picking up speed, and they stumbled inside as the caboose swung around a curve. The conductor said his name was Joe, told them to sit on a pair of unmade cots, and shook their hands, except for Doc, whom he punched lightly in the arm, saying, "Told you we'd get you, didn't I?" He handed around scalding coffee in chipped, greasy cups, said he'd warn them when Gauley Bridge was near.

"We'll be slow enough?" Doc Booker asked.

"Slow enough to climb on, wasn't it?"

"Tell Calvin thanks. And you too."

"Ain't nothing." The conductor disappeared through a wooden door scored with curlicues carved by a penknife.

Fred tried to sip the hot coffee, but the caboose lurched and he burned his upper lip. He grabbed the edge of a battered desk to keep from toppling over and knocked off a stack of papers. Everywhere there was clutter, untidy stacks of ink-smeared forms that hid the desktop, piles of rumpled clothes in the corner, a hot plate and skillet crusted with the remains of scrambled eggs.

"We could have bought a ticket," Fred said.

"No. I don't want anybody to see us stepping out of a passenger car." Doc Booker sipped his coffee. "Anybody know where we're going?"

"No. You acted like this was some big secret, so I didn't say a word to anybody at church."

Dietrich asked, "Why are we so careful?"

"Let me put it this way," said Doc Booker. "Me and Earl and Fred don't mean a thing to white people, and if they think we're poking our noses where they don't belong, watch out. A few Negroes disappear, nobody asks questions. How you think all these people dying at this tunnel and nobody raised hell yet? On the other hand, nobody pays much mind to hoboes these days. They think we're just after work at the tunnel, or passing through, then they'll leave us alone. So danger depends on what they see when they look at us. They see a doctor and a preacher and a white man being nosy, we're in trouble. They see three shiftless niggers and a piece of poor white trash, that's safer. Unless we're just unlucky."

"And if in danger," Dietrich asked, "from whom?"

"You tell me who," Doc Booker said. "Du Pont providing the explosives.

Westinghouse building the dam and the turbines at the power station. Ingersoll-Rand planning the tunnel and Rinehart and Dennis overseeing construction. All of them working for Union Carbide and Carbon Corporation. And who are all those companies? Wealthy, respected men. Churchgoing men. Pillars of their communities. Not a one that would harm a hair on our heads. Don't even notice themselves. Don't even be troubled, else they might feel bad. So who wants to be a colored man accusing them of murder?"

Fred poured another round of coffee from a fresh pot. Doc Booker took a flask from his pocket and added a shot to three of the cups. Earl Harvey crouched on the end of a cot, knees drawn up to his chin. He began to rock back and forth, said, "Not me. Don't drink. I'm going to heaven."

"Right," said Fred. He moved to the cot, huddled close to Dietrich, and whispered, "Wake me up, man. Wake me up and let me be back on Broadway."

They shut their eyes and tried to nap.

The train slowed to a crawl half a mile before Gauley Bridge, and they jumped off. Fred slipped and fell on the loose gravel beside the track, scraping his knee, but scrambled up at once. They walked the track with stiff legs and a reluctant, awkward gait, pulled along by the receding lights of the caboose. Dietrich stumbled. They trudged on in silence and stopped by the riverbank just before dawn, when the sky thickened even as it grew lighter. Doc Booker opened his pack and passed around fried egg sandwiches. Two men passed them in the gray stillness with scarcely a glance.

"Should we be laying low?" Fred asked.

"No need now we're off the train. People are used to hoboes. Suffocated with hoboes."

Dietrich chewed his fried egg sandwich slowly, savoring the crackly brown at the edge of the white. To be hungry and to eat an egg under trying circumstances brought back memories of childhood during the war, when eggs were so scarce they were saved for birthdays. Dietrich had such a craving then for eggs that he hoarded his pfennigs until he could buy a hen to share with the family. The family, he thought. Two weeks from this moment I shall be in Berlin.

The river emerged in the gray light. It was broad as a small lake, scored by ragged falls and islands spiked with trees. Fog sprites danced across the milky surface. The green wall of mountain beyond seemed to move closer as if borne on the water. Dietrich was reminded of the Thuringian valleys he had hiked with Sabine. Or at least it was like a Thuringian valley if all that was comfortable and German was stripped from it, and only the land remained. His head swam from lack of sleep, so he shut his eyes and thought again of Germany. His chin dropped to his chest and he was there.

Then he saw peasants crossing a field, wooden clogs breaking through crusts of ice, as sharp as gunfire.

He shook his head to clear it and brushed crumbs from the bib of his jeans. Doc Booker had provided his clothes, faded cotton shirt and denim overalls held up by copper-reinforced straps that chafed his shoulders. He kept plucking at the stiff, unfamiliar material and shrugging to adjust the straps. It was already so warm his face was moist beneath his glasses. He took them off and wiped them on his sleeve.

Fred said, "You need those to see?"

"I use them for distance," Dietrich said.

"You better take them off. They don't look like the kind of thing a tramp would wear."

Dietrich folded the thin gold frames carefully and put them in the breast pocket of his shirt, beneath the overall bib. It depressed him to hide them, as though he were putting away the last piece of his old self.

Doc Booker was watching him. "Know what I think? You better pretend like you can't talk."

"Why?"

"Look here. You'll call attention anyway, being a white man with us. You got a strange accent, very stiff. Nothing like American. If you pretend you can't talk, you won't stand out so much."

"Good idea," said Fred. "That's even an excuse to be hanging around us. We'll say you needed help and we took you in. You and Earl. Looking after you."

Earl said, "Why you say that? I don't need nobody taking me in. I get by all right."

"Sure," Fred said impatiently.

"You do fine," Doc Booker said more gently. "We wouldn't be here without you, Earl."

"Damn straight," said Earl. He rocked back and forth, fingernails digging into his knees.

"So here we are," Fred said, "thanks to Earl. What the hell do we do now?"

"Don't cuss," said Earl.

"You cussed! You said damn!"

"That's different. You a preacher. But you the least preacher-acting thing I ever did see."

"Is that so? How's a preacher supposed to act?"

"You supposed to be nice to peoples. Help 'em out. Act all the time like you in church."

Fred waved his arm. "I don't see any church around here, Earl. I don't see any church."

Dietrich noticed Fred's overalls were torn at the knee, where he had fallen, and the skin was scraped and bleeding. Fred had turned his back and was looking out over the river. "Can we get on with this?" he said softly.

They followed the riverbank past the cluster of six or seven brick and wood buildings that were the entirety of downtown Gauley Bridge. A small hotel. A drugstore. Grocery. Five-and-ten. A restaurant called the Grill, because everything on the menu would be fried on a grease-spattered sheet of hot metal. They crossed a stone bridge over a smaller stream. "This," Doc Booker said, "is where the Gauley joins the New. Where the big river starts. The white water and the tunnel are on up there."

A row of shotgun shacks built of dust-streaked unpainted boards huddled on the narrow scrap of flatland between mountain and river. Doc Booker knocked on the door of the third house, and they listened, feeling the thin floor of the porch sag beneath their weight. The front door was open, no doubt because of the heat, and through the haze of the screen came a woman's voice—"You feel like seeing who it is, Raymond, I ain't done with your brother"—a man's answering mutter, and the approach of slow, shuffling footsteps.

The man who came to the door was as wizened and stooped as a wood-carving of a character in a Grimm tale. He was also young, his pale skin smooth and hair thick and blond.

"Raymond," Doc Booker said.

Raymond stood a moment, swaying, his breathing loud as a whistle.

"Good to see you still getting around," Doc Booker said.

"Barely," Raymond wheezed. He held his head at an angle so they could not see his eyes. His thin fingers fumbled with the latch on the screen door. He led them into the small, close front room, through a kitchen that smelled of sour milk and pork fat, to a room at the rear. A small electric fan whined from the windowsill, swiveling futilely from side to side. A heavy woman in a cotton housedress leaned over the man on the bed, propping up his head and shoulders with one arm and spooning broth into his mouth. The man, his face tight and shrunken as a cadaver's, stared at the ceiling. In between spoonfuls of broth, he took short, rattling breaths. The woman nodded briefly to Doc Booker, who entered the room first, knelt by the bed, and pulled a stethoscope from his battered knapsack.

"He's still yet here," the woman said, watching the face of the man on the bed. He never blinked, only stared, swallowed, opened his mouth to the air.

Doc Booker didn't answer, just listened through the stethoscope, held a limp wrist between his fingers, and counted. Earl went to a spiderwebbed corner, slid to the floor, and drew his knees to his chin. A trickle of sweat tickled the small of Dietrich's back. He felt queasy. Fred turned and left.

Dietrich followed him to the front porch, where Raymond sprawled listlessly on a wooden swing.

"I'm next," Raymond said. The exertion of his breathing carried the swing back and forth. Soon his mother came outside and sat on the swing beside him.

"Doc's looking after Ed," she said. She put her arm around Raymond's bony shoulders, and he leaned against her.

Fred sat motionless on the steps, back against the banister. "So what is there to do?" he asked. He watched the road.

The woman grimaced and rested the back of her head against the swing chain. "Ain't nothing," she said. "My boys both worked the tunnel. Muckers. Six months they was in there. And this is where it landed 'em. Ed in yonder will last a few more days maybe. Raymond here, he's got a couple months if he don't take the pneumonia." She patted Raymond's arm, and he stared unblinking at something across the road. "He knows it, don't need to hide anything from him. Ain't that right, Raymond?"

Raymond nodded his head and stared.

"This hit Ed worse than Raymond, for some reason," the woman continued. "Ain't no sense to that part, that I can tell, because Raymond was a more sickly youngun than his brother. I hear tell they's a few fellows been up there right on. Not many, but a few. They're sick to death but they're still yet working. Others didn't last a month. Shack rousters go to rouse them, find them dead in their beds."

"Why do they keep drilling this tunnel?" Dietrich asked.

She looked at Fred. "Where's this fellow from? He talks funny."

"You aren't supposed to talk," Fred said to him. Then, "He's a visitor from Germany."

"Oh," she said. "Well, I don't know about Germany, but here they'll do anything if they's money in it. Take this here silica. That's what that doctor in there calls it. Ain't sure what that is myself. What I do know is my boys claim they couldn't hardly get their breath inside there. That right, Raymond?"

"Burns eyes," Raymond wheezed. "Burns nose."

The woman said, "Them supervisors know it. They wear masks when they go in, but they ain't give my boys none."

"Can't see for the dust," said Raymond. "White in there. They want the white. For something. What we haul out, they keep."

His mother said, "My boys told me when the men come out of there after a shift, everybody's white as chalk. Even the colored boys is white."

"How many dead so far?" Fred asked.

"We don't rightly know. Somebody falls out, they hire on a new one."

"From where?"

Raymond lifted his hand as though to wave, then dropped it in his lap.

"Walk up yonder. They're camped out in the bottom. Waiting. Somebody dies, they take their place."

Dietrich started. "Don't they know what is happening?"

"Hell yes. Means they don't wait long for a job."

"But why in the name of God—"

Raymond had fixed his deathstare on him. "People got to eat. Don't they eat in Germany?"

"But if they know they will die—" Dietrich began, and stopped, understanding suddenly that the man in front of him would have gone back himself if he had the strength, if there was nothing else. And there was nothing else.

Fred stood and walked to the end of the porch. In the field beyond, black men hunkered in bunches or walked about aimlessly. The grind of a bluesy harmonica sounded faintly.

"Yes," Fred said. "They'll make what they can. Send it south. Buys food while it lasts."

"Won't send much," the woman said. "Twenty-five cents a day, but they're paying scrip up there. Running a commissary, and that don't leave much to send to your people. They bring in bootleg liquor too, on the weekend. Get them boys drunk on Saturday night, call in the sheriff and keep them in jail until Monday morning, then take the fine out of their pay. Tell you what they're making up there. Making a bed and beans and cornbread from the cook tent. That's what they're making."

"Least they ain't no burden," Raymond said. "Not like me and Ed."

"No, now." His mother patted his arm, pulled him closer.

"Wisht we'd got took with this a way far off," said Raymond. "Mommy wouldn't work herself to death like she is."

"I couldn't stand if you was way far off," she said.

The harmonica speeded up. Raymond coughed, leaned over, and spat. "Boy ain't gone in yet," he said. "Nobody gone in can spare breath for a mouth organ."

Fred turned. "Let's take a walk up there."

"You watch out," the woman said. "Them shack rousters is mean as striped-ass snakes. And they don't let white people in the colored camp, or the other way around."

Fred stood close to Dietrich. "What you say? Pretend like we're looking for work."

Dietrich took a deep breath. "All right," he said.

"Only don't you say a damn word, you hear?"

"Yes."

Fred stood for a moment, thinking. Then he went into the house. Dietrich sat on the porch steps and mopped the sweat from his forehead with the red bandanna Doc Booker had provided. Raymond and his mother stayed on the swing, she rocking back and forth and cradling him as if he were a child, despairing and yet somehow satisfied.

Fred returned. "Doc's going to see some other people up Gauley a few miles from here that worked the tunnel and need a doctor. So he's giving us twenty-four hours." He held up the sack of provisions they'd brought. "Doc and Earl will eat where they're going, so we get the ham biscuits. Let's go."

He went down the steps.

"Go?" Things were moving very fast. "Twenty-four hours? What are you thinking we shall do for twenty-four hours?"

Fred stood in the road with his fists on his hips. "You want to stay with Doc and Earl?"

"No."

"Then come on. And keep your trap shut."

The men in the field watched them come on, looked away, watched, looked away. They were Negroes who sprawled on the ground beside the morning's dying cookfires. Wandered aimlessly. Or peeked over the shoulders of other men hoarding crackedgray playing cards, men who flipped the dog-eared cardcorners with ragged fingernails, holding their hands close beneath their chins, fanning themselves with clutches of diamonds and clubs that might win them an extra leaf or twig. Two white men with lank brown hair huddled apart in the shade of a rock on the riverbank and passed the stub of a cigarette back and forth. They watched the Negroes intently, despising them, and longing to join them.

Dietrich followed Fred, who moved toward three men in the shade of a willow near the river's edge. One was the musician they'd heard. When he saw them, he gave the shiny harmonica a quick, loving rub and slipped it into his shirt pocket.

Fred said, "You waiting to get on up there?"

The man with the hidden harmonica said, "You think of any other reason to wait under this tree?"

"How you get on?" Fred asked.

"Go up there and ask for McCloud."

"McCloud," Fred said.

"He the butt kicker," another man said. "White man who keeps order. Take your name, come down here and call you when they need somebody. But you got to take your turn."

"Then you go in the tunnel?" Fred asked. "What's it like in that tunnel?"

They stared at him. They stared at Dietrich.

"Who's this white man?" said the one with the harmonica.

Dietrich opened his mouth, remembered, and strangled what he was about to say with a vague "Aaaah."

"My buddy," said Fred. "Can't talk. Not real smart, you know. I look after him."

"How come?"

"Just feel sorry for him," said Fred.

"Yeah?" said the man with the harmonica.

"Well," said Fred, "he come in handy when we go asking. You know. Send him to white people's door with a poke and he stand there holding it open and looking pitiful. They put something in the poke. I stay back. You know."

The men looked away, which meant *Go on and join us*. They sat, and Fred opened the faded cotton sack.

"Ham biscuit?" he said. "Cigarettes?"

They leaned forward as Fred took the biscuits from the sack.

"Where you get them?"

"Woman in Boomer fix them for me this morning."

"Yeah. What you do for her?"

"Said it was best loving she had in a year. Didn't even charge."

Dietrich felt as though he had never seen Fred before. Fred handed out biscuits laced with brown salty ham. The men took this offering as though it were sacred, turned the biscuits over, touched the crusty edges, sniffed the meat.

"Damn," one said.

"Mmm. Good woman," said another.

"I always been lucky," said Fred.

When they had eaten, they lay on their backs amid the weeds. The sun was directly above them and they drew close to one another to share the shade. Beyond their tree a greenscum backwater choked with weeds washed back from the river. Dragonflies, spindly black sticks with invisible wings, flitted over the stagnant pool.

"Snake doctors," Fred said, and pointed at them.

Dietrich tried to ask *What* by opening his eyes wide.

"He *is* dumb, ain't he," one man said.

Fred showed him dandelion weeds topped by clumps of bubbly spittle. "Snake doctor sign. Means they's a sick snake around here. Sickness everywhere."

Dietrich tested the wet white mound with the tip of a finger. It was like human spittle, and yet too thick. He didn't trust it.

Fred was looking off toward the river. "You sure they ain't nothing for a man to do here without waiting?" Turned back suddenly. "How you earn them beans?"

"Aw, man. You want to know?"

"I want to know. Ham biscuits gone, we need beans too."

They rubbed their heads, poked the dirt with sticks.

"You want to know."

"I said, ain't I."

"Ghost shacks up there. Hire you to work them. Nobody does it but once though. So you might get on."

"Ghost shacks?"

"Mens that's dying, they keep them in there. Feed them a little. Clean up after them. When they dead, put them on a truck and haul them off somewhere."

"Where?"

Shrug. "Up the hill. Don't ask, man."

Fred said, "This a strange job, I do believe."

"You right there."

But they would say nothing more. Fred passed around cigarettes. They smoked and then, dulled by the heat, lay down to rest.

Through the whole of that day Dietrich did not believe he slept. At all times he knew where he was, flat on his back in American weeds and white heat, ants crawling beneath his collar and cuffs. He dug at them and turned his head back and forth. Then he did not move. He dreamed. He saw unspeakable visions. Father walking naked through the house in the Wangenheimstraße. The house aflame and a sister or brother screaming from every window. Himself standing in Unter den Linden calling out in a language no one could understand while he was jostled and spat on by passersby. Snake doctor spittle. Above him loomed the smothering green dome of the willow melting in the heat. He saw it always.

And yet it was sleep. When he woke, he did not know he had rested.

But it was suddenly dark and Fred was shaking him into groggy wakefulness. He shoved a plate of food in Dietrich's hands and said in his ear, "Eat, but remember—don't talk."

Dietrich tried to get his bearings and gestured *Spoon*.

"Use the corn pone," Fred whispered, and showed him how to rake clumps of beans into his mouth with torn bits of stale cornbread. The others watched closely.

"Pitiful," said one, and the others said, "Mmm-mm."

"He strong in the shoulders?"

"Strong," Fred said. "Man can move."

"He be all right," they said. "They love him in that tunnel."

Fred looked at Dietrich and smiled, touched his hand. "You hear?" he

said, but when he saw Dietrich's inclination to answer, pinched the skin of
his wrist. "You can lift anything, can't you man?"

Dietrich choked the dry cornbread and beans into an *Aaaaah*.

So they trudged upriver to the Negro camp. Dietrich kept behind Fred,
tried to pretend he wasn't even there. Fred seemed to like it that way. They
came to a rough stand of fence topped by barbed wire. A large white man,
bare to the waist, sat on a stool at a gate, two chins resting on his hairy
chest, rifle propped against his thigh.

"Yeah?" he said.

"They told us ask for McCloud," Fred said.

The man didn't move. "Got a waiting list. And this is Negro camp only."

"That's all right," Fred said. "We want to work while we wait."

The man curled his lip. "What kind of work you think—"

"We heard tell," Fred said, his voice low and deliberate, "you need some
cleaning and some hauling."

"That right," said the man.

Fred gestured toward Dietrich. "This boy here is white but dumb. I look
after him. He strong. Do anything you ask and not say a word."

"Yeah? And what about you?"

"What you think?" Fred said.

He looked them over a moment, then turned and gestured toward a
group of white men gathered in front of a makeshift wooden structure.
"Call McCloud!" he yelled.

They passed through the ragged gate. Dietrich noticed he was not the
only white man in the Negro camp, but the only white man with no
authority. They followed kerosene lanterns, festive orange in the bluedark,
to a row of wood shacks, where shovels and moldering buckets were thrust
into their hands. They were warned to tie bandannas across their face.

The smell hit as soon they stepped inside. They scraped feces, satin in
the lantern light, onto their shovels and slipped the dark globs into their
pails. Dietrich retched and turned away to grasp the wall but grabbed Fred
instead, who had also bolted for the door. They held on to each other and
breathed through the open doorway for a moment. Then, knowing what to
expect, they returned to their labor. And that was the easy part.

Because the waste seemed living matter, but it had issued from dead
men.

They left the bodies on their rough pine bunks draped with stained tattered cotton while they scraped with their shovels, then threw buckets of
water against the walls of the windowless shacks. Finally they grasped
corpses by the wrist. These came flopping from the bunks with such an

unexpected heaviness that Fred toppled to the floor. Dietrich helped him up. The leg of Fred's overalls was stained dark where he fell.

Outside a truck with a wood-frame bed had drawn up and the driver sat smoking in the open cab door. His face was hidden by shadow. Perhaps, Dietrich thought, the man had no features at all. He didn't move as they carried the corpses between them, one at a time, and laid them in the back of the truck. There were five bodies in all, three rigid and unyielding, two that sagged when lifted as though they were turning to liquid, so that Dietrich feared they would pour from their clothes.

"That it?" said a voice from the truck cab as they hoisted the last one. It flopped onto its stomach, one dead hand flung palm-up across its buttocks.

"Yes sir," said Fred.

The truck door slammed, the engine rumbled and caught, and the wheels skewed with a scraping noise in the dry dirt.

"Come on," Fred said and ran after the truck.

Dietrich was too startled to protest and thought only of keeping up so as not to be left alone. They just managed to clamber aboard as the truck, bouncing along the rutted dirt track, picked up speed, and they fell forward, their fall broken by the nest of corpses. Dietrich lay still, trying to catch his breath despite the rank smell, his cheek pressed against the dusty hair of the dead Negro beneath him.

"Where are we going?" he gasped.

"What they do with them." Fred moved close to him. "I have to know what they do with them."

"And then?"

Fred turned away and hid his face in his sleeve. The truck paused, then pulled with a final lurch onto pavement and picked up speed, its engine whining with relief. Dietrich twisted around to stare up at a blurred wedge of moon moving away from black shreds of cloud. The truck was soon climbing steeply, gears slipping and then catching with a low grind. Tentatively Dietrich moved his hand along the cheekbone of the dead man who cushioned him, and over to his forehead. He drew an invisible cross on the man's forehead with the tip of his finger and whispered a prayer. Felt this to be ludicrously inadequate, and yet Dietrich reached for another of the dead to bless. Instead he touched living flesh.

"It's me," Fred said.

Dietrich's hand rested at the base of Fred's neck, glad of the warmth. "Where do you think we are going?" he said.

"Bury them someplace out of the way, I guess. In the woods. I find out where, maybe I can report it." He raised up and peered between the wood slats. Then he said, "Way we turned, I'd say we're going up the big mountain behind the camp. Same mountain they're drilling the tunnel through. Only the one paved road up here."

"Take care the driver doesn't see you."

Fred craned his neck to look into the cab, then lay back down. "No problem. He's got a flask in there. Big worry may be he doesn't take us over the side of the mountain here. Doc says it's cliffs. Straight down."

And that was no small concern. For the man drove fast and twice edged onto dirt before skittering back to the pavement. Dietrich fished for his glasses in the pocket of his shirt and wrapped them across his face. Beyond the wooden fence he glimpsed silver flashes of river far far below.

"Best not to look," said Fred.

Rather than fear, it was peace Dietrich felt as he stared into that abyss. To plummet to his death while riding upon a pile of murdered corpses (it was quite clear they were dealing with nothing less than murder) seemed either so absurd as to be impossible, or fate. Either prospect was strangely comforting. He relaxed back upon his unquiet bed, felt anonymous bone slip beneath skin thick as rubber each time the truck lurched around a bend in the road.

They turned at last up a sharply climbing dirt track. Atop their shifting load, they slid to the back of the truck, feet pressed to the gate. Then the truck leveled abruptly, lurched and relaxed, its engine cut. They pitched forward, sprawled across the dead.

The door of the truck cab opened. Fred twisted around and pulled on Dietrich's arm. They leaped from the truck and landed hard just as the door slammed. Fortunately the man walked away instead of coming to the back of the truck. They stumbled and ran to a ditch just beyond the road, where they threw themselves flat. Only then were they able to get their bearings. The truck had drawn up at the edge of a cornfield. The man who had driven the truck leaned against a fence and smoked a cigarette. He took a watch from his pocket, held it up to the moonlight, then put it back and turned to look toward a house at the far edge of the field. He began to hum.

They stayed quite still except to peer cautiously above the ditch line, for they were unprotected except for the muddy depression they lay in. After a time, two more men appeared, walking one behind the other along a row of corn. They carried shovels.

"How many you got this time?" one asked the truck driver.

"I think they's five."

"Jesus Christ. I'll be pulling out another row at this rate. Won't be able to use any of this field."

"Rich dirt other ways," the driver said.

The men laughed.

"Let's get 'em then," said one man. "I got to be up with the chickens tomorrow."

They came to the back of the truck, and the driver lowered the gate. One of the men turned away, dragging a corpse by the legs. He stopped.

"Hey! They's somebody in that ditch!" He dropped the corpse and came toward the ditch. "Get your gun, Daddy!"

They were up and running down the road even as he called out, dropping out of sight when the track dipped over the hill, pounding around a curve, the precipitous drop propelling them faster and faster even as there came a sharp cracking sound and a whine above their heads. They leaped from the road and went over the embankment, sliding and tearing through the woods with a terrible racket, stumbled across a level shelf, followed it until their way was blocked by a thick stand of rhododendron, then dropped over the edge again, twisting, leaping, falling over roots, and at last sliding to rest against a broad tree trunk.

Dietrich rested his cheek against the rough bark, air slicing his lungs with a painful whistling sound. Fred was on his knees, arms wrapped around the trunk. Little by little they breathed more slowly until they could hear another, more delicate rushing sound, far below. It was the river. Dietrich slid to a sitting position.

"I think we are near a cliff," he said.

"Don't look," said Fred. "I think we almost went over a cliff."

Gingerly, for every bone in his body ached, Dietrich edged around the trunk and peered out into the darkness. A fresh breeze cooled his scratched and burning face. Just beyond a large flat rock at the base of their tree was a precipice above the band of river, black in the changing nightlight.

"Shit," Dietrich said. He felt faint.

Fred started to laugh, a bit hysterically. "Where did you learn that word?"

"From you, of course." Dietrich started to laugh as well.

"Sssshh!" Fred said. "Listen."

Dietrich raised his head, afraid the men might have found them. The river sang like the airy rush of a seashell pressed to the ear. Then he was aware of a distant steady pounding. He realized he had been hearing it all along but thought it was the beating of his heart.

"It's the tunnel," said Fred. "They're down there right now. Drilling."

They sat in silence for a time. Dietrich thought that Fred wept, but couldn't be sure, for his face was turned away, and in shadow. At last they got up and made their painful way down the mountain.

The Word of the Lord

THEY LAY ON THEIR BACKS in the cattle car, which was empty save for scattered bits of straw and dried dung from a shipment of Florida livestock unloaded in Winston-Salem. They were bone-weary, for one had been tending the dying and two had spent the best part of the night climbing down the labyrinth of Gauley Mountain. They sprawled, heads resting upon meager piles of straw husks, half-dreaming though afraid to dream.

Except for Earl Harvey. He paced and sliced shafts of moonlight with bony arms in one of the fits of frenzy which periodically overtook him.

Doc said, "Stand still, Earl."

"Can't." Earl slung his arms, pushed off the wall of the cattle car. "Got to move. Moved since I was little, under the trains. Lived right by the railroad tracks, me and my momma. Used to go out there, me not four years old. Laid down under the trains when they stopped. Stayed there till they started up again. Then moved in and out, behind the wheels. Loved to roll. Rolled over top the rails. Always behind the wheels though."

"Earl," Fred said, "you're crazy."

Back and forth, Earl crashed into the side of the boxcar, pushed away and propelled himself across to the opposite wall. "My momma found out, she whipped me all the way home. Tied me to the bedpost to keep me inside. Always got away though. Couldn't stop rolling under trains. How I learned to move. *Had* to learn how to move. What I come on this earth to do. Preacher, you know what you come on this earth to do?"

"No," Fred said. He stood abruptly and went to the far end of the boxcar, where he stood with his back to them, squinting through a wide slat that let in the white dawn.

Doc had risen stiffly and took Earl—who turned docile at his touch—by the elbow and led him to a corner. Earl slumped sideways with his head resting on Doc's thigh, muttering beneath his breath.

Dietrich said, "What is happening in that tunnel?"

"I hear they run into silica in there," Doc said. "Company didn't expect to find it when they started drilling, but now they found it, they want it. Valuable stuff. But it's fine-ground glass those men are breathing in. Cuts their lungs to pieces. Sometimes fast, sometimes slow."

"And these companies know this?"

"Don't let their own people in without masks," said Doc. "Hell, they know what it is. Indians in South America dug silica for the Spanish four hundred years ago."

Dietrich joined Fred and began to tell him what Doc had said, but Fred raised his hand and shook his head. "I'll know soon enough," he said. And he turned on Dietrich a face filled with fear. "When we arrived yesterday I told Earl there wasn't any church here," he said. "What if there is? What if it's my church?"

Dietrich felt his mouth go dry. "You have a church," he said.

"A church that never has felt right. Never felt the hand of the Lord on my shoulder when I walked in that church. I felt it back there. Heard the voice in my inner ear. That's what a call is, and it's a terrible thing. I don't want it, not at all."

"Can this all be in your head?" Dietrich put his hand on Fred's shoulder. "It has been a shocking day, and you haven't slept."

Fred shook his head. Dietrich watched him for a time and then said, both skeptical and wistful, "How do you hear such calls? Why do you receive them and not I?"

"I hope you never get a call," Fred said. "I wouldn't wish it on you. Go on back to Germany. You've had your little adventure. Go on back home to your rich family where it's safe."

"And what are you going to do?"

"I don't know how just yet," Fred said, "but I'm coming back here."

He turned and pressed his cheek against the wide-set slats of the cattle car. The new morning was so bright the train seemed to hurtle through a tunnel of flashing light.

Domine deus, rex caelestis

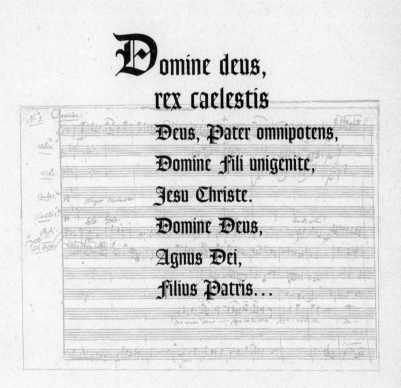

Deus, Pater omnipotens,
Domine Fili unigenite,
Jesu Christe.
Domine Deus,
Agnus Dei,
filius Patris...

Lord God, Heavenly King
Almighty God and Father
Lord Jesus Christ, only Son of the Father
Lord God, Lamb of God,
Son of the Father...

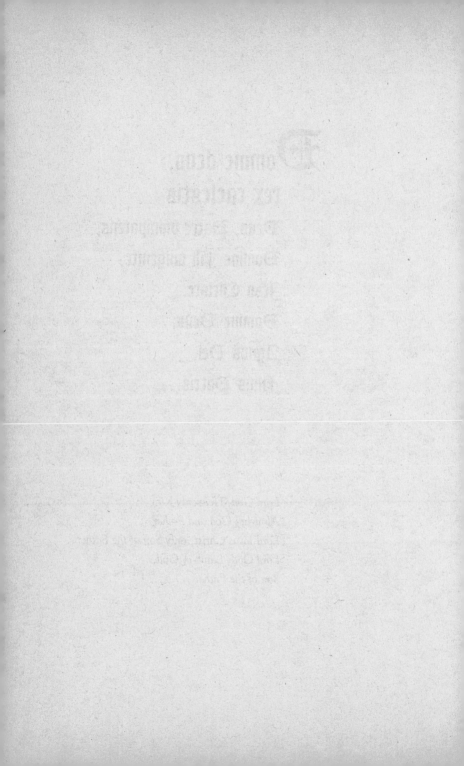

Doppelgänger
1924

THE DOG is long dead, and the boy Alois is a man who has entered a meeting room in Berlin for the first time. He finds the city appallingly cold and ugly, and the room is a relief. It is plain, like the schoolroom at home in Schönberg, the walls peeling here and there, the floorboards scuffed, all in a lived-in way. The only decoration is the bright red-white-and-black flag on the wall. He stands with the other new members up from Bavaria, afraid to look for a seat until told to do so. Then Hitler enters the room and moves down the line, stopping to talk to each recruit. He moves slowly, as if he has all the time in the world for them.

"And what is your name?"

"Alois."

He clenches his fists to keep his hands from shaking.

"Alois. It's my brother's name." A shadow passes over Hitler's face, as though a cloud has passed over the sun. "And my father's."

Some blessed impulse causes Bauer to blurt, "I despise my father!"

Hitler nods. His face shows he is greatly moved. "Never mind, Alois. Tell me, what are your gifts?"

"Gifts?"

"Everyone has a gift. What can you offer the Fatherland? Sport? Public speaking? Music?"

Bauer brightens. "I adore music."

"Wagner?"

"Mozart!"—then adds, thinking quickly, "And Wagner as well!"

He wants to say, Actually I'm not a real musician and I knew nothing of music until I joined the party, I simply love to listen. But Hitler has already passed on to the next man.

Berlin, September, 1932

ON DIETRICH'S RETURN from America, the family noted the changes. He had lost weight, and shiny patches of scalp showed through the carefully arranged hair on the crown of his head. More alarming, the periods of melancholy which had always afflicted him seemed to come more frequently, and he spent a great deal of time to himself in the room at the top of his parents' house, his light burning long into the night. Old von Harnack next door, who often saw the squares of light on the tiles of his lavatory wall when he got up to relieve himself, inquired after Dietrich to the elder Bonhoeffer.

"America," Dr. Bonhoeffer said curtly, "seems to have turned Dietrich's brain to porridge."

He was the only one of the children who still lived at home. Sabine, whom Dietrich missed sorely, was in Göttingen with her husband, Gerhard, raising their first child. Dietrich saw Baby Suse most often, though in his absence everyone else had stopped calling her Baby Suse, since it was clear she was the most worldly of them all. Suse had disregarded her family's advice and taken a flat of her own.

One day, on the first afternoon that possessed a bite of autumn chill, Suse stopped to show off her new hat. It was gray felt and cut like a man's, except it sported a spray of baby's breath at the band. The butler said Frau Bonhoeffer had gone out to play bridge with friends in Dahlem. Suse was standing in the hall, trying to decide whether to wait or come back later, when a distant thumping, rhythmic and insistent, wafted from above. She looked up and began to climb the stairs. The two housemaids, Elli and Maria, drifted along the first-floor landing, caressing the dark oak railing with white cloths. They were also listening. Maria, the younger, smiled at Suse and said, "He plays this music every day." Still above, but quite distinctly, they heard the creaking of floorboards, accompanied by *Wat-dat-do Wat-dat-do Wat-dat-do wat-dat-do wat-dat-do*.

Suse crept up the stairs, but she needn't have worried about being overheard, for the music was loud enough to drown out any other sound. She peeked into the room.

Dietrich was dancing. His back was to the door, his arms raised to grab and twirl an invisible partner. He moved deftly, hips swaying slightly to the growl of a throaty saxophone, eyes shut and fingers stroking the back of a phantom companion. Suse retreated quickly, as embarrassed as if she'd interrupted him making love.

She wanted to tell someone. But it was not a thing to share with the brothers and sisters, much less their parents. Sabine would understand, but she was so rarely in Berlin. Gerhard was being harassed at the university in Göttingen. Many students refused to attend his classes, so that his voice echoed around near empty lecture halls, and death threats garnished with crudely drawn swastikas had been slipped beneath his office door. Sabine, with the same protective instinct that led her to lie awake at night for the child Dietrich, would not leave her husband, even for a few days.

Then Suse thought of Hans.

Hans von Dohnanyi, Christel's husband, was Dietrich's favorite brother-in-law. Because his own family had disintegrated when he was a boy, Hans had pursued the Bonhoeffers like a starving man. And yet the lonely years of avoiding his mother had schooled him. He was working at age fifteen to pay his mother's debts, worked still longer to put himself through university, and had recently become the most prominent young lawyer in the Justice Ministry. All without the help of a single Bonhoeffer. So Karl and Karl-Friedrich were never able to bully him.

Suse invited herself to dinner at the Dohnanyi home in Sacrow. After the roast pork and stewed prunes, while Christel was putting the children to bed, she sat on the veranda with Hans, sipping coffee and admiring the sunset across the flat mirror of the Jungfernsee. Suse told him what she had seen in Dietrich's room.

Hans smoked his pipe and thought for a moment. "How does he pass his time when he isn't hiding up there?"

"He's teaching at the university, so there are lectures to prepare and papers to read."

"Still in his room."

"Yes. And Karl-Friedrich says he's a reputation for being very demanding, so his classes are small. Not that theology is a terribly popular subject anyway. At least he seems to enjoy his writing. He's doing something on the nature of the church."

"Ummm."

"He preaches now and then. But he never tells us ahead of time. It's as though he were ashamed. I found out by accident last month he was to be at Trinity Church and went to hear him. Without telling him, actually, and

I hid behind a pillar. I'm afraid—" she hated to admit this—"the church was nearly empty, and I heard people grumbling about the sermon as they left. I gather he's got a reputation for being difficult, so people stay away."

Hans chuffed away on his pipe like a locomotive, and stared at the lake, his eyeglasses glowing a light orange in the sunset. He rubbed the tip of his nose—a most marvelous nose, sharply delicate but with a pugnacious tilt— as was his habit when deliberating. Then he sat up straight. "What our Dietrich needs," he declared, "is a woman."

"That," Suse said with satisfaction, "is what I concluded as well."

"And who better," said Hans, "to find a woman for Dietrich than Suse?"

"Ah." She smiled. "I even have someone in mind."

He laughed. "Of course you do. Tell me, what sort of woman *would* come to mind for our Dietrich?"

"She's intelligent. A few years older than Dietrich, but he won't mind. Jewish, but he won't mind that either. Besides, her grandfather converted to Christianity years ago. And she studied theology in Bonn. He'll like that very much."

"But what does she look like?"

A man's question. "Brisk," Suse said. "Full of energy."

"Which means homely," Hans said.

"It does not. It means she's not pretty, but not unattractive either. She has a friendly face. Yes, that says it best. Friendly."

"Friendly."

"What? Do you want Marlene Dietrich? She's perfect for him."

"And what is this friendly person's name?"

"Elisabeth Hildebrandt. Her father is a surgeon at the Charité. Father knows him."

"And of course you've thought how to bring Elisabeth and Dietrich together?"

"That is the easiest part. Elisabeth and I are helping start a new club for underprivileged youth. Actually we're bankrolling most of it between us. And Dietrich has been saying how he misses his work with young people in Harlem. He taught that confirmation class in Prenzlauer Berg last year too, and you recall how he enjoyed it. Naturally he'll want to become involved."

When she came downstairs, Christel saw them through the French doors, leaning against one another on the wicker couch, giggling. In some families, this might suggest a flirtation, but no Bonhoeffer would assume such a thing. Though if pressed, Suse might have admitted she did fancy Hans. If her sister hadn't grabbed him first. But such thoughts passed quickly through her mind. It was Dietrich she planned to seduce.

He knew right away what Suse was about. She had always been an open book, the kind of child who dropped so many hints about what she was giving for Christmas presents that everyone had to pretend to be surprised. He was tempted to turn down her invitation, except that he didn't want to hurt her feelings. So he left the university after his afternoon lecture and walked up Unter den Linden amid a shower of lime leaves. New York had altered the way he looked at Berlin. As claustrophobic as he had first found the crowded canyons of Manhattan, the prairielike vastness of Unter den Linden with its monstrous piles of stone seemed more ominous. Ranks of sculpted sentries, ever vigilant, surveyed the boulevard from the low rooftops and dispatched riders in chariots pulled by tireless horses. Berlin was a city of shadows lurking behind gates, under perpetual surveillance by those who had never drawn breath.

He entered the Café Bauer and looked around, relishing the mingled smells of coffee, cinnamon, and amaretto that lightened his mood. Suse had suggested the Romanische Café, but he had resisted. The Romanische was a hangout of artists in black clothes and garish makeup. The Café Bauer, on the other hand, was a fantasy of glass cases and mirrors, mahogany cabinets, crystal chandeliers, gold-faced clocks, and hand-painted vases. Gray-haired men and women in tweed conversed over pots of coffee, sturdy walking sticks propped against their chairs and small dogs on leashes curled beneath the marble tables. The Café Bauer would be a great consolation of old age.

Then he saw Suse. She was seated beside a window with a couple who did not fit at all. The man wore a cloth cap and threadbare jacket, as though to disavow a lean, aristocratic face that could have comfortably carried a monocle. The woman had unruly brown hair cut short in bangs across her forehead and wore a plain gray coat. They were already sipping coffee and passing around plates of Linzer torte, double chocolate bars striped with cherries, and shortbread with almonds.

Suse looked and called, "There you are! As you can see, we waited for you."

"Sorry, so sorry. I was held up arguing with some students."

The man was standing and offering his hand. "Falk Harnack," he said. "You probably don't recall, but we met once, years ago, when we were boys. My old uncle lives next door to your parents."

Dietrich did remember, and noted the family resemblance. He also understood why Harnack was dressed like a workingman. He and his brother Arvid were notorious for their Communist sympathies, rare in men of their social class. They were entitled to style themselves *von* Harnack but refused to use this aristocratic prerogative out of principle.

"Oh, yes," Dietrich said. "Your uncle was my first professor of theology. It has been a long time since we met. You're not from Berlin?"

"No, no. I grew up in Munich. But I've been in Berlin the past year. The atmosphere in Bavaria is intolerable just now." Harnack had sat back down and was pouring coffee. "Cream?"

"Yes, please," Dietrich said, and sat awkwardly, but it was the woman who passed him the tray of cream and sugar, so he was forced to look at her more quickly than he had planned. He felt he must be blushing, and wished Suse had not been so clear about her intentions. He also wondered if the woman and Harnack had come together. He glanced at his sister, who was looking very pleased with herself.

"This is Elisabeth," Suse said. "Elisabeth Hildebrandt, my brother Dietrich."

He realized he had blundered by sitting so quickly, not like him at all to forget his manners, and stood quickly, knocking his napkin off the table. He took her hand, bowed over it, and hastily retrieved the square of white cloth. Elisabeth pushed her bangs back from her forehead, rested her elbow on the table and put a hand to her chin, and smiled. A face comfortable with smiling, he thought.

She said, "And what sort of argument were you having?"

"What?" It was so different from what he expected her to say that he wasn't sure what she meant. "Argument?"

"You said you'd just had an argument with some students."

"Ah, yes. I've just begun a series of lectures on the nature of the church. It happens at the beginning of each term—the new National Socialist students don't know me and sign up for my lectures, then realize right away that I am not one of them." He sipped from his own cup, and began to warm to his subject. "When I speak on the nature of the church, I make it quite clear that the church, and indeed God, should not be challenged to offer anything to twentieth-century man; rather we must ask how we may serve God, and that is how the church—"

Suse kicked him beneath the table.

He looked down quickly, pretended to choke on his Linzer torte, said, "Pardon me," and dabbed at his lips with the napkin. "I'm sure I am boring you. Anyway, several students challenged me afterward and I had to make my own position quite plain. The long and short of it is, most of them won't be back."

"What is the theological position of a National Socialist student?"

"That the church exists to serve the Fatherland. That the Fatherland is a gift to us from God, and that God has blessed the Fatherland by raising up Adolf Hitler to lead us to our divinely ordained place at the head of the nations."

Elisabeth was watching him closely. He liked her eyes, which were very dark, brave eyes that met his without looking away.

"And what," she asked, "is your response?"

"That God does not play favorites with nations, and anyone who claims a divine blessing for his country is guilty of blasphemy and idolatry."

She nodded, her smile gone. "You are in for something, aren't you."

It was Harnack who laughed. "As if there were a God who could fix the mess we're in."

"God isn't a handyman," Elisabeth said back. She looked at Dietrich. "Falk," she said, "is an atheist and a Marxist."

"And you," said Harnack, stifling a yawn, to Dietrich, "remind me of my uncle. A Christian. How comforting in times like these."

"No," Dietrich said. "I am a theologian who would like to be a Christian. And it is not comforting at all."

"Funny," Elisabeth said. "I am a Christian who would like to be a Jew."

Suse, who had been fidgeting at the beginning of this exchange, looked happily around the table. If she and Falk were put off, it was clear Elisabeth and Dietrich were not.

"Well," she said, "whatever our views, we all have an interest in this youth club. I've told Dietrich a little about it and he'd like to help, wouldn't you, Dietrich?"

"Yes," he agreed. "But one thing has been bothering me. Suse says you've found some rooms in the Schloß Straße. But why Charlottenburg? Why near the palace? Wouldn't it make more sense to have it in Prenzlauer Berg or Wedding? Charlottenburg isn't exactly a working-class quarter."

"That's just the point," said Harnack. "The presence of our club will be a calculated insult thrown into the face of the bourgeoisie. Poor youth should be able to congregate in Charlottenburg, or anyplace else they damn well please."

"But isn't it out of the way for them? Can they afford the S-Bahn?"

"Are you concerned it's out of the way, or that they'll offend bourgeois sensibilities?"

Dietrich had been about to bite into a square of shortbread but he set it down on his plate. "My concern," he said, "is that we reach as many of these young people as possible. Or do you have a different agenda?"

"Actually," said Elisabeth, "I agree with Dietrich. But there's another consideration. You should have mentioned it, Falk, instead of waving your Marxist rhetoric like a bloody flag. Look at Hamburg, seven thousand storm troopers attacking working-class homes in Altona, and it's happening in P-Berg and Wedding as well. We thought we might more easily avoid that in Charlottenburg."

"It may be no different in Charlottenburg," Dietrich said. "It's the middle-class youth who are most caught up in this brownshirt frenzy. I see it every day at the university."

"Then why not confront them where they live instead of the other way around?" Harnack leaned forward. "These working-class young people are our only hope. They see through the fascist lie. Ask them who they support in the elections. Thälmann and the Communists. They adore Thälmann, they name babies after him. And the few who aren't for Thälmann are Socialist. Although those few are getting fewer as they watch this government sell out over and over to the rich, and cower before Hitler and his thugs."

Elisabeth said, "Falk, we've told you the club will be open to everyone. We want open discussion and tolerance. You said you would work with us on a theater project. That's it. No pushing ideologies."

"You are an actor?" Dietrich asked, glad for a change in subject.

"And a director," said Harnack. "I've worked with the National Theater in Leipzig, but I've started to feel that's all irrelevant. I want to bring art to the masses, and use theater as a weapon against fascism."

Elisabeth glanced at Dietrich and rolled her eyes. He relaxed. "And where," he asked, "do I fit in?"

"Anywhere you like," Suse said. "You're a wonderful musician, and you can tell stories, or give tennis lessons—"

"Tennis lessons!" Harnack chortled.

"Shut up, Falk," Elisabeth said.

"Sorry." He was suddenly contrite. "I don't mean to rag you so much, Bonhoeffer. Suse here is such a good sport, and she does speak so well of you."

Dietrich wondered if Suse had kicked Harnack beneath the table.

Then Suse looked at her wristwatch, as though suddenly remembering something, and announced, "Oh, dear, Falk and I must run. He's taking me to a rehearsal of his latest play. Dietrich, can you see Elisabeth home? Oh, and can you get the bill as well? There's a dear."

Elisabeth, Dietrich noted, looked as startled as he. Harnack and Suse were already standing, pulling on their coats, waving goodbye.

"I think," Elisabeth said, "we've been set up."

"Suse means well," Dietrich said miserably. "I hope you don't mind."

"No," she said, "I don't believe I do."

It was not until he walked beside her that he realized how tiny she was. The top of her head did not quite reach his shoulder, and when she brushed the hair from her forehead, which she did often, he noted the slenderness of her hands. He guessed he could circle one wrist easily with his thumb and forefinger.

She lived alone, in a flat at the top of a building on the Ludwigkirchplatz. The weather was fine, so rather than take a tram, they wandered through the Tiergarten, past the Neuer See and across the Landwehrkanal to the zoo.

"Let's go in," she said. "I haven't been in years."

Dietrich hesitated. He always felt uneasy in the zoo, for it reminded him of his childhood and the war.

"You don't have time?" she asked.

"I do," he said. "Why not?"

Inside, they stopped on a small bridge and leaned against the rail, watching ducks dive beneath the surface, as though obliterating themselves, and then bob back up.

"They may be the luckiest creatures in the world just now," Elisabeth said. "They have everything they need, including safety."

He said nothing, remembering the distant screams of starving animals. The ducks would not have suffered long. They would have been among the first creatures to be caught and eaten.

She was watching him. "You look very sad. Are you often?"

"Sometimes," he said. "Not always."

She was quiet for a while. He liked that. Many people would have pressed him to share what was on his mind, but Elisabeth moved away a step and brushed fallen leaves from the railing into the water. He glanced at her to see if she was put off by his mood, but she was smiling to herself, watching the ducks dive and reemerge as new creatures. After a time he placed his hand on her elbow. She looked up at him, and he led her off the bridge.

She invited him to eat with her. Upstairs in her flat, she set out plates of bratwurst, cheese, bread, and sliced cucumbers in sour cream while he stood in the front room and studied the spire of Ludwigkirche. When she brought the plates of food to the table, she said, "Suse told me you were in America last year, at Union Seminary."

"Yes," he said.

"Then we have a friend in common, I believe. You were there with Jean Lasserre."

"Good God, yes. You know Lasserre?"

"I worked with him one summer, four years ago. When I was at the university in Bonn, I used to spend summers in the Ruhr. It's a branch of the institute Jean works with in Artois, a mission to mining villages, and once I went to Bruay instead of the Ruhr, as a sort of exchange. Trying to promote better understanding between Germans and the French."

"That sounds like Jean. What kind of work did you do?"

"I taught literature classes to miners' wives in the Ruhr, but in Bruay my French wasn't good enough, so I had an art program for children." She pointed to a row of framed charcoal drawings. "The students did those, and the one above the fireplace is mine."

He stepped closer to examine her drawing. The stooped figures of the miners were faceless, their clothes a pastiche of black melting into light gray. But their helmeted heads were pierced with shafts of light like the halos of angels.

"I used to watch them emerge from the pits in the evening, after dark," she said. "Their lamps would still be lit to show the way home. I've always been drawn to miners. I'm in awe of the way they work underground, always in darkness, always in danger. And yet they come out of that place and go on about their lives as if it were nothing. They eat their supper, bounce their children on their knee, play chess or drink beer with their friends, make love. As though there were nothing at all to be afraid of. And the next day they are back underground never knowing which breath will be their last. You would think they'd go mad. But they don't."

Dietrich was once again in the back of the truck, riding on a mattress of dead men. "I know something of what you mean," he said.

"I used to think their lives terribly different from mine," she said. "Until the last few months."

"Perhaps the government will hold firm," he said.

"I'm not sure the government wants to hold firm."

She led him to the table and passed him a plate of food. They ate awhile in silence, then she said, "You know I am Jewish."

"Suse mentioned it." He tried to sound nonchalant.

"Does it bother you?"

"I wouldn't be here if it did."

She set two wineglasses on the table, handed him a bottle of Riesling and a corkscrew, and said, "My grandfather Nathan converted to Christianity, and my father was baptized when he was ten years old. I myself was baptized as an infant. I think they are ashamed of the religious Jews, the poor ones who cling together in the Scheunenviertel and wear black hats and earlocks, still eat kosher, and speak Yiddish. Those are the backward ones, they think, the fanatics. They themselves are rational men. Physicians. Their Christianity is not passionate, but practical. When I decided to study theology, they were appalled."

Dietrich tugged at the bottle, enjoying the release of pressure as the cork came away. "This does sound familiar."

"Yes. Suse told me how it is with your family."

"It seems Suse has laid the groundwork very well."

She poured the wineglasses half full. "Did she tell you I studied with Karl Barth at Bonn?"

"You're fortunate. Barth is the greatest theologian in Germany."

"Perhaps. But in the end I have been more interested in Martin Buber."

"Buber. Ah. *I And Thou*. I must admit I have not read Buber closely. He is very much the fashion these days, and that tends to put me off a bit, though I know it is unfair."

"A Jew." She sipped her wine. "Though many of the Orthodox don't care for him."

She did not tell him that she often walked through the Scheunenviertel, past the gold-domed New Synagogue in the Oranienburger Straße, bought a pickle and a thick salt beef sandwich in a grocery and ate her lunch on a bench across from the Old Cemetery. She watched the passersby, most of them poorly dressed working-class Jews, and tried to catch snatches of conversation in Yiddish, which she only partly understood. She felt like an eavesdropper, a spy. She would always be a Jew with no one in the Scheunenviertel. But though the Scheunenviertel seemed a world away, she did not live far from the synagogue guarded by stone lions in the Fasanenstraße, lions more imposing than their flesh-and-blood counterparts in the nearby zoo. She was often tempted to enter and worship, but she did not tell Dietrich this either. Instead she continued to speak of the theologian Buber.

"So you avoid what is fashionable," she said, "even though it may have great worth."

"I admit that it may. But this is my mood of late."

"So where do you turn?"

"To scripture," he said. He made a sandwich of meat and cheese and ate without tasting his food. "I read the Bible constantly. I have been preaching sermons quite often. Not very good ones. And just now it seems to me more important than anything to preach a good sermon."

She rested her chin on her hand and watched him. "Why?"

"Because in America I worked at a Negro church in Harlem where I encountered the power of the spoken word. Because since I have been back in Berlin I have been unsettled by what is happening in Germany. The instability of the political situation, the terrible hardship caused by the economic depression. People are frightened and hungry, and yet what they truly need is spiritual. They need to hear the Gospel preached." He stopped. "You will think me a fanatic," he said.

"No," she said. "I think I know what you mean."

"Do you?" he said, not believing her. He had grown used to assuming that he was unfathomable.

When they had finished eating and she poured the coffee, he asked, "Would you like some music?" and nodded toward the gramophone which stood against the far wall.

"Certainly. You choose something. The records are in the cabinet."

He opened the oak door, pulled out a sleeve, and saw he was holding Mozart's Great Mass in C Minor. At once he was back on the sofa at the Berlin Conservatory, Kreuzer complaining Dietrich played with no passion while the parents nodded their heads.

Elisabeth had turned to watch him.

"That one is lovely," she said.

"Yes," he lied, "but I heard it just the other day," and replaced it quickly. He fingered a few more, Bach, Handel, Mendelssohn.

Elisabeth said, "If you want something new, look at the other end."

He removed another record and brightened. "You like American music?"

"I love it. What do you have, Gershwin? Marvelous!"

He laid the shiny black disc flat and swung the arm above it. The cool metal rested upon his fingertip for a delicious moment, and then he let it drop. He asked shyly, "Do you dance?"

They circled the small room to "Embraceable You." Neither tried to look the other in the face, and when the song ended, each took a step back. Dietrich clicked his heels and gave a small bow.

To his surprise, Dietrich was invited to preach the Reformation Day sermon at Kaiser Wilhelm Memorial Church before Hindenburg and other members of the government. He owed the honor, it turned out, to a government minister whose wife had been successfully treated for hysteria by Karl Bonhoeffer.

"Her idea altogether," said Dr. Bonhoeffer as he and Dietrich sat smoking in the library. "You know I've never asked favors on behalf of my children. If I had, certainly Walter would not have—" He shut his eyes and leaned his head against the back of the chair.

"I won't tell them what they want to hear," Dietrich said.

"What would they want to hear?"

"Nothing. They'll want to digest their breakfast in peace."

Karl Bonhoeffer stared at the empty fireplace. "There's a chill this evening," he said. "I'll have Elli light the fires. And what will you speak about?"

"The church."

His father shrugged. "I don't see how that could upset anyone."

He thought back on the only sermon he had preached at Abyssinian Baptist. He had been nervous then as well, for he knew he could never match the preaching style of the Powells, the scaling of emotional heights that caused people to call out from their pews.

He therefore had started slowly, preaching on a text from the Gospel of Luke, concentrating on speaking clearly so his accent would not make his words incomprehensible. They had listened in polite silence until he quoted from his Gospel text

The Spirit of the Lord is upon me, because he hath anointed me to preach the gospel to the poor

and he had no sooner uttered *poor* than a woman's voice shouted

AMEN!

He was startled but continued more slowly and emphatically
heal the brokenhearted
AMEN BROTHER!

deliverance to the captives
PRAISE JESUS!

to set at liberty them that are bruised, to preach the acceptable year of the Lord

BLESSHISNAMEPRAISEJESUS!

they cried out from all parts of the sanctuary, the call and response continuing through the rest of the sermon. He found himself anticipating his words, even in midsentence, leaving out arid phrases, even entire paragraphs, repeating everything that seemed full-blooded.

It was nothing like a sermon by Pastor Powell, people would say as they filed out of the sanctuary, and the white man had seemed more moved than they, and yet they honored his effort. He had been trembling visibly when he sat down, and his face was wet with sweat though it was February. He wiped his eyeglasses on the sleeve of his cassock.

Back in his room at Union he had gone over the sermon, striking out everything he hadn't said with red ink, rewriting what remained.

As the day of the sermon approached, Dietrich had difficulty sleeping. He would stay up late working, making painstaking notes in a small, neat script. Then he would be too keyed up to sleep and mentally review what he had written, trying to imagine how it would sound from the pulpit. Turtledoves settled on the eaves above his open window, muttering to themselves. From the Halensee came a distant squabbling of ducks, interrupted by a passing automobile, then silence. He switched on the bedside lamp and scanned his notes once more, then took a sleeping pill and lay back on the pillow. As he drifted off he heard a thin wailing of sirens, perhaps police rushing to a brawl between Communists and Nazis. The Nazis must be getting the worst of it, or the police would not be so anxious to intervene. He turned on his stomach, then back again, and in that borderland between waking and sleep Dietrich would be back in the boxcar hearing Fred Bishop say *I hope you never get a call I wouldn't wish it on you* and Dietrich wouldn't answer, would just try to listen.

He had been writing a treatise on the nature of the church, and writing about the church he had felt himself falling in love with his subject in all her hideous corruption. As a man falls in love with a whore, as did the prophet Hosea, he told Elisabeth, who was the only person he could speak with of such things. The sermon he would deliver at the Kaiser Wilhelm Church must convey this somehow, along with his own awkward groping toward personal faith.

He wanted to tell Elisabeth what had happened to him at the end of his stay in America but found he could not yet speak of it. He nursed these memories like a fresh wound. He had written once to West Virginia, the week after returning to Germany, and received no reply. He meant to write again, but he was held back by some sense that it was easier not to know what was happening to Fred, who was becoming somewhat unreal, a part of imagination rather than memory. The blurring of his face helped Dietrich sleep at last.

Amid the faux-Gothic splendor of the Kaiser Wilhelm Memorial Church, the trumpet voluntary sounded beneath nineteenth-century gargoyles who had never watched over bubonic plague or witch-burning. Dietrich surveyed the tightly packed rows of beribboned officers, women in autumn colors of brown, gold, and green, government ministers in frock coats and starched collars. President Hindenburg, corpulent and dyspeptic, sat in the front pew, his monocle glinting in the morning sun like a photographic flash.

Dietrich ascended a pulpit of fantastically carved oak, enclosed like a small house and roofed with a crown of gold. From the middle of the church, where Elisabeth sat beside Sabine, he looked blond to the point of transparency, and very young.

"He's frightened to death," Sabine whispered.

Elisabeth nodded. She was grateful Sabine had spoken to her. Though not normally a shy person, she, an only child, had felt overwhelmed by the vast tribe of Bonhoeffers—and especially the beloved Sabine—at the breakfast in honor of Dietrich's sermon. She had thought, They know exactly who belongs to them and who does not, or will not be allowed to. Meeting them is like standing before a choir of angels while awaiting the disposition of one's soul.

Dietrich was reading a part of the appointed lesson, his voice low at first but gaining strength as he went.

"From the second chapter of Revelation we hear these words: *Nevertheless I have somewhat against thee, because thou hast left thy first love.*"

He looked up, searching for the family. Halfway back he glimpsed his mother's green hat.

He took a deep breath and said, "The church has reached the eleventh hour of her life. Before long it will be decided whether a new day will dawn, or whether the church is done for. It is high time we realized this."

They sat as though transformed into pillars of salt.

"The trumpets sound on this Reformation Sunday. We celebrate Martin Luther and the courageous stand he made. But a fanfare of trumpets is no comfort to a dying church, much less can it bring her back to life. A fanfare of trumpets is a shout down the cold silence of a still colder clamor, where funeral marches hide the stench of mortality. Such fanfares are known to all of us in the church, and they are a proclamation of death."

He did not want to see their faces. They were before him briefly, and then he saw them no longer. He was at Abyssinian Baptist. He leaned forward, beating the pulpit gently with his fist, trying to recover the cadence, to hear the ghostly call and response.

"The church which celebrates Reformation Day cannot leave poor Luther in peace. He is called on to support all our fearful practices. We prop up this dead man, cause him to stretch out his hand, fingers bloated as overripe fruit, point to this church and cry, with religious fervor, over and over again: 'Here I stand, I cannot do otherwise!' And we do not see that this church is no longer the church of Luther. It was in fear and trembling, driven by Satan into his last stronghold, that Luther spoke in the fear of God his 'here I stand.'

"What has this to do with us today? No one here has stood in that place from which he can only say to God in prayer, 'I cannot otherwise, so help me God!' Thousands of times today it will be proclaimed from the pulpits: *Here I stand, I cannot do otherwise!*

"But God answers, 'I have somewhat against thee. . . .'"

He removed his glasses, wiped them and placed them in his pocket, looked over the congregation with blurred vision. He gripped the sides of the pulpit.

"Leave the dead Luther in peace," he said, "and hear the word of God."

Then he stepped down.

The family left immediately after the service, so that they might prepare for the reception at the house in Wangenheimstraße 14, supervise the handing out of nosegays, lay out the plates of smoked herring on ice, place the string quartet in an appropriate spot. Only Elisabeth stayed behind. She caught him as he left the church alone. He stopped, bowed his head, and she grabbed his hands.

"What you did today," she said, "was what you were put on earth to do."

He reached out and drew her close, squeezing the breath from her, then walked with her out the arched stone door.

From Morn to Midnight
1933

THE BUILDING WAS one of the more nondescript in the Schloß Straße, four floors of peeling brown stucco and crumbling stone steps. A sign above the bell read

CHARLOTTENBURG YOUTH CLUB
Open 6:00 p.m.–10:00 p.m.
Everyone under 25 WELCOME

It had once been home to an expatriate Church of England congregation which had moved on to more ecclesiastical surroundings. The basement was kitchen and social hall. The ground floor had a large room—painted in drabgreen and dimly lit—with a stage. The Anglicans had used this room for Sunday worship. A gothic IHS was carved into the movable podium and embossed in frayed gold on the purple drapes above the stage. The ground-floor windows were streaked with grime, and the carcasses of flies littered the sills between iron bars and glass panes.

The first and second floors had smaller rooms for classes and meetings. Falk Harnack taught acting and public speaking, Elisabeth art, Suse literacy, and Dietrich—in addition to a sparsely attended course in ethics—gave piano lessons. The piano was an upright that had once served a vaudeville hall, and three keys, including middle C, were missing their ivory. He developed a callus on the side of his right thumb.

He had fallen into an agreeable routine, morning at the university, noon meal at home with his mother, afternoon study and writing in his room, and a light supper with Elisabeth before going together to the club. They sometimes held hands on the tram but were otherwise no more demonstrative in public than a couple married half a century. In the drawing room of Wangenheimstraße 14—he rarely allowed himself to be alone with her in her flat—they sat side by side on the sofa. The Bonhoeffer parents had never permitted their daughters to be alone with their young men until their engagement, and though Dietrich was a son and therefore allowed more freedom, he feared to act on it. He had only recently been ordained, and he was his parents' child.

One evening when he had accompanied Elisabeth to her flat, he allowed himself to stand in the doorway and kiss her briefly. It was the greatest pleasure he had ever experienced, placing the tip of his finger beneath her chin, shutting his eyes so that he might have been dreaming as he leaned forward, tasting her lips and then a fleeting touch of her tongue. Afterward he held her for a moment, his cheek resting against her hair, which smelled slightly of soap. Then he pulled away, looking at his watch and mumbling that he had nearly forgotten he must meet with a student in half an hour. He knew this abrupt withdrawal confused and hurt Elisabeth, but he had felt a surge of desire so fearfully strong he knew nothing to do except flee.

At the club, Suse and Falk noted the budding romance with winks and nudges. They were themselves lovers, Suse having shared Falk's bed in his Magdeburger Platz flat. No one in the family knew, of course, since the parents would have been scandalized. Suse and Falk both knew this would not be a lasting relationship. Falk would not settle down with one woman, not for years anyway. As for Suse, he often drove her wild with his politics, since she liked to laugh about everything and he would not be teased about his Communist sympathies.

"If he'd talk like a human being instead of a bloody pamphlet," she complained to Elisabeth, "he might be bearable."

She doubted the times or his personality lent themselves to such a transformation. Still he was good-humored otherwise, and an excellent lover. She would wait until they tired of sleeping together, and then decide if the time had come to tend a home and family.

It was an unquiet New Year. Rumors flew that President Hindenburg was dying, that the chancellor, von Papen, was scheming to replace him with Hitler, that von Papen's enemy Schleicher had suffered a nervous breakdown, that the Communists were plotting to murder businessmen in their beds and ravish their wives, that the Jews, wealthy to a man and stingy as packrats, would hoard the nation's riches in foreign bank accounts until Germany was brought to her knees, that poor men who entered the green cast-iron public pissoirs at night were being castrated by Nazi gangs, that the poor women who waited in line for hours to buy a scrap of rancid meat were being poisoned by the fascists were being abducted from the line into white slavery were being sold the flesh of their own children instead of pork. Hitler and his followers were conspicuously present at Holy Day services across Germany, praying visibly and piously. In many churches, the crosses on Christmas altars were flanked by the national flag and the swastika, in thanksgiving for the gifts of Baby Jesus and Fatherland. On

New Year's Eve, torchlight parades wound through Nuremberg Munich Weimar Regensburg Cologne Heidelberg Düsseldorf Bremen Passau . . .

At the Charlottenburg Youth Club, Falk Harnack posted a notice announcing auditions for the club play. He would be directing *From Morn to Midnight,* by the expressionist Georg Kaiser.

Dietrich read the script and objected.

"This," he said, "is the most cynical piece of work imaginable."

"What would you suggest?" Falk said. "The man is brilliant. He even collaborates with Kurt Weill."

They sat in the basement kitchen sipping coffee and smoking after locking up for the night, surrounded by cheap wood cabinets that had once held heavy crockery, pots and pans, but now stood empty, their bottoms littered with old mouse droppings.

"I had thought," Dietrich said, "perhaps Hofmannstahl."

Falk blew smoke at the ceiling.

"He's good for young people," Dietrich said. "We performed his plays when I was a schoolboy. His work has a moral center."

"As if a moral center exists. Hofmannstahl is crashingly old-fashioned. Worse than that. He's positively medieval, a monk writing morality plays. And my God, the man was a librettist for Wagner! I'd rather die than do Hofmannstahl."

"Falk *does* want something up to date," Suse said in what she hoped was a conciliatory tone.

"To say the least," Falk said. "If Georg Kaiser is cynical, he reflects our times."

"But it does no good," said Dietrich, "to go on and on in a nihilistic way. That leads only to inaction."

"I have another objection," said Elisabeth. "I don't care for the scene in the velodrome with the identically dressed Jewish gentlemen. I think it's anti-Semitic, and the Jewish young people won't like it any better than I do."

"Why don't we do Brecht instead?" Suse asked.

"But you don't like Brecht either, do you?" Falk said to Dietrich. "You don't care for anyone who's penned a play since fucking 1914."

"I won't apologize for my taste," said Dietrich.

But it was Falk's play, and after this initial protest they acquiesced. They agreed to help with the audition and handed out mimeographed copies of the script—at least with the reference to the gentlemen in the velodrome as Jewish scrupulously marked out with black ink—while Falk stood on the low stage. The young people—Dietrich and the others always thought of them as the young people even though they (Elisabeth was the oldest, at twenty-nine) were not much older—sat on the folding chairs or in cross-legged Red Indian style on the floor. They had narrow faces and eyes bright with cunning and hunger. The boys had only thin jackets despite the winter cold, the girls wore plain dresses with torn stockings and scuffed shoes.

"Here's the play in brief," Falk said. "The central character is a Cashier in a bank. It's the most difficult part, since it demands the mastery of several long speeches and soliloquies. The Cashier is a symbol of our times. He exists in a bourgeois society where life has absolutely no meaning. Only money counts."

The young people listened and hungered.

"The Cashier," Falk was saying, "is trapped in a capitalist world, literally behind the bars of his teller's cage."

Dietrich and Elisabeth stood with Suse in the back. Suse sighed loudly. "He *will* work in his politics," she whispered.

"A beautiful woman enters the bank at the same time another character, the Stout Gentleman, is depositing a large sum of money. The Cashier, certain the woman is attracted to him, believes she will only run away with him if he is wealthy, so he steals the money. When he realizes he has misunderstood the lady's attentions, he flees alone into a larger world just as devoid of meaning as the bank. He escapes his tiresome family, wanders for a time in a wilderness, throws away vast sums in a velodrome and a restaurant, pursues women in a hedonistic way. None of this satisfies his longings. Then he meets a girl from the Salvation Army who takes him to a meeting where he is urged to repent of his supposed sins. As if he, and not society, were the perpetrator of his misery. He trusts the girl, who seems to represent what is good and spiritual, but she betrays him to the police. He sees there is no place for him in this corrupt world. And so he shoots himself, gasping 'Ecce homo' as he dies—ah, that means 'Behold the man'—a last declaration of his fleeting and futile existence."

The young people nudged one another, whispered among themselves, the low murmuring punctuated by titters.

"What's wrong with a nice love story?" one of the girls called out.

"Yah," a boy yelled at her, "just because you want to be the one who gets laid!"

Laughter erupted, and Falk's face reddened. He called for attention. When they had quieted, he said, "These are serious times. Love, sentimental love at least, is a luxury we cannot afford just now."

At the back of the hall Suse moaned, "Oh, God."

"In any event," Falk continued, "you have the wrong idea about art. Art, true art, is a weapon. A play like this can open your eyes, open the eyes of your audience, to what is happening in the world."

When the young people had left and the doors were locked for the night, only thirteen had signed up to audition.

"Each scene has a different cast of characters," Suse commiserated, "so it is possible with thirteen if some take on double roles."

"It's their lack of purpose . . ." Falk complained.

Elisabeth was studying the sign-up sheet. "No one has asked for the Cashier."

Falk threw up his hands. "Only the most important part."

"They're just shy," said Dietrich. "I mean, look at the script. The Cashier's speeches aren't just long, they're very dense. If you'd never performed in public before, would you want to take it on?"

Suse clapped her hands. "I've an idea! You could play the Cashier, Falk."

"I didn't plan on acting, Suse. It should be their play."

"But listen. If they see you perform, they'll learn so much just from watching you. You can teach by example."

He hesitated. "Well. What do you lot think?"

Dietrich and Elisabeth had moved away and begun discussing where to go for cake and coffee. They stared at him.

"Falk to play the Cashier," Suse said, making gestures behind Falk's back to her brother.

"Of course," Dietrich said. "Why not?"

"No one's signed for the Stout Gentleman either," Falk said.

"They're all far too starved to play a stout man," said Suse.

Falk said, "You could do it, Dietrich."

"Me?"

"Suse told me you loved to act when you were in school."

"Yes, but—"

"Dietrich is not stout," Elisabeth said loyally.

"He's a large man," said Falk, "and he has the face for the part. You could wear a bit more padding, Dietrich, and be the very image of a greedy capitalist."

"Thanks very much," Dietrich said.

It was settled. Suse would help with costumes and lights, and Elisabeth would be stage manager. They exited the front door, stepped through a curtain of snow into a circle of streetlight, faced one another, each couple aware of the other as audience. Falk and Suse stood apart, feigning indifference as they began to imagine the approaching pleasures of the bed. Dietrich folded Elisabeth's arm through his, formally, said goodnight, and led her away. It was as though the eighteenth century bid farewell to the twentieth.

Dietrich and Elisabeth walked in silence. Beneath each streetlamp she glanced at his illumined face, hoping to see something in it she had been longing for, something she had seen in the faces of Falk and Suse just now. But instead the familiar melancholy was there.

"Did Falk hurt your feelings?" she asked.

He shook his head slightly.

"You never tell me how you really feel," Elisabeth said.

He didn't reply.

"I want to be close to you," she said, "and you make it so difficult."

They stopped at the top of the steps at the U-Bahn station in Sophie-Charlotte-Platz.

She said, "You draw into yourself and won't let anyone near. I have an acquaintance who teaches at the university. He says there's more than your politics to isolate you from others. The students who do come to you, who are drawn to your theology, are also in awe. They think you feel superior, that you won't deign to grow close to anyone inferior. It puts people off."

He turned his face away from her.

"Why can't a person be who he is?" he said.

She reached out and touched his arm. "I told you this because I care about you. Dietrich, I believe I'm falling in love with you."

He didn't move, didn't answer. After a moment, she left him, making her way down the concrete steps to the train platform. He didn't follow.

HE SOMETIMES THOUGHT his depressions were not limited to his own mind but were part of the times. The economy was depressed, the German people were depressed, the government was paralyzed by depression. Where once his moods had only driven him to his room, he now took to the streets, as though searching for the causes of his infirmity, or perhaps for fellow sufferers. So he went out on the night Hitler was named chancellor, the night Berlin seemed to throw off its ennui and exult, even the doubters, even the enemies, to come alive again because everything had begun.

No one in the family accompanied him. Sabine and Gerhard were lying low in Göttingen, frightened. Very few Jews would go abroad that night in Germany. Suse was with Falk, who was equally cautious, for he was known in some circles for his Bolshevik sympathies. The other Bonhoeffers would not associate themselves with so vulgar a show, and the mother and father retired early to read Dostoevsky in bed, secure in the knowledge that a buffoon like Hitler could not last long. Only Hans von Dohnanyi had seemed consumed by events. He returned home early from the Foreign Office and, while Christel gave the children their cocoa and biscuits, sat in the study of the house in Sacrow, before a blazing fire, and committed a foot-high stack of documents to the flames. As he watched the white sheets turn livid and then shrivel into black wafers, he laid his plans.

Dietrich would know nothing of this yet, not as he traipsed to the Grunewald station and took the train to Friedrichstraße. The cars were jammed with revelers, many of them sporting swastika armbands or waving the red-white-and-black flag. He had not supposed there would be so many. At Friedrichstraße the crowds swept him up and carried him to Unter den Linden. Everyone seemed to know there would be a parade, though none had been announced, and that it would pass beneath the Brandenburg Gate. They jostled and pushed for a place along the sidewalk, or climbed stone horses and perched on their rumps, holding on to the frozen riders for support.

Then he entered a sorcerer's fantasy. A lake of torchlight rippling like the Havel in a high wind, filling the width of Unter den Linden. The chants *Sieg-heil Sieg-heil Ju-den raus Ju-den raus* and above all the drums, which lodged inside his head, and ran down his spine like a pointed finger. The door of the university thrown open and light streaming from within, blotted out now and then by faceless gnomes, backs bent, entering and leaving with stacks of books in their arms. The bonfire in the university courtyard.

He drew closer and saw the gnomes were students casting volume after volume on the fire, reveling in their newfound freedom. From now on, they would read what they liked. When Dietrich grabbed a young man laden with books and asked what in God's name he was doing, he was shoved rudely against a stone pillar and hit the back of his head so hard he nearly blacked out. But an SS band was passing by and the music brought him around.

He would never admit to anyone, not then or later, that he loved the drums, that they stirred him and roused him and made him long to join the marchers just as Fess Williams and his Royal Flush Orchestra had once led him to the Cats Corner. For the first time in his life as he leaned against that pillar and watched the students rush past him and felt the drums raise a lump in his throat and draw him toward the street, he began to distrust music.

After a while he wandered to the Ludwigkirchplatz. He had not seen Elisabeth for weeks, except at the club (where they were civil and restrained, to the disappointment of Suse), not since that night she left him standing in Sophie-Charlotte-Platz. She was a long time in answering his knock, and before opening the door, asked in a low voice, "Who is it?"

When he answered she opened the door quietly and stood looking at him, but did not move to let him in. Her face was drawn with worry, and there were dark circles beneath her eyes.

"What do you want?" she asked. "I would have thought you'd be safe and sound in the Grunewald."

"I didn't want to be safe tonight," he said.

Only then did she step aside and let him enter.

Even in her flat, windows shut against the cold, they could hear the drums.

"My head is throbbing," he said.

She sat beside him. He huddled, seemed to invite comforting. When she pulled him close, her fingers touched the sticky patch on the back of his head.

"What happened?"

"I was shoved against a pillar and hit my head."

She went for a cloth and a bowl of hot water. He leaned against the sofa and shut his eyes. When she returned she pressed the wet cloth to the back of his head without speaking, then pulled his face to her lap while she gently wiped the caked blood from his blond hair.

"It's not very deep," she said. "But you've got a lump."

He didn't try to sit up. She watched him for a time, then put aside the wet cloth and stroked his temple, traced the outline of his mouth with the tip of a finger.

"I have never meant to keep things from you," he murmured. "I sometimes feel I have nothing to give anyone. It's this damned melancholy. My father says it has to do with the chemistry of the brain, but to me it seems a spiritual illness."

Her fingers smoothed the damp hair from his forehead. "You keep saying that. Can anyone be spiritually whole?"

"I don't know. I have a friend in America, a Negro, who is faithful, or seems so to me. Though he is no saint."

She considered this. "Do you love this man?"

"Yes."

"What of me?" she asked. "Do you love me?"

He sat up, embarrassed, and began to adjust the spindly gold frames of his glasses.

"This is not the time," she said, a hint of coolness in her voice, "to love a Negro in America or a Jewess in the Fatherland. And yet if you are to find what you seek, Dietrich, you shall have to face up to love."

He turned from her, his body hunched forward. "There is love," he said, "and there is desire. I'm trying to discern the difference."

"Both are gifts from God."

"And yet love does not threaten chastity, whereas desire can confuse—"

She reached out and placed her hand on his cheek. "Sometimes," she said, "you think too much. And on such a night as this—"

He suddenly pulled her to him, sliding down until they lay full length upon the sofa. He gasped like a man being pulled underwater. "What are we doing?"

She unbuttoned his shirt and hid her face against his shoulder. "Making a safe place," she said.

ON THE MORNING of February 1, Elisabeth Hildebrandt turns on her radio. Dietrich is to broadcast a talk as part of a regular series of university lectures. Elisabeth sits at her dressing table, before the mirror, arranging her hair. The radio crackles and she twists the knob slightly. She hears an announcer from Reich Broadcasting, the RRG, then Dietrich's voice enters the bedroom.

. . . *my subject is "The Younger Generation's Changed View of the Concept of Führer."* . . .

Elisabeth brushes her hair back from her forehead.

. . . *the narcissism which often accompanies youth can be corrupted by old men* . . .

She pictures him at the Broadcasting House in the Potsdamer Straße, seated before a bank of gauges with waving needles, hunched over his notes.

. . . *authority is necessary but must be properly constituted. It is a necessary corrective to both selfish individualism and smothering collectivism* . . .

She smiles. "Falk will hate that part," she says to the radio.

. . . *but when a people, a nation, make an idol of authority, then the leader shall become a misleader—*

She has just caught her hair above her ear with a barrette when the radio crackles and falls silent save for a low hiss. The room is suddenly bereft of Dietrich.

In the Broadcasting House he is still talking intently, anxious not to stumble over a word.

. . . *The leader who makes an idol of himself and his office mocks God.*

Then he looks up and sees the needles are frozen and the red light on the board has gone out. He looks through the glass wall at the technician in the next room. When Dietrich gathers his notes and leaves, he stops beside the man's desk.

"Was I cut off?"

The technician shrugs without removing his headphones. "If you were, it was done upstairs," he says. "Don't complain to me." He turns away and begins to sort through a stack of record albums. Without looking up, he says, "It may be just as well for you if you were."

Doppelgänger

SS-Obersturmführer Alois Bauer, having grown with the century, turns thirty-three in February of 1933. He believes this, coinciding as it does with the coming to power of the Führer, is auspicious, and celebrates with a visit to the Prussian State Library in Unter den Linden.

He has been once before, in 1931. Then he made the same request he proposes for today, to view the original manuscript of his favorite work of Mozart's, the Mass in C Minor. In 1931, the request was denied.

Now he enters once more and asks for the curator of the manuscript collection. He is ushered at once to a long table beside a window overlooking the courtyard. A small, balding man in a gray suit approaches nervously.

"The Mass in C Minor," Bauer says. "Mozart. You have the original manuscript in your possession."

"We do, Herr Obersturmführer."

"I would like to look at it. It's a special favorite of mine, you see."

The curator notes the death's-head ring on the left hand, which rests comfortably on the tabletop, the black-handled knife and pistol in the belt, the officer's insignia and double S's like bolts of lightning on the uniform collar.

"Certainly. You may wait here."

Bauer smiles and nods his thanks.

The manuscript, when it arrives in a plain white folder, has turned the color of old butter and is brittle with age. Bauer touches it reverently. "Shouldn't it be under glass?" he asks.

"We haven't room to display everything in that way. It is kept in a climate-controlled vault, and of course it is rarely handled."

Bauer lays the folder flat on the table and carefully slides out a manuscript page with the tip of his finger, admiring the shapely notes like spiders in the web of treble and bass staffs. At the Domine he begins to hum softly, nodding his head slightly in time to an internal rhythm. He pauses at the end of the Et Incarnatus Est.

"Where's the Sanctus? The Benedictus?"

The curator shrugs. "No one knows. They did come into the library's possession with the rest of the manuscript, but they disappeared sometime before the turn of the century."

Bauer whispers, "But it is the most beautiful part of the Mass."

"It has been reconstructed using the notes of Johann Anton André, a famed musical historian who owned the manuscript before it came to us."

"Reconstructed! Then it might not be as Mozart meant it to be. And yet . . ." He stands suddenly. "You have not guarded this treasure, Herr Curator. Not as you should."

The curator turns pale. "It was before my time," he stammers.

"Nevertheless. The Mass in C Minor deserves better than this—" he waves his arm—"this dusty sepulcher."

And he walks out, near tears, leaving the shaken curator to gingerly return the manuscript to its folder.

The playbill read

FROM MORN TO MIDNIGHT
A drama of modern life by
Georg Kaiser

Saturday, February 12
8:00 p.m.

CHARLOTTENBURG YOUTH CLUB
Schloß Straße 63

Admission 10 pfennigs; free for the unemployed

The young people were dispatched to post the notices on sidewalk pillars in every neighborhood from Neukölln to Tegel. There the thin gray sheets buffeted by wind and sleet melted into layers of old playbills and political posters, announcements of art exhibits, concerts, lectures, rallies. The tattered thirteen-year accumulation of the Republic. Some playbills, Falk Harnack noticed on his walks near the Technical University, had been defaced by swastikas.

He mentioned this to Otto Linke, a young Communist from a tenement in Marsstraße whose father had built locomotives for Borsig but was now unemployed. Otto was an exceptionally homely young man, with splayed ears peaked at their crests like a bat's, but with a gift for ignoring his odd appearance. He would be playing the roles of the Manager in Scene One and the Policeman in Scene Seven. He said, "I know who is drawing swastikas on posters in Tegel. They come here as well."

"Not here to the youth club?"

"Of course. Some of them live in my building."

"Why would workers support a party that despises them?"

"The Nazis have been helping with our rent strike. Not as much as the Communists, but almost. And they bring food. Some people say they're after the same thing as the Communists, but they're more patriotic. They don't answer to the Russians."

"That's preposterous!"

Otto shrugged. "I'm just telling you."

That was why Falk announced without warning at rehearsal, "Is anyone in this cast a Nazi sympathizer?"

There was a moment of stunned silence as they looked up from their dog-eared scripts. Elisabeth was the first to recover.

"You know we don't bring politics into the club," she said.

"This is not about politics," Falk said, "this is about fascism. I will not have a fascist in this play." He looked around. "Any admirer of Hitler in this room should leave now."

Two boys in the back who had the parts of soldiers nudged each other and stood up. One walked to the door with his head down. The other stopped near Falk, dropped his script on the floor, and said "Heil Hitler" in a low, taunting voice.

"Get out," Falk said.

Dietrich said, "Wait. We must talk about this."

The boy, who had joined his friend at the door, turned and glared at Falk. "It's a stupid play anyway. Enjoy it while you can, Bolshies. Your days are numbered." Then they stalked out.

Everyone began to talk at the same time, the young people among themselves, Dietrich Elisabeth and Suse remonstrating with Falk. Four other youths slipped out, one of them flipping a Nazi salute behind Falk's back.

"How do we reach them if they aren't here?" Suse was saying.

"Reach them? Suse, you're so goddamn naive. You can't convert a Nazi."

Dietrich said, "Why then did we begin this club?"

"To reach out to working-class youth, to keep them out of the hands of the fascists. The Nazis are inside the barricades. If we don't fight them now, we'll never be free of them."

"You can't believe Hitler will last. The German people have much more sense—"

Suse tugged on Dietrich's arm. "Stop it, you two." She nodded at the young people, who had grown quiet and begun listening.

Falk turned away and ran his hand through his hair, stared at the ceiling a moment, then said, "All right, we lost two members of the cast."

"Six," someone said.

He shut his eyes. "Six, then. Never mind, we'll recruit new people. The fascists will not stop this production."

Dietrich loved play-acting. He was good at it, capable of stepping out of his own skin and losing himself in a character. At play's end he would feel as refreshed as though waking from a deep and pleasant dream. That, at least, had been his boyhood experience, in school productions of Goethe and Hauptmann and E.T.A. Hoffmann. He was surprised to learn it was true for the hideously modern Georg Kaiser as well. As he rehearsed the part of the Stout Gentleman, he secretly baptized his anonymous character with a Christian name, Fritz. Fritz was Stout because he ate too much. He ate too much because he was lonely. Though greedy and facile, he was also painfully aware of his own repulsiveness. In short, Fritz suffered. Though bored by the Stout Gentleman, Dietrich was glad to present Fritz to the world.

None of the family, save Suse, of course, was faintly interested in attending the play. So they would not see Dietrich in his oversized trousers held up by suspenders and stuffed with a large feather pillow, suit coat barely buttoned over his bulging stomach. Nor would Elisabeth's father and grandfather be present. Grandfather Nathan tended to fall asleep after seven o'clock, and her father would be on call at the Charité, waiting at his surgeon's table to receive the slashed, beaten, and blasted offerings of the new regime.

Dietrich would have been happy to act before Leo Hildebrandt, to offer another side of himself for inspection. He had been once to the physician's spacious home in a quiet tree-lined street in Dahlem. Nathan Hildebrandt, eighty-five years old and frail, had not come down from his room, but Dietrich and Leo had smoked cigars companionably in the study while Elisabeth looked in on her grandfather. The two men had been wary of each other, since each knew of the other from Karl Bonhoeffer. To his colleague, Dr. Bonhoeffer had once complained of his youngest son's choice of vocation and melancholy reserve—"though Dietrich has a marvelous sense of humor once you know him, and he is unfailingly kind. But he's lost when it comes to such hardheaded matters as politics and finance—" an embarrassed glance away—"and women. He's quite shy." His opinion of Leo Hildebrandt, he told his son after meeting Elisabeth, was one of "the greatest admiration for his professional ability, one of the finest surgeons in Germany. But an emotional man, enjoys the pleasures of the flesh. He's had several affairs since the death of his wife. And he's raised the girl as though she were a son. Rather unconventional. You might be careful how deeply you become involved with her."

Dietrich stood now in the small room off the stage, which was actually a janitor's pantry, and waited for his cue. He had the first lines, and felt the responsibility of pulling the audience—heard through the curtain talking loudly and rattling chairs—into the story as though plunging them into a deep pool of water. Elisabeth was watching Falk the Cashier take his place behind a counter with iron bars, her face calm as if her mind were elsewhere. Then Falk pointed at her. She turned to Dietrich, blew him a kiss, and reached for the rope that hung beside her, reached high with her head thrown back, as though ringing a church bell, and drew the curtains open.

THE CURTAINS PART, the lights—such as they are—go up. The Stout Gentleman strides onto the stage, flinging his arms as though casting off Dietrich. He sits upon a wooden chair near the Cashier's counter, hands cradling his pillowed belly to keep it from shifting. His trousers are ill-fitting, and he plucks at the material where it binds him across the knees, pulling the pant legs up to show brown socks, garters, and an inch of milk-white flesh. He looks around impatiently while the Cashier completes a transaction with a Messenger Boy—Falk Harnack and a skinny twelve-year-old urchin named Ernst after Thälmann the Communist leader. The Messenger Boy leaves and the Stout Gentleman lunges forward, briefcase in hand.

Now the fat fellows take their turn, he announces.

But he is interrupted by the arrival of a Lady—though no lady but a buxom raven-haired baker's daughter from Prenzlauer Berg—and gallantly gives way to her, saying, The fat fellows can wait.

Though he ogles her in an ungallant manner.

Her transaction is questioned, for she wishes to withdraw a great deal of money on an account in Florence. The Manager—Otto Linke in the first of his roles and quite uncomfortable in the only high starched collar he has ever worn—enters and arrogantly refuses her the money, insinuating she might instead sell herself in her hotel. She leaves in tears.

STOUT GENTLEMAN: Three thousand marks is not bad. I guess three hundred wouldn't sound bad to her either.

MANAGER: Perhaps you would like to make a lower offer at the Elephant? In her room?

The audience titters. Dietrich feels very hot, and despises the Stout Gentleman. He has forgotten Fritz.

STOUT GENTLEMAN: Now it's time for fat fellows to unload.

MANAGER: What are you bringing us this morning?

STOUT GENTLEMAN: [sets his briefcase on the counter and flips it open to reveal stacks of bills. A flourish] With all the confidence that your elegant clientele inspires.

MANAGER: In any case we are immune to a pretty face when it comes to business.

STOUT GENTLEMAN: [counts money in briefcase] How old was she, at a guess?

MANAGER: I haven't seen her without rouge—yet.

STOUT GENTLEMAN: What's she doing here?

MANAGER: We'll hear that tonight at the Elephant.

The young men in the audience hoot. Dietrich retreats backstage, where he unbuttons his jacket and pulls the sweat-drenched pillow from his trousers. The Lady is in her hotel room, explaining that she wanted the money so her son could purchase a painting; Falk the Cashier arrives with the Stout Gentleman's money, which he has embezzled; the Lady rejects the Cashier, who sets off on his round of meaningless adventures.

Dietrich watches for a time, his arm around Elisabeth's waist. Then she shrugs him off.

"Sorry," she says, "I've got to close the curtain."

"It should stay closed," he says.

She pokes him in his smaller but still fleshy midsection and says, "Very funny."

SS-Obersturmführer Alois Bauer is drunk, as are his twelve comrades. They are visiting beer gardens and cafés, starting beside the duck pond in the Tiergarten and moving to the Romanische Café, which quickly empties as *artistes* with white-painted faces and black mascara slip out the back door. *You're dead Bol-shie ghosts,* the SS boys chant, and pound the tables with their death's-head rings turned palm down while they wait for their brandy. After several rounds they graciously leave the place intact and wander on up the Fasanenstraße, where they throw paving stones at the doomed synagogue, not yet doing damage, since their aim is so erratic. They stagger on beyond the Savignyplatz, so tipsy and raucous they are turned out of a beer garden despite their black uniforms by a handful of cautious policemen, into Kantstraße, where they pile onto a tram and slide off at the bottom of Schloß Straße, though they know nothing of where they are. (Someone has suggested this is where a lot of Jews live.) There they sprawl on the front steps of a house—two of the youngest tussle happily on the sidewalk and roll into a bank of frozen old snow—singing "Deutschland, Deutschland über Alles" at the top of their lungs. They take turns pissing against the front door to watch the steam rise from their urine. Across the way a shade is slowly drawn and a light blinks out.

Inside the Charlottenburg Youth Club, the audience is restive. The Cashier has just ended a long soliloquy—

The earth is in labor, spring gales at last! That's better! I knew my cry could not be in vain. My demand was urgent. Chaos is insulted and will not be put to shame by my colossal deed of this morning. I knew it. In a case like mine never let up. Go at them hard—pull down their cloaks and you'll see something etc. etc. etc.

—delivered in a snowstorm of shredded cotton balls blown about by electric fans. In the audience, flasks of peppermint schnapps are drawn from coat pockets and passed surreptitiously. When the flasks are empty, some young people in the back—four boys and two girls—slip out the door, determined to find a bench in a cozy pub and drink more schnapps. Outside, the cold air rouses them and drives them into one another's arms. They are linked together singing "Wem Gott will Rechte Gunst erweisen" when they happen upon the drunken SS. Taunts are exchanged, a few paving stones thrown. The young people, realizing they are outnumbered and yet more sober than their opponents, flee laughing down the Schloß Straße. But Obersturmführer Alois Bauer, though drunk as anyone, has leadership qualities, and has noted which house they came from. His comrades, squaring their shoulders and locating the blackjacks that hang from skewed belts beneath their greatcoats, leaning against one another for support, gather around him outside the Charlottenburg Youth Club.

The Cashier, on the run from the Authorities, has placed his life in the hands of a Salvation Army Lass. Of course he believes she will save him, since she represents Christian charity; of course because she represents Christian charity she will betray him. The Cashier staggers across the stage in the midst of a demonic revival meeting shouting his protests while demented penitents confess their sins. He is pursued by the Salvation Army Lass, who lusts for his bloody soul as though possessed of a vampire's fangs.

So Dietrich thinks, rather melodramatically he admits to himself, as he watches the final act. Falk Harnack, he would say, should stick to directing rather than acting, assuming his taste in plays improves.

The Cashier is screaming something like *the beginning and the end Maiden and man fullness in the void Maiden and man the seed and the flower send and aim and goal*

and the Lass flings open a plywood door to reveal Otto Linke, now the Policeman, whom she sets on the Cashier like a bellowing foxhound.

The Cashier reaches in his pocket as the drunken SS in black greatcoats stagger into the room waving their cudgels above their heads and whooping like the Red Indians in a Karl May potboiler. The Policeman is crying *Switch off that light,* which is his line, but the room has erupted and Falk who is now living only for the play has the gun out, the gun which he should press to his chest and do away with himself in a grand statement of existential angst except Alois Bauer spots the pistol which threatens harm to his own boys and finds his own gun and while Falk stands unsure whether to shoot himself or flee, fires at the Cashier hitting him in the shoulder and sending him sprawling across the stage just before one of the young people knocks the gun from Bauer's hand and another brings a folding chair down over his head.

Falk raises himself up, imagines his lines *why did I hesitate why take the road whither am I bound from first to last you sit there naked bone from morn to midnight I rage in a circle,* then a wave of white heat emanates from his shattered shoulder to his scalp to his toetips and Dietrich and Elisabeth are lifting him and he begins to sing as loud as he can something that seems more himself *stand up ye victims of oppression for the struggle carries*

They wait at the bottom of the basement stairs—Dietrich with an arm under each of Falk's shoulders, Suse and Elisabeth each clinging to a leg—while several young people flee past them. Then they carefully climb a stone stairway limned with black ice, and stop, listen to the frantic bleating of an SS whistle.

"We can't stay here," Dietrich says.

They move along the alley and into deserted Zillestraße, as frightened as if tracked by a spotlight, and slip into another alley. They creep into a shadowy tunnel behind a row of garbage cans and lay Falk Harnack down in a nest of snow.

"He'll catch pneumonia," Suse frets.

Elisabeth is already kneeling beside him, stripping off her sweater and wrapping it around his chest. "He's fainted. That's just as well. He'll be in shock. But the cold is better for the wound."

Dietrich would have given her a jacket of his own to cover herself, but they have come away without their coats. Instead of his Shetland wool from Schneiders in the Pariser Straße he wears only the shirtsleeves and cheap baggy pants of the Fat Gentleman.

Suse holds Falk's head in her lap and strokes his hair. "What shall we do? Dietrich, can't you call for Father's car? We'll take Falk to the Charité."

"No," Elisabeth says. "Father told me the Nazis have been watching the emergency room and sometimes they kidnap people they suspect were hurt in street fighting."

Dietrich says, "We could take him to his aunt in the Wangenheimstraße."

"That's the first place they'll look for him," Elisabeth says.

"What makes you think they'll be looking?"

"Did you see, before we got out of there? The SS were getting the worst of it. They'll make inquiries to save face if nothing else."

"We'll take him to our house," Suse says.

"It's next door to the Harnacks," said Elisabeth. "They may inquire there too. Do you want to place your parents in that position?"

"Then we'll take him to Hans and Christel in Sacrow," says Dietrich. "They'd never think to look there. And Sacrow is so isolated, it will be easy later to slip him out of Berlin all together."

"Yes," Suse agrees. "Yes, that's good."

Elisabeth presses her fingertips against Falk's neck. "His pulse is steady," she says. "I think he'll make it if Father can see him soon." She is so numb with cold she scarcely notices when Dietrich kneels and places his hand on her shoulder.

"I'll find a telephone," he says.

The women are hovering over Falk like a twinned pietà when Dietrich makes his careful way over the packed snow toward the street, slipping twice as he goes.

He knows where he is in the dark streets, and yet still feels disoriented, for he is being drawn inexorably back toward Schloß Straße. It is as though he were the one in shock. Blank stone facades seem to stretch forever, marked here and there with a muted light. He stops at a corner shop. A screen of iron bars have been drawn across the entrance, but there is a light in the back. He starts to bang on the window, then notes the name painted on the glass—Abramsöhn and Sons. How does he dare ask a Jew to put himself at extra risk?

He moves on down the street, notices for the first time that he is limping. The sign beneath the corner street lamp confirms his location—Schloß Straße and Bismarckstraße. There is a telephone booth, and Dietrich reaches into his pockets for a coin, then remembers he is wearing the clothes of the Fat Gentleman and his own wallet is at home in a drawer in the Wangenheimstraße. He goes on, resigned to his fate.

The door of the youth club stands open, a goldbrick of light that promises warmth. Carefully he climbs the steps and peers inside. The foyer is empty. He enters. A floorboard creaks just as he reaches the doorway of the auditorium. He stops.

A man in a black uniform lies prone on the floor amid a wreckage of chairs and tables. Two others in SS uniform kneel over him. They look up alarmed, pulling their guns from their holsters and pointing them at Dietrich even as he somehow finds the presence of mind to shout *Heil Hitler* and thrust out his arm. He expects the bullets to take him in the chest, just below the vulnerable armpit.

Instead, one Nazi asks, "Who are you? What do you want?"

"I—I was looking for a telephone. I've been attacked, you see, by a gang of Reds. They robbed me so I haven't even the money for a phone call. If I can reach my family, they'll come for me."

They lower their weapons. Dietrich now sees they are very young, sixteen or seventeen, perhaps. One has been weeping, and Dietrich smells the sour stench of vomit as well.

"The same bastards who jumped us, I'll bet," says one.

The younger of the two wipes his eyes. He has the thin, homely face of a boy who has been the butt of classroom pranks. "We've sent for help but no one has come. And the Obersturmführer is badly hurt." He looks down at his fallen leader. "We can't let him die. He'd do anything to save us."

Dietrich takes a cautious step forward.

The older one says, "Why are you dressed like that?"

Of course he wears the huge pants of the Fat Gentleman, now missing their pillow and barely held up by suspenders, and the cheap cotton shirt, stained and torn, and nothing else.

"Those Communist bastards took my trousers and coat and left me to freeze. If I hadn't found these in a refuse pile behind a haberdasher's, I'd be standing before you in my underwear. Not a pretty sight, I assure you."

They smile despite their worry.

"How was your friend wounded?"

"Some Bolshie hit him in the head. His scalp's bleeding here, you see."

Dietrich comes closer, kneels beside them. "My father was a doctor," he says, "and I picked up a bit from him over the years. May I?"

They back away and Dietrich leans over the fallen SS man, whose eyes are closed. His light brown hair is matted with dried blood, but his breathing is regular. Dietrich finds his pulse.

"His heartbeat is strong." He turns to the youngest. "Do you have a torch?"

After some fumbling, the boy removes the electric torch from his belt. Dietrich lays his hand across the Obersturmführer's forehead, places a fingertip on each eyelid. The eyes, when he opens them, are pale gray and unmoving, so wide and clear of thought or guilt the stricken man seems the most innocent of innocents.

Dietrich holds the torch over the blank face and flips the switch. The pupils, caught suddenly in a halo of light, shrink to tiny black points. So, Dietrich thinks. Something there after all.

He turns the man's face toward the two boys and moves the torch back and forth. "See how the pupils dilate and contract? That means there's no serious damage. A concussion, most likely. I'd guess he'll gain consciousness before long, and be none the worse for it except for a bump on the head."

The youngest boy rocks back on his heels, sighs, and smiles.

"You're certain?" the other asks.

"Yes. But he should be seen by a doctor."

"Shit! Where are the others? They've been gone long enough."

"Probably passed out in an alley," the youngest moans.

Dietrich stands. "Why wait for your companions? Surely a building such as this will have a telephone. You stay with your officer and I'll find it for you."

Thank you, they say, thank you thank you.

Once out of their sight he moves quickly up the stairway to the second-floor office. He glances out the window into the street. No sign of more Nazis. He turns on a light and dials his parents' number. Paula Bonhoeffer answers, and he tells her Keppel must bring the car at once to the corner of Zillestraße and Fritschestraße.

"Something's wrong," she says.

"Yes, but it involves someone else. Suse and I are fine. If Keppel comes, everything will be all right. And Mother? Once you send for Keppel, phone Elisabeth's father and have him go at once to Hans and Christel's in Sacrow with his medical bag. Tell him he'll be treating a shoulder wound."

"Good heavens, Dietrich. Who's injured?"

"Falk Harnack. Now hurry, Mother."

After hanging up, he rifles the top desk drawer, finds the building lease signed by himself, the receipts for expenditures in Elisabeth's name, the blackbound ledger. He stuffs the papers in his oversized pockets and slips the ledger into his underwear against his backside. He goes downstairs.

The younger boy is still tending the Obersturmführer, but the other greets him at the bottom of the stairs.

"Herr—?"

"Schmidt," Dietrich says.

"Herr Schmidt! He's coming around! He opened his eyes and tried to speak."

Dietrich pats the young man on the shoulder. "Good, good. Now go up to the second floor. There's a telephone in the front room. I've left the light on for you. And when someone comes for you, go to the Charité. That's the best hospital, and the closest."

"Yes! The Charité!" The young man pumps his hand and bolts up the steps two at a time.

"I've made my own call," Dietrich says to the boy who has remained behind. "I'll be going now."

"Yes, of course," the boy says. Then he calls after Dietrich, "The Obersturmführer will be most grateful. If you need anything, anything at all, you must let him know. SS-Obersturmführer Alois Bauer."

Dietrich waves farewell and heads toward the alley behind Zillestraße as fast as his trembling legs will allow.

HANS VON DOHNANYI WOKE from a restless sleep to the jangling of the front doorbell. When he slid out of bed and pulled on a dressing gown, Christel sat up and asked blearily, "Is it the children?"

"No," he said, and added, "Something I forgot to do for work. Go back to sleep."

Most likely nothing at all, he thought as he felt his way down the dark stairs. Someone's automobile has broken down.

When he turned on the hall lamp the hands of the grandfather clock stood at midnight. Perhaps a ghost, then. He hurried to open the door.

He did not know the man who stood before him, black leather surgeon's bag held in front of his chest as though for protection.

"Herr von Dohnanyi?"

"Yes?"

"Dr. Leo Hildebrandt, a surgeon at the Charité. I am a colleague of your father-in-law, and my daughter is a friend of Dietrich and Suse Bonhoeffer."

Dohnanyi stood aside and gestured for the doctor to enter. "But no one here is ill." In the hall light he took note of the man's dark curly hair and beard and wondered if he might be a Jew. "Or are you yourself in some sort of trouble?"

"There is trouble, but it is not yet mine."

Leo Hildebrandt was describing the telephone call he'd received from the Wangenheimstraße when the Mercedes pulled into the drive. At the sound of the engine, Dohnanyi opened the front door to see the door of the motorcar burst open and Suse jump out crying, "Hans! Christel!"

Hans gestured for quiet even as Dietrich and Elisabeth dragged a blood-spattered Falk Harnack from the car. Falk was yelling, "*Call my brother! A telephone, damn you! Warn my brother!*" as though the only energy left him lay in his lungs. An upstairs window bulged suddenly with light.

"Quiet, for God's sake!" Dohnanyi was shouting as well even as he herded them inside.

In the house Dr. Hildebrandt took over, helping carry Falk, dripping blood through the hall, into the kitchen, where the cook's board would do the office of an examining table. While Leo Hildebrandt spread his instruments on a cupboard shelf, Suse and Christel, come from upstairs in her dressing gown, set pots of water on the stove to boil. Elisabeth cut away Falk's bloodcrusted shirt with a butcher knife.

Dietrich hovered in the doorway, trying to decide how to help, but Dohnanyi grabbed his arm.

"You'll only be in the way. Come with me."

In the hall, Dohnanyi stooped to examine the bloodstains on the beige carpet, then opened the front door and listened for a time.

"Hear anything?" he said to Dietrich beside him.

Dietrich listened. "A dog somewhere around the lake," he said. "A breeze rustling tree branches."

Dohnanyi closed the door and led Dietrich to the study, chilly since the hearth fire had long since died out. Instead of turning on a light, Hans went to the French doors that looked out on the garden. A skein of moonlight sliced across his face.

"How did this happen?"

Dietrich explained, pausing now and then in expectation of a question, a comment, but Hans only stared into the darkness.

When Dietrich fell silent, Dohnanyi said without looking at him, "Don't ever, *ever* involve me in something like this again. Do you understand?"

"What—what are you saying?"

"I believe I spoke plainly."

"We didn't know where else to turn," Dietrich said. "Sacrow is quiet and the house is isolated—"

"I," Dohnanyi said as he turned to face Dietrich, "am not isolated. I am personal assistant to the justice minister, and shall continue to be so in this new regime."

"But you can't—"

"And you," Hans continued, "are an amateur. Do you understand?"

"Saving a man's life has become amateurish? God save us then. And you speak as if you mean to go along with these thugs."

Hans shook his head impatiently and pointed to a safe set in the wall beside the fireplace. "In there," he said, "is a journal. I began it on the night of January thirtieth. In it I write down the crimes of this regime, names and dates, victims and perpetrators. Some have been reported in the papers, but most haven't, especially as the press is feeling threatened by the Nazis. I write in a very small hand, but I already have filled pages. Supposedly random and unsolved killings. Jews, Socialists and Communists, trade union leaders, journalists, artists. Beatings and maimings likewise. Jailings. There's a camp going up near Munich, at Dachau, did you know that? Of course you didn't. It's a place into which people may disappear. A record of all this is vital, because in a few years this government will fall, and when it does it will be faced with an outcry such as never has been seen in Europe. In the meantime, you bring into my house a known Communist who has been wounded in a street brawl with the Nazis—"

"They attacked us!" Dietrich interrupted.

Hans threw up his hands. "Do you hear a word I say?"

"You think they watch this house?"

"I don't know what they do," Hans said. "Or will do. I only know they trust no one. And neither must I."

"Not even family?"

"Of course I trust your integrity, Dietrich, your character. But not your judgment. I don't mean that as an insult. Few decent men will comprehend what's happening. But look what you've done. You bring this man into the house—"

"A family friend—"

"His blood stains my carpet. You've involved a family servant who may or may not report what he has seen. You may or may not have been observed or followed. And you haven't any idea what to do with this wounded man."

"I thought you might," Dietrich said gamely.

Dohnanyi sighed and rubbed his face, then went to his desk and fumbled in the drawer for his pipe. He thrust a pouch of tobacco across the desk toward Dietrich.

"My pipe is at home," Dietrich said. "I'm in costume, you know."

"Ah. I thought perhaps you had another fugitive hidden inside your trousers."

"I could use a cigarette."

They shared a match and sat quietly for a time, filling the darkness with milky smoke. Then Dietrich said, "It's dangerous, what you're doing."

"Any act of integrity will be dangerous the next few years."

"That's not what I meant," Dietrich said. "I meant morally dangerous. Can you really fight this from within?"

"The only way to stop a runaway train," Hans said, "is to be on board and try to pull the brake."

"And if a failed brake is the problem?"

Hans blew smoke at the ceiling. "God knows."

Elisabeth joined them, sank wearily onto Dietrich's lap, and rested her cheek against the top of his head.

"How's the patient?" Dohnanyi asked as if he and Dietrich had been discussing nothing more serious than the weather.

"Resting at last. Father's just finishing. He says the collarbone is broken but the bleeding's stopped and there's no other damage except a few torn tendons."

"Does your father think him fit to travel?" Dohnanyi still spoke casually.

"He didn't say. But before Falk fell asleep he said he wanted to go to his brother in Munich. And Father said, 'We'll see about that.'"

"Then I think," Hans said, "that we should. Do you know how to reach the brother?"

"Suse does," Dietrich said.

"Then she should call him as soon as possible. But not from this house. Find a public telephone. Then cover him with blankets in the back of the Mercedes and drive Harnack yourself, Dietrich, to Friedrichsbrunn."

Elisabeth sat up and asked, "Why can't he stay here until—"

Dietrich squeezed her arm and interrupted, "Friedrichsbrunn will be fine. You'll like it, Elisabeth, it's our family's house in the Harz Mountains. Arvid Harnack can meet us there."

She started to speak again and he continued, "You and I can take turns, drive straight through, and be there before dawn."

She was watching Dohnanyi. "All right," she said, and stood up, smoothing the front of her skirt. "I'll tell the others." She went to the door, then hesitated. "Dietrich and I rented the hall," she said to Dohnanyi. "They'll find the records."

"No," Dietrich said. "I managed to take everything." He patted the packet of papers at his backside.

Dohnanyi shook his head. "That's not much good. It will be easy enough for the SS to trace you. Give everything to me." He held out his hand. "I know someone who can take care of this."

Dietrich handed over the papers, feeling a bit sheepish. And when he and Elisabeth had left, Dohnanyi sorted through the papers, then picked up the telephone and called the minister of justice.

He longed to be a scholar hidden away in a dormered attic room lined on all sides with books, so that no matter which way he swiveled in his chair—and of course the chair must swivel—he would see thick volumes of theology. He wanted to emerge from this room groggy from his studies and wander to Berlin University, where he would deliver lectures of such density his students would not be able to look up from their note-taking. They would whisper about him afterward, shake their heads and wonder what sort of life he must lead. He would enjoy the speculation. He wanted to be wildly, luxuriously eccentric, instead of what he was becoming—practical, organized, and a writer only of pamphlets.

He began to think of the students as his enemies. When he posted notices of meetings on the Christian response to the new government, they were ripped down. More and more university scholars sported shiny gold-and-enamel swastika pins on their lapels. They stood in the middle of Dietrich's lectures with a great show of slamming notebooks, and walked out. He tried to ignore the interruptions, though his face reddened as he bent over his notes and sought to control his voice. But the most disconcerting challenge came in the customary way. A young man with the face of an angel and bearing on that face the look of aggrieved youth smitten with divine knowledge raised his hand at the end of a lecture.

Dietrich paused as he straightened his notes. "Yes, Herr ah—?"

"Bielenberg."

"Herr Bielenberg. Your question?"

"In fact, a complaint, Herr Professor."

Dietrich noted the swastika pin on Bielenberg's lapel and held his breath.

"You speak of theology as an intellectual pursuit, Herr Professor, which implies openness to ideas. Yet you consistently trample upon the sensibilities of your students."

"In what way?"

"You have no respect for our opinions. And no openness toward the new thinking in Germany."

"Hear, hear," someone called from the back of the lecture hall.

"You wish to force everyone to think as you do," said Bielenberg. "You are narrow-minded. In addition you are unnecessarily negative when you speak of the Fatherland. We students want open-mindedness, not a simplistic parroting of liberal nonsense. Is that too much to expect from the lecturers of this university?"

These remarks were greeted by thunderous applause. Dietrich searched for a response, but his mind seemed to have turned to glue. He, narrow-minded? An enforcer of prescribed opinion because he appealed to reason and tolerance and Christian charity? As he groped for an answer the students were leaving the lecture hall, filing out with loud guffaws and much back-slapping, or moving in small packs toward Bielenberg to pump his hand.

Dietrich navigated the marble staircase to Unter den Linden and crossed to the garden beside the State Opera House. There he slumped on a stone bench in the growing darkness, gulping the winter air like a thirsty man at a cold stream, and knew he would not stay much longer at the university.

Although his pamphlets were not at all what he would have liked to spend his time writing, he tried to think of them as theology of a practical sort. This was something of a comfort. He neglected his other work, for always he was attending meetings, organizing meetings, speaking at meetings, in an effort to prod the Church into some response. Day after day he sat in drab parish halls, dragging on one cigarette after another and blowing smoke toward ceilings mottled with brown watermarks while this one fretted, "Hitler may be a bit hard on the Jews," and that one responded, "Of course he's only huffing and puffing, it plays well to the crowd and makes for a colorful speech," and another said, "Doesn't hurt to have a bit of a shaking all round, wake everyone up."

Sometimes resolutions were passed. Most of the time nothing was done and more meetings were called.

One saving grace was that Elisabeth often accompanied him. He enjoyed her company most when they traveled together, driving from town to town in Brandenburg and Saxony and Thuringia with bundles of pamphlets stuffed in the boot of the family Mercedes. At the end of a meeting they escaped whatever stuffy parish hall they'd been in and headed to a café for strudel dredged with cream, and coffee. As though the Political Situation, as they called it, had taken on the role of organizer of their social calendar. Dietrich liked to be seen with her, especially when she laughed at him, covering her mouth with one hand and opening her eyes wide, or leaned back in her chair so that her short dark hair fell away from her face. They held hands beneath the table. He imagined other men might be envious, that elderly women sitting across the room watched them with pleasure and recalled their own first love.

Their time alone was different. Dietrich enjoyed holding her close, liked to kiss her and run his fingers through her hair, around her neck, and down the curve of her back before undressing her and taking her into his bed. But when all was done he felt a nagging emptiness in the pit of his stomach, even as he held her close. For he wasn't certain he loved her enough to marry her, and in such circumstances he thought it wrong, very wrong, to be sleeping with her.

He admitted this to himself at Friedrichsbrunn, though he hadn't the courage to tell Elisabeth then. The drive to the Harz Mountains with the wounded Falk Harnack, hidden beneath a bearskin rug so not even the top of his head showed, had been quiet and tense. Exhausted even before setting out, they were forced to take turns resting and driving, so that whoever was awake had no company but the sounds of the road and the sleep-heavy breathing of the other. Dawn broke well before they arrived. Outside Quedlinburg they ran low on petrol, but Dietrich was afraid to pull up to a pump. Instead he stopped a quarter of a mile past a station and hiked back, purchased petrol in a can, and returned to the Mercedes.

Friedrichsbrunn was not what Elisabeth had expected. When Dietrich had talked of the Bonhoeffer vacation home in the Harz Mountains, she had imagined a half-timbered lodge nestled in an isolated hollow. But the Friedrichsbrunn house was ugly, a squat structure of brick studded with gables, one of several houses in an open field between the village and the woods. Dietrich drove the Mercedes across the frozen garden and pulled up beside the back door. Falk was awake and summoned enough strength to stumble into the house supported on either side by Dietrich and Elisabeth. It was broad daylight, impossible to hide their arrival, but no one in the village seemed about, and no one stopped by, even after Dietrich built a fire in the bedroom grate.

"They'll notice the smoke," Elisabeth said, "and know someone's here."

"Yes," said Dietrich. "But to be honest, we keep mostly to ourselves here, and people in the village have never paid much attention to us. Except for the families who run the guesthouses, they're rather insular."

As are you Bonhoeffers, Elisabeth thought. She went downstairs to search for food. In the cellar she found a bin of potatoes and onions, butts of crusty ham and salt beef suspended from rafters, and a rack of dusty wine bottles. The pantry held a round white cheese, tins of herring, and bottles of brandy and schnapps. Back upstairs, where Dietrich had changed Falk's dressing and put him to bed, she said, "I was afraid there'd be no food. But it looks as though we could survive here all winter."

Falk, groggy again, mumbled, "Something hot to drink?"

Elisabeth patted his blanket. "You'll have a toddy very soon, and something to eat. And your brother will come as well." She looked at Dietrich. "Won't he?"

"I hope. If Suse has got hold of him."

Arvid Harnack arrived sooner than expected. Suse had quickly reached him, and he had driven through the night with his American wife, Mildred. Mildred possessed the blunt optimism and aura of self-sufficiency Dietrich had noted before—and been disconcerted by—in American women. When she saw the haggard-looking Falk, she said quite cheerfully, "Oh dear, our boy will need some rest, won't he."

Falk blinked up at her. "Mildred," he croaked, "where will you take me?"

She sat on the edge of the bed and patted his hand. "You'll come home with us to Munich, of course. We'll fatten you up, and then you can get back to your work in the theater. How does that sound?"

He nodded and shut his eyes. "It's not so bad then?"

Arvid, a taller, thinner, and bespectacled version of Falk, said, "It's still Germany, of course, no matter who's chancellor."

"Of course," Mildred said briskly. "All this will blow over soon enough. The German people won't be ruled by such idiots."

They ate sandwiches, huddled around the hearth in Falk's room for warmth, then carried Falk to the Harnacks' waiting car. Arvid and Dietrich shook hands, Mildred kissed Elisabeth on the cheek, and the Harnacks were gone. Dietrich and Elisabeth stood arm in arm in front of the house.

"Are Americans always so cheerful?" she asked.

Dietrich laughed. "They're in love with happy endings. And the women can be a bit pushy."

"Oh?" Elisabeth looked up at him. "I didn't think so. I quite liked her, actually."

They walked through the garden to the back of the house. A clear midwinter sun lit the pasture with a brown glow, and the dark looming woods were shot through at the edges with threads of light. In the distance the carpet of forest ran up the haphazard folds of the Harz.

"I'm beginning to understand the attraction of Friedrichsbrunn," Elisabeth said.

"They're wonderful woods to walk in," said Dietrich. "All rises and ravines. One expects at any moment to encounter a goblin or a Walpurgis Night witch."

"Are there lonely cottages?"

"Oh, yes, and abandoned pilgrims' crosses and bears who once were princes. Shall we stay a day or two? Or do you want to go back to Berlin tonight?"

"I'm so tired," Elisabeth said. "Let's stay."

Dietrich had daydreamed of bringing a new wife to Friedrichsbrunn on honeymoon. Most women he knew (of the few women he knew) would have wanted to go to Paris or Rome. But Elisabeth was the Friedrichsbrunn type. She liked the outdoors and had a vigorous way of walking, head up and footsteps loud as she plowed along paths crusty with old snow. The cold air quickened her face behind the white veil of her own frozen breath. Elisabeth should fit very well in the Friedrichsbrunn daydream.

Except Dietrich was not happy. He put it down to guilt. He was deeply old-fashioned where marriage was concerned. The teachings of the Roman church on divorce seemed admirable to him, much to the dismay and amusement of his brothers and sisters. Marriage was a sacrament, he argued, a sign of grace, and once undertaken with vows to one's partner and to God, it must last forever. How then, Suse once asked, would anyone dare to marry? Perhaps, he'd answered, few *should* marry. And he'd thought what a frightening responsibility it was, to commit to a single person for the rest of one's life. Suppose one's chosen mate failed in some terribly important way? Suppose she, for example, proved shallow, had only pretended to love Bach so as to impress the other, or read only trivial romantic fiction, or became a hypochondriac, or secretly admired Hitler? Or, or, or? There were a thousand ways to disappoint Dietrich.

And if marriage was sacred, how dare he sleep with his future wife without the benefit of the sacrament, especially at Friedrichsbrunn, his family's home?

When they came in from their late walk in the Friedrichsbrunn woods, he said, "Since we're both so tired, perhaps we should sleep in separate rooms. It would be more restful."

She looked surprised. "Why? Is something wrong?"

"No. Of course not."

She would not be put off. "What is it? One of your depressions? If you're wanting time alone I can entertain myself. But we'd be warmer sleeping together. You'd have to build another fire otherwise, and we may not have enough wood."

He was suddenly angry that she would reduce the situation to a practical level, and saying nothing, went across the hall to the doorway of the room he slept in when the family was in residence. It was a long, narrow alcove that lay in shadow, and the windows were laced with hard frost.

She came to stand behind him. "It looks as though it misses the sun," she said.

He reluctantly admitted that the room was one of the coolest in the house because it sheltered beneath the close-standing oak and lacked direct sun, making it much prized in the summer months. And as he spoke she reached beneath his jacket and ran her hand up his spine and let it rest beneath his shoulder blades. He pulled her close and rested his cheek on the top of her head, knew he would give in to desire once again.

Back in Berlin they visited the service at Elisabeth's home parish of Annenkirche in Dahlem. They sat in the last pew. During the lessons, Dietrich's attention wandered. He studied the walls, tried to imagine the former glory of the faded medieval paintings which hovered ghostlike just beneath the thin surface of whitewash. Elisabeth interrupted his reverie to point out this or that distinguished parishioner. "General von Hammerstein-Equord," she said in his ear. "Friedrich Dietlof Graf von der Schulenburg. Major Hans Oster."

Dietrich studied Hans Oster with mild interest, because he had heard Hans von Dohnanyi mention him recently. Oster, Dohnanyi thought, might be One of Us. But Oster was also in disgrace for conducting an affair with the wife of a senior officer. He sat now beside his own wife (no farther away from her than Dietrich sat from Elisabeth), eyes on the pulpit, with an iron-straight posture that can only be achieved by a military man or a fanatic.

Pastor Martin Niemöller was preaching. His sermon, which Dietrich carefully evaluated, was noncommittal (taking its text, as required, from one of the many verses in the Gospel of John which meditated on Jesus as the bread of life). The ending was more to the point—there is only one God, and He is already known to us. After the service, as Niemöller shook the hands of departing parishioners, he grabbed Dietrich by the arm—"Ah, yes, Pastor Bonhoeffer, I know why you are here"—and motioned him aside. Dietrich and Elisabeth waited outside, at the edge of the crowded cemetery with its maze of snow-capped headstones and shrubbery. When the crowd had cleared, Niemöller, a thin man with a wizened face that made him look older than his years, came to them and said, "I would take you home with me"—a large comfortable-looking brick house with a bay window that overlooked the church—"but my wife has influenza and I don't like to disturb the quiet. However, the Café Luise is just down the street."

So they ended in the front room of the Luise, overlooking the frozen beer garden, which in summer would be filled with shirtsleeved men and women in cotton frocks talking over round iron tables. They ate plates of schnitzel and buttery noodles washed down with red wine.

"Now," Niemöller said, chewing his words as vigorously as his meat, "we must deal with this Hitler fellow. He must be made to understand he can't dictate to the church as he does to those brownshirts of his."

Dietrich nodded.

"On the other hand," Niemöller continued, "I look for some good in him. Do you know what I hear from my parishioners?—and many of them are highly placed in government, as I'm sure you know. Hitler will soon take us out of the League of Nations." He hefted the bottle of burgundy. "More wine?" And smiled. "That will be something, anyway."

Elisabeth drove back to the Grunewald while Dietrich stared moodily out the window.

"He was a hero in the Great War," Elisabeth pointed out. "A U-boat commander. Not that that excuses him. But you have complained about the Versailles Treaty yourself."

"When was the last time you attended one of his services?" Dietrich asked abruptly.

"It's been a while," she said. "Over a year. We've been all over the place on weekends, you and I—"

"That's not the only reason," he said.

"No," she said, "not the only reason. I'm not comfortable in church. I only go with you for the company, and because I believe in our work. But I'm not so sure, Dietrich, what I believe anymore. Or who I am."

"Who you are?"

She drove for a time, careful to avoid the rims of hard snow on the shoulders of the roadway.

"Every day," she said, "I feel more like a Jew. I'm not sure about the rest."

That night they went to bed in her apartment and lay without touching, their faces turned toward the window, watching clumps of snow flutter against the pane.

At last she said, "We don't have to go on, you know. Not if you don't want to."

"You're moving away from me," he said. "You're becoming a different person."

She sat up and pulled the quilt tight around her. "Don't dare blame me."

"I don't mean—" he stammered, trying to think how to continue. "Elisabeth, I do care about you."

"I know you care about me," she said. "I'm not sure how much."

"You know how I feel about marriage."

"God knows we've argued enough about that," she said. "You're the most old-fashioned man I know."

He raised up on one elbow and said almost eagerly, "Then doesn't it seem strange for me to be here in bed with you?"

She shut her eyes.

"That first night—" he searched for words—"it was as though the world had turned upside down. As though normal ways of behaving had gone out the window. At least normal for me. But I'm getting my bearings again."

He waited for her to answer. When she was silent he continued, "I can't sleep with you again. At least, not until we're married. And I'm not ready to marry."

She turned her face away and nodded.

"I'm sorry," he said.

She put her hand to her face and sobbed. He stroked her arm, feeling miserable, and said, "I still want to see you. I want everything else to be exactly the same. Except, a step back please, from this. At least, for now. And I need your help because God knows I find you attractive and it is easy for me to give in to that. So I must ask you not to initiate any physical—"

"Then you should go," she managed to say.

He dressed quickly, after stepping away from the snow-lit window into shadow, as though modesty would erase past intimacy.

When he went to the door she said, "We may not be able to go on as before. Men who feel bad usually blame the woman."

"I won't," he said. He came back then and sat on the edge of the bed, pushed the hair from her forehead with one large hand. "There is no blame, only gratitude." He bent and kissed her forehead. "And there is a future. I just need some time."

She touched his cheek and shook her head. "We'll see," she said. And used the rest of her tears when he had gone.

IN HIS ROOM HIGH UP in Wangenheimstraße 14, in the privileged quiet of the Grunewald, Dietrich listens to the radio. It is not what he should be doing. He should be writing. Instead he sits at his desk, sips a glass of wine.

He turns the dial ever so slowly. The radio crackles and squawks—interrupted now and then by a low, soothing voice, a wisp of violin music or quiet French horn—

Except for the clearest frequency, the RRG, which erupts with Adolf Hitler in full cry, answered by the clamor of a cheering throng—a broadcast from the Sportpalast. It is the first political rally to be carried live on radio.

Dietrich listens, chin resting in hand. He is alone and yet he is not, for the Nazis have provided radio receivers at nominal cost to anyone who can scrape together a few marks. This is the idea of Goebbels, who dreams of millions of Germans, even the poorest Germans, sitting with hands on chins before their new receivers. Next Goebbels will imagine everyone listening to the same thing.

Unlike Dietrich, who quickly tires of Hitler's tirade despite a desire to learn more about what the Nazis are up to. He shakes his head and decides this new tactic will fail, for how will anyone be able to bear the stale jokes and forced humor, the historical inaccuracies, spiritual vapidity, and up-side-down logic that characterize Hitler's speech?

He concentrates again on the dial and at last picks up a distant thump and wail. He turns up the volume. Swing music from the BBC. Chick Webb and his orchestra.

Dietrich shuts his eyes tight, and the wine and the music bring him to tears.

Doppelgänger

EVEN AS DIETRICH LISTENS to Hitler live from the Sportpalast, the Nobel laureate Thomas Mann addresses a gathering of Social Democrats amid the baroque splendors of the Schauspielhaus. The author cuts an appropriately melancholy figure, dwarfed as he is by the massive podium imported into this musical theater for the occasion, and backed by a massive red banner of the Social Democratic Party embossed with 𝕾𝕻𝕯 in bold blackgothic letters. He surveys the gathering from his wooden battlement, then speaks in a voice so low the front rows lean forward to hear him and the others shake their heads and look questioningly at one another: *What can I say to you. I only write books. You are the political leaders. And you don't know what to do.*

Outside the Schauspielhaus the black-uniformed SS gather around their beloved leader, Obersturmführer Alois Bauer, who is soon to be promoted to Hauptsturmführer. They clutch truncheons in their hands and carry their pistols loosely in their belts. Their orders do not allow them to kill or harm in any way the famous Thomas Mann. No one reads him anyway, they have been told, except intellectuals with shriveled balls, and good German students forced to read him at university are only too glad to pitch his work on the bonfires. They want something practical, something that will get them a job when they leave school. Send Thomas Mann away and no one will die for missing him.

Only Social Democrats should have their heads broken. *Their* abiding sin is muddled thinking, so their brains must be cleared of nonsense once and for all. This is how Alois Bauer views his work, as the promotion of clear thinking. He is himself an intellectual. He is a student of history, after all, and a defender of true German art and music. Bauer has no uncertainties about what to do. He has a firm grip on his truncheon.

Betrayals

IF BERLIN WERE A CITY OF HILLS, like London or Paris, people would have gathered on Hampstead or Montmartre to watch the Reichstag burn. As it was, those at some distance only knew the pulsing red glow on the horizon and the wail of fire trucks. Then came the explosion beneath the dome of the Sessions Chamber which broke glass in nearby buildings and rattled windows for miles around. In the music room of Wangenheimstraße 14, where Dietrich Bonhoeffer had just finished a piece by Mendelssohn for his parents, the crystal chandelier quivered and the strings of the grand piano hummed.

"Dear God," Paula Bonhoeffer said.

Dietrich said, "A bomb, do you think?"

"Perhaps an airplane has crashed at Tempelhof," said his father. "We'll find out soon enough from the morning paper. Now, shall I begin the Dostoevsky? If there is some type of alarm, it should ruin the effect of Dietrich's playing anyway." And he began the literary reading, this time from *The Idiot*, which always followed the evening's music. The clamor of distant sirens lent an eerie atmosphere to Prince Myshkin's monologue.

The telephone rang. Dr. Bonhoeffer removed his reading glasses, laid his book aside, and picked up the receiver. He listened for a time without speaking, then said, "I see. Of course. Goodbye," and replaced the phone on its cradle. He looked at Dietrich. "Where is Suse this evening?"

"I believe she's at her flat. What is it?"

"That was Hans. The Reichstag is burning. He thinks we should lock the doors and stay inside, and that it might be best for Suse to join us here for a few days, if she can come quickly. And he said we mustn't involve Keppel this time."

Dietrich stood up. "I'll go for her myself," he said, and then, "What is Hans afraid will happen?"

"He thinks," said Dr. Bonhoeffer, "that the Nazis will be out and about tonight. Will be quite busy. So take care and come home at once."

Paula Bonhoeffer sat with her eyes shut and one hand covering her mouth. Dietrich kissed her on the cheek and left. In twenty minutes he was ringing the bell of Suse's flat in the Magdeburger Platz. She opened the door at once.

"Father telephoned," she said, her face pale. "It's something to do with Falk, isn't it?"

"It's anyone on the Left, apparently," said Dietrich.

"Or anyone with friends on the Left?"

"Hans is only being cautious, I'm sure."

In the darkness of the car, she began to sob. "I've been seeing someone else, anyway. It's over between Falk and me. It was over even before he was shot, actually, and we'd both meant to tell everyone after the play was done. Only now he's in trouble and I feel I've abandoned him."

"He's in good hands with Arvid and Mildred," said Dietrich. Careful to avoid the Kurfürstendamm and other avenues leading to the Tiergarten, he drove cautiously down darkened side streets until he reached the Pauls-borner Straße. At one intersection he caught a glimpse of the distant dome of the Reichstag, brightly lit as a Japanese lantern, but turned the Mercedes in the opposite direction and hurried homeward.

Suse went to bed in her old room, the room she had shared with Sabine after Dietrich's childhood expulsion. As she lay on her back and stared at the moonlit window, Dietrich rapped three times from the other side of the wall as he had done long ago. But Dietrich was not thinking of God. He was thinking of Sabine.

Sabine was safe that night. But while the family slept, or pretended to sleep, thousands of Communists the length and breadth of Germany were hauled from bed at gunpoint and shot, or merely disappeared. The next day's newspapers cried

REICHSTAG BURNS!
COMMUNIST THREAT TURNED BACK!

**HITLER DECLARES EMERGENCY DECREE
FOR PROTECTION OF STATE AND PEOPLE**
to save the German people from excesses of speech and an irresponsible press, from threatening assemblies and associations, from conspiracies utilizing the national postal service, telegraph and telephone; and authorizing searches of houses and confiscations to protect the public welfare...

Old Mrs. Harnack next door received no word of her nephews for several days. Then came two notes from Mildred Harnack, one addressed to Suse Bonhoeffer. It bore a Vienna postmark. *Falk had nearly recovered his health,* she wrote. *But while Arvid and I were out visiting friends, other friends called at our flat and took Falk home with them. He is staying with these friends in Munich, but we hear he will soon be going to a new town close by, when it is finished. You know the place. We hear he is as well as can be expected. As you have guessed, we have decided on a trip abroad. Only for a time, we hope.*

Your American friend, Mildred.

"He'll be in that new prison camp Hans told us about," Suse said, her voice bleak.

When Hans von Dohnanyi saw the letter he agreed. "They'll take him to Dachau soon; it's nearly finished. Clever of Mildred, and most considerate, to write so obliquely." He addressed the family assembled around the dining room table in the Wangenheimstraße. "Where politics are concerned we must all be careful what we put in our correspondence, what we say on the telephone—" he stood and went to the door, looked out in the hall and came back to the table—"even what we say in this house as long as the servants are close by."

"Oh, surely not," said Dr. Bonhoeffer. "We've employed these people for years."

"Even here in front of the servants," Dohnanyi repeated.

"Hans is right, dear," said Paula Bonhoeffer. "I deal with the staff more than you do, and I know how sometimes an unsuspecting slight or silly grudge can upset them. And who knows what sort of ideas Hitler will put in their heads."

"Damned fool man," grumbled Dr. Bonhoeffer. "Gallivanting around the country with a riding crop in his hand. As if he were a Prussian gentleman. I doubt he sat a horse in his life."

Dietrich and Dohnanyi glanced at each other and stifled their smiles.

"The thing is," said Karl-Friedrich, who'd driven over with his wife Grete, Hans von Dohnanyi's sister, "the thing is to look after the family. If the times are as unsettled as Hans believes, and certainly he is in a position to know these things, we must circle the wagons, as they say in America."

Dietrich folded his napkin and sat back from the table. "I have been thinking of the family," he said, "and it's Sabine I'm worried about now."

"Won't you go to Göttingen?" Paula Bonhoeffer said quickly. "Just to make sure they're all right."

"That's exactly what I was thinking," Dietrich answered.

He invited Elisabeth Hildebrandt to accompany him. But first there was the election to be got through. It was a depressing affair. In the days leading up to the balloting, the radio waves were inundated with Nazis—the shouts of Goering, the velvet-voiced Goebbels, who could have been hawking cigarettes or fine liqueurs, the heartfelt emotion of Adolf Hitler, who loved his country lived for his country would sacrifice all for his country. The Communists were jailed, the speeches and posters of the Socialists were officially banned, and the remaining parties seemed shrunken and pale.

Dietrich and Elisabeth cast their ballots and then headed for Göttingen. They barely spoke until they had left the city and emerged onto a long straight highway that cut across the barebrown rise of the Märkische Heath.

"Who won, do you think?" Dietrich asked.

"No one," Elisabeth answered shortly. Then after a time of squinting at the first line of hills to disturb the horizon, "The middle class has gone mad."

"They've suffered with this depression," Dietrich said, "and we haven't."

"It's no excuse," she said. "If it weren't for the Socialists, the middle class would have disappeared in 1919."

"Who'd you vote for?"

"The good old timid SPD," Elisabeth said with a sigh. "For whatever good it will do."

"I voted for the Catholic Center Party," Dietrich said.

She laughed then. "A Protestant voting for the Catholics? Won't the ancestors be spinning in their proverbial graves?"

"The Catholic Center's been as outspoken against Hitler as the SPD," he said. "And they've got support outside Germany. Something we may need, I'm afraid." He reached across and took her hand, laced her fingers through his. He said, "Don't dare tell Father how I voted."

Elisabeth had seen childhood photographs—sepia-tinted formal portraits in silver frames—of Dietrich and Sabine. They stared at the camera with large expressive eyes, rosebud mouths, and silken hair, though one was dark and the other fair. They were the most enchanting children she'd ever seen.

The physical beauty had not lasted, she thought as she studied brother and sister across a Göttingen café table. The childhood delicacy was gone. Dietrich, though not fat, was a large man, broad-faced and thick-necked. His white-blond hair was so thin, patches of scalp shone through despite careful combing. Sabine's features had sharpened, and carrying two daughters to term had cost her her figure. But the siblings still possessed lovely eyes, though Dietrich's hid behind thick glasses, and the quick intelligence so evident in the childish faces still dominated the personalities of both. It was also clear they were twins, for despite lengthy physical separation they fell at once, on meeting, into a state of relieved completeness. Elisabeth would have been uncomfortable to have someone else so totally at home in her skin, and she had noted the night before, at supper, that Sabine's husband, Gerhard, also looked on brother and sister with bemusement. As they left Dietrich and Sabine with their heads together over the supper table and cleared the dishes, Gerhard said to Elisabeth with a smile, "She writes him once a week, but there's no need really. I believe they talk to each other in their dreams."

Elisabeth had laughed. "Perhaps they do." She took up an apron. "Do you ever feel left out?"

"Oh, no. Sabine and I talk often enough when we're awake."

In the Stadtcafé, seated at a window where they could watch the passersby, Sabine handed around plates of *Zweibelkuchen*.

"Forty-four percent of the vote," Dietrich said, studying a newspaper he had purchased from a stall in the market square.

"It's not a majority, thank God," said Sabine.

"But the Nazis are the largest party now. The other conservative parties will go along with anything they want."

"They can't say they have the will of the people behind them."

Dietrich sipped from a blue cup. "Nevertheless, they will say it."

Sabine turned to Elisabeth. "You're very quiet."

"I find it all too depressing," Elisabeth said, "that people can be so beastly stupid."

"This won't be the first unjust government in the world," Dietrich said, "or the last. God knows I won't be happy living under it, but it will come to an end."

"Will it?" Elisabeth stared out the window.

"Everything does." Dietrich folded the newspaper neatly and laid it on an empty chair. "But it will be unpleasant in the meantime."

They had stayed up late the previous night hearing the latest from Sabine and Gerhard. The day after the Reichstag fire, Gerhard had arrived for his lecture in constitutional law, head in the clouds as usual, shuffling his notes and reminding himself which points to emphasize so that he hardly watched where he was going, when he nearly bumped into a student dressed in the brown shirt of Hitler's SA who barred the door to the lecture hall.

"The Jew Leibholz will not lecture today," the student said.

Gerhard had been so surprised he stepped back and looked around. Students arriving for the lecture took one look at the guard, heard his repeated announcement—*The Jew Leibholz will not lecture today*—and left. Gerhard tried to make eye contact with the young man, to no avail. Finally he cleared his throat and said, "Pardon, but I am Professor Leibholz, and I most certainly will lecture today."

The SA guard still would not look at Gerhard, but said (in what Gerhard called a heartbreakingly young voice), "The students of this university are not interested in Jewish lies."

"I am here to lecture on constitutional law," Gerhard persisted.

"The constitution has been perverted by Jews. It has been used to deny German men their birthright."

At this point Gerhard gave up trying to reason with the stone-faced youth and resolved to enter the lecture hall. He had expected resistance, was prepared even to receive a blow, but was surprised to slip effortlessly by the young man, who did not follow Gerhard or even deign to look around, but held to his post at the door. Gerhard straightened his tie and strode to the front of the hall, opened his briefcase, and arranged his lecture notes on the podium. The guard continued issuing his warning to approaching students.

Fifteen minutes later, the young man left. Gerhard was alone in the lecture hall. He waited ten more minutes, then put away his notes and went home.

"So," Sabine said as she drank the last of her coffee, "we are very tenuous here."

"Will Gerhard be dismissed?" Elisabeth asked.

"I don't know if it would come to that," Sabine said. "But he must find enough open-minded students to attend his lectures. How can there be a professor without students?"

"At my father's hospital, there is a rumor that Jewish doctors will get the sack," Elisabeth said.

Dietrich looked surprised. "At the Charité? I don't think Father's heard that. He would have mentioned it."

"Perhaps he hasn't paid attention to the rumors. It wouldn't affect him."

"It most certainly would affect him! And of course he would protest."

"Much good that would do," said Elisabeth. "If it's going to happen, it will."

"She's right," Sabine said. "When another law professor protested Gerhard's treatment, he was censured by a vote of the faculty. If Gerhard is dismissed, we'll have no recourse here. But at least we aren't on our own like so many others. We have the family."

"Of course you do," Dietrich said. "And Father and Mother want to assure you they shall help in any way possible. You mustn't be too proud to ask."

"No," Sabine agreed. "Gerhard and I have spoken about that. These are not times to stand upon false pride." She lowered her voice. "One thing you should know. Gerhard has purchased an automobile."

"But he always hated to drive," Dietrich observed, then realized the import of what she was telling him.

"He rarely uses it," agreed Sabine as she watched his face grow even more serious, "but we sleep so much better now."

They were to meet Gerhard at the hospital where his father lay dying from cancer. The elder Leibholz had not been happy to leave Berlin, where he owned several textile mills and served as a councilman from Wilmersdorf. But his doctors gave him only weeks to live, and he had no wish to burden his son and daughter-in-law with numerous journeys to and from Göttingen, especially in such troubled times. Nor did he wish to introduce a deathbed into the shadow of his young granddaughters' nursery by moving in with his son. Gerhard and Sabine protested that the girls must not be sheltered from a natural part of life. But Jacob Leibholz was adamant. So the widower's mansion on the shore of the Königssee was sold and its invalid resident lodged in a private suite in Göttingen's finest hospital, where his family took turns sitting at his bedside.

A damp March wind whipped off the Hainberg, rattling the awnings of the Stadtcafé and sending a single scrap of paper—a poster from the recent election—skittering across the cobbles of the Marktplatz. As Sabine led her two visitors into the open square toward the iron-lace canopy of the Goose Girl Fountain, an elderly gentleman approached, waving a cane with one hand and holding his hat against the wind with the other.

"Frau Leibholz!" he called. "Frau Leibholz!"

"Ah, Professor Örtmann," Sabine answered. She introduced Dietrich and Elisabeth, and told them, "Professor Örtmann teaches theology at the university. Perhaps, Dietrich, you know his work?"

"Oh yes," Dietrich said politely. "I especially enjoyed your treatise on the christology of Adolf Harnack."

"Good, good," Örtmann said in a distracted manner. He spoke in a loud voice and cupped a hand to his ear. "Now, Frau Leibholz, I must tell you how appalled I am by the recent treatment of your husband at the hands of our students."

"Why thank you, Professor," Sabine said, looking around.

"I beg your pardon?" Örtmann said.

"I—said—thank—you—," Sabine repeated, more loudly.

"Yes, yes," Örtmann continued, more loudly still, so that passersby turned to look at him. "Most appalling! When students at a distinguished university can behave so abominably, one wonders what is in store for our poor country! This new man is a barbarian!"

Sabine patted his shoulder, took his arm in hers, and led him away from the open square to a sheltered doorway, where after a few more minutes' conversation, Professor Örtmann took his leave of them.

"Hard of hearing," Dietrich observed.

"Terribly," Sabine agreed, watching Örtmann stump his way across the square. "And also a very dear man."

"But he's no idea what's coming," Elisabeth said.

"I don't know about that," Dietrich said. "His judgment of the Nazis was accurate enough."

"Yes, he's worried," Elisabeth replied. "But he's not yet afraid."

Dietrich bit his lip and looked after the departing Örtmann.

"Perhaps," Sabine said, "he is too old to be afraid."

Elisabeth said, watching Sabine carefully, "Then you think he has reason to fear. You were trying to quiet him."

Dietrich turned and said in a sharp voice, "You seem to think, Elisabeth, that you are the only person in Germany who guesses these people may cause problems."

"Dietrich!" Sabine admonished. "There's no reason to take that tone with Elisabeth."

"Sorry," he said contritely. "You're quite right. Forgive me, Elisabeth."

Elisabeth had folded her arms across her chest and was surveying the Marktplatz, her lips pressed tight in a thin line and her eyes half-shut against the wind. Dietrich took his watch from his waist pocket and pretended to study it, said, "We'd best be going to the hospital."

Sabine guided them across the square. When they reached the southeast corner, now warmed somewhat by the afternoon sun, she stopped. "Here, let me show you this. Local people call this spot the Vierkirchenblick, the View of Four Churches. Because look, you can turn in a circle and have a view of all four of the town's medieval churches. See?" She turned in a circle, shading her eyes with one hand and pointing with the other. "St. Jakobi's. You can tell it by the wonderful gargoyles. The Johanneskirche, you see the towers don't match. The Albanuskirche to the east, there in the sun. And to the south, St. Michael's."

Dietrich and Elisabeth turned around obediently.

"Surrounded by churches," Dietrich said, trying to lighten the mood with small talk. "One wonders why they were built so close together. There must have been some rivalry among the parishes."

"They probably hated each other," Elisabeth said. "Christians must have someone to hate, after all."

They had begun to walk again. Elisabeth stopped.

"I would like to see the synagogue," she said. "Is it close by?"

"It's in the Untere Maschstraße, in the opposite direction," said Sabine.

"Oh," Elisabeth said. "Never mind."

"It's a lovely building," said Sabine, aware of some tension in the air whose source she couldn't divine, "though not nearly so old as the churches. Rabbi Berman is a nice man. He visits Papa Leibholz quite often."

Elisabeth gave some barely polite answer, and was silent for the rest of the walk to the hospital. Dietrich was annoyed with her, as one is annoyed with a peevish child. They waited in the hall outside Jacob Leibholz's hospital room while Sabine went in to see if he felt like receiving visitors. Dietrich whispered, "Why are you angry with me all of a sudden?"

"I don't know," she whispered back. "Why are you angry with me?" And went inside at Sabine's welcoming gesture, crossed to the old man's bedside and said, *Shalom, Herr Leibholz.*

When the Dutchman Marinus van der Lubbe was arrested in Berlin and charged with burning the Reichstag, all Europe took note. Van der Lubbe was a vagrant, an unemployed bricklayer whose eyes had been injured when lime splashed into his face. In the newsreels which flickered on movie screens around the world, he was seen to have a perpetual squint, and to shield his eyes with a hand held tight against his forehead as though he perceived all the world to be aflame.

When he was sixteen, van der Lubbe had joined the Communists in his native Netherlands. Then he left the Communists for the anarchists. Such shifts of allegiance suggested a young man's dabbling in politics. In fact, Marinus van der Lubbe was searching for someone to stop the burning in his eyes. On the last day of January, when he heard of Hitler's accession to power, he knew at once who was responsible for his terrible pain. He determined to go to Germany and warn everyone about Adolf Hitler. Once in Berlin, he came under the scrutiny of the SS, who could not help but notice the scruffy foreigner who muttered to himself about the Führer. Especially when he bought naphthalene-and-sawdust packets from street vendors—packets used to start fires in coal furnaces—and proceeded to set small ineffectual blazes at the state welfare office in Neukölln, the Schöneberg town hall, and the Bellevue palace.

When Marinus van der Lubbe was charged with setting the Reichstag fire as part of a Communist plot, political lines were quickly and efficiently drawn. The Left from Birmingham to Barcelona saw van der Lubbe as a fall guy, a stooge to cover fascist crimes. The Right from Madrid to Milan boasted that the Bolshevik menace would now be laid to rest once and for all. Dr. Karl Bonhoeffer, as the leading psychiatrist in Germany, was assigned the task of determining the sanity, or insanity as might be, of this dangerous Bolshevik who according to the prosecution had masterminded the infamous attack on Germany's hallowed symbol of democracy.

Both Left and Right deposited messages inside the iron gate of Wangenheimstraße 14. The offerings of the Left were quasi-literary. Each morning, the maid Elli opened the front door to find pamphlets rolled and stuffed between doorknob and lock. These were earnest appeals, badly written and printed in almost unreadably dense typeface, to protect the working class from its fascist persecutors.

The Right was more imaginative, as Karl-Friedrich dryly noted. At the bottom of the steps of Wangenheimstraße 14, piles of human excrement were placed delicately on sheets of newsprint bearing van der Lubbe's picture, accompanied by a sign that read BOLSHEVIK FILTH. Skinned rats were arranged on sheets of stained paper, and the sign THUS TO ALL RED SYMPATHIZERS. Then the body of Widow Harnack's old tabby cat, garroted with a twisted clothes hanger, appeared with a similar warning. (Paula Bonhoeffer, unable to tell the entire truth to her neighbor, removed the metal and went next door to say that the old cat had been run over by an automobile.)

In the midst of these upsets, Uncle Rudi came to call.

General Rüdiger Graf von der Goltz, husband to Paula Bonhoeffer's sister, had not set foot in Wangenheimstraße 14 since the marriage of his niece Sabine to a Jew. Suse was stretched across a bed reading when Elli knocked at the door and informed her of the visitor's arrival. Suse sat up and slammed her book shut.

"Good God, whatever is he doing here? I suppose I must go down?"

"Your mother is asking for you," Elli agreed.

"Oh, Lord," Suse moaned.

She met Dietrich on the stairway. He was hastily knotting a tie beneath his chin.

"Interrupted your writing, has he?" Suse said. "Poor Dietrich. Don't tell him you've been hunched over your desk all day or you're in for one of his lectures on the joys of the military life." She puffed out her chest and lowered her voice. "'The army, my boy,'" she proclaimed. "'That's the life for you!'"

Dietrich rolled his eyes. "Think he's come to gloat over the election results?"

"What else?"

"I wonder if he still has that ridiculous monocle."

Suse laughed. "Do you recall how he always fidgeted with it while he sipped his coffee? Karl-Friedrich said he was afraid it would fall into his cup. But Christel said the monocle was a spigot and if he turned it the wrong way, he'd suck the coffee up his nose!"

They giggled all the way to the sunroom, then paused at the door to collect themselves. Suse straightened Dietrich's tie, and they entered arm in arm. Paula Bonhoeffer and Uncle Rudi sat at a white wicker table which held a plate of pastries and coffee in a silver urn. Uncle Rudi, still monocled and wearing an impeccably tailored suit, stood at once and bowed at the waist over Suse's extended hand. He then greeted Dietrich with a fierce handshake. (Suse later claimed she'd heard the crunch of metacarpals.)

"Susanne! What a beauty you've become. And Dietrich, good to see you, my boy. You've certainly grown into a strapping fellow."

Suse plopped into an empty chair and mouthed at Dietrich *the ar-my,* then flashed her sunniest and most dangerous smile. He tried to ignore her and, after holding his mother's chair, sat down.

Uncle Rudi placed a yellow napkin across his knee, and turned his full attention on Dietrich as a more appropriate person to address than the women. "Well, my boy, you see I'm in civilian clothes. Gave up my active commission. Had a good run, but I'm getting older. Time to practice law again, what with all the activity in Berlin. Found a spot in the Justice Ministry. Perhaps I'll run into young Dohnanyi, eh?"

"Hans is at Justice, yes."

"What about you? Still mucking about with philosophy?"

"Theology," Dietrich said.

"Yes, yes. A bit slow, isn't it? How old are you now, twenty-six, twenty-seven? Not too late to consider the military. Lots going on these days, and it would be a shame for a young man in his prime to miss out."

"It's too bad," Suse interrupted, leaning forward, "that Sabine isn't in Berlin just now. She'd love to see you."

Uncle Rudi's smile froze and his eyes were still.

Paula Bonhoeffer raised warning eyebrows at Suse, who ignored her and continued, "We don't see much of Sabine ourselves. Her father-in-law is very ill."

"Ah yes, Leibholz," Uncle Rudi said. As though being ill was the sort of thing he had expected from the Jew Leibholz.

There followed an uneasy silence while Elli hovered over the table, pouring coffee from the silver urn. Dietrich pretended to watch a robin in the back garden as his mother handed round the cups and saucers. Uncle Rudi, after a nod of thanks, clapped his lips onto the edge of his cup and, as though turning a valve, grasped his monocle and in one smooth motion tipped his cup.

Suse covered her mouth and made a strangled noise.

Uncle Rudi looked at her uncertainly. "*Gesundheit,*" he said, lowering his cup.

Suse glanced at Dietrich and then began to giggle.

"Suse," her mother said. She also looked imploringly at Dietrich, then at Uncle Rudi. "Really, I don't know—"

Dietrich covered his face with his napkin. Something like a honk came from behind the thick linen.

Paula Bonhoeffer tried a diversion. "More coffee, Uncle Rudi?"

"I'm sorry," Dietrich gasped, and dropped his napkin. His face was bright red. "Ever so sorry."

Suse was leaning against the table, her face hidden in the fold of her arms. Her shoulders quivered uncontrollably. Then she gave up the effort and leaned back in her chair, crying with laughter. Dietrich turned toward the French doors and pretended to clean his eyeglasses. His lips were pressed together and he sucked his cheeks and bit hard on the soft flesh inside his mouth.

Paula Bonhoeffer turned to Uncle Rudi. "I assure you, Rüdiger, this is most unlike my children. They aren't themselves these days, none of us is. The times are so distressing."

"The times!" Uncle Rudi bellowed. He stood and threw down his napkin like a gauntlet. "Nothing wrong with the times! Nothing except impertinent young females like the daughters of this house. No wonder, since you allowed one of them to marry a Jew, that the youngest is undisciplined as well!"

Dietrich stood as well. "How dare you insult this family! All because we don't share your joy over this bunch of thugs who've taken over the country."

"And how dare you insult the legitimate government—"

"A government which suppresses the freedom of its citizens can only be called illegitimate, however legal its institution."

Uncle Rudi stepped so close Dietrich could count the hairs in his mustache. "Only those who would suppress freedom will have their freedom suppressed. So you should have nothing to fear. Or have you?"

"Your views are despicable," Dietrich said. "They always were, and they haven't changed."

Uncle Rudi turned and fixed a stern eye on Paula. "My dear, your son needs a good thrashing! If he were mine, I'd administer it myself, by God!"

"Sir," Dietrich said, "I am not your son. And now I must ask you to leave."

Uncle Rudi stalked to the door, then turned once more. "Paula, I know you and Emilie meet often and talk. I shall forbid such meetings in the future. As for this afternoon's events, of course you need fear no repercussions from this quarter. But I warn you, not everyone will be as tolerant of such unruly young people as I am."

When he had gone, Paula sank back into her chair. "Dear God," she said, "my sister's husband."

Dietrich knelt beside her chair. "I'm so sorry, Mother."

"I'm not sorry," Suse said. "Uncle Rudi hadn't been here in years anyway. And Aunt Emilie will find a way to see you, Mother. Anyway, I thought Dietrich was magnificent."

Paula sighed and touched her son's cheek. "And so you were, Dietrich. I recall when you were children. If anyone dared bully Suse or Sabine, you were their staunch defender."

"And he still is," Suse said.

Which made what came next all the more inexplicable.

April in Berlin was cool and damp. It was too early for cafés to break out their sidewalk tables, but the air had grown clear and pale, as though drained of the heavier humors of winter. Dietrich, like many others, ventured outside more and more often. He especially enjoyed the walk from the university in Unter den Linden through the Tiergarten and home to the Grunewald. Street after street, square and park and market, all at odd angles and teeming with humanity, unfolded one after another like an inhabited kaleidoscope. Nothing, not even the swastika flags draped everywhere like a multitude of funeral palls, could quell the energy of Berlin.

Dietrich returned home from such a walk to find his mother in the garden, tending her flowers. She wiped her hands on her apron and held them out to him.

"Sabine telephoned. Papa Leibholz has died."

"Oh, oh." Dietrich held her close. "Poor Gerhard. I must call them back at once."

"Yes. Sabine said Gerhard wants to speak with you. But they have gone out to make the funeral arrangements. They'll ring us tonight. They're bringing him back for burial tomorrow, and I believe they are going to ask you to help with the service."

"But wouldn't they want a rabbi?" Dietrich asked.

"Of course they would. But I gathered from Sabine that Gerhard has you in mind as well."

"I'm very honored," Dietrich said. He paused to kiss his mother's cheek before dashing upstairs. "Now, I'm on my way to a meeting with Niemöller in Dahlem. He promises a large turnout of pastors to discuss the political situation."

She patted his hand. "Go on then. You can talk to Sabine tonight."

The meeting in Niemöller's spacious study in Dahlemdorf drew three dozen pastors from around Berlin and as far away as Brandenburg. Niemöller himself served as chair.

"Everyone is of course aware," he said, "of the latest measures concerning what the government calls 'racial conformity.' According to Pastor Bonhoeffer—" a nod toward Dietrich—"whose brother-in-law is highly placed in the Justice Ministry, the civil service is soon to be purged of Jewish employees. This will of course include our church employees who happen to be Jewish. And we are all aware of the call for a boycott of Jewish-owned businesses. These measures are meeting with little resistance."

"There is some resistance to the boycott," Dietrich said. "Some women, I have heard, passed through the SA lines to shop without incident."

"Yes," said Paul Schneider, a young pastor from Potsdam, "but a woman has more freedom to be defiant. Of course the SA will not attack women. Have you yourself crossed a boycott line, Pastor Bonhoeffer?"

"No," Dietrich admitted.

"Nor could any of us here without being beaten," said Pastor Braun from Tegel. "I would suggest this group confine itself to matters we can address with some hope of success. In any event, the government will soon see that its more extreme measures, such as economic boycotts, are highly impractical, and will drop them."

"I agree," said Niemöller. "I would also suggest that as churchmen, our most pressing concerns are those which directly affect the church. I met yesterday with Pastor Müller, who as most of you know is leading the efforts of Christians who support the new government. Pastor Müller's group plans to issue the following statement, which he was kind enough to share with me in advance."

Niemöller cleared his throat and read a list of indictments against the liberal Republic, including economic chaos, the promotion of internationalism over patriotism, and the corruption of morals among the young, especially young women. "'In conclusion,'" Niemöller read, "'should the state find it necessary to use its ordained powers against those who undermine order—especially to oppose those who would corrupt marriage and the family, undermine the Christian faith, and mock dying for one's country—then the state is acting in the name of God.'"

Niemöller folded the document and laid it on the mantel. "They're calling themselves 'German Christians.' They intend to present candidates for all the most important church offices at the election, and they propose Müller himself as Reich Bishop. Müller also informs me the new civil service legislation would deny ordained ministry in the state church to any baptized Christian of Jewish ancestry. The German Christians agree with this position as well.

"As for myself, in my conversation with Müller, I assured that gentleman that those of us critical of his efforts are in no way unpatriotic; in fact the best way to ensure a strong Fatherland is to ensure a strong church."

They were silent for a moment, then Paul Schneider said, "I'm as patriotic as the next man. But I'm concerned about such direct government interference in church affairs. A political test should not determine who leads the church. Nor should the government decide who we may or may not ordain."

There was a murmur of assent. But Braun said, "I agree on the whole. But as to the question of ordaining baptized Jews, is it worth a schism? After all, we're talking about how many clergy—perhaps a dozen in all of Prussia?"

Dietrich listened, tapping his fingertips together and thinking of Elisabeth. Then thinking of Papa Leibholz.

"Most Jews," he said, "are *not* baptized, and yet they are bearing the brunt of these new measures. What of them?"

"As Pastor Niemöller has stated," Braun said, "we must confine ourselves to church matters."

After some discussion they agreed to produce a pamphlet to be distributed in churches throughout Germany taking issue with any attempt to interfere in church elections. Dietrich, acknowledged as the finest writer, would author the pamphlet. Then they shook hands all around and chatted over glasses of wine before departing. Dietrich was the last to leave. While a maid fetched Dietrich's hat and overcoat, Niemöller said, "There is an opening for a pastor at Johanneskirche in Friedrichshain. I'd like to put in your name. We need more energetic men like you out in the churches."

Dietrich flushed with pleasure. "I'd be most grateful. I've decided to leave the university anyway. So many of the faculty and students support the German Christian movement it is becoming uncomfortable for me there." He paused, then said, "I've something else on my mind, Martin, and would appreciate your advice. I received word from family in Göttingen. My sister's father-in-law has died and I may be asked to conduct the funeral."

"My condolences," Niemöller said.

"The father-in-law," Dietrich said, "was a Jew. Not a Jewish Christian."

Niemöller shook his head at once. "No, Bonhoeffer. Oh, no no no no. It won't do, not at such a critical time. In a few months perhaps, when all this foolishness has died down and we can go about our normal business, then there would be nothing wrong with it. Of course not. But the timing is wrong. Imagine if Müller and the German Christians learned that one of our members was participating in a non-Christian ceremony. They would certainly use that against us to sway opinion during the church election."

"This," said Dietrich, "is my family."

"And I doubt any member of your family would wish to place you in such a difficult position, once they understand the circumstances." Niemöller patted Dietrich on the back as they walked to the door. "Of course, do as you must. But think hard, and pray hard, my friend. There is more at stake here than a Jewish funeral, which after all is most properly performed by a rabbi, is it not?"

Outside a light rain had begun to fall. Dietrich buttoned his overcoat and put on his hat. Niemöller stood at the top of the flagstone steps. "I look forward to your pamphlet," he said. "Your writing is always a joy to read. So lucid."

At home in his room, he awaited with dread the ringing of the telephone. When he heard the faint jangling sound far below, he pretended he hadn't, and continued to immerse himself in his work on the pamphlet. But then Suse was tapping on his door. "Dietrich, it's Gerhard and Sabine. Of course, they want to speak with you—why haven't you come down?"

He followed her downstairs and picked up the receiver. It was still warm where Suse had held it, and the mouthpiece smelled of her breath. She had retreated to a chair and sat watching him expectantly.

"Hello? Gerhard? Gerhard, I am so sorry. It is difficult to know what to say, except that our prayers are with you all."

Gerhard's voice was faint. "Sabine and I feel you all very close, very close. I shall put Sabine on, but first I wanted to speak to you. We'll accompany the body by train to Berlin early tomorrow morning, and the funeral will be at the Fasanenstraße synagogue at three in the afternoon. Rabbi Hartstein will be present, but it would mean so much if a member of the family conducted the service. Well, there are no rabbis in the Leibholz clan, so you are our minister. It's what Papa wanted, he specifically asked about it before he died, and Rabbi Hartstein has agreed gladly."

Dietrich tried to speak. After a moment, Gerhard said, more faintly still, "Dietrich?"

"Gerhard. Gerhard, I'm sorry, but I can't do it. Please let me explain. I've just come from a pastors' meeting. The situation is very sensitive in the church just now, very sensitive. The timing is not—" Dietrich paused and searched for words. "I raised the issue. It was thought this would not be a good time, with church elections approaching—"

And he could not go on. He turned and leaned against the wall, listening to Gerhard, who was saying *yes, yes, of course.*

"The times," Dietrich said again, trying not to hear the hurt in Gerhard's voice, and then he was talking to Sabine, repeating himself so that he seemed to be talking inside his head, wanting to cry *Sabine Sabine.*

When he finally replaced the receiver in its cradle, Suse said, "You refused to do the funeral."

"Yes. You heard me say that."

She turned away and went upstairs.

He went straight to his parents in the music room. Paula was embroidering while her husband read aloud from Stifter.

"I can't do the funeral," he said. "I've told them. Niemöller believes it would be very ill-advised at this time."

Karl Bonhoeffer removed his reading glasses and looked at Dietrich. "That is regrettable," he said.

"Yes," Dietrich said, steeling himself for his father's disapproval. "But we've national church elections coming up and we must avoid unnecessary controversy."

"Sabine will be disappointed," Paula said.

Karl turned to his wife. "Yes, my dear. But Sabine is quite as strong as anyone. I'm sure she and Gerhard didn't stop to consider the larger situation when they made their plans. For a while we must learn to adjust our expectations of what can and cannot happen. I know Hans was very concerned about the incident with Uncle Rudi."

"Yes," Dietrich said. "I suppose that was foolish of me to antagonize Uncle Rudi." He sighed, stood, and walked to a bookshelf, ran his finger distractedly along the spines of the leather-bound volumes.

His father said, "Why don't you play for your mother and me? That would be soothing for us all."

"Yes, all right." Dietrich went to the Bechstein and raised the lid. "What would you like? Mother?"

"I always enjoy Mozart," she said.

He would not have chosen Mozart, whose work always seemed to ask more of him than he could give. He made a halfhearted attempt at the Piano Concerto in C Major while his mother sewed and his father leaned back in his chair with eyes shut, smoking his pipe. When Dietrich had finished he stood and said, "It's been a trying day. I believe I will go to bed."

He bowed to his father, and kissed the pale cheek his mother offered him. On his way upstairs he passed the open door to Suse's room. She was listening to a phonograph recording of Schubert's *Trout* Quintet, and he wondered if she had turned it on to drown out the sound of his playing.

With the family he sat in the front row while Rabbi Hartstein chanted the Kaddish. Now and then he glanced sidelong at Gerhard and Sabine, pale but dry-eyed, and themselves as still as the dead. Dietrich imagined himself stumbling through the unfamiliar service. See, he told himself, it is best this way.

Afterward they followed the coffin to the Jewish Cemetery in Weißensee. Dietrich watched the pedestrians en route, imagined heads turning to stare after the hearse with its menorah displayed on the grille. In fact, at one corner in Prenzlauer Berg, as they waited for the change of a traffic signal, a group of black-uniformed SS pointed and, laughing, began to applaud. Dietrich looked quickly at Gerhard, but his brother-in-law had either not seen or refused to notice. Nor did Gerhard pause to take note of a crudely painted graffito on the cemetery wall that proclaimed

A BLESSED DAY FOR GERMANY
WHEN ALL JEWS LIE WITHIN THESE WALLS

Dietrich moved close to Hans von Dohnanyi and whispered, "It's outrageous! Before, that sign would have been quickly painted over."

"This is not before," Hans said. "And I'll tell you, soon such a sign will not be done by hand."

"What are you suggesting?"

Hans didn't answer, just nodded toward Rabbi Hartstein, who had begun to say the final words over the coffin.

The family gathered for supper back in the Wangenheimstraße, but Dietrich had no appetite. He had barely spoken to Gerhard and Sabine (Gerhard was polite; Sabine had kissed him for greeting, and briefly squeezed his hand as they entered the synagogue, but had otherwise been quiet and withdrawn). While the others gathered in the library, he went miserable to his room, pleading one of the moods which had often sent him away from company to seek solitude. Even that didn't help. He had an unbearable need to stand face to face with an accusing angel. He slipped downstairs and out the front door, heading on foot for the Ludwigkirchplatz.

He had not seen Elisabeth Hildebrandt since their return from Göttingen. They had barely spoken on the return journey, and Dietrich had been angry at her silence. Of course she was on edge, everyone was, but it was ridiculous to blame him, as she seemed to do.

Now he wondered.

He walked fast, flinging his arms as though warding off invisible attackers. After striding along at such a pace for half an hour, he encountered a drunken brownshirt, a fat and balding SA Oberschütze who staggered and leaned against a wall. He passed so close to the shambling creature he caught the sour smell of beer and urine and heard a low mumbling singsong as the Nazi comforted himself. Dietrich was taken with a sudden urge to throw this pathetic excuse of a man to the pavement and stomp his head against the cobblestones. He forced himself to hurry on.

When he entered the Ludwigkirchplatz, he walked once around the perimeter, then twice more encircled the church with its ghosts of pilgrims and penitents who had gathered there in ages past. He could see the light in Elisabeth's apartment each time he passed the south transept. Finally he gathered his courage, climbed the stairs, and pounded on the door. Hearing no answer, he decided she must be out. Then a frightened voice within said, "Who is it?"

"Elisabeth. It's Dietrich."

The door swung open. Only partially open.

"It is you," Elisabeth said. "You frightened me, knocking so loudly at this hour."

"Why? Has someone threatened you?"

Elisabeth held on to the edge of the door with white-knuckled hands.

"Not personally," she said. "But I hear things. In the streets. I suppose it's much more quiet in your Grunewald." She stood back. "You'd better come in."

He went inside, but when she gestured toward the couch and asked if he wanted something to drink, he shook his head and remained standing, looking at the floor.

"Well?" she said.

He told her everything. Admitted as well that he hadn't invited her to the funeral because he'd been afraid of what she would say. Only when he had finished speaking did he dare look at her. She was staring at him, arms folded across her chest. He longed to touch her, to kiss her as he slipped a hand inside her blouse, to carry her to bed.

He reached out a hand, and she stepped back.

"My God," she said, "how can I trust you? If you can do this to Sabine of all people, what would you do to me?"

"Elisabeth, it isn't as though I refused because I support what the government is doing!"

"Why did you come here tonight? For absolution? You'll not get it from me!" She studied him for a moment, then said more softly, "No, it's not absolution you want, is it? You've already received that from Sabine, without even asking for forgiveness. And that isn't fair."

He sank onto the couch and covered his face with his hands. "What should I have done? Niemöller said it would hurt our cause in the church election if—"

"The church election! As if your side has a chance of winning that. And as if it would matter if you did."

"Why wouldn't it? Do you think the church so unimportant?"

"Dietrich, these people aren't going away. And they'll kill us all if they have to."

He stared at her.

"It's not just a transfer of power," she said.

"The German people will—"

"The German people will love it. Germany is like a wound swollen with corruption, and the German people are ill with the need to puncture it. You and your church elections. I've been with you, remember, to your meetings. I've seen how you all talk and talk and talk. It's futile. But you know that, deep down. You know it, and that's why you've come here, to hear me say it." She lit a cigarette and gave it to him, but moved away again as she lit another for herself and blew smoke at the ceiling.

"I'm leaving," she said.

"What? Leaving Berlin?"

"Leaving Germany. I've written to Jean Lasserre and he has a position for me. So it's coal miners again, in France this time."

"But what shall I do—"

"—without me," she finished, and shrugged.

"Why are you mocking me? After our friendship, after our—"

"What would you call it?" she said.

Such a look of pain came over his face that she relented at last, stubbing out her cigarette, sitting beside him and resting her head on his shoulder. He took her in his arms and they sat very still for a time. Then she stood once more.

"Go away," she said. "I don't want to see you again. I hope someday you find some courage. That's what you need, you know."

She went into her bedroom and shut the door.

He waited, smoking another cigarette, but she didn't come back out, or call to him. Finally he let himself out the door and made his way home.

Time of Trial

THE NOTORIOUS COMMUNIST charged with setting fire to the Reichstag is on hunger strike in Tegel Prison. Marinus van der Lubbe's complaint is that he has been lied to. The SS men in their black uniforms have not healed his eyes as they promised. So he has decided he will refuse to eat until he receives satisfaction. If that fails he thinks he will hire a lawyer and bring suit.

He lies in a fetal position on a narrow cot. When the guards slide a metal tray of food through the slit in the door, he looks away. He holds his breath. He bangs his head with the butt of his hand. Anything to keep from eating until the tray is removed.

One day the guards carry him unprotesting—though he will not help them by walking—to a small room on the ground floor, where he sits head down on a chair in the middle of the whitewashed room. For a time he is alone. Then two men enter and sit opposite him. One of the men, who has gray hair and a neatly trimmed goatee, speaks slowly in German, then waits for the other to translate.

"Herr van der Lubbe? May I call you Marinus? I wonder if you would be more comfortable if I address you by your given name?"

Marinus van der Lubbe nods, without speaking, without looking up.

"Marinus, I am Dr. Karl Bonhoeffer."

At the word "doctor" Marinus looks up, squinting against the light. He grabs the translator's hand imploringly. The man gestures toward the other. "There, Marinus, there is Dr. Bonhoeffer. You should address him."

His head bobs ups and down and he tries to focus his eyes. "Dr. Bonhoeffer, you have come to heal my eyes?"

"Marinus, I'm so sorry. I'm told you've been examined by an eye specialist since you've been in prison, and nothing can be done for your eyes. The damage is irreversible. I'm sorry."

Van der Lubbe covers his face with the sleeve of his striped prison uniform. Nothing can coax him to look at the men again, or speak to them.

Finally he is hauled back to his cell, where he will be strapped to his cot. A tube will be inserted into his nostril and snaked through the esophagus into his stomach and so he will be fed.

The visitors return in a week, after Marinus has forgotten them, and Dr. Bonhoeffer patiently tries a different approach to his examination, careful to avoid mention of the prisoner's eyes.

Dietrich Bonhoeffer stands in the pulpit of the Johanneskirche in Friedrichshain. It is solidly middle-class, a church of shopkeepers, managers of rail stations and canal operations, clerks in various government ministries, and their wives and children, all dressed in their best clothes and anxious to judge the newest candidate. After the service they will shake hands with the blond young man who is hoping to become their pastor, the third in a month who has stood the test. They await the sermon with relish, pleased to know that these earnest applicants must curry their favor, pleased they can decide who shall have a position and who shall not.

Dietrich has not preached in several months. He glances nervously at his notes, which seem suddenly to have rearranged themselves from the orderly paragraphs over which he labored so diligently the night before. He holds tight onto the oak pulpit and wishes it were the Abyssinian Baptist Church he stood in, longs for a congregation that will call out.

He preaches on Moses and Aaron at the foot of Sinai—one fresh from the presence of Yahweh, the other paying homage to a gold calf—brothers arrayed one against the other.

He says, "Aaron's Church of the World stands against the Church of the Word. Moses waits, while his brother worships the god who is no god. This strife at Mount Sinai is repeated over and over throughout history, even unto our own day. Sunday after Sunday we come together as a worldly church, a church which has no interest in the invisible and mysterious. We come together as a church which creates its own gods. We come as a church which looks for pleasing gods to worship rather than asking how to please God. We are a church which will sacrifice to idols but will not sacrifice *for* the true God.

"I must tell you, our current idol already lies smashed on the ground, scattered in pieces about us. Therefore we must be patient, like Moses. We must go away to listen, and come back again, ready to worship the true God."

They listen in puzzled silence, and afterward shake hands politely with the candidate before filing outside into the bright September sunshine. They gather in clusters on the sidewalk in front of the church, and agree among themselves that they have likely seen the last of Pastor Bonhoeffer.

Fatherland

WHILE HE AWAITED THE DECISION of the good burghers of Friedrich-shain, Dietrich daydreamed about what it would be like to have his own church. To stand in the pulpit Sunday after Sunday, charged with the care of souls. To lean close while listening to the lonely ramblings of an elderly woman, to hold the parchment hand of a dying man or comfort a woman who had lost her child. To teach young and old alike, not as the sort of academic lecturer he had been at the university, but as a storyteller. To direct and deepen the spiritual life of the parish, which would become a community, an extended family.

He thought of all this with both awe and pleasure as he sat inside a window in the Gaststätte Pilsen and watched Pastor Martin Niemöller emerge from a leaf-strewn path in the Tiergarten onto the Budapester Straße. A wind had kicked up, forcing Niemöller to hold on to his hat. Once inside the restaurant, Niemöller waved as he handed over his hat and coat, and smiled as he approached the table, shaking Dietrich's hand and saying, "You managed the most pleasant table in the place, I see."

Dietrich shrugged. "I come here often and the *maître d'* knows me."

"Then the chef must know you as well," Niemöller said, "and so I shall be most grateful you suggested we meet here."

Dietrich ordered a bottle of Riesling, and when it had been decanted and tasted, Niemöller grew serious.

"I'm afraid I have bad news," he said.

Dietrich squeezed the stem of his wineglass and looked down. "Johannes-kirche," he said.

"I'm afraid so. You'll receive official notification from the superintendent, of course, but I thought you'd want to hear from me first." Niemöller noted the look of pained disappointment on Dietrich's face, and then said, "I knew you wanted this position, but I didn't realize quite how much."

"It's just I've been thinking for days now how nice it could be to have my own church. I'd just about decided it was what God had in mind for me."

Niemöller said gently, "Perhaps you're hearing a call. But Johanneskirche isn't the only church. I don't know of any other openings in Berlin at the moment, but vacancies show up with some regularity."

"Yes," Dietrich said, "but."

"But?"

"Was it politics?"

"Who knows?"

"They gave no reason for rejecting me?"

"Well." Niemöller hesitated.

"I'd like to know," Dietrich said. "It might be useful in the future."

"The written evaluation of the search committee states that your preaching style was too demanding, and your message depressing."

"Good Lord," Dietrich said. He fought off a sudden craving for a cigarette.

"I hope I haven't ruined your appetite," Niemöller said, gesturing at a just-arrived plate of oysters on the half shell.

Dietrich shook his head, took up a fork, and dislodged an oyster. "Nothing ruins my appetite," he said. Then the fork paused in midair. "What am I supposed to do, Martin? It was a good sermon. It was biblically sound and addressed our current situation."

"There are a few congregations which will appreciate that," Niemöller said dryly. "They just aren't available right now."

"I must find something," Dietrich said. "I don't want to go back to the university."

"Would you be willing to leave Berlin?"

"If I have to."

They discussed possibilities while enjoying the trout with capers and wild rice. Hamburg was mentioned, as were Ulm, Regensburg, and Aachen. (Dietrich recalled how close Aachen was to the French coalfields, and silently crossed it off the list.) When the apple charlotte arrived they moved on to small talk, Niemöller describing his wife's prize roses and Dietrich explaining how he enjoyed searching for wild mushrooms when he walked in the woods.

Over coffee, Niemöller took a folded sheet of paper from inside his jacket.

"I have some business of my own to discuss before I go," he said. "It seems definite now that Hitler will take us out of the League of Nations. Very soon, perhaps a week or two. I've the text of a telegram here which I propose our pastors send, congratulating him on this move."

He handed the paper to Dietrich, who made no move to take it.

"You can't be serious," Dietrich said.

Niemöller reared back in his chair. "Of course I am. There's no reason to allow the Nazis to corner the market on patriotism. Just because we don't support their entire program, that doesn't mean we don't love Germany. We're the true patriots, Bonhoeffer. Why, we're better National Socialists than they are."

He offered the paper again.

Dietrich stirred cream into his coffee and shook his head. "Taking Germany out of the League is a belligerent move," he said. "It will be perceived that way abroad."

"So? Does it matter if the countries who humiliated us at Versailles are displeased?"

"Yes," Dietrich said.

"You're young, Bonhoeffer. Too young to have fought in the war as I did. You don't realize—"

"I lost a brother in the war," Dietrich interrupted. "Germany bears a responsibility for the war. Perhaps no greater responsibility than any other nation, but a great responsibility nevertheless. And surely you can't wish to lend credibility to Hitler?"

"I believe," Niemöller said, "that Hitler is surrounded by fools and charlatans, and that he receives bad advice. But he's also quite obviously an intelligent man. He wouldn't have got as far as he has otherwise. Who knows, perhaps he's capable of listening to other voices as well. If so, we can do a great deal to alleviate the harsher measures the Nazis have proposed."

"That," Dietrich said, "is terribly naive."

He was angering Niemöller, he realized, and he did not enjoy it. His hand shook slightly as he lifted his cup of coffee.

"If you oppose me, you'll be outvoted," Niemöller said.

"That may be. But I'll not have my name attached to such a document."

Niemöller stuffed the paper back into his pocket. "If your sermon had this tone of intransigence, I can understand why the parishioners of Johanneskirche were put off."

Dietrich flushed. "I must admit it is new to hear myself called intransigent. Most recently I was called a coward."

"By Elisabeth Hildebrandt. Yes, don't look so surprised. Her father spoke with me. He was concerned, because he likes you very much and doesn't want Elisabeth to lose your friendship. Listen to me, Dietrich, Elisabeth is a bit hysterical just now. You know how emotional young women can be. There's no need for you to try to live up to some false notion of heroism just because she's made you feel guilty for your earlier prudence with regard to the Jewish funeral."

Dietrich folded his napkin and laid it beside his plate. "You're wrong," he said. "About everything you've just said."

"Then let me warn you," said Niemöller, "no church in Germany will have you with your present opinions. There is a vacancy in London which has been open for more than a year, because it's a dreary low-paying position and few clergymen want to leave the country now, not with the excitement here. But if you persist in isolating yourself, it's the only type of position you'll be able to find, now or in the future."

Outside the restaurant they parted awkwardly and walked in opposite directions, Dietrich turning his collar up against a brisk autumn wind. But he stopped before he'd gone half a block, turned, and hailed Niemöller. The older man approached him with a tentative smile, as though expecting an apology.

"Tell me more," Dietrich said, "about the position in London."

Niemöller's smile faded. "There are two German-speaking churches," he said, "one in a poor area of the East End, the other in south London. Both with congregations so sparse they must share a pastor. The position carries a special charge for ecumenical work with the Church of England. Not exactly a relevant way for a German pastor to spend his time these days, is it?"

"I'm going to consider it."

"If it's courage you're looking for," Niemöller said, "you won't find it abroad."

On the way home, Dietrich stopped outside a Jewish bakery whose window bore a sign reading **Deutsche! Kauft nicht bei Juden!** A brown-shirted member of the SA loitered nearby, looking bored. Dietrich made eye contact and the man stared back. Dietrich walked to the door. "Jewish shop," the man said. Dietrich ignored him and went inside, purchased two berliner doughnuts from the nervous baker, and went back out. He stopped and held a doughnut out to the Nazi, who shook his head quickly and turned away, as though pretending he hadn't seen. Though he wasn't at all hungry, Dietrich ate one of the berliners as he walked down the Konstanzer Straße. Close to home he took a detour into the Grunewald woods, following golden paths beneath beech trees whose remaining leaves fluttered in the breeze. As he walked, he prayed. With each step he felt gradually lighter, like a man carrying a heavy pack through a desert who decides what he once thought essential no longer is, and begins to cast aside his burden, piece by piece.

A few days later, Dietrich came downstairs to find his father having breakfast with Hans von Dohnanyi in the morning room. He moved along the mahogany sideboard, filling his plate from crystal bowls of cucumber and herring in sour cream, a platter with paperthin slices of smoked salmon arranged in the shape of a rose, soft-boiled eggs perched on tiny china cups, Schwartzbrot and a slab of fresh butter on a silver serving dish. When he had taken his place at table, Karl Bonhoeffer said, "I'm going to court with Hans today. Since I'll be offering my own testimony soon, I thought I might acquaint myself with the surroundings."

Hans von Dohnanyi had been observing the trial of Marinus van der Lubbe as a representative of the Justice Ministry.

"How is it going?" Dietrich asked as he tapped his egg with the side of a spoon.

"I've been surprised," Hans said with a sidelong glance at his father-in-law, who was attacking his food with relish. "Hitler has allowed a very fair judge, and there's been no interference with the defense."

"Not everything is rotten in Germany," Dr. Bonhoeffer said cheerfully. "And Hans says Goering has made an absolute fool of himself in cross-examination. That doesn't hurt either."

"Have you decided," Dietrich asked, "what you will say in your testimony?"

"I have. There's no question van der Lubbe is sane and competent to stand trial."

"But some of the encounters you've described—"

"Not insanity. He's definitely a disturbed young man. But within the context of his past and present, his actions make perfect sense. His reasoning is sensible, within the framework of his own world and values. That wouldn't be true with an insane man. You can't make any sense at all out of the actions of the insane."

"But he was set up by the Nazis."

Dr. Bonhoeffer shrugged. "I don't know that."

Hans said, "Do you believe that on his own he scouted out the Reichstag and laid twenty-eight fires, as the forensic experts reported?"

"That's not the point. I'm being asked to give psychiatric testimony, nothing more. It's up to the defense attorney to bring out other points."

Hans persisted. "What if you declare him insane, even if you believe otherwise? Think what it would mean. If van der Lubbe is declared insane, then the case has been robbed of its political significance. After all, the Nazis are playing on public fears of a Communist conspiracy to push through their programs."

"Yes," Dietrich said, "and if you, Dr. Karl Bonhoeffer, declared van der Lubbe insane, you would pull the rug from under the Nazis!"

Karl Bonhoeffer threw down his fork. "I don't believe what I'm hearing from the pair of you. It is precisely because I am Dr. Karl Bonhoeffer that I could never do what you suggest. You're asking me to lie, and to betray my professional integrity."

"Perhaps your diagnosis is wrong," Dietrich said, and received such a look from his father he felt he'd been struck.

"Would you do what you are asking me to do? Would you as a Christian minister commit an immoral act in order to address what you perceived as a political problem?"

Dietrich looked at his plate.

"My duty," said his father, "is to testify to the mental condition of the accused. I shall discharge my duty."

And assuming the end of the discussion, Karl Bonhoeffer resumed eating.

"When I was in America," Dietrich said, "I studied ethics under a man named Reinhold Niebuhr, who believed that ideas and ideals should not be separated from the reality of the situations in which we find ourselves."

"Am I to be expected to allow theological speculation to induce me to perjure myself in court?" his father said curtly. "And don't start talking about some new ethic to me. It's this mania for change that's at the root of our current troubles." Then, "Is something the matter, Dietrich? You've been in a strange mood the last few days."

"I didn't get the appointment to Friedrichshain," Dietrich said.

"Ah. Well," Dr. Bonhoeffer said with an air of being let down. "You'll apply again elsewhere?"

"I thought of applying for a post in London. Two churches and liaison work with the Church of England."

"Good Lord. Why leave the country?"

"Never mind. I've decided against it. It would be cowardly to leave Germany just now."

Nothing more was said, and Dr. Bonhoeffer excused himself to send for Keppel and the car. Hans von Dohnanyi, who had been smoking quietly at the far end of the table, regarded Dietrich through half-closed eyes.

"I think you should apply for that vacancy in London," he said.

"You do?"

"Yes. Who knows. I might find something for you to do."

PASTORS FROM ACROSS THE FATHERLAND have gathered in Berlin to plan for the church elections. They discuss other news as well as they sip coffee and nibble on pastries in the fellowship hall of the Kaiser Wilhelm Church—that Catholic priests and bishops have stopped criticizing Hitler's policies now that the Vatican has recognized the Nazi government. That withdrawal from the League of Nations is imminent.

Dietrich Bonhoeffer approaches Pastor Martin Niemöller and requests permission to address the gathering. Niemöller gives him a hard look but nods his head. "Certainly," he says. "You've as much right to defend your position as I have. Suppose I put you on the schedule for eleven-thirty, just before we eat? Is that enough time?"

"Yes. Thank you."

Niemöller knows nothing Bonhoeffer can say will persuade the majority of pastors to oppose withdrawal from the League. But when Dietrich stands at the lectern and speaks to the pastors perched uncomfortably on their folding chairs, he does not so much as mention the League of Nations.

He grips the sides of the lectern as though to keep from toppling over and says, "There is more at stake today than government interference in church affairs. More at stake than the government's refusal to allow converted Jews to serve as pastors. The vast majority of Jews are not baptized and have no wish to be, no wish to deny the faith of their fathers. Their shops are being boycotted. Many have been turned out of their jobs, particularly in the civil service and the army. And yes, I hear reports of random beatings, and even killings, which go unreported and unpunished. This is monstrous. The German Christians support this attitude toward the Jews. In doing so, they are no longer able to truly call themselves Christians. If we refuse to speak out against these outrages, we also will no longer be able to call ourselves Christians."

A low murmuring has broken out, but Dietrich ignores it.

"What, you may ask, should we do? The church does not, of course, rule the state. Nor should it seek to. But when the state uses its power to destroy Christian faith and teaching, then the church must act.

"We can act in several ways. First, we Christians can challenge the state's actions and ask the state to live up to its responsibilities. Second, we must do everything we can to help those who have been victimized by the state. That includes those victims who are not part of the Christian community. 'Do good to all people,' scripture tells us.

"Third," he raises his voice as the grumblings grow louder, "and finally, if these first two courses of action do not achieve satisfactory results, we are obligated not just to bandage those who have been broken beneath the wheel of the state, but to jam a spoke in the wheel itself. This of course will involve direct political action—"

"It will involve sedition!" someone cries from the back. And there is a general hubbub as many in the audience stand and begin to walk out. Dietrich raises his voice even more, so that he is shouting.

"One course of action might be a pastors' strike. Suppose, in response to the measures taken against the Jews, the pastors of Germany refused to perform their duties. No weddings, no baptisms, no funerals until the anti-

Jewish measures are dropped. Consider what a powerful statement to the German people."

More pastors leave the audience, some talking angrily as they exit. Dietrich finishes quickly, stumbling a bit over the last of his speech—". . . a national church which accepts Nazi policies may be popular, but it will never be Christian. The choice before us is clear, Germanism or Christianity"—then steps away from the lectern and nearly runs into the waiting Niemöller.

"Have you gone mad?" Niemöller demands.

"Someone must begin to say these things."

"Someone must call for rebellion against the government? Good God, Bonhoeffer, how the German people would take such a message! And to ask pastors to walk away from their responsibilities? An easy decision for a pastor without a church."

"I have two churches," Dietrich says. "I've been offered the posting in London, and I have accepted."

Before Niemöller can respond, a furious Pastor Braun pushes his way in and wags a finger at Dietrich.

"How dare you, young man? Some of us may disagree with Hitler's tactics, Bonhoeffer, but we still love Germany."

"Yes," says Dietrich, and hears the voice of Fred Bishop whispering in his ear, "but do you love Jesus?"

Braun stares at him, face purpling, then turns on his heel. Niemöller folds his arms and says coolly, "Well, it will be easy enough to defend the Jews from the safety of London, won't it? Think of the rest of us here, from time to time, when you're feeling judgmental."

And Dietrich is left alone with the jumble of papers that is his speech.

Later in the autumn he climbs aboard a train bound for Ostend. He is on board a ferry crossing an English Channel enclosed in white mist when a guillotine in Berlin slices off the head of the dangerous Communist Marinus van der Lubbe.

Qui tollis peccata mundi
miserere nobis
suscipe deprecationem nostram

Thou who taketh away the sins of the world
have mercy on us
and receive our prayer

(Double chorus with French double dotting)

4 Feb. 1934

23 Manor Mount S.E.
Forest Hill

My dearest Sabine,

How I long to be with you on our birthday, but this year it shall not be. For me it is a time to contemplate my weakness, and separation from you is part of my penance. I am speaking of your father-in-law's funeral, and my refusal to participate in it as you and Gerhard requested. I am tormented when I recall this betrayal. How could I have been such a coward? Sabine, I no longer understand myself. Worst of all is the knowledge that one never makes up for something like that.

Still one cannot become paralyzed by past failings. I want you both to know I constantly pray for the courage to speak out against our new government. Here in London, I have made quite a nuisance of myself, popping up at meetings wherever so-called Christians who support the fascists put in an appearance. At one such gathering last week, I met an English bishop, a most extraordinary man. . . .

London
1934

THE PLACARDS in Lancaster Gate announce

PASTOR J.G.W. HOSSENFELDER
Missionary to the slums of Berlin
will speak about
EXCITING NEW DEVELOPMENTS IN GERMANY!
2:00 P.M. SUNDAY, MARCH 14
Opening remarks by Dr. F. Buchman!
Come find the Answers to Life's Questions!
Sponsored by the Oxford Group

From the dark gray London street, the windows of the Victorian hall offer an invitingly warm glow on this late winter's afternoon. In the foyer, neatly dressed young people come and go. These are Dr. Frank Buchman's converts, clean-living young men and women who have accepted the Lord as their personal savior and turned everything over to His guidance. If questioned at this very moment, each would acknowledge that knowing the Lord so intimately is a very great advantage. In a world threatened by economic depression and political upheaval, they are safe as houses. Their satisfaction is evident in the confident way they cover the long tables with white linen and set out trays of cucumber and butter sandwiches and scones and shortbread biscuits and steaming pots of tea flanked by urns of cream and sugar. They fold white cloth napkins with razor-straight edges and arrange stacks of cups and saucers. But they have grown a bit subdued, pausing from their tasks now and then to glance anxiously at one another. Because beyond the open doors, the meeting hall has erupted into a shouting match.

The source of agitation is a tall blond man who speaks a sort of Americanized English with a German accent. This man, who claims he is a pastor, has dared to challenge the beloved Dr. Buchman, the great moral leader and saver of souls come from America to transform a godless Europe. It is an ironic challenge, since the German looks like a younger version of Dr. Buchman, sharing with him a round face, rimless spectacles masking intelligent eyes, and thinning hair (gray in Dr. Buchman's case).

"I most certainly will speak to this gathering," the German declares, "since I have been invited to do so. I have in my pocket the letter which invites me to join other Germans in publicly welcoming Pastor Hossenfelder to England."

"A strange idea of welcome!" Dr. Buchman interrupts.

"A strange idea of a representative of Christ!" the German replies, and many of those in attendance gasp at such rudeness. In the foyer, the young people duck their heads in embarrassment and go back to the business of readying the reception.

The afternoon program began innocently enough. Hundreds of well-educated and prosperous Christians—a goodly number of clerical collars sprinkled among them—had come to hear Pastor Hossenfelder, a leading spokesman of the new church leadership in Germany. (Pastor Hossenfelder had himself hoped to be sponsored in his visit by the Church of England, but when such an invitation was not forthcoming from the skeptical Archbishop of Canterbury, he accepted Dr. Buchman's invitation with good enough grace.)

The audience had first been treated to a rousing introduction from Dr. Buchman, the great saver of souls himself, in the following vein:

"As many of you know, I was raised in Pennsylvania, a child of German immigrants. I have continued to carry with me a great *love* for Germany, that land of my parents' birth. No wonder I feel such *emotion* today. We are at a critical time in history, when England and my own United States are *seething* with *Communism*. What personal *joy*, then, to see hope arise in Germany. The new government of that great nation offers *infinite*"—he stands a-tiptoe and stretches his right hand toward eternity as he often does in mid-speech—"possibilities for remaking the world and putting it under *God* Control."

In the foyer, the young people paused to listen and murmur their approval.

"The world needs the *dictatorship* of the *living spirit* of God," Dr. Buchman proclaimed. He smiled and adjusted his glasses, which meant a familiar and well-loved expression was forthcoming. "I like to put it this way. God is a perpetual radio broadcasting station and all we need to do is *tune in*. What we need is a network of live wires across the world to every last man, in every last place, tying us all together, giving us all the same *divine commands* to live by. God has a plan for *every* person, for every nation. The liberals like to talk about the *economy*. But the world's problems aren't *economic*. The world's problems are *moral*, and they can't be solved by immoral measures. The world's problems *can* be solved within a *God-controlled* democracy. And some would like to call Herr Hitler's government a fascist *dictatorship*. Well, the world's problems can be solved through a *God-controlled* fascist dictatorship. Because if *God* is in control, that's all that matters."

No one had paid attention to the tall German sitting at the back of the hall who squirmed on his chair, crossing and uncrossing his legs and folding and unfolding his printed program into an accordion. After Dr. Buchman's glowing introduction of the man who had labored long and hard in the missionary field of Berlin's worst slums, fighting with great success against the godless Communists, Pastor Hossenfelder had himself taken the lectern and delivered a rambling address about the great future of Germany under Hitler and the enthusiasm of German Christians for their new government. He was met with polite applause, interrupted almost at once by his fellow countryman in the back row.

"Let me tell you," announced the tall German, "about this man who stands before you. This is no great missionary. This man served a tiny church in a poor district in Berlin, where he was noted for his lack of attention to pastoral duties. When Hitler began to interfere in church affairs, Hossenfelder's own congregation turned him out, because the poor of Berlin still know the difference between a Christian and a fascist. Were it not for his new role as apologist for Nazi arrogance, this man would have no platform to speak to anyone."

Hossenfelder had turned pale and stammering, but been championed at once by Dr. Buchman, who was never at a loss for words.

"And what platform do you claim?" Dr. Buchman demanded, to a smattering of applause.

"I am Pastor Dietrich Bonhoeffer, lately arrived from Berlin. I am in charge of the German-speaking congregations of Sydenham and East London."

And so the donnybrook commenced, and continues even though it is time to disperse and enjoy the refreshments the young people have prepared.

"You call Hitler's measures harsh," Dr. Buchman is saying to Bonhoeffer. "They don't seem so harsh to me, but rather good common sense. You seem to forget that your country was close to being overrun by Bolsheviks."

"You tell me of my own country? You dare? What do you know of the climate of fear that has arisen in Germany in the present day?"

"I was recently in Berlin," Dr. Buchman says. "I enjoyed a stroll along Unter den Linden, and through the lovely Tiergarten. I saw the young couples strolling hand in hand, the mothers pushing prams beneath the trees, the pretty girls reading books on park benches. I know quite a few young men here who would enjoy such a climate of fear."

There is general laughter and more applause. Dr. Buchman beams.

"You trivialize this crisis! Germany is not a Christian nation and Hitler stands for everything that is unchristian!" Dietrich cries to no avail, for there are now scattered boos and calls of *Sit down!*

"If Hitler is no Christian," Dr. Buchman says, "then we—" gesturing around him—"shall convert him."

This raises an excited murmur until the voice of Dietrich Bonhoeffer breaks in. "That is a laughable sentiment. It is we who are in need of conversion—you and I and everyone in this room—before we can speak of Hitler."

Which is a statement so breathtakingly absurd, this declaration to a people who know the Lord, that the hall falls silent for a moment.

There does not live the man or woman who can cost Dr. Frank Buchman his composure for more than a few seconds. He bows his head and raises his right hand palm out. His broad forehead collapses in wrinkles of holy forbearance. When he prays—and he knows prayer will not be interrupted—it is in a voice fraught with forbearance. "Lord Jesus, we are in the presence of an unruly spirit. But we know You to be the Lord and we know You have a plan for the nations of the world. Lord Jesus, we are part of Your plan or else we are cast into darkness. Bless You Jesus for Your presence among the good Christian people of Germany." He looks up, nods to the pianist cowering in the corner. "Let us close with hymn number 316."

Despite his agitation, Dietrich automatically reaches for the tattered brown hymnal on the rack in front of him and stands along with everyone else. They launch into a rousing version of "Onward Christian Soldiers."

He stares at the page for a moment, reads *Onward Christian soldiers, marching as to war, With the cross of Jesus going on before,* and slams the book shut.

"Arrogant song," he mutters in German.

Then he realizes someone has come to stand beside him. It is a man with neatly combed gray hair and piercing blue eyes who wears a purple shirt and white clerical collar. The man studies Dietrich for a moment, then closes his own hymnal as well and replaces it in the rack. Dietrich swallows hard, suddenly embarrassed at the scene he has caused, and looks down at his big white hands clutching the back of the chair in front of him. His companion begins singing the tune of "Onward Christian Soldiers," but with different words.

> Lloyd George knew my father.
> Father knew Lloyd George.
> Lloyd George knew my father.
> Father knew Lloyd George.

Dietrich stares at the man, who smiles back and continues to sing, more loudly now and with a sort of thumping gusto so that others turn to look at him.

Dietrich joins in on the chorus.

> Lloyd George knew my fa—ah—ah—ther,
> Father knew Lloyd George.
> Lloyd George knew my fa—ther.
> Fa—ther knew Lloyd George. AH—MEN.

The man leans toward Dietrich and says in a low voice, "My favorite hymn from the Great War." Then he offers his hand. "George Bell. I'm the Bishop of Chichester."

DIETRICH HAD LIKED TO THINK himself sympathetic to the plight of the poor, had even dreamed of becoming poor himself, but London called these ideals into question. One of his parishes was St. Paul's Goalston Street, a pile of soot-blackened brick wedged into a Whitechapel neighborhood bereft of trees. The warren of streets, home to an assortment of Cockneys, Jews, and recent immigrants, smelled of fish and garbage. Canvas market stalls fronted tenements and cold-water flats that seemed little improved since the days of Dickens.

The south London suburb of Forest Hill, where he chose instead to live, was by contrast modest and middle-class, a scattering of yellow brick houses whose parlors, Dietrich imagined, housed conversations given over to football matches and the latest neighborhood gossip rather than evenings of music and intellectual discourse. Not that he inquired what went on behind the mass-produced white lace curtains. He mostly kept to himself in two rooms of the shabby manse that stood at the top of Manor Mount. He only had the first floor, since the ground floor was given over to a German-speaking school. The wainscoting in the entry hall, an elaborate prefabricated etching of entwined leaves, birds, and butterflies, was covered over with a hideous salmon-pink paint. Dietrich's rooms at the top of the stairs had high white ceilings, peeling wallpaper, and windows that whistled with each gust of winter wind. One room was dominated by the Bechstein grand piano from Wangenheimstraße 14. His mother had ordered it crated and shipped by rail to Bremerhaven, then put on board the same steamer that bore her son across the North Sea. It had been a great comfort during the rough passage to imagine the Bechstein sleeping in its darkened bed in the hold, its silent keys awaiting his touch to call them to life. On its arrival in Forest Hill he sat down amid the splintered wood of the crate, played a Schubert sonata while imagining his family joining in with violins and cellos, then rested his head on the music stand and wept.

He was done for by a Mrs. Potts, another present from his mother. "When your brothers and sisters were married," Paula Bonhoeffer told him, "your father and I helped each of them for a time, because we didn't wish them to start out on their own without at least one servant. Why shouldn't we do the same for you? After all, you're starting a household, even if you do persist in remaining a bachelor." Mrs. Potts was engaged at long distance on the recommendation of a pastor of Paula's acquaintance who had served the London parishes for two years in the 1920s. (A far longer time in the wilderness than Jesus endured, the man confided to Dietrich's mother, but she did not mention this to her son.) Mrs. Potts proved to be a bedraggled woman whose thin gray hair, sunken cheeks, and poor teeth made her seem far older than the fifty-odd years she claimed. She kept her head down at all times (except for quick, random glances over her shoulder) and often talked to herself. Her main contributions to the upkeep of the house were to chop awkwardly at the floor with a scraggly broom and to present Dietrich each morning with a limp greasy kipper, a fried egg whose hard crusted yolk crumbled beneath the edge of his fork, and a weak pot of tea. He got the rest of his meals himself.

He also learned to make his own fires, dragging a sack of coal up the frozen back stairs, shoveling and poking around the maw of the stove, washing the black dust from his hands, digging it from beneath his fingernails with a file, wiping dust from the furniture each morning, especially from the precious Bechstein, which he took to covering with a blanket. Then, at night, by the weak light of an electric lamp, he would whip off the blanket with a flourish for invisible eyes, sit carefully on the stool, and play. By turning his head he could glimpse the flailing of his shadow arms on the illumined wall. He heard the voice of the respected Kreuzer charging there was no passion in Dietrich's playing. If only Kreuzer were in the mean rooms of the Forest Hill house listening while Dietrich brought forth thunder and anguish from the Bechstein, sometimes until three in the morning so that Mrs. Potts, who was cowering in the basement, swore to the butcher that the German gentleman she did for was possessed by the Devil.

So he found himself as though awakened from a nightmare in the library of the Athenaeum, one of Pall Mall's most exclusive clubs, seated before a blazing hearth in a soft red leather chair and sipping ancient Scotch. He held the smoky glass at nose level, studied the man across from him, then glanced at the letter in his other hand, the letter he had received only a week earlier from Hans von Dohnanyi. *Uncle Rudi is still ailing, and the doctors fear worse news in the coming months. As for what you can do, of course you cannot heal Uncle Rudi from England. You mustn't feel bad; after all, you aren't a physician. But I am advised it could be helpful to establish contact with the Rt. Rev. George Bell. He is the Bishop of Chichester and not only one of the most respected clergymen in England but a founding leader of this new international ecumenical movement. I would think his prayers and support might be of some benefit to poor Uncle Rudi at this time. With affection, Hans v. Doh.*

"Amazing coincidence," Dietrich said, "that I should stumble upon you at that meeting when you're just the person my brother-in-law suggested I see."

He handed the letter to Bell, who scanned it with raised eyebrows and said, "Uncle Rudi?"

"A sort of family joke. Uncle Rudi is a Nazi relation, a horrid man altogether. Whenever we refer to the political situation at home by telephone or letter, we use his name as a code word." Dietrich paused and then said by way of a test, "Perhaps you think we are too cautious?"

Bell shook his head. "Not at all. I was there, you know, in '33. The very night Hitler came to power, watching from a room in the Hotel Adlon as the parade went past."

Dietrich set down his glass. "I was there as well," he said in a low voice, "nearby in Unter den Linden."

"Mesmerizing, wasn't it?" said Bell. "The drums and the trumpets, the uniforms, all that rage and joy commingled."

"Yes," Dietrich said. "I know I was not myself that night, and perhaps have not been since." He watched the fire for a moment. "What were you doing in Berlin?"

"A meeting of the World Council of Churches, some of the executive committee. Berlin's a convenient location, or was."

"This ecumenical movement, is it worth anything more than a lot of pious speeches? Will stands be taken?"

Bell offered a cigarette, then struck a match for Dietrich, who leaned forward as though to kiss the bishop's ring. "Will stands be taken?" Bell said. "That's up to us, isn't it? I've seen enough of Dietrich Bonhoeffer in action to think stands will damn well be taken if he becomes involved."

They smoked for a while in companionable silence. Dietrich was warmed by the older man's mixture of amiable generosity and bracing toughness, by the glints of humor in the blue eyes. He judged Bell to be in his fifties, nearly old enough to be his own father, but a more genial father than he had ever known. He had not thought of a father as someone to confide in, and yet he felt he could tell anything to this man. Not that this was necessarily admirable, he reminded himself sternly, anxious to avoid disloyalty to Karl Bonhoeffer.

". . . not so amazing," Bell was saying, "that we met as we did. I've been watching with a great deal of interest how Buchman and these pietists of his have embraced your more conservative countrymen. I've been to several meetings before this one and established myself as a bit of a *persona non grata*. Not just because of Germany. Buchman hates the trade unions, thinks they're all a front for Communism, has no time for the poor except to patronize them with claptrap about saving their souls, as if that were Buchman's work instead of God's. No, Buchman doesn't like it when I show up. Not that he'd ever ask me to leave, too cagey for that, but I'm no longer called upon when I raise my hand to speak. Nor will you be from this point on."

"Perhaps I shall not be so polite as to raise my hand," Dietrich said. "Not that I'm used to making a scene. But I find now that I am angry, always angry. It's not just the bullying and the threats. It's the way all logic and knowledge and reason are twisted into their exact opposites. So that it is no longer possible to converse with these people. Only to scream at them, even to—"

Bell watched him closely.

"When I saw Hossenfelder there, that desiccated skeleton, claiming to speak for Germany, claiming to speak for Christians in Germany, I could have struck him. I could have pummeled him, trampled him until he was senseless. Which of course is not Christian either. Is the opposite of Christian. And so I wallow with them in this cesspool of evil."

After a moment Bell said, "In the last war, I lost two young brothers. Donald and Benedict."

"And I an older brother, Walter."

"For a while I hated Germans."

"And I the French and English."

"The forgiveness and grace of God relieved me of that sin."

Dietrich nodded.

"But I have never stopped hating the Great War, Dietrich. I try to practice charity toward my fellow man, but I shall never stop hating the viciousness and pettiness and meanness in humanity that led to the war, and that feeds this new monster." Bell leaned closer. "It is new, you know. Not tyranny, of course. Tyrants have always been with us. You've only got to look at the Soviet Union. My friends here—" he waved his arm at the half-dozen graying men slumped in armchairs reading their newspapers or sleeping beneath them—"think there's the great threat. Not because it's tyranny—they can live with all sorts of tyranny. Because it's Communism. They're cautiously optimistic about your new government. 'Well, this Hitler fellow will throw a good scare into the Reds.' You know the sort of thing, you hear it at home."

"Things have gone beyond throwing a good scare into anyone," Dietrich said.

"Oh, to be sure. I've no doubt of Hitler's methods, though your well-off Englishman is pleased to overlook them. But there's more going on in Germany, you know there's more going on. There is joy in Germany! Excitement!" Bell was growing more excited himself. "No, my boy, this is much more insidious than Communism. Communism denies man's spiritual nature. But this new thing, this attacks man's spiritual nature and turns it inside out. So that people can believe they live as they always have. They can believe they maintain their ancient virtues and religions. They can hate and truly think it love. Oh, we're not immune to the modern disease here in England, not by any means."

They were interrupted by an elderly man, also wearing the purple shirt of a bishop. "Ecclesiastical visitor, George?"

Dietrich stood quickly, clicked his heels, and offered his hand to the newcomer.

"This is Pastor Dietrich Bonhoeffer, Arthur," Bell said. "And this is the Rt. Rev. Arthur Headlam, the Bishop of Gloucester."

"German, then?" Bishop Headlam beamed. "Would have guessed it by your greeting. You Germans are the only race who do manners better than we English."

"You are very kind," Dietrich said.

"Will you join us?" Bell inquired.

"No, no time just now," Headlam waved at him, then turned back to Dietrich. "Interesting man you've got now, this Hitler. Giving the trade unions a good scare, I understand. Could use a bit of that in this country, eh George? 'Course he won't agree," Headlam continued good-naturedly. "George here is a bloody socialist himself, aren't you, George? Only one in the Athenaem. Wonder you don't just pitch it all and go off to live in a tenement somewhere. Doubt you care much for Hitler either."

"Of course I don't care for Hitler," Bell said pleasantly. "I've never cared for bullies."

"Bosh! Good discipline, that's all. Germany was on the brink, after all, wasn't it, Pastor—"

"Bonhoeffer," Dietrich reminded him. "Of course there were problems, but I assure you, sir, Hitler is not the answer to them. He's jailing Communists and Socialists without cause. And he's persecuting Jews."

"Yes, well," said Headlam, and looked at his pocket watch. "Got to run, I'm afraid. Meeting my wife in half an hour. Going to some damn concert or other."

When he had gone, Bell did not sit back down. "He's right about one thing, you know. It is hypocritical for a trades union supporter to inhabit the Athenaeum. But I don't come here often, actually, just when I have to stay in London overnight. I spend most of my time at home in Chichester. You must come to visit."

"I would very much like that. But until Easter, at least, I'm afraid I am stuck here. You know what a busy time it is for the clergy."

"Why not come down in May after our respective Easter duties are over? That's always a fine time for a clergyman to take a vacation. And Chichester is lovely in the spring."

Dietrich smiled at the thought of escaping Forest Hill. "Perhaps I will visit in May."

"Good. And now come along to dinner. They serve a very good leg of lamb downstairs, and I want to hear more about Germany."

Back into exile in frigid rooms on Manor Mount. He decided he would fill his time by writing a book. A book about what it meant to live an authentic Christian life in the modern world, a book that would challenge the hypocritical pieties of the Buchmans of the world and expose the heresies of the Hossenfelders, the complacencies of the Bishop Headlams. But each attempt at a start ended with a few empty phrases scratched out, paper crammed into balls and tossed in the wastebasket. He took to drinking more wine than he was used to, and sleeping in the afternoons. He scratched his name on icy window panes with his fingernail, like a forlorn child.

HE THOUGHT HE MIGHT BE GOING the way of Mrs. Potts, whom he found one morning curled in a fetal position beneath the kitchen table, muttering to herself. She had been collected by her nephew and a doctor and taken to a hospital for the insane. Not that Dietrich was going mad. But the melancholy which had touched him now and again throughout his life seemed to have taken up permanent residence. He found little to inspire him in his pastoral duties. His congregations were small, their members drawn together on Sunday mornings less for spiritual guidance than to sastisfy their longing to hear German spoken. They tolerated Dietrich's sermons with bland equanimity, and even the subject of Hitler did not rouse them into any sort of spirited discussion. Dietrich wondered if his own state of mind might be to blame. For a time his only interest lay in firing off letters to Martin Niemöller in Berlin, urging him to push the church to some action against Hitler. He received a few testy replies in response, which plunged him deeper into despair. Then he could not write, could not even read, could summon no more energy than was necessary to plod through his pastoral duties. In the evenings he slumped beside the telephone, wondering if he should call Berlin, hoping someone there would ring him. He could sit without moving for an hour, two hours.

He contemplated suicide. In his darkened rooms he lay on the bed staring at the cracked ceiling and clutching a bottle of sleeping pills. He was using the pills nightly; the bottle was half empty. But also half full. He shook it. Stared at the ceiling. Tried, without success, to pray.

The telephone rang on the bedside stand. Dietrich cradled the receiver to his head as a small child will pillow a favorite stuffed toy. Pastor Martin Niemöller spoke from behind a curtain of light static. "Bonhoeffer? I took the liberty of tracking you down through Uncle Rudi. He didn't think you'd mind."

"Uncle Rudi?" Dietrich sat up in the dark. "I've been longing to hear something from Uncle Rudi. Anything."

Niemöller laughed. "You'd not want me to call if I had nothing to tell you. If I called with no news, I'd soon be getting another of those damn letters of yours."

Dietrich said nothing.

"Still there, Bonhoeffer?"

"Yes," he said.

"We've a meeting scheduled with Hitler himself. Next Thursday."

"Good God," Dietrich said, and thought, Are you also going mad, my friend? "Why? What could that accomplish?"

"Probably nothing. But it seems prudent to me to at least try to reason with the man. Otherwise the church can be accused of refusing to be open to his point of view."

"The church *should* refuse to be open to Hitler's point of view," Dietrich said sharply.

Niemöller's sigh was audible.

"What do we accomplish," Dietrich said, "by treating him as if he were legitimate?"

"Damn it, man, he *is* legitimate. He's running the country, in case you've forgotten!"

"He has no moral standing, he—"

"Dietrich, listen to me. Stop trying to turn me into an opponent. I agree with you. I agree so strongly I may be putting my head in a damn noose here."

Dietrich lay back on the pillow. "Sorry," he said. "You're taking risks and I'm not. You're quite right to upbraid me."

"I didn't call to upbraid you. I called to say it's your turn."

"Ah."

"I expect, to be frank, that Hitler will refuse to stop interfering in church affairs."

"What about the Jews?" Dietrich interrupted. "You must challenge him about his persecution of the Jews."

"I'll try to convince the other pastors who'll be accompanying me," Niemöller said. "They won't be happy about it but I'll try anyway."

"Good. Good for you Martin."

"As I was saying, Hitler will probably refuse to listen to us. We will then proclaim our good faith, and our love of the Fatherland. He will still refuse, or at least will give us no direct answer. In that case we will have done all we can. We will go away, and we will call a meeting to separate ourselves once and for all from the state church and set up our own denomination. I'm beginning to see now you were right about that. It's the only way."

"Thank God," Dietrich said. "It's past time."

"Not so easy, though," Niemöller continued. "Most of our bishops and pastors, most of our members, are not happy at Hitler's interference but won't be happy either at an outright break. That's why this meeting with Hitler is important. It has to be clear he's given us no other choice."

"Take care. He'll try to outmaneuver you, try to co-opt you. He's cagey."

"So am I," Niemöller said. "Besides, I'm going to have your help. Uncle Rudi says you've made friends with an English bishop who's active in the ecumenical movement."

"Yes. George Bell."

"Is he influential in London as well? Enough so that the newspapers will notice when he speaks out? Enough so the government will notice?"

"I think so. He seems very well respected, and it's assumed he'll be the next Archbishop of Canterbury."

"Good. Have him primed and ready. As soon as we've met Hitler and received no satisfaction, let's have a letter from your bishop in the *Times*. Let's have your bishop telling the world that Hitler is persecuting the true church in Germany and that the state church is a sham. Let's have him saying Christians in Germany have no choice but to oppose this government. And let's have your bishop writing all his fellow church leaders in Sweden and France and Switzerland and urging them to say the same things in their own countries."

"Actually, he's already been doing the latter, at my urging."

"Good. If Hitler knows the world is watching him, perhaps he'll think twice before going any farther than he has. Perhaps he won't come after us."

"So you believe he *will* come after us?" Dietrich asked.

"Who knows?" Niemöller replied. "If he does, you'd best stay where you are."

That was how Dietrich came to stand beneath the timetable in Victoria Station, suitcase in hand, feeling happier than he had in weeks. The shrill whistles and slamming doors that proclaimed a departure set his heart to thumping, and he nearly ran to the train. Though he was traveling in the opposite direction from Canterbury, he felt as though he were on pilgrimage. Alone in his compartment and yet for once not lonely, he pressed his face against the window glass and dreamed himself into the landscape. He played Noah as the train passed through the green Sussex countryside, plucking this creature and that—sheep and bull and white-tailed rabbit, horse and dog and swan—from landscape to mind's Ark. At Pulborough the ridge of the South Downs broke the horizon. Three girls in black long-skirted uniforms emerged from a copse of trees into a lush clearing, walking arm in arm, then vanished as though dissolved by sudden smoke.

He stepped down in Chichester to find Bishop Bell himself waiting.

"This is a great deal of trouble for you," Dietrich fretted.

"Nonsense. It's only a short way to the cathedral and I often go for a stroll this time of day. Here, we shall send your bag on by a porter and I shall take you home by way of the close gardens."

They skirted a city wall and passed through a stone gate into a green parkland lined with hedges and flower beds and lit by sprays of yellow and purple and red blossoms. The spires and towers of the cathedral hovered just beyond. Bell stopped. "My favorite view," he said. "I never tire of it."

They walked on through the gardens and along the cloisters, the mellow stone enveloping them as comfortingly as a blanket. "There is something here," Dietrich said, giving himself over to the graceful lines of spire and nave. He stopped to admire a pastel sundial high on a tower. "Something I feel."

"What do you mean?"

Dietrich said, "When I visit an ancient place, I often pick up a mood, an aura. In the Lambertikirche in Münster, Anabaptists were tortured to death and their rotting corpses suspended from the ceiling in iron cages. When I visited Münster, I could not bear to stay in that so-called sanctuary more than a few minutes. All I felt was dread."

"And here?" Bell asked.

"Peace," Dietrich said. "It is as though some heart of goodness resided here."

Bell thought a moment and then exclaimed, "Ah! I know just what it is, the heart of goodness that resides in Chichester. It will be my secret until tomorrow. But now you'll want to rest and wash up before dinner. And I'm afraid I haven't warned you. We've another guest this week."

"Oh," Dietrich said, a bit disappointed, for he had hoped to have the bishop to himself. "Who is it?"

"A very fine poet, Tom Eliot. American, but he's been in this country for years. I've asked him to write a play, you see, for a church festival next year at Canterbury. Poor fellow's been having a rough time lately. He's separated from his wife, a mentally unstable woman. She's taken to following Tom around, staring at him through restaurant windows, denouncing him in the street, interrupting his poetry readings. Very sad for them both. He's had the best doctors trying to see her, but she isn't the most cooperative patient. It's driving him to distraction and he hasn't been able to write. He called me up, desperate to get out of London for a few weeks, so I invited him here. I feel somewhat responsible, since he's writing this play at my instigation and he's miserable if the work isn't going well."

"I understand," Dietrich said.

"Well, the palace is quite spacious, as you can see"— gesturing at a rambling stone lodge at the end of a gravel drive. "You and Tom needn't disturb one another, unless it turns out you enjoy one another's company."

Dietrich didn't meet Tom Eliot that evening, since the poet was, according to Bell's wife, Hettie, "on a writing tear that he doesn't want to interrupt."

"Not even for dinner?" Bell asked as they sat down to eat.

"He requested a tray be sent to his room. And if I've guessed his mood, I doubt he'll taste a bite of it." Hettie Bell, a tall dark-haired woman with a blaze of white at one temple, smiled at Dietrich. "Do you write, Dietrich?"

"I've written a few short theological volumes," he said shyly. "Nothing major yet. As a matter of fact, I've a book in mind that I think could be important, but I've not been able to make myself start it."

He sipped an excellent consommé and took note of his surroundings. The Tudor dining hall was large enough to feed a school of small boys. A massive fireplace at one end was empty now that the weather had turned warm and the tall milk-paned windows stood open in their stone casements. Two servants brought plates of salmon in dill sauce and asparagus and new potatoes. They finished with a strawberry tart in cream. Mrs. Bell poured the coffee herself from a silver urn. "Tomorrow I suppose George will give you a tour of the close, won't you, George?"

"Oh, yes," Bell said. "We saw a bit today, didn't we? Dietrich had a most interesting observation. He believes there's a mysterious good presence here at the cathedral. What do you think it might be, my dear?"

She thought a moment. "The Fitzalan tomb?" she suggested, then, seeing this was not the right answer, thought some more. "Oh!" she exclaimed, and her eyes lit up.

"No, no, don't say yet," Bell wagged his finger at her.

"In the—" *chapel,* she mouthed.

"Yes, that's it."

She smiled, pleased with herself, and took her husband's hand across the table. Dietrich looked enviously from one to another.

"Our secret is a quiet one," Bell was saying. "This cathedral has not been the site of momentous events, no martyrdoms at the altar or tombs of kings. We've a few bishops and knights buried in our vaults. People living and marrying, giving birth and dying. Only the shades of everyday life haunt Chichester."

"Nothing like Canterbury," said a voice from the door. The man who stood there was thin, with a shock of brown hair that he pushed back from his forehead in an almost gallant gesture. He walked delicately to the table, pulled out a chair, and sat ramrod straight with his hands folded in his lap, looking down a long, sharp nose at Dietrich. "Chichester," he continued, "is certainly nothing like Canterbury with its blood-spattered altars and rifled treasures and hordes of foul-smelling, fornicating pilgrims. No fat King Henry the Fourth rotting in his sarcophagus in Chichester, no Black Prince dreaming on his stone bed about the wondrous times he had while dashing babies against walls. No Becket at Chichester. Good evening, Pastor Bonhoeffer. Tom Eliot. Sorry I have been so impolite as to miss dinner."

All this before anyone else could breathe.

"And how did the writing go?" Hettie Bell asked indulgently, as though quite used to such flights.

Eliot turned his head to answer without moving his body. "My waste-basket," he said, "is full. All in all, a frantic evening."

"Oh dear," Bell said. "Perhaps we'd better retire to the library and hear about this over a drink."

"Scotch," said Eliot, "would clear the head marvelously."

Dietrich was himself feeling a bit muddle-headed. He followed the others down the oak-paneled hall and into the library, where a pair of auburn-haired retrievers lay before the hearth. Bell poured drinks from a crystal flask on the sideboard while Dietrich settled on the sofa beside Hettie Bell. Eliot perched on the edge of an armchair.

"Another man of the cloth," he said, "and unlike the good bishop here, come from a place of turmoil, eh?"

"Rather more turmoil than in England, I'm afraid," Dietrich said wearily.

"Fascinating, absolutely fascinating. We must spend some time together, Bonhoeffer. I'd love to hear about your adventures."

"I'm not sure I consider the crisis at home adventurous," Dietrich said sharply. "Rather tragic, I'd say."

"Ah, yes," Eliot said, covering his mouth with one hand but not looking the least bit abashed.

"Really, Tom," Bell admonished, "it is a very difficult and delicate situation."

"Perhaps," Eliot said with a wave of his hand, "but you must indulge me a bit, George, if you want me to write this damned play of yours." He turned back to Dietrich. "Martyrdom of Thomas Becket. The last play the church festival had was John Masefield's *The Coming of Christ*. Really, George, it's not fair to me." He pressed a hand to his chest. "Masefield gets the Divinity and I'm left with poor little Becket."

"But Becket is my favorite saint!" Hettie said.

Eliot sniffed. "Ah, yes. 'The hooly blisful martir.' But I can't help think of him as a mountebank. Quarreled with Henry the Second over church funds and archbishop's privileges. Is this the stuff of martyrdom?"

"Next you'll be telling us Saint Francis was really a vagrant who fed pigeons and talked to himself," Hettie said.

Bell said, "There is more to Becket than Tom lets on."

"There is indeed," Eliot cried, "but what is it? I must know! I'm the one who has to write the damned thing!" He turned to Dietrich. "What do you think, Bonhoeffer? How does an ordinary man like Becket become a saint? Is sainthood truly the fruit of a holy life? Or is it stubbornness, or pride, or sheer luck? And would that be good luck, or bad luck?"

Just then a telephone rang at the far end of the room. The dogs raised their heads. Bell answered, then said to Dietrich with his hand over the mouthpiece, "It's for you. From Berlin."

While Dietrich was answering the phone, Hettie whispered to Eliot, "Really, you shouldn't harass the poor man. Imagine, calls from abroad at this time of night. He's having a very hard time just now."

"And so am I, Hettie. I'm trying to find my archbishop."

"Does it help to press poor Dietrich?"

"Probably not at all," Eliot said cheerfully, "but I'm desperate."

When Dietrich spoke into the phone, Niemöller's voice said, "Bonhoeffer. Sorry to call so late, but I've just come from a pastors' meeting. Trouble, I'm afraid, with your request to address the Jewish question."

"Trouble, of course," Dietrich said tersely. "You and I both know it will mean trouble."

"Listen to me. We've got bishops and pastors from all over Germany, finally willing to confront Hitler on Thursday. It's been a massive effort to get them out, just to rouse them at first, and then to give them courage. But they're here, and they've come to accept that something must be done."

"But," Dietrich said, and waited.

"But it's government interference in church affairs that concerns them. They don't want to take up the Jewish question except as it pertains to Christians of Jewish ancestry. They're adamant on this point. I couldn't change their minds, and if you were here, you couldn't either."

"Then why are you bothering to call me?" Dietrich said.

"Believe it or not," Niemöller said testily, "I thought you might have

some idea what to do next. I thought perhaps if the meeting with Hitler
goes well, you might want to fly to Berlin and try to persuade the other pastors that taking up the Jewish question is the next logical step. Once it is
clear that the church is safe, of course."

"Safe!" Dietrich's voice rose. "The church cannot be safe! In fact,
Martin, the church no longer exists in Germany. This safe congregation of
yours, it no longer interests me. The battle lines have moved elsewhere."

"Then I take it," Niemöller said coldly, "there is no need for me to telephone after our meeting with the Führer."

"That is up to you," Dietrich said. "I still plan to speak to Bishop Bell.
But not on your terms."

When Dietrich replaced the phone on its cradle and turned, he realized
the others were watching him. Bell stood close by, a look of concern on his
face.

"Forgive me," Dietrich said, "but I am very tired. I would like to go to
my room." He turned to Bell. "If I might speak with you about this tomorrow at your convenience?"

Bell patted his shoulder for answer.

Dietrich bowed formally to Hettie and Eliot. "Then I shall say goodnight."

When he had gone the others fell silent. Eliot rubbed his chin, lost in
thought. When Bell offered him a cigar, he looked startled, then said, "No.
No, I think I may do some more work tonight," and took his leave.

In his room, Dietrich changed into pyjamas and climbed into bed with his
Bible. Though he'd had a good dinner, he felt ravenously hungry and was
pleased to find a tin of biscuits at the bedside. He munched on shortbread,
turned to the Gospel of Matthew, and read and reread the Sermon on the
Mount. *Blessed are the peacemakers. . . . blessed are those who are persecuted
for righteousness sake. . . . You have heard that it was said 'An eye for an eye
and a tooth for a tooth.' But I say to you, do not resist an evildoer. But if anyone strikes you on the right cheek, turn the other one also. . . .* He ate more
biscuits and talked to himself, murmuring over and over, "It cannot mean
to do nothing, it cannot mean that." Love and nonviolence, but in what
cause? He flipped frantically through Matthew, through Mark with a piercing fear that he had been wrong, that no action was called for but only
silent suffering, yet appalled at what seemed the inherent selfishness of
such a notion, "For how," he said aloud, "can one justify one's own suffering for the good if it leaves the other's suffering unaddressed?"

At last, unable to keep his eyes open, he let the Bible slip from his grasp
and fell asleep, forgetting even to turn off the bedside lamp and insensible
to the glow of light.

Tom Eliot did not make an appearance at breakfast. Bell himself served eggs and bacon and grilled tomatoes and mushrooms from the sideboard. Hettie poured the tea and handed around triangles of buttered toast in a silver rack. When they were done eating, Bell said, "Now to the chapel for morning prayer, where Hettie and I shall reveal to you Chichester's good heart."

The chapel was on the ground floor, a small plain room with oak beams. Dietrich was admiring the simple proportions when Hettie plucked his sleeve and led him to the near wall. Beyond her was a faded round painting, a Virgin and Child in gold and pale blue.

"The Chichester roundel," Bell said. "Mid-thirteenth century. Painted over by the Puritans sometime in the seventeenth. What impulse, do you think, could lead anyone to see this as the work of the devil? Thank God it was found and returned to the world."

"What do you think of it?" Hettie Bell asked like a proud parent at a recital.

Mother and Child were surrounded by acolytes flinging ghostly thuribles at wild angles. Crusted gold adorned the illumined crown of Mary and the halo of the baby Jesus, and golden wisps clung to the Child's sleeve as He reached for Mary's neck. Mother and infant bestowed on each other a look of pure love.

"What do I think of it?" Dietrich whispered. "It's so lovely one doesn't know what to say."

"In so many paintings of this type," Bell said, "the infant Jesus is already looking to heaven and Mary is anticipating her loss. But these faces! No fear of the future, no grief, not even pride of purpose. Nothing here but sheer joy in one another's company."

"So sad it's hidden away where few can see it," Hettie said.

"Yes," Dietrich said again. He wished he could be alone.

When he turned, Bell caught his eye and put his hand on his shoulder. "You must visit the chapel on your own whenever you like."

Dietrich nodded his thanks. During Morning Prayer he sat with Hettie at the front of the chapel and felt as though Mother and Child were whispering behind his back.

For the rest of the morning they went their separate ways, Bell to tend to diocesan business in Brighton, Hettie to the meeting of some town charity. Dietrich took his notebook to the garden and tried to write, but nothing would come. Nor could he concentrate on any sort of reading, so he slipped back into the chapel and sat before the roundel, trying to pray. But even the roundel had lost its magic, and the smiles of Mother and Child seemed like indecent smirks. Dietrich felt himself as crabbed and sour as any

Puritan. He wandered on through the cloisters, immune to the charms of light upon stone, and into the cathedral. Behind the altar he lit a candle and waited as clear wax wept into gummed sand. He tried to pray for the pastors' meeting, but knew he was going through the motions.

When he emerged into sunlight he glimpsed Tom Eliot striding—no, prancing—through the garden. Dietrich stepped behind a wall. It was no good. When he looked again, Eliot was headed toward him.

"I thought that was you lurking among the primroses," the poet exclaimed happily. He threw himself on a bench and motioned Dietrich beside him. "What have you been doing with yourself?"

Dietrich reluctantly sat down. "I have been wrestling with the Sermon on the Mount."

Eliot laughed. "Wrestling, and losing of course. 'Blessed are ye,' et cetera et cetera. 'Course, when you read that blessed list, none of *us* is."

"No," said Dietrich, warming to the American cadences, "None of us is."

Eliot crossed his legs, leaned back, and continued to smile. Dietrich imagined his own face fixed in a scowl, the stubborn brow and arrogant chin, the clenched fists. He felt ashamed. This man had done nothing to him and did not deserve to be made the butt of his bad humor. He turned to Eliot and said, "I must apologize. I have not been civil to you. I have allowed my concern for what is happening at home to get in the way of common courtesy."

Eliot shrugged and, as if Dietrich hadn't spoken, asked, "On what points do you wrestle with the Sermon on the Mount?"

"Well. I had been thinking of the Sermon as a call to action. A proclamation that turns the world upside down. It is the poor, after all, who are blessed, not the rich. It is the meek who shall be rewarded, not the grasping and coarse. The weak who are to be championed, not the powerful."

Eliot nodded.

Dietrich took a deep breath. "Of course, I have been relating all this to the situation in Germany. For months I have been talking, writing letters, trying to get the church in Germany to be the church of the Sermon."

"With little success," Eliot guessed.

"None. My colleagues in Germany are a contemptible collection, some cowardly, some shortsighted, some naive, some bigots, some doddering old fools. Hardly a single principled stand among the lot of them."

"Dear, dear," Eliot murmured, looking pleased, unaccountably pleased.

"Then last night," Dietrich said, "after that telephone call, I read the passage again. I was stricken with terror. The text offered nothing. No call to action, none, only a call to refuse resistance. I began to search elsewhere in the Gospels. Nothing. Whenever I thought I had found some call to act on behalf of the oppressed against an oppressor, it turned out to be God who would do the acting. Not man. God says *He* has filled the hungry with good things and the rich *He* has sent empty away. God says *He* has brought good news to the poor and proclaimed release to the oppressed."

"Well?" Eliot asked.

"He hasn't!" Dietrich flung his arms wide. "Look at the persecution, the starvation, the injustice throughout the world! God has done nothing! Yet only suffer, the Gospel says. We are to be a pack of impotent bystanders. I can't bear it."

"To act and to suffer," Eliot said. "Perhaps they're the same."

Dietrich looked up to see if he was being mocked, but saw the other man was no longer smiling.

"'You know and do not know what it is to act or suffer,'" Eliot said. "'You know and do not know that action is suffering and suffering action.' A line from my play. I read it to some friends in Bloomsbury who didn't understand a word of it, and I wasn't able to explain it myself. That's the way of writing sometimes, you know. The words come and we stand back and wonder what the hell! Anyway, I'd gotten no further, until last night."

He offered Dietrich a cigarette, shared a match.

"Tell me, Bonhoeffer, have you ever acted? In a play, I mean?"

Dietrich saw the black-uniformed SS flailing their batons, the drawn pistol, Falk Harnack writhing in agony. "Yes, but the last play I was in didn't go especially well."

"Here's what I'm thinking," Eliot said eagerly. "In a couple of days I'd like to gather you and the Bells together for a reading. In the meantime, I'll play the hermit and write some more. If you don't mind?"

"No," Dietrich said. "God willing, I'll be doing much the same."

But he could not write until he had spoken with George Bell. He awaited the bishop's afternoon return as eagerly as he had waited for his parents to return from journeys in his childhood. From the window seat in his bedroom he watched the drive for a sign of the blue Austin, and when it arrived, turning in a graceful half-circle in front of the house, he bounded down the stairs and reached the doorway at the same time as the bishop's retrievers. Bell laughed when he saw them, and called, "You're nearly as quick as the dogs, my boy."

Dietrich blushed. "I've so much on my heart," he said, "that I think I shall burst with holding it in."

"Then by all means, let's have our talk."

"May we go to the chapel?" Dietrich asked. "I'd also like to make a confession. If you'd allow me."

Bell studied him a moment. "I'll see we're not disturbed," he said.

They sat side by side before the altar, Dietrich leaning forward with his hands clasped between his knees, Bell with his elbow on the pew back and his head resting on the heel of his hand. Dietrich recounted his first conversation with Niemöller, including the role Bell might play.

"The meeting with Hitler is—?"

"Thursday," Dietrich said.

"Day after tomorrow. Yes, I can call Bishop Söderblum in Stockholm this afternoon, and Henriod in Geneva. They're already at work on this, as you know, and I think they'll be ready to move. I can certainly have a letter of my own ready to go to the *Times*. But there's more to this, isn't there? You were quite upset last night."

"The church in Germany won't take a stand on the Jewish question."

"I see."

"It's worthless, all worthless. The church cannot preserve itself in Germany unless it goes into open political opposition. And if we don't place ourselves between Hitler and the Jews, we are not worthy of being called the church."

"I don't suppose," Bell said gently, "you could see this as a first step, as Niemöller suggested. The first risk taken is always the hardest. If Hitler sees the pastors are in earnest, perhaps he will negotiate—"

Dietrich shook his head. "No, no, no. Hitler negotiates as a tiger negotiates with its prey. He cannot be trusted, and that is that."

"And you base this judgment on your own instincts?"

Dietrich stood. "I base it on what my brother-in-law tells me of the methods the Nazis are using to crush dissent. Neighbors denouncing neighbors, arbitrary imprisonments, random murders of Jews and leftists with no attempt to find the perpetrators. And yes, I base this judgment on my own instincts. I can smell the rot. If you of all people don't believe me, then I have been wasting my time here."

He turned to leave.

"Dietrich!" Bell said sharply. "You said you wanted confession."

Dietrich hesitated, then returned and knelt before the bishop, resting his forehead against the older man's arm. "Father forgive me," he said. "I betrayed my twin sister, whom I love more than anyone in the world, by refusing to conduct the funeral of her Jewish father-in-law. And a young woman I—of whom I've grown quite fond, who is also Jewish, has broken off all contact with me as a result of the pain this caused her. Worst of all, God has deserted me. I cannot write or pray. I have nowhere to go, I have no home."

He began to sob. Bell leaned forward, hugged him tightly, and said,

Almighty God have mercy upon you; pardon you and deliver you from all your sins; confirm and strengthen you in all goodness; and bring you to everlasting life; through Jesus Christ our Lord. He made the sign of the cross over Dietrich's bowed head.

They remained there until Dietrich grew calm. Then Bell reached down and picked up the gold-rimmed glasses, which had fallen unnoticed to the floor. He wiped the moist lenses on his sleeve and handed them back to Dietrich.

"You will need these to see clearly," he said.

Dietrich put his glasses on and sat down wearily. Outside the cathedral clock tolled in the bell tower.

"The absolution was for your betrayal of Sabine," Bell said, "and her husband and his father. As for the rest, you're right. Absolutely right. The church cannot be anything less than the church, and only a suffering church can face down Hitler. Don't allow yourself to be dissuaded."

"Absolution isn't enough," Dietrich said.

"It should suffice. Don't ever turn your back on grace, Dietrich. It's a free gift."

"Not free for me," Dietrich said. "I am a debtor, and I must somehow make up what I owe. But I can't go back to Germany. Even if I find the courage, no one listens to me there. The other pastors think I'm mad. What shall I do?"

"You have a part to play in all this. You must pray to find out what it is. But first I suggest you write to Sabine. When was the last time you corresponded?"

Dietrich sighed. "I haven't written Sabine since our shared birthday on February fourth, over three months ago. I've been too ashamed."

Bell began to laugh softly and clapped Dietrich on the shoulder.

"What?" Dietrich said.

"February fourth is also my birthday. It would seem my connection with you in some way partakes of the mystical."

Back in his room, Dietrich took out his notebook and sat at the small writing table. He wrote, *Cheap grace is the deadly enemy of our church. We are fighting today for costly grace.*

He read this over, scribbled EXPAND in the margin. Below he wrote, *Costly because it costs a man his life and grace because it gives a man the only true life.*

This he also read over several times. At the top of the page he scrawled DISCIPLESHIP. Then, feeling somewhat easier, he stretched out on the bed and slept until teatime.

THEY HAVE COME FROM AFTER-DINNER DRINKS, in evening dress, to
stand before the high altar of the cathedral.

(Dietrich unwillingly, for he has hoped all day for a call from Martin
Niemöller, waited in vain for news of the day's meeting with Hitler. Only
the lateness of the hour and the promise of a summons from the butler tears
him away from his room.)

The cathedral gates have long since been shut against tourists and the
odd soul who might wander in to pray. The altar is lit by banks of candles
bending and wavering and throwing up shadows twenty feet high that leap
across stone and dart between ancient pillars.

Eliot has insisted upon the setting even though it is only dear dull Chichester rather than bloody Canterbury. He has insisted upon the evening
dress as well. He must see his first act because he is stuck again, unsure how
to proceed, and so he wants a performance, needs the intensity. He is
responsible for the casting. Dietrich must be Becket. Nothing else will do.
And Dietrich must not read the script beforehand, must come to it as fresh
as Becket himself.

He stands alone, typescript dangling forlornly from his hand, while Eliot
and the Bells confer in the transept, hears voices like the distant scurrying
of mice. When he turns toward them his glasses flash like a signal in the
candlelight.

All is silent.

Hettie Bell approaches slowly, almost luxuriantly, with a rustle of her
skirt. She speaks in a light, fluting voice, tosses her silver hair, urges, *Be easy
man! The easy man lives to eat the best dinners.*

Dietrich has been thinking how much younger she looks in the candlelight. He glances at his manuscript, mildly disconcerted. "'You come
twenty years too late,'" he tries in his best actor's voice.

He has begun to like Becket and waits with more enthusiasm for the
Second Tempter. Eliot himself, slinking from the shadows with glowing
red cigarette in hand, a sly courtier come to urge complicity in the King's
intrigues. He speaks his lines from memory, staring Dietrich directly in the
face.

*Think, my lord, Power obtained grows to glory. Power is present. Holiness
hereafter.*

Dietrich/Becket looks away from the script and leans forward.

"'No! Shall I, who keep the keys to heaven and hell, descend to desire
a punier power? No! Go.'"

Leans back, satisfied. Eliot leaves him with a look that says, Yes, very
nice.

In comes Bell, sauntering, jacket askew, tie loosened and top button of shirt undone. Third Tempter.

I am no courtier. I know a horse, a dog, a wench; I know how to hold my estates in order, a country-keeping lord who minds his own business. It is we country lords who know the country and we who know what the country needs. It is our country. We are the backbone of the nation.

Becket gathers himself majestically, declares, "'Pursue your treacheries as you have done before: No one shall say that I betrayed a king.'"

Bell exits with a bow and an ironic flourish.

A Fourth Tempter. Eliot again, nonchalant this time, slow with his approach. An unexpected visitor, Dietrich learns from the script.

"'Who are you?'" he asks, and thinks (growing a bit bored), These nocturnal visitors smack too much of Dickens. "'Say what you came to say.'"

Eliot comes closer. His eyes glitter in the candlelight. Sets out Becket's plight, claims there is no hope of reconciliation with the state yet opposition will lead to sure death.

"'What is your counsel?'"

Fare forward to the end.

Dietrich looks down at the script, feels a sudden thrill of fear.

Think, Thomas, think of glory after death. When king is dead, there's another king.

Dietrich waits. Does he hear a voice say, softly, *And there'll be another Hitler after?* He looks up. Eliot watches him, shadows stealing across his face.

Saint and martyr rule from the tomb. And think of your enemies, in another place.

(Along with your fellow pastors? Eliot whispers. Or does Dietrich imagine it?)

He clutches the manuscript, forces himself to stare at Eliot, says, "'I have thought of these things.'"

Eliot's voice rolls on, cajoling deriding. Of course time will pass, and even the most revered martyr be forgotten. Who cares now about Becket? A dreary name for bored schoolchildren to memorize. That's all. Nothing left.

Becket asks, "'What is left to be done? Is there no enduring crown to be won?'"

The Tempter circles so close behind, his breath warms the back of Becket's neck.

Yes, Dietrich, yes; you have thought of that too.

Dietrich pulls away at the sound of his own name and flings down the script. "What are you doing?" he cries. "What the *hell* are you doing?"

Eliot calmly rescues the scattered sheets of typescript. As the Bells hasten from the shadows of the transept, he is reading, "'Seek the way of martyrdom, make yourself the lowest on earth, to be high in heaven. And see far off below you, where the gulf is fixed, your persecutors, in timeless torment, beyond expiation.'" He looks at Dietrich. "Then you say, 'You only offer dreams to damnation' And I answer, 'You have often dreamt them.'"

Dietrich cries, "You know nothing of me, or the state of my soul, to judge me like this!"

Bell steps in. "By God, Tom, you've gone too far."

"Don't misunderstand," Eliot says. "I owe you a debt, Bonhoeffer. You're teaching me what I need to know to write my second act, and by way of penance I'll tell you what I believe. True martyr after all, Becket. In the end, he wins through because he stops trying to be right and simply is. Suffering is action, and action suffering. There. Have I made amends?"

"What does this have to do with me?" Dietrich says angrily. "I have no desire to be a martyr, nor do I expect to be one."

"No," Eliot agrees, "it's not likely. But you're no stranger to spiritual pride, are you? And that's what I needed at the moment. Now if you'll excuse me—" bows over Hettie's hand—"there are a few more writing hours left before sleep overwhelms me. Good night."

He disappears into the darkness, footsteps receding along the nave. A distant door creaks open, then shuts with the finality of a coffin lid.

MARTIN NIEMÖLLER SITS BESIDE THE TELEPHONE in the brick parsonage in Dahlem. He longs to ring Bonhoeffer but is afraid to pick up the receiver. He sits for hours, despite his wife's entreaties to come to bed. Now and then he rises to peer out the window, careful not to disturb the lace curtains in a manner that might draw attention. The black Mercedes still lurks in front of the Annenkirche.

At last he takes a sheet of paper and writes in a circle of lamplight.

> *Dear Dietrich,*
> *You will be wondering why you have heard nothing from me, and will think it is because I have lost patience with you once and for all. That is not true. Here is what has happened.*
> *We had our meeting with the Führer. Thirty bishops and pastors, torn between fear and admiration, squirming on folding chairs in a tiny room in the Prinz-Albrecht-Straße. We had hardly begun to raise our concerns when Hermann Goering burst into the room, brandishing a sheet of paper.*
> *"My Führer," he cried, "I must make a most astonishing report, though—" pausing to survey the room contritely—"it is upsetting to expose wicked deception before such reverend company."*

He handed the paper to Hitler, who made a show of studying it carefully, his face variously registering curiosity, concern, and astonishment. (The man really should have gone on the stage.) Then he looked up and said in the most injured tone, "My dear gentlemen, I hold here a scandalous communication concerning one of your members"—and fixed his gaze upon me. "The authorities have intercepted a telephone conversation between Pastor Niemöller and another of your number who disdains to live in the Fatherland." Of course, I knew this must be you, Dietrich. Hitler continued, "These two talked at length about their plans to bring about a break with the state church. To such renegades it does not matter if our talks succeed today. They have already made up their minds to this rupture. What motives could they have other than to embarrass Germany before the world?"

He proceeded to read, word for word, excerpts of our conversation. Then he turned his full attention to me. "Shame, Pastor Niemöller! Shame! I have come to these talks in all good faith, at risk of ridicule from my own supporters who would have me take a harsher line, and you have stabbed me in the back."

The others were stunned, of course. As was I, since I hadn't the least idea it was possible to record someone's telephone conversation. We live, it seems, in peculiar times.

The consequence was immediate chaos. The others, especially the bishops, declared themselves "shocked by the insolence and duplicity of Pastor Niemöller." The result is not only the collapse of the talks. I have been dismissed from my post. I am no longer pastor of the Annenkirche and I am forbidden to hold any other pastorate in Germany or to preach from any pulpit. Don't concern yourself about that. I have my naval pension, and my wife has a modest inheritance. We shall be comfortable financially. I am well aware that if I were a country parson with eight children I would not have the luxury of defiance I now possess.

For I am defiant. There shall be a new church, I promise, without the bishops if necessary. There are still dissenters, more than Hitler realizes, who will come out of Babylon with me.

I must close by giving you your due. You saw this coming, my friend. I thought you a radical. Now it is I who look to you.

I am sending this letter by diplomatic post through your brother-in-law Hans von Dohnanyi, so that it will escape the eyes of the Gestapo.

Your brother in Christ,
Martin Niemöller

Doppelgänger

SS-Hauptsturmführer Alois Bauer is on retreat at the Windberg monastery with a new friend, SS-Scharführer Adolf Eichmann. The retreat is Eichmann's idea. He is beginning work on a pamphlet for Section II 112 of the SS, a treatise about Zionist plots to revive the League of Nations and create a one-world government. He knows from experience that the retreat will be just the thing to get the creative juices flowing.

"I go on retreat at least twice a year," he tells Bauer, who steers the rented Daimler along a narrow road through the Bavarian Forest. "Though this is my first time at Windberg. Usually I go someplace alone, on silent retreat. But with you along, well, we'll want to converse. The other monasteries I visit won't allow that."

Their rooms are at opposite ends of the cloister but are otherwise identical, bare save for a bed, chair and desk, washstand, pitcher and basin, and crucifix on the wall. Eichmann spends his mornings in meditation and works on his pamphlet in the afternoons. Bauer, whose only motive for the retreat is to escape the noise and pressure of Berlin for a few days, takes long hikes through the woods. He has brought a pair of binoculars for bird-watching, and two books, Gibbon's *Rise and Fall of the Roman Empire* and *Moby-Dick* by the American Melville. Eichmann has glanced at the covers, said, "Good Lord, you've got patience to plow through such stuff."

In the evenings after attending Compline with the monks, they sit on a bench in the refectory garden and smoke until dusk.

"The only thing I miss right now," Bauer says, "is my phonograph."

That is when Bauer tells Eichmann of his passion for Mozart.

"Mozart?" Eichmann thinks a moment. "You know he was a Freemason."

Bauer shrugs.

"I've just been writing about them. 'A worldwide conspiracy of Jews, Freemasons, and Bolsheviks lurks at the dark edges of the world, waiting for a hint of German weakness,' or some such thing. I can't recall now exactly how I phrased it. Of course, the Freemasons of Mozart's day were probably another thing altogether. Harmless."

"No doubt."

"I must confess," says Eichmann, "I once considered becoming a Freemason myself. Joined the SS instead, and that's when I learned it's not a good idea to espouse Freemasonry these days. Didn't realize that at the time, you see."

They smoke awhile in silence. "What about this?" Bauer asks, and waves his arm to take in the monastery. "Do you take it seriously?"

"Oh yes," Eichmann says, surprised at the question. "Oh, absolutely. Don't you?"

"I don't believe in God," Bauer admits. "Or at least, I don't think I do."

"How can you not believe in God? How can you go for your walks and enjoy nature and not believe in God?"

"Of course there's beauty in the world," Bauer agrees. "But look at the rest. So much evil. If there's a God, why does He allow it?"

"That's not ours to know," Eichmann says. "Not ours to question."

"But I do question it," Bauer says. "And the lack of an answer is a bar to my belief. Do you pray?"

"Of course," Eichmann says.

"I've tried, now and then. But it's like facing down the wind. Nothing behind it. And look at those who claim to be our spiritual leaders, the clergy. My section is having to deal with a pack of them this week, preparing for a meeting with the Führer. I was only responsible for background, thank God, that part's done. One reason I was glad to get out of Berlin. There's a pack of charlatans for you, the clergy, and useless to anyone. You should include them in your pamphlet."

"Perhaps I shall," Eichmann says. He looks around quickly to see if they've been overheard. "But not the monks. Actually, I'm quite fond of monks."

"I'll tell you where I find spiritual solace," Bauer says. "In music. Nowhere else."

"Mozart again," Eichmann says. He is losing interest, but stifles a yawn so that Bauer won't guess. He is pleased to have been befriended by a superior officer and anxious to remain in the good graces of the Hauptsturmführer.

In this manner they pass a pleasant enough week. On Saturday Eichmann will not leave until he signs the monastery guest book.

A. Eichmann. "Faith for faith." *May 7, 1934.*

GERMAN CHURCH

GROUNDS FOR FOREIGN UNEASINESS

TO THE EDITOR OF THE TIMES

SIR,—— In Germany today we are witnessing
the cruelty of a regime based not on democratic
principles but upon a leadership principle supported by force and intimidation. The German
government is undertaking disciplinary measures against dissenters and has employed measures of racial discrimination against its Jewish
citizens. Such practices are now being extended
to the German Church in a manner without
precedent, and in direct opposition to true
Christian principle. . . .

> Yours faithfully,
> GEORGE CICESTR. †
> The Palace, Chichester, June 15, 1934

BISHOP BELL AND DIETRICH BONHOEFFER met once again over drinks
in the library of the Athenaeum.

"I've had a letter from Niemöller," Dietrich said. "It's official. There has
been a separation, and those who have come out of the Reich Church are
calling themselves the Confessing Church. They're moving now to set up
their own institutions, find places to worship, train their own pastors. Niemöller's very grateful for your support, and, needless to say, so am I."

"Glad to help," Bell said with a wave of his hand. His letters to the *Times*
had cost him little, he reflected, except patience with some of his fellow
club members, who chastised him for scaremongering. He also wondered if
the letters had done any good. He shrugged, said, "We'll keep pounding
away. Now tell me, how have you been keeping yourself?"

It was a question that needed no answer. Dietrich was thinner and his
face was drawn with weariness. There had been no relief from his spiritual
malaise.

"Still writing?" Bell asked.

"A little," Dietrich said. "I've got two chapters roughed out, that's all."

"That's something," Bell said.

Dietrich smoked, forgot to tip his ash, and a white nub fell into his lap.
He swiped his leg absentmindedly.

"I've been to hear Gandhi's people speak," he said, "at the Albert Hall.
I met C. F. Andrews afterward. He says he knows you."

"Charlie Andrews? Good Lord, yes, known him for years. And Madeline
Slade, Mira Bai she calls herself now. Her father's an old friend."

"You never told me you'd met Gandhi."

"Well." Bell coughed. "You never asked. Only met the man twice, actually. But we've corresponded through Charlie. Gandhi's interested in the ecumenical movement, thinks it has great potential. A very ecumenical faith, you know, Hinduism. A natural for them."

"I want to meet him," Dietrich said.

"Meet Gandhi?"

"Yes. Not just meet him. I want to go to India and study his movement, stay a year or two, then take what I learn back to Germany."

Bell considered this.

"Andrews suggested I should study at the University of Rabindranath Tagore," Dietrich continued, "but that's not good enough. I thought with your help I could get straight to the man himself. Look here, the Indians are trying to throw out the British, yet two of Gandhi's leading supporters are English. They should be the enemies of Gandhi, and yet they've been to prison with him. Imprisoned by the authorities of their own country. Here they are now, touring Britain to gather support for the cause of Indian independence. Traveling freely—"

"Not everyone's pleased about that," Bell said. "Just bring up the subject here at the club and you'll see. But this is a free country."

"That's not the point," Dietrich said, growing agitated. "It's the method of opposition that Gandhi preaches. Nonviolence. Turning your enemy into your friend, or at least into a nonviolent opponent, by practicing love rather than using violent tactics. Surely there's something there, something more Christian than what we Christians have been doing. If the Confessing Church is to have a chance of opposing this regime, this might be the answer. What else can be done? The word from home is that Hitler is more and more popular. The affections of the German people must be turned—"

There was a hubbub outside the library, voices raised, then the door opened and a servant entered with copies of the evening newspapers. Bell took the *Evening Standard*, scanned the front page, and handed the paper to Dietrich. Ernst Röhm of the SA, a potential rival to Hitler, had been murdered, along with several army generals deemed troublesome to the Führer and scores, perhaps hundreds, of other Germans whose bodies were still being discovered. The victims appeared to be trade unionists, intellectuals, government officials, and a random assortment of Jews. Dietrich handed the newspaper to Bell, said in a strangled voice, "I must call home at once."

"I'll take you to a phone," Bell said.

In Wangenheimstraße 14, the phone rang but no one answered. Hans von Dohnanyi had ordered the family to stay away from the telephone for fear of a wiretap. But when Dietrich returned to the manse in Forest Hill a telegram was waiting.

UNCLE RUDI UPSET STOP FAMILY CONCERNED BUT ALL WELL
STOP HANS

George Bell caught the night train home to Chichester. He found
Hettie in the library reading the latest Dorothy Sayers mystery. She offered
her cheek to be kissed without looking up.

Bell poured himself a glass of sherry and sat beside her.

"Dietrich is in a state," he said. "He's talking about chucking everything
and heading off to India to live in an ashram with Gandhi."

"Oh, dear." Hettie tore herself away from the adventures of Lord Peter
Wimsey. "It's something every week with Dietrich."

"I think he's serious about this. But what a damned mistake." Bell
stretched out on the sofa with his head in Hettie's lap. She massaged his
temples. "He wants a letter from me to Gandhi."

"Then you should refuse."

"On what grounds? I can't deny the man a reference. But first I'm going
to insist he go to the ecumenical conference in Denmark with me."

"You said if Dietrich went it might put him in conflict with the official
German delegation."

"Yes," Bell agreed. "Perhaps that is what he needs."

YEARS LATER WHEN HE THOUGHT BACK on the Danish island of Fano,
Dietrich could only recall bits and pieces of the place. Glints of light reflecting off water and sand like chipped glass. Dim rooms in the conference
center, thick-aired in the August heat. Flash of gull wheeling through glim-
mering mist, arm tallying votes on luminous chalkboard. Rumble of surf and
murmur of voices. People gliding past, faces never coming into focus.

Except for a few.

The Fano retreat center, a cluster of white wood structures trimmed in crisp
red, is nearly empty. Soon all the languages of the world will sound through
the buildings and along the walkways, Swedish and Japanese, English and
Dutch, Hungarian and Urdu. Only the leaders of the international ecumenical movement have arrived early (as well as Dietrich Bonhoeffer, who
accompanied Bishop Bell and sits alone in his room brooding, trying to
write, filling up ashtrays). The place seems haunted, despite the newness of
the buildings, which have been kept spic-and-span clean by an attentive
staff. It is the emptiness, the echo of solitary footsteps down long hallways,
the slamming of distant doors, that causes the early arrivals to start and
look over their shoulders when they are alone.

Night. The doors and windows of a ground floor room are wide open onto a black sea, open to saltbreeze and the sound of tumbling surf. The men are seated in the light of a single lamp. Each cradles a mug of hot coffee in his hands. Bell, England. Ammundsen, Norway. Leiper, United States. Söderblum, Sweden. Henriod, the general secretary from headquarters in Geneva, and Visser't Hooft the Dutchman, his assistant. Shadows loom large in the lamplight.

"Here it is, gentlemen," Bell says. "In Germany a number of Christians have separated from the state church and are calling themselves the Confessing Church. They say they are the true Protestant church in Germany, and ask their delegates be recognized at this conference as the only legitimate representatives of German Protestantism. On the other hand, a delegation representing the Reich Church will be arriving tomorrow and they expect to be the only German delegation."

General Secretary Henriod. "Like it or not, there is a state church in Germany, and Hossenfelder and his delegation are its representatives," he points out. "If we deny them a seat, how do we justify ourselves? On what grounds do we exclude them?"

"Where I come from," Leiper says, "when a church suffers a schism, there are two ecclesiastical bodies. Why not two delegations? Wouldn't that be simplest? After all, we're hardly equipped at this conference to sort out the mess in the German church."

"I'm uncomfortable with the extremist language of the German dissenters," Henriod adds.

Visser't Hooft, soon to be general secretary, says, "What are your thoughts, George? You've had your ear closer to the ground than anyone."

"My thoughts," Bell says. He shuts his eyes and rubs his forehead against the heel of his hand. "Under ordinary circumstances, I would raise the same questions you have. On what grounds can one denomination claim to be the true church and declare another false? On what grounds exclude a delegation, especially the official delegation of a state church?" He opens his eyes. "These are not ordinary circumstances. And one sign of these unusual circumstances, gentlemen, is that the leaders of the Confessing Church in Germany were afraid to attend this conference, and the young man who is here on their behalf is squarely in the sights of his so-called fellow Christians of the Reich Church. At great cost."

Sometime after one in the morning, there is a knock on Dietrich's door, and George Bell enters. Bell places a hand on the younger man's shoulder, then removes it.

"It's not everything you wanted," he says. "It's something."

Hossenfelder stands at the registration table, suitcase in hand, flanked by several other pastors from the German delegation. With them is a man with light brown hair and pale eyes who looks vaguely familiar to Dietrich. But he is no clergyman. He wears an expensively tailored gray suit and sports a swastika pin on his lapel. He does not bother with the demeanor of fake humility employed so effectively by Hossenfelder and the others. Instead he is bored, even slightly contemptuous. He fixes on George Bell, who has approached the registration table and waved aside the woman passing out forms.

"Gentlemen, welcome," Bell says. "Go ahead and register for the time being, make yourselves comfortable. But I must inform you there has been a challenge to your credentials. The executive committee of the council met last night to take up the matter, and a final decision will be made this afternoon before the convention officially opens."

"Challenge to our credentials?" Hossenfelder twists his thin body like a stricken snake. "What on earth can you mean? We are the duly elected delegates of the Reich Church."

"Nevertheless," Bell says politely, "there has been a challenge. You will learn more at this afternoon's meeting. Now if you'll excuse me," and takes his leave with the aplomb that Englishmen of a certain class seem to possess as a birthright.

Dietrich has been standing near the front door. There has been no mention of his name, and Bell has not even glanced in his direction. But Hossenfelder spies him before he can duck out, and the impeccably dressed man with the light brown hair turns to stare at him as well. Dietrich forces himself to stare back. Hossenfelder whispers something to the other man, who smiles at Dietrich, gives a slight nod, then turns his back.

Hossenfelder is in a fury. "Two German delegations! There is only one Reich Church!"

George Bell stands at the head of the executive committee, who hover close behind him as though for protection. "The Confessing Church—"

"A minority of malcontents," Hossenfelder interrupts. "Even their representative—" a disdainful wave toward Dietrich—"if you call him that, must admit that most Germans have remained faithful to the Reich Church."

"The Confessing Church," Bell continues, his voice growing harder, "claims to be the only true Protestant church in Germany—"

"Claims to be!" Hossenfelder roars. He paces the length of the conference room, then back again. "These renegades can *claim* to be anything they want."

"And many of us support that claim," Bell says quickly. He steps toward Hossenfelder and backs him toward the wall so that the German is forced to stop pacing. "The question last night was never whether to exclude the Confessing Church. The question was whether to exclude your delegation."

"How dare you?" Hossenfelder demands. "How dare you pretend to represent the Church of England and tell me that Germany's state church is illegitimate? How dare you attempt to interfere in the internal affairs of my country!"

"We dare," Bell says, "because we are members of the body of Christ. That comes before country, mine or yours."

"Before your country perhaps," Hossenfelder sneers, "but we in Germany do not hesitate to offer ourselves as the instruments of a divine mission to the world, and we have no doubt that offering will be accepted by God."

"You blaspheme!" cries Dietrich Bonhoeffer. He has been standing behind a chair, clutching its back to steady his trembling legs, but now he comes forward. "The Reich Church does not exist for God, it exists for Adolf Hitler. And to dare claim that as Christian! My God, if no one opposes you then Christianity is finished in the West!"

"You are no patriot, Bonhoeffer!"

"And you are no Christian!"

"Gentlemen," Bishop Ammundsen of Norway waves his hands, "this rancor is most unbecoming. Is personal defamation necessary to settle this dispute?"

"I am willing to be civil," declares Hossenfelder, "but I will not have my faith called into question by this—this failed pastor no parish in Germany would call. And to grant him the status of a delegation, this lone malcontent—"

"You know very well there are others," Dietrich says, "and they are not here because they are afraid to leave Germany."

"Hah! Why should they be afraid?"

The man in the gray suit smiles. He glances at his watch and stifles a yawn. He says in a pleasant voice, "If it is so dangerous, Pastor Bonhoeffer, why are you here?"

Dietrich wheels around to face his questioner. "You're SS, aren't you? Why are *you* here?"

The man laughs and doesn't answer.

Dietrich turns to the committee members. "There you have the answer to Hossenfelder's question. I must say, gentlemen, I am as unhappy with your decision as is Hossenfelder. By seating this delegation of so-called churchmen, you only delay a decision. The ecumenical movement, like the church in Germany, must choose sides. Now if you'll excuse me, I've work

to do to prepare for this convention. I am writing resolutions which I hope
will merit your support."

Bell follows him out the door, catches him down the hall. "Good Lord,
Dietrich," he says, "what have I done by bringing you here?"

"What do you mean?"

"It would have been safer not to call attention to you. It's one thing to
talk about all this, but to see you among those others. My God, I didn't
expect the SS at this conference."

"I did," Dietrich says. "George, you may think you brought me here, but
you haven't. You've helped me these last months to see what my direction
should be, and for that I'm grateful. Now, I'm going to my room to work on
my resolutions. I'd appreciate your help persuading the other delegates to
support them."

He leaves Bell standing in the hall. Visser't Hooft comes out of the
meeting room.

"Hossenfelder is still angry," he says, "but I think he's decided to make
the best of things. They're staying."

Bell watches the departing Dietrich. "Frankly, Willem, Hossenfelder can
rot in hell for all I care."

Other faces. Reinhold Niebuhr, his professor from Union Theological
Seminary in New York. Laughing at the look of surprise on Dietrich's face.
"Well, what did you expect, Bonhoeffer?" American accent evocative as a
long-forgotten tune. "You knew I'd have to get involved in this mess eventually." Niebuhr, sitting with Dietrich on the seaside veranda of the conference center, bottle of mineral water in hand, the tip of his sharp nose
turning red in the sun. (Dietrich has already taken to wearing a tatty straw
hat when outdoors to keep the top of his fair, balding head from blistering.)

"Do you hear anything from Fred Bishop?" Dietrich asks.

"Fred—? Oh, Fred Bishop. No, not a word. Don't know that anyone has.
Lots of fellows leave Union and don't keep in touch. Going back South,
wasn't he?"

Dietrich doesn't answer, instead says, "I'm thinking of going to India.
I've already written to Gandhi."

"Really? Why?"

"To learn about his movement. Perhaps it can be applied to the situation in Germany."

Niebuhr squints at him. "You've got to be kidding! What do you expect
Hitler would do, faced with a Gandhi?"

"Of course it would be dangerous," Dietrich says. "Especially at first. But
as the movement gathered force and the German people were confronted
with the sacrifices of the opponents of the regime—"

"Bullshit. You've already got opponents of the regime rotting in detention camps, Bonhoeffer. Dying too. Do the German people give a damn about their sacrifices?"

"But if a moral force were the obvious impetus—"

"Moral force my ass. Are those poor souls rotting in Dachau because they're immoral? Of course, they're only left-wingers and Jews. You didn't answer my first question. Dietrich, Dietrich," Niebuhr rubs his scalp in the old familiar gesture, "you wouldn't last a week as a German Gandhi."

Dietrich stares straight ahead, says, "Of course I don't see myself as a Gandhi. I am not so arrogant as to imagine that," and makes awkward small talk before escaping from Niebuhr.

He encounters Jean Lasserre soon after in a hallway, hugs the Frenchman and receives a kiss on both cheeks.

"Jean! What are you doing here?"

"I'm on the panel for Ministry to the Working Class," Lasserre says. "And you?"

"I'm representing the church in Germany, the Confessing Church," Dietrich says. "You'll be proud of me. I've become a pacifist. And I'm writing a book about the Sermon on the Mount."

Lasserre beams. "*Très bon!* Stand back and let me look at you. Thinner than you were in New York."

"I've been away from my mother's table too long," Dietrich says. "I'm living in London at the moment."

"I know, I know. I have heard this from a mutual friend."

"Elisabeth Hildebrandt," Dietrich says. His smile vanishes. "How is she?"

"Well, as far as I know. Actually, she's no longer in Bruay. She's gone on to Wales. We're setting up a new branch of our mission for miners in the Rhondda Valley, and she's gone to help out. Then she plans to travel. She's working on a collection of drawings from coal mining regions. She's been to the Ruhr, the Saar, and France and Belgium. Now it's Wales and the north of England. I believe she'd like to go to America eventually, but it may not be possible."

"Why not?" Dietrich asks, pretending only mild interest.

"Her father's situation is precarious. You know he lost his position at the Charité?"

Dietrich shakes his head. Karl Bonhoeffer has failed to mention this in his letters.

"He's trying to leave Germany. It's the only way he can continue as a practicing physician. Also there's the fear of violence against the Jews."

"Yes," Dietrich says, thinking of Sabine and Gerhard.

"So Elisabeth's making inquiries for him as she travels about. Nothing so far, according to her last letter. It isn't easy when there's a shortage of medical vacancies and you only speak German."

"I might be able to help. I've become friends with the Bishop of Chichester. He's a very influential man in England." Dietrich scribbles his address inside a matchbook. "Here. Have Elisabeth write to me at this address. And give her my regards."

Lasserre nods. "I shall. She speaks quite highly of you."

"She does?"

"Of course. Don't look so surprised."

Dietrich knows he is blushing. He is relieved to see George Bell waving to them from the doorway.

"Come on," Bell calls, "I want you to meet the Japanese delegation."

The delegates from around the world meet and debate, break into committees for more meetings, listen to panels, meet, debate, meet, debate. At last they pass resolutions, among them the offering of the delegate from the German Confessing Church:

Resolved. That the church must proclaim the Word of God. To do so, the church must remain independent of purely nationalistic aims. In particular, the church may under no circumstances lend its spiritual support to a war. In the face of the increasing claims of the state, the church must abandon its passive attitude and proclaim the will of God come what may. This conference urges the churches to refuse to recognize as Christian any church which denies its own universality and which sees itself as an instrument for furthering the policies of the state.

Reinhold Niebuhr of the American delegation opposes the sentence on war as an oversimplification which ignores the possibility of future wars which may be just and necessary. Bishop George Bell of England defends the sentence on war, noting that while he is himself not a pacifist, he believes violence is always evil in some degree, and it is the burden of those committing violent acts to justify them. Thus, Bell says, while Christians may find themselves at some point engaged in acts of violence, including warfare, it is never the purpose of the church to bless the organized and premeditated violence that is war.

On Sunday, Pastor Dietrich Bonhoeffer is invited to deliver the sermon. This is understood to be a rebuke to the Reich Church delegation, which chooses not to attend (except for the very well dressed SS man, who sits in the fourth row).

Pastor Bonhoeffer speaks so forcefully that many of the delegates are drawn to the edge of their seat.

How does peace come about? Through a system of political treaties? Through the investment of international capital in different countries? Through the big banks, through money? Or through universal peaceful rearmament in order to guarantee peace? Through none of these, for the sole reason that in all of them peace is confused with safety. There is no way to peace along the way of safety. For peace must be dared. It is the great venture. It can never be safe. Peace is the opposite of security. . . .

Niebuhr shakes Dietrich's hand afterward. "Powerful sermon," he says and adds with a wry smile, "but I can't help wondering, what if everyone wants peace except Hitler?"

"That is the risk we bear as peacemakers," Dietrich says. "I am a Christian and a German. Hitler is my cross to bear."

"Yes, well." Niebuhr sighs. "Here's hoping he doesn't become mine too."

The Nazi Party newspaper *Völkischer Beobachter* carries stories of the Fano conference, and editorializes, *The World Council of Churches is a liberalistic body devoted to forcing the one-world ideology of the League of Nations down the throat of freedom-loving nations such as Germany. The German people defy this meddling in the affairs of the Fatherland. Germans know what is best for Germany, and true Christians in Germany are thankful for God's gift of the Nation.*

Late night. Dietrich goes to his room hot and weary, for a parched breeze is blowing off the sandy beach and he has spent the evening talking to delegates, answering questions, cajoling, persuading, encouraging. Sucked dry to the marrow. He shuts his door, leans against it, and realizes he is not alone.

"A good speech," says the SS man. "Very impressive." He is sitting at the table near the window with a bottle of brandy and two glasses. He replenishes his own glass, offers the other to Dietrich, who doesn't move.

"Not a speech," Dietrich says. "A sermon."

"Ah. Whatever. Very fine. I especially liked the line *Peace is the opposite of security.* I've always felt that way myself. If I heard more of that sort of thing from the clergy, I might start attending church myself."

He offers the glass again, waves it enticingly. "It's not drugged. That sort of thing only happens in the cinema."

Dietrich sits and accepts. "What do you want?"

"I want to tell you what I know. I've the transcript of your telephone conversation with Pastor Niemöller. Bit of luck we caught it. We aren't that organized. Yet." His voice is almost apologetic.

Dietrich says, "What is your name?"

The man looks surprised, considers the question, decides there's no harm in answering. "Alois Bauer. SS-Hauptsturmführer Alois Bauer."

It is Dietrich's turn to hesitate.

"What?" says Bauer.

"I believe I know that name."

"You believe?"

"You were injured once, in a raid on a youth club in Charlottenburg. Hit on the head. Am I right?"

Bauer's eyes narrow. "What do you know about this?"

"I came to your aid. The two young men with you were frightened. They happened to mention your name. I examined you, assured them you weren't seriously hurt, and helped them call an ambulance."

Bauer rubs his chin, stares at Dietrich. "The young men told me. I don't recall the name Bonhoeffer."

"Of course I didn't use my real name. When dealing with the SS—" Dietrich shrugs.

Bauer seems pleased at this admission of fear. "Of course. And it seems I am in your debt."

"It was the Christian thing to do."

Bauer laughs. He replenishes their glasses.

"I'll tell you why I'm here," he says. "I have in my pocket a paper to be signed by you that states you promise to cease your work with the ecumenical movement. But what I have seen of you these last few days, I realize you will not sign. A compliment, by the way, Pastor Bonhoeffer."

"Taken as a compliment." A most fearsome compliment, Dietrich thinks, for now he must live up to it.

"And as I owe you a favor, I shall not waste your time with such nonsense. Instead I shall tell you this." Bauer leans forward as though they were conspirators. "Stay in England, or go back to Germany. Either way, all will be well for you, as long as you limit yourself to these church matters. The church is no threat. The SS knows this, Hitler knows this. A lot of talk, even defiant talk, but nothing more. Stick with the church, Pastor Bonhoeffer, even the Confessing Church, and you'll live a long life."

He stands, pats Dietrich on the shoulder, and leaves, taking the bottle of brandy with him.

FOUR DAYS BEFORE CHRISTMAS, Dietrich returned home from a visit to an elderly parishioner in a Whitechapel High Street boardinghouse. He had taken his midday meal alone at the restaurant Czardas, which specialized in the cuisine of Mitteleuropa, had lingered over the roast duck and dumplings and stewed prunes. Regent and Oxford streets had been a fantasia of Christmas lights. But in Whitechapel High Street, mounds of sharded green glass decorated the streetgutters and tatty bits of tinsel drape fluttered from telephone poles and streetlamps. He took the train to Forest Hill, tramping up the London Road from the station with his coat collar turned up against a brisk wind. Outside the house he grabbed a gunnysack, stuffed it full of coal with a wedge of shovel, and huffed up the stairs to the first floor, stamping his feet. A woman sat at the top of the landing, leaning against the door and hugging herself against the cold.

It was Elisabeth Hildebrandt.

"You should have let yourself in." He handed her a steaming mug of coffee. "I never lock the door."

"I supposed you would get enough of a start as it was without me rising from your couch like the ghost of Christmas past."

He smiled. "I could never take you for a ghost."

She wore her hair longer, thin black feathers draped across her shoulders and held back from her forehead with a brown plastic clip. The long hair gave her a slump-shouldered appearance, as though she were weary, but her face had the same quick intelligence he remembered. She sat on the edge of his couch and sipped the coffee, then looked around at the room, bare save for the piano and a shelf of books, and chilly despite the coal fire.

"Dietrich, what is this? Some sort of mortification of the flesh?"

"Perhaps it is."

"And how long does your penance last?"

"God knows. I may be going to India soon. I'm awaiting a letter from Gandhi."

Her face clouded. "India. More penance, or something else?"

He didn't answer, instead asked, "Where are you staying?"

"I was at the YWCA last night. I've been traveling quite a bit and I'm afraid I'm low on funds."

"You're a fine one to talk about penance," he said. "You must stay here. You can have my room and I'll sleep on the sofa."

"My art supplies and drawings are at the Y, and my clothes."

"We'll go get them."

"I'd like to stay here," she said shyly. "It's not a good time of year to be alone."

"No," he agreed. "For either of us. Now, tell me about your father."

"He's no longer in Germany. I know Jean told you he'd lost his position. It seems Jews are no longer allowed to continue as doctors or lawyers or teachers."

"It's appalling," Dietrich said. "And yet no great outcry?"

"Outcry? I believe most Germans are quite pleased. More positions for them, after all. Besides what does an outcry get you? Some months in Dachau."

"Where is your father now?"

"Amsterdam. His sister and her husband are there. It's only a temporary solution. He's no money coming in. But I've had a letter from your Bishop

Bell. There's an opening at a hospital in Southampton, and Father's German might actually come in handy, because they're treating quite a lot of refugees these days."

"Yes," Dietrich said. "They've even built camps to hold them. I often receive letters of inquiry, people stuck in a camp and hoping someone in my congregation can provide a job, or connections of some kind. It's very difficult."

"It's just the beginning."

She took out a cigarette and he leaned forward to light it, then one for himself. They smoked for a time, watched each other warily.

"What are your churches like?"

"Very small," he said. "Fifty parishioners here, thirty in Whitechapel. The organist at St. Paul's only knows three hymns, and plays them over and over, week after week. It's always a relief when she misses a service because then I can play the organ myself and we have something different."

She laughed, then said, "You can't mean to stay here much longer?"

"No," he agreed.

"God," she said. "India."

Dietrich took her to the YWCA to collect her belongings. Then they bought a Christmas tree, placed a belated Advent wreath on the mantel, and lit all the candles at once. Elisabeth baked a loaf of stollen and a gingerbread house while Dietrich was out on his pastoral rounds. On Christmas Eve she sat in the congregation of St. Paul's Goalston Street and heard the three hymns, none of them appropriate to the season, and smiled behind her hand as Dietrich stubbornly led the congregation through an a capella rendering of "Stille Nacht." His voice, loud and fine, carried throughout the church and he was soon several notes ahead of the dawdling congregation.

Afterward they walked through the black night to the Aldgate tube station. At the bottom of the stairs Elisabeth stepped sideways to avoid a broken bottle and bumped into Dietrich. He took her arm to steady her, and didn't let go.

"I've missed you," he said.

"And I've missed you."

He leaned down and kissed her forehead, then led her along the platform with his arm around her shoulder. Back at Manor Mount he lit the coal fire and they snuggled close to the stove until the room grew warm. They drank hot wine spiced with cloves and cinnamon while decking the tree with gingerbread cookies and white candles and strips of tinfoil, pausing to play carols on the Bechstein, and four-handed Bach, and sometimes—arms around waists—two-handed Bach.

They exchanged gifts, the collected works of Shakespeare for Dietrich, a silver necklace with a single pearl for Elisabeth.

At midnight they held hands and went into the bedroom. Nor did Dietrich sleep on the sofa thereafter.

On the Twelfth Day of Christmas, all seasonal duties done, they went together to Chichester. By this time the way was familiar to Dietrich. He had been meeting George Bell on a regular basis, either in London or at the bishop's palace, to talk about Germany, about the ecumenical movement, or simply to enjoy each other's company. This trip was different, and not just because he delighted to share it with Elisabeth. In his vest pocket he carried two letters. One was from Gandhi, inviting him to the Mahatma's ashram. The other was from Martin Niemöller.

. . . You should have seen the crowd. The arena holds twenty-thousand and there were people standing at the back, sharing seats. We'd have let more in but didn't want to give the Gestapo an excuse to shut us down for breaking fire codes. I managed to see some foreign press reports thanks to an American journalist, William Shirer, who has been most helpful. It seems the Confessing Church has just held the first major anti-Nazi protest since the new regime took over.

In the library of the palace, George Bell looked up from reading Niemöller's letter. Dietrich sat across from him, on the sofa beside Elisabeth.

"Your faces," he said. "You should see your faces. I have never seen such longing. You would have loved to be there."

He continued reading.

It was a prohibited meeting yet they did not shut us down, even though Paul Schneider and I were most pointed in our criticisms of the regime. Many people did report seeing Gestapo agents in the crowd, ostentatiously taking notes. As though the note-taking was their only weapon. I believe they were afraid to do anything more. Afraid of what? Public opinion? The German public has in general seemed reluctant to express any opinion, one way or the other. Even most of the people in the pews, we are finding, are waiting to see which way the wind blows before committing themselves to either state church or Confessing Church. Everyone wants to keep his nose clean.

Some of our pastors have been arrested, over a hundred at last count. They're usually held in jail a few weeks, then released. Nothing more serious than that. Yet. We continue to work and wait.

Yours in Christ, Martin

P.S. Let me say once again, I hope you are sufficiently convinced of our commitment to accept the offer we have made. We need your stubbornness in Germany.

"Well," Bell said, folding the letter and handing it to Dietrich.

"The offer," said Dietrich, "is not exactly a call to the front lines. They want me to head a new seminary training pastors for the Confessing Church. It will be a quiet place in the woods of Pomerania, away from the public eye."

"India would be far more daring and romantic," Elisabeth said. "I'm sure the Gestapo have Pomerania on their maps, if you're wanting so badly to be arrested. And if it's publicity you're worried about, well, Pastor Niemöller has a friend in the American press. Who knows, he may be as famous as Gandhi some day."

Dietrich twisted around to face her. "That is most unfair! And coming from you when—" He stopped and glanced at Bell, who was looking a bit embarrassed, as though he had been caught eavesdropping. Dietrich blushed.

What Dietrich did not know was that Elisabeth carried a letter of her own, which she had held for three days while she tried to decide how to share its contents. She felt herself to be standing upon a cliff overlooking a cold blue lake. Now she took a deep breath and stepped off the ledge. "I have to tell you something, Dietrich. Something very important but very difficult."

Bell stood. "Perhaps I should leave you two alone."

"No," Elisabeth said quickly. "I want you to hear. I know how important you are to Dietrich, and I am in your debt as well for helping my father. He's had word of his appointment to the hospital in Southampton, and he's most grateful, as am I. Dietrich has assumed, I know, that this means I shall be remaining in England. But that is not the case." She turned to Dietrich. "I've an offer of my own, as a result of my own inquiries, to work with an organization that is helping Jews to leave Germany. It's being run by Jews out of the Scheunenviertel. Not yet underground—" she raised her hand as though to stay his objections—"and not so morally pure either. The Nazis are cooperating. They want rid of us. I'll be dancing with the devil, it seems. But people are desperate to leave Germany. So I'm going back to Berlin to help them."

"When people are trying to leave," Dietrich said, "you are going back?"

"Yes. Why not? You're thinking of the same thing."

"It's different with me. I'm not Jewish. And I'm not a woman. You can't go back. I would be so worried about you."

"Then you will have to worry. As I shall worry about you. Don't think you will change my mind. I have decided, as you will decide. Neither of us can escape that, can we?" She stood. "And now I shall go for a walk in the close. I want the two of you to talk and then, Dietrich, I want you to come to me, out there." She put her hand on his shoulder, the lightest of touches, and left.

Dietrich said to Bell, "Did you know about this?"

"Heavens no! I'm as stunned as you are. Well, I admit to being stunned by everything, including Elisabeth. When you asked me to help her father, I'd no idea she was so close to you."

"I hadn't said much before this because Elisabeth and I parted on bad terms and I didn't expect to see her again. Then she appeared on my doorstep just before Christmas. One thing led to another—" He blushed again.

"You needn't apologize, my boy. The love between a man and a woman is a beautiful gift. Indeed a sacred gift. I often wonder what I'd do without my Hettie."

"It isn't so simple for us. The circumstances— My God, even if we both go back to Germany, who knows how much time we could spend together. I know Elisabeth. If her heart is set on this work in Berlin, then that is that. But the uncertainty! How could a marriage survive under such conditions?"

Bell shook his head. "I don't know."

"Better if I go to India as I planned."

"I would be happy for you to go to India."

"Really? I was expecting you to talk me out of it. Faithfulness and discipleship and all that."

"Is that what returning to Germany would mean?" Bell leaned forward. "Would it mean being faithful to the call of God?"

Dietrich shut his eyes. "Yes," he said.

"Then you should listen to what you just said. And listen very carefully to what I said. I would be happy if you went to India. Because I would be happy to see you clear of that mess in Germany. For purely selfish reasons. I love you, Dietrich. Hettie and I have no children, you know, and I've come to think of you as the son I never had. Not easy to admit without sounding a sentimental old fool, but true. And suppose I say to you, By all means, Dietrich, you must return to Germany, that is the way of a true follower of Jesus Christ. And then suppose something happens to you. How could I forgive myself?"

Dietrich was too moved to speak. He looked out the window. Snow had begun to fall from a gray sky. After a time he regained his composure and said, "It will be lovely in the Harz Mountains just now. My parents have a country house at Friedrichsbrunn, and the family often goes there after Christmas. There will be snow on the ground, and from the kitchen the smell of venison stew and plum cake. When you walk in the hills there, you expect to round a bend and come upon Rumpelstiltskin grumbling along his way, or Hansel and Gretel scattering their breadcrumbs. It's so very German, so—"

Bell seemed to shrink in his chair. He put a hand to his forehead, then stood and went to the window, his back to Dietrich. "Why don't you go to Elisabeth?" he said.

Dietrich found her in the close leaning against a wall, her red coat vivid against the gray stone. He leaned beside her and tilted his head back to take in Chichester Cathedral towering above them, rimed with new snow like a frosted cake.

She said, "When you go back home to visit you'll find that all the Jews you knew in Berlin, all the friends of your family, are gone. They are the ones with money enough to leave and be welcomed elsewhere. For the others, the ones you don't know, it isn't so easy. Few countries will give entrance visas to Jews, not unless they're bringing money with them. I've learned quite a bit about emigration while trying to help my father. I've traveled and made contacts. I speak French and English. All that makes me a valuable person to Jews still trying to get out of Germany. How could I refuse to go back and help?"

"You couldn't refuse," he said. "Nor can I. I never truly believed in India."

"I know."

He took her cold hand. "You've come without your gloves," he said.

She smiled. "So have you."

"Elisabeth, I want you to marry me. But only after everything has been sorted out. Only after we see how things are, and know there is a way for us to make a home together."

"Yes. It makes no sense to marry just now. But it isn't fair, is it?"

"No," he agreed. "Not fair at all."

George Bell, still standing at his high window, watched them embrace. He turned away just as Hettie entered the room.

"It looks as if we're losing Dietrich," he said in a rough voice.

"I knew it the second I saw you," she said, reaching for his handkerchief, "because your eyes are so bright."

IN THE SPRING Dietrich took the train to Canterbury. Tom Eliot's new play was in rehearsal at the cathedral chapter house. Dietrich had a note from the poet, a special invitation to attend, along with an apology for the hurt feelings of the previous year. Elisabeth had been in Berlin for nearly two months, while Dietrich had been delayed, tying up loose ends at his churches. He was lonely, and apprehensive, he sometimes admitted to himself.

At the train station he noticed the handbills.

MURDER IN THE CATHEDRAL
A play in verse by
T. S. Eliot
featuring Robert Speaight
as Archbishop Thomas à Becket
June 3 - 24, 1935
8:00 p.m.
THE CHAPTER HOUSE
Canterbury Cathedral
Admission 1s.6d. free for the unemployed

Before seeking out the chapter house, he entered the cathedral itself. Once he had told George Bell he was sensitive to atmosphere. He paused now inside the entrance. Before him, green light of spring dimmed by stained glass, the nave of Canterbury Cathedral stretched to a distance, choir and apse beyond, each higher than the next, up and up and up. He climbed to the lofty chapel which held the tombs of Becket, the Black Prince, and King Henry the Fourth, and looked back down along endless arches. Should he seek out the spot of Becket's murder? Everyone who visited the cathedral was apparently required to stand upon the spot and imagine the deathcries of Becket, the grunts and hiccups of his murderers, the sword thrusts, the streams of blood.

Dietrich was afraid of such specifics. He would not look. He hurried down the chapel steps and out of the cathedral.

In the chapter house Eliot greeted him warmly (*Bonhoeffer! Oh jolly good!*— Eliot was more English than ever) but was soon distracted. "Sorry," he explained, "it's bitching time just now," and went off to argue with the actor playing Becket, who complained that certain thumpings at the door were not happening at the right time.

Dietrich slipped into a seat near the front and settled down. Eliot joined him. The actors disappeared as though waved away by a magic wand, the lights went down, and the chapter house dissolved in medieval gloom.

The first act was much as Dietrich remembered. He cringed when the Fourth Tempter taunted Becket for his spiritual pride, and glanced at Eliot, who studied the actors intently, now and then whispering a line along with them.

Then there was a sermon preached by Becket. The Archbishop shared his new understanding that martyrs do not choose their deaths but are cho-

sen by God. Becket told his congregation, with a catch in his voice, that
he would not likely preach to them again.

"Very good," Dietrich said during the break. "The sermon is quite moving."

Eliot nodded, pleased, and went off to share notes with the actors.

Act Two.

Eliot had not returned to his seat, and Dietrich sat alone in the dark.
Four knights entered, threatened Becket and his priests. The Archbishop
gave no ground and the knights left.

Dietrich found himself drawn to Robert Speaight, the actor playing
Becket. An intelligent, mobile face shining with self-awareness. When the
Chorus of women appeared, lamenting the violence they feared was coming, Becket calmed them, his countenance alive with pity. *Humans cannot
bear too much reality*, he said.

Then there came a violent crash at the rear door and all fled save
Becket. The door burst open and Dietrich, struck with fright, leaped from
his seat and turned, expecting to face SS-Hauptsturmführer Alois Bauer
and his blackshirts. . . .

Instead, armed knights baying for the blood of Becket, and Becket waits,
in his face fear and resignation and expectation and courage and compassion and pride and pity as he faces his drunken accusers.

Dietrich sank back onto his chair, feeling foolish and yet still unnerved.
He could barely watch the inevitable murder, flinched when drawn swords
flashed in candlelight and Becket was sent sprawling before the altar.

Eliot was back beside him for the rest of the performance.

The lights went up. Eliot watched Dietrich, who nodded and tried to
smile. "Good, very good. Powerful."

"Something upset you," Eliot said. "I assure you, it wasn't intentional
this time."

Dietrich shrugged. "It's only that I was reminded of something that happened before I left Germany."

"George says you're going back. And that you've become involved with
a young woman. A Jewess, he says. Good Lord, Bonhoeffer! Your own tempt-
ress eh?"

Dietrich who had begun to put on his coat, paused for a moment. "No,"
he said. "My conscience."

He went out beneath an ancient stone arch and pulled the heavy oak
door shut behind him.

Three days later Dietrich took ship from Harwich to Bremerhaven, standing upon a deck lashed by North Sea wind. He wished he could descend
into the bowels of the vessel and curl up in a shipping crate, cozy and safe,
with the Bechstein.

Quoniam tu solus sanctus

tu solus Dominus

tu solus Altissimus

For thou alone art holy
thou alone art the Lord
thou alone art the Most High

Olympiad
1936

IN STORIES, people come together and are torn apart and come back together. Events double back on one another.

Twins, a boy and a girl, hike through the Thuringian Forest and are lost in a snowstorm. Together they find their way home. Years later, they lose not only home, but each other. Will they live happily ever after?

Sabine is not happy now. She has a Jewish husband who has been dismissed from his university position in Göttingen. She and Gerhard and their two daughters would not be able to survive if not for money sent from her family in Berlin. They are afraid to answer the doorbell. Sometimes the SS pass the house and hurl insults, sometimes they bump Sabine in the street and call her obscene names, and once the house was searched and some books confiscated. But nothing else has happened. Yet.

In the middle of the night when Gerhard and the children are asleep, Sabine creeps downstairs to the study at the rear of the house. She pulls back the curtain and looks across the veranda past the beds of white geraniums shimmering at the edge of the moonlit orchard. More than the Göttingen house she loves its orchard, a tangle of cherry, plum, apple, and pear trees. One summer night she opens the French doors and wanders out beneath a full moon. The silver-leafed trees have been shedding their fruit. Sabine drifts from tree to tree, swaying, drunk with the fragrance of fermenting fruit.

Then the distant flailing of sirens, and perhaps (she is not certain) screams. She hurries back inside and locks the doors behind her.

Dr. Karl Bonhoeffer is still the preeminent psychiatrist in Berlin, still conducts his medical practice at the Charité. He and his wife, Paula, have sold the house in Wangenheimstraße 14, the splendid house in which they raised their children. The new house, Marienburger Allee 43, is much smaller, only eleven rooms. Not enough space for servant quarters, but this is just as well, since it had become a strain to always worry about what the help might see or hear. Or report. Most of the staff has been let go, even Keppel the chauffeur (with an adequate pension for many years of service, of course), and the elder Bonhoeffers, despite their age, have taken driving lessons and obtained their licenses. A cook and housemaid still arrive each day to manage the chores, but return to their own flats in Wedding at night. In the evenings now, the family and their frequent visitors can talk freely, without peeping around corners or closing doors.

The neighborhood is tucked away in a secluded corner north of the Grunewald, near the new Olympic stadium but far enough away to be spared the traffic and noise. Now and then, when a German athlete has made a spectacular throw or broken the tape at the finish line, a faint whoosh like the rush of a seashell held to the ear reaches Paula Bonhoeffer through the open windows of the sunroom. The house hides in a short cul-de-sac surrounded on three sides by woods so that Paula has taped black silhouettes of birds to the windows to keep the finches and swallows from crashing into them.

Dietrich has his own room at the top of the new house, a spacious alcove with dormers which he uses whenever he can get away from his seminary duties. The other children are married with homes of their own. Christel and her husband, Hans von Dohnanyi, are still above the Havel in Sacrow. Karl-Friedrich and Grete are settled in Leipzig, where he has accepted a chair in physical chemistry. It is a new field for Karl-Friedrich, who has abandoned nuclear chemistry to avoid being drafted into atomic weapon research. Even Baby Suse is married, to a Confessing Church pastor named Walter Dress with a church in Dahlem. It is difficult to imagine Suse in a manse parlor, entertaining the women of the parish sewing circle over coffee and cake. But that is just what she does. Though she mildly scandalizes these same women with her comments in favor of degenerate music and art, and her habit of tooling around Berlin on her bicycle with her skirts hiked to her knees. Sometimes she thinks of Falk Harnack, but since her family moved from the Wangenheimstraße she no longer sees his aunt. She has heard Falk was one of the prisoners released from Dachau because of the Olympics, but she doesn't know where he is.

All the world is caught up in the pageantry of the most spectacular Olympic Games ever staged—the immensity of the stadium, the lavish opening ceremonies with their searchlights and orchestral arrangements of Wagner and splendid Teutonic costumes. There has been the threat of a boycott by the United States over Germany's treatment of the Jews. But this is avoided after U.S. Olympic officials and business leaders visit the Reich before the Games and come away greatly impressed. One delegation headed by the publisher of the *Los Angeles Times* meets with U.S. journalists, including William Shirer, the friend of Pastor Martin Niemöller. They accuse the American foreign correspondents—known leftists, most of them, and probably anti-American or they wouldn't be so anxious to live abroad—of exaggerating reports of German wrongdoing. Look how peaceful, they say. No labor troubles, no strikes, no agitators, no Reds. The Nazis are putting people back to work and making them stand on their own two feet instead of spoon-feeding them as Roosevelt is doing back home. No one is in trouble here who doesn't deserve to be. As for the Jews, of course there's prejudice. Maybe even discrimination, like that new law banning marriage between Jews and Aryans. And we hear some Jews have lost their jobs. That's too bad.

No one says it, but in the back of the visitors' minds loom the American Negroes, who they will admit when pressed by their German hosts have even more cause for complaint than German Jews. Though the Negro is a special case, the American visitors argue uneasily, the Negro cannot handle equality, while the Jew has proved quite capable in the past . . . Nevertheless, the Germans reply, it is hypocrisy to fault us. And if you criticize us in public, why, should we not respond in kind? Finding no answer, the Americans shrug their shoulders and change the subject.

Dr. Frank Buchman, the great American evangelist, is in Berlin for the Games. At the Adlon Hotel he attends lavish receptions, holds private meetings with Himmler ("a great lad") and Goebbels, and even talks briefly with Hitler himself. The Führer assures Dr. Buchman his work is appreciated and no roadblocks will be placed in the way as he preaches the Gospel. Dr. Buchman glides along the marble floors of the Adlon ballroom, catches satisfying glimpses of himself in the gilt-edged mirrors before yet another Nazi official pumps his hand and praises him for his outspoken opposition to Communism.

Dr. Buchman is interviewed by a reporter from the *New York World-Telegram*. He announces there is no persecution of the church in Germany. He suggests that the Nazis, like Franco in Spain, are making the world safe for true Christianity and protecting the West from godless Communism. "Compare Germany today to England, which is seething with Bolshevism," he says. His rimless glasses glint in the pop of a flashbulb. "I thank God for a man like Adolf Hitler, who built a front line of defense against the Antichrist of Communism. My barber in London told me Hitler saved all Europe from the Red menace. That's how he felt. Of course I don't condone everything the Nazis do. Anti-Semitism? Bad, naturally. I suppose Hitler sees a Karl Marx in every Jew. But think what it would mean to the world if Hitler surrendered to the control of God. Or Mussolini. Or any dictator. Through such a man God could control a nation overnight and solve every last, bewildering problem."

What of Pastor Niemöller and the Confessing Church? the reporter asks. They claim the church is being persecuted.

Dr. Buchman turns somber. He leans forward in his chair. "Is the spirit of God really at work there?" he asks. "Or is it the spirit of egoism and unrest and dissension?"

During the Olympics, the Confessing Church is allowed to hold a series of worship services throughout Berlin. At first Dietrich refuses to participate.

"It's propaganda," he says to Niemöller over coffee in the Dahlem parsonage, where the congregation has maintained its pastor despite his banning from the pulpit. "Window dressing. We'd never be allowed to speak so freely without the Olympiad. But visitors from abroad will think this is normal in Germany."

"Of course," Niemöller says, his chronic exasperation with Dietrich flaring, "but who knows when we'll have such an opportunity again to reach so many people? And if the public responds well, perhaps the regime will realize it has nothing to gain by interfering with the church. Wait until the Games are over, and then we'll see. Perhaps it will be better."

Dietrich is asked to submit a photograph for the publicity posters. He refuses. He has no wish to see his face plastered at street corners as an advertisement for the new order. But he finally agrees to speak from the pulpit of the Pauluskirche. It is a sweltering summer evening. A few hours earlier, the American Negro Jesse Owens broke the tape in the hundred-yard dash. (*So like the Americans to cheat by running a Negro*, Eichmann complains that evening to SS-Hauptsturmführer Alois Bauer. *Perhaps we Germans should have entered a racehorse.*) Under Dietrich's black robe sweat stains half-moons at each armpit, trickles down his backbone, spreads beneath his leather belt, and pools at the top of his buttocks. As he surveys the crowded sanctuary the congregation settles back with a collective sigh, waving their programs in a vain attempt to cool themselves. Dietrich looks for Elisabeth but doesn't see her.

He glances at his notes and says, "When Judas came to betray Our Lord, Jesus asked him, 'Friend, why are you here?' Listen to the love in that question, consider that Jesus knows his hour is upon him and still he calls Judas 'friend.' Jesus will not part with Judas. He allows Judas to kiss him and does not turn away."

In the evening shadow their faces are turned up to him like flowers reaching for the light.

"A final declaration of love, this kiss, and at the same time, a betrayal.

In the end, Judas's love for Jesus is not as strong as his hate. Yet both are present."

Dietrich leans over the edge of the pulpit.

"Who is Judas? Does not Judas stand for the people? Who is the traitor? Is it you?" Points at the congregation. Slowly bends his arm and jabs his own breast with the accusing fingertip. "Is it I?"

Outside the Pauluskirche, the foreign visitors stroll along the Grunewaldstraße, duck into the shops and cafés and bars, pause to buy sausages or Italian ices from vendors sheltered by bright yellow and green umbrellas, stop to talk or flirt, all the colors of humanity, all the languages, all the flags worn as patches on shirts or pins on lapels. Some expect Jews to approach furtively and complain of ill treatment. None does. So. Everything must be all right after all.

The young people of the world praise their German hosts. The Olympic Village, the living quarter for the athletes, is pleasant and comfortable, the beds firm, the rooms quiet, the food bountiful and well prepared.

Nearby, though no one notices, the prison camp at Sachsenhausen is being enlarged. When the Games are over the Olympic Village becomes a barracks for the SS guards who work at the camp. The beds remain firm, the rooms quiet, and the food bountiful and well prepared, at least until the last year of the war.

Dietrich Bonhoeffer is back at his duties in Pomerania. He is in charge of a seminary for aspiring pastors who wish to serve Confessing Church congregations. They have taken over an old house in the village of Finkenwalde, a bare, drafty place with cracked plaster and leaking ceilings. It is seldom visited by outsiders and surrounded by woodland, secluded and private. Here twenty seminarians sleep in one large room. In the classroom, once the preserve of a governess and her charges, a faded portrait of Bismarck hangs above a chalkboard. The seminarians eat common meals, usually soup and potatoes or cabbage. Their only books come from Dietrich's private library. It pains him to see his precious theological volumes with pages dog-eared and covers battered from constant passing back and forth. But he decides his fretting is sin, an unseemly worldly attachment. He is trying to set a spiritual example. He runs the seminary as strictly as a monastery, with regular hours for meditation and prayer and silence. The students grumble that their teacher is too strict, that he is an enthusiast, a Roman Catholic masquerading as a Protestant. But they must admit that he does not set himself above them, that he chops wood as they do, washes dishes and tends the vegetable garden as they do. He also takes them into the village and regularly beats each and every one at tennis.

Even here, surrounded by his students twenty-four hours a day, he is lonely. When there is talk of meetings between the Reich Church and the Confessing congregations to resolve differences, Dietrich declares, "There can be no communion between church and unchurch." The students are amazed at his rigidity. Dietrich circulates a paper in church circles that proclaims, "There is no salvation outside the Confessing Church." Of course, this raises a scandal. (In Berlin Niemöller hears complaint after complaint about Bonhoeffer's narrow-mindedness.) Though the seminarians have grown fond of their teacher, they have concluded he is something of a fanatic. At night in their beds, though they are supposed to maintain silence, they wonder in whispers why their teacher is so obsessed with the Jewish Question. Did the Jews not crucify Christ? Did not Martin Luther himself chastise the self-proclaimed chosen people? Hadn't the Jews in general been entirely too self-satisfied? And if privation and discipline are so beneficial for the students of the Finkenwalde seminary, might they not be beneficial for arrogant Jews as well? After all, one gets weary of hearing people complain about how they are mistreated.

In his own room—the one privilege he has allowed himself—Dietrich lies awake on a lumpy mattress listening to the creakings of the old house. Sometimes he thinks of Elisabeth, longs for her so painfully he is near tears. But this happens less and less often. In the past year, Dietrich and Elisabeth have spent thirteen days together. And just as well, perhaps, for thanks to the Nuremberg Laws, they can no longer make love without committing a capital offense.

Stille Nacht

WHEN THE FINKENWALDE SEMINARIANS dispersed for the Christmas holidays, Dietrich went home to Berlin. One morning he opened the *Berliner Börsen Zeitung* to a short notice at the bottom of page 4.

U.S. CONGRESS INVESTIGATES INDUSTRIAL DISASTER

Washington DC (Reuters)—The House Sub-committee on Labor will hold public hearings into allegations of an industrial disaster in Fayette Co., W.Va. Hundreds of workers are reported dead or seriously ill as a result of the construction of a hydroelectric facility and tunnel at Gauley Mountain. The workmen are said to have died from breathing pure silica dust while drilling the tunnel. If the reports are true, said subcommittee chairman Glenn Griswold (D-Ind.), it would be "the worst industrial disaster in the history of this nation." Griswold said he expected the subcommittee to conduct "a thorough investigation." He and Rep. Vito Marcantonio (R-NY) also plan to introduce legislation designed to improve workplace safety. Marcantonio has called for the establishment of a national agency for occupational safety and health.

Although work on the tunnel was completed by the end of 1931, the magnitude of the disaster is just becoming known. Rep. Marcantonio criticized "the neglect of worker safety under previous administrations."

Dietrich's hands trembled as he cut the story from the newspaper with his mother's silver sewing scissors. He folded the clipping and slipped it into his wallet, then put on coat and hat and headed for the Scheunenviertel.

The sidewalks of the Oranienburger Straße were as crowded as a tram at rush hour. All the Jews of Berlin and the surrounding region seemed to have congregated beneath the shadow of the gold-domed New Synagogue. In the Oranienburger Straße they found safety in numbers. Not like the Ku-Damm or Friedrichstraße, where a Jew might be refused service in a shop by a surly clerk wearing a swastika armband, or spat upon by passersby, or accosted by a Gestapo patrol and dragged into an alley for a beating. In the Oranienburger Straße, the warming crush of fellow Jews was as comforting as a blazing hearth on that December day.

Dietrich made his way slowly, studied the faces around him, the worried, weary faces of people who had lost jobs, who had registered their property with the state, who had grown used to looking over their shoulders. Not like other Berliners in and out of shops bright with Christmas lights hugging packages wrapped in red and green and gold pausing at the corner butcher shop to inspect whitefeathered geese hanging by webbed feet dragging Christmas evergreens fresh from the country, treetips like tails tracing patterns on snowdusted sidewalks.

Elisabeth worked in an office two blocks from the New Synagogue, a large ground-floor room crammed with desks and chairs and people standing in lines between the desks and along the walls. Dietrich had to push his way to the center of the room before he could see her, rummaging through piles of paper at a desk in the far corner.

When he squeezed past the line of people waiting to see her, she said without looking up, "Wait your turn, please," pulled two forms from the pile, then, "Dietrich!" while a pregnant woman with a little boy in tow watched anxiously. "You know I don't have time to talk here."

"Have lunch with me."

"I scarcely have time to go to the toilet." She shoved the forms toward the woman, handed her a fountain pen and bottle of ink.

"You must eat sometime," he insisted.

"I ate a sandwich at my desk," she mumbled and pointed to the middle of one form. "Write the names and ages of the children there, and the grandmother down here."

"I'll be at the Café Bauer when you get off work." When she didn't answer he said, "I'll be there every night until you come."

The woman across from Elisabeth pressed one arm against her large belly and leaned over the desk. Her dark hair fell across her face and she pushed it back impatiently, then began to write. Elisabeth sighed and shut her eyes. "I'm always so tired after work."

"Please. I'll buy you supper, and a good bottle of wine, and afterward I'll rub your neck."

"Here," the woman pointed at the form, "should I mention the little one on the way?"

Elisabeth waved Dietrich away. He made his way out, stopped at the door, and put on his hat. He looked back. Above the slumped shoulders of the writing woman, Elisabeth was watching him. She smiled then and held up seven fingers.

She was not at the Café Bauer at seven. Dietrich called for a bottle of peach brandy. He sipped two tiny glasses and was about to leave at quarter to eight, but the door swung open and Elisabeth entered in a whirl of new snowflakes, pulled off her gloves, and looked around. He waved. She sat across from him, pulled off her black knit hat, and shook out her hair. Dietrich noticed the tight dry skin across her cheekbones and nose, her pale lips.

"You do look tired," he said. "Now I feel guilty for keeping you from your rest."

"No," she said, and placed her hand on his. "It's good to see you." She took her hand away and looked around. "This is the place we met," she said. "Ages and ages ago."

He handed her a glass of amber liquid. "Peach brandy. I've ordered a Riesling with dinner." He raised his own glass. "To you and your work."

She sipped the brandy with her eyes closed. "I hope it doesn't put me to sleep."

"You've lost weight," he said.

"So have you."

"I'm eating mostly potatoes and cabbage. I've become a regular peasant."

"I'm too tired in the evenings to eat much," she said.

He lit a cigarette and handed it to her, leaned close and touched his own to hers.

"We never see each other," she said.

"No. I can't get away. Even when we take our breaks, Niemöller keeps me busy. And when I do have some free time, you—"

She looked away. "You see how it is with me. People are desperate to get out of Germany. And we've nowhere to send them. No one wants Jews. So. Everything is worse and worse."

"You don't write as often," he said.

"I go to work at seven and there are nights I don't get home until eleven. There are nights I fall asleep on the tram and miss my stop."

A waiter offered as tenderly as a newborn child the Riesling cradled in white linen. "Ja," Dietrich said and accepted the bottle. "Never mind pouring. Just bring two orders of the goulash and leave us be."

He filled Elisabeth's wineglass. She said, "You don't write so often either."

"No," he agreed. "You are very far away. Sometimes it's difficult to believe you exist."

Her eyes filled with tears. "It's no good, is it?"

"I don't know." He laid his cigarette against the red ashtray, read worlds of possibility in the glowing ash. "Come home with me for Christmas. We'll have Bach and Schubert on Christmas Eve, and then to the Annenkirche at midnight. A big dinner on Christmas Day, the entire family there—"

"Dietrich." She placed her hand across his lips. "Dietrich. I'm not having Christmas this year."

"Not having— You mean you have to work?"

"I mean I'm not a Christian anymore. Dear, dear Dietrich. Please try and understand. I can't be a Christian in the Scheunenviertel."

The waiter descended on them with steaming plates of goulash and a basket of bread.

The plates sat untouched.

"What does this mean for us?" Dietrich managed to say.

She shook her head. "I don't know, I don't know. Sabine married a Jew. Does it matter to you?"

"Of course not. But it's going to be difficult whichever religion you observe. I'm afraid Gerhard and Sabine will have to leave soon. You'll have to leave soon."

"I won't leave."

"Elisabeth, you must be reasonable. You don't know what will happen."

"What don't I know? What is there I don't get a whiff of every day?"

"Hans says—Hans says it's going to get worse. He's seen the new laws they're drawing up. Jews will be banned from theaters and concert halls and public schools. You'll be treated the same as the Negroes in America."

"I don't see the Negroes leaving America."

"It may get worse still."

"Will it? And what do you plan to do about it? That's your responsibility, isn't it? You and all the other Christians? What will you do?"

"I don't know. But I'll do something. I promise I'll do something."

They picked at the food growing cold on their plates, finished off the bottle of wine, and went out into the winter night. In Unter den Linden they caught a tram to Weißensee, where Elisabeth had three rooms on the second floor of a house owned by a Jewish couple she'd helped emigrate to Hong Kong. Outside the house in the Charlottenburger Straße, they stopped and looked up at the dark windows. "Why did you come today in particular?" she asked.

He remembered the newspaper article and took out his wallet, handed her the clipping. She held it up to the light of the streetlamp.

"You were there," she said.

"Yes. With Fred. I've often wondered if he went back to the tunnel."

"Why did this bring you to me?"

"It reminded me how much you and I need each other."

"Funny," she said, "because this was a friend who had his own road to travel."

He didn't answer, could not find his voice.

She lingered a moment with her hand on his sleeve as though about to invite him upstairs, then seemed to think better of it, kissed him on the cheek, and went inside.

Two months later he sat at his window staring out at the spring-green woods of Finkenwalde. Paper and pen were spread out before him. He picked up Elisabeth's latest letter, read, *You seem so far away. In a different world. There is much I want to tell you but how can I begin? Are you doing anything besides writing your book and teaching your students? Dietrich! How long can we wait? Of course I cannot say more in a letter. But I'm tired of excuses. Some people find a way to do what they have to do.*

He recalled their most recent conversation, a hasty meeting on a cold bench in the Tiergarten. They hadn't even held hands.

"All I hear from Christians is excuses," she'd said. "I'm tired of excuses. Hitler doesn't have to be obeyed. He's banned marriages between Aryans and Jews. Does that matter? People still make love. He's banned abortions, but women still have them. Why must others hide behind their decency?"

He had been embarrassed by the baldness of her examples and hadn't answered.

She'd said, "You're uncomfortable, aren't you? You don't like to be reminded how most people have to survive. It doesn't fit the clean world of the Wangenheimstraße."

"We no longer live in the Wangenheimstraße," he'd reminded her, aware of the lameness of his response.

She'd shaken her head in frustration, then said, "I have to go, there's so much work waiting for me."

He took up his pen and dipped it in a bottle of blue ink. He wrote, *You know how I struggle with ambition. Spiritual ambition. I thought I learned something about that in America. But I continue to fail, as you like to point out. I am often quite pleased with myself and unhappy with others. If you look in your heart you will find you are not unfamiliar with such feelings.*

I have a path I must follow, and so do you. All that is clear. You are responsible for the way you choose. I am also responsible for my decisions, though my way is not so clear to me just now. I cannot feel, as you seem to, that it is unimportant to train future pastors. And there are other matters about which I may not speak.

The government has made it illegal for us to marry each other. Even without that we seem to be moving apart. Perhaps the times are to blame. Perhaps we shall never know. In any event, I see no future for us as a couple.

I don't want to lose touch with you. But it is clear we must both be free. I do still love you, dear Elisabeth. You must believe that. And you must promise that if you find yourself in any kind of trouble, you will come to me at once. In that, at least, you will find me faithful.

Yours,
Dietrich

He held the letter for three days—reading it over and over—before he posted it. There was no response.

Disappearances
1937–38

After the Olympiad, paintings disappeared from museum galleries, leaving pale rectangular ghosts upon the walls. Books disappeared from library shelves. The works of Mendelssohn and other Jewish composers disappeared from concert halls. Bookstores and theaters closed. Writers and artists and musicians vanished, some into the camps, some abroad.

Pastor Martin Niemöller also disappeared. Twice. Each time Frau Niemöller telephoned Dietrich in a panic and he left his post in Pomerania to return to Berlin and wait with her. A few days would pass and Niemöller would reappear, disheveled and tired and hungry but otherwise no worse for wear. Each time he had been taken to Gestapo headquarters in the Prinz-Albrecht-Straße, questioned about his activities on behalf of the Confessing Church, and then let go.

Dietrich wondered why he had himself not been detained. Of course, he would not enjoy being taken in by the Gestapo. But was he being ignored because he was in fact doing nothing important? He shared this fear with his brother-in-law Hans von Dohnanyi when the family had gathered in the Marienburger Allee for Easter dinner. Hans looked at him oddly, then led him out onto the veranda.

"God knows I can't tell you what to do," Hans said, "but this is a very sensitive time for me just now."

"Is it?"

"I'm being eased out of the Justice Ministry. It seems I'm not enthusiastic enough for the Nazis."

"You expected that," Dietrich pointed out.

"Yes. But now that it's here, I've a decision to make. You know General Hans Oster?"

"Not personally. But I know he's a member of Martin Niemöller's parish in Dahlem, and Martin thinks highly of him."

"Oster has just been made second in command of the Abwehr. Military intelligence. He wants me as his assistant."

"Will you accept?"

"Yes. I can't think of a better position for keeping an eye on what's happening, perhaps even undermining the Nazis from the inside. I believe that's Oster's idea as well."

"And what has this to do with my concern about my own work?"

Hans placed his hand on Dietrich's arm. "Only this. Don't take any unnecessary risks right now. Stay in Pomerania with your students. Please."

"What do you mean? I'm just—"

Hans raised his hand. "Please. I can't say any more, but perhaps in a few months, if this appointment goes through, I'll know where we all stand."

"We all?"

"The family will stand together. Won't we?"

Dietrich swallowed hard. "Of course," he said.

"Good." Hans went back inside.

No unnecessary risks, Dohnanyi had said. And what of necessary risks? Dietrich pondered the question as he finished writing the book he had so hesitantly begun in England. It was a study of Jesus' Sermon on the Mount, written with Elisabeth's final accusations ringing in his ears. On his visits to Berlin he walked the streets with Jews casting frightened glances about them as they hurried along. He would go straight to his desk and write, and even as he set pen to paper he knew himself as one whose only response to the call of Jesus was this solitary act. It was not enough, not nearly enough, and as he wrote he accused himself. *Cheap grace is the deadly enemy of our church. We are fighting today for costly grace. Cheap grace means grace sold on the market like cheapjacks' wares. The sacraments, the forgiveness of sin, and the consolations of religion are thrown away at cut prices. . . . In such a church the world finds a cheap covering for its sins; no contrition is required, still less any real desire to be delivered from sin. . . . Cheap grace is not the kind of forgiveness of sin which frees us from the toils of sin. Cheap grace is the grace we bestow on ourselves. Cheap grace is the preaching of forgiveness without requiring repentance, baptism without church discipline, absolution without confession. Cheap grace is grace without discipleship, grace without the cross. . . .*

To endure the cross is not a tragedy; it is the suffering which is the fruit of an exclusive allegiance to Jesus Christ. When it comes, it is not an accident, but a necessity. . . . The cross is there, right from the beginning, one has only got to pick it up; there is no need to go out and look for a cross, no need to run deliberately after suffering. . . . Thus it begins; the cross is not the terrible end to an otherwise God-fearing and happy life, but it meets us at the beginning of our communion with Christ. When Christ calls a man, he bids him come and die.

These words materialized, it seemed, without thought or plan, and he was frightened to have penned them. When he had read them over he stood and went to his shaving mirror, stared at himself for a very long time. "Now I must do something," he said aloud, "to make myself an honest man."

As the director of the Finkenwalde seminary he was often summoned to Berlin for meetings of the Confessing movement, meetings which were more and more discouraging. Martin Niemöller's expulsion from the pulpit had both frightened and awed many of the other pastors. "When in fact there should be only contempt and defiance," Dietrich complained to Niemöller.

Niemöller, who since his banishment was thought by many to have become as unreasonably intransigent as Dietrich, said, "It won't happen. Most of the laypeople and clergy, even those supportive of the Confessing movement, are desperate for a compromise with the Reich Church."

"Like children caught in an act of rebellion against their parents," Dietrich said, "who retain a facade of defiance even as they prepare to break into tears and beg for pardon."

At church meetings he found himself speaking out despite Dohnanyi's plea for caution. As the government was extending its discriminatory measures against Jews, he stood before a convocation of clergy in a church hall in Wilmersdorf. His audience waited his words with dread, now and then casting sidelong glances at one another. A few took notes.

"Now we are offered compromises," Dietrich declared. "We shall be allowed to go our own way in what is called peace if we recognize the Reich Church and drop our opposition to it. There must be no such compromise. The national church has cut itself off from the Christian church. The national church has embraced heresy. It has done so by its treatment of the Jews. And if we refuse to concern ourselves with any Jews other than baptized Jews, then we too shall have fallen into heresy. Only those who cry out for the Jews may sing Gregorian chant."

There were gasps at this statement, and one or two of those scribbling notes did so carefully. Not long after, the state church announced that Dietrich Bonhoeffer had been banned from teaching in German universities.

In the summer his study of the Sermon on the Mount was published. He had titled it *Discipleship*, and the dedication page read

For Pastor Martin Niemöller
He would have written this book much better

He set out for the Dahlem parsonage with a copy, signed and wrapped, and wished he could boast of what he carried to other passengers on the train. But as he walked past the Annenkirche and turned in the gate a weeping Frau Niemöller threw open the door and waved for him to hurry inside.

"They've come for Martin again! The Gestapo!"

"Again?"

"The children are out hiking in the Grunewald with the dog. They don't even know." She dabbed at her eyes with a handkerchief. "I'm so frightened. The men who came this time were very rude. Not like before when the officers were respectful, even if they weren't particularly friendly. These men shoved Martin several times, and when I tried to kiss him goodbye, one of them pushed me so hard I nearly fell."

"How long ago?"

"They only just left, not ten minutes ago. I haven't had time to think what to do."

Dietrich went instinctively to a phone before he remembered it was not wise. He set down the receiver and put his hat back on. "Look here, I'd best go to see Hans at once. Maybe he can find out something."

"It's so good of you, Dietrich," Else Niemöller was saying, and threw open the door just as a black saloon car pulled up. She blocked the way and grabbed Dietrich's arm. "Quick! Out the back before they come in!"

But Dietrich had been seen, and even as he sprinted through the house and out the back door a Gestapo agent with drawn pistol turned the corner into the garden.

"I wouldn't be leaving just yet," the man said pleasantly. He noticed the package still under Dietrich's arm, put his gun in his pocket, and held out his hand. "May I?" He ripped off the wrapping paper and dropped it on the ground, studied the book's jacket, opened it and read the inscription. He looked up. "You are the author?"

Dietrich nodded.

"Congratulations. Now—" with a jerk of his head—"back inside."

In the house a team of six Gestapo agents emptied the contents of drawers onto the floors, slit cushions and rummaged inside trailing stuffing like spoiled entrails, held books upside down to see what might fall out, then tossed them into piles. Else Niemöller stood by, her face a mourner's mask, but she no longer wept. Dietrich went to her and held her in his arms.

"Might as well make yourselves comfortable," said the man who'd detained Dietrich. "We'll be a while. It's a big house, after all."

"Where are we supposed to sit," Dietrich said, "if you're destroying the furniture?"

"What's wrong with the chairs in the kitchen?" the man asked impatiently, then, "Fritz, go upstairs with Albrecht. Anton and Erwin can handle the papers down here." He took a slip of paper from his jacket pocket and smiled at Dietrich. "Before you retire to the kitchen for a nice cup of coffee, Pastor Bonhoeffer, I must thank you for saving us from tracking you down to give you this message. You've been banished from Berlin. Since you're here just now, we'll hold you until we're done and then send you on your way back to whatever woodsman's cottage you're holed up in. Unless, of course, we find something incriminating here in the house or—" He tapped the book.

Dietrich led Frau Niemöller to the kitchen, where a maid and cook waited nervously. A pot of coffee was soon brewing, and the cook, a woman so thin she seemed not to have taken a bite of her own food, set out plates of sliced ham and cheese, hard-boiled eggs and herring and onions in sour cream, thick slices of black bread and butter. The Gestapo ransacked the house for eight hours, sending men in teams to sort and haul away books and papers, tapping walls and chopping through plaster with pickaxes at suspiciously hollow places. (And pausing now and then to invade the kitchen and eat large helpings of the food without a word of thanks.) The Niemöller children came home from their outing with their pet schnauzer, Max, and were shepherded, frightened and distraught, into the kitchen, dragging the yapping dog with them. When the youngest boy was allowed upstairs to the toilet he returned in tears to report the family goldfish and hamsters had been flushed. Everyone feared for Max and he was shoved beneath the table and tied to a post so tightly he couldn't move, but the Gestapo ignored him. "There, there, they'll not hurt the little dog," the cook reassured the children. "The Führer wouldn't allow it. He loves dogs."

At last Dietrich was told to leave. When he protested that someone must remain to help Frau Niemöller, he was manhandled and shoved toward the door.

"Never mind, Dietrich," said Frau Niemöller, "we shall go tonight to my sister in Zehlendorf."

"You, Bonhoeffer," said the officer in charge, who'd since identified himself as Hauptsturmführer Sonderegger, "have forty-eight hours in Berlin. Then get out, or else you'll find yourself in Sachsenhausen."

And Dietrich was in the street, picking up his hat where they'd tossed it into a puddle.

Dr. Karl Bonhoeffer and Hans von Dohnanyi sipped brandy and smoked pipes in the study in the Marienburger Allee house, while Dietrich went through an entire pack of cigarettes.

"I doubt it will matter what they found or didn't find," Dohnanyi was saying. "It looks like they mean to hold him this time, no matter what." For he had learned that Niemöller was already lodged in the concentration camp at Sachsenhausen.

"It matters to Dietrich," Karl Bonhoeffer said, as though his son were not in the room, were not pacing back and forth across the Persian rug. "If there's anything incriminating I may not be able to help further."

Dietrich stopped short. "There won't be anything. Martin was very discreet after that run-in with Goering and Hitler. As for helping me, you've done quite enough, thank you."

Dr. Bonhoeffer and Dohnanyi looked surprised at the tone of his voice. They'd just told him that his banishment from Berlin had been lifted after only a few hours. The ban on teaching and preaching remained in place, but he could otherwise come and go unmolested.

"I would have thought gratitude a more appropriate response," Karl Bonhoeffer said, "since I have worn myself out and used a great deal of political capital to get this banishment rescinded. I would be hurt, except that I know you've had a stressful day."

"I? It is Else Niemöller and her children who've had a stressful day. Not to mention Martin himself. I've suffered nothing. After all, my father is the renowned Dr. Karl Bonhoeffer, who has great influence with our government."

Karl Bonhoeffer said nothing, for it was his policy to hold back his words until his anger had passed.

Hans said, "Actually, Uncle Rudi made most of the contacts."

Dietrich threw up his hands. "Fine! Uncle Rudi! I suppose now I must throw myself at his feet in gratitude and pledge to be a good boy."

"You talk as though you'd prefer to be in Sachsenhausen with Niemöller," said Karl Bonhoeffer. He tapped the bowl of his pipe on the edge of an ashtray and reached for a pipe cleaner. "This is childish, Dietrich."

"It's not what I wish," Dietrich said, "it's what I fear. I doubt I would have the courage to face what Martin is about to face. But pardon me if I feel guilt that he is bearing this burden without me."

He went to stand at the open window. It was a pitch-black night with no moon, and a light breeze that smelled of rain. Dohnanyi went to Dietrich's side and pulled the window shut.

"Isn't it a bit warm for that?" Dietrich said grumpily.

"Someone might be within earshot."

"And what is it they mustn't hear?"

"Dietrich," Hans said, "there is a plot to overthrow the government. Your father and I are both involved."

Dietrich stared from one to the other. He sagged onto a chair. There was no need to ask what the consequences would be if they were caught. "Who else?" he managed to ask.

"Mostly people in the Foreign Office, and military men. The army is the only institution in the country that could really carry this off, you know."

"And why would they want to?" Dietrich asked. "Weren't they ecstatic when Hitler moved into the Rhineland? With all this sword-rattling about Austria and the Sudetenland, I'd think the army would be thrilled."

"Some of the generals are pleased. But many of them believe Hitler is reckless enough to take us into war with France and Britain. They don't believe we could win, and the result would be worse than the Great War. With the blame falling on them, they fear. So they want rid of him."

Dietrich shook his head in disbelief. "Can you trust them? Hans, you've never cared for the military."

"I despise the military," Dohnanyi agreed. He pulled a chair close and said in a low voice, "I hate the regimentation and the arrogance. But they're afraid, the bastards, and we need them. Besides, General Oster—Oster is different. A renegade, but a respected one. He's the real force behind this. He's been recruiting the other generals."

"Recruiting them? And what if someone reports him?"

"He doesn't believe they will, if he's careful who he approaches. It's a matter of honor, *esprit de corps*. Something these people are very good at, I will admit."

Dietrich looked at his father questioningly.

"My own part is small," Dr. Bonhoeffer said. "Using evidence Hans has provided, I'm drawing up a psychological profile of Hitler. As evidence to be used in court, to show the man is mentally unfit to govern, if such justification is needed."

"You'll arrest him then?"

Dohnanyi looked away.

"Arrest him," Dr. Bonhoeffer said, "and either lock him away for crimes against the state, or commit him for insanity."

"Of course, the evidence for insanity must be medically sound," Dietrich said bitterly, recalling the wretched Marinus van der Lubbe.

Dr. Bonhoeffer ignored him and said loftily to Dohnanyi, "I wonder if we were right to tell Dietrich? This is a bit beyond his scope." Then he stood slowly, and the two younger men hastened to their feet. "It's been a long day. Paula will wonder what is keeping me."

They bowed stiffly, and stared at the closed door after Dr. Bonhoeffer had gone.

"There'll be no arresting Hitler," Hans von Dohnanyi said softly. "We'll have to kill him."

"Good God," Dietrich whispered.

"It's the only way. He's too popular to leave alive." Hans waited, then asked, "Do you want to know more?"

Dietrich took a deep breath and shut his eyes. He shook his head. "No," he said.

Pomerania beyond the Oder was a land of marsh and forest, of dense woods choked with blackthorn and hawthorn. A treacherous place whose paths might lead the unwary into bogs impassable save in the dead of frozen winter. A land of bittern and stork and nightingale and turtle, whose people—at least those who were wealthy—lived in the saddle and hunted wild boar.

Dietrich preferred the city. Or if he must be in the country, he would choose the gentle Harz Mountains where the Bonhoeffers had their summer home of Friedrichsbrunn. He loved to climb in the Harz, to hike a stony path up onto an ancient crag, or down into a secluded cove. The flank of a mountain could be drenched in sunlight at one moment and covered by a dark cloak the next as clouds walked across the surface of the earth. In Pomerania one was either enveloped in smothering woods or stranded in a vast open field smelling of manure. For a long time Dietrich could not imagine wandering there, could not understand how people got their bearings.

But after two years of exploring in his free time, he had begun to make his peace with this landscape. Like the Harz Mountains, the old forest of the East was a place where the practice of magic was still recalled. In his solitary walks beyond Finkenwalde, Dietrich discovered a small lake which he visited with knapsack stuffed with book, bread and cheese, bottle of wine. And there were other times, not so solitary. For Dietrich had been "adopted" by some local gentry, the von Wedemeyers.

They were an old family, Prussian and conservative but down on their luck, which went a long way to curb haughtiness. The once-grand estate at Pätzig, Kreis Königsberg, was a trifle shabby, with peeling wallpaper, plumbing that clanged and banged, and here and there a leaking roof. The west wing was closed off entirely in winter, because the von Wedemeyers could not afford to heat it. But Wedemeyer was reckoned by his tenants a fair man as landlords go, not mean and gouging as others might be in his straitened circumstances. When a peasant fell ill, Frau von Wedemeyer visited the sickbed with a jar of chicken stew and a bottle of homemade plum brandy, as von Wedemeyer women had always done. Each Christmas she directed the church Nativity play and distributed packages of toys and nuts to the village children. Her own children, seven in all, carried themselves with the well-mannered assurance of aristocrats. They were usually to be found in riding habits and jodhpurs, whips in hand, clambering onto the back of a horse with a hand up from a groom. For Dietrich, visiting Pätzig was like escaping into a nineteenth-century novel.

He did not like everything about Pätzig. He was often reminded how country people, even the most aristocratic, could be unsophisticated in their outlook. When he sat before the hearth with Herr von Wedemeyer in the great hall, trying to ignore the antlered head of a stag glowering over them, he often grew bored with hearing how everything would be set right in Germany if only the monarchy were restored and government turned over to the ancient nobility. He could recite by heart how Wedemeyer got the news of Kaiser Wilhelm's abdication on his wedding day and wept so fiercely his bride-to-be tried to call off the ceremony. ("But she went through with it. Thought if the Reds actually won they'd have more sympathy for a newlywed couple and leave us be, eh?") And the stories of how two years earlier Herr von Wedemeyer defied the local Nazis who accused him of "antisocial behavior." ("They wanted Pätzig, you see," Herr von Wedemeyer explained. "I mean, that must have been it, because what had I done to antagonize them? I don't drink with them, or invite them to my house. Why should I? Bunch of shopkeepers. None of them from good families, not a one can sit a horse or bring down a deer. Except Goering, I hear, but he's titled. No, it was the land they wanted, clear it and make some money. Might have got it too, if your Uncle Rudi hadn't come through. One of the best lawyers in Berlin, von der Goltz, that's what everyone round here said. And he did the job. Told me he had a relative moved hereabouts, and when we heard you preach in Stettin I said to my wife, 'That's the very fellow, old Rudi's nephew.'" Dietrich sighed and reminded himself that his own dear mother did indeed hail from these Prussian gentry.)

At Easter Wedemeyer's middle daughter, Maria, came home on vacation from her boarding school, the Magdalenen-Stift in Thuringia. "Our school is for girls of the Protestant nobility," she informed Dietrich, who was to instruct her for confirmation now she had turned thirteen. She folded her hands in her lap and sat very straight. "Don't hesitate to be strict with me. I'm used to it."

He quickly realized this bit of pomposity was play-acting. She reminded Dietrich of his sisters at that age, bright and good-natured, with light brown hair and pale skin dusted with freckles like Christel's. Maria was constantly called down by her mother for her high spirits, but her father, who adored her, was another matter. When she stood before the altar of the village church in Pätzig to be confirmed, she made a face at Wedemeyer, who grinned back from the front pew and received a nudge from his wife for reproof. At home afterward, they played at croquet on the lawn. Wedemeyer pretended to mistake Maria's ball for his own and sent it with a loud whack into a clump of alder bushes. Maria yelled. Wedemeyer grabbed his daughter and pulled her braids while she stomped his foot in a pretend fury.

"Isn't this one a ridiculous little Miss Mouse! Eh, Pastor Bonhoeffer?"

"Papa!" Maria shrieked. "You are so bad, Papa!" And leaped onto her father's back, arms around his neck, until both sank to the ground, laughing.

Which was nothing like Dr. Karl Bonhoeffer and Dietrich's sisters.

Dietrich's students, most of them respectably middle-class, teased him about his newfound aristocratic friends. He accepted their banter good-naturedly, for he admitted there was something funny about a rather dry academic (so he saw himself) taken in by the family of a country squire. In a time of quiet, it might make an amusing film.

This was not a time of quiet. In the evenings after study was done, the seminarians gathered around the radio in the parlor. The German army had marched unopposed into Austria, whose citizens gathered in the hundreds of thousands to celebrate their inclusion in the Reich.

It's only right, the seminarians agreed. After all, they're really Germans. Like us.

Dietrich insisted the radio dial be tuned to the BBC, where the reports of the Anschluss were considerably less exultant.

"The British are frightened," Dietrich said.

What? Frightened of us? The German people don't want war with Britain. As long as we are not provoked . . .

When Hitler returned from Austria the joyous scenes of welcome were repeated. In Stettin, where the seminarians took in a film together, the newsreels ran on for half an hour. Screaming women threw flowers at the soldiers, and burst into tears when Hitler passed by in an open car. Hitler kissed children, accepted nosegays from little girls with neat braids, inspected ranks of Hitler Youth. It was an exciting time to be German, and young.

Back at Finkenwalde seated before the radio as though deep in meditation. The gas lanterns had not been lit, to save fuel, and the faces of the listening seminarians dissolved in the gloom of the summer evening. The news reports claimed that ethnic Germans were being mistreated in the Sudetenland, a region of Czechoslovakia. Hitler demanded that the Sudetenland be turned over to Germany, or he would make war on the Czechs.

The seminarians talked among themselves. No one wanted war. "But if there is a call-up," one said, "it would be a blessing for us in the Confessing Church. Then we should have a chance to prove we are as patriotic as the pastors of the state church."

There was general agreement. Dietrich, who had been seated near the window, crushed his cigarette in an ashtray and stood. The students fell silent and looked toward him. "Do you agree, Herr Professor?" one asked.

"No. I don't agree. It is not our patriotism we must prove, but our faith as Christians. If Germany's cause is not just, and I believe with all my heart it is not, then to serve in the army would be to crucify Christ once again."

Why must you always be in opposition? they asked. With due respect, Herr Professor. So wearying to be always in opposition. Can we not make a greater effort for the good if we are also good citizens?

"If you are traveling to Berlin," Dietrich said, "will you get there by boarding a train going in the opposite direction and walking backward?"

They stayed up until three in the morning, arguing by moonlight. Most of the students were firmly against their teacher's position. How could one's country, one's homeland, be left defenseless? How could anyone see brothers and fathers and friends march away to war and refuse to support them? A minority agreed with Pastor Bonhoeffer that it would be wrong to serve the Nazi state in wartime, but what could one do? To refuse would be punished by death.

What will you do? they pressed him.

"I don't know," he replied.

A few weeks later, the Confessing Church council, caught up in the wave of patriotism sweeping the nation, voted to begin closer cooperation with the state church and issued a statement thanking the government for its revitalization of German life. With Niemöller in Sachsenhausen and Bonhoeffer largely ignored, there was little objection. Soon after, an agent of the Gestapo in Stettin arrived in Finkenwalde. Dietrich and the students received the man in the dining room, offered him coffee and biscuits. He declined politely and said he would not take much of their time. It had come to the attention of the government that the Confessing Church was training pastors apart from the state church seminaries. Given the new state of affairs this would no longer be necessary. A fine thing for the Fatherland to have peace among church people, they would all agree. Therefore the Finkenwalde seminary was now closed.

It was somewhat of a relief, everyone agreed, to be thrown back out into the world, away from the hour of silence at the start of the seminary day, away from the dense lectures of Pastor Bonhoeffer, away from his high expectations. Though he was a lovely man. A man to make you stop and think, to challenge you. Indeed, a man you might count on in a real scrape. But a relief nonetheless to be shed of him.

Dietrich was the last to leave. As he walked along the gravel drive, suitcase in hand, a carload of Gestapo agents arrived and, ignoring him, entered the house.

At home in Berlin, he found his brother Karl-Friedrich had come up from Leipzig. After supper Paula Bonhoeffer said, "Father and I are very tired. We'll go to bed and leave you two boys to talk."

And Dietrich was left at the table across from Karl-Friedrich, who leaned back and took out his pipe.

"Shall we sit someplace more comfortable?" Dietrich asked.

"I'm fine here. What I have to say won't take long."

"What you have to say? You mean this visit was no coincidence? Am I to receive some brotherly lecture and then go to my room like a bad boy?" Dietrich said. "And whom do I have to thank, Mother or Father? Or you?"

"All of us, if that's your attitude. The fact is, Dietrich, we're rather worried about you. On several counts. I know Father and Hans have told you something about the current political situation and their involvement in it. I won't say much about that, since I've asked to be left out. But we thought it had been made clear that you must not draw attention to this family just now. Yet Father and Mother say you plan to go to the Confessing Church council to protest its recent actions and to ask for more outspoken opposition to the government's military buildup."

"And its treatment of Jews, which worsens every day."

"Whatever noble reason you may have, it would be best if you remain quiet. There is your own safety to consider. No one wants to see you in prison with Niemöller, and Mother especially is distraught at the prospect. But if that doesn't concern you, you might consider Sabine and Gerhard. They've been harassed by the Gestapo and may have to make a run for it at any time. If you bring notoriety to the family, it won't do them any good."

"Notoriety. Good God." Dietrich drummed his fingers on the table. "Hans asked me to stay in Pomerania with my students. Well, there are no more students in Pomerania. And perhaps no more Confessing Church unless the council is moved to reverse its actions. Is that worth a risk? You and Walter risked your lives in the Great War. Hans is risking his life now. May I not risk my life for my church?"

"But the sensitivity of the times—"

"I am not stupid, Karl-Friedrich. I know what the times are, and I have no intention of drawing any notice to Hans and what he is doing. But if the plan is to dispense with Hitler and bring in someone else to rule, do you or anyone else believe that will succeed if the church has gone over to the side of Satan in the meantime? Can you ask the German people to turn against the Nazis if even the church will not do so?"

"And the rest of the family? We have no feelings, no concerns?"

"No one is more concerned about Sabine than I am," Dietrich said angrily. "If the danger is so great, and it is, then it is time for Sabine and Gerhard to go. Much as I shall miss them, I will tell them so myself. As for Mother and Father, I am sorry they are worried. But if my parents want to spare me the fate that thousands of others are suffering every day, there is nothing I can say to them. We are no better than the others."

"And nothing will change your mind?"

"No. My mind is made up. But I'm curious. You said you have asked to be spared knowledge of the conspiracy. Why?"

"Some man of the family must stay clear of all this for the sake of Mother and our sisters and children," Karl-Friedrich said. "It seems clear that role has fallen to me."

"Then take that role by all means. But leave me another."

Karl-Friedrich watched him through a curtain of smoke. "You also refused more knowledge of the conspiracy," he said. "Hans told me. I ask you as well, why?"

Dietrich felt himself suddenly run to ground. He searched for words. "If they try to kill Hitler—"

"—you don't want your hands dirty? For the sake of your religious convictions, I suppose." Karl-Friedrich laughed. "You Christians. You'll make sure you don't endanger the salvation of your precious souls, but you don't mind if someone else does the dirty work for you. Give me an atheist any day." He stood up and stretched. "I'm going upstairs. Go out and rouse your church council if you want. But stay away from Hans."

He went, having heard the council would be meeting at the Kaiser-Wilhelm Memorial Church. Went knowing that those likely to be most sympathetic to his plea were either in concentration camps or under surveillance. Was met at the door of the meeting room by Pastor Braun, who said, "Bonhoeffer. We know why you are here, and we don't want to hear it. We're tired of you sowing dissension in this church."

And shut the door in Dietrich's face.

SS-Hauptsturmführer Alois Bauer longed to talk with his friend Adolf Eichmann, but Eichmann had been away since the Anschluss. He had a new job in Vienna organizing an Office of Jewish Emigration. Jews from all over Austria were forced to register and receive exit visas, so that the Reich's new territories might be rid of them once and for all. Eichmann was in contact with governments all over the world, even traveled himself to Palestine, in search of a place to ship the Austrian Jews. *It isn't so easy*, he had written Bauer, *as Britain and France and the United States don't want more Jews. Certainly the Russians and Poles and Ukrainians don't want more Jews.* He thought he might find some land in the interior of Argentina and ship

entire boatloads there, but nothing was firm yet. Still Jews were leaving
Austria in greater numbers than in Germany, and Adolf Eichmann was
becoming known in Berlin as a man who could get things done.

Bauer was happy for his friend. He had himself been sunk in a strange
ennui whose source baffled him. These were, after all, heady days, as the
Führer bluffed and threatened and cajoled and schemed and made bloody
fools out of Germany's enemies. It looked as though the British would fight
over Czechoslovakia. Bauer found the prospect rousing, but did not trust
the British to carry through. In any event, he had begun to suspect his problem was metaphysical and therefore not easily resolved. For him, despite his
commitment to National Socialism, something was missing. Then he discovered the Future.

When Eichmann finally visited Berlin, Bauer was a rejuvenated man.
They met in the dining room of the Adlon. Bauer was carrying a book
under his arm. He clapped Eichmann upon the back, pointed out that
other officers in the dining room were staring at them.

"You know what they are saying, my friend? They are saying, 'Isn't that
Eichmann up from Vienna? The chap we've heard so much about?'"

Eichmann waved a bashful hand and laughed, his face pink as a broiled
salmon.

"And how is your wife?" Bauer asked.

"Fine, fine. She went to Jerusalem with me, enjoyed it immensely. And
you? Anyone special these days?"

"Me? No. No time for that right now. No matter. There are some damn
fine whores in this town."

Then a pack of waiters descended. A pale Moselle was decanted and sil-
ver covers were lifted from platters of roast pork, and eels in green sauce.
Dumplings and stewed apples and sauerkraut arrived, and dark green
Brussels sprouts drenched in butter were ladled onto plates. The food was
so hot that steam rose to cloud the window looking out on Unter den
Linden, and traffic passed outside in a misty haze.

The talk over dinner was of the latest SS gossip and the Czech crisis.
Eichmann thought there would be war, Bauer disagreed. Later they retired
to the hotel bar. Only then did Bauer show Eichmann the book he'd
brought with him. Eichmann turned the book over several times and
frowned.

"*The Futurist Manifesto*," he said in a puzzled voice. "By some Italian."

"The Führer is very keen on Italy as an ally," Bauer said defensively.

"Yes, but what's this all about? Can't even pronounce the fellow's name."

"Marinetti. F. T. Marinetti. Don't worry, he's a good fascist. Mussolini
admires him immensely."

"But it's not *Mein Kampf*."

"Is *Mein Kampf* the only worthwhile book in the world?"

Eichmann shrugged good-naturedly. "I suppose not. But it's the only one I have to like."

Bauer took the book and began flipping through dog-eared pages thick with underlining until he found what he was looking for. "Listen to this. *We stand at the apex of time! We glorify war, which purifies the world. We will destroy the museums and libraries and places of dull study which sap the spirit of humanity. Today, we proclaim Futurism, so we may free our nation from the rot of professors and archaeologists and critics. We will free Italy from the number-less museums that cover her like so many graveyards.*" He shut the book with a clap. "Not just Italy! The Fatherland as well! When all else is done, it's what we will lack for perfection. Look here, Hitler has given us the political vision, the racial vision, even the artistic vision where content is concerned. But this is one step further. This is the spiritual vision."

Eichmann was staring at him with a bewildered expression. "It's all very interesting, I'm sure. But I don't see—"

"The museums!" Bauer leaned forward. "The museums and the universities. They're destroying the culture of the Fatherland. Even the Führer, wise as he is, hasn't grasped it yet. All this art tacked onto museum walls like the corpses of frogs in a dissecting room. Precious manuscripts locked away in vaults like—like—"

Eichmann waited, glass of whiskey in hand, nodding. "Like?" he encouraged.

Bauer ran his hand through his hair and glared at the ceiling, then looked at Eichmann. "We treat our great art worse than we treat our Jews. "Yes," he nodded his head emphatically, "that's it. Jews run here and yon across the Fatherland spreading like vermin and we lock up our great art." He picked up the book and laid it in his lap, comforted by the feel of the smooth cover against his thigh.

"So." Eichmann looked thoughtful. "I see some of what you are getting at."

"The Mozart manuscript," Bauer said softly. "The Mass in C Minor I saw in the Prussian State Library several years ago. So sad. Do you know what I've decided? I'm going back to look at it again. Often, so those damned curators will know I've got my eye on them. And someday, by God, I'll see the Mass out of that place. Art should live among the people. If it is worth anything, the *Volk* will see that it is preserved. Otherwise let it go down the sewer."

"You're sure the Mozart would survive if it were taken from its vaults?"

Bauer smiled. "There is nothing on this earth of which I am more certain. The German people would die for Mozart."

"Well, then." Eichmann raised his glass. "To Mozart. But Alois, not to worry about the Jews. That's why I've been called to Berlin this week. There's a change of plan."

Dietrich dreamed often of Sabine and she of him. They dreamed of losing their way in the Thuringian Forest, losing their way in the Harz Mountains, losing their way in Sabine's garden in Göttingen, wandering beneath the fruit trees calling out each other's name. They even dreamed of losing each other in the marshes of Pomerania, though Sabine had never been there. She knew the place somehow, or at least a dream version of it.

When Sabine and Gerhard sat in their parlor one September night, listening to the BBC, she knew it was not the Gestapo who disturbed them with a knock at the door. Even though Gerhard switched off the radio and looked frightened.

"No," she said. "It's Dietrich."

She opened the door without hesitation, and he brought the crisp autumn air inside with him. He kissed her on top of the head.

"I left the car several blocks away and walked here," he said. "I didn't want your neighbors to see a visitor this late." He shook hands with a relieved Gerhard and glanced at the darkened stairs. "The girls are in bed?"

"They go to bed at nine on school nights," Sabine said.

"Good." He took off his hat and jacket, hung them on the hall tree. "Make a pot of coffee, Sabine, there's lots to do."

They did not need to ask if it was time to leave, but over coffee and cake, when the initial packing was done, Dietrich explained why.

"Hans has just found out. In two days Himmler will announce all Jews are required to have a large J stamped on their passports. After that it will be much more difficult for Gerhard and the girls to leave."

"But they've been encouraging people to leave," Gerhard said.

"Yes. Something's changed. We don't know exactly what, but Hans believes it may be too late if you wait longer. I've sent a telegram to George Bell in England, a coded message, of course. He'll be expecting you, just as we've planned all along. I'll drive with you to Switzerland, and you can wait there until we know for sure. But we've got to leave tomorrow morning."

"So soon," Sabine said. "No time to say goodbye to anyone."

"No one must know you're leaving for anything except a short holiday."

"Of course." Gerhard took Sabine's hand. "None of this is a surprise. In a way, we've been saying goodbye for years."

"But I'll miss this house," she said. "And of course the family. Dietrich—"

"I'll visit you in England," he said. "I've got no wife or children to keep me from traveling, not even a position just now. I'm free as a bird to come

and go, at least unless there's a war. Who knows, if they push military conscription, I may be joining you."

They spent the rest of the night packing. The most difficult task was
choosing what to leave behind, for they could take no more than what
would seem normal for a holiday. One group of boxes, books and personal
mementos, was set aside to go with Dietrich back to Berlin.

"And Mitzi," Sabine said, bringing out a cage for the family cat. "Suse
promised to take her in if need be. The children will be heartbroken to part
with her. And can we even allow them to take their dolls?"

"One each," Gerhard suggested, "if they promise to be responsible for
them."

"And we must all wear several pairs of underclothes." Sabine planned as
she spoke. "And as many layers of clothes as we can bear."

By six they were ready. While Gerhard and Dietrich packed the family
car, Sabine went into her daughters' bedroom. Mitzi, the gray-striped tabby,
slept in the curve behind little Christine's knees. Marianne, the elder,
opened her eyes. "Is it time to get up for school?" she asked.

Sabine leaned over and kissed her. "Darling, you're not going to school
today. We've decided to go on a little holiday."

Marianne sat up. "Where?"

"We'll tell you later. Right now I must help you dress. Oh, and Marianne. Uncle Dietrich is here. Isn't that lovely?"

It was lovely, for Dietrich was the favorite uncle of all his nephews and
nieces. Because he had no children of his own, he spoiled them, forever
taking them to the zoo or the symphony, buying them books or bringing
them sweets hidden in his pockets. When the Leibholz family set out from
Göttingen on their outing to Switzerland, the girls rode with Uncle Die-
trich in the Bonhoeffer Mercedes, following close behind the Leibholz
Daimler. They sang and played games, and every time they crossed a bridge,
Dietrich gave them a gingersnap from a box sent by Grandmother Paula.
But when they grew tired of all this, and Christine had fallen asleep,
Marianne said, "We're not coming back, are we?"

Dietrich glanced at her. She was staring straight ahead as though afraid
to let her parents out of her sight. But he saw no tears.

"Someday," he said. "But not for a long time."

"Not until Hitler stops being mean to Jews?"

"Yes. But you mustn't say that aloud to anyone."

"You needn't tell me that," she said. "We've been to school, you know.
The others call us dirty Jews. And my teacher doesn't like me either. She
never calls on me in class. Mummy and Papa won't let us say anything
about Hitler at school, or about our family. So we don't talk at all."

He glanced at her again, heartbroken at the worldliness, the hardness, in the nine-year-old face.

"What will happen to Mitzi?" Marianne asked.

"I'll take Mitzi to Aunt Suse's house."

Marianne nodded her head. "Aunt Suse has a nice big garden, and she likes cats. But you must tell her that herring is Mitzi's absolute favorite thing. She gets a bite every night. And Mitzi's afraid of the telephone when it rings, so she should have someplace quiet to sleep where she needn't hear it. You tell Aunt Suse."

Dietrich put his hand on the girl's shoulder, and she turned to look at him.

"Aren't you coming with us, Uncle Dietrich?"

"Only as far as the border."

"What will you do with Mummy so far away?"

He said, "Oh, don't worry about us. Your mummy and I can talk to one another just by shutting our eyes."

"That would be magic," Marianne said suspiciously.

"It is. It's twin magic."

Ten miles from the border they pulled off the road near a grove of trees and a clear rushing stream, opened a hamper, and spread out a picnic of bread, cheese, and sausages. The children ate quickly and then began to tease each other.

"Girls, this stream will be going to the Rhine," Gerhard said to distract them. "So if you toss in a twig, it may reach Basel before we do."

"We're going across the Rhine," Marianne said.

"Yes," her father said. "Now, go. Find some twigs."

When the children were busy, Sabine said, "Dietrich, Gerhard and I have been talking. We don't think you should go to the border with us. If something goes wrong, we don't want you caught up in it. And even if everything is all right, there's no need for you to be seen traveling with us. It can't help anyone, and it may call needless attention."

"But how shall we know you've arrived safely?"

Gerhard said, "Go back to Göttingen and wait there. Assume the best. Once we're across the border, we'll either call you there or send a telegram."

"But—"

"If we're detained," Sabine said, "there'll be nothing you could do anyway. Hans will have to look into it."

They finished eating and walked slowly back to the cars.

"Mummy, Daddy!" Marianne cried. "I've an idea! If we want to send a message we won't have to telephone. You can call Uncle Dietrich with your twin magic."

"My what?"

"Twin magic, twin magic!" Marianne skipped to her parents' car, flung open the door, and plopped down on the backseat as though she'd already forgotten ever having lived in Göttingen.

Dietrich said, "I was telling her how we sometimes anticipate each other. Only I'm afraid I made it sound more spectacular than it is." He looked away, fighting back tears. Gerhard tactfully busied himself making the car ready and settling the girls in back while Sabine took Dietrich by the hand and led him away.

"We've seen little enough of each other," she said. "Your work has kept you so busy."

"This is different. You'll be out of the country."

"Yes, but it's not the country I'll miss. It no longer feels like my country. Or yours." She put her arms around him. "If things get worse, promise me you'll leave too."

"I promise. You'll like George and Hettie Bell. They'll be good to you. George shares our birthday, you know. Perhaps he's our triplet."

"Do you remember when we were children and we used to hang out our windows and talk to each other after everyone had gone to bed?"

"Of course I remember. Do you remember when we were lost in the snowstorm and slept in the peasant barn?"

They said nothing more and clung to each other. Then Gerhard, as from a great distance, said, "We'd best be going, dear. It's nearly four o'clock."

Gerhard embraced Dietrich, helped Sabine into the car. Then he got in the car and started the motor, and they left Dietrich standing desolate beside the road.

He arrived back at the Göttingen house around midnight and spent what was left of the night with Mitzi the cat sprawled on his chest. Sometime after daylight the bedside telephone rang and the cat was away like a shot. Dietrich fumbled with the receiver, nearly dropping it, then holding it upside down before he finally woke enough to right it and recognize Gerhard's voice saying, "Dietrich? We're having a lovely time in Basel. A beautiful city. We're staying at the Hotel Drei-Könige-am-Rhein and we've an incredible view of the river from our room. Yes, everyone's fine. We'll be waiting to hear what the weather is like before we proceed with our trip."

The weather was stormy. Next day the government announced the stamping of Jewish passports with the J, and the restriction of travel for Jews. Passports of Jews without a J would no longer be valid. Dietrich sent a telegram to G. Leibholz care of the Hotel Drei-Könige-am-Rhein in Basel, Switzerland: YOUR RETURN NOW UNSUITABLE STOP GO TO GEORGE STOP GODSPEED STOP

Kristallnacht

DIETRICH MADE THE LONG LONELY DRIVE back to Berlin with the personal effects of the Leibholz family in five boxes and the cat, Mitzi, in a wire cage. As though Sabine and her family had died and he must dispose of their goods.

He counted his other losses. The Confessing Church swallowed up by the state church, the will to fight weaker than the longing for acceptance. He tried to imagine what it must be like for Niemöller in Sachsenhausen. Had he any idea what was happening without him?

Elisabeth. Was she well? Had the new restrictions convinced her she should join her father in England? Had she been able to leave?

Why didn't the Gestapo agents who came to Finkenwalde take him away with them? Not that he wanted that. It was in fact his greatest nightmare, for he knew all too well how he loved creature comforts—a glass of wine and a thick cut of meat, a warm fire, a firm bed with clean sheets. He recalled sitting with Niemöller late at night and hearing the story of a young pastor who had just emerged from a year in Dachau after preaching an anti-Nazi sermon. Dietrich had forced the man to describe everything in great detail—the drafty huts with a single stove to keep out the winter cold, the moldering bread and thin fetid soup, the slop buckets, the sounds of beatings, screams of pain, and now and then a gunshot.

Dietrich took to his room in the Marienburger Allee in such a deep depression that he could not get up in the mornings. At night he swallowed pills to sleep. He told his worried mother that he was nursing a strained muscle in his back.

News reports of the deepening crisis over the Sudetenland drew him downstairs sometimes. Each evening the family ate a quick supper and then gathered around the radio. They listened to the BBC, for unlike most of their countrymen they did not trust the German state radio, the RRG. Christel brought her children to visit, because her husband was often working at his new office in the War Ministry. Dohnanyi arrived as late as ten or eleven, worn out and worried. Then the radio was switched off and he shared his own news. He told them the Nazis were fabricating the stories of atrocities by Czechs against ethnic Germans in the Sudetenland. (These atrocity stories were being repeated indignantly in shops and on the street by Berliners who were stunned, *stunned*, that the Czechs could bear Germans such ill will.) He told them German troops were massed at the Czech border, ready to move at a word from Hitler. Propaganda Minister Goebbels had taken surreptitious soundings of the mood of the German people. Despite the atrocity stories, the people seemed to be against a war. It was not that anyone feared the Czechs or thought it wrong to intimidate them. No one wanted to fight the British.

Dohnanyi said nothing to the family about the plot. But when Dietrich took him aside one night and asked, he said, "We have a man in London right now, trying to get to Chamberlain. That's all I'm at liberty to tell you."

SS-Hauptsturmführer Alois Bauer was visiting the Prussian State Library. He wanted to see the manuscript of Mozart's Mass in C Minor and was ready to threaten and swagger as on his first visit, but with the added bravado of a Futurist. On he went, past the iron gates, past the nightmare of a fountain with its greenscum water, across the chipped tile floors yellowed with age. To the same scrawny curator with pocked skin.

But something was different. The curator, pitiful specimen of Aryan manhood though he was, no longer cowered at the sight of the black SS uniform. Because this time Alois Bauer was not an unexpected visitor from a new and unpredictable conquering army. The new order had long been firmly established and the curator himself had found a place in it. He had his own orders and they came from someone higher than a middling officer in the SS.

"The Mozart manuscript," he said unctuously, "the manuscript of the Mass in C Minor," speaking even more slowly, "which you request," preening a bit, brushing back a stray lock of hair with one finger, "is no longer available for your perusal."

"And why not?" Bauer demanded.

"Because, my dear Hauptsturmführer, like our other great treasures—" Bauer's stomach turned at the smugly possessive *our*—"it has been packed for transportation to a safe place far from Berlin. In view of the growing international crisis. We would not want Germany's cultural heritage to fall into enemy hands—" he realized his mistake and quickly corrected himself—"not that any enemy could ever set foot in the Fatherland. But there is the destructive nature of modern warfare to consider. I'm sure the Hauptsturmführer will agree totally with the judgment of the Führer in this matter." Strong emphasis on Führer, followed by a triumphant smile.

"Where has it been sent?" Bauer managed to ask.

The curator spread his hands. "I am not at liberty to disclose that information."

Bauer was so distraught he could say nothing else. He rescued himself with a sudden straight-armed salute and a quick exit.

Dietrich was alone in his room when Suse came upstairs. She sat on the edge of his bed, where he was propped on a pillow and reading by the light of a small metal lamp. She touched the book.

"Shakespeare?" she said.

"*Macbeth.*"

"Why don't you come downstairs? Christel and the children are here and we haven't seen you for days."

He said, "One of my strange moods. I've been reading the scene of Lady Macbeth's madness. *Out, damned spot! Hell is murky. Yet who would have thought the old man to have so much blood in him.*"

"You've missed the horrible news. It's just come over the radio. Chamberlain has caved in to Hitler's demands for the Sudetenland. Our troops are already crossing the Czech border. Papa says Hitler won't stop. It's just a matter of time before he controls Prague as well."

Dietrich closed the book and stared at the ceiling.

"Everyone is desolate downstairs. Won't you come console us?"

"Me? What can I do?"

"Simply be with us. We miss you when you go off by yourself like this. Besides, you are our pastor."

Dietrich laughed bitterly. Then he asked, "Is Hans with you?"

"Hans is in his office. Christel says he's been there for two days and nights, and she doesn't know when to expect him."

"So I am not the only anchorite in the family."

"No one is forcing you to stay up here."

"No." He grabbed her hand and held it. "I love you, Suse."

She kissed him on the forehead. "I love you too, silly goose. Now come downstairs. We're going to console ourselves with some *Apfelkuchen* fresh from the oven. Mother says we must enjoy what we can of life, no matter how gloomy the news."

Hans von Dohnanyi made an appearance two days later. He was thin, and his cheeks were pale with the fresh-scraped look of someone who's only just shaved after several days of stubble. But he was neatly dressed in cotton sweater and trousers. He went straight to Dietrich's room.

"Come on," he said. "I need to be outdoors. Let's go out in the boat."

Hans and Christel kept a sailboat at a dock below their Sacrow house. They liked to wander along the Havel and its connecting lakes, ranging from Potsdam to the Wannsee to the Tegelersee. Dietrich was not comfortable with boats. As a boy he had fallen into the Landwehrkanal while climbing out of a punt, to the great amusement of Karl-Friedrich and his friends, who were watching him from the dock. But he enjoyed going out with Hans and Christel as long as he need only sit back enjoying the water and fresh air without worrying about being knocked overboard. He settled onto a pile of cushions in the bow while Dohnanyi trimmed the mainsail and then sat hunched at the tiller.

The sloop, propelled by a brisk October wind, sizzed across the Havel toward the Wannsee. The day was a chameleon of colors and moods. Sky and water merged in a flat gray, and the tips of cedars on Pfauen Island seemed to float on a layer of creamy white fog. But after half an hour the mist had burned away to reveal the onion dome of SS. Peter and Paul on the far shore. Banks of clouds moved like herd animals across skeins of pale skylight. The Wannsee, now mauve now azure now Prussian, churned as though the water were the skin of some leviathan flexing its muscles.

Dohnanyi lowered the mainsail and they drifted, waves slapping the boat gently. Dietrich lit a cigarette and handed it on.

Hans said, "Can't anything be done about your depressions?"

Dietrich was startled. He had expected a conversation about the political situation. He held the cigarette in one hand and covered his eyes with the other to keep out the sun. "Father says no. He doesn't believe in Freudian therapy. Someday there'll be a cure, he says; some kind of medication perhaps. In the meantime I endure my melancholies. Only—"

"Only what?"

"Only I don't see how any medicine could cure spiritual sickness."

"And is that what you're suffering? Spiritual sickness?"

"It's what we are all suffering. We display different symptoms, that's all."

A blue heron glided toward the stern rail, sensed it was not alone, and flapped off. The men were silent for a time, each lost in his own thoughts.

"Why do you ask?" Dietrich said suddenly.

"Hm?" Hans stirred. "Oh, about the depression? Because I've been mulling over your dilemma in my mind, and trying to find a solution."

"My dilemma?"

"Very simple. War is coming. Nothing can stop it now. Hitler has acquired a taste of blood, like a young shark."

"Who will be next?"

"The men in the know at the Abwehr say Poland. Very popular in Germany to beat up on Poles, and even better, their army is no match for ours. But if Hitler keeps going, someone will fight him. Stalin perhaps, or the British sooner or later, the goddamn fools."

Dietrich wanted to ask about the British, but first reminded Hans, "And my dilemma?"

"There'll be universal conscription. Soon. You've three choices, brother-in-law. Serve in the army. Follow Sabine out of the country. Or be arrested and likely shot."

"And the latter option would not only be most unhealthy for me, but for your plotting friends as well. Not that they're doing anything, are they?"

Hans didn't rise to the bait. "I've had an idea. But I don't know how you would respond. I could find you a position with me in the Abwehr. As a way of fulfilling your military service."

Dietrich sat up. "Me? In military intelligence? My God, I'm no spy. Nor a soldier. I can't even handle a weapon. Not that I want to."

"And then there are your depressions," Hans continued in an even voice, "which don't at first glance seem to indicate mental toughness. Except I fancy myself a good judge of character. Unlike your father, who thinks you naive and lacking in common sense, I have a great deal of respect for both your judgment and your courage. You could be quite useful to us."

"Useful to Hitler's war effort?"

"You know that's not what I'm about," Hans said.

"What are you about?"

Dohnanyi rummaged around in a cabinet beneath the tiller, found a flask of brandy, and handed it to Dietrich, who unscrewed the cap and took a swallow.

"Oster has been in London," Dohnanyi said. "Ostensibly to brief the German vice-consul, who is one of us. In fact, they were trying to get to Chamberlain. The stupid bastard wouldn't meet with Oster. But we did get to Churchill and Vansittart in the House of Commons. Those are the hard-liners in the Conservative Party. Oster convinced them of the seriousness of the plot, and in turn they begged Chamberlain to hold fast, to stand up to Hitler and threaten war if he went after the Czechs." Dohnanyi took the flask of brandy from Dietrich, his voice rising as though he were hearing the story for the first time himself. "Do you know what Chamberlain's people said? They told Churchill and Vansittart they couldn't believe that German diplomats and officers would actually undermine their own government. Said if the plot was genuine, we were a bunch of traitors and not to be trusted. And that was that. The goddamn fools."

Dietrich shook his head. "I know the type. Honorable English gentlemen. As bad as honorable Prussian gentlemen. So what has happened?"

"The plot is off, of course. My God, we had generals ready to call out their regiments, generals ready to arrest Hitler and Goering and Goebbels and Himmler. All waiting on the word from Chamberlain. And now all for naught."

"Why? It's not too late to stop Hitler without the British."

"It is for the generals. They're scared to death of public reaction. It's one thing for them to arrest Hitler and claim they have saved Germany from a devastating war. Quite another thing to try to put the man in prison when everyone in Germany is exulting over the return of the Sudetenland and draping our soldiers with garlands of flowers and prostrating themselves at his feet. If Hitler were jailed now he would be freed in short order by a popular outcry and we would all be executed. Anyone who tried to kill him, even if he succeeded, would go down in German history as the worst sort of villain."

"Well," Dietrich said. "Perhaps someone must risk that."

Dohnanyi gave a short, bitter laugh. "Yes, well, you can imagine the generals are standing in line ready to play *that* part."

"And you?"

Dohnanyi stared at Dietrich. "And you?" he echoed.

Dietrich was the first to look away.

"Well then." Hans stood and stretched, then raised the mainsail. At the tiller he turned and said, "Sabine was the first to go, and you must be next. There is no shame in that, just a plain statement of fact."

They faced into the wind, and Dietrich squeezed his eyes shut, his cheeks wet with spray and tears.

"It is true I must go," he said. "But before I do, there is one more who must be got out."

The storefront in the Oranienburger Straße had been boarded with plywood and daubed with anti-Jewish graffiti. Dietrich peered through a crack and glimpsed the interior, dusty and bare save for a litter of paper and a single broken chair.

Next he rode the streetcar to Weißensee, found Elisabeth's house, and climbed the stairs to the second floor. No one answered his knock. Then he noticed a new nameplate pasted onto the oak door. *B. Zinn.*

He stood a moment, gripping the wood rail of the stair, fighting down a wave of fear. Then he knocked on a doorway across the landing. A small gray-haired woman answered.

"Pardon me," he said. "I'm looking for the young lady who used to live across from you. I—I used to know her, and as I was in the neighborhood I thought I'd say hello."

"Well," the woman said in a thin voice that could have quavered from either age or fear. "She doesn't live here any longer."

"Do you know where she's gone?"

"No, she didn't tell anyone. She left in a great hurry. You see—" The woman plucked at his sleeve, drew him closer, and lowered her voice. "I believe she had to leave because she was mixed up in something she shouldn't have been. She was a Jewess, you know."

"I see," Dietrich said. He felt ill. "Can you tell me how long she's been gone?"

"Not long. A month, perhaps. A man came and helped her pack. A Jew himself, by the look of him. That's all I know, and more than I should say." She shut her door.

Through Dohnanyi's office, Dietrich learned that no one by the name of Elisabeth Hildebrandt had been allowed to emigrate. Then came Kristallnacht, the Night of Broken Glass, when the windows of Jewish homes and stores across Germany were smashed, and Jews were dragged into the streets and shot and beaten. Thousands of Jewish men were arrested and sent to concentration camps.

Dietrich made one more attempt to find Elisabeth, inquiring among Jews he encountered on the street, but they were too frightened to talk to him. He wandered the Oranienburger Straße, past the ruins of the great synagogue which had burned on Kristallnacht, past street sweepers pushing shards of glass with their brooms, past more storefronts covered with plywood. He went every day for several weeks, but caught no sight of her.

Elisabeth had vanished into the Scheunenviertel.

...Jesu Christe
Cum Sancto Spiritu
in gloria Dei Patris.
Amen.

...*Jesus Christ*
With the Holy Spirit,
in the glory of God the Father.
Amen

(Double fugue)

New York
Summer 1939

THE HEAT AND HUMIDITY of Manhattan were already unbearable, though it was only the middle of June. New Yorkers seemed not to notice. Street venders tended their hot dog carts with shirtsleeves rolled to their armpits. Negroes with fluttering shirttails hawked newspapers on Broadway and long-legged girls lounged on Central Park benches in cotton dresses, eating ice creams.

But a German used to Berlin's mild summers who felt naked if not properly dressed and would not dream of wandering the streets of the world's largest city with jacket and tie off and shirtsleeves rolled like a navvy . . .

In his own room, it was another matter. At first Dietrich tried to remain fully clothed, afraid someone would knock and find him undressed. But he finally gave in, after letting it be known that he preferred not to be disturbed in the afternoons. His writing time, he said. And after the noon meal he would take a cold shower, then bolt the door and lounge in his undershorts. At first he felt foolish, but soon he could hardly wait for the meal to be done so he could slip away.

Dietrich Bonhoeffer was living in the Prophets' Chamber. In his own case the name was a bitter joke, he thought. Better to call it the Cowards' Chamber. A large corner room on the second floor of Union Theological Seminary, it was reserved for the use of distinguished visiting lecturers. Thus the name, bestowed by students. A huge room, more chapel than bedchamber, with a twenty-foot-high ceiling and a bank of five Gothic windows at each end, one set facing inward to courtyard, chapel, and cloisters, the other overlooking the intersection of Broadway and 121st Street.

He had planned to begin a new volume of theological ethics, but he was not writing. He was not even preparing the lectures he was scheduled to deliver at Union's late-summer term. He paced the length of the room into the night, filling up ashtrays, stopping now and then to jot random notes on loose sheets of paper. Lay sleepless on his bed. Read the notes he'd written the night before, crumpled the scraps of paper and tossed them in the wastebasket. Tried to pray and instead found himself facing the void.

His old professor Reinhold Niebuhr had been waiting on the dock when he stepped off the boat. Niebuhr embraced Dietrich, then stood back and looked his former student up and down. "Safe then," he said with obvious satisfaction.

"Yes," Dietrich agreed, and tried to smile. "Thanks to your very hard work."

Niebuhr waved him off. "Baloney! Couldn't let Adolf get his hands on you, could we?"

He relived the scene over and over. Strange to have felt no joy. Not even gratitude. He was certainly an ingrate, as he feared Niebuhr had come to view him. Though there were no accusations. Only a questioning look now and again.

"I seem to recall," Niebuhr said once, when Dietrich sat in the refectory absentmindedly picking at a plate of meat loaf and mashed potatoes, "that you aren't too fond of American cooking."

"Oh, you mustn't think that," Dietrich said, and blushed with embarrassment. "I am not particular about food. I am most grateful for it. It is the heat, that is all. It puts me off my appetite. Anyway, it wouldn't hurt me to lose a few pounds." He rambled on about nothing in particular while Niebuhr watched him again with the quizzical look but said nothing.

He had been fortunate to get out of Germany. Travel outside the Reich was more and more difficult, and his own passport was due to expire in a few months. There would be no possibility of renewing it when it did. Nor was it easy to gain entry into the United States. People were turned away every day (he thought guiltily of Jews trying to get to New York). His family had relied on all their contacts, and Niebuhr worked hard on his end to convince the Americans that Dietrich would find gainful employment when he arrived, that he was a specialist in his field whose scholarly work would reflect well on his new country. At last the visa had come through, just as he had received notice he was being conscripted into the German army. Hans von Dohnanyi had dealt with that, gaining an extension so that Dietrich might go abroad indefinitely to enhance Germany's academic reputation. And if he was stranded in America after the start of the war which Dohnanyi expected to come within the next few months, well, what could be done about that?

On board the *Bremen*, Dietrich tried to read, stretched on a deck chair wearing a white skullcap to protect his balding scalp from sunburn. One of the crewmen had slowed down as he walked past and muttered, "Getting out, Jew scum? Taking the Reich's money with you, I'll bet." Dietrich had started to protest, but the man had moved on.

He kept a letter from Sabine on top of his desk, and read it over and over.

So glad you are safely out of Germany, she wrote. *My greatest fear has been the thought of what would befall you if the situation at home worsens. I know how you feel about fighting for Hitler, and what the consequences of refusal would be. There is no sense in your being caught up in something you have no hope of successfully opposing. Now I can sleep well at night. Please express my gratitude to Professor Dr. Niebuhr. Your loving twin, Sabine.*

He read the note, then switched off his desk lamp and stood at the windows overlooking Broadway and facing the rise of 121st Street, a tunnel between buildings disappearing over the hill. It was three in the morning, and fog drifted in from the Hudson so that the melting gold of the streetlamps had begun to smudge the black night.

Seated in the cubbyhole of an office which held the seminary telephone, Dietrich managed to reach the exchange in Charleston, West Virginia. But an operator told him there was no telephone listed in the name of a Fred Bishop. He hung up and sat thinking a moment. It was no surprise if after eight years Fred had moved on. Perhaps he had gone home to Alabama after all to serve at his father's church, or had landed the longed-for teaching position at Morehouse. But in that case wouldn't someone at Union Seminary have heard?

He tried the Charleston exchange once more and asked for the First Baptist Church. On the fourth ring a deep voice answered, "First Baptist, Reverend Johns speaking."

Dietrich hesitated, then said, "Pardon me, but I am Pastor Dietrich Bonhoeffer from Berlin, Germany. I am calling from the Union Theological Seminary in New York City. I was a friend of a pastor at the First Baptist Church named Fred Bishop. We were students together here in New York. Is it possible you would know how I might get in touch with him?"

It was the turn of the man on the other end to hesitate. Then he said, "Pastor Bonhoeffer? My name is Vernon Johns. There was a Fred Bishop at this church, yes. I took his place just before Christmas of 1931."

"But that was only—" Dietrich stopped, trying to calculate the time.

"Reverend Bishop only served here a few months," said Vernon Johns. "You say you were friends? Close friends?"

"I visited him in West Virginia when he first arrived there," Dietrich said, suddenly dreading to continue the conversation. "Then I returned to Germany and have heard no more of him these past eight years."

"I see. I'll tell you what I know. But there's also much I don't know. Reverend Bishop was fired, sorry to say. There were rumors in the church that he was drinking, and then he spent one Saturday night in the bar of a local hotel. The next morning he showed up drunk in the pulpit. Very drunk, I'm told, although of course I wasn't here."

"My God," Dietrich said.

"Yes. You know how Baptists are about drinking. He'd been pastor a little over three months and he was let go soon after. The elders started the search for a new minister and I was called in early December."

"You don't know where he went?"

The phone line crackled and the voice of Vernon Johns faded, then returned: "—what's so strange. Nobody knows for sure where he went. The only story anyone heard comes from a fellow name of Earl Harvey. White people here in town call him Lightning because he can do all these fancy mathematical equations. But the poor fellow is touched in the head, you might say."

"Yes," Dietrich said. "I met Earl Harvey when I visited Charleston."

"You did? Then you know he's not what you might call a reliable witness. But if there's any truth to Earl's version of events, I hate to say it, but Reverend Bishop is probably dead."

Dietrich sat slumped on a swivel chair, legs crossed and head bowed and telephone receiver pressed hard against his ear.

"With Earl," Vernon Johns was saying, "you have to listen hard and then read between the lines. But since I've known him, he's never changed his story where Fred Bishop is concerned. And he claims Reverend Bishop didn't tell anyone else where he was going, that he was going to tell a local doctor but the doctor had just died of a heart attack. Reverend Bishop told Earl that First Baptist was no longer his church, that he had a new church. Earl says a tunnel they dug a few years back up at Hawks Nest was Reverend Bishop's new church and that he went to preach to what Earl calls the skeletons there. He says Reverend Bishop went to be with the skeletons, that he went into the tunnel with the skeletons and never came out. That's what Earl says. And if you act like you don't believe it, he'll say, 'That Reverend Bishop he never was no preaching acting thing.'"

PRAYING PACING DRINKING SMOKING SWALLOWING SLEEPING PILLS PASSING OUT then again and again.

One day Dietrich can no longer stand the Prophets' Chamber and goes out into the heat of Manhattan.

He does not wear coat or tie and his shirtsleeves are rolled to his armpits.

He sits on a bus bound for Harlem hot as an oven and mops the sweat from his face with a grimy handkerchief.

At 138th Street he steps off and wanders for blocks, past a storefront church hidden behind an iron grille, past a Jamaican restaurant that smells of coriander and ginger and nutmeg. Studies the window of a shoe repair shop for a quarter of an hour as though it held the answer to the mystery of life.

He slips into a dimly lit bar and orders a beer. The only white man present. No one speaks to him. He drinks the watery beer and listens dreamily to the click of pool balls in the next room. Back out into blinding afternoon light. He thinks he would like to find the Savoy ballroom, would just like to look at it, but he has forgotten the address.

He strays along St. Nicholas for a time, no longer sure if he is walking north south east or west. Then he sees the man. He is nearly a block away, across the street. His back is to Dietrich. He is tall, wears a gray suit and hat. From behind, he looks like Fred Bishop. He pauses to buy a newspaper, glances at the headline, then folds the paper beneath his arm and walks away. Dietrich tries to follow, keeps the man in sight for several blocks. But it is hot and Dietrich feels very tired. The man walks quickly, turns along 145th Street, and by the time Dietrich is there, the man is gone.

He rides a bus across town to Yorkville. Enters the 86th Street Garden cinema. A German comedy is showing. *Das Ekel*—"The Jerk," according to the English translation on the marquee. Nothing safer than comedy. He sinks into his seat, sipping an iced Coke, and gives in to his homesickness. The film is mindless and he doesn't laugh once, but he sits through it because he could be in Berlin. In more ways than one. For newsreels follow, with reports on the growing tension between the Reich and Poland. Goose-stepping German soldiers pass before Hitler in review, and the audience cheers. When a Pole appears on the screen, people in the audience cry, "Kill them! Kill them all!"

Dietrich flees the theater and emerges into white-hot sunlight.

The American newspapers carry stories of lynchings in the South. Of government troops firing upon striking workers. Advertisements for jobs, for resort hotels, with the blatant stipulation "No Jews." Writes in his diary. *In this country the conflict bubbles beneath the surface. Someday it will break out as it has at home. Woe to those who are alien here. It is not a place to seek to avoid one's destiny.*

He skips supper in the seminary refectory and retreats to the Prophets' Chamber with two bottles of wine. He is determined to drink as much as

Fred did when he was banned from the pulpit of First Baptist Church. He does, and the floor spins and he sprawls facedown on his bed. But there is no one to expel him from his new safe haven and force him back to Germany. The ribbed oak walls of the Prophets' Chamber close in on him like the bars of a prison cell.

Fred is beside him.

You got yourself fired on purpose, didn't you? Dietrich says. So you'd have the courage to go in.

Fred is transparent, seems to waver and fade, returns for a second, then disappears. Without saying a word.

Perhaps Dietrich has dreamed all this. When he wakes, head throbbing and stomach sour, a breeze is blowing across the room from the open windows. It is morning, humid, but with a tangy promise of rain. The sun has burned away the early mist on Broadway, but 121st Street, facing east toward the sea, toward the Fatherland, remains a tunnel of white fog. Dietrich leans against the casement. A voice inside his head says, *Go on in go on in. You should see inside. Walls blasted out of rock, ribbed walls. Like arches in a church. White dust flying like cut glass. First breath is the hardest. First breath burns. But after that it isn't so hard.*

Dietrich whirls around to grab his tempter and flails the air

THE PRESIDENT OF UNION SEMINARY, Dr. Coffin, owned a house on the water at Lakeville, Connecticut. On a weekend when the Coffins were away, Reinhold Niebuhr drove Dietrich there, "to escape this damned city heat," he'd said, but he sensed his German friend was at the end of some sort of tether. So haunted and exhausted did Bonhoeffer look, in fact, that Niebuhr feared a nervous breakdown might be imminent.

They passed the journey in near silence. Dietrich stared moodily out the window yet barely noticed the scenery. Close to their destination the road narrowed and followed the shore of Lake Wononskopomuc. Patches of water glinted between stands of birch and fir trees. Here and there the peaked roof or gabled porch of a lakeside home could be seen. Then they skirted the wrought-iron fence of a small hotel. Niebuhr slowed the car and pointed out a sign posted on the gate that read

**No Dogs
or Jews allowed**

"Land of the free and home of the brave," Niebuhr said.

Dietrich didn't respond except to look even more glum. He continued his silence at dinner, a splendid meal of fried lake perch and new potatoes, string beans, corn on the cob, and tomatoes from the backyard garden, all prepared and served by the Coffins' Negro servant. After dinner they retired to a pair of rocking chairs on the veranda. The sun had set behind the black ridge of mountains and the lake was a pool of spilt ink.

"Two weeks until the beginning of your summer lecture series," Niebuhr said casually, as though nothing was wrong. "Will you be ready?" When there was no answer, he lost patience. "Damn it, Dietrich. What's going on?"

Dietrich didn't stir, but he said, "You must find someone else to give the lecture series. I'm going back to Germany."

Niebuhr stopped rocking. He had expected some sort of physical illness or family problem, even homesickness, but certainly not this. "What the hell are you talking about, going back! You can't go back! War could break out at any time."

Dietrich shut his eyes and thought of the telegrams that had flown back and forth between himself and Dohnanyi the last few days.

IS UNCLE RUDI COMING SOON STOP DIETRICH

UNCLE RUDI COMING VERY SOON STOP DEFINITE STOP HANS

DOES PREVIOUS OFFER STAND STOP DIETRICH

PREVIOUS OFFER STANDS STOP HANS

CONFIRM POSITION STOP DIETRICH

COMFIRM STOP HANS

RETURN NEXT BOAT STOP DIETRICH

"I have to get back to Germany before the war starts," Dietrich said.

"But you're safe now!"

"Yes. But Germany is my home. I live there, not here. And I love my country."

Niebuhr stood and began to pace. "Let me get this straight. You're going back to Germany even though you'll be conscripted into the army. Even though you've claimed to be a pacifist and even though you've declared a Christian can't serve a fascist regime. Do you really think you could refuse to serve and survive?"

"I've changed my mind," Dietrich said. "I'm joining the army."

Niebuhr stopped pacing and stared at him.

"My brother-in-law is arranging it," Dietrich said. "I can't say anything more."

"You've said quite enough," Niebuhr said. "My God."

The tone of Niebuhr's voice, rather than his words, stung Dietrich. "You must trust me," he said.

Niebuhr shook his head. "I remember when you first came here in 1930. Then you were Bonhoeffer the patriot, fretting over the Fatherland's defeat in the Great War. Quick to take offense at any slight to Germany. I suppose George Bell filled your head for a time with those notions of Gandhi and peace and the brotherhood of man and so forth, but push come to shove you haven't changed, have you?"

"How dare you judge me so? You don't know what it's like at home!"

"Spare me." Niebuhr looked at his watch. "Nine-thirty. I think I'll turn in, and I'd suggest we head back in the morning. If you don't mind, I'd rather not listen to this drivel all weekend."

Niebuhr went inside, slamming the screen door behind him, and climbed the stairs to his room, where he began to stuff his scattered clothes back into a small suitcase. Dietrich clattered up the stairs behind him and leaned against the doorframe. "After such work to bring me to the United States, are you so quick to dismiss our friendship?"

Niebuhr laughed. "After such hard work—and damn straight it was hard work to get you into this country, no telling what poor fellow got left out because you're here—you're going back to join the goddamn Nazi army. Why should our friendship mean anything? After all, I'm an American and you're a German."

"I was wrong," Dietrich said. He felt short of breath. "I was wrong to come here. A mistake. Please understand."

Niebuhr folded his arms and waited.

"I've known it was wrong all along. On my first morning in New York I began my daily devotions from a prayer book I brought from home. The scripture that day was Isaiah 28:16. *He who believes does not flee.*"

"When I was a kid," Niebuhr said, "I tried to make an important deci-sion by opening the Bible at random and pointing with my eyes shut. My inspirational verse said, *Amon was twenty-two years old when he began to reign.* Second Kings."

Dietrich sat wearily on the edge of Niebuhr's bed, took off his glasses, and wiped them on his sleeve.

"What do you suppose life in Germany has been like these past few years?" he asked.

Niebuhr waited.

"What do you think it will be like when war comes?" Dietrich asked.

"A hell of Germany's own making," Niebuhr replied.

Dietrich nodded. "I don't dispute that. But my family is there, and our neighbors and friends. The people I have known all my life. In Germany."

"Or in Germany's concentration camps."

"Yes. Of course that. All the more reason. And beyond people, there is the land itself, the mountains and rivers and farms. The cities. All facing a devastating war. I'm sorry, Reinie. I must live through whatever my coun-try lives through. Someday this nightmare of ours will end, and Germany will be made new. But I shall have no right to take part in that new day unless I face the trials of this time."

"Serving in the army," Niebuhr said.

"Yes. It's the only way I can go back without being killed at once. But I won't be your enemy or the enemy of any nation. You must trust me."

"The situation is past compromise, you must know that. You are taking sides. How should I trust you when you wear Hitler's uniform?"

"By what you know of me. And by what I am about to say. I'm facing a terrible choice. When I return, I can work for the triumph of Germany and thus the destruction of civilization. Or I can work for the defeat of Germany in hopes of saving civilization. I promise you. I shall be working for the defeat of Germany."

"That would be treason," Niebuhr said.

"I can't tell you more and you mustn't ask."

"You can work for the defeat of Germany here, in the United States. In safety."

"In safety," Dietrich echoed. "I can't make such a choice in a safe place. It would be too easy, and it would not be Christian."

Niebuhr shook his head, started to speak, then turned away. Dietrich stood still, head down and hands in his pocket.

"My God," Niebuhr said. "You're so damned arrogant. You think you're going to save civilization by some wild heroic act, don't you?"

Dietrich smiled and shook his head for answer.

Niebuhr sighed. "Sonofabitch," he said.

On July 7, Dietrich Bonhoeffer took ship for England aboard the *Bremen*. He stood at the rail as the ship moved past the Statue of Liberty and out of New York Harbor, felt wistful, nostalgic even, as the city skyline slipped off the edge of the horizon. Goodbye to Reinie. Goodbye to the ghost of Fred Bishop.

Five days later, George Bell met him on the dock at Southampton. They embraced, and Bell said, "Sabine is waiting for you in Chichester. Gerhard has a temporary job in London and couldn't get away. I have to warn you, your sister is worried and upset with you, and so am I. We're all of us determined to talk you out of returning to Germany."

"You must allow me get back my land legs," Dietrich protested as they walked to the boat train along a platform that seemed to pitch and roll. "Then we'll talk."

He found Chichester little changed from five years earlier. The same modest market town. The same cathedral precinct, ancient stone surrounded by the darkgreen of late summer. Hettie Bell in a floppy straw hat, rising from her knees in a bed of roses and removing her dirt-stained gloves before taking Dietrich's hand and offering her cheek to be kissed. What was new was to follow the Bells into the bishop's palace and find Sabine in the morning room. When she saw Dietrich she gave a little cry and ran to him. George and Hettie slipped out while the twins embraced and closed the door quietly behind them.

Sabine wept against Dietrich's chest, while he shushed her and brushed the hair from her damp forehead as though she were a small child. When she had regained her composure she said fiercely, "I shall give Hans a piece of my mind when I see him again!"

"You mustn't blame Hans. This is my decision and mine alone."

"It's homesickness. That's all it is. Stay with us in England a few weeks and it will pass. You'll see. I miss the family and Germany as well, but it's not unbearable. Stay with us. You don't have to go back to America. You can find something to do here. George will help you."

He shook his head. "I can't stay, Sabine. I know that would be easiest for us all, but I could never live with myself."

"You don't think less of me for being here."

"No, of course not. But you have a husband and children. God has given me something else."

Sabine pulled away from him. "You can't believe God wants you to die."

"I don't expect to die anytime soon," he said. "But if that is what happens, then so be it. Death is inevitable, after all."

She put her hand to her mouth. "I recall when we were children," she said. "At night in bed you were certain you were about to die. You'd panic and I had to talk to you and talk to you until you fell asleep. You've always been terrified of death, Dietrich, and half in love with it as well."

"Sabine."

He moved close to her, but she waved him away. "No, no, don't expect to comfort me. I know something you don't. We only just read it in the *Times* yesterday. A pastor named Paul Schneider—you knew him?"

"Yes, Paul attended Martin Niemöller's meetings."

"He's dead," Sabine said. "Tortured to death in Buchenwald."

Dietrich turned pale. He seemed to have trouble catching his breath. "Tortured to death?"

"The government doesn't try to hide it," Sabine continued. "They're no longer ashamed of such things. An example. That's what they call it. What chance do you stand with them, Dietrich? And soon the war will begin and we shall be caught on opposite sides. We won't be able to speak on the telephone or even to write. I'll have no way of knowing how you are. I tell you, I won't be comforted."

When they joined the Bells for a late lunch they had composed themselves, but barely. Dietrich tried to speak calmly of his time in New York.

"What do the Americans say about the situation over here?" Bell asked.

Dietrich shrugged. "Most Americans aren't paying much attention. They don't know or care what's happening in Europe. Many of the conservatives, the business people, are sympathetic to Hitler, but they don't want to see him fight England. People on the left hate the Nazis, but they're a minority. No one wants to see America in a war, although Roosevelt seems inclined to help England any way he can short of calling out troops."

"That's something, I suppose," Bell said.

Dietrich said, "Sabine will have told you that I'm taking a position in the German army."

There was an awkward silence. Sabine picked at the food on her plate and said nothing.

"We would seem to be made enemies very soon," Dietrich said. "But you mustn't think that is what we really are. I apologize, as I did to my friend Reinhold Niebuhr, for I can say little more. Only I hope in the future you will think of me as you have known me, and not as I may soon seem from afar."

"You have never been my enemy," Bell said, "nor ever shall be."

The two men stared at each other as though exchanging silent vows. Sabine suddenly began to sob, and left the table. Dietrich stood, but Hettie Bell said, "I'll go to her. You and George need to talk."

Dietrich sat down slowly.

"She'll be all right," Bell said. "She needs time."

Dietrich shut his eyes. "I seem to have a gift for bringing pain to the people I care for most. Tell me, George, am I wrong to go back?"

"Only you can answer that."

Dietrich nodded. "Then I have answered it. Only I would ask you one more question. What would you say to a man who fears he must sin, and sin to the point of endangering his own soul, in order to help others?"

Bell was silent for a long time, then asked, "What sort of sin?"

"Lying. Blasphemy. Betrayal. Killing. The denial of everything one has believed in."

"And the benefit to others?" Bell asked, then quickly added, "No, don't answer that. I know. I can think of no greater sacrifice for a man like you."

Dietrich flushed. "A man like me?"

"Why be hypothetical? We both know this is no intellectual game. I'll tell you what I think. You're right not to say any more to me. I mustn't know, and you must learn to keep your own counsel. As to the final disposition of your soul, that is in God's hands. Is that your conclusion?"

"My conclusion," Dietrich answered, "is that it would be self-serving to allow concern for the disposition of my soul to push me off this course."

"In that case," Bell said, "you have stepped off the edge of a high precipice and are beyond human aid. God help you."

Evensong in the cathedral. Choirboys robed in white and black sing the psalms like angels and, when no one is looking and they are hidden behind their benches, trade toy soldiers they have stashed inside their voluminous sleeves. Dietrich and Sabine sit side by side on uncomfortable high-backed seats while George Bell, wearing his bishop's vestments, reads the collects and lessons. When he delivers the second collect—*Give unto thy servants that peace which the world cannot give; that our hearts may be set to obey thy commandments, and also that by thee, we, being defended from the fear of our enemies*—he pauses deliberately and looks at Dietrich, then continues—*may pass our time in rest and quietness; through the merits of Jesus Christ our Saviour*—while two of the smallest choirboys nudge one another, anxious to be done and home for supper.

Credo

in unum Deum

I believe in one God

V·Mann
1940–41

MEMEL, EAST PRUSSIA. JUNE 14, 1940. Falk Harnack, in the uniform of a Wehrmacht officer, strolled along the Memel harbor on a fine summer afternoon. A breeze blew in from the Baltic and set the water glittering like a cache of jewels. The ferry from Stockholm emerged from behind a pack of gray minesweepers. Passengers thronged the railing, waving their arms gaily or holding white arms to their foreheads to ward off the glare of the sun. Falk paused a moment to enjoy the scene, smoking a cigarette as he rested one foot upon a wooden pile. Then he checked his watch and walked on, leaving the harbor and heading into the heart of the city until he reached a quiet street bordering a green park. Here he turned into the beer garden of the Café Weiß Schwan, removing his cap and tucking it under his arm as he passed beneath a flowering arbor. He stopped and surveyed the crowd, enjoying the mild weather and the good local beer. Many were men in uniform—sailors, soldiers of the Wehrmacht, and officers of the SS, on leave now that the Polish campaign was done and attention had shifted to the troops fighting in the West. Four merchant sailors from neutral Sweden sat near the bandstand and flirted with some pretty Memel girls at the next table. Here and there a businessman in shirtsleeves read the afternoon paper over plates of sliced ham and hard-boiled eggs and a stein of beer.

Then there was the man Falk Harnack was looking for.

Dietrich Bonhoeffer sat alone in a corner that had already lost the afternoon sun. The nearby tables stood empty, the other patrons happy to avoid the shade as long as possible. Falk sighed and wished he could ignore Bonhoeffer and sit close to the Swedes and their giggling quarry. But he had an assignment. It was a strange business. When asked by his brother, Arvid, to make contact, he had expected to travel to wherever Bonhoeffer might have been posted. Instead he had learned from his aunt in the Wangenheimstraße, who had contacted her former neighbor Paula Bonhoeffer, now living in the Marienburger Allee, that Dietrich was spending several weeks in East Prussia. This was convenient, since Falk was stationed in Warsaw and need not use so much of his leave. But it was also odd. What was Bonhoeffer doing all the way over in East Prussia? And it seemed, according to his aunt, that Dietrich was still a civilian. How, in the middle of the invasion of Norway and the Low Countries and France, had he managed that?

Bonhoeffer stood, offering his hand. He was a large man, though thinner than seven years earlier, and looking more fit, tougher somehow. "It's been many years," he said.

"Yes," Falk agreed, "and for me some years were longer than others." He referred, they both knew, to Dachau.

"Well," Dietrich said, "now you have a chance to atone for all that."

Falk sat down, pretending to smooth his uniform jacket in order to hide his surprise at the remark. When he looked at Bonhoeffer again, the other man was smiling.

"An Oberleutnant, I see," Bonhoeffer said approvingly. "And where are you serving?"

"In Warsaw just now, though I've heard I may be transferred soon to Vienna. I'm a cultural officer. Responsible for entertaining the troops, and also liaison with cultural organizations in cities under our, ah, jurisdiction."

Dietrich nodded. "Good, good. Things getting back to normal in the East after so much upset. And you are able to use your talents as well."

Falk said nothing, just studied Bonhoeffer through narrowed eyes.

Dietrich continued, "So. How did you find me in Memel of all places?"

"Through my aunt, of course. I was quite surprised to learn you were here. And not in uniform," Falk added significantly.

Dietrich shrugged. "The Wehrmacht wouldn't have me. A medical problem."

"But a chaplaincy, surely?"

"No. I applied, but they only take you on as a chaplain after you've got in the Wehrmacht. Still, I am able to serve the Fatherland in my own way."

Which is? Falk longed to ask. But he reminded himself to be patient. Arvid had been most emphatic. As a senior civil servant in the Reich Ministry of Economics, Arvid had his ear to the ground. And as members of a clandestine Communist cell reporting to the Soviet Union, Arvid and his wife, Mildred, were also very much in danger. In Berlin at the beginning of Falk's leave, Arvid had said, "Something has to be up with Dohnanyi in the War Ministry. I know it. I remember Hans from the old days, and so does Aunt. I can't believe he's just going along."

"But what am I looking for?" Falk had asked.

"Anything. You know the younger Bonhoeffer brother better than I do. Isn't he the best bet?"

"It's been years," Falk had said. "But if you're wanting information from someone, then yes, he might know some of what Dohnanyi knows, and he'll be much more approachable."

"An innocent," Arvid said. "At least that's how he struck me the few times we met."

The innocent Dietrich had ordered two steins of beer. Falk tipped his until he got past the head, wiped a line of froth from his upper lip with a discreet knuckle. He asked, "So what are you doing in East Prussia? It's a long way from home."

"Last night I delivered a sermon to a local congregation. Twenty people in attendance. Today I addressed a church conference. Three elderly clergymen and four laypeople."

Falk laughed, lightheartedly, he hoped. "And did you come all this way only for that?"

"I have never before seen this eastern corner of the Reich," Dietrich said. And added amiably, "And why did you come all this way to see me after all these years? Perhaps you want news of Suse. She's married and has a child. But then you would know that from your aunt, wouldn't you?"

Falk felt as though he were standing on one leg and trying to keep his balance, had felt that way ever since he sat down. "You've changed," he said, for lack of anything better, and felt a complete fool.

"Have I? You haven't. You seem to be getting on. And why not? After all, Comrade Stalin and our own Führer are now partners, are they not?" And Bonhoeffer raised his stein in a mock salute.

So it was Falk who must be reminded of his past and defend himself, at a risk, or else deny everything and pretend he had come all this way on a social call. "Unlike some of my acquaintances," he said, "I take no pleasure in the present coalition."

"Ah," was all Dietrich said.

A band of elderly men dressed in folk costume—white blouses, brightly embroidered belts and suspenders—had climbed onto a low stage and launched into a rousing rendition of "Rosamunde," playing so loudly it was difficult to talk. Falk drummed his fingers on the table in irritation and considered his next move. But it was Bonhoeffer who leaned close and said, "People here are very nervous. The rumor is that Stalin is going to move into Lithuania soon. So close by. But our armed forces don't seem particularly concerned, do they? All these men on leave. Therefore the Soviets will stop at the border. I imagine it's all been agreed upon, don't you? There will be no unpleasantness between ourselves and Stalin, at least for now. Other more pressing matters to tend to."

"You mean the war in the West."

"I mean—" Dietrich leaned closer still—"what do your Wehrmacht comrades in Poland say about the atrocities being committed by the SS?

Civilians murdered. Jews especially, but also a wholesale slaughter of the Polish clergy and professional classes. Lawyers, doctors, teachers. People forced to dig mass graves, then lined up and shot. Do your fellow officers like what the SS is doing, and would they obey orders to intervene? It would be interesting to hear this from a man who has just claimed to oppose the Führer's friendship with Stalin. Some people would be upset to hear you question the actions of the Führer. As if he might be mistaken."

And so. Falk patted his pocket to see if it had been picked as well. Dietrich, mistaking the gesture, offered a cigarette.

"Morale is low," Falk said, and dug in his pocket for a book of matches. "Even in the SS. Some of their men are going mad and are being shipped back to Germany in straitjackets. But most of them carry on, though they drink like fiends in order to do what they're being asked to do. There's a joke you can tell how long an SS man has been in Poland by how much he drinks. The army stands by and watches, like useless children. Some of my superiors are upset, but they're also afraid. Until some general gives an order, they won't intervene."

"Names," Bonhoeffer said. "I want names of the officers who are upset."

And soon he had names, scanning the list Falk scribbled inside a matchbook and handed to him. But before he could offer any thanks, the band stopped playing, shushed by the manager of the café, who was waving his arms frantically and calling for attention.

"The official announcement has just come over the radio!" the man cried. "Paris has fallen to our glorious armed forces!"

People cheered wildly, some jumping up and down, some climbing onto chairs, all offering the Nazi salute. Dietrich Bonhoeffer was among them, leaping up with arm outstretched, calling *Sieg heil! Sieg heil!* He pulled a stunned Falk Harnack to his feet, grabbed his arm, and forced it up in the air. And as the band broke into *"Deutschland, Deutschland über Alles"* and the crowd began to sing, he said in Falk's ear, "There are things worth dying for, my friend, but a salute is not one of them."

"WHAT DO YOU THINK YOU ARE?" Hans von Dohnanyi said, his voice edged with anger. "Some kind of *V-Mann*? A secret agent in a film?"

"I was trying to help," Dietrich said. "I didn't plan this, you know. But when Falk turned up, I thought why not see what I can learn."

They sat alone on the veranda of the Sacrow house watching the sun set beyond the Havel, sky and water stained dark orange. In the dense light Dohnanyi seemed a figure in a Renaissance painting. He had delicate, sharp features, a boy's face grown canny rather than middle-aged. "You will be most helpful when you do what you are told and only what you are told."

He picked up the matchbook cover, squinted at it in the waning light, and slipped it into his shirt pocket. "Think if you'd lost this or if it had somehow got into the wrong hands."

"Anyone working for the Abwehr would have to be careful with names," Dietrich said stubbornly, "not just me. And I am not a careless person."

"The point, Dietrich, is that you took a chance for this information when it wasn't necessary. We have our methods of identifying sympathetic officers. In fact, every name on your list except one is already known to us."

"Then that is one more name I have got for you," Dietrich said, but more sheepish now, for he knew Hans was right.

"This is no game," Dohnanyi said. "You don't know anything about Falk Harnack's activities these days. He may have been taken in by the SD, Gestapo foreign intelligence, for all you know. Or he may be working for the Soviet Union. Certainly I have my suspicions about Arvid, though I don't tell anyone. If the Harnacks are undermining the regime I don't give a damn who they're working for. But I don't want them anywhere near our operation. Is that clear?"

"Yes," Dietrich said. He thought a moment. "Though I must say, I don't think you need worry about Falk. I got the impression he's more of an amateur than I am, if that's possible."

Dohnanyi laughed. "It's possible. And you're probably right. My guess is Arvid sent Falk to see what he could get out of you. It seems he didn't get much. So. Stay away from them in the future, agreed? Not so much as a good morning, how are you."

"Agreed," Dietrich said. "But it remains . . ." His voice trailed off.

"Yes?"

"You give me nothing to do. No, don't deny it."

"If I were only interested in your protection I'd never have agreed to your return from America. You were already safe there, and a lot less fuss about it."

Dietrich ignored this. "You knew I'd return no matter what you said, so you had to think of something safe for me. Well, you've certainly found it. You send me to Pomerania and Königsberg and Memel and tell me to keep my eyes and ears open. I live on the hospitality of the Prussian gentry and pick up a little about troop movements here, which you will already know from other sources, and a little peasant gossip there, which can never be believed, and if any of it were useful, most of it will only help the government and not hurt. Meanwhile those families I'm visiting, the von Kleists and von Tresckows and von Wedemeyers, all have husbands and brothers and son and cousins in the army, they've already buried some of them, and there I am, safe. You can imagine what they are saying about me. Why is Bonhoeffer here instead of serving in Poland or France? My own students from the Finkenwalde seminary are serving with the army. Two of them have died. And I don't know what would be worse, to serve alongside them knowing that I served evil but might comfort the afflicted, or to be where I am now and not doing a damned thing to help anyone."

Dohnanyi was silent for a time, then said, "You mustn't think I am unsympathetic. You do us great good by being our pastor, by giving us counsel and encouragement. Most of us are religious men, though we may not show it."

Dietrich understood what he meant. He had been allowed to attend many of the meetings of the resistance, a motley collection of Abwehr operatives and officers, attorneys and men from the Foreign Office. He had been present when Oster came to discuss the most delicate matters. He was trusted, was acknowledged one of the conspirators, that he could not deny. On a number of occasions after a hard decision had been taken, one or another of those present—a lawyer or a junior officer—would seek him out and ask for prayer, or wonder in a voice taut with worry what Dietrich as a pastor thought of God's judgment or God's mercy or God's compassion. Or simply ask for a passage of scripture to meditate upon.

Dietrich thought upon all this, was grateful for it, but now he said, "It is not enough."

"Not enough," Dohnanyi echoed. He was himself still keeping the diary of Nazi crimes, a log he kept hidden in a Wehrmacht safebox along with grainy film of SS troops committing murder in Poland, obtained from a sympathetic communications officer. "There is little enough for any of us to do just now. All these damned victories. A general trains all his life to win a war, and suddenly he is master of the entire continent. Even the ones who despise Hitler are stunned."

"Must we wait on the generals?"

"Without them a coup would be hopeless." Dohnanyi sighed. "It is a terrible thing to stand against one's own country in time of victory."

"Somehow we must," Dietrich said. He looked out over the darkening mosaic of water and forest. "Because in the meantime, the Jews—life in Germany is becoming impossible for them. Can we do nothing?"

Dohnanyi waved his hand. "Things will get better for the Jews when Hitler is gone. That is what we can do."

"What you can do," Dietrich said. "I can do nothing, it seems."

And he found himself back at the beginning of the argument.

They had already lost one opportunity, their best chance, Dohnanyi feared. Before the invasion of the West, Oster had been secretly negotiating with Churchill's new government in London. He was convinced that had Churchill and not Chamberlain been in charge in 1938, the British would have stood firm on Czechoslovakia and Hitler could have been brought down. With the conquest of Poland complete and the invasion of the West not yet begun, Churchill was at last in charge and Britain had finally taken a stand.

The German generals were frightened again. It was one thing to attack a weak Poland, quite another to take on the greatest power in Europe. Even the pact with Stalin did not calm their fears, for who trusted either Hitler or Stalin? They were ready to listen to those who spoke quietly against the government. Even the commander in Chief, Generalfeldmarschall Walther von Brauchitsch, sat down with Oster and pledged his support to over-throwing Hitler.

On Dietrich's return from New York, he had met with Dohnanyi and Oster at the War Ministry in the Tirpitz-Ufer. The building overlooked the pleasant Landwehrkanal on the edge of the Tiergarten. But the demands of the war effort had brought an influx of new employees crammed into make-shift cubicles in a series of row houses connected to the main building. Most of the cubicles had no windows to enjoy the view of the canal. Die-trich maneuvered from cubbyhole to cubbyhole, past women hunched over typewriters in artificial light, haunted by invisible lindens above slow-mov-ing green water. At last he came to a room slightly larger than the broom closets of the typists, but it at least had a window that let in a meager after-noon light. There Dohnanyi waited with Oster. It was the first time Die-trich had seen the Abwehr second-in-command since that long-ago day at Niemöller's church in Dahlem, when Elisabeth had pointed out a man accused of cheating on his wife, a man ostracized by his fellow officers for this sexual indiscretion. A world away. Oster had made his way back to power by sheer ability and his deep roots in the old Prussian ruling class. He had the taut, tanned look of a man used to the saddle, the hunt. Fit, alert, not inclined to show age.

Dohnanyi said little, let Oster do the talking.

"Welcome, Pastor Bonhoeffer. We are pleased you have chosen to serve the Fatherland through your affiliation with the Abwehr." This with a sig-nificant glance at the door, but no change in the expression on his face or the inflection of his voice. "Our work is most sensitive, as I'm sure you appreciate. Intelligence gathering is highly specialized. The expertise you bring is not easily come by, so we believe you will fill a niche that will be most useful to the Reich. You have contacts among religious organizations in the West which should prove useful both for gathering information and for spreading disinformation through counterintelligence work. Though we don't have an immediate assignment for you. Meanwhile, we will introduce you to our agent in charge of liaison with the Vatican, Dr. Josef Müller. You shall be his Protestant counterpart. We also understand you are familiar, through your work with the Confessing movement in the 1930s, with many of the established families of Pomerania. Of course, we have no doubts about the loyalty of these families, but their lands in the East put them in a position to see and hear things that may be useful. Many of these estates are now in the hands of women, since their husbands are off serving in the Wehrmacht. It would be a great comfort to those families, and possibly useful to us, if you would visit Pomerania and East Prussia from time to time. Simply to reassure, and to assess the situation there. Who more trusted for such a task than you, Pastor Bonhoeffer? After all, you have preached to these families, instructed their children for confirmation."

And on and on. . . .

"Well?" Hans had asked after the meeting.

Dietrich had little to say, for he was thoroughly depressed. On board ship from New York he had allowed himself a few daydreams. Dietrich delivering a fiery sermon which would rouse the good Christians of Berlin to throw themselves between the Gestapo and the suffering Jews. Dietrich the faithful assistant to Hans von Dohnanyi of the Abwehr, lurking in dark alleys at midnight waiting for the clandestine message which would save the world from Hitler. Dietrich standing beside the engineer of a locomotive pulling a trainload of Jews to freedom.

Of course, all that was foolishness, but it had helped him to sleep at night.

He contemplated his immediate assignment. Life in a country house. Eating fresh eggs and homegrown vegetables. Having coffee with the middle-aged wives of Prussian officers suffering at the front.

"What do you think intelligence work is?" Dohnanyi had asked. "It's boredom, mostly. Waiting for something to happen. And something usually doesn't happen, except that if you aren't alert, you miss that small detail that brings down empires."

Dohnanyi also said, as they ate roast duck at the Hotel Kempinski, confiscated from its Jewish owners and now boasting swastikas over every glittering entrance, "Safe? You think you will be safe? I assure you, brother-in-law, even in these small things you are committing treason. Though to the outside world it will look like collaboration. All your erstwhile admirers abroad, in America, in England, the ecumenical movement, will wonder. 'What about Bonhoeffer?' they'll say. 'Has he truly gone over to Hitler?' But I assure you, your name is now irrevocably linked with ours. If Oster falls, you and I fall. We'll see the inside of a Gestapo prison and be lucky to get out alive. That is intelligence work. Boredom on the one hand, death on the other."

Reports of events in Poland arrived daily in the War Ministry and were carried on to the Bonhoeffer and Dohnanyi homes. Then the Abwehr's Vatican liaison, Dr. Josef Müller, had arrived in Berlin after a trip to Warsaw, Kraków, and Czestochowa. Late at night in the Sacrow house Dietrich had listened while Müller, a large man with a long head and white hair thick and wavy as cake frosting, dictated an account of his travels. He paused now and then to accept a suggestion from Dohnanyi, while Christel sat at the dining-room table hunched over a typewriter in a circle of light. Müller's voice was flat, matter-of-fact, as he described what he had seen in Poland.

Refugees bombed in the roads as they attempted to flee. Children in the fields strafed by low-flying Luftwaffe planes, their twisted bodies found along with their companions—dead horses, cows, dogs. Churches looted. Priests, schoolteachers, gentry, attorneys, and physicians identified in villages and towns, and lined up before firing squads, an entire educated class eradicated.

And the Polish Jews, murdered out of hand or rounded up into detention camps or city ghettos.

From time to time Christel stopped to rub her forehead and run her hands through her hair, not tired so much as overcome by the words she was putting to paper. Sometimes Dietrich took her place, but he was not nearly so competent a typist and she would soon be back at it. Dietrich felt his own uselessness. He had nothing to contribute. He had not been back to the War Ministry, or visited Poland. Nor would he go to Rome, as would Dr. Müller, with a copy of the report hidden in the false bottom of a valise, to tell the Pope how his Polish flock was being treated. He only hovered, replenished the coffeepot, brought out plates of cheese and sausage, rubbed Christel's back and shoulders while she threaded pages through the typewriter.

They had called this the X Report. A ridiculous name, pretentious without meaning a thing. And yet the lack of meaning was crucial. That was espionage, Dohnanyi would say. The X Report was more than a catalog of horrors in Poland, and copies would go not only to the Vatican. The X Report included the assurance that a coup was being planned, that Hitler would be overthrown. Oster had made contact with Churchill's government, which agreed it would treat with a new German regime if Hitler was disposed of before he could attack the West.

"We must also say we'll withdraw from Poland and Czechoslovakia," Dietrich had said, "and make restitution. The British will demand that, and they've every right to."

"Yes," Dohnanyi agreed, "but we only talk about that with the civilians in the resistance. We can't say it to the generals yet, including Brauchitsch. Except for the atrocities, they're very proud of the Polish campaign, God help them."

"How do they make an exception of the atrocities?"

"When human beings do well at their work, they can overlook quite a lot." Dohnanyi sighed. "It's an argument for later, when Hitler is gone."

"Suppose, when that is accomplished, Goering or Himmler or someone simply steps in?"

"Civil war," Hans said in a flat voice. "The army against the SS. But believe me, that would be no contest. The army wins the battles. The SS are not a fighting force, they're a damned murdering mob. Anyway, I hope it won't come to that. When we take out Hitler, we'll take out Himmler and the others at the same time. Oster knows how to do it."

Oster had made his plans—which divisions would take over which facilities, which would arrest Hitler and the others and stand them before a firing squad. Dohnanyi was in charge of civilian unrest. He had managed to make contact with trade union leaders inside Dachau and build a modest network that reached outside the camp. He thought he might be able to pull off a general strike to coincide with the army takeover.

One thing had remained. Oster went to East Prussia, where he spent an afternoon with Generalfeldmarschall Walther von Brauchitsch. In tweed jackets and corduroys, the two of them accompanied by water spaniels rather than aides de camp, carrying rifles. Duck hunting.

Oster flew back to Berlin that night and was met at Tempelhof airfield by Hans von Dohnanyi. His face was drawn with worry, and he said not a word. Dohnanyi had known at once.

"Are we dead men?" he asked when they were alone in the car.

"That depends," Oster said, "on whether Brauchitsch talks. Walther and I have known each other since we were boys. I appealed to his honor. He's from the old school, you know."

"Oh yes," Dohnanyi said. "So."

"So." A light rain had begun to fall, and Oster stared at the windshield wipers, clicking steady as a metronome, while Dohnanyi drove. "So he has changed his mind. He said, 'My God, man, you should not have brought this to me. This is nothing less than treason.' I told him if it was treason, I was the only one to blame. And I reminded him I had come to him in the strictest confidence. Did he hear that? We shall know soon enough."

Dohnanyi drove for a time without speaking. Then he asked, "Why did Brauchitsch change his mind?"

"That's the worst part. It's because he's been helping draw up the plans to invade Scandinavia and the West. I've seen the plans as well. And he believes, as I believe, that they will succeed."

They had spent several anxious days until it became clear that Brauchitsch had told no one of Oster's activities. All that could be done now was to warn the British and Dutch and Belgians that the Wehrmacht would turn its attention away from a coup and toward them. The dates of the invasion were confirmed, and Oster sent couriers to London and Amsterdam and Brussels and Oslo. *Be prepared on November 12, 1939,* the message said. *This information comes from the underground opposition in Germany. We are highly placed, we are not loyal to Hitler. Please trust us.*

The day came and went, without an invasion. Hitler had changed his mind. Again after the New Year an attack was planned, and Oster sent word to the West. Again Hitler delayed. When through clandestine channels a third message from Berlin announced the invasion on May 10, 1940, it was ignored. The western governments had decided the earlier dates were deliberately planted by the SD and the Abwehr to keep them off guard. It was highly doubtful, Churchill's cabinet agreed in Whitehall, that anyone placed highly enough in Germany to have access to the actual date of an invasion would blatantly betray his country by passing it on, especially in light of the earlier misinformation. Reports of a coup and leaks of German military secrets, it was agreed, should henceforth be treated with a great deal of skepticism.

But this time Hitler did not waver. Belgium and Holland were quickly overrun and the British army nearly trapped at Dunkirk. Then Paris fell.

Dietrich traveled to Memel, to Königsberg, delivering dull lectures on scripture to gatherings of elderly church people, lectures that must be devoid of political content so as not to draw attention to himself. Spent much of 1940 at Pätzig, the von Wedemeyer estate, beginning work on his new book. Waiting for a word from the Abwehr that he was needed. A call which did not come, because the German generals were deliriously happy, the German people were deliriously happy, and no one except a few fools wanted to talk about overthrowing the government.

POMERANIA. SUMMER AND AUTUMN 1940. The Junker estate of Pätzig was bereft of men. Herr von Wedemeyer was now an officer serving in Poland, and son Max, only eighteen, was stationed in France, had marched jauntily into Paris and posed for a snapshot in front of the Eiffel Tower. Frau von Wedemeyer displayed the photograph on the mantel in her breakfast room, a place where she could often be found seated by the window in the warm summer sun, sewing and mending for the estate and for her men in the Wehrmacht.

Sometimes she was joined by Dietrich Bonhoeffer, who would take a break from writing in his room and come downstairs for a cup of coffee. Dietrich could not bear to look at the photograph of Max, his former confirmation student. A sweet young man as Dietrich recalled, kind and generous, now handsome in his uniform with a proud face, arms folded and legs apart, a colossus astride the world. Frau von Wedemeyer, on the other hand, often looked up from her sewing to study her son's image, as though such close observation would keep him safe.

Once Dietrich said, "You have no photo of your husband."

"No," she said, "he keeps forgetting to send one. Besides, I have our family photographs, and I don't need him in uniform. Poland is safe now."

Safety in Poland, Dietrich thought, depended upon your perspective. "The Jews," he said cautiously, "are coming in for some rough treatment there."

"Yes," Frau von Wedemeyer said with a wave of her hand. "Father wrote something about it. The SS are misbehaving. They have no discipline, he says. But the generals have complained to Hitler and so it will be dealt with."

Frau von Wedemeyer was a stern woman with a face whose features often seemed as frozen and studied as if she posed for a portrait. In the past she and Dietrich had not warmed to each other. He seemed an odd bird to her, for he did not ride or hunt, indeed had never sat a horse or discharged a firearm, and what else were men good for? He sensed her antipathy, and on his part had thought her especially hard on her daughter Maria, a cheerful child who seemed to wilt in her mother's presence. But with husband and eldest son in the army and the other children away at boarding school, Frau von Wedemeyer was lonely. When it was suggested to her by a von Kleist cousin in the War Ministry that Pastor Dietrich Bonhoeffer needed a place to live while pursuing his writing and ministry in Pomerania and East Prussia, she had readily invited him to Pätzig.

They settled into an odd domesticity. She was suspicious of his idleness—he was the only man of his social class and age in the entire district who was not in uniform. There had been some hint of a medical disability, and indeed she judged he would make a most awkward soldier. But surely he might serve in some capacity, a chaplaincy or a desk job. He himself seemed embarrassed by his lack of involvement in the war effort, grew markedly uncomfortable when the subject arose, and if she made remarks which were too pointed—she could not resist now and then—his ears turned pink and he would not hold her gaze.

But the presence of a man in the house, especially a man who could converse intelligently and escort her on her walks through the woods and play the piano in the evenings, was a comfort. For several months, they got on well enough.

As time passed, though, Dietrich grew more and more moody. When he returned from the trip to Memel shortly after the fall of Paris, she greeted him exuberantly, overjoyed that the fighting was at last over and her Max was safe.

"I've just had a letter," she said as they walked from the railway station. "He is billeted at Versailles, can you imagine, and he's already been into the city several times. Of course, the museums are closed as the paintings have all been hid for safekeeping. Still, Paris is Paris, he says, and he's always longed to see it."

"Surely he won't enjoy seeing it in such circumstances," Dietrich answered shortly.

She was stung nearly to tears, and said little the rest of the way. It was a walk of nearly three miles, and she had not brought the car because of the rationing of petrol. But she wished now she had used the fuel, for she wanted to be away from this man who strode beside her, healthy as an ox, while her darling boy risked his life in France for the Fatherland.

Through the rest of that summer and into the autumn, Dietrich kept more and more to his room. Frau von Wedemeyer saw him only at mealtimes, and sometimes he even asked for a tray to be sent upstairs. Once he went to Stettin to preach at a church, and returned in an especially morose mood. At breakfast the next morning, he asked, "Have you been to town lately? The SS is rounding up the Stettin Jews and transporting them to Poland. Why, do you think?"

She patted her mouth with her napkin. "I'm sure you must be mistaken," she said.

"No, I'm not. I telephoned Berlin, and nothing is happening there. But in Stettin Jews are being forced from their homes and put on board trains. Not passenger trains, Frau von Wedemeyer, but cattle cars."

"I don't believe it."

"I saw it with my own eyes."

She stood up suddenly. "If you'll excuse me, Pastor Bonhoeffer." At the door she turned and faced him. "Perhaps Polish Jews who came to Stettin as refugees are being sent back. The Reich cannot be expected to take care of everyone, you know."

"No," he said. "They are German Jews."

She left the room without another word.

He had returned from the trip to Stettin with a shortwave radio. Sometimes at night when Frau Wedemeyer retired and walked softly along the corridor past his room she could hear the crackle of static and then voices speaking in a foreign tongue which she recognized as English. So Dietrich was listening to the BBC. It was an offense punishable by death according to laws enacted at the beginning of the war. At Pätzig, at night, there was no one to hear except Frau von Wedemeyer, and certainly she would not dream of reporting him. But she was angry nonetheless, and had less and less to say to him.

At night in his room, Dietrich turned out all the lights and lay on his bed, listening to the BBC. *This—is London.* Air-raid sirens wailed like a Greek chorus. The Luftwaffe was sending squadrons of bombers over London and Coventry and Exeter and Southampton and all those places whose names had become so familiar to Dietrich during his time in England. London's East End was on fire, the BBC said, block after block destroyed, thousands dead. The dome of St. Paul's Cathedral dark against the flaming sky. Londoners spent nights in backgarden shelters, or crammed together in tube stations. A band of actors, according to one broadcast, went from shelter to shelter performing the play *Murder in the Cathedral* by the poet T. S. Eliot.

Dietrich wept. He wondered if quiet, dull Forest Hill had been bombed. Knew in his heart that St. Paul's Whitechapel, whose organist knew only three hymns, was no more and wondered if the organist was no more. Wondered if George Bell's club, the Athenaeum, still stood. Wondered about Chichester. Coventry Cathedral was a pile of rubble, and the city of Portsmouth, only a few miles from Chichester, had been reduced to ash.

And where was Sabine?

It was a relief to both Dietrich and Frau von Wedemeyer when the telephone call came from Hans von Dohnanyi.

"Things are changing," Dohnanyi said, without explaining what "things" were. "We want you closer to Switzerland. Come back to Berlin and we'll explain your new assignment."

He packed his bags with a full heart, Sabine ever before him, and George and Hettie Bell, and Elisabeth Hildebrandt lost somewhere in Berlin while trains idled in rail yards.

Frau von Wedemeyer made sure that a basket of sandwiches was packed for his journey, but she did not walk with him to the station.

KLOSTER ETTAL. WINTER 1940–41. When he had planned, years before, to write a study of Christian ethics, he had envisioned it as a multivolume affair, and as long ago as his stay in England he had carefully set down an outline. The Foundations of Christian Ethics. Guilt. Justification by Works. The Commandments of Christ. Eschatology. Personal Ethics. Governmental Ethics. Community Ethics. The Church. The Family. One by one his list had grown until he had known that to complete this study would be his life's work, the crowning achievement of his theological career. It would moreover be, like his earlier book *Discipleship*, a statement of profound assurance, a call to spiritual arms. *When Christ calls a man, he bids him come and die.*

And now?

And now he was becoming a theologian of ambiguities. He worked on his *Ethics* at a desk in the library of the Benedictine monastery of Ettal, deep in the German Alps. The words he seemed to discover on the pages of his manuscript evoked a furtive sense of shame even as he was compelled to keep writing them.

Being evil is worse than doing evil. Better for a lover of Truth to lie than for a liar to tell the truth.

Which is worse? To stay clear of political conflict for fear of compromising the church, or to become involved out of love of neighbor and sin greatly in the process?

To escape sin may be the ultimate guilt.

A far cry from his earlier writings, he sometimes thought. Then he had been an arrogant young fool enamored of his own goodness and more interested in personal perfection than living for others. Whatever he had now become, he was no longer proud of his own virtue.

He had been dispatched to Ettal by the Abwehr because it was isolated, and near to Switzerland and Italy if it was judged necessary to send him there. But no call to travel was received, and fretful months passed in a remote landscape. It was a fairy-tale place. The baroque fantasy of Kloster Ettal with its bluecopper domes and turrets, creamy marble walls dashed with ocher, roofs of red tile. Entering the monastery church was like stepping into a world made of Meissen porcelain. A pulpit of beaten gold, surrounded by fantastic creatures, hung suspended from one wall, and all around was more gold, more statuary, cherubs, saints, demons, creatures half-human half-animal. Frescoes of sacred scenes were set at intervals around the walls. Inside the dome, an observatory for probing the celestial world, a landscape of heaven swarmed with angels.

Sometimes Dietrich went to confession, in part because he had a morbid fascination for the confessional box itself. Above the door a stone angel clutched a cross and played with a golden skull like a child handling a ball. Beside the screen a frescoed skeleton posed with legs crossed at ankles, left arm extended to proffer a skull that rested on its bony palm, right hand on hip. The skeleton wore a robe which opened seductively. A coquette.

Dietrich said to the abbot of Ettal, Father Johannes, "Protestants do not treat death so lightly. No leering skeletons for Protestants, only fear of the gaping jaws of Hell."

"Yes," said Father Johannes. "You Protestants set yourself such a hard task, trying to do everything for God. No wonder you're frightened, and worn out. Catholics believe God has already completed the hardest work. So we can sneak up behind the Devil and pull his tail."

The Ammergau Alpen—Laberberg, Laberjoch, Mühlberg, Notkarspitze, Ziegelspitz—loomed above the monastery walls. Beyond ragged spits of rock and ice, the Swiss border beckoned.

In November an unusual warm spell gave way to a freakish thunderstorm. Dietrich went out, climbed the meadow above the monastery, daring lightning to strike in winter. He scattered a herd of goats who fled in alarm to their leader, a sturdy brown billy. The billy warned the intruder away with a belligerent stance and a series of bleats, but the man scarcely noticed and trudged on up the steep slope until he had a view of the valley. The Ammergau, lit by flashes of lightning, were like great hag's teeth.

That night in his room he wrote, *Today there are once more saints and villains. Instead of the uniform grayness of the rainy day, we have the black storm cloud and brilliant lightning flash. Outlines stand out with exaggerated sharpness. Shakespeare's characters walk among us. The villain and the saint emerge from primeval depths and by their appearance they tear open the infernal or the divine abyss from which they come and enable us to see for a moment into mysteries of which we had never dreamed.*

He slept and was visited by demons.

CHRISTMAS EVE 1940. A season when people gather to eat and drink well, and make music. Not unusual for Catholic leaders from across Germany to gather at Kloster Ettal in the Ammergau. Not unusual—especially since Italy was a revered ally of the Reich—that they would be joined by colleagues and diplomats from Rome. Or that a few Protestant friends would be invited. Of all places, one would want to spend Christmas in Ettal. A quiet, remote valley deep in the mountains. A tiny village, its inhabitants dependents of the monastery. Like the old man who tends the goats and his wife who works in the monastery laundry. A village with quaint cottages lit by lantern, the sort of place to illustrate a child's Christmas story. The monks of Ettal are famous for their beer and liqueur, distilled inside the walls, and fresh meat and cheese and eggs are also provided by the admirably industrious brothers and their dependents. Much of the produce goes now to the war effort, but some of the first fruits stay close to home. A single road in and out, a snow-covered road that must be traveled with care. In Ettal, the war seems very far away. The men in charge of the war seem very very far away.

In the common room of the guesthouse, Dietrich Bonhoeffer is playing the piano, and everyone is singing Christmas carols. *O Tannenbaum, wie treu sind deine Blätter . . . O du fröhliche, o du selige . . . Es ist ein Ros'ent-sprungen . . .* Hans von Dohnanyi stands behind Dietrich and sings, his hands resting on the shoulders of his son and daughter, who have come down with him from Berlin. Everyone sings—the abbot of Kloster Ettal, Father Johannes, along with Abbot Hofmeister of the monastery at Mettin, Fathers Leiber, Schönhöfer, and Zeiger from the Vatican, Schmidhuber from the Portuguese consulate, Bishop Neuhäusler, Dr. Josef Müller, and an assortment of officers from military intelligence, the Abwehr.

At ten the children are put to bed. Platters of black bread and goat cheese are passed around and tiny glasses filled with pastel Ettaler liqueur. Father Johannes offers a blessing, and the good bishop proposes a toast to the monks who provide this bounty.

They will talk all night, sharing military secrets to be sent on to the Pope, hearing of resistance movements in France and Belgium, of plots against Mussolini. And Hans von Dohnanyi says, "It is time to resume our own work here in Germany."

"It is one thing to resist in France or the Netherlands or Denmark," Father Dr. Zeiger of the Vatican points out. "There the resisters are heroes. They can count on at the least the silent support of the majority of their countrymen. They have networks to provide food and shelter. But here you face something quite different, my friend. You are no hero, you are a traitor, and the German people are dead set against you."

"We know all that," Dohnanyi says, "and yet it must be done."

"Events have been against us," Josef Müller adds. "One victory after another. But the British are now holding firm. That changes everything. People begin to see this will be a long war after all. More important, the Wehrmacht begins to see. For a time we lost the generals, but one by one we begin to regain them. Will the Pope help us?"

"The Holy Father assures us," says Father Dr. Schönhöfer, "that if a coup occurs he will call on all German Catholics to support the new government. He will also act as a mediator between the new government and the British, if that is requested by all parties."

They drink to that. But much is not being said, and everyone knows it. The details. No one wishes to consider the details. Dohnanyi tries to think how to declare what must be declared. But it is Dietrich—who has not raised a glass to any sort of success—who stands and goes to the door, turns back, and says, "I have never handled a weapon in my life. But I swear before God, I will kill Hitler with my bare hands if necessary."

He leaves. Dohnanyi looks around. "It is what must be done. You must tell the Pope, it is what must be done. And will be done. If that is not acceptable we go on without Rome."

At four in the morning the meeting breaks up. Dohnanyi finds Dietrich in his room, looking out the window and smoking a cigarette, a full ashtray beside him.

Dietrich says without looking at him, "When this is over, I shall never be able to be a pastor again. It isn't possible." He stubs out the cigarette and lights another. "My God," he says. "Christmas Day."

GENEVA. AVENUE DE CHAMPEL. FEBRUARY 27, 1941. A stiff, icy wind blew off Lac Léman and the man walked straight into it, head bent and gloved hand planted firmly on his hat. A sheet of discarded paper leaped at him, clutched briefly at his leg, and then danced on past.

The Avenue de Champel was empty of shops and galleries. No cafés where people might take refuge from the attacking wind, huddling for warmth over steaming fondue pots and platters of raclette. The Avenue de Champel was a plain block of blank-faced official buildings and large houses converted into the headquarters of a variety of organizations. At that time of day no other passersby were about, no automobiles trundled past, and the man could imagine himself the only living creature in the world. He stopped outside Number 25, studied a slip of paper clutched in one gloved hand to check the address, then noticed the bronze plaque which read WORLD COUNCIL OF CHURCHES. He struggled with the heavy door, then slipped gratefully inside, where he stood, bundled in coat and scarf, before the receptionist, a small thin woman of about sixty.

For a moment he could not speak, then the warmth of the room began to send prickles through the muscles of his face and he said as though waking from sleep, "I have an appointment with General Secretary Visser't Hooft. My name is Dietrich Bonhoeffer."

Willem Visser't Hooft was a trim man in a pinstripe suit, with a hairline that receded in a V of perfect proportions. He stood and shook Dietrich's hand, offered a cup of coffee, which was accepted with gratitude, then sat and studied his guest, making no attempt to hide the wariness in his face.

"So," said the General Secretary, "you have survived the *bise*, I see."

"The *bise?*"

"Our lake wind. The Genevois proclaim it the worst in Europe and are very proud of it."

"I won't dispute them," Dietrich said.

"An unfortunate season for a holiday," Visser't Hooft continued. His voice held a sharp, challenging edge that caused Dietrich to shift uncomfortably in his chair. "You would enjoy the city more in spring or summer. Then there are pleasure boats on the lake, and people sit on the terraces in the afternoon. On a clear day one can see Mont Blanc. A peaceful contrast to the rest of the continent."

Dietrich took a deep breath and said, "Perhaps you don't recall, but we met at the ecumenical conference in Denmark in 1934, when you were assistant secretary. You were most sympathetic to the cause of the Confessing Church."

"And you were an effective advocate," Visser't Hooft said with a nod. "But that was years ago."

"George Bell always thought very highly of you."

"And I think highly of George," replied Visser't Hooft. "That is why I wrote him as soon as I received word of your coming."

"Ah. A check of my credentials?"

"Of course."

"And have you received a reply?"

"Not yet. The mails between Switzerland and Great Britain are not so reliable these days, as you well know." This said with a discreet, but angry, cough. Then, "I must tell you, Bonhoeffer, no one in this organization thinks I should have anything to do with you."

Dietrich bowed his head. "I'm sorry. That would be unwise."

"Would it? Their reservations are legitimate, it seems to me. They wonder why you are allowed to travel freely from Germany to a foreign country. They wonder how you got into Switzerland, since it is nearly impossible to come by a visa these days without some very powerful friends. In fact, we all wonder about your relationship to your government."

Dietrich bit his lip, considered how much he should give away. Visser't Hooft waited, fingertips touching.

"I'm working for German military intelligence," Dietrich said, and held his breath.

"The Abwehr," said Visser't Hooft.

"Yes."

"And why should I not show you the door here and now?"

Dietrich said, "Because I have come to tell you that we are planning to overthrow Hitler."

Visser't Hooft raised his eyebrows but said nothing for a very long time. Dietrich looked away. Out the window a thin ridge of snow-capped peaks was visible above the gray sky.

Visser't Hooft stood suddenly. "Go away," he said. "Now. But don't leave the city. Leave your address with my secretary. I shall be in touch."

Dietrich stood as well, so startled he knocked over his cup of coffee.

"Never mind." Visser't Hooft waved his hand at the brown stain spreading across his blotter. "Just go."

Dietrich ate steak and *pommes frites* in his hotel room and contemplated his failure. It seemed that Hans Bernd Gisevius had been right.

"Gisevius is the German consul in Zurich," Hans von Dohnanyi had explained when he briefed Dietrich on his Swiss mission. "He's also the most important member of the resistance in Switzerland, and he's got access to the British embassy. Though so far it hasn't done us much good, because they don't trust him. They still can't seem to conceive of high-ranking Germans who would betray their country. Can't blame them—at this point, we've damn little to show for ourselves. Anyway, I have to warn you Gisevius doesn't want us using you in Switzerland. He considers the country his bailiwick and thinks you're a rank amateur."

"Which I am," Dietrich pointed out.

"Aren't we all? Not something we're taught in school, is it? Anyway, just wanted you to know who Gisevius is. He'll stay out of your way, since we convinced him it can't hurt to establish a channel of communication with the churches in the West. And in that sphere no one has the credentials you do. So you see, you're going to prove useful after all."

"But won't I need some sort of training? Don't people involved in espionage need to learn how to set up secret meeting places or tell if they're being followed?"

Dohnanyi laughed. "You've seen too many films. No, you don't have to go skulking around Switzerland. No need to pretend to be anything other than you are."

"And that is?"

Dohnanyi's smile vanished. "You are a patriotic German pastor in the service of the Abwehr who is attempting to influence the World Council of Churches to support the German war effort, or at least to remain neutral. That's what you must never forget. It isn't the other side we must fool, it is our own people. As far as anyone must know, even most people you meet abroad, you are a loyal subject of the Fatherland. Pick and choose carefully whom you attempt to convince otherwise."

Now his first attempt to "open lines of communication," as Dohnanyi put it, had ended in failure. His memories of Visser't Hooft at the Fano conference had led him to believe the Dutchman would be his most receptive target. Apparently not. Dietrich held on to some hope, thanks to the request to remain in Geneva. He was staying at the Beau-Rivage, the finest hotel in the city, as befitted a representative of the German government.

Despite attacks of remorse that he should be so comfortable, it was a pleasant sojourn. The weather relented, and Dietrich enjoyed strolling along the lakeshore. Days turned into weeks. He browsed bookstores, visited art museums and ancient churches in the Old Town, and ate in restaurants well fortified with foodstuffs that were growing scarce in Germany. In Geneva people went about their normal lives, and Dietrich became one of them. Only the bustle of relief activities coordinated by the International Red Cross gave any indication of the scope of suffering and dying only miles away.

One evening in mid-March, when he had taken refuge from a rainy night in his room with a bottle of kirsch and a German translation of *Don Quixote*, the telephone jangled.

"Bonhoeffer," he said into the mouthpiece.

"Visser't Hooft here," replied the voice on the line. "Can you see me tomorrow at eight o'clock? We can have breakfast in my office."

"Of course," Dietrich said eagerly.

"I've heard from our friend," Visser't Hooft said. "I'd like to discuss it." Then he hung up.

Dietrich hurried along the Quai du Mont-Blanc once again facing into a lake wind, this one warmer than the last. Gray ice floes drifted past. In the Avenue de Champel a few hardy robins plied patches of thawing ground, so hungry they ignored the passing man. Once again Dietrich met the gray-haired receptionist, who was far more friendly this time. He was shown into the empty office of Willem Visser't Hooft and told the general secretary would be with him shortly. Dietrich tried to fight his nervousness by looking around the room. It was a nondescript office. A bulletin board held family snapshots and postcards of religious artwork. On the desk a cigarette box incongruously topped by an American buffalo provided the only decoration.

Visser't Hooft entered, this time himself carrying a tray with coffeepot and cups and a plate of croissants and slices of Gruyère. The two men shook hands, shyly but with some warmth. Dietrich settled back in his chair and began to relax.

"You may have guessed," said Visser't Hooft as he sat, "I've received a letter from Bishop Bell. A long letter which you will be able to read for yourself in a moment." He held up the envelope and Dietrich glimpsed the familiar emblem of the Diocese of Chichester on the stationery. "George says that you are to be trusted completely, despite any doubtful appearances."

Dietrich nodded. "Thank you, and George."

"I must tell you," Visser't Hooft continued, "my most trusted advisers are still urging caution. They're extremely skeptical that elements of the German armed forces might be disloyal, and that you would take the risk of sharing secrets with outsiders. But I have decided to trust George. First, however, you will want to know the good bishop sends greetings from your sister Sabine, who he assures you is well, as are her husband and daughters."

This sudden good news after so long a silence brought Dietrich near to tears. When he had composed himself he said, "I am so grateful. And I understand your caution. No German can expect to be trusted after what we have done. The suffering of your own country of Holland under German occupation must be very painful to you."

"Yes," said Visser't Hooft. "I still have family and friends there."

"Therefore I must earn your trust by telling what I know."

Dietrich then traced the history of the plot since 1937, careful to emphasize the obstacles which existed. "I do not wish the situation to sound more hopeful than it is," he said, "or to make those involved more heroic than we are. Caution and fear continue to overcome courage and resolve, and there is the very painful question of betraying one's country. The Wehrmacht's successes in the field have brought opposition to a halt for the time being. But as the war drags on, General Oster and my brother-in-law have grown more hopeful once more. We are a long way from accomplishing anything, but we want to open channels to the West so that if something should be accomplished, we shall be able to communicate with the West at once. Since the World Council of Churches is an international organization whose leaders are well-respected churchmen in their own countries, it seemed wise to approach you."

"I believe we can help," Visser't Hooft agreed. "For example, Bishop Berggrav in Norway, as you may know, has become a leading figure in the opposition to the German occupation of his country. We've also been able to use the neutrality of Sweden and Switzerland to great effect. And we have contacts inside the detention camps in France. Do you know the group CIMADE?"

Dietrich shook his head.

"George says in his letter you are a friend of Jean Lasserre. Jean is involved. CIMADE smuggles food and money to Jews in the French camps and to people in France and the Low Countries and Germany who are hiding Jews."

"In Germany?"

Visser't Hooft smiled. "Oh yes. There are a few brave and good souls, though not many."

Dietrich flushed. It was something like this that Elisabeth had wanted from him, and he had turned his back on her. He studied his hands, ashamed to meet Visser't Hooft's eyes.

"When I sit before the fire at home with my books and my cup of hot chocolate," Visser't Hooft said gently, "I must remind myself that we are given different tasks, each of us. I do not go into the camps myself; it is not a risk I assume. I oversee the operation from this office and I am very good at it. That is important. It is what I do now. As to what any of us must face in the future, God knows."

"Perhaps you are right," Dietrich said.

"Anyway, you see why I have been so cautious with you. We are a lifeline to many people and the work is dangerous and confidential. Nothing must interfere with it."

"And so," Dietrich said, "the rest of what I have to tell you has added import." He opened his briefcase and removed a folder, which he glanced at before handing it across the desk. "This is information so sensitive I crossed the border with it concealed in a false bottom of my valise. But now that it is here, you must share it with anyone who will listen to you."

Visser't Hooft scanned the sheets typed by Christel far away in Sacrow. As he read his face grew pale, and now and then he murmured, "My God, my God." He was reading an expanded version of the X Report which included not only atrocities in Poland but the euthanasia of the sick and infirm and mentally ill inside Germany.

"As you see," Dietrich said, "anyone who does not fit into some category of ethnic purity is judged unworthy of life. In Poland there were random killings at first, and mass executions by firing squad. Labor details with such hard work and little food or shelter that people drop dead. And here is something new. Jews are being transported in closed vans which are pumped full of exhaust fumes as they travel. Women and children and the elderly, those who cannot do hard labor, seem to be particular targets. The mentally and physically infirm in Germany are also being dispatched by gas and by lethal injection."

Visser't Hooft continued to read and shake his head.

"We estimate that by the end of 1941, if nothing changes, a million people will have died." Dietrich's voice was steady, a concerted effort not to sound hysterical. "Jews are also being removed in Austria and Czechoslovakia, along with gypsies and homosexuals. There are rumors that people now being deported from the Reich are being taken to special camps. Not just for detention. There are rumors, though so far as we know nothing has been confirmed, rumors that more efficient methods of mass murder are being tested at secret locations. If this is the case, food and money will do the Jews no good."

Visser't Hooft swiveled his chair toward the window. "What's to be done?"

"On our side, we must get rid of Hitler. On yours, pressure on member nations to accept refugees. Especially Switzerland and the United States."

Visser't Hooft laughed bitterly. "You know these Swiss I live among turn Jews away at the border every day. They don't want to anger dear Herr Hitler, and, if truth be told, they're as anti-Semitic as the average German. As for the Americans, Henry Leiper shares some of his mail and press clippings with me. It seems the World Council of Churches is a godless Communist front duped by Zionist propaganda that is trying to draw the United States into a war. Those are the catchphrases of the American right wing. Leiper says he's had to hire security guards for the office in New York because they've been firebombed."

"Still we try," Dietrich said.

Visser't Hooft rubbed his chin and stared out the window. A light snow had begun to fall. "Of course."

"And we pray," Dietrich said.

"Pray. And for what, Bonhoeffer, do you pray?"

"I pray for the defeat of my country. It is the only way to atone for our sins."

"Do your fellow conspirators share your views?"

Dietrich hesitated. "No," he admitted. "Most of them are patriots. They blame the freedoms of the Weimar Republic for Hitler. They hope that the war will end soon but that the Reich will remain intact, will even continue to include Austria and the Sudetenland and Poland. As a buffer against the Soviets, they will claim, and because before the Great War much of Poland belonged to the Prussian Empire. No. Most of my fellow conspirators dislike my views."

Visser't Hooft shook his head. "Indeed, you are the loneliest man I know."

Operation 7
September 1941–May 1942

DIETRICH BONHOEFFER RETURNED to Geneva at the end of August 1941 with little new to report. He, like everyone else, had absorbed the shock of Germany's June invasion of the Soviet Union and seen in it a conclusion one way or the other. The military successes there and in North Africa would make it difficult to stir up the generals to revolt. But Oster was cautiously optimistic. He believed not even Hitler with his perverse luck could hope to defeat the Soviet army in winter, and a stalemate, with the British continuing to hold firm, would make for a restless Wehrmacht. Dietrich tried not to think about how many would die in the meantime. He willed himself to be hopeful. So he told Willem Visser't Hooft. Visser't Hooft had little news except that it was more and more difficult to gain access to the labor camps in France. Dietrich returned to Germany, once again discouraged at how little he could accomplish.

He boarded the train in Geneva on a September morning when Lac Léman glinted in the sunlight that abruptly broke through the dense alpine mist. Dietrich wished his departure had come a day later, for he would have enjoyed a walk by the lakeshore. In fact, he wished he did not have to return at all, wished he could go back to Visser't Hooft and beg him for a position in Geneva. He thought this all the way to the station, thought it as he climbed on board his car and wandered the corridor to the compartment he had reserved. As long as he thought about it, he felt he would not do it, and when the train left the platform he found to his relief that he was still on board.

He changed trains at Basel, and soon after faced the border crossing at Weil. All went smoothly enough: he possessed the proper papers identifying him as an important military official, and he was carrying no incriminating documents, having left everything of a sensitive nature behind with Visser't Hooft. There was still the most uncomfortable sensation of hearing the distant clanging of an iron door at his back when the train lurched and slowly began to move across the frontier into the Reich. He shut his eyes in the hope of escaping into sleep, and was successful for a time. He woke as the train pulled into Karlsruhe and watched dreamily while passengers moved past the window. Beyond a group of soldiers carrying duffel bags, a thin dark-haired woman wearily pushed a broom along the platform. On the front of her tattered sweater she wore a large yellow star.

Startled, Dietrich turned to the middle-aged woman who had shared his compartment since Freiburg. "What is that badge?" he asked.

"You don't know?" the woman said suspiciously.

"I've just returned from a week-long business trip to Switzerland," he said.

"A new decree from the Führer just two days ago," the woman said in a more friendly tone of voice. "All the Jews must wear a yellow star. So we know who they are and can keep an eye on them. Who knows what tricks they might pull otherwise? It does make it easier, doesn't it?"

Dietrich looked back out the window. The woman had passed the soldiers, who were laughing and shouting something after her. Then the train moved and they disappeared from view.

"No," said Hans von Dohnanyi. "Absolutely not."

Dietrich paced back and forth before Dohnanyi's desk in the study of the Sacrow house. "Something must be done," he said.

"Not by us. It's far too risky."

"So we just stand by—"

"Do we risk all," Hans interrupted, "to save a few? We save those few and so thousands more are condemned to die because we are found out before we can finish this? Ah, the lucky few! Who shall they be? No. I don't want to discuss this further."

"Don't want to discuss it," Dietrich said, "because your conscience can't bear it?"

"Yes, that's it. Call it whatever you like. But I will not put the larger conspiracy at risk."

"The larger conspiracy! What conspiracy? A pack of vain, two-faced generals too busy invading the Soviet Union to bother with Hitler. I'm sick of it, I tell you. I want out."

And Dietrich stopped, jarred at the sound of his own voice.

"If it's what you want," Dohnanyi said quietly, "I'll not stop you. But what will you do?"

"Perhaps I'll go to Geneva and volunteer to work with CIMADE. Visser't Hooft might send me to France."

"You'd be spotted as a German national in a minute. Anything Visser't Hooft has for you will be in an office in Geneva, far safer than here."

Dietrich turned away and went to the window. It was a clear autumn

Saturday morning and Christel and the children were raking leaves into heaps.

Dohnanyi said, "You've learned quite a lot about the treatment of Jews in France and the Low Countries. Perhaps you can use what you are learning to encourage the generals."

"Another report? What will this one be, the Triple X Report?"

"You won't be reasoned with?"

Dietrich sighed and said, "Of course I will be reasoned with. I am more reasonable than brave, aren't I?"

He continued to work on his *Ethics*, writing about *a world where success is the measure and justification of all things. When a successful figure becomes especially prominent and conspicuous, the majority give way to the idolization of success. They become blind to right and wrong, truth and untruth, fair play and foul play. It is not even seen that success is healing the wounds of guilt, for the guilt itself is no longer recognized.* But wondered if it was easier for a failed man to make such an indictment.

His parents had given him a room at the top of the house in the Marienburger Allee, a pleasant attic space that held a small bed, desk, bookcases, and his clavier. The desk stood near a double window set in a casement, and he paused often at his work to look out. He had asked for the room at the front of the house rather than the back, even though the rear view was of a pleasant grove of trees. But the back windows also showed the air-raid shelter in the garden, freshly dug and piled with sandbags. Dietrich found the sight depressing. Besides, he wanted to keep an eye on the street.

He wrote, *The only appropriate conduct of men before God is the doing of His will. The Sermon on the Mount is there for the purpose of being done. Only in doing can there be submission to the will of God.*

He read these sentences over and over until he could shut his eyes and see them written across the darkness.

Autumn passed. Rommel was sweeping across North Africa. In the Ukraine, Kiev fell to the advancing German army. Then Orel fell, halfway between Kiev and Moscow. It took a great deal of fortitude just to open a newspaper. For solace Dietrich continued to listen to the BBC, to share an imagined companionship with the beleaguered voices drifting across crackling airwaves from London. Thought of Sabine and Gerhard, and George and Hettie Bell hearing the same words, the same music. Benny Goodman. Artie Shaw. Vera Lynn.

He only dared listen at night when the maid, Katherina, had gone home. Katherina seemed kind, not the sort to go to the Gestapo, but she had been with the family for only two years, and one never knew. She was a plain, dull-looking young woman with a round face and thick eyebrows. If she wondered why the youngest son was allowed to secrete himself in his room all day, reading and writing while other men his age were fighting and dying on the Russian front, she never let on. She had been told not to disturb him at his work, and enough was said to give her the impression that he was performing some service for the government. Sometimes when she cleaned his room, she glanced at the papers scattered on the desk top, from idle curiosity rather than any sort of suspicion. A dense, obscure text thick with biblical quotations. She could make nothing of it, and so came to pay it little mind.

Then, on a cold day when Paula Bonhoeffer had gone out to visit Suse and Dietrich had just begun to think about his noon meal, his writing was interrupted by hurried footsteps climbing the stair and a sharp urgent rapping at his door.

"Come in," he said, startled.

Katherina flung open the door and stepped inside, a frightened look on her face.

"Pardon, sir," she said, "but there's a woman at the front door asking for you."

"Well, Katherina, did you show her in? Did she say what she wants?"

"Sir—" Katherina put her thumb to her mouth and bit it nervously— "it's a Jewess. I didn't want to let her in, so she's still at the door. What should I do?"

But he was on his feet before she had finished speaking, clattering down the stairs to throw open the door.

Elisabeth Hildebrandt stood beside the front gate as though poised to run, the yellow star vivid as a flame against her gray coat.

"My God!" he called and waved to her. "Come in, come in!"

She approached hesitantly, and he pulled her inside the door and slammed it shut. She stood for a moment as though unsure what to do or say, and then turned a distraught face to him.

"I shouldn't have come, I don't want to get you in trouble, but I didn't know where else to turn."

For answer he reached out and pulled her close. She buried her face against his chest and said, "I'm afraid to go home."

She had come by bicycle, since Jews were no longer allowed to use public transport. He found the bike leaning against the outer wall beside the gate, wheeled it to the back of the house, and stashed it inside the air-raid shelter after first looking around to see if he was observed. Back in the house, he went to the kitchen, where Katherina sat at the table. She stood, but he motioned her to sit and pulled up a chair beside her.

"Katherina, I must ask a favor of you."

She stared at him, and he leaned closer and said in a low voice, "I must ask for your discretion. The young woman who has just arrived, the Jewess as you could plainly see, is here on a matter of some urgency." He took his wallet from his pocket and opened it to his Abwehr ID. "Do you see what this is? I work for military intelligence."

Katherina looked frightened, he was pleased to see.

"Even Frau Bonhoeffer knows little of what I do," he continued. "It is highly confidential. The Jewess upstairs is an informer, and she has come to tell me about troublemaking by some other Jews she has been observing. She would not normally come here to the house, but she has lost her own safe-conduct pass. I must now take her report and attempt to obtain another pass for her."

He sat back, wondering if any of this seemed remotely plausible, and waited for Katherina to absorb what he had told her.

"Do you understand?" he asked.

Katherina nodded her head and said, "Yes, Herr Bonhoeffer," in a small voice.

"Good. Now, I shall need to talk with the Jewess undisturbed, and then try to get rid of her before my mother returns. I don't want to frighten or worry Frau Bonhoeffer, you understand?"

"Of course not," Katherina agreed.

"If Frau Bonhoeffer returns and sees you are upset, she will wonder about it. So why don't you go home now? I shall tell my mother you've been taken ill and that I excused you."

"What about Cook? She'll be here this afternoon to do supper for your parents."

Dietrich thought quickly. "She hasn't seen the Jewess either, so we needn't worry her any more than my mother. Do you understand? Discretion is everything. Not even your own family must be told about this."

"What if the neighbors saw her?"

"We must hope the Jewess wasn't seen, but if she was, well, there's nothing one can do to prevent a Jew from knocking at the door. And Katherina, if you hear any gossip in the neighborhood, you must say that she is a former student of mine at university who came to ask a favor and was turned away. It is a lie, but for the Fatherland—"

Again she nodded. "But it's all very worrying," she said.

"All the more reason to go home and try not to think about it." He patted her hand. "Let me do the worrying. I shall take the report from the Jewess and then deal with her. Tomorrow it will be as if she were never here. *Ja?*"

Katherina smiled at his cajoling tone, and he patted her shoulder, helped her collect her belongings, and showed her to the door. When she had gone he went back to the kitchen and made a plate of sandwiches.

Upstairs he found Elisabeth standing close to the radiator warming her hands. He noticed for the first time how thin she was, how threadbare her coat. She looked at the tray of sandwiches, then at Dietrich, and back to the sandwiches. He set the tray on the desk and pulled out the chair.

"Sit, eat," he said. "It's all for you."

Without a word she did as she was told, gripping a sandwich with both hands and showing her teeth as she tore at the bread's tough crust. She chewed very fast. Dietrich retreated to the clavier bench and watched her. A lock of hair fell across her forehead, and he longed to push it back but he remained still.

She paused at her eating and looked up. "Sorry," she said with her mouth full.

"I'm aware that rations for Jews are not what they should be," he said.

She glanced uneasily at his bedroom door.

"It's all right," he said. "We're alone in the house and no one seems to be about outside."

"The maid who answered the door?"

"I made up some story and sent her home. My mother is spending the day with Suse and my father is at the Charité."

He had made three sandwiches of sliced ham and cheese, and after finishing the first she pushed one toward him. "No, for you," he said, but she said, "I'm not used to so much at one sitting. You haven't had your midday meal, have you?"

He admitted he hadn't, and accepted a sandwich for himself. Elisabeth ate her second sandwich more slowly. She still kept her coat on, though the room was warm, and now and then she shivered, her shoulders hunched tightly together.

"I wish I could offer you some coffee," Dietrich said, "but we're out until we receive more rationing coupons. I'll go down and warm some milk. And there," he pointed to a door in the corner, "I have my own bathroom. It's early in the month—you could draw a small tub of hot water."

She looked down at her half-eaten sandwich. "Baths are restricted," she mumbled.

"I don't care. I'll make do with water heated on the stove."

"I shall get you in trouble. I must leave soon or your neighbors will think you're up to something."

"Perhaps you weren't seen."

"Someone will have seen. It's quiet here. There won't be many yellow stars about."

"Elisabeth," he said firmly, "you must tell me where you have been living, what your circumstances are, and what brought you here this morning. Then together we shall decide what to do."

He left her to draw a bath and went downstairs to heat the milk, taking his time so she wouldn't feel rushed. He remembered a bar of chocolate in the pantry he'd been saving for the Dohnanyi children, and went to his mother's room and slipped a heavy cotton nightgown from the bottom of a drawer. Back in his room he knocked quietly on the bathroom door, then handed in the gown and chocolate and cup of milk without entering.

She emerged a few minutes later wearing the nightgown, hair wet and skin rosy. He gave her a pair of his socks and insisted she bundle herself in a blanket and sit on the bed, propped up on a pile of pillows. She laughed and said, "Dietrich, you are spoiling me."

"Something you've been denied lately," he said.

She stopped smiling and settled back on the pillows.

He said, "I did look for you. I swear it."

"I knew you would look," she said. She sipped the hot milk. "But then I didn't want to be found. Anyway, I thought you would leave Germany. I assumed you'd got out before the war began. It's something I've held on to, actually, the thought of you living safely abroad."

"I went to New York, but I didn't stay. I couldn't bear to be away at such a time. But if you thought I was gone, why did you come here?"

Elisabeth looked embarrassed. "I suppose it was some sort of desperate gesture. An act of nostalgia. Or perhaps I wanted to reassure myself that you, at least, were safe. If I'd known you were actually here, I probably would have stayed away."

"Are you still so angry with me?" he asked. "If I could only tell—" But he went no further, could not stand before her and plead—as he had to Reinhold Niebuhr and George Bell and Willem Visser't Hooft—Trust me, for there is a reason why I am not helping Jews.

But Elisabeth was saying, "We've grown apart in so many ways. But I still care for you very much, and there's something you don't know."

He waited.

"Dietrich, I'm married."

She was no longer Elisabeth Hildebrandt, but Elisabeth Fliess, wife of Dr. Hermann Fliess, a pediatrician. She had married in June of 1940, even as Paris was falling, even as Dietrich was sparring with Falk Harnack by the Baltic in Memel.

"Hermann and I have a lot in common," she explained. "He interned at the Charité and knew my father. He grew up only two blocks from the Leibholz family in Wilmersdorf and went to school with Gerhard and his cousins. He met Sabine once at a party. So we even had you in common. We worked together in an underground Jewish organization. We've had to run our own medical clinics."

"I see," he said, only half listening. He felt as though he'd been kicked in the stomach, was thinking selfishly of what he'd lost.

"Hermann and I agreed we wouldn't resist if we were rounded up. If Jews from Pomerania and East Prussia are being resettled in the East to do war work, as we hear, you can be sure there is a need for doctors. And there will be plenty for me to do as well. But Hermann and I always assumed we'd go together when—" Her voice broke and she pressed her hand to her mouth.

While she composed herself, Dietrich went to the window and looked out. Nothing moved in the street.

"They've begun the roundup in Berlin," she said. "This morning."

Dietrich turned, surprised. "Today? I've heard nothing of this."

"Nothing has been announced publicly. But word was spreading throughout our building before dawn, and Hermann went out to see if it was true. While he was gone the Gestapo came with eviction notices. We must be ready to leave for the East in three days. We're only allowed to pack what we can carry onto the train. I waited for Hermann to return, but he didn't come back, so I went downstairs. A neighbor told me he'd been talking to some men on the street corner when a van came up and the SS took them all away at gunpoint. So I didn't pack. I went out looking for him but I couldn't find him and I was afraid I'd be picked up so I came here."

"Do you have any idea where they would have taken him?"

She shook her head. "I tried to ask questions at first, but I was afraid to linger on the street too long, especially once I left the Scheunenviertel. I saw the vans myself, taking people who stopped to talk. It's as if they want to keep people from gathering in public."

She fell silent. Dietrich remained standing near the window. He seemed to have gone a long way away. Elisabeth waited a moment, then pushed away the blanket.

"I must go. It was wrong of me to bother you after all these years when it can only cause you trouble."

She stood and looked around for her coat, but Dietrich was beside her, pulled her to him and rested one large hand on top of her head. "No," he said. "I'm going out to look for your husband."

"Dietrich, you mustn't—"

"Hush, now. You will stay here. Be very quiet, take a nap if you like, or read one of my books. Cook will come in around two, but she'll stay downstairs. My mother will be gone for hours yet, and she never enters my room without knocking first. All I ask is if she comes up here, hide in the bathroom or under the bed. It will be easier for my parents to behave as if nothing has happened if they know nothing to begin with. I'll be back tonight at the latest, and I'll bring you something to eat then. Who knows, perhaps I shall bring your Hermann as well. All right?"

She tried to smile and nodded her head. "Yes," she said. "But Dietrich, if they have already sent him East, I want to go there and find him. Only I need to know where he has gone. If you can learn that, I would be so grateful."

"I'll try my best," he said, and left her, closing the door to his room softly behind him.

Downstairs he put on his coat and hat, then hesitated, thinking hard. He left a hastily scribbled note on the hall table explaining he had gone out on "some business for Hans" and might not return until after dark. Then he took a small bottle of cognac from his father's liquor cabinet, slipped it into his coat pocket, and walked to the Grunewald S-Bahn station. From the platform he could look toward the forest past a row of idle trains that extended out of sight.

In the Oranienburger Straße he felt as if he stood on the bank of a fast-moving river. Thousands of people wearing yellow stars flowed past him—some carrying suitcases and boxes, others wandering confused and empty-handed—beneath the watchful eyes of armed SS guards. Dietrich plunged through the stream, dodging one here, jostling another there, stopping to make way for a woman leading five small children like a gaggle of geese. At the corner of Krausnickstraße he asked a guard, "Where are these people going?"

The SS guard, a corporal, gave him a cold stare and said, "Who wants to know?"

Dietrich held his breath and dug out his identification. The corporal studied it a moment with a bored expression, then said with a sideways nod of his head, "The Jewish Home for the Elderly at the Old Jewish Cemetery in Schönhauser Allee."

Dietrich clicked his heels and thrust out his arm.

The Jewish Home for the Elderly occupied a pleasant campus on the edge of the cemetery. This proximity to a burial ground had given rise in the past to right-wing jokes about the efficiency of dispatching aged Jews. The grounds of the home as well as the open spaces of the cemetery were now filled with people spreading their belongings on the ground, huddling in forlorn groups, or wandering aimlessly in search of friends or relatives. Impossible, Dietrich realized, to identify a man he'd never set eyes on. Not without help. He patted the bottle of cognac in his pocket and went in search of an officer.

Near the cemetery gates a row of tables had been set up to process the deportees—for that was the fate Dietrich assumed awaited these Jews. Clerks searched through sheaves of paper, checked off typed names, paused now and then to sharpen pencils, shouted their questions above the crying of children and general din of confusion. Dietrich pushed his way through the crowds, despairing of finding anyone in authority who would take the trouble to help him. In the end, he was himself found. He was the only person about in civilian clothes who was not wearing a yellow star. In not a quarter of an hour he had been accosted by a black-uniformed private who demanded to know his business. Once again Dietrich flashed his Abwehr ID and asked, "Who is in charge here? I would like to speak with him." The private led him toward the home. As they were about to enter, there came a racketing of gunfire from inside the cemetery. Dietrich stopped.

"What was that?" he asked.

The private shrugged and adjusted the strap of his own rifle. "Just some of the troublemakers," he said. "We try to catch them early."

As he followed the private along the hall, Dietrich realized there was nothing of what one might expect to see in a home for the elderly: no nurses in white uniforms, no attendants pushing meal wagons or medicine carts. No elderly people. Had the inmates already been evacuated? But for what purpose? What sort of war work could be done by frail octogenarians?

SS-Hauptsturmführer Josef Hubertus sat at a cluttered desk in what had once been the supervisor's office of the elderly home, according to the faded lettering on the glass door. He studied Dietrich's papers, then looked up. "And how may I help you?" he asked in a not unfriendly tone of voice.

"I am looking for someone," Dietrich said. "A Jew who has been useful to me in the past."

Hubertus motioned for him to sit. Dietrich remembered the bottle of cognac and took it from his pocket. "Um, I hope you will not be insulted, but I thought I might offer you a glass while we talk."

The Hauptsturmführer looked amused. "Really, Admiral Canaris should teach his men to be a bit more subtle." But he rose readily enough, produced two glasses from a sideboard, and accepted the proffered bottle. When he had filled the glasses and handed one across to Dietrich, he raised the other in a jaunty toast.

"Now," said Hubertus. "This useful Jew of yours. His name is?"

"Hermann Fliess."

Hubertus called to an adjutant in the next room. "Alex. Check today's lists for a Hermann Fliess."

"It is also possible," Dietrich said, "that he may not be on your lists. It's my understanding he was rounded up on the street. A random pickup."

"Oh, that may very well be," Hubertus agreed. "It is our policy to discourage the Jews from gathering in crowds during the roundup. Otherwise there might be some ugly confrontations. Best for all concerned to avoid that."

"Of course," Dietrich said.

"Which raises an important question. There is only one way to keep a Jew from being caught up in such a sweep. Did yours carry a safe conduct from the Abwehr?"

"No," Dietrich admitted. He felt his stomach tighten.

Hubertus shook his head and made a tut-tutting sound. "Very sloppy, Herr Bonhoeffer. If he is such an important asset of the Abwehr, you should take better care of him. How exactly has he helped you?"

Dietrich felt a trickle of sweat between his shoulder blades. "Dr. Fliess is a well-respected physician in the Jewish community," he said. "People confide in him, and he has from time to time passed on the names of troublemakers. Especially saboteurs, people working in the factories who might harm the war effort. That is our special concern in the Abwehr. The rest we leave to the Gestapo."

"Of course," Hubertus agreed, helping himself to a second glass of cognac. "A doctor, you say? In that case, there is nothing I can do for you, even if we locate him. No physicians will be allowed to stay in Berlin, I can tell you that, Abwehr informers or no."

"Why not?"

"In future a physician will either be very useful, in certain situations and if he is cooperative, or a great deal of trouble. Once the transports arrive at their destination, all physicians will be evaluated on a case-by-case basis. That is all I can tell you. But the only Jews who will remain in Berlin are essential defense workers. A very few, as you will guess." He shrugged good-naturedly. "Here is what I would do. Forget your doctor and find an informer inside the factories. A Pole, perhaps, or a Russian. And if you want them left alone, issue them a safe conduct. I tell you this because from here on everything is going to be much more tricky." Hubertus nodded and pursed his lips. "Much more tricky."

The adjutant returned to report that the name Hermann Fliess did not appear on any of the current lists. Hubertus stood, said, "So," and shrugged. Dietrich realized he was being dismissed. He stood, his mind racing, but he could think of nothing else. Hubertus picked up the bottle of cognac as though to hand it back, but Dietrich waved him off. "May I ask," he said, "where you are sending these Jews?"

"This lot is going to the ghetto in Smolensk," said Hubertus. "After that?" He held out his hands, palm up.

Dietrich thanked him, exchanged a straight-armed salute, and left.

Hubertus patted the bottle of cognac, a very good brand he had noticed at once, and said to the adjutant, "God, the Abwehr! Aristocratic bloody amateurs! Why the Führer doesn't just turn all the intelligence work over to us, I'll never know."

By the time Dietrich reached the Tirpitz-Ufer it was growing dark. In peacetime the streetlamps would be coming up, but now there was a blackout because of the occasional air raids by the British. People were leaving their offices in darkness and heading home, bundled against the cold. But Hans von Dohnanyi would certainly still be in his office, and there Dietrich found him, blackout curtain in place over his window, working in a circle of light at his desk. He looked up questioningly when Dietrich entered.

"We have to talk," Dietrich said.

Dohnanyi looked at the papers spread before him.

"I know you're busy," Dietrich said, "but it can't wait. And I don't want to talk about it here. I don't trust—" He looked around.

"Very well," Dohnanyi said. "Over a beer?"

"If there is someplace we can speak quietly without attracting attention."

Hans smiled. "I know just the place."

Dohnanyi drove with his headlights shrouded because of the blackout, but this was not especially difficult, since vehicles were increasingly rare. As a high-ranking official, Dohnanyi was one of the few people who had access to an adequate supply of petrol. He navigated the Daimler like a bat through the darkened city to a beer cellar off the Alexanderplatz. It was a warm, smoky place, loud, but with high-walled oak booths conducive to private conversations. When they had their steins of dark beer, Dohnanyi said, "See the proprietor over there?" and nodded toward a stout, red-faced man talking with the bartender. "He's Hitler's half brother Alois."

"No!" Dietrich exclaimed, craning his neck to have a look. "And you bring me here to talk confidences?"

"Can you think of a safer place?" Dohnanyi said.

Dietrich laughed then, for the first time in what seemed ages.

"Sometimes," Dohnanyi said, "we must be defiant. Of everything."

"Yes," Dietrich agreed, and wondered if Hans could read his mind. He sipped his beer and surveyed the room, which was filling up with a variety of low-ranking functionaries of the SS and the government ministries, the clerks who could not afford the Adlon or the Bristol but were happy enough basking in the refracted light of the Führer's brother.

"What is it then?" Dohnanyi asked.

"Elisabeth has turned up. She's waiting in my room right now." Dietrich waited for the expected outburst, but Dohnanyi said nothing, so he continued, "They've begun to round up Berlin's Jews for deportation. Perhaps this is not news to you."

"We knew it would come soon," Dohnanyi said, "though we only got the dates today. We now expect more transports on the twenty-third and twenty-eighth of October."

"You might have told me."

"You knew something like this would happen," Dohnanyi answered. "You knew of the deportations in Stettin. As we agreed in our previous conversations, the saving of Jews is not your assignment. I didn't think the exact dates should be a concern of yours."

"They have become my concern," Dietrich said, and told Dohnanyi everything that had happened that day, speaking quietly but never taking his eyes off his brother-in-law. "You see, the die has been cast," he concluded, "and I cannot go backward. I will do what I can for Elisabeth, whatever the consequences."

He had expected Dohnanyi to interrupt, but he remained silent, rubbed his face wearily with one hand. Dietrich offered him a cigarette, lit one for himself. When Dohnanyi did speak, it was to ask quietly, "Have you given any thought to what you can do with her? It isn't so easy, you know."

"She's safe enough in my room for the time being," Dietrich said. "If she isn't there long, my parents won't even have to know. Father is hard of hearing, though he won't admit it, and Elisabeth knows to be very quiet when my mother is on the first floor. Besides, they seldom come to my room, because they don't like to disturb my writing. And I often take my meals there, so that will not surprise them. Elisabeth can eat the food sent up for me, and I'll find something elsewhere. Meanwhile I thought you might know how I can locate her husband. If she insists on following him, we must make certain he is in Smolensk and that she will be able to find him without difficulty once she arrives. Otherwise it would not be safe to let her go—"

"Dietrich," Dohnanyi broke in. He twisted uncomfortably on his bench. "Dietrich, she must not go to Smolensk."

"But she insists that they stay together."

"I don't care what she insists. The Jews of Smolensk won't remain there very long. They'll be moved into some new camps being built in Poland and Czechoslovakia."

"Labor camps? Will the conditions be worse than in the ghettos?"

Dohnanyi stubbed out his cigarette. "I have some information that I have been waiting for the right time to share. Not because I don't trust you, but because I know of your desire to help the Jews and because what I have to tell you is so unbelievable and appalling I was afraid it would cause you to do something rash. The details have not been officially decided upon yet, and won't be until after the New Year. But the government is making plans to kill the Jews. All of them."

Dietrich stared at him.

"They're meeting in January at Wannsee to come to a final decision. You already know about the mass executions in the Ukraine, the shootings, the vans filled with carbon monoxide. That's all too slow for them. They're building camps where they hope to be able to kill thousands of people a day using lethal injections and gas chambers and crematoria. They plan to 'cleanse' Europe of Jews. Their terminology. If the government is convinced that the plan is efficient it will go into effect immediately after Wannsee. And since I have seen a report from our office which demonstrates that the Wehrmacht will be able to incorporate such a plan into the war effort, I see nothing to prevent them trying to carry it out."

Dietrich's stomach churned. He shoved away his glass of beer and pushed his way through the drunken crowd, up the steps, and outside into the cold night air. Dohnanyi tossed a couple of Reichsmarks on the table and followed, found Dietrich leaning against the wall outside. Dietrich began to walk away very fast.

"Dietrich! All the more reason to push ahead with—"

"Don't come near me! Don't— Just leave me be! I want nothing to do with any of you!"

Dohnanyi caught up to Dietrich and grabbed his arm. Dietrich turned and shoved Dohnanyi so hard against a wall that his hat rolled into a gutter. Dietrich retrieved the hat and handed it to the shaken Hans, then walked away and left him standing there.

He took the tram, so crowded he had to stand on a running board, to Adolf-Hitler-Platz. At a corner market about to close for the evening he was able with his coupons to buy a small loaf of black bread, a sliver of Mainzer cheese the size of two fingers, and a six-inch-long *Leberwurst*. He walked up the Heerstraße with this treasure, Elisabeth's supper, bundled in his arms. By the time he reached the Marienburger Allee it was after eight o'clock. His mother heard him on the stairs and opened her bedroom door.

"Dietrich? Is that you?"

"Yes, Mother." He stopped and she came into the hall wearing a bathrobe.

"There hasn't been any trouble?"

"No, don't worry." He kissed her on the forehead. "You're going to bed early."

"Yes, it was a tiring day. Suse dug a straw pit, just as we did in the Wangenheimstraße during the Great War, and we spent the day filling it with cabbages and potatoes and apples from their garden. I expect there'll be shortages this winter, don't you? Suse says Christel and the children have put up quite a bit as well. Your father's gone to bed. He has a cold and didn't want to aggravate it." She noticed the food he was carrying. "You haven't eaten?"

"Not yet. I stopped at the market, since I missed supper."

"There's potato soup in the icebox, and some nice bits of bacon in it. You must heat it up."

"Thanks, I will. Good night."

He hoped Elisabeth had heard him coming, for his mother would wonder if he knocked at his own door. He pushed it open slowly and whispered, "It's Dietrich."

She was sitting in the dark at the desk.

"Don't turn on the lights," she said. "I was afraid to put up the blackout curtain. I thought your parents might go out and notice and wonder who had done it."

He covered the window and she turned on the desk lamp. She had put on her own clothes and looked tired and worried.

"Sorry I was so long. It must have been terrible for you sitting here in the dark alone, and without any supper."

"Being hungry wasn't the worst part. You didn't find him, did you?"

He shook his head. "No. Though I've learned some things."

"You must tell me! You may think it best to spare me, but that would be the worst of all, not to know the truth."

"Won't you eat first? You'll feel much better."

"How can I feel better, not knowing what is happening to Hermann?"

He had been agonizing all the way home over how much to tell her, how much she needed to know to make a wise decision, how much to sustain hope, how much to survive. He held out his hands and led her to sit by him on the edge of the bed, put his arms around her and held her close. She began to tremble as though expecting the worst.

"I have been to the Scheunenviertel," he said. "I have seen the deportations underway. I spoke with the SS officer in charge, and have been to Hans as well. Here is what I know."

And he told her everything he had seen and heard at the Jewish Home for the Elderly, including the shots in the cemetery, including the assertions of Hubertus about the extent of the deportations and the impossibility of trying to release a doctor. He told her the destination, Smolensk. And he told her the deportations would continue through October until most of the Jews of the Reich had been sent East.

He did not tell her about the death camps.

She listened. Only once did she interrupt, to ask, "Do you think they have shot him?"

"I don't know," he had said. "How would he have acted at the detention area?"

"He is a brave man," she had said proudly. "He would have spoken up if he thought it necessary. He would have told them he is a doctor and would have asked if there were sick children who needed tending. He would not have acted afraid." Then her pride had given way to fear and she had listened again until he was done, when she said, "I must go to Smolensk. I must try to find him. It cannot be any worse there than in the Scheunenviertel."

"It may be," Dietrich said cautiously.

"Not if I am to be alone here."

"Elisabeth, we must think of alternatives. You must help me."

"You don't understand." She stood up. "There's something else I haven't told you. I don't know for certain—perhaps it's too early to say—but I believe I'm pregnant." She paced back and forth. "If it is true, I have to tell him. I have to be with him when I have our baby." Then she saw Dietrich's face.

"What?" she said.

"You can't go to Smolensk. Especially if you are pregnant."

"But I'm probably not even two months along. There shouldn't be any danger in traveling. You said yourself there will be more transports at the end of the month."

"Yes. That is the horror of it. Elisabeth, you can't go to Smolensk. You must hide. You must save your life, and if you don't care about that you must save the life of your child. Hans has told me. The trains for the East are death trains. The Nazis are building new camps especially for killing Jews in gas chambers. They don't want a Jew left alive."

She would have shrieked had he not caught her and clapped his hand over her mouth. She fought him, beating against his chest, kicking him, dragging him onto the bed until the need to breathe at last exhausted her and she began to gag and gasp for air.

Elisabeth lay on her back with the bedclothes pulled to her chin. She had refused the food Dietrich offered, refused to speak. Dietrich was on the floor in the sleeping sack he took on hiking trips in the Harz Mountains. He listened for the sound of her breathing, to know if she slept or wept, but she seemed determined not to let him hear anything.

"Elisabeth?" he said.

She didn't answer.

He turned on his side and shut his eyes but did not sleep. After a time she said in a flat voice, "Are you still writing?"

"Yes," he said.

"And what do you write about at a time like this?"

"The same things I would write in more normal times, except with more urgency."

"Nothing more? My God, at least the Nazis are taking risks."

"What would you have me do?" he asked wearily.

"Be as good as my husband," she said in a hard voice.

"That, it seems, is impossible."

"Ah! I am making you angry! Good. I want you to hate me as much as I hate Germans. And you."

"You don't mean that."

"I do."

"Will hatred save your child?"

"I don't want to save my child. Who wants to bring a child into such a world?"

"Would you say that to Hermann?" When she didn't answer, he raised up on one elbow and asked, "Suppose there were Germans who, after a great deal of soul-searching and cowardice, got the nerve to do away with Hitler?"

"It's too late," she said fiercely. "Don't expect me to weep for you. Or to stay here any longer. I'd rather die among my own people."

She threw off the covers and began gathering up her clothes. Dietrich scrambled from his sleeping sack.

"Wait!" he cried. "You can't leave!"

"You can't prevent me!"

"No! Listen to me! Only a few days. I shall go out tomorrow and find a place of my own that's suitable and conceal you there myself."

"No!"

"Hate me if you want, I don't care! But you and your child—"

They were both stopped by the creaking of the stairs. They looked at each other, then Dietrich went to the door and cautiously opened it. His mother stood there, holding a steaming kettle between two potholders.

"I doubt either of you have eaten a bite, have you?" she said as she came into the room. "It would be a shame to waste such lovely potato soup. Especially since I found us short of milk and Cook had to improvise with water and flour. Dietrich, did you think I wouldn't notice? Now go downstairs and get some bowls and spoons. I couldn't carry everything."

Elisabeth leaned against an armchair, weary as an animal run to ground. The blouse she had been clutching fell to the floor. Paula Bonhoeffer set the kettle of soup on the desk and held out her arms. Elisabeth began to sob. Paula drew her onto the chair, cradling Elisabeth on her lap like a mother comforting a small child. She caught Dietrich's eye and nodded sharply. He went out at once, closing the door behind him.

Hans von Dohnanyi arrived just after dark the next evening and climbed the stairs to the attic, where he found Dietrich working at his desk and Elisabeth reading a book. She started when she saw him and watched warily while he took a chair and sat down.

Dietrich said, "I must apologize for last night. I had no business to treat you as I did."

Dohnanyi nodded, said, "I have forgotten it." Then, to Elisabeth, "I have tried to find out more about your husband, but without luck, I'm afraid. It may be possible to locate him once the transports arrive in Smolensk, but I'm not hopeful. In any event, if he were able, I'm sure he would advise you not to try and follow him. He would want you to look out for your own safety."

"And how am I to do that?" Elisabeth asked.

Dietrich wondered as well, and said to Dohnanyi, "Elisabeth believes she may be pregnant."

"All the more reason," Dohnanyi said. "It would be better for all concerned if we could get you out of the country. I needn't tell you that will be difficult, but it may be possible. I have been meeting with Admiral Canaris and General Hans Oster all morning at the War Ministry. It seems they also have Jewish friends they would like to help out of the country. I have also been in touch with an old law professor of mine who is now in hiding with his wife. Seven people altogether, counting you, Elisabeth."

She looked away. "Only seven out of so many millions. And because we are fortunate enough to know people in the Abwehr."

"I'm aware this is a pitiful response. But your seven deaths will not save the millions. And what we propose in this situation won't work with a large group. Dietrich, the idea is yours, really. I told Oster what you had done yesterday. He thought your actions, while rash, were basically quite sound. You see, the only way we can openly protect a group of Jews in full view of the SS is if they are working as confidential agents for the Abwehr."

"I will not work for you," Elisabeth said sharply.

Dohnanyi raised his hand. "I have just been to see my professor friend on the way here. He said the same. But it will be a ruse. We will get you into Switzerland, ostensibly to spy on the emigrant community in Zurich. But in fact you will do nothing of the sort. You will have to report to the German consulate from time to time, but you needn't tell anything of substance. And the consul there, Gisevius, is one of us."

Elisabeth looked at Dietrich. "It will work," he said. "I'll do everything I can to help."

"And Hermann?" she asked, her eyes filling.

"As a physician, he would be useful in a camp," Dohnanyi said, "and that gives me hope that he would not be killed right away. Perhaps he can survive long enough for this ordeal to be over. But there's no question of your joining him."

"I want to think about this."

"You needn't decide for a few more days." Dohnanyi reached into his jacket and pulled out a square of paper. "But first, something essential. This is a safe-conduct pass from the Abwehr." He handed it to her. "You must carry this with you at all times, even indoors. If you are picked up, or harassed in any way, show it at once." He stood. "I would recommend you stay here a few more days, but continue to keep out of sight. For reasons I won't go into, we can't have you living here very long."

"Hans," Dietrich interrupted. "Shouldn't the family have some say in that?"

"We'll relocate you as soon as possible," Dohnanyi continued as though Dietrich hadn't spoken. "I warn you, this will not be easy or quick. We may have to put you in one of the factories for several months, perhaps in a barracks with Russian slave laborers, until we can sort out all the red tape. But it's better than the alternative."

"And there is no question of her remaining in this room?" Dietrich insisted. "She has the safe-conduct pass now, and Mother and Father say they are prepared to take the risk."

"I'm not," said Dohnanyi. "You can't even tell me for certain that none of your neighbors knows of Elisabeth's presence, and when the transports are finished, there may be house-to-house searches for those in hiding. It's a large enough risk to carry out the plan I'm proposing. If the least thing goes wrong, we shall all be lost, and more than we. Please allow me to do this as safely as possible."

"Hans is right," Elisabeth said, to Dietrich's surprise. "I've learned something about survival these last few years. There's no sense in taking needless chances. I'll go wherever you send me."

"Thank you," Dohnanyi said. He took Elisabeth's hand and bowed over it. "It would be best if we don't meet in person again, but I shall stay in touch through Dietrich. Keep faith."

When he had gone, Elisabeth said, "You're involved in something, aren't you?"

Dietrich sighed. "So I'm told."

"What you said last night, about an overthrow—"

"—should be forgotten," he finished for her.

She looked at him steadily. "It is."

Once the servants were gone and the windows covered for the night, Elisabeth was invited downstairs. She shared the Bonhoeffers' frugal supper of cabbage and carrot soup and the *Leberwurst* left from the night before. Suse, who often came to visit because her husband was serving a chaplaincy with the army in Greece, was there as well with her small son. After the dishes had been cleared, Dietrich and Suse played duets on piano and violin and Paula sang, while Elisabeth sat at the chessboard with Karl Bonhoeffer and little Michael. Then Suse and Michael went home, the elder Bonhoeffers retired for the night, and Dietrich and Elisabeth climbed the stairs to the attic like an old married couple.

Except they were not.

When Dietrich turned on the desk lamp, Elisabeth saw his face just as he was composing it.

She said, "Oh, Dietrich. This is very painful for you, isn't it? Personally, I mean. And I haven't given a thought to that."

He shook his head and turned away, pretended to be searching through the papers on the desk.

"I'm so sorry," she said.

"No, no. It was over between us years ago, and it would be a very great sin for me to resent your life with Hermann. There is much more to be concerned with than any leftover feelings of mine."

He sat at the desk, took off his glasses, and wiped them with his handkerchief. Elisabeth watched him fondly, recalling his shyness and awkwardness when they made love, as though he was amazed each time to find himself with her.

"I should never have slept with you," he said. "It was wrong. Perhaps I have been punished for that."

"Don't say that."

"My views of the sanctity of marriage. You know my views—"

"Don't wish the past away. I've never regretted it. You mustn't either. Besides, you'll find someone else to love."

He shook his head. "In times like these, better for me to remain celibate."

She laughed. "Silly goose! I've always suspected you were a Catholic at heart, but don't go turning priest on me. You'll make a wonderful husband and father, and as for the times, well, all the more reason we need each other." She went to him and put her arms around him. "Dear, dear Dietrich," she said. "You don't stop caring about one person just because you grow to love another."

He stood and put his hand on top of her head, as he had always liked to do.

Neither was ready to sleep. Time for that when all this is over, Elisabeth said. Dietrich went downstairs and returned with a pot of weak tea and two slices of poppyseed cake Suse had brought from Dahlem. He turned on the shortwave radio. A strident-voiced announcer was proudly proclaiming that German troops had reached within eighty miles of Moscow, and went on to play an excerpt from the Führer's speech in Cologne that day.

Dietrich said, "Shall we break as many laws as we can?"

"Why not?" said Elisabeth.

He twisted the needle to the BBC. They listened to the news, which included a report that the Rt. Rev. George Bell, Bishop of Chichester, had addressed the House of Lords on the plight of Jewish refugees being held in internment camps in Britain. *These people suffered greatly under the Nazi regime, the bishop said, and came to our shores to escape persecution. Britain has nothing to fear from them, and it is hypocritical to hold them in detention camps while criticizing Hitler's policies toward the Jews. . . .*

Elisabeth said wistfully, "I wonder how it is with Papa."

"George will look out for him," Dietrich said.

The BBC switched to a concert live from the Palladium—subject to interruption by bombing, the announcer said jauntily, as though warning of showers at a cricket match. *And now Carroll Gibbons and his Savoy Hotel Orchestra, accompanied by that lovely young songbird Anne Shelton.*

The sweet sound of piano and horns filled the room.

> *I'll be seeing you in all the old familiar places*
> *That my heart and mind embraces all day through. . . .*
>
> *I'll find you in the morning sun and when the night is new*
> *I'll be looking at the moon, but I'll be seeing you.*

Dietrich stood in the middle of the room and offered Elisabeth his hand. He took her in his arms, and they danced.

WHEN THE JEWS MOVE INTO THE LARGE OLD HOUSE in Dahlem, there is gossip in the neighborhood. The house itself stands apart, partly hidden in a grove of beech trees on the edge of the Grunewald. It remained empty for five years after its owner, an eccentric old woman who lived alone, died without heirs. A jumble of brick and stone, it is somewhat derelict, with a leaking roof and unreliable plumbing, but good enough for these Jews, since the rest have been sent East to help with the war effort. This bunch is also engaged in some sort of war work. No one knows how this bit of information got out, but if Herr Graber, who owns the butcher shop in Königin-Luise-Straße, thought hard enough, he might recall a local pastor's wife, Susanne Dress, mentioning it. What sort of war work no one knows, but it is obviously confidential, and these particular Jews are too valuable to be sent to some munitions factory in the East. The most likely

rumor is that they are scientists—one knows how bright the Jews can be—
or cryptanalysts engaged in cracking top-secret British codes. After several
weeks pass, and it is clear the Jews are keeping to themselves as much as
possible, interest in them dies down. The Japanese have bombed Pearl
Harbor and the United States has entered the war. Much more pressing
matters to discuss.

Though the code name remains Operation 7, there are now fifteen Jews
involved. Six of them, who had no place to go, live in the Dahlem house,
which Suse noticed was large, isolated, and empty. The other nine are scattered throughout Berlin. Elisabeth Fliess has been allowed to keep her cold-
water flat in Fürstenburgstraße, since the government has not yet decided
what to do with all of the newly empty living quarters in the Scheunenviertel. Hers are the only occupied rooms except for an elderly couple on
the third floor. During the air raids, which are fortunately infrequent, she
is not allowed into the basement shelter with them, but must huddle in the
ground-floor stairwell. She does not see Hans von Dohnanyi or Dietrich,
who has been ordered to stay away from her, but once a month an envelope containing food coupons and a few Reichsmarks is slipped beneath the
door of her flat. She also finds a book or two outside her door on occasion,
and suspects Dietrich is responsible, but she never sees who leaves them.
She keeps her safe-conduct pass in the pocket of her skirt and stays indoors
as much as possible, thinks of herself as under house arrest.

Helping the Jews of Operation 7 has been more difficult than even Hans
von Dohnanyi expected. The SS has grudgingly accepted the explanation
that these Jews are to be used in intelligence work (*Why not?* Dohnanyi has
argued. *We use Jews in other countries, why not German Jews?*), but Hans has
seen the raised eyebrows, even among some of his Abwehr colleagues, and
knows he is the subject of skeptical gossip. Even with the protection of the
head of the Abwehr himself, Admiral Canaris, he is terrified by what he has
undertaken.

Then there is the red tape. Dohnanyi must deal not only with the Reich
Security Office but with the Labor Office. He must be vigilant lest the
names of the fifteen inadvertently show up on the transport lists (The
Dahlem group has already come close to being picked up.) The Jews must
have food coupons and a bit of cash. There is the foreign currency exchange
to consider, since there will be restrictions on taking Reichsmarks out of
the country. And the Swiss. Will they even issue entry visas? Nothing has
been agreed to, though Dietrich has traveled to Zurich about the matter
and Gisevius at the consulate is helping as well. But how will the new
arrivals live? Dietrich has a personal promise that Willem Visser't Hooft
will help Elisabeth, but what of the others? All this takes time, and

Dohnanyi must not let it seem that Operation 7 interferes with the rest of his work.

Christmas is approaching, but Berlin is not festive. Though the city has been bombed only sporadically, people are worried. The blackout and other restrictions preclude any seasonal decorations. Food shortages are not yet severe, and there are even some luxury items available to those with money, because the bounty of France and the other captive nations is flowing into the Reich. But rationing is tight. A hedge against the future, and well advised, since the German army is retreating from Moscow through snow and bitter cold, leaving thousands of fallen comrades behind. It is the first setback of the war, after people had come to believe there would be no setbacks.

Dietrich hears of the deaths of several former Finkenwalde students who were serving with the army. Even as he mourns them, he hopes. Hitler, as stunned as the German people at the setback, has dismissed General Brauchitsch and taken personal command of the armed forces. For many generals it is the last straw, and talk of a coup has begun again. Dietrich has told Visser't Hooft it is the light at the end of the tunnel, that the war will be ending soon.

At Christmas he agrees to accompany his parents to a concert. The Bonhoeffers have been boycotting most concerts because so many include a selection by Wagner and they will not hear Hitler's favorite composer, nor do they like the conductor von Karajan. But this night Wilhelm Furtwängler will conduct selections by Handel and, in its entirety, Mozart's Great Mass in C Minor.

All his life, Dietrich has avoided the Große Meße as assiduously as he now does Wagner. He cannot hear the Kyrie without being transported back to his childhood and the failed audition at the Berlin Conservatory. But his parents want his company and he has not attended a concert for some time, so he relents. Silly to avoid a piece of music because of childish disappointments.

At the intermission, after the Handel, Dietrich remarks on the warmth of the concert hall.

"Warm?" his mother says. "But it seems quite cold to me, despite the crowd. You know they barely heat public buildings these days." Then looks at her son more closely. "Your cheeks are red." Touches his face with the back of her hand. "Dietrich, you're burning up."

Indeed he is growing aware of an ache in his limbs and a tenderness of the skin which presage a fever.

"When we get home," he says, "I shall go straight to bed."

"Should we leave now?" asks his father.

"No. I'm not that sick. Furtwängler is in top form. You must enjoy the music."

He shuts his eyes at the beginning of the Mass and feels as though the Kyrie is taking the top of his head off, that he is leaving his body and floating above the music.

Afterward, on the way out, he stumbles and bumps into an SS officer who wanders carelessly in front of him. They stare at each other, each with unnaturally bright eyes, each thinking the other looks vaguely familiar. They say I beg your pardon in dreamy voices, and move on.

The next morning Dietrich has a fever of 102, and it continues to climb. The doctor is called and diagnoses double pneumonia. When the fever fails to abate, Dietrich lies near death and the family keeps a vigil at his bedside. In her chilly flat, Elisabeth stares out the grimy window at electrical wires scabbed with frost and waits for news.

Top government officials meet at a resort overlooking the Großer Wannsee to decide once and for all how to deal with the Jewish Question. Alois Bauer, newly promoted a Sturmbannführer, is present. He receives congratulations from all sides for his fine work against the underground in Poland. Alois Bauer has become an expert in counterintelligence investigations. Since November he has been called back to Berlin to deal with a rumored Communist spy ring in the heart of the Reich. He believes he is making progress.

Despite his own bright prospects, Bauer is gloomy, and says so to his friend Adolf Eichmann over breakfast in the terrace restaurant above the lake. There is a single black spot on the pristine white surface below, a duck held fast by rapidly freezing ice.

"I don't like it," Bauer says in a low voice. "It's the middle of a war, goddamn it, and we've suffered a serious reverse this winter. Now America joining in. Can we spare the resources for this?"

Eichmann shrugs. "It seems to be a priority."

"A priority, perhaps, but what's wrong with waiting until after the war? It's not as though the Jews are going anywhere. Besides, they're providing free labor."

"Himmler thinks we've enough Russians to take their place."

"That can't be counted on to last. If you want my opinion, the Führer is getting bad advice."

"Perhaps," Eichmann agrees, "but you must admit a good man is now on the job."

"Well," Bauer says, "if anyone can pull this off, you can, my friend."

Eichmann smiles at the flattery and orders two fried eggs and a rasher of bacon.

"An American breakfast," Bauer says.

"Have you been there?"

"America? No. I should like to go sometime. After we've beaten them. Or at least made peace with them."

"A lot like us, the Americans," says Eichmann. "Bold. Expansive. Know who they are. Damn the Japanese for dragging them into this. If I could, I'd trade the Japs for the Americans any day."

Bauer shakes his head. "Can't always choose your friends."

The fever breaks. Dietrich soaks two sets of bedclothes with sweat before settling into a deep, exhausted sleep. Now and then he slides into consciousness, notes the faces of his mother, then Suse and Christel, then his mother again. Then Hans von Dohnanyi.

"Good news and bad news," Dohnanyi says as from a great distance. "The Swiss have given us the entrance visas, and it appears exit visas will also be available. At least, the Gestapo aren't blocking us so far. The bad news. The Swiss will let them in but they won't let them work. Which means I have to come up with enough funds to sustain them indefinitely. How, I don't know. It will take several more months to arrange."

Dietrich sleeps.

He sits up in a pile of pillows and sips a bowl of oxtail soup. The spoon rings against the bottom of the bowl. Dohnanyi takes the bowl and Dietrich settles back on the pillows. He shuts his eyes and asks, "How are you managing?"

Dohnanyi shrugs. "It's complicated. Shifting funds from one account to another. Playing with the figures. Changing currency on the sly."

"Is it legal?"

"Of course not." Dohnanyi lights a pair of cigarettes and hands one over. "Do you have a will?"

"No."

"I'd draw one up, if I were you."

Dietrich blows smoke at the ceiling. "It's so bad?"

Dohnanyi says, "I have a friendly informant at Gestapo headquarters in the Alexanderplatz. He told me last week an order has gone out to tap my telephone, and yours, and to intercept our mail."

"What else?"

"Nothing yet, he doesn't think. But they're just waiting for something to make them more suspicious. And I must warn you, I've got some enemies within the Abwehr as well. As the war goes badly, the patriots grow restless."

"I'm sorry. This is all my fault."

"Don't be ridiculous," Dohnanyi says. "You didn't create the Nazi policy toward the Jews."

"You warned me not to become involved."

"And you were right to ignore me in this case. When someone you love stands before you and begs for help, you can't turn away. We wouldn't deserve to succeed if we did that. Besides, the plot is taking on a life of its own. If something happens to you and me, it will go on without us. We've passed beyond caution. From now on, we travel light."

"Any news of Elisabeth?" Dietrich asks.

"I post someone outside her building now and then. She goes out now and then to the shops. Her pregnancy is beginning to show."

"We must get her to Switzerland before her baby is born," Dietrich says. "It isn't just that she will need medical care. If there's a child involved, the paperwork will be delayed even more."

"Yes," Dohnanyi agrees. "I'm going to send her out ahead of the others."

THE JEWESS ELISABETH FLIESS FOUND HERSELF BEFRIENDED by the elderly couple in her building, the Holzers. The situation with the air-raid shelter—the "ridiculous situation," as Frau Holzer called it—broke the ice. For when Frau Holzer went down the stairs to the basement upon hearing the warning sirens, she could not ignore the sight of the pregnant woman huddling forlornly in the stairwell. "So it's against the law for Jews to be in the shelter with Aryans," she said to her husband, a retired bank clerk, as they waited below. "Who ever comes to our basement? Who will know? And are we to live for seventy years only to turn our backs on a poor girl trying to hide from the bombs? What would Seppi think, who has always been such a thoughtful boy?" (Seppi was their only child, a corporal in the Wehrmacht who, though they did not know it, lay in frozen purity beneath four feet of ice somewhere west of Moscow.)

The invitation to the shelter led to a sharing of rations. Elisabeth reciprocated, for, thanks to her mysterious visitors from the Abwehr, she sometimes had foodstuffs unavailable to the Holzers. The Holzers offered to do Elisabeth's shopping so she need not be out in the streets. There followed an invitation to sit with the old people in the evening. Theirs was a plain flat, one room holding an iron bedstead and battered wood chest, the other a stove, table and chairs, and threadbare sofa. The walls were decorated with out-of-date calendars with rural winter scenes, and photographs of

Bismarck, Kaiser Wilhelm, and the Führer. The Holzers learned enough about Elisabeth to realize she was a Special Case of some kind. A ward of the Reich. Not that this mattered so much. While they would not openly risk their lives for her, they had never considered themselves anti-Semites, indeed, would never have lived in the Scheunenviertel in the first place if they had been. They didn't understand all the fuss over the Jews, said this to Elisabeth over and over, and they trusted the Führer. If the Führer had allowed Elisabeth to stay in Berlin, there must be a good reason.

So the Holzers, attuned as they had become to Elisabeth's presence, were surprised when she left the building on an early morning in May, wearing the threadbare coat with the vivid yellow star, the coat which now could barely reach across her large belly. Elisabeth had stayed off the streets as much as possible. Even though she was a Special Case it was better not to court trouble, she believed, and the Holzers had agreed wholeheartedly. Frau Holzer stood at the window, holding back the thin green curtain with a dryskinned hand, and watched the small lopsided figure hurry along the Fürstenburgstraße, looking right and left as though expecting to be accosted at any moment.

"Something has happened," Frau Holzer said fretfully.

Her husband sat near the kitchen stove reading the morning paper. "Sit down and drink your tea," he said. "She'll tell us when she returns."

Elisabeth was on her way to Gestapo headquarters in the Alexanderplatz to pick up her passport. She kept her head down in what she hoped was a deferential attitude, but constantly glanced to the right and left. People stared, as she had expected. A yellow star was not often seen in Berlin these days, had not been seen for months. She had dreaded this walk, feared being accosted. But for many blocks no one approached. In fact, people shrank from her as though she were a leper, a carrier of contagion, turned from her as if by averting her eyes they might render her invisible. Not until she reached Unter den Linden was she approached by a swaggering officer in uniform, a tall thin man with a large mole on his cheek. Before he could speak she had her Abwehr safe-conduct pass out of her pocket and was waving it in front of him as though confronting a vampire with a crucifix.

He looked disappointed, made a show of studying the pass with his lips pursed, then said, "Where are you going?"

When she gave the address of Gestapo headquarters he said knowingly, "Ah. You are in trouble."

"If I were," she replied, forcing herself to meet his eyes, "I would not go voluntarily. In fact, my job is to report on other Jews who are in trouble."

He smiled slightly and inclined his long head toward her as though he wished to bow but would not dare do so in a public street. "You will come with me, then. Safer for you that way. Not everyone stops to ask questions first, as I do."

And so they proceeded to the Alexanderplatz, the lanky policeman and pregnant Jewess, and the stares this unlikely couple provoked were of course furtive.

The Holzers heard her return just as they were sitting down to their midday meal. Frau Holzer knocked on the door and invited her to eat with them. Elisabeth gladly agreed and when she joined them, brought with her a large bratwurst, a wedge of cheese, and her food coupon booklet. The Holzers stared at this offering in surprise.

"You must have it all," Elisabeth said. "I've no use for it now."

Frau Holzer was the first to recover. "But what will you do, my dear?"

"I can't tell you much," Elisabeth said. "But I'm going abroad. I leave first thing tomorrow morning and I won't be back."

"Oh dear," said Herr Holzer. "Nothing terrible has happened, I hope?"

"No, no," Elisabeth reassured them. "I am going on an assignment for the government." She showed her new passport. "You mustn't fear that your kindness to me has brought you any trouble. Everything is aboveboard. I have even been cleared by the Gestapo."

"But you will be safe?" Frau Holzer asked, even as she fingered the food coupons.

"Oh, yes," Elisabeth said. "You mustn't worry."

"I'm so glad," said Frau Holzer. "It's kind of you to leave us your coupons. Do you know, I think I will save some of them until Seppi comes home on leave. Then we shall have a feast."

"Lovely," said Elisabeth. "When you do, please remember me."

Then Frau Holzer began to weep, and Herr Holzer, to the surprise of everyone, followed. At last they managed to say they would miss Elisabeth, that she had been a great comfort on the cold winter evenings and it would be lonely without her, that they would like to have seen the birth of the little one.

Elisabeth did her best to comfort them. Finally they sat down to a dinner of sausage and potatoes and bread, not good *Schwartzbrot* but a pasty wartime concoction that still filled the belly.

Again Elisabeth left in the gray light of early morning, this time for the Swiss consulate to get her visa stamped. Because she also had a train to catch, she would have to take a tram. Except Jews were not allowed on trams. She did as Dohnanyi had instructed, carried the coat rolled up so that the star didn't show. This looked odd, since the spring mornings were still chill, but when the woman she sat beside on the tram asked, "Aren't you cold, my dear?" Elisabeth replied, "Between the baby and the suitcase—" pointing to the valise at her feet—"I was carrying so much weight I became warm. Anyway I've grown so large the coat doesn't fit very well."

The woman nodded, having already lost interest, and Elisabeth stared out the window, clutching the coat tightly to her chest. The streets were filling with people on their way to work, most of them on bicycles because of the scarcity of petrol. Despite the presence of spring flowers the city looked shabby, the shop windows bare, the crowds glum and weary. Perhaps she hated these people, she thought, these same people she had grown up among. Or perhaps it was only pity mixed with contempt at their smallness. One way or the other she would be glad to be away from them, not only on account of her safety but because of the way they made her feel.

Near the consulate she slipped into an alley and emerged wearing the coat. Her documents showed her to be Jewish and they would be examined carefully, not only by the Swiss but by the police stationed outside. She held her breath each time she handed over her papers, safe conduct always on top, to officers who studied her with cold eyes. Through the gate, struggling through the heavy doors which no one held open for her, past the guard desk in the lobby, along the corridors to the office where her visa was stamped, the fresh ink pale blue beside the large red **J**. The Swiss clerk with the stamp looked at her a moment through thick glasses and then smiled.

"Good for you," he said quietly.

She nodded and turned to leave.

"Wait," he said. "I'll see you to the front door."

Another tram ride, again with coat off, to the Lehrter Bahnhof. The morning had grown warmer, and carrying the coat no longer drew attention. At the station she tucked it carefully under her arm. As long as you don't drop it, she reminded herself. Inside she walked past a row of kiosks which before the war would have been filled with candies, sandwiches, books and magazines, newspapers. Now a single stand sold pretzels, and the Nazi newspaper *Völkische Beobachter*. Fortunately Elisabeth had a book with her, a translation of Emily Brontë's *Wuthering Heights*. A novel from an enemy nation, but safe because it was old.

The noise in the vast main terminal was a shock after months of silence in her rooms. Fortunately she already had her ticket from Dohnanyi, tucked as carefully into her pocket as her official papers. She set down the suitcase underneath the large clock and timetable board in the center of the terminal, leaned against a bench to ease the weight of her swollen belly, and looked up. It was nine-twenty. Still half an hour to catch the next train to Nuremberg, where she would change for Stuttgart and then Basel. The

Nuremberg train would leave from Track 4, according to the board, and Track 4 still stood empty. Elisabeth sank onto the bench and took a deep breath. She must not allow herself to relax, but must also try to avoid calling attention to herself by appearing too tense, too nervous. She looked around. The waiting area was crowded. People were traveling by train instead of automobile, and many were leaving the city, for the bombing raids were more frequent now that the Americans were in the war. Many of those waiting were children, perhaps going to relatives in the country where there were fewer bombs and more fresh produce. And there were soldiers on leave, most looking gloomy, probably on the way back to the front.

Then she saw Dietrich.

He was seated on a bench about twenty yards away, watching her above the open pages of a newspaper. Their eyes met, but he gave no sign of recognition, and she resisted the urge to smile. He went back to his paper.

When the Nuremberg train was announced, Elisabeth hoisted herself up from her seat, one arm pressed against her stomach, and glanced toward Dietrich. He was ignoring her. He leaned over and picked up a small bag. In his other hand was a railway ticket.

Elisabeth walked along Track 4 to her car, knowing that he was behind her. When she reached her compartment, a soldier who was already there took her bag and placed it in the overhead rack. He would have taken her coat as well, but she said, "No, it eases me to put it behind my back." She sat down and wedged the rolled-up coat behind the small of her back.

The soldier smiled. "You're carrying quite a load," he said. "Heavier than my backpack, I'd guess."

"And in a more awkward position," Elisabeth said and smiled back, but her eyes were on the corridor outside. Dietrich walked past, gave her a small nod as one sometimes does to acknowledge the glance of a stranger. She could just see his shoulder as he stopped at the next compartment and then the door opened and he disappeared inside.

At Nuremberg, Elisabeth left the compartment while the soldier and an elderly gentleman who'd joined them in Leipzig stayed aboard. When she climbed awkwardly down the narrow steps to the platform, she saw that Dietrich had already exited and was walking slowly ahead of her. He glanced back once to see that she followed.

On board the next train she bought a cup of ersatz coffee and ate the food she'd brought with her, the scanty remains of the previous night's feast of sausage and cheese. Then she had to use the toilet and left the compartment—which held an elderly woman, a young woman with two small children, and a businessman in his fifties—with great anxiety. It would look foolish to take her coat with her, but she was afraid someone might move it while she was away.

On the way back from the WC she noted Dietrich in the compartment beside hers. Again their eyes met, and she knew he was watching closely as she went to her own compartment and hesitated at the door. The rolled-up coat was still in its place. She breathed a sigh of relief and went inside.

At Stuttgart there was a layover of over an hour while the cars were separated and new engines brought in to tow them in different directions. Elisabeth took out her book and tried to read. The elderly woman in the compartment nodded at the cover and said, "Brontë, eh? *Sturm und Drang.* Like our Goethe."

"The English aren't so different from us," the businessman chipped in. "Why they want to fight us is beyond me. Think what we could do together against the Russians."

"In peacetime," complained the elderly woman, who turned out to be a retired schoolmistress on her way to visit her daughter in the mountain town of Waldshut, "in peacetime"—to the bored children who squirmed on the seat across from her—"we would have reservations in the dining car, and be escorted to our seats by a steward, and we would have wine and schnitzel or perhaps roast chicken and dumplings and a pastry to end. With a pot of real coffee."

"Madam, you make this journey more difficult by reminding us," muttered the businessman, who worked for a timber concern in the Black Forest.

"I think they should know," sniffed the elderly woman, "it will not always be like this."

The mother of the children was sleeping, head thrown back at an angle and mouth slightly open. One of those people who can sleep anywhere, no matter how noisy or uncomfortable the surroundings. The children, a boy and a girl, fidgeted and poked one another.

The businessman got off the train at Freiburg. Elisabeth looked out the window. She would have to act soon. The train would pull into Weil, the last station before the border. At Weil, customs officials would come on board and she would be asked to present papers. Her papers identified her as a Jew, and yet she wore no star. She twisted in her seat, trying to ease the aching in her calves and thighs caused by the pressure of the weight she bore. The baby responded with its own twisting and turning, pushed so strongly she gasped.

The two women, young and old, looked at her.

"A lively one," said the schoolmistress, and smiled.

"Yes," Elisabeth said. "A long journey for us both."

"Where are you going?" asked the young mother.

"Switzerland," said Elisabeth.

Ahs all round. Switzerland was a destination now closed to most Germans because of currency and travel restrictions. Their curiosity was roused. And their envy. It was clear they wanted to ask more questions. But as the train pulled into Weil, where the others stood to gather their belongings, Elisabeth unfurled her coat and put it on. They stared at the yellow star.

"This is *verboten!*" exclaimed the schoolmistress. "You should not be on this train."

"Nevertheless I am on this train," said Elisabeth. "The border guards will deal with my papers. The outcome doesn't concern you."

The schoolmistress jerked open the compartment door and hurried out. But the young mother still sat, pulling on her children's jackets, brushing their hair from their forehead, wiping their faces.

"You have papers to get out," she said without looking at Elisabeth.

"Yes," Elisabeth said.

"Good," the woman said. "I hope you have a beautiful baby. In Switzerland." She stood and faced Elisabeth. "My husband died outside Kiev. We are going back home to my family in the mountains."

Elisabeth nodded. "I wish you well."

"In the mountains," the woman said, "life goes on. Always."

The woman and her children left and the compartment was flooded with men in a variety of uniforms. They pushed in, stared at the pregnant Jewess who huddled in the far corner, holding her belly with one hand and offering her papers with the other. The papers were passed back and forth, then taken away.

One of the men had worn a Swiss uniform, and Elisabeth prayed his presence would keep the others from hauling her off. She wondered where Dietrich was. She stared out the window. Night had fallen, and her car had stopped past the station so that there was nothing to see except a black square of cold glass.

An hour passed. The lights inside the compartment were dimmed because of the blackout. Another hour passed. Then the men returned. They stood in the half-light of an electric torch and one said, "Well then, Frau Fliess. You will come with us."

She followed, her trembling legs barely able to carry her, to another car and was put in an empty compartment that smelled of pipe smoke. No one came to her. Then the car gave a backward lurch and stood still. Then moved smoothly forward. The compartment lights came up, so she lowered the blackout curtain and peeked cautiously out one corner. For a long time there was only darkness.

Then a flash of gray, an outline of trees on a hillside, a wedge of three-quarters moon. A man in uniform came along the corridor. A Swiss uniform. Returned her papers, said *Danke schön*, and moved on.

And lights. Elisabeth had not seen anything like it since the beginning of the war. A floodlit hillside church flashed by and was erased by a wall of black trees. Then houses with lights in their front windows, and streets lined by lights, and lights everywhere, flying and floating past like good fairies.

She stepped onto the platform at Basel to a distant echo and call of porters, of doors slamming, of engines chuffing banks of smoke.

She carried her valise along the track, weaving back and forth from weariness, finally reaching the terminal waiting area, which was deserted.

Except for a well-dressed man, a sturdy balding man who wore wire spectacles. Who strolled over to Elisabeth brandishing an open penknife.

He stopped in front of her, leaned close, and began to carefully cut the threads which held the yellow star to the front of her coat. When he was done, he held the limp yellow rag aloft like a prize of war, then flung it into a nearby waste can.

"Dearest Elisabeth," Dietrich said, "you don't have to wear that star anymore."

V-Mann
Summer 1942

SASSNITZ–TRELLEBORG FERRY. MAY 31, 1942. The lounge of the ferry is packed with German businessmen on their way to Sweden and Norway. They line up at special counters to buy cigarettes and liquor, or sit around tables over platters of herring and sardines. They drain amber glasses of aquavit. They are a loud, jovial bunch, with good reason, for money is being made hand over fist in Scandinavia.

One man in the lounge keeps to himself. He is tall and, unlike the others, solemn. He is wearing a trench coat and broad-brimmed hat, and carries a briefcase, which he keeps close at hand. He stands in line for cigarettes—craves a good smoke as much as the next man and suffers from the shortage of tobacco in Berlin—but exchanges no pleasantries with those around him. Once he has bought his cartons he flees the lounge for the open air on deck, where he chain-smokes furtively, as though he would be embarrassed to be seen. The porters speculate about him. A loner, obviously. "He would not make a good *V-Mann*," one says. "He sticks out too much. And he looks far too mysterious."

"Gunther," warns another, "is it wise to talk about a *V-mann* in such dangerous times? Even when joking? Besides, I've spoken with the man. He's a professor. An egghead."

"Ah," says Gunther. "That explains it."

Dietrich Bonhoeffer had not expected to be sitting on the deck of the Trelleborg ferry, fretfully smoking one cigarette after another. Only a few days earlier he had been in Switzerland with Elisabeth. They spent the first night in Basel in adjoining rooms at the Hotel Drei-Könige-am-Rhein. After a quiet supper they stood upon a balcony overlooking the Mittlere Rheinbrücke. The Rhine in late spring was black and swift, so that had it not been for the anchor of the stone bridge supporting a procession of pedestrians and bright green trams, the city might have been a boat carried away on the current.

"It's almost more than I can bear," Elisabeth said. "Such a lovely view, and a good meal, while Hermann is suffering God knows what. Or perhaps is dead."

Dietrich did not know what to say.

"You will go back?" Elisabeth said after a time.

He nodded. "I must." Though he could not admit that he had not yet summoned up the courage to return to Germany. Each time was harder than the last.

In the end, George Bell, without knowing it, gave him the resolve he needed. Dietrich and Elisabeth had gone on to Geneva, where it was agreed she would stay with Visser't Hooft and his wife until her baby was born. Then she would work with refugees, and if possible join her father in England. Visser't Hooft met their train, took them to lunch, and over plates of rosti, almost as an afterthought, pulled a crumpled telegram from his pocket and handed it to Dietrich.

"From George," said Visser't Hooft. "He's in Sweden. Been there a week and will be there two more."

"Whatever is he doing in Sweden?" Dietrich asked.

"Some sort of cultural exchange between the British and the Swedes. The poet T. S. Eliot is with him."

"Eliot!"

"You know him?"

Dietrich smiled. "We've met."

"Why don't you find some excuse to go to Sweden?" Elisabeth said. "It would be lovely for you to see George again after all these years."

"Of course," Dietrich said and laughed. "Wartime enemies meeting in a neutral country. Wouldn't the SS love that!"

"You're meeting me now," Visser't Hooft pointed out.

"That's different. We aren't at war with Holland, we've conquered it. You're one of ours now, in their eyes, and besides, I'm supposed to be spying on you, remember?"

"Oh, yes," Visser't Hooft said.

"You could spy on George," Elisabeth offered.

"Yes, I could spy on good old George. I could——"

Dietrich stopped, and a shadow passed over his face.

"What?" Elisabeth asked.

Dietrich shook his head distractedly. He looked around, glanced at his watch, put his hand to his mouth. Elisabeth glanced at Visser't Hooft, who was watching Dietrich closely.

"Dietrich," Elisabeth coaxed.

He seemed to recall where he was, sat up straight. "I've got to go back to Germany," he said, "on the first available train."

"Just like that?" said Visser't Hooft.

"Yes. I can't say any more."

Elisabeth was staring at her plate.

"Of course I must go back," he said.

"But not so soon," she whispered. "I thought you might stay for the birth of the child."

"Not possible in any case," Dietrich said, and realized guiltily he would be relieved not to be present when the baby was born. He still loved Elisabeth and longed to be away from her once and for all.

"Well," said Visser't Hooft, "we'd best get you to the train station," and he called for the bill.

There had followed the overnight trip to Berlin, and after a hurried consultation at Abwehr headquarters, Dietrich was in his room in the Marienburger Allee packing a suitcase. Hans von Dohnanyi appeared in the door and held out a sealed envelope.

"Last-minute decision. Will you give this to Bishop Bell to post when he returns to England?"

Dietrich took the envelope from Hans. It was blank. "Memorize this," Dohnanyi said. "When you meet the bishop, address this to E. P. Harrison, 45 Whyke Lane, Chichester. Not before. That address in the possession of a German would call attention."

"What on earth?"

"Better if you don't know," Dohnanyi said.

For the first time in his Abwehr career he had to make use of the subterfuge of spies familiar to reader and cinema-goers—the constant awareness of whether one was being followed and the precautions of misdirection that would cover one's trail. Except for an hour's hurried conversation with Oster he had had no "training" for espionage. He would simply rely on his own common sense, and if his activities were noticed by German agents in Sweden, he would produce an excuse that his mission had been undertaken to confuse the British. He carried in his jacket Special Courier Pass No. 474 from the Foreign Office, which declared he was engaged on important business on behalf of the German Reich and must be protected from interference at all cost.

He arrived in Sassnitz four hours before the ferry was scheduled to depart and took advantage of the delay to play the foggy-headed academic on his way to deliver a theological paper in Stockholm. (The paper was an old one on Christology hastily dug out of a desk drawer.) This was his answer to polite inquiries from others waiting to make the crossing. It was also a good excuse to take a walk through the beech forest toward the cliffs of the

Stubbenkammer. This was what academics did—they communed with nature in an addle-brained sort of way while all the world warred and burned around them. He walked, head down, and tried not to think of his final parting with Elisabeth, of her face, filled with love and concern, as she stood beside Visser't Hooft and his wife. Dietrich had watched her out of sight when the train pulled out of the station. Only then had he turned away his face and wept.

After Berlin, Stockholm was as lovely and well provisioned as any fairy city, its weather as clear and mild, its inhabitants as well disposed. Again Dietrich wondered where he would find the strength to return home. Home, he repeated to himself to ward off fear. Home home home home.

He found the hotel in the Riddargatan where Bell's telegram to Visser't Hooft had been posted, but learned the bishop and Eliot had checked out two days earlier.

"Where have they gone?" Dietrich asked the desk clerk, a thin bored young man who in Germany would have been at the front.

"They left no forwarding address," said the clerk. They were speaking in English, since Dietrich knew no Swedish.

"But they are still in Sweden?"

"I believe it was their plan to remain in the country for a time, yes."

Dietrich chewed his lip, thinking hard. Then he asked where he would find the offices of the Swedish state church and was soon back in a taxi, glancing warily out the rear window for signs of pursuit.

SIGTUNA, SWEDEN. JUNE 1, 1942. T. S. Eliot, fresh from a triumphant reading of his poems at the ancient university in Uppsala, was scheduled to repeat the performance at the Nordic Ecumenical Institute in Sigtuna. The institute was entirely too Protestant for Eliot's taste—indeed, the same could be said for the whole of Sweden. But the audiences so far had been large and enthusiastic—word had it that once the war was over Eliot would be in line for the Nobel in literature, and everyone wanted to catch a glimpse of him. Eliot heard the gossip and was keenly aware the committee which picked the prizewinner was based in Stockholm. He was at his best.

But being at his best took a great deal out of him, and he spent the afternoon napping in his room in the wood-frame guesthouse of the institute. He would rather have been walking along the shore of the Skarven, contemplating this venerable seat of Scandinavian royalty, as he would have done if he had more energy. But there it was, he was not so young as he used to be.

At half past three he woke, slapped cold water from an enamel basin in his face, and went in search of the good Bishop Bell, who was taking his own nap. Bell would be sharing theological reflections on the poems as his contribution to the evening's event. But just as Eliot stepped into the hall there was a sharp rapping at the front door. He waited to see if a servant was about, and when none appeared, went to answer the door himself. Outside Dietrich Bonhoeffer stood stiffly clutching a briefcase. Eliot stared in astonishment.

"Hello, Tom," Dietrich said. He was relieved rather than startled, for he knew Eliot was traveling with Bell.

"My God!" Eliot exclaimed, recovering his voice. "What on earth are you doing here?"

"Official Reich business. I can't explain. But I must see George." Dietrich was keenly aware of Eliot's reaction—the sudden chilly set to his features, the surprise turning to cautious distaste, even contempt. Dietrich tried to pretend he didn't notice. "May I come in?"

"*Jawohl, mein Herr,*" Eliot said, and clicked his heels. Then he stood back and Dietrich stepped inside.

At that moment George Bell appeared in purple bishop's shirt, fidgeting with the clerical collar dangling loosely around his neck and saying, "Tom, who is it? Did I hear—" and stopped when he saw Dietrich.

"George!" Dietrich cried. "Oh, George, thank God!"

"I've been taking a nap," Bell said slowly. "Can it be I'm still dreaming?"

"No dream," Dietrich said. "I can't say how glad I am to have found you."

Eliot stood watching them with his arms folded across his thin chest. "Our friend is here on official business for the German Reich," he said pointedly.

"Ah," Bell said. "You aren't here, Dietrich, because you've escaped and want asylum?"

"No," Dietrich said. "I can only stay a few hours. I must return to Stockholm this evening and take the night train back to Trelleborg."

Bell studied Dietrich a moment, then held out his hand, which Dietrich grasped as though he were being swept out by a tide and Bell were the lifeline.

"My room is at the end of the hall," Bell said. "We can talk there. I'm sure Tom will excuse us, won't you, Tom?"

Eliot looked suspicious but said, "I wouldn't dream of interfering." He watched them go slowly along the hall, the bishop steady and deliberate, Bonhoeffer, still clutching the briefcase, seeming to totter back and forth as though carrying an iron weight. Then they went into Bell's room and closed the door.

"What are you doing in Sweden?" Dietrich asked.

Bell laughed. "I'm the one who's supposed to ask *that* question. Tom Eliot and I are over here putting on a dog and pony show. Don't tell him I said that. We're supposed to show the Swedes that British culture is alive and kicking despite the war. Anyway, what a joy to see you, my boy, after these terrible years of separation, but whatever are *you* doing here?"

"Do you trust me still? Tom obviously doesn't. Neither did anyone in the Swedish archbishop's office. At first they wouldn't tell me where you were."

"I would trust you with my life," Bell replied.

"Then I hope to keep that trust," Dietrich said. "My credentials are from the Foreign Office, but my mission is on behalf of elements in Germany who are planning the overthrow of the Nazi regime."

Bell nodded without surprise. He looked around the plain room, then pulled a pair of hand-carved wood chairs to the window. The two men sat close together and turned their faces toward the late-afternoon sun.

Dietrich asked, "Do you recall whom Dante consigns to the deepest circle of his Hell?"

"Those who betray their country," Bell said.

Dietrich sighed as though relinquishing his last breath. "That is why I am here."

Bell reached over and placed his hand on Dietrich's arm. He waited, knowing Dietrich must talk awhile.

"All my life I have listened to the teaching of Luther," Dietrich continued. "The state is ordained by God and therefore is sacred and must be obeyed. Loyalty to one's own country comes before anything else. But I no longer believe this. Germans, Americans, English, Italians, Russians, all believe it and all are wrong. The nations have become idols, and I will not worship them. I have brothers and sisters everywhere on earth. I have another country."

"The kingdom of God," Bell said. "Remember Isaiah. *All the nations are as nothing before God. They are accounted by Him as less than nothing.*"

"Yes," Dietrich said. "Tell me, George, do you believe that too?"

"I believe it," Bell said. "I love Great Britain, but God comes first."

"And so I have come to you. We are going to kill Hitler."

"I guessed as much."

"There have been setbacks. The German military successes were devastating to us. But now—things move forward again."

"And what do you want from me?"

"I have told my fellow conspirators in the Abwehr that you have the ear of top British officials."

Bell blanched and looked away. He thought, with a stab of fear, Despite

Dietrich's time in England, he does not understand how things work there.
"Perhaps not so—"

"I visited you in your club, the Athenaeum. I saw who dined there. And
now you sit in the House of Lords."

"Dietrich, the House of Lords is not so powerful as some might think."

"The Archbishop of Canterbury. You are close to him. And you will
yourself be archbishop someday soon. Everyone said it when I was in
London."

"The archbishop is listened to, of course, but when it comes to military
policy—well, it's quite a bit different from having the ear of Churchill
and—"

"Eden," Dietrich said. "That is who we would like you to approach."

"Anthony Eden?"

"He is the foreign secretary and he is a member of the Athenaeum, so
you could easily speak with him."

"Yes, but that doesn't mean he'll listen to me."

"I have names!" Dietrich broke in desperately. "I have told my brother-
in-law and Oster and the others that you have influence, that you will
speak with Anthony Eden, and they have given me names. A death list,
these names, if the Gestapo gets hold of them. These are the men who will
govern Germany once Hitler is removed. And they need help from the
British government. Only this—"

"Dietrich!" Bell tightened his grip on Dietrich's arm. "I will do what I
can. But I do not sit at the right hand of the prime minister. Do you understand?"

Dietrich sat back his chair. "Yes," he said. "I understand. But you can get
to Eden?"

George Bell took stock of the situation.

"I promise," he said, raising his hand. "I can get to Eden. Whether he
will listen is another matter."

"It is all we can ask. Here is what you tell him. You must write this down
and then keep it safe."

Bell took out his notebook and fountain pen and wrote quickly as
Dietrich spelled out the names. Generals Beck and von Tresckow and
Hammerstein and their allies in the Army. Goerdeler, the conservative
mayor of Leipzig. Leuschner, the socialist trade union leader who had survived a stint in Dachau, and Kaiser, of the Catholic Trade Unions. Schacht,
Nazi minister of economics and head of the State Bank, who had secretly
turned against Hitler at the start of the war.

"These are the men who will form the backbone of a new government.
It is also possible, even though few of the resisters are monarchists in principle, that the monarchy will be restored to lend legitimacy to our efforts.

Louis Ferdinand, the grandson of the old Kaiser, is a commendably open-minded young man, and very popular in the country. His presence would do much to undermine the efforts of any Nazi who might seek to succeed Hitler. But we are under no illusion that an overthrow will be welcomed with open arms. Most Germans support the government and the war effort. Because of this it could make a great difference if we receive certain assurances from the British. From a distance it will not for a time be clear to the rest of the world what is happening in Germany. There will be chaos. Even worse, the new government won't be able to make known its friendly intentions toward the Allies until the situation is secured. You must make this clear to Eden."

Bell nodded, absorbed in writing.

"We would also like to ask that if possible there might be a pause in the fighting. The Wehrmacht will be much easier to control if the Allies are not taking advantage of the situation."

Bell looked up. "That will be tricky."

"I know. But you must ask. If the German people feel the life of the nation is at stake they will support Hitler whatever he has done. That is a sad fact." Dietrich took a deep breath. "There is one other complication. Even within the resistance there are those who supported Hitler's aggression in the East. They believe Poland and the Sudetenland and Austria are rightfully German and should remain in German hands, even though they believe we must get rid of Hitler. Many of us in the resistance find this attitude repugnant. And you know my views. We Germans must repent our many sins and be punished for what we have inflicted upon humanity. But all this must be sorted out later, after Hitler and the Nazis have been destroyed. Until that happens, nothing else matters."

Dietrich fell silent and watched Bell's pen scratch the notebook page. When he was done, Bell went back over his notes with Dietrich to make sure they were accurate.

"When do you return to England?" Dietrich asked.

"In a week. Is that soon enough?"

"It will have to be." Dietrich hesitated, then opened his briefcase and thrust his fingers into a small, nearly invisible slit in the edge of the lining. He drew out the blank envelope, addressed it, and handed it to Bell.

"Who is this?" Bell asked.

"I don't know," Dietrich replied. "Hans asks that you post it when you return. Only first I must tell you. To do so will directly involve you in our activities. For better and for worse. Whatever the result, even the loss of life, you will be at least indirectly responsible. So. If you refuse to post this, we shall both of us understand."

"Do you know what is in it?"

"No," Dietrich said. "Hans would not tell me."

Bell held the envelope for a long time, his eyes shut as though he prayed. Dietrich thought he would refuse. Then Bell took a deep breath and said softly, "Into Thy hands, O Lord." He slipped the envelope into the notebook, which he hid in his suitcase beneath a pile of underclothes.

They talked together awhile longer, first about Chichester, which had so far been spared serious bomb damage. "We're a bit too sleepy for the Luftwaffe, I expect. Thank God. We've got quite a few youngsters from London sheltering in the area. And it would break Hettie's heart, and mine, if we lost the cathedral as they did in Coventry."

Dietrich told Bell about Elisabeth.

"I'm happy Elisabeth is safe," Bell said. "But I'm sorry for you."

"Oh." Dietrich shook his head. "It was over between us years ago. Still, I'm sad. There is something about this predicament I am in that makes me long for a family of my own. I don't know why. I'd only be sick to death with worry for their sake." Then he glanced at his watch and stood. "I must leave now."

Bell stood as well. They shook hands, but that was not enough, so they embraced. Dietrich picked up his briefcase and went to the door. He stopped and looked back.

"George, if we should never meet again," he said, "I want you to know you are one of the finest men I have ever known. Thank you for everything you have done for me."

Then he was gone.

LONDON. JUNE 1942. The Athenaeum had survived the Blitz with only the loss of windows and several holes of a width of three to five feet in the attic. Still, the upper floors were little used. There was a decided draft. And most of the members liked to gather, after a long round at Whitehall or Parliament or Lambeth, at twilight. Just about the time the first warnings sounded. So the wine cellar downstairs had been expanded to include a lounge complete with carpet, electric lamps, billiard tables, and the overstuffed chairs which were as indispensable as a good brandy. The rules were bent so that many members even took their meals on trays while seated in the chairs, like middle-class American men in their rumpus rooms.

So it was a simple matter for the Bishop of Chichester and the foreign secretary to find a quiet corner in the first-floor reading room. They sat with legs folded and exchanged pleasantries while a servant poured the brandy and arranged the blackout curtains. When the sirens went off, the men ignored them. The German raids had been lighter of late, and what little activity there was seemed to focus on the docklands to the east.

"It seemed to dawn on Jerry," Anthony Eden observed, "that the bombing was getting them nowhere. We'd lost so much, what's a bit more. No one here caved in because of it."

"Let's hope so," Bell said. He was aware Eden was regarding him amiably but a bit warily.

"That was quite a speech you gave in the House of Lords last month," Eden said, referring to Bell's attack on the internment camps set up to hold German nationals living in Britain. "I don't have to tell you Vansittart was beside himself. You always were a man of strong opinions, George."

Bell didn't answer, waited for the question he knew would be next.

"And what strong opinion led you to request a 'discreet meeting on a subject of the most urgent importance,' as you put it?"

Bell sent up a quick, silent prayer, took the list of names from his pocket, and handed it to Eden. Eden scanned the list and looked up quizzically.

"The next government of Germany," Bell said. And he told Eden everything, reading from his notes, that Dietrich had related. When he was done the two men sat in silence staring at the fire. A lump of burning coal fell from the grate with a sizzling pop.

At last Eden said, "This is not the first feeler we've received from the Germans, you know. There is more than one group which calls itself the resistance, and most of these groups are probably the SS trying to either seduce or confuse us."

"This one isn't SS," Bell said. "I'd stake my soul on it."

Eden raised his eyebrows. "Do you know what Vansittart would say? He'd say you are soft on the Germans."

"There was a time," Bell said angrily, "when Churchill and Vansittart and I were the only men in the kingdom who wanted to take on Hitler. As I shall not hesitate to remind anyone who dares call me a Nazi sympathizer. But not all Germans are Nazis."

"Are you suggesting the German people don't support their government?"

"No. Like people everywhere, most Germans support their government in wartime. Even if the war is terribly wrong, unfortunately. What is it—what quality of humanity—that allows for such blindness? But these men—no. They're prepared to commit treason—have already committed treason—to end this war and overthrow the Nazis."

"We've heard from another resistance group within the German Foreign Office," Eden said, "which claims the same thing, and yet wants to retain Poland and Czechoslovakia for the Reich."

"That is unacceptable to the people I am speaking for. And yet these men are aware there are some in the resistance who would want to keep conquered territory. They believe once Hitler is eliminated this question can be dealt with more satisfactorily."

Bell felt himself to be a bundle of nerves, had stood and begun to pace to ease the tension. Eden waved him back to his chair and refilled their glasses. "I'm not unsympathetic to what you are proposing," he said.

Bell stopped and sat, took the offered glass with a trembling hand.

"In fact," Eden said, "I am the best person in the cabinet you could have approached with this. But for my sake and the sake of your cause, I must play devil's advocate."

Bell nodded.

"There is some skepticism," Eden continued, "because some of those Germans, especially in the Foreign Office, who have approached us clandestinely have done so through acquaintances in the English upper classes who were known to be, if not sympathetic toward, at least tolerant of the German government before the war."

"I know the type well," Bell said. "We could include members of this club in that group, couldn't we? In fact, if you mistrust every member of the upper classes who was tolerant of the German government before the war, well, you'd have lost most of your cabinet, wouldn't you?" (Including Eden, Bell thought.)

Eden smiled. *"Touché,"* he said. "But that isn't the most serious sticking point. These contacts of yours have had plenty of time to declare themselves. All the most outspoken opponents of the Nazis went into the concentration camps in the thirties. Anyone else is suspect."

"The trade union leaders on this list spent time in Dachau," Bell pointed out.

"But the others," Eden said. "Beck and the other military men are prosecuting the war—quite successfully, I might add—even as we speak. If the Germans take the Middle Eastern oil fields, the game is over. And some of these men on your list, like Goerdeler and Schacht, have held positions in the Nazi government."

Bell said, "People learn. They change their minds."

"Yes, but where are the results? The war has been going on for three years. What have these people been doing? Where are the assassination attempts, the other overt acts to show they are serious?"

"All I can say in their defense," Bell said, "is that their position is difficult. I do believe they are serious and will act with or without the British government. But if we don't help them, they may very well fail. The Nazis, as you yourself agree, are still very popular, and any attempt to dislodge them must be quick and decisive. Otherwise these—these very fine Ger-

man patriots will give their lives for nothing and millions more innocent
people around the world will continue to die."

Eden had worked the sheet of paper with the names into a tight roll and
tapped it on the arm of his chair. "One thing more. We have pledged our
word to the Americans and the Russians to keep up this fight. We can't just
unilaterally pull back without consulting the Russians especially, even if
there is a coup. Stalin would be furious. Not that there aren't many people," he added significantly, "who wonder privately why we are fighting
Hitler instead of Stalin."

"I don't wonder about that," Bell said sharply. "Hitler must be fought. As
for how this can be done without offending the Russians, I'm no diplomat,
I'm not privy to discussions with the Allies. I only ask you to do your best."
He sighed. "It's not much good, is it?"

Eden shook his head. "I doubt it. But I'll see what I can do." He stood,
glanced at his watch, and offered his hand. "Now it's back to the salt mines.
And George—" he held the bishop's hand between both his—"take care of
yourself. Of your reputation, I mean. You're on dangerous ground."

WHITEHALL. ONE WEEK LATER. Anthony Eden sits at his desk in the
Foreign Office with Sir Robert Vansittart, the permanent undersecretary,
and Stuart Menzies, head of the British intelligence service, MI6. Eden
hands round a box of cigars. "Well," he says.

Menzies says, "We've had other peace feelers in the last three weeks,
from Madrid and Istanbul. Are any of them legitimate or trustworthy?" He
shrugs. "My top expert on this is a fellow named Philby. He's most skeptical of all these communiqués, but especially this latest one, which he sees
as a typical counterintelligence ploy."

"At least this one's creative," Vansittart says, rolling his eyes. "I mean, an
English bishop."

"Yes, well, perhaps old George is turning fascist on us," Menzies says.

"I don't think so," Eden says. "If this is a fake it's only because George
has been suckered in. I like him. I think he's sincere."

"Because you like him?" Vansittart says acidly.

"Because he strikes me as a man of great integrity," Eden answers plac-
idly, "and because he is one of the most respected clergymen in the Church
of England. But in any event, I quite agree we must see some action in
Germany before we can take any of this seriously."

"Winston's position exactly," agrees Vansittart. "Give us a dead body.
Namely, Hitler's. Then we'll see what we shall see."

They finish their cigars and go their separate ways, Vansittart to speak
with Churchill, Menzies to file away the recommendation from MI6 agent

Kim Philby, who unbeknownst to him is a double agent in the service of Stalin's NKVD and who has orders to keep Great Britain and Germany fighting one another at all costs.

BISHOP'S PALACE, CHICHESTER. JUNE 15, 1942. George Bell sits at the desk in his study. Through the window he can see across to the sundial on the cathedral's west transept. He holds the letter from Anthony Eden in his hand and reads it several times.

> Without casting any aspersions on the bona fides of your informant, I am satisfied that it would not be in the national interest for any reply whatever to be sent. I realize that this decision may cause you some disappoint-ment, but in view of the delicacy of the issues involved I feel that I must ask you to accept it.
>
> Yours,
> Anthony Eden
> Whitehall

The bishop takes out pen and paper and writes the text of a cable to be sent as arranged to Willem Visser't Hooft in Geneva.

Undoubted interest, but deeply regret no answer possible. Bell.

Doppelgänger

SS-Sturmbannführer Alois Bauer sits in his spacious corner office on the second floor of the massive stone pile in the Prinz-Albrecht-Straße. A well-appointed office with bookshelves (mostly bare), a painting by Barthel Bruyn the Elder that before the war hung in a Belgian museum, an antique cherry liquor cabinet, an adjutant and a typist in the adjoining room. The desk is large, of solid oak, polished to a sheen that reflects the glow of the overhead lamp. A file folder lies on the green blotter. Bauer picks up the folder in both hands. The folder is more precious than the painting and the contents of the office; indeed, everything else is the result of the folder. Bauer smiles across the desk at his boss, Heinrich Himmler.

"I have them now," Bauer says. "The end of the Rote Kapelle, the Red Orchestra. And not too late, I hope, to correct the damage that has been done. We could bring these people in at any time, but we are just now in the midst of using them to send false information to Moscow. A sort of parting gift."

Himmler nods and accepts a glass of brandy from the adjutant, who bows discreetly and leaves, closing the door softly behind him.

"How did you do it?" Himmler asks.

"We used new electronic equipment to pick up the signals of their radio transmissions from Paris. And then the code-breakers went to work. The Soviets were foolish enough to include names and addresses in one of their transmissions, if you can believe that."

Himmler says, "It's always the most simple mistake that brings down the fortress."

Bauer's expression changes, grows more serious. "One thing is very bad. These are people in sensitive positions. Members of the old Prussian elite, highly placed in the government as if by some sort of birthright. Not because of loyalty, certainly." He opens the folder. "Harro Schulze-Boysen, a leading official in the Air Ministry and the grandnephew of Grand

Admiral von Tirpitz. How can the same family produce a military hero and
a traitor? Then there's Arvid von Harnack, from a family of distinguished
academics. Harnack is a senior official in the Ministry of Economics. Imagine, a Communist spy in charge of the Reich's economic policies."

"God," Himmler mutters. "I detest these old families. They think they're
just below the Almighty. Never trust anyone with two last names, I always
say."

"One wonders," says Bauer, "how many more traitors there are."

Himmler nods. "So do I. My guess is there are more traitors in the
Foreign Office and War Ministry than lice on a Jew."

"My guess as well," says Bauer. "Because here's what is most disturbing.
Not only did the Red Orchestra pass on military secrets to the Soviets.
They also sent dispatches claiming many of our generals are seriously disil-
lusioned with the Führer."

"I have heard such rumors from other quarters. And I believe we have
found the man to look into the matter."

Bauer bows his head modestly, just after he glimpses his own reflection
in Himmler's monocle.

"I'm suspicious of the Abwehr," he says. "Even though army intelligence
was helpful in catching out these traitors. The best men I spoke with in the
Abwehr believe their own ranks are tainted. I've been wanting to investi-
gate army intelligence for some time. But one has gotten the feeling it is a
sacred cow."

"Because of Heydrich, poor fellow," Himmler replies. "I liked Reinhard.
But he and Admiral Canaris were old friends, lived next door, and Canaris
was like a father to him. Both fanatics about dogs, and so Heydrich would
never hear a word about the Abwehr, would take your head off if you suggested something might be very wrong there. But Heydrich is dead"—the
head of the SD, the intelligence wing of the SS, had been assassinated by
Czech partisans—"and there is now no one between the Abwehr and me.
Do I make myself clear?"

"Quite," Bauer says. "My colleagues will be very pleased to hear this." He
was thinking especially of Sonderegger of the Gestapo, who had barely
been kept on a short leash when the report of disloyalty on the general staff
had been transcribed by the cryptanalysts.

"This mustn't be botched!" Himmler said sharply, as though reading
Bauer's mind. "Any warning will send these people running for cover."

"I'm aware of that," Bauer agreed. "I know how to handle this. One can
keep very still while looking—as you said—for details."

Himmler nods, pleased. "You have already done a great service to the
Reich," he says. "The Führer has informed me you are to have a reward."
He turns to the painting on the wall. "A work of art from his private col-

lection. A Vermeer perhaps, or a Brueghel. Though if the bombing worsens everything will be going underground for the time being."

Bauer coughs discreetly. "I am honored," he says, and places his hands in his lap to keep them from shaking. "But I must admit my artistic passions lie in a different direction."

"Oh?" Himmler leans back so his chair creaks.

"I adore Mozart," says Bauer.

Himmler looks puzzled. "But surely recordings of Mozart are available. If there is something you lack for your collection—"

"A manuscript!" Bauer breaks in, dismayed at his own boldness.

But Himmler is not offended, only bemused. "A manuscript?"

"Mozart's Mass in C Minor. The original manuscript is in the possession of the Prussian State Museum and, I understand, stored underground somewhere in the Reich."

"And you want this manuscript?"

"Yes," Bauer whispers. "Oh, yes."

"Well—" Himmler claps his hands on his knees. "After all, it's only a few scratches on paper. Not the actual music itself. I don't see why not. I shall tell the Führer."

"Would you?" Bauer's eyes are shining. "Oh, would you?"

When Himmler leaves, Bauer stands and salutes so vigorously that he nearly wrenches his shoulder out of joint.

Himmler is as good as his word. Three weeks later, Alois Bauer's saloon car draws up outside a potash mine deep in the Thuringian Forest. A dwelling place of dwarves, Bauer thinks as he is led deep into the bowels of the earth by a guard, their gargantuan twisted shadows preceding them along the passage. The depths of the mine hold the collections of the Prussian State Library, carefully crated and labeled, perhaps by the same officious curator Bauer has come to think of as an ogre guarding an enchanted treasure. Now there are no curators present, only armed guards, who have their orders from the top. The specific crate has already been located, to save the Sturmbannführer time, since he is an important and busy man. His visit is off the record; no one has noted it in the repository ledger.

The crate is carefully pried open. Bauer stands over it and beholds the object of his desire, the parchment a pale illumined gold beneath the glow of the electric torch. He does not move for many minutes, head bowed so no one can see his tears. The guards wait patiently; nothing better to do anyway. At last he looks up.

"You are certain it is safe here?"

"Oh, yes," says the SS Hauptsturmführer in charge of the potash mines. "Only the Führer is more secure."

"But at any time—"

The man nods so that he doesn't have to finish. "Whenever you wish, it will be waiting for you. We have the orders on file."

Bauer sighs. He would like to take the manuscript with him, but he loves it too much to expose it to the bombs which are falling with increasing frequency on Berlin. "*Auf Wiedersehen,*" he says to the crate, in a voice so low no one else hears. "Until we meet again." He salutes the guards, and leaves the mine, his boots echoing along the stone chamber.

Maria
August–November 1942

AFTER DIETRICH BONHOEFFER'S CLANDESTINE TRIP to Sweden he began to daydream about children. Not just any children but his own. Though they of course did not exist. Perhaps it was because of the news sent through diplomatic post that Elisabeth Fliess had given birth to a daughter. Dietrich thought of Hermann Fliess, who did not know he was a father, who might know nothing more of this world. Meanwhile Dietrich loved the child even without having met her, but she was not his. He thought of Hermann Fliess and himself as half-men, each possessing what the other lacked.

Thus the dreams of children. Waking, he longed for children. Not children with Elisabeth, for alive or dead Hermann Fliess stood foursquare between them. Dietrich could not explain this; he would not attempt it. Elisabeth must go to England to be with her father, as should be. And Dietrich must move on. That was all.

In the late summer of 1942, in North Africa, Rommel launched an offensive. In the east, the Wehrmacht captured the Maikop oil field from Soviet troops and pushed on to the Volga. But it was another period of quiet for Dietrich. After the clandestine trip to Sweden, Oster and Dohnanyi thought it wise for him to "disappear for a time," as they put it. Not to hide, but to go back to the countryside to write his *Ethics* and not call attention to himself. It had become increasingly obvious to the resisters inside the Abwehr that they were being watched more closely. The SS and Gestapo were regular visitors to the Tirpitz-Ufer. It was not unusual to bump into a black-uniformed officer in a hall or walk past the open office door of an Abwehr hard-liner and glimpse an SS officer reared back in a chair smoking a cigarette and chatting amiably. Dohnanyi waited nervously for word from England. When the telegram from Bell arrived, he became ill with disappointment, could not keep down food for two days. But what could one expect? The British had every right to be cautious. They would not believe in the resistance until a dead body had been produced. Very well then. The plotters would try to deliver, even though the increased surveillance had everyone on edge. At least the mysterious letter Dietrich carried to Sweden had received a positive response.

Dietrich knew that his mission had failed, that the SS was closing in. He would have expected this knowledge to crowd out thoughts of family, of children, but instead his longing grew more intense. It was difficult to concentrate on his writing, despite the pleasant surroundings. He had once more been remanded to the care of the Prussian gentry. Not to Pätzig this time. He had pleaded with Dohnanyi, explained how he and Frau von Wedemeyer had parted on such unhappy terms. So he was sent instead to Klein-Krössin, a larger, more prosperous estate owned by the von Kleists, relatives of the von Wedemeyers and distant kin of Dietrich's mother. Unlike the von Wedemeyer family, the von Kleists were members of the resistance, and while Frau von Kleist did not know the details of Dietrich's work, she did not judge him for lacking a uniform.

Dietrich had special cause to appreciate the new arrangement when word came that von Wedemeyer, a cavalry officer serving in the Ukraine, had been killed in action. His commanding officer wrote the grieving widow that Rittmeister von Wedemeyer had died valiantly after being struck by a shell. He had been buried in the Ukraine. Dietrich, reflecting on the damage that could be done by an exploding shell, wondered if there had been much to bury.

In the absence of a body, a memorial service was held in the little church at Pätzig. Dietrich walked over through the woods from Klein-Krössin. Although he was one of the few clergymen in the region, he had not been asked to help with the memorial service. Instead he sat near the back of the church while a retired pastor from Stettin delivered the eulogy.

He dreaded to meet Frau von Wedemeyer. And she treated him as coldly as he had expected, though she was, of course, polite. A Prussian lady would always be polite. When he passed through the receiving line after the service, she offered him her hand—which he bowed over and pressed in sympathy without receiving any response—and turned a dry cheek to him to be kissed. She did not meet his eyes, but directed his attention to the young woman standing beside her.

"You will recall my daughter, Maria," she said. "Maria, this is Pastor Bonhoeffer, who lived nearby before the war. Remember he confirmed you and your brother."

Maria. She had been thirteen when last he saw her and in his memory remained thirteen. But this was no child, he realized with a shock that ran from the tip of his toes to his scalp. She was now eighteen, a pretty, full-figured girl with light brown hair and a delicate complexion. Her tears deepened the blue of her eyes. She took his hand automatically, tried to smile politely but failed and bowed her head. He held her hand tightly.

"I am so sorry," he said. "I recall how close you were to your father. I especially loved to watch the two of you at games."

"Yes," she murmured. "Papa loved games."

"I'm afraid he always spoiled Maria," Frau von Wedemeyer broke in. Then she turned pointedly away and greeted the next visitor.

Dietrich thought it an incredibly cruel remark at such a time. Maria raised her eyes and met his. "He loved me better than anyone," she said fiercely.

"He did," Dietrich agreed. He realized with a start that he was still clutching the girl's hand. He tried to let go but she was holding on just as tightly.

"He liked you," she said. "Papa liked you very much. I remember. He used to say you were one of the few clergymen he could talk to like a normal person."

Dietrich winced inwardly but said, "I also liked him. He was a good man."

"Thank you," she said. He was being forced along, as Frau von Wedemeyer had finished with the guest behind him. The handclasp was broken. But as he moved away Maria called after him, "I should like to talk with you again. About Papa. Will you call?"

"Of course," he said. "I can come over next week if you like, after you've had time to rest."

"Oh, sooner. I don't need rest so much as comfort."

Because of the distance they had to raise their voices. Dietrich supposed Frau von Wedemeyer had heard this exchange and would disapprove. Too bad, he thought. He wandered away to a table of refreshments set beneath a grove of trees and pretended to be occupied with his teacup and plate of cakes. But he could not keep his eyes off Maria. He saw all his own sisters in her. The flaxen hair and clear complexion of Christel, the high spirits of Suse evident despite her grief, the full figure of Sabine. He imagined taking her in his arms, taking her into his bed. At this he blushed and tried to distract himself, sipped his tea, then squinted at a squirrel on a branch above his head. Then back at Maria. A wisp of hair had escaped the clip above her ear and straggled against her cheek. He longed to brush it back. As if reading his thoughts, her hand went to the stray lock and pushed it behind her ear. She turned her head, caught him watching her. He looked quickly away. When he raised the teacup to his lips, his hand was trembling.

Because of the loss of her beloved father, because she could not avoid imagining what had happened to him, how the shell had torn him apart, how what was left of him had been tossed into a muddy pit and hastily covered over, because of all this, Maria did not at first guess the nature of Dietrich Bonhoeffer's interest in her. He was a pastor concerned for a daughter mourning a father. Her state of mind was much too fragile, the pain of loss too fresh, to consider anything else. The desperate clinging to his hand, the desire to throw herself in his arms and be comforted, she simply accepted. If her brother Max had been killed, her father would have been there to hold her tight while she wept. But with Papa himself dead— There had been no one else she wanted to hurl herself at and beat upon the chest, certainly not her mother (as likely throw oneself upon an ironing board), no one she longed for until the tall, rather stocky Pastor Bonhoeffer appeared. Only Pastor Bonhoeffer was the same size as Papa.

Of course, she could not actually throw herself upon him in the garden at Pätzig, where he sat two days after the memorial service and allowed her to pour him a cup of camomile tea.

"It's beastly stuff," she complained, eyeing the yellow liquid in the cup, "I should like to serve you Darjeeling, but with the war—" And the thought of the war brought Papa to mind, and her eyes filled with tears.

Dietrich offered his handkerchief and took one of her hands in his own, even though he was sure Frau von Wedemeyer watched from some window of the house. He said little, for he had begun to feel that words, however eloquent, were mere foolishness in the face of great sorrow. At last Maria composed herself and said, "Mother says that Papa is in Heaven. But I don't know what I think about Heaven. I believe Papa still exists, that he is here right now. He's glad I'm sitting here with you, as if he's whispering it in my ear. Do you think that's silly?"

"Of course not," Dietrich said. "And while I can never be as special to you as your father was, I should like very much to be your good friend. If you'll allow me."

"Oh, yes," she said. "I need a good friend ever so much."

A maid arrived with two plates, each holding a slice of poppyseed cake. Of course Frau von Wedemeyer would not send out the entire cake, Dietrich thought. A clear message—or was he overly sensitive?—eat this bit, then be gone. He obliged, lingering only a little over the crumbs before making his way back through the woods to Klein-Krössin. But first Maria walked to the edge of the trees with him, just out of view of the house, and promised that they would soon ask him to dinner. Then just as he was about to take his leave she flung her arms around his neck, held on for a few seconds as though drowning, and just as abruptly let go and ran away.

The dinner invitation never materialized, and two weeks later, a telegram arrived from Hans von Dohnanyi recalling Dietrich to Berlin. He packed his bags and left Pomerania once and for all, with no idea of ever seeing Maria von Wedemeyer again. But waking or sleeping, staring out the window of a train or sitting up late with his fellow conspirators smoking cigarette after cigarette, the girl appeared to him. He saw the two of them married, strolling arm in arm through the Tiergarten or the woods at Pätzig. Pushing a baby's pram. Making love. That above all. In his mind's eye Maria was naked and he explored every part of her.

He accompanied Dohnanyi to Rome for consultations with the Vatican. While his brother-in-law huddled with Fathers Leiber and Schönhöfer over the report they would give the next day to the Pope, Dietrich could not keep his mind from conjuring the phantom Maria, who drew him into bed and wrapped her legs around his waist. He sat hunched on his chair, his body turned away from Dohnanyi and the priests, fighting an erection.

On the return trip he shared his feelings with Dohnanyi, stammering and blushing like a schoolboy, seeking relief rather than advice. Dohnanyi listened without interrupting while Dietrich babbled on—"Perhaps it's because of our situation. I'm sure danger is an aphrodisiac. One is frightened of death and what better way to assure one is alive than to fall in love. If it is love. Probably only lust. She's very young, isn't she? Eighteen to my thirty-seven. Good God, I must be mad. I mean, I'm not thinking clearly. Am I?"

Dohnanyi said, "It's natural. You're a healthy, normal man and you've met a pretty girl. Why shouldn't you be attracted to her?"

"At such a time," Dietrich continued distractedly. "Such an awful time."

"All the more reason. Who among us doesn't yearn for love, and especially in times like these?"

Their train was crossing the Brenner Pass, climbing laboriously up and around hairpin turns past artillery placements set against raw cuts in the mountainsides.

"We'll be back across the border soon," Dietrich said, thinking he was changing the subject. But he came back to Maria. "It would be criminal for a man in my situation to take a wife now."

"Do you think it's better for a man to be without attachments?" Dohnanyi said. "I don't agree. Perhaps it would be easier for Christel and the children if they didn't know me. But I wouldn't want to have missed our life together all these years. That is where I get my strength. And if the worst comes, their love will be what helps me face it. You could do far worse just now, brother-in-law, than fall in love."

Dietrich felt a surge of hope. "You think so? Then what should I do? I'm such an idiot when it comes to such things."

Dohnanyi laughed. "It's not as though you've never been with a woman."

"Yes, but with Elisabeth, it seemed we were thrown together as friends and then just fell into a relationship. Ultimately I was no good at it. And this is different. I would have to court this girl. She would expect it, wouldn't she? She's so young, and she knows nothing of me. And such a pretty girl must have admirers her own age, young men in the army perhaps, who will seem very heroic to her. How could I compete with that?"

"She's been away at boarding school," Dohnanyi pointed out. "And I'd guess her mother keeps a close eye on her. She's probably been very sheltered."

"That's true, but it may do me more harm than good. Her mother detests me."

The conversation continued sporadically throughout the trip. Dietrich feared Hans would be bored but, except for an obvious bemusement, he seemed to enjoy Dietrich's predicament. As if he had been taken away from the war and the plot and dropped into the world of schoolyard gossip where boys shared smokes and swapped stories of real and imagined conquests. After the conductor entered to pull down their sleeping berths they continued to talk, lying on their backs and blowing smoke at the ceiling, savoring the cigarettes hot in their mouths as the tip of a woman's tongue.

He nursed his desire for Maria through other journeys—to Switzerland, where he oversaw the safe arrival of the remaining Jews of Operation 7, to Munich, where Josef Müller was arranging the illegal transfer of currency to support the refugees in their new Swiss homes. In September he gathered up his courage and wrote a letter, composing four drafts before sending it off, striving for just the right blend of affection and distance, and finally deciding to err on the side of caution. *Dear Maria, Amid all the dreariness and sorrow of this war, I have continued to treasure the memory of our meeting at Pätzig, even as I mourn the circumstances. I think of you often and wonder how you are bearing up to the burden of your father's death. It is often in the weeks after such a loss, when friends have gone on about other business, that sorrow is most difficult to face. Please know if you ever need a friend to confide in, I am here.*

I recall some details of our conversation apart from the talk of your loss. You told me that you long to study mathematics at university when the war is over, and that your mother laughs at such an ambition as a silly whim, a course of action not suitable for a young woman. I happen to think it is admirable that you should want to pursue such a difficult subject, and I encourage you to continue with your plans. The war will not go on forever, and we all need something to hope for. As for the field's unsuitability, I don't see why a fine mind should be wasted whether it is possessed by a woman or a man. Certainly there is no question of any sort of work marring the feminine charms which you possess in such abundance. . . .

He read this draft over and over, aware that except for the last sentence it might be a missive from a fond uncle. And yet after mailing the letter, he turned away from the postal box certain that this single sentence had completed the final act of a short-lived infatuation. She would laugh at him, perhaps show the letter to her younger sisters at night, reading his parting words aloud to the accompaniment of girlish giggles. Or even worse, she would write to a lover at the front about the balding old man who had sent her such a ridiculous letter.

Her response arrived ten days later, a short polite note thanking him for his concern, his offer of friendship, and the list of Bible verses he had so thoughtfully included for her comfort in dealing with her recent bereavement. Her mother had, of course, read his letter as well, and had helped compose this response. The note was signed *With kind regards, your young friend, Maria.*

At the bottom of the page, a hasty scrawl had been added. *Mother will have surgery on her eyes at the Franziskus Hospital in October. Shall I see you?*

Frau von Wedemeyer lay on her back in the white iron hospital bed. Two sandbags, long and slender like pillowcased sausages, were packed tight against the sides of her head. Her eyes were swathed with bandages and her thin hands splayed limply across her chest.

Maria put a finger to her lips. "Shh. She's been asleep for over an hour. Or at least she doesn't answer when I speak softly to her."

She took Dietrich by the arm and led him into the corridor. He glanced back into the room and said, "I would have brought her flowers from my mother's garden, but this last cold spell has taken them all."

"She couldn't see them anyway," Maria said. "The doctor says the bandages won't come off for a week. And she isn't allowed to move her head because the stitches are so delicate."

"What is it? Cataracts?"

"Yes. She'd had more and more trouble reading, but she kept putting off doing anything about it. Since Father's death, she has missed more than ever being able to read, so she decided on the surgery at last."

"Would you like to go out for a walk?"

"I can't just now. They'll be bringing the midday meal in fifteen minutes and I'll have to help her eat."

"Perhaps we could stroll the corridor?"

Maria smiled and took Dietrich's arm. They went along past ranks of doors. The hospital was built like a large square around an open courtyard, and they could make a circuit, pausing at each corner before a high window that overlooked a garden turning brown in the autumn sun. Some of the windowpanes were missing, casualties of the ever more frequent bombing raids.

"I was very pleased with your letter," Maria said, "and I would have liked to come visit you."

Dietrich flushed with pleasure.

"Only," she continued, "Mother didn't think it would be appropriate. She said we haven't known each other very long, and you are, after all, a mature man." She turned on him a look with such a strange mixture of shyness and knowingness that he stopped walking and leaned against a wall.

"If you are in Berlin for several weeks, we can remedy our lack of acquaintance," he said. "I would like very much to get to know you better."

"Mother will have to be told," Maria said.

"Of course."

"But not at first. I'm staying at my aunt's house in the Brandenburgische Straße. Mother doesn't expect me to be with her every minute—in fact, she sleeps quite a lot, which is only natural. She needn't know everything I do."

"Maria, I don't want to deceive your mother or take advantage—"

"I'm not talking about deceiving her," Maria interrupted. "I'll tell her very soon that you've come to call. But I want to get to know you better first. That way I can face her more easily. You know how she is. She interferes. But I'm a grown woman now and I must make my own decisions. She will come to accept that in time."

They continued along the corridor, Dietrich thinking furiously what he should do. The daydreams he had harbored for the past few months seemed surprisingly more likely to materialize than he could have imagined. Maria's fair skin betrayed a passionate warmth as easily as did his own, and the pressure of her fingers on his arm had been unmistakable. So. He must ask himself, did he truly wish to pursue this, especially in the face of the mother's opposition?

They reached Frau von Wedemeyer's room just as the food cart approached. Maria turned to him. "Come back at two o'clock," she whispered. "She'll certainly be resting again and we can go to lunch."

She disappeared inside the room. From a distance he heard, "Mother, dear, it's time to wake up and take some soup," then Maria's voice was drowned out by the rattling of the food cart along the long linoleum corridor.

He took her around the corner to the beer garden run by Hitler's brother. When he pointed out the name of the proprietor painted in Bavarian letters beside the door, she laughed. "This will be something funny to write my friends. I bet the Führer would be just as glad if his brother changed his name."

"I do believe our great leader is ashamed of his relation," Dietrich agreed.

The day was warm, one of the last of the season, and so they ate outside at a wooden table beside a linden tree. The garden was crowded with officers, and when Dietrich on a whim flashed his own Abwehr ID, they were treated to portions of bratwurst and red cabbage which were larger than any Dietrich had seen since the beginning of the war, along with thick slices of *Schwarzbrot* and a square of butter. Maria looked at Dietrich curiously.

"I'm very impressed," she said.

"Don't be," he answered more sharply than he meant. "Intimacy with this regime is not a reason to be impressed."

She studied him carefully a moment, went back to her food, then looked up. "Why aren't you a chaplain? Why aren't you at the front?" When he didn't answer at once she added, "Mother says you are a coward. A slacker."

He looked down at his plate, stunned with anger and embarrassment. "Your mother is quick to judge," he managed to say.

"She thinks she has a right. She has lost a husband, and her son is on the Russian front."

"Max? I thought he was in France."

"There was more need for men in the East. Max's unit has reached the Volga. They've been quite successful, according to his letters, but then you can't always tell by that, can you?"

"No," Dietrich agreed. He did not tell her that the Abwehr had been warning Hitler of disaster threatening the Sixth Army on the Volga as Soviet forces regrouped.

Maria seemed to read his thoughts. "For the first time," she said, "Max sounds frightened. He tries not to write anything gloomy, of course. But I know him so well." She leaned closer. "You were a great comfort to me when Father died. I'm sure you would be a comfort to boys like Max as well. If you were a chaplain, I mean."

"Why do you press me on this? Do you want me to go away?"

"No. But I want to admire you."

He met her eyes. "Maria, I must be very honest with you. I cannot serve in the field. It is a matter of personal principle. This does not mean I am unpatriotic, nor does it mean that I despise the men like your father and Max who are fighting this war. It is a tradition in our country that men will fight when called upon, even if they do not believe in the cause. But sometimes a patriot chooses a different course of action. I have, for reasons of conscience, chosen to serve Germany in a manner that will not be clear to you, nor can I make it so. You will have to trust me. That is all I can say in my defense."

She considered this. He felt a sudden rush of tenderness for her, for the way she had confronted him so forthrightly, for the way she so seriously weighed what he had told her. Only eighteen, he thought, but not immature, not by any means.

She said, "I think I am a good judge of people And I do trust you."

He took her hand across the table. "My family will gather tomorrow night at my parents' house for an evening of music. I would be very happy if you would accompany me. If your mother can spare you, that is."

"Yes," she said, and squeezed his hand in return. "I should like that very much."

He met Maria at the hospital after her mother had taken her evening meal. He felt compelled to speak to Frau von Wedemeyer, for it went against his upbringing to escort a young woman about town without her mother's knowledge. Frau von Wedemeyer answered him in a tremulous voice, as though she was overwhelmed by the blackness of the world in which she lay and by her inability to even turn her head toward him.

"In my day it was considered inappropriate for a single man and girl to be alone together until they were engaged," she said to the black void.

"That was my family's custom where my sisters were concerned," Dietrich replied. "Though times have changed. The old ways seem very far off now."

She longed to answer him sharply, but the slightest tensing of her muscles caused pain to shoot through her eyes to the back of her skull. She merely pressed her lips together and said, "As far as my daughter is concerned, I still decide what is appropriate and what is not."

"Of course, Frau von Wedemeyer," Dietrich said. "I didn't mean to imply otherwise. I promise that my parents will be present throughout the evening, as will my sister Christel and her husband, Hans von Dohnanyi. I shall have Maria back at her aunt's in the Brandenburgische Straße by ten-thirty, and both Dohnanyis will travel with us as chaperons. Your daughter will be very safe with my family."

And knew he was not telling the truth, though in a very different way from what Frau von Wedemeyer imagined.

He saw Maria every day, neglected his writing to be with her whenever her mother slept. They walked in the Tiergarten just as Dietrich had dreamed, though with Paula Bonhoeffer in tow instead of a baby pram. The park had been damaged by the bombing; craters pocked the greensward, trees were snapped in two or split as though struck by lightning. A shell had fallen in the zebra compound of the zoo, killing all but one of the banded animals. Dietrich scarcely noticed. Nor did he pay much attention to the music when he escorted Maria to a performance of *The Magic Flute* at the Opera House. They had gone out with Hans and Christel, since Dietrich was still scrupulously trying to keep his promise to Frau von Wedemeyer. He tried to think of a way to be alone with Maria, but the closest he came was in the hospital corridor, always in view of passing nurses and attendants.

He decided he might manage a chaste kiss in her mother's room, while Frau von Wedemeyer slept. He considered this possibility over and over. Unless Maria herself protested, it would work, he thought. Best done when he was taking his leave. Then there would be no question of further expectations until Maria had a chance to sort out how she felt about such an advance in their relationship.

But when he arrived the next morning at the Franziskus Hospital, Frau von Wedemeyer was sitting up in bed, bandages off. Her eyes were red, the cheekbones beneath them swollen and with a bluish stain, but she could see. She greeted him with the news that she would be returning to Pätzig the next day.

"Is—is that wise?" he stammered.

"Normally it would be another week," she said. "But new casualties are arriving from the front, soldiers with eye wounds. They're setting up cots for the poor boys in the corridors, and I can't bear to take up a bed under such circumstances. Besides, Pätzig is such a comfort, I'm happy to return as soon as possible. My own physician can tend me quite well there, and of course Maria will be with me."

From a chair in the corner of the room, Maria gave him a helpless smile.

Frau von Wedemeyer said, "After all, dear, you did say Aunt Spes was beginning to wear on your nerves."

"Yes," Maria agreed. "She's quite an anti-Semite, you know, Dietrich, and she blames the Jews for the war. I really weary of hearing it. And I do miss the woods at home. But you will come visit us?"

"I'm sure Pastor Bonhoeffer is quite taken over with his duties here in Berlin," Frau von Wedemeyer answered for him, making no effort to conceal her contempt.

"But you will come when you have a chance," Maria insisted, refusing to be intimidated.

"Of course," Dietrich said. "When Hans can spare me."

He saw them off at the Anhalter Bahnhof, pushing Frau von Wedemeyer in a reclining wheelchair while Maria walked beside them. Several railway attendants hoisted the chair onto a sleeping car, and Dietrich lingered on the platform, hoping Maria would hesitate as well and he could kiss her goodbye. But Frau von Wedemeyer was calling for her daughter, one hand clutching a rail to keep her chair from moving, and Maria turned only long enough to give him a fleeting peck on the cheek before climbing aboard.

ON OCTOBER 26, 1942, Max von Wedemeyer was killed in the early days of the Russian offensive that would overwhelm the German Sixth Army at Stalingrad. When his remains arrived at Pätzig, it fell to his sister Maria to escort them from the station. Likewise it was Maria who arranged the funeral service, for Frau von Wedemeyer had been so devastated by news of her son's death that she kept to her bedroom for a fortnight. Trays of food were returned to the kitchen barely touched, and though she was usually fastidious, it was several days before Frau von Wedemeyer could summon the strength even to bathe. When a parcel of Max's effects arrived on one of the last German trains out of Stalingrad, it was Maria who opened it.

The package contained a torn and bloodstained leather pouch. Maria fought back a wave of nausea, then opened the clasp, dumped the contents on her bed, and called for a servant to dispose of the pouch with instructions that her mother must know nothing of it. Then she turned to all that remained, the few items Max had carried on his person. There was a small Bible. A locket she recognized as a gift from his girlfriend Anna. A dog-eared pack of playing cards. A penknife. And an envelope stamped with a Berlin postmark and addressed in a familiar hand. She opened the letter, smoothed out the pages, which appeared to have been folded and unfolded many times, and read the words of comfort Pastor Bonhoeffer had written her brother on the death of their father. She read it through three times, could hear Dietrich's voice, gentle and soothing. Then she stretched out on the bed, the letter beneath her, and cried herself to sleep.

The memorial service was delayed until Frau von Wedemeyer had gained enough strength to leave her room. Not until her mother had appeared at the dinner table, thin and silent, did Maria write Dietrich and invite him to attend. She was afraid he wouldn't receive the letter in time, for she knew from his own letters that he traveled often between Berlin and Munich. (Though she did not know the reason—that the position of the conspirators was so precarious they no longer dared communicate except through trusted couriers like Dietrich.) When there was no word from him and the day of the memorial service approached, she forced herself to speak with her mother.

"I'm sure he'll answer as soon as he receives my letter," she said at the breakfast table, as Frau von Wedemeyer picked at a soft-boiled egg. "I'm sorry to be so uncertain. But of course there's plenty of room here in the house if he is able to come, and Dietrich isn't a demanding houseguest. It would mean a great deal to me if he could say a few words at the service."

"I don't want him," Frau von Wedemeyer said without looking up.

Maria stared at her. "But—well, if you don't want him to speak, I still—"

"I don't want him under this roof," her mother interrupted. "I won't have it. Not when Max—" She broke off, then stood abruptly and left the table.

The rest of the day Maria busied herself with household chores. She finished in her father's study, sitting in his old leather chair close to a west window, where she mended stockings in the waning afternoon light.

Frau von Wedemeyer appeared, a shadow in the doorway. "You have already written to invite Pastor Bonhoeffer," she said.

"Yes," Maria answered with relief, assuming her mother had bowed to the inevitable.

"I thought I understood as much. I've just sent Fritz to post a telegram to Pastor Bonhoeffer withdrawing the invitation. I'm sorry if this is awkward for you, but next time you shall consult me before inviting people to my home."

Frau von Wedemeyer left the study and climbed the back staircase. Maria could hear the floorboards creak along the upstairs hall to her mother's room.

Maria wrote at once to apologize for her mother and declare her own innocence in the matter, and Dietrich, his initial hurt assuaged, responded with relief. Frau von Wedemeyer could do nothing about their continuing correspondence, indeed knew little of it, for Maria daily walked the two miles and back to pick up the mail and post her own letters. Dietrich had grown more bold, proclaimed his affection more plainly, the words coming easily because they were addressed to the unseen Maria of memory. In one of his letters he enclosed a snapshot. It was several years old, taken before the war. He was leaning back in the front seat of a Mercedes, striking a carefree pose, smiling broadly and looking much younger than he at present felt. Maria wrote her own letters to this dashing Dietrich. She imagined him in just such a car, driving through the night to a clandestine meeting in Munich whose purpose remained for her cloaked in shadow. Never mind. Whatever he was about, it must be good and right.

A few weeks after Max's memorial service, Dietrich wrote

> My dearest Maria,
> I can no longer hold back but must tell you all. I love you above anyone. More than this, I want to marry you. Of course, it would be best to ask you in person, but as we are kept apart, that is impossible. I must have

your answer, and if it is what I hope, I shall arrange to come speak with
your mother at once.

    Yours always,
    Dietrich

Maria read the letter once and hid it away inside her desk drawer. She was too shaken to look at it again for several days. When at last she retrieved it she carried it downstairs and dropped it on the table in front of her mother as though it burned her hand. Frau von Wedemeyer looked at the envelope, then at her daughter. She took her reading glasses from the pocket of her skirt, opened them carefully, and read the letter. When she was done she looked away without a word. Maria burst into tears and ran from the room.

They didn't speak of the proposal until after supper, when a fire had been lit in the sitting-room hearth and the family dogs brought in for the night.

"I suppose," Frau von Wedemeyer said, "you have taken great pleasure in defying me."

Maria began to cry again. "You are so unfair! To both of us! Papa loved him! He did!"

"Your father was fond of Pastor Bonhoeffer. But after all, he didn't know him that well. Really, they had little in common."

"It's not true. He tells me something about Papa in every letter. Every one."

"He is old enough to be your father."

"I don't care. He's ever so much wiser than the boys my age, ever so much wiser."

"My dear child, with the war, you've hardly had a chance to know any boys your age, except for your cousins."

"I don't care," Maria repeated. "If you refuse us, you will make me miserable for the rest of my life." She stood up as though to leave the room.

"So," her mother said, "you will go about weeping and accusing me because you believe I am treating you unfairly. Is this what I shall have to endure, on top of losing your father and brother?"

"You aren't the only one who lost them!" Maria cried.

Frau von Wedemeyer said nothing, and once more Maria turned to leave. Behind her, her mother said, "Very well, write Pastor Bonhoeffer. Tell him I wish him to come to Pätzig so I may speak with him." And when she saw the joy spread across her daughter's face, she said, "It may not be all that you hope for."

"You will refuse us?"

"I shall propose a compromise. But that, Maria, is not where the disappointment may lie."

She would later remember the shock of that winter meeting after weeks of separation. That afternoon she stood on the platform and greeted the man who emerged from the Stettin train, the sturdy, solemn man—older than her dream Dietrich—who kissed her cheek under her mother's watchful gaze. She could scarcely look at him, found it hard to keep her mind on the conversation as they walked back to Pätzig. He gave her a small package, after assuring Frau von Wedemeyer that it was not an engagement ring. Maria felt as though someone else fumbled with the wrapping, exclaimed with gratitude at the necklace which had belonged to Paula Bonhoeffer's mother. Someone else listened calmly, almost gratefully, as her mother agreed to a marriage only on condition that Dietrich and Maria see nothing of each other for a year before becoming engaged, so that Maria might "settle down." Someone else attempted to whisper words of comfort to a disappointed Pastor Bonhoeffer.

That night, seated at her desk wearing the necklace over her nightgown, she wrote in her diary

It's true I don't love him. But I know I will love him.

Christmas 1942

MUNICH. Dietrich Bonhoeffer walked down the Ludwigstraße past the Ludwig-Maximilian University. His hat was jammed tightly on his head because of the stiff wind, and the lower part of his face was hidden by a gray scarf. He was on his way to Abwehr headquarters with papers from Hans von Dohnanyi, but his mind was not on his mission. He walked with his head down and allowed himself a furtive glance at the wall on his right. A trio of women prisoners were busy scrubbing at the plaster beneath the watchful eye of a guard, but had not yet been unable to obliterate the words, three feet high, scrawled in black paint

DOWN WITH HITLER!!

At the end of the block Dietrich turned and retraced his steps. Again the furtive glance. The words were no mirage, were real, even though the DOW was fading beneath the application of turpentine. The other letters would soon vanish as well, but their ghosts would remain unless the wall was painted. Dietrich's eyes narrowed to slits and tears caught at the corner of the lids. He turned his head and walked on. Other people passed him, walking quickly with heads down, whether from fear or anger he could not tell.

Three hours later he stepped into a phone booth in Munich's Am Platzl and spied the corner of a mimeographed sheet protruding from the telephone directory.

A CALL TO ALL GERMANS!
Leaflet of the White Rose

Nothing is so unworthy of a civilized nation as allowing itself to be "governed" without opposition by an irresponsible clique that has yielded to base instinct. It is certain that today every honest German is ashamed of his government.

He looked around quickly and then slipped the sheet of paper into his pocket. Not until he was back in his hotel room did he smooth out the crumpled page and read it carefully.

> If the German people are already so corrupted and spiritually crushed that they do not raise a hand; if they surrender man's highest principle, that which raises him above all other God's creatures, his free will; if they are so devoid of all individuality, have already gone so far along the road toward turning into a spiritless and cowardly mass—then, yes, they deserve their downfall.
>
> If everyone waits until the other man makes a start, the messengers of avenging Nemesis will come steadily closer. Therefore every individual, conscious of his responsibility as a member of Christian and Western civilization, must defend himself as best he can at this late hour, he must work against the scourges of mankind, against fascism and any similar system of totalitarianism. Offer passive resistance—*resistance*—wherever you may be, forestall the spread of this atheistic war machine before it is too late. Do not forget that every people deserves the regime it is willing to endure.

Dietrich arrived in Berlin just before dark the next day and went straight to the Dohnanyi house in Sacrow. Dohnanyi was usually at home in the evenings. Events were moving quickly now; a definite plan for Hitler's assassination had been developed and would soon be set in motion. Dohnanyi preferred to busy himself with mundane affairs while under the watchful eyes of the SS and Gestapo men who now seemed omnipresent in the Abwehr offices at the Tirpitz-Ufer. At four he would pack his briefcase and go home. He would share a light supper with Christel and the children, then retire to the quiet of his study overlooking the Havel for his real work.

He was smoking his pipe and writing a new report for the Vatican when Dietrich entered and handed him the leaflet. Dohnanyi glanced at it and turned pale, sat up straight with one hand gripping his eyeglasses, and read it more slowly.

"My God," he said at last. "The Gestapo will be going crazy."

"God have mercy on whoever wrote this," Dietrich said. "If they're caught it will go hard."

"They'll be caught," Dohnanyi said, "especially if they keep at it."

"There's something else," Dietrich said, and told him about the walls near the university and the English Garden covered with the slogans DOWN WITH HITLER and FREEDOM.

"Students," Dohnanyi said.

"I wondered."

"Just the sort of thing young people would do."

"But the leaflets. It would take resources to print and distribute them."

Dohnanyi shook his head, lost in thought.

"Whoever did it," Dietrich said, "it means something's stirring."

"Yes. Unfortunately the Gestapo will be so on edge they'll be shooting at their own shadows. A dangerous time for us already, since they've just smashed the Rote Kapelle. Poor Arvid and Mildred." He paused, thinking of the Harnacks, who were awaiting execution for espionage. He could feel the rope about his own neck but shook the thought away as though shooing a bee. "I'll have to talk to Oster first thing in the morning. Funny no one in the Tirpitz-Ufer has mentioned anything about this."

"It even caught Müller by surprise," Dietrich said, "and he's had his ear to the ground in Munich."

In fact the leaflets were the talk of the office when Dohnanyi arrived the next day. They had been found in Hamburg and Saarbrücken and Cologne as well as all over Munich, in libraries and public rest rooms and telephone booths, were even turning up in the mail, addressed to attorneys and members of university faculties. The Gestapo was analyzing the paper and ink to determine their source, inventorying large-scale purchases of stationery and stamps, and searching for unauthorized mimeograph machines. Hitler was said to be in a rage. No wonder, Oster pointed out. It was the first word of public dissent since the Olympic Games of 1936.

Arvid and Mildred Harnack and their fellow Communist conspirators were waiting to be hung by the neck with piano wire. With the knowledge of their fate looming over him, Dietrich Bonhoeffer decided to write a Christmas message to his own fellow conspirators. He sat for hours at his desk in the attic room of the Marienburger Allee house, scribbling a few lines and then marking them out, pausing to scratch aimlessly at the frosted windowpane with his fingernail, or wander to his pianoforte and play a few bars of Bach. He thought almost constantly of Maria. He heard again Frau von Wedemeyer stating her opposition to the engagement, demanding that he not see Maria for an entire year.

A year he might not survive.

Only when he had forced himself to face this possibility could he write his Christmas gift to the conspiracy.

Death has become familiar to us, he wrote. *We calmly hear of the deaths of our acquaintances. We come to expect our own deaths and welcome each new day as a gift. Life is too precious for us to romanticize its ending. But death cannot take us by surprise now, and we have seen enough of it to know that goodness and life can come from it. And it is after all better to die while living fully than in some trivial way.*

Something else we have learned that we might otherwise have missed. We have learned to view life from below, from the perspective of the outcast, the transgressors, the mistreated, the defenseless, the persecuted, the reviled. It is impor-

tant that we are not bitter or envious. For we have learned that personal suffering unlocks more of the world than does personal good fortune.

And when he had written these words, he also knew he could not agree to Frau von Wedemeyer's demands. When he had done with the Christmas message, he took up another sheet of paper and posted a letter to Pätzig, asking Maria von Wedemeyer to become secretly engaged to him. She agreed.

The White Rose
December 1942–February 1943

MUNICH. THREE MEDICAL STUDENTS hurried along blacked-out streets in the university quarter of Schwabing. One cradled a bottle of schnapps inside his coat. Though the hour was late, no one noticed these particular young people, for many others like them were out celebrating the end of the winter term, blundering through the blackout in drunken bliss as students are wont to do, war or no.

The medical students slipped into an alley off Leopoldstraße and stopped before a large wooden door set in what looked like a garage. Shurik, so nicknamed because his dead mother was Russian, produced the key and in a moment they were inside, drawing blackout curtains, turning on lights and gas heaters. It was an artist's studio belonging to a friend of Shurik's who was a corporal with the army in France. Paintings hung on plaster walls and a half-finished canvas, livid with reds and purples, stood on an easel in one corner surrounded by metal pails crammed with tubes and bottles and brushes. Shadows draped the room like blankets.

"Music?" Shurik asked, going to the phonograph.

Hans Scholl shook his head no. He shrugged out of his coat and set the bottle of schnapps on the edge of a table littered with magazines. Willi Graf found four glasses, wiped them with the tail of his shirt. They pulled four chairs into a circle and sat, stared nervously at the empty seat. Willi took out a pack of cigarettes and offered it around.

"Will you pour then?" Shurik asked.

"No," said Scholl. "Not yet. We want clear heads."

"I'm telling you, he's okay. Lilo says—"

"Lilo says, Lilo says."

Shurik was mad about Lilo (among a number of other women he was mad about), and the others were weary of hearing about her. Lilo, an artist like most of Shurik's friends, who daubed great swatches of color on canvases ten feet high from a homemade pallet of berries and roots since oils were scarce, who wore her black hair straight and her fingernails purple, who could find hashish even in wartime.

"He's an old friend of hers," said Shurik—and thinks, An old friend she's been sleeping with.

"Another artist," said Scholl.

"He's in theater," Shurik corrected. "He once directed the National Theater in Leipzig."

"So of course he's okay."

"He has been in Dachau," Shurik said.

"And he got out," said Willi Graf. He spoke so seldom that they usually stopped and paid attention to him. He looked from one to the other. "I'm not saying anything against him. But there may be a reason."

"He got out during the Olympics," Shurik said testily. "Dear old Adolf let everybody out during the Olympics."

"Not everybody." Scholl leaned back and blew smoke at the ceiling. "They didn't change Dachau into a resort during the Olympics."

"You know what I mean," Shurik said. "They let a lot of people out. He was lucky enough to be among them."

They were interrupted by three soft knocks at the door, followed by two louder raps.

"Him," Shurik said. He jumped up and went to the door. Willi Graf leaned forward expectantly, and Hans Scholl watched with narrowed eyes through a curtain of smoke.

A man in the uniform of a Wehrmacht officer stepped through the door, blinking as he came into the light.

"Gentlemen," Shurik said, announcing the newcomer's name for the first time, "I'd like you to meet Falk Harnack."

He brought a whiff of death with him. When they studied his thin face with its long, aristocratic nose, they could not help see the face of his brother staring at them from the newspaper photographs. Arvid Harnack and his American wife, Mildred, were only days away from their execution in Plötzensee Prison for their part in the Red Orchestra conspiracy.

Falk rubbed his face wearily. "I only have two hours," he said. "Then I have to catch the night train to Vienna."

Even Hans Scholl was awed. Here was a man who not only slept with Lilo the Artist but traveled to Vienna in military uniform despite being brother to the most famous traitor in Germany.

"Lilo says—" Shurik's voice broke and he cleared his throat, embarrassed. "Lilo says you know things."

Falk almost smiled. He accepted a glass of schnapps from Willi. "And if I know 'things,' why should I tell them to you?"

"Lilo has spoken to you," Shurik said.

"Yes, of course, or I wouldn't have come here. But are you serious? Or are you little boys looking for an adventure?"

They glanced at one another. Hans Scholl would have to make the decision. He took a deep breath and said, "That chair you're sitting on. Is it comfortable?"

"It's hard for a chair with a cushion," Falk said, "and there's a sort of ridge pushing on my balls. Most *un*comfortable, I would say."

"Because there's a mimeograph machine inside," Hans said.

"Surprise surprise." Falk twisted his rump to a more comfortable position. "And possession of a mimeo machine is a capital offense. But of course you know this."

"So our lives are in your hands. Would you like to see the machine?"

"I know what one looks like," Falk said. "But I would like to know what you do with it."

"Tell us something first," Hans Scholl demanded. "Something that would put you in danger. To show we can trust you."

Falk studied his fingernails, then looked up. "Someone is going to kill Hitler," he says.

To a young person who had only known Hitler as sun and moon, it was as though someone said *The sun and moon will be extinguished tomorrow.* They clutched the arms of their chairs.

"Who?"

Falk Harnack smiled, pleased at the effect he had created, as though they were onstage and a line of dialogue had sent a thrill through the audience.

"Why should I say anything more?" he asked.

They produced a copy of an old leaflet from inside a book on a shelf. ("What a rotten hiding place," Falk said, "and why would you endanger your absent friend this way?" They blushed.) With trembling fingers they spread the yellowing sheets on the table like sacred parchments.

Falk bent over the table and read

Nothing is so unworthy of a civilized nation as allowing itself to be "governed" without opposition by an irresponsible clique that has yielded to base instinct. It is certain that today every honest German is ashamed of his government.

traced the margins with his finger while trying not to laugh because he pitied the young people for their naiveté

If the German people are already so corrupted and spiritually crushed that they do not raise a hand; if they surrender man's highest principle, that which raises him above all other God's creatures, his free will; if they are so devoid of all individuality, have already gone so far along the road toward turning into a spiritless and cowardly mass—then, yes, they deserve their downfall.

straightened, eyes at the door.

"What have you done with these leaflets?"

They had bought envelopes and stamps in many small batches, mailed the leaflets to people who owned bookstores, people who were artists and intellectuals and professors and pastors. People in the telephone book. Left batches of leaflets in phone booths and toilets and empty classrooms at the university.

The leaflet called for an uprising of the German people.

"Any response?" Falk asked.

Their faces, eager as they explained their work, changed. "No response," said Shurik.

"People are so uncertain," Willi Graf said. "They need an example."

"No response," said Hans Scholl. "Yet."

They were interrupted by a pounding at the door.

"Jesus Christ!" they cried, shuffling leaflets into hiding places frantically until they heard a woman's voice on the other side of the door.

"Hans? Shurik?"

They opened the door to Hans Scholl's sister Sophie, a first-year philosophy student, who rushed in clutching a cloth bag to her chest.

"My God, Sophie!" Hans cried. "What are you doing here?"

"I followed you." She set the bag down with a thump and took out cheese and a bottle of wine.

"Something's going on," she said. "Something's going on and I won't leave until you tell me. If I were a man, you wouldn't leave me out of this. Would you? Would you?"

"It's not something women should be involved in," Shurik said.

She glared at him, her short hair sticking out at odd angles beneath her kerchief.

"I won't go away," she said.

Before Falk Harnack left to catch his train, he wrote the address of his aunt in the Wangenheimstraße and gave it to Shurik, who handed it on to Hans Scholl. "If it's an emergency you can write to this address. Otherwise wait until I contact you."

"Remember," Scholl said, "we want a meeting. We don't want to be left out. If there's an uprising, German students must be involved. There can't be a revolution without students."

"I'll do what I can," Falk said, and slipped out into the night.

Falk decided to try once more to draw on his old connections to the Bonhoeffers. Not so much for Shurik and the other students but for himself. With Arvid and Mildred dead, he was left isolated and despairing. He was frightened as well, but driven more than ever to act, to do—something. Arvid had wanted him in the Rote Kapelle, but despite his earlier predilections, Falk no longer felt comfortable working with the Communists. Stalin's pact with Hitler had shaken him, as had the stories of the persecution of Jews in the Soviet Union that had filtered into Poland, stories that led him to condemn the Russians and Ukrainians and Lithuanians and Poles as bitterly as he did his fellow Germans. Falk now considered himself to be a democratic socialist and a citizen of the world. Nothing else. In Poland he drifted into the orbit of the few Wehrmacht officers who had defied the expectations of their class to harbor socialist sympathies of their own. It wasn't so hard to find them. A few veiled references to the Weimar trade unions and one could very quickly size up the lay of the land.

Through these same officers he learned enough of the resistance to consider himself a part of it. He guessed there was a cell in the Abwehr working toward a coup. He'd never been given names, but he could guess. Still he didn't dare show his face at the War Ministry in the Tirpitz-Ufer. The sudden appearance of the brother of an executed spy would have sent them all running for cover. The same would happen, he believed, if he went to either the Dohnanyi or Bonhoeffer homes.

Instead he began to frequent the concert halls. The men he sought were music lovers. Concerts would be among the few diversions they would allow themselves, and he guessed they would seek the solace of music as often as possible. He was right. On his third attempt, a performance of the Berlin Philharmonic, he ran into both Dohnanyi and Dietrich Bonhoeffer at the interval.

Dohnanyi was coolly polite, and obviously keen to get away. Dietrich seemed more hesitant and for a moment resisted Dohnanyi's tug at his sleeve.

"I'm so sorry," he said, referring to Arvid and Mildred but afraid to say their names aloud.

Falk nodded. "I'd like to talk to you."

"Not possible." Dohnanyi intervened quickly. "Come, Dietrich."

And they were gone. But Falk was able to see where they were sitting. And when the concert was over he got close enough to jostle Dietrich and slip a note into his pocket. Their eyes met briefly and then Dietrich turned away.

The note had asked for a meeting the next day at the Renaissance hunting lodge built by the Elector Joachim II on the shore of the Grunewaldsee. It was a spot they had frequented long ago, Dietrich and Elisabeth and Falk and Suse, because they considered its irregular towers and turrets romantic. Falk still had a snapshot taken one winter, all of them bundled in coats and hats and scarves. Smiling at the camera. So young. He smoked a cigarette and watched Dietrich make his way toward him. They stood for a time, watching a pair of loons on the lake, not so close as to seem to be together.

It was a bitterly cold day and it was soon apparent no one else was about. Dietrich was the first to move closer. An act of generosity, Falk thought.

"So?" Dietrich said.

Falk said, "I have friends in Poland." He mentioned names. "I know what you're about."

"Do you?" Dietrich said.

"Not the details," Falk admitted. "Nor do I want to know. I only wish to pass on that I have information about a resistance movement that is growing among university students. Independent of your own activities."

"Ah."

"They are responsible for the Munich leaflets. You know what I'm talking about?"

"Yes. I've seen them."

"I know the leaders of this movement. They want to make contact with the larger resistance. I don't know that it's possible, but I promised I'd ask. They mean well. They're obviously very brave. And very bright, if a bit foolish the way young people can be. You understand?"

"I understand. But I must tell you the others will not want to bring them in, because of the very foolishness you have mentioned."

Falk offered a cigarette and lit one of his own. "Do you agree?"

Dietrich hesitated. "No," he said after a moment. "I think the young people put us to shame."

They smoked awhile in silence. The loons had flown away, leaving the lake flat and empty. Dietrich said, "You must tell them to be very careful. No unnecessary risks."

"Yes," Falk said.

"I will speak with my brother-in-law."

"You know what he will say."

"What else can I do?"

"The leaders are some young medical students named—"

Dietrich put up his hand. "Don't tell me."

"Very well. I'd like to bring them to Berlin to meet you. You wouldn't have to tell them much, just enough to let them know you're legitimate. They're impressive young men, the sort who could lead the nation someday. There's another bunch of students in Hamburg who are just as active, and they've got contacts at universities across the country. Perhaps you could suggest some ways they can help that run less risk of drawing attention from the Gestapo, such as preparing for the moment when—" Falk dropped his cigarette butt and ground it beneath his feet. "For the moment that is so hard to imagine just now."

"It seems to me," Dietrich agreed, "it would be useful if students were prepared to take to the streets. My brother-in-law has contacts with former trade unionists still working in the factories who are ready to step down when word comes. Why not students as well? But as for a meeting, I don't—"

"Please," Falk interrupted. "Next month." He suggested a date in late February. "I'll be back in Berlin then for a meeting. I could bring them to you here, at this very spot."

"All right," Dietrich said. "But only if you don't use my name."

They shook hands. Falk left first, strolling at an easy pace, a soldier on leave enjoying a bit of fresh air and quiet. Dietrich watched until he disappeared into a stand of birch trees.

The Americans flew over Munich by day and the British flew by night. The young people waited in the garage studio off the Leopoldstraße. Hans Scholl and his sister Sophie, Willi Graf, and Alex Schmorell, called Shurik. Outside the sirens commenced their plaintive wailing. Hans Scholl smiled. He went to a cabinet and brought back a bottle of wine and four glasses, passed them around. Shurik was pulling up planks from the floor of a closet and hauling out cans of paint. A present from his sometime lover Lilo, who had once filled canvases with great slashes of black and purple and green but claimed now the muse had deserted her. End the war, she told Shurik, and I shall buy more paint.

Willi took brushes from jars of water, wiped them, and handed them around. Outside there was a distant barking of flak, and then a series of irregular concussions.

"Too far north," Shurik said.

They sipped their wine. The young men talked, made jokes, but Sophie was silent, staring at the blacked-out window, lips moving as though praying. The explosions were louder and closer. The edges of the blackout curtain glowed like white neon. A concussion set a tremor along the floorboards, then came a slow tearing sound as houses crumbled a few streets away.

Hans set down his glass and stood.

"The party begins," he said.

They had learned when to go out, just when the wave passed. When everyone else still cowered in shelters and would do for another hour or so. When the whoosh of heat blast had subsided, and the fires gave enough light to see by but the worst flames could be avoided. Of course, it was dangerous. A shift in the wind and a firestorm would blow right over them. Willi Graf looked up just in time to call them away from a collapsing wall. Flying debris cut Shurik's cheek. Dangerous, but lovely as well. They dodged and darted about like enchanted creatures, sprites or fairies, in the yellow light of the flares which blossomed in the sky above and drifted down like falling petals.

They sprinted with the cans and brushes to the university, to the main gate in the Ludwigstraße, and by strobelike light they painted

FREEDOM

in letters four feet high.

Falk Harnack had always loved Munich. Compared to the granite pile of Berlin, Munich was a pastel paintbox, a stage set for a fantastical opera. Or was before the bombings. Now the effect was of a smashed pastry shop. Swirled confections of rococo white and gold littered the streets, and plaster like fine powdered sugar sifted over ruins of pink and green and Esterhazy yellow.

The streetcars no longer ran because the tracks had been ripped from the pavement, so Falk shouldered his duffel bag and hiked north toward the student quarter. Until he reached a wall at the southern end of the English Garden. A gaggle of Russian conscripted workers scrubbed halfheartedly at purple graffiti.

FREEDOM!

Falk had started to turn away when he realized an SS man guarding the prisoners had noticed him. Falk approached, shaking his head.

"What sort of scum would do this?" he said, offering the man a cigarette.

"Scum is right," the guard replied. "It happened last week too. And it's peacetime paint—hell to get off." Gestured toward the scrubbing women as though they were draining his energy.

"So I see."

"How the hell they got hold of real paint, I don't know. Anyway, a lousy welcome home if you've been at the front."

"Yes, for me it is," Falk agreed. Since his meeting with Bonhoeffer he had been at his cultural post in Poland, not at the front, but pretended otherwise, lingering awhile longer making small talk about the crisis at Stalingrad, so he could continue to enjoy the wall. Even as he considered what he would do to make sure it didn't happen again.

Hans and Sophie shared rooms in a courtyard off the Franz-Josef-Straße, and that was where Falk Harnack found them. Studying. Sophie had been to visit the mother and father in Ulm and brought back a cinnamon cake. She cut a slice and offered it to Falk.

"Are you mad?" Falk said.

She froze, wondering why he would react so to the cake, but he was talking to Hans as though Sophie were not present. Like her brother and his friends, Falk did not quite take Sophie seriously.

"Sophie," Scholl said. "Leave the room."

"I want to listen. I have a right. I take the same risks."

"And I want to spare you at least some of those risks. Leave the room."

She went out to the kitchen, but stood just behind the closed door, her ear to the crack.

"Yes," Scholl said, turning back to Falk. "We are mad. It is what this regime does to decent people."

Falk stepped closer. "I thought you wanted to know about the resistance."

"I do," Hans answered defensively, "since we happen to be part of it."

"Let me tell you something. My brother and sister-in-law are dead. Mildred was gang-raped. Her breasts were burned with lit cigarettes. Arvid received electric shocks to his genitals and was beaten so badly his eye was dislodged from its socket. They were hung with piano wire, which nearly decapitated them."

Behind the kitchen door, Sophie put her hand over her mouth.

Falk continued, "I learned all this from a guard I bribed at Plötzensee. I'm telling it to you because you seem to think this is some kind of game we're playing."

"You're referring to the graffiti." Scholl's voice held a slight tremor.

"Yes."

"Do you know what kind of stir it's creating? I bet they know in Berlin."

"Of course they do. The resistance knows. And they'll not let you within a mile of them as long as this sort of thing continues, because the Gestapo also knows. It's a childish gesture. It's not worth the risk. It's so easy to get caught."

"No, it's not. We only go out during bombing raids."

"Bombing raids!" Falk threw up his hands.

Sophie came back in the room. "It's not just that the bombs cover what we're doing," she said. "It would be so easy to hate the British and Americans. The bombs are killing thousands of people. Old people, children. But when we use the air raids, I can even be thankful for the bombs. Then I don't hate anyone. Except the Nazis. I would shoot Hitler myself if I met him in the street."

Hans looked at Falk and shrugged, as if to say, *This is how a woman reasons.* He lit a cigarette and began to pace. "At least we're doing something. In Berlin they only talk. The leaflets are a risk as well. What about the leaflets? Do we stop that too?" He paused. "You've spoken to someone in Berlin. About us."

"Yes," Falk said.

The day after Falk Harnack returned to Poland, Hans Scholl visited a sec-
ondhand bookseller, Herr Söhngen. Herr Söhngen was antifascist and had
agreed to pass messages between Hans and his contacts. This time he whispered to Scholl, "I am so sorry, but the book you requested, *Totalitarianism
and Utopia*, is out of print." Shaken, Scholl stared at Herr Söhngen, unable
to speak. It was the message agreed upon if the Gestapo hung around asking questions. He glanced around at the customers browsing the meager
supply of books on the shelves, caught the eye of a middle-aged man in a
well-made raincoat and gray hat. The man smiled—or so Scholl thought—
and went back to browsing. Scholl thanked Herr Söhngen and went out,
taking a circuitous route back to the university while glancing back often
to see if he was being followed.

That evening he told Shurik and Willi Graf, "We must step things up.
There may be nothing to lose." Then he began to weep uncontrollably.

Later Shurik and Willi sprinted through empty streets while the sirens
warned of incoming British bombers. Before they ducked into the shelter
in Theresienstraße, Willi grabbed Shurik's arm and said, "Perhaps we
should lie low for a while. Hans is liable to snap."

"He isn't the only one," Shurik answered as he turned away.

The next leaflet boasted a new title. Instead of the more modest **Leaflet of
the White Rose**, it was emblazoned across the top

LEAFLET OF THE RESISTANCE

"They'll be angry in Berlin if we claim this name," said Willi Graf, ever
the cautious one.

"I'll have the meeting with Falk's contact soon after we distribute it,"
Hans Scholl said, holding up the thin black stencil to the light. "This will
let them know we mean business."

The text of the leaflet had also been a source of friction. Professor Huber,
an anti-Nazi member of the faculty, had helped with the writing. The students were fond of Huber, a professor of philosophy who often dropped
veiled barbs at the Nazis into his lectures. But Huber was a Conservative—
his distaste for the Nazis stemmed from his belief that they had brought dis-
honor and defeat to the great German nation. He inserted a sentence
which read, "The youth of Germany must learn to emulate our glorious
Wehrmacht, not the butchers who have taken control of our beloved
nation." But Hans and Shurik would have none of it. They had been at the
Russian front, they had seen the atrocities of not only the SS but the "glorious Wehrmacht" as well; Professor Huber had not. "We are not national-
ists," Shurik said. "We are internationalists, democratic socialists."

"This is a new time," Scholl told his stunned professor. "A time when students teach their teachers."

FEBRUARY 3, 1943. The students are drinking tea in the Scholls' flat and Mozart is playing on the radio, which suddenly falls silent.

Shurik looks up from the chessboard he is sharing with Willi. "Has the electric gone?"

Then the radio spits static and emits a metallic drumroll. A bleak, distant voice says *The Battle of Stalingrad is over. The Sixth Army under the illustrious command of Feldmarschall von Paulus has succumbed to the enemy. Three hundred thousand of our brave men have been lost on the field of battle. Our beloved Führer declares three days of national mourning. . . .*

The students sit still as the gloomy second movement of Beethoven's Fifth fills the room. Then Hans Scholl goes to the radio and switches it off.

"The next air raid, more graffiti," he says. "No matter what they say in Berlin. This is the end. The people will rise up now."

Sophie is weeping; so is Willi. Everyone knows someone from school who has been serving with the Sixth Army at Stalingrad. Only Shurik is strangely happy, because he is remembering his long-dead Russian mother. "The Russians," he says several times. "I knew it would be the Russians."

The leaflet is printed.

LEAFLET OF THE RESISTANCE
Fellow Resistance Fighters!

Stunned and distraught, we behold the loss of the men of Stalingrad. Three hundred thousand German men have been senselessly done to death by the inspired strategy of a World War I private. Führer, we thank you!

The German people are in turmoil. The day of reckoning is here, the day German youth demand restitution from the most horrible tyrant our people has yet endured. For us there is one slogan—Fight against the Nazis! We want true learning and true freedom of expression.

The name of Germany is dishonored for all time if the young people of Germany do not rise up, take revenge, and establish a New Europe, a Europe of the spirit. The dead of Stalingrad implore us.

The leaflets are hidden beneath the false floor in the studio closet, the stacks growing as the students acquire more and more paper, at great peril. They have agreed these leaflets will be sent first to universities in the hope they draw students into the streets. And in order to do that, Hans Scholl decides, they must not be distributed singly through the mail and phone booths. Instead they will be left in piles around the university buildings, so groups of students will find them and discuss them together.

Shurik objects strenuously. Too dangerous, he says. There must be some other way to distribute them, at night perhaps. But Scholl can think of no other way. And since the danger is very real, he decides to take it upon himself, without telling the others.

But he has never been able to fool Sophie.

FEBRUARY 17, 1943. The weather is unseasonably warm, more like April than February. The trees, tricked by the heat, have begun to show green buds. Sophie takes a walk in the English Garden and then, back in the flat, throws open the window of her bedroom. White curtains billow out like beckoning arms. She turns on the phonograph, searches through her albums, and takes Schubert from its dust cover. The *Trout* Quintet. Sophie dances around the room, turns into a trout, wriggles and purls through cold clear water with open eyes.

FEBRUARY 18, 1943. The main entrance of the Ludwig-Maximilian University is in the Ludwigstraße. Across a courtyard and through heavy doors into the marble central hall. A decapitated Medusa with her head-dress of snakes is depicted in the floor tiles. A strange decoration, Sophie has always thought. She can't think what it has to do with learning, has never liked to look at it. Instead she peers up through three floors of open space, past marble balustrades, to the skylit dome.

Usually the hall would be echoing with footsteps, conversations, laughter, friends calling to one another. Now there is silence, for lectures are in session. In ten minutes or so, the dismissal bell will sound. Hans and Sophie Scholl must move quickly. Her brother will be glad she is along now, Sophie thinks. He has no choice, for she laid in wait for him at the studio, caught him just as he was stuffing leaflets in his briefcase, and showed him her own satchel already filled and ready. No time to talk her out of it, and so here she is.

They climb the stairs to the first floor, pausing at window ledges and benches to leave little stacks of paper. The leaflet of the resistance. Sophie's heart is pounding as they split up, head for staircases on opposite ends of the hall, race up to the second floor. They pause at doorways, glance around, drop the leaflets, hurry on.

When they are done, they rush downstairs, out of breath. They look at each other and begin to laugh. Then Hans cries, "No, look, here are some more!" and points to an outside pocket on Sophie's satchel where she has stuffed dozens of leaflets. "We mustn't waste any!" And back upstairs they run, laughing, exhilarated by what they are doing, the audacity of it. They are just at the top again when the bell rings and doors fly open, but not before Sophie has the leaflets and flings them over the balustrade, where they flutter like white butterflies down to Medusa's head three floors below. For a moment she has vertigo, feels as though she might slip over the railing herself, but she takes a deep breath and pushes herself away.

Hans and Sophie are swallowed up by the mass of students flooding into the halls. They hold hands while around them people find the leaflets, cry out in surprise, or drop them in fear, or stuff them into their pockets. They follow the crush down the stairs to the ground floor, but when they reach the door their way is blocked by a janitor clutching a sheaf of leaflets. He grabs Sophie's arm roughly.

"You!" he cries. "And you!" to Hans. "You threw them from above. I saw you with my own eyes, didn't I? You can't get out, I've locked the doors." Hans tries to pull Sophie from the man's grasp, but a security guard appears, drawn by the hubbub. "Call the police! These two are under arrest!"

FEBRUARY 19, 1943. Dietrich Bonhoeffer waits beside the Grunewaldsee. From time to time he glances at his watch. Because the weather is fine there are more people around, women walking in pairs, small children flying kites or pushing wooden boats along the water's edge. Dietrich waits for three hours. Falk Harnack and his promised visitors from Munich never appear. At last, Dietrich turns and trudges home to the Marienburger Allee.

In Munich the Gestapo ransack the flat in the Franz-Josef-Straße. They rip open cushions and strip books from their binding. They interrogate neighbors, and are led to the studio in the Leopoldstraße. They find paint and brushes. They find the mimeograph machine. They find names. Professor Huber. Willi Graf. Falk Harnack. Alex Schmorell, AKA Shurik.

Shurik is a wanted man. His face is on posters going up all over Munich. A reward is offered. He goes the only place he knows to go, to Lilo.

He has identification papers stolen from the body of a dead Russian laborer near the front, papers he has held on to for just such an emergency. He speaks Russian fluently, and thinks he can lose himself inside a labor camp. A hard life, but better than the alternative. Lilo helps him forge the papers, sleeps with him, sends him on his way with a warm meal.

But just as he reaches the train station, the air-raid sirens go. He reluctantly follows the waiting passengers who jam their way down the steps into the shelter. It would not be wise, after all, to call attention to himself by trying to get away. He sits on a bench and tries to relax. Then he hears his name. "Shurik."

He doesn't look up, pretends he hasn't heard. But after a moment he glances furtively to his left. A young woman is staring at him. Marie Luise, a fellow student he seduced several months ago. He looks away, doesn't hear his name again, tries to ignore the whispers and exclamations coming from the direction of Marie Luise. Until a man in a gray overcoat edges close and withdraws an identification badge from inside his coat.

"Herr Schmorell, I believe? Hauptsturmführer Mohr of the Gestapo. The young lady was sure she recognized you. When the all clear is sounded, you will come with me, please."

Sophie Scholl knows nothing of this. She thinks Shurik has escaped, that he is safe. She does not know that Willi Graf and Falk Harnack and Professor Huber have been arrested. She and Hans are brought before Hitler's favorite judge, Roland Freisler. He harangues the brother and sister, calls them scum, traitors, degenerates. Hans and Sophie stand silent.

"How?" Freisler cries. "How could any German commit such heinous acts against the Fatherland?"

Sophie looks up as though surprised at the question. She says, "Someone had to start."

FEBRUARY 23, 1943. Hans von Dohnanyi stands before the hearth at Sacrow, stares into the flames. Dietrich Bonhoeffer sits with his head in his hands.

"Late last night," Dohnanyi is saying. "Beheaded on the guillotine at Stadelheim, outside Munich. The girl went first. As a courtesy. Then her brother and the other students. And a professor from the university."

"Falk?"

"They can't place him in Munich on any of the days the leafleting and painting took place. He was always at his post in Poland. They're suspicious because they found his name among the students' papers, and then he's Arvid's brother. So, a life sentence in Dachau."

"And us?"

"They've found no connection. How could they? There is none."

Dietrich looks up, takes off his glasses, and rubs his forehead.

Dohnanyi watches him closely. "Is there?"

Dietrich shakes his head.

London
February 1943

THE RT. REV. George Bell was late in accepting that position which is the prerogative of a bishop of the Church of England—a seat in the House of Lords. As a man of the middle classes with more than a little sympathy for socialist programs, Bell instinctively bridled at automatic inclusion in such a bastion of privilege. It was the ever practical Hettie who pointed out that his club, the Athenaeum, was an equally exclusive old boys' retreat and that he had never raised a moral quibble about joining *it*. "Because you enjoy your club," she pointed out. "And the House of Lords, on the other hand, is an absolute bore."

When the war started he took Hettie's advice, set principle aside, and accepted his seat in the chamber of peers and clerics. It was a larger pulpit, he decided, and one that might prove useful for advancing his concerns about the treatment of German refugees in Britain. The warmth of his personality made him many new friends; his persistent speeches on behalf of the refugees caused the members to shake their heads over their schedules and mutter, "Oh God, George again."

But there was no such good-natured consternation in late February when Bell was once more set to address the chamber, because word had it the subject would not be refugees at all. Bell, it was whispered incredulously, planned to take the government to task for the bombing of German cities. The bishop himself did not deny it—he was most anxious that the tenor of his speech be known ahead of time so that it might draw the widest possible attention. Nor was he surprised to receive an urgent summons, the day before the speech, to meet with the Archbishop of Canterbury at Lambeth Palace.

Archbishop Lang was dying. Though the nature of his illness was not discussed in public, it was presumed that he had cancer, and that he would not live out the year. Lang was understandably sensitive about the subject of his imminent demise, and it was customary among his clergy not to remark upon the archbishop's health unless he himself introduced the subject. He did so now, seated stubbornly at his desk, his back cushioned by several pillows.

"A bad day today," he said. The hard edge of his voice and the skin drawn tautly over his cheekbones left little doubt that he was in pain. "I'll be brief for your sake and mine. This speech you plan to deliver to the House of Lords is extremely ill-advised."

"Yes," Bell agreed. "I suppose Jesus got the same advice when he decided to go to Jerusalem."

Lang looked momentarily angry, then a spasm of pain wiped his face clean. He said, "George, you aren't Jesus."

"No," Bell said. "I beg your pardon."

"Spiritually arrogant, George. Bishop Temple has described you that way. And quite frankly, in this instance, I'm inclined to agree."

Bell waited.

"The general assumption for quite a few years has been that when I am gone, you will be named the next Archbishop of Canterbury," Lang continued. "If you give this speech, you can forget about sitting at this desk. The see will go to Temple instead."

"That is most likely," Bell said. "But it can't be helped."

"Can't it?"

Bell leaned forward. "I had hoped I might have your support. A slim hope, I realize. But you are as familiar as I am with the teachings of the church concerning war. The killing of noncombatants is never to be allowed, and yet our bombers are specifically targeting civilian areas of German cities. I had hoped you might join me in expressing concern about the deaths of women and children."

"I am not at all disposed to be the mouthpiece of this concern of yours, because I do not share it. And when I am asked by the press to respond to this issue, as I surely shall be, that is what I shall say. You'll stand alone, George."

"Women and children, Gordon. Old people. Sick people."

"*German* women and children and old people. The Germans started this war, and the Germans have certainly shown no compunction about taking the lives of British civilians."

"Jesus didn't say we should do unto others as they do unto us."

The search for words sent shocks of pain from the base of Lang's skull down along his spine. He shut his eyes. "We are at war. And I am no pacifist. Nor can you expect most Christians to be pacifists, and most especially you cannot expect pacifist behavior from the government which is charged with protecting us all. And my God, what of those brave young men who are dying every day in their airplanes just to keep you safe?"

Bell bowed his head. "I have nothing but the utmost love and admiration for those young men. I baptized some of them, you know, confirmed them, counseled them, performed their weddings. I bury them, too, Gordon. Nothing I say will in any way condemn them. But their leaders should be sending them against military targets. I doubt that many of those young air-men enjoy burning people alive in the streets of Hamburg and Munich."

Lang shook his head. "Those young men will be appalled by your speech. They will feel personally attacked, and so they should. They know you don't fight a war from a pacifist position."

"I'm not a pacifist. Have you ever known me to call myself a pacifist? And you know as well as anyone I have been consistently anti-Nazi."

"Then your position makes no sense," Lang said. "How do you destroy the Nazis and the threat they present if you deny the means of that destruction?"

Bell sighed. "I'll admit the inconsistency of my position. But people have to come first, and they come first in different ways, depending upon the situation. We're being consistent now, responding with the immoral methods the enemy has chosen first to use against us. When all is over, this country will be the worse off for having done that. The world will be worse off. When one is consistent, Gordon, there's no going back."

Lang turned his head gingerly and stared out the high Gothic windows of Lambeth at the gray Thames. "There's no reconciling our positions, George, and I'm growing very weary. I must leave you to make your deci-sion."

"It is already made," Bell said.

He walked to the podium amid a low murmur. Every eye followed. Sir Robert Vansittart, who had clashed so often with Bell over the refugee question, had a conspicuous seat on the front row. There was only one half-friendly gesture when a man he vaguely knew as a retired naval admiral plucked at Bell's sleeve as he passed. Bell paused, and the admiral whis-pered, "Every man here knows what you are going to say, and every man here wishes you wouldn't say it. But of course, you must do your duty."

Bell nodded gratefully at this small kindness and pressed on through the thick still air of the upper chamber. At the podium he took his reading glasses from a coat pocket and set them on his nose, looked down at his notes, then up.

"I have been fond of saying," he began, "that every good sermon should contain a shot of heresy. It may be true as well that every good speech, in time of war, should contain a shot of treason."

There was a gasp, and the low murmur began again. He waited calmly for it to die down.

"We are in the midst of waging a war for survival against a vicious enemy, the Nazi government of the Third Reich. As I hope you all know,

I have been an outspoken opponent of the Nazis since their accession to power in Germany in 1933. I as much as anyone long for the day when this war ends, and it must end with the utter defeat and destruction of Adolf Hitler and his cohorts. But I must say to you, Hitler's defeat will do no good if his legacy is passed on to us."

Mutters, and a few scattered boos.

"Step by step, we on the Allied side have become numbed to what is right and wrong, so that which seemed unacceptable in 1939 or 1940 is now commonplace. The targeting of civilians for bombing was called barbaric when Hitler did it at the beginning of this war. And rightly so. Now we ourselves have taken on the mantle of barbarism as we return bomb for bomb, firestorm for firestorm, death for death. If we do not stop now, we shall never see an end, not in our lifetimes, not ever."

He was speaking more and more loudly to be heard over the rising catcalls. He paused to catch his breath and cried, "Can we truly fight fascism with the methods of fascism?"

The outcry was so loud he could no longer be heard. He stood for what seemed an eternity until the din subsided into a sudden, eerie silence. Bell removed his glasses and looked straight at his audience.

"Gentlemen," he said, "I am speaking to you as a churchman. The gospel is a gospel of redeeming love. Though all the resources of the state are concentrated on winning the war, the church is not part of those resources. The church must preach the gospel of redemption."

He stuffed his notes in his pocket. In a relentless silence broken by his own footfalls, he left the hall.

Hettie tried to hide the newspapers from him but soon gave it up. Headlines and editorials in the *Times*, the tabloids, even the *Guardian*, called him a fool at best, a traitor at worst. The Archbishop of Canterbury denounced him, as did a host of other bishops, clergy, military chaplains. He tried to ignore the chilly disapproval he met, or fancied he met, as he went about his pastoral rounds in the diocese. For solace he turned to Sabine and Gerhard Leibholz. And of course to Hettie, who remained outwardly unfazed, even when her ladies' book circle asked her to stop attending meetings.

The only time he broke down was at the third anniversary of the Battle of Britain, when the dean of his own Cathedral of Chichester informed him he would be unwelcome at the memorial service commemorating fallen fliers. Bell nodded and turned pale, but said nothing. At home, when he tried to tell Hettie, he began to weep. She sat beside him on the sofa and cradled his head to her breast.

When he could speak, he said, "I wonder if Dietrich listens to the BBC?"

𝕍-𝔐ann
𝔐arch 1943

DIETRICH WAS LISTENING to a report of the Bishop of Chichester's speech on the BBC, along with Christel and Hans von Dohnanyi. They were in the Dohnanyi bedroom watching Hans pack a suitcase. He was to travel to East Prussia on the night train and wanted Dietrich to drive him to the railway station in Dr. Karl Bonhoeffer's automobile. As a physician, Karl Bonhoeffer was one of the few civilians with access to petrol. But Dohnanyi's position in the Abwehr meant he too had a car. Dietrich wondered why he was needed, but didn't ask. Hans would tell him in good time.

"Your friend the bishop is right," Christel was saying. She had been doing volunteer work in the underground wards at the Charité, reading books in badly lit bomb shelters to children with shattered limbs and critical burns. The bomb damage in Berlin was still relatively light, but the Dohnanyi and Bonhoeffer families often spent the night in their own sandbagged shelters dug into back gardens.

"Yes," Dietrich said, "but the moral responsibility is ours. We started all this."

"The children didn't," Christel insisted.

"No," Dietrich agreed.

Hans seemed to be only half listening as he took the folded clothes Christel offered him and arranged them in the small suitcase. "The blue socks," he said. "The brown ones have a hole in the toe."

"You should have told me before," said his wife. "I would have mended them."

"I kept forgetting," Dohnanyi said absently. Then, "It's also true, you know, that the bombing makes our task more difficult. Even people who despise Hitler are afraid to turn against him. They think he is their only protection."

Dietrich shook his head. "I'm sick of making excuses for the German people and for myself."

Dohnanyi looked up. "Are you?"

"My dear, what are you doing?" Christel scolded. "You've shoved your clothes to the edge of the suitcase and left a hole in the middle. Everything will be wrinkled."

"I'm making a nest," Dohnanyi said.

She laughed. "A nest? Are you laying eggs, then?"

"Precisely. A nest for this." He opened the drawer that held his underwear and took out a small package wrapped in plain brown paper.

"What is it?"

"Guess."

"Soap," Christel said. "Real soap. Not for some East Prussian mistress, I hope."

Dohnanyi groaned. "So little faith. But it's a bad guess anyway. Why would soap need a nest of clothes?"

"It's breakable then," Dietrich said. "A bottle. No, two flasks wrapped together, you can see where they meet. Liqueur, I'd bet."

"Right you are," said Dohnanyi. "Very good liqueur. Cointreau."

"A very special mistress," Christel teased.

"Not a mistress. They're for General von Tresckow." He laid the package in the middle of the clothes. "And now, my dear, if you don't mind, I should like to talk with Dietrich alone."

She kissed his cheek and went out, closing the door behind her. Christel was used to being dismissed, not because Dohnanyi distrusted her but because he feared they both might be arrested and tortured as the Harnacks had been. For the sake of the children, they had agreed, she should know as little as possible so that one of their parents at least might have a chance to return to them.

When she had gone, Dohnanyi remained looking at the package. "Not Cointreau," he said softly. "A bomb."

Dietrich started and took a step back.

"Though I'm glad it fooled you," Dohnanyi added. "It must pass as Cointreau."

"My God!" Dietrich managed to say. "Here at the house? What if it goes off?"

"It's supposed to be quite safe until I activate the fuse. Then it has thirty minutes."

They stood side by side looking down at the suitcase.

"Did you mean what you said earlier?" Dohnanyi asked. "No more excuses?"

"Yes," Dietrich said.

"Then I would appreciate it if you could drive me to the railway station with this. It's not necessary, of course; Christel could take me. But I'd as soon not involve her, and your company would mean a great deal to me. To know that someone else is responsible as well. You see, we're going to blow up Hitler's plane. That means everyone on board will die."

Dietrich imagined the plane exploding, plummeting to the earth in flaming bits. Perhaps the men on board would be caught in one last thought seconds after their bodies ceased to exist.

"Who?"

"Whichever of his aides he brings along. Several army officers not involved in the plot. The pilot and copilot. Men with families. Blood on my hands, and yours."

Dietrich said, "There comes a time when it is a great relief to sin. At last, at last. But you must tell me what is going on."

They talked while Dietrich drove. He maneuvered the automobile carefully through the gray streets quickly emptying of pedestrians. Soon it would be dark and a clear night, so the Allied bombers were expected. There was little traffic, since not even the trams could make regular runs now, but the pavement was so damaged that it was difficult to make more than thirty kilometers an hour without damaging a tire or breaking an axle. Dietrich glanced at his watch. He would just have time to drop off Dohnanyi and get back to the Marienburger Allee.

"Couldn't you shoot him?" he asked. "To spare the others on the plane, I mean?"

"It's very hard," said Dohnanyi. "He's become a virtual recluse, and very paranoid. He's under heavy guard at all times. The sight of a gun would bring an instant response, probably before he could be shot. We have to strike now. Everything is ready at this moment for the coup. The troops we need within the Reich are in position. In a week something may change."

Dietrich had already known something of this. Within the family they had continued to refer to the plot as "Uncle Rudi" after their Nazi relative. The word for the past several weeks had been that Uncle Rudi would soon be coming for a visit. But it was a shock to think of the means of accomplishing Hitler's demise so close at hand. When Dietrich glanced in his rearview mirror he could see the brown leather suitcase perched on the backseat.

"This is not your first involvement with the explosive," Dohnanyi was saying. "You recall the letter you gave Bishop Bell to post? That's how we got the fuse. It's something new the British have developed, and we used a German agent to steal one. Our own fuses make a hissing noise after the bomb is set to go off. Someone on the airplane might notice. But this fuse is absolutely silent."

"But why are you going to East Prussia?"

"Because since Stalingrad, Hitler is very worried about the rest of the Eastern Front. So he's going to Rastenburg for a high-level conference three days from now. I'm taking the bomb to General von Tresckow. He's responsible for seeing the bomb is on board the return flight to Berlin. We thought it best to try for the return. That way Tresckow and his aides can use the visit to determine the exact situation in the rest of the army. As soon as word comes that the plane is on its way back, those units will move into a state of alert. They'll be in position to surround Berlin and arrest Goering and Himmler and the top SS brass. Negotiations with the Allies will begin at once."

Dohnanyi fell silent and twisted in his seat to look out the window, back toward Sacrow. An orange glow tinted the western sky.

"If this fails," he said, "you and I only have a few more days to live."

"Then," Dietrich said, "we should make the most of them. When you return from East Prussia, we shall have a family celebration."

Last Things

The family gathered to celebrate the seventy-fifth birthday of Karl Bonhoeffer. Karl-Friedrich and his wife, Grete, came up from Leipzig, and Suse's husband, Pastor Walter Dress, obtained a leave from his army chaplaincy in Italy. The cellar of the house in the Marienburger Allee held a number of smoked haunches carefully stored before the war and drawn upon for such special occasions. Cook retrieved a large ham, and Suse and Christel provided jars of homemade preserves, the last of the previous summer's vegetable gardens.

After dinner a deputation consisting of the administrator and chief physician arrived from the Charité. They brought with them an official proclamation from the Führer himself, bestowing the Goethe Medal for Art and Science upon Dr. Karl Bonhoeffer in honor of his long and distinguished career. But they didn't stay long. The gathering was a private, family affair, they sensed. So after an hour of good cognac—also taken from prewar stock—they bowed, shook hands with the good Dr. Bonhoeffer, and departed with stiff-armed Nazi salutes all round and *Heil Hitlers* shouted with good-natured exuberance. The family concert began. The Bonhoeffer children and in-laws presented a cantata by Walcha, one of Karl Bonhoeffer's favorite composers, which they had been rehearsing for several days. Dietrich was at the piano, Karl-Friedrich played the violin, Christel the cello. Paula, Suse, Hans von Dohnanyi, and the children formed the chorus. Dohnanyi, the least musical of all the family, kept forgetting his cue—he was the only bass—and received a dig in the ribs from his youngest son. Outside the front door the Dohnanyi car waited with the keys in the ignition. When the phone call came, Dohnanyi planned to drive at once to the Abwehr office in the Tirpitz-Ufer.

Hans strained to listen, and missed another entrance. He lost his place and looked up from the music momentarily. Dietrich continued to play, his face placid. He was also listening for the telephone, but one would never know it, for he played with marvelous concentration. A good quality if we get into trouble, Dohnanyi thought, this ability to focus.

When the music was done the family gathered around Karl Bonhoeffer to offer their birthday kisses, the only kisses allowed for the year, a light brushing of lips against the dry cheek of the old man. Dietrich and Hans drifted over to the radio. Christel, who shared their secret, watched, her hands resting on the shoulders of her daughter. Almost reluctantly, Dohnanyi turned on the radio. They waited fifteen minutes for a Schumann *Lied* to finish playing, the rest of the family laughing and talking all around them, and then an announcer brought the news. *The Führer's plane has landed at Tempelhof after a successful trip to East Prussia for consultation with his top generals. Despite the setback at Stalingrad, the war effort progresses satisfactorily in other areas of the Eastern Front, according to the general staff of the Wehrmacht. The Führer will remain in Berlin for several days in anticipation of the ceremonies on Heroes' Memorial Day. . . .*

Dohnanyi switched off the set and straightened slowly. He could not look at his wife or Dietrich.

"Back, is he?" said Karl-Friedrich.

He received no answer.

The bomb had simply not gone off. General von Tresckow had set the fuse himself and seen the package onto the plane, handing it over to one of Hitler's aides with a promise to deliver the "Cointreau"—a birthday present—to a fellow officer in Berlin. That officer, a fellow plotter, had the unenviable task of receiving the package and defusing it while wondering if the bomb might decide to work at any moment.

"Too cold perhaps," he suggested to Dohnanyi when he had regained his composure. "Some of these explosives are quite sensitive to temperature."

"Would it be so cold on the plane?" Dohnanyi said.

"Perhaps they put it in the baggage compartment. Or perhaps Hitler likes it cold when he flies. He has some quirks, you know."

Dohnanyi took a deep breath. "No matter," he said. "It didn't work. So. We try again. Immediately."

Newly appointed SS Judge Advocate Alois Bauer sits in his bare office in the Prinz-Albrecht-Straße. The expensive furniture has been removed, the wall which once held the painting by Barthel Bruyn the Elder is bare. Because of the air raids, everything of value has been removed for safekeeping to a secure underground storage facility outside central Berlin. Bauer has been assured that once the war is over his possessions will be restored to him. He has some doubts about this. Though the war in the East is going well again and a great victory has been won at Kharkov, though the liquidation of the Polish ghettos is proceeding, the situation in Italy is unstable. Mussolini cannot last, it is rumored, and the Abwehr reports the Allies are preparing to mount an invasion of the peninsula.

The Abwehr. More than once Bauer has heard an SS colleague complain, "Can we believe anything that comes from the Abwehr?" Bauer tends to think the Italian reports are reliable, if only because it is the gloomiest Abwehr intelligence which seems to prove the most accurate. Bauer is loyal, but also practical. And a creative man. No one could speak openly about losing the war, but one could well imagine. So Bauer is cultivating contacts in Italy, Czechoslovakia, and Hungary, making use of those intelligence officers he has found to be most congenial.

One of these officers, a station underling in Prague, appears in his office in mid-March unannounced.

"I have something for you," the man says.

"Something worth a long train journey," Bauer observes, and motions to a chair.

The man sits. He never takes his eyes from Bauer's face. "Worth a reward," he says. "A promotion."

Bauer nods. "Then you will not mind if I ask a colleague to share in this conversation."

The man looks startled but has no choice but to agree. Bauer has learned, as he has been drawn deeper and deeper into the world of agents and counteragents, that it is never wise to listen alone when sensitive information is passed on. He picks up his telephone and calls Hauptsturmführer Franz Xaver Sonderegger of the Gestapo.

The bomb, no longer disguised as a package of liqueur bottles, was refitted with a new fuse and was being worn by a young officer of the Wehrmacht, Rudolf Gersdorff, inside his uniform jacket. Gersdorff's wife had recently died in childbirth and they had no other children. He decided he had the strength to join her. The ever-reclusive Hitler, at the invitation of the Abwehr, would visit an exhibit of captured Russian weapons at the Old Arsenal Museum for half an hour; Gersdorff would escort Hitler around the exhibit, stay as close as possible during the time the fuse was set to go off, and blow them both up.

(Gersdorff went to his elderly father for a last visit and told him of this plan. The old man looked away from his son and said, "Yes, you must do it.")

When Gersdorff unbuttoned his uniform just before the arrival of Hitler's entourage and activated the fuse, he saw his father's face, lean and ancient and ready to offer a son to the god of death for the sake of honor. The face of a Roman nobleman prepared to open his veins and those of his family, of an Aztec baring his child's chest beneath the blade of a priest. Gersdorff shuddered and tried to think instead of his wife, six months in the ground along with their stillborn child. As he shook hands with Hitler and followed him into the museum, he stroked once more the silken blond hair of his Beate, looked into her eyes, and said, I shall be there soon. Gersdorff checked his watch. As Hitler stood indecisively in the middle of the exhibition hall, Gersdorff motioned and said, "Over here, my Führer. There is something I would especially like you to see."

Hitler looked around quizzically. Gersdorff, glimpsing the Führer's face, had the momentary impression of pouches of decaying flesh ready to slip from the skull. Hitler glanced at his watch, then said, "There is nothing here to see except Russian junk," turned on his heel, and stalked out of the hall trailing a gaggle of anxious SS security guards. Gersdorff stared after him, then realized with a start he must rid himself of the live bomb. He hurried to a toilet, praying no one else would enter, and defused the bomb. Afterward his hands shook so badly he could not undo his fly to urinate, and he wet his dress trousers.

Again Dohnanyi waited, this time at the Tirpitz-Ufer. When at last the phone rang, it was the hopeless voice of the supposed-to-be-dead Gersdorff.

Gersdorff steeled himself for one more attempt at getting close to Hitler but was wounded in an air raid and confined to hospital. In the meantime, a cache of SS uniforms Dohnanyi had squirreled away for possible use as disguises was destroyed in another fiery raid two days later.

"It is as though God protects him," a distraught Dohnanyi said to Dietrich.

Dietrich had difficulty answering. "No," he said after a time. "God must play some other part in the workings of this world."

"Currency violations?" says Gestapo Hauptsturmführer Sonderegger with a puzzled look on his face.

Bauer nods and leans back in his chair with an air of satisfaction. The visitor from Prague has just taken his leave, and Sonderegger is struggling with the implications of his information. Bauer likes working with Sonderegger, who has no imagination and knows it, but compensates with tenacity and loyalty. The perfect subordinate.

"Wouldn't you consider Prague a backwater?" Sonderegger says. "I mean, where our work is concerned?"

"It's the Abwehr," Bauer says. "No matter which office laundered the currency, it's a violation. And I'll guarantee, follow this up and the path will lead to Munich at least, and perhaps here to the Tirpitz-Ufer."

"A minor violation," Sonderegger says, "all things considered."

"Yes," says Bauer, "but one which will allow me to make arrests and interrogate at my leisure."

"You think the Abwehr is harboring a Communist cell like the one at the Ministry of Economics?"

"I don't know. But there's something going on there."

Sonderegger yawns, a bit disappointed that his colleague is so vague. "Like what?"

Bauer shakes his head. "I've been told by some of my informants in the Abwehr to keep an eye on Hans von Dohnanyi. And now this fellow from Prague mentions his name in connection with the exchange of large amounts of currency for some scheme to use Jews as intelligence agents. Doesn't that seem odd to you?"

"Of course it does. Anyone who thinks Jews are useful to the Reich as intelligence agents has a screw loose, or is incompetent."

"Not incompetent," Bauer says. "Something else."

"So he's a Jew lover. How much is that worth?"

"It won't take much time or effort for us to find out."

So over the next few days Bauer begins to take a closer look at Hans von Dohnanyi. He soon turns up confirmation of massive currency exchanges related to the removal of a party of Jews to Switzerland, ostensibly as Abwehr agents, though there seems little evidence of their usefulness. He also learns of a number of trips to Rome and Poland in the company of an Abwehr agent in Munich named Josef Müller. Meetings at the Vatican. And trips to Switzerland and Sweden on behalf of army intelligence by a brother-in-law of Dohnanyi's, Pastor Dietrich Bonhoeffer. Bauer dredges his memory for details of Pastor Bonhoeffer, digs through his files. An ecumenical conference before the war, an outspoken attack on the Führer and the Reich government. A late-night conversation in Bonhoeffer's room. Bauer rubs his head as he reads the report. A handwritten note in the margin reminds him of the assault in Charlottenburg. A debt incurred and repaid long ago, Bauer thinks. And am I now supposed to believe that so outspoken a man should be trusted abroad with the best interests of the Reich?

Still, a little too close to Dohnanyi for a first move. He would rather strike a bit farther afield and watch the reaction. He telephones Sonderegger and says, "This Josef Müller in Munich. Have your men bring him in."

April 5, 1943

THE WEATHER PROMISING TO HOLD FAIR and warm, Dietrich Bonhoeffer determined to take a day away from his writing and go cycling in the Grunewald with his nephew. But when he rang the Dohnanyi home in Sacrow, a strange man said, "Hello."

Dietrich froze, then set the phone slowly back on its cradle. He stared straight ahead for a time, seeing nothing. A dull thud at the back of the house brought him back to himself. He went outside and found a robin lying on the veranda. It had crashed into the glass windows of the sunroom. Dietrich picked it up and its head fell limply across his finger. A broken neck. He laid it off on the grass and, on an impulse, covered it with dry leaves. Then he went inside and climbed the stairs.

His parents were taking their afternoon naps, so he tiptoed onto the landing outside their rooms and on up to his attic. He glanced out the window, then went to his desk and methodically checked the drawers for incriminating papers. Nothing. From the mattress on his bed he took a sheaf of papers, fakes all of them, pertaining to his trips abroad, and placed them in a drawer where they would be easily noticed by the Gestapo. Then he went back downstairs and ate a large meal.

"Hungry already?" Cook said. "But you ate only two hours ago. And your mother's butter she was saving for Sunday—"

He looked up from slicing bread. "She'll understand," he answered gently. "It may be the last for a while."

"The last?" The woman was puzzled.

"Yes, Frau Brandt. I'm going away for a time."

Back upstairs he washed up quickly and stood by the window. He removed his glasses and examined the frames. The right earpiece was slightly bent and the edge of the lens chipped where he'd dropped them in the bathtub a few months earlier. He cleaned them carefully and put them back on. Soon after, the black saloon car came slowly along the Marienburger Allee and pulled into the drive. Two men got out and came to the door. Just before ringing the bell, the man in front looked up at the window where Dietrich stood. Their eyes met. Then SS Judge Advocate Alois Bauer knocked on the door.

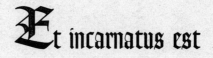

Et incarnatus est

was born and became man

Tegel Wehrmacht Interrogation Prison

DAY 0. The prisoner is placed in a holding cell where he will spend the night while his arrest papers are processed. SS Judge Advocate Alois Bauer has explained this to him already, in the rear seat of the black Mercedes on the way to Tegel. A hand resting gently on the prisoner's arm as he spoke. *Not very comfortable, I'm afraid. But it's only overnight until they can move you to a permanent cell.*

The prisoner repeats *overnight overnight* tries not to hear *permanent permanent*.

In the holding cell a slop bucket overflowing with clumps of feces stands in the corner. There is a cot and a single blanket so stiff and vile-smelling he cannot bear to touch it. He nudges it onto the floor with the toe of his shoe. The cot has no mattress, only a frame of metal mesh. Just as well if one could imagine the state of a mattress.

He stretches out on his back with his jacket folded into a neat square for a pillow. He works a long time to make the corners of the jacket just so. Determined to be neat. The cell is chilly but the blanket doesn't tempt him. He folds his arms across his chest for warmth. The grid of the metal mattress frame bites the flesh of his back.

A single light bulb hangs suspended from the ceiling above his head. He turns his head to one side so the light won't hurt his eyes and looks toward the door. No switch to turn off the light.

A slot in the wooden door. After a time—he has no idea how much—the slot opens with a crack and he sees part of a man's face. The nose first. Eyes meet his. The slot slams shut.

Suicide watch.

He closes his eyes.

The slot opens. A hunk of stale bread is shoved through and falls to the floor.

The effects of the large meal Cook made him have passed, and his stomach growls. But the bread lying on the grimy concrete floor tempts him even less than the blanket. He looks away. He is not desperately hungry. Yet.

The slot opens and closes at regular intervals. The light stays on. He cannot sleep even though he feels he will die of weariness. The light bulb burns his skull.

The room buzzes. The light bulb throbs. He squeezes his eyes tight but he can still hear the buzzing. Voices shoot around the cell, disconnected disjointed voices. Karl-Friedrich. *Think of the family Think of Mother and Father What will happen to them if you?* Karl-Friedrich is a physicist, he knows about light and air. How much they can bear. Karl-Friedrich investigates the mechanism of rhythmic reactions. He knows how little the mind can apprehend. Of lights and their buzzing. The family. Mother. Elisabeth. No. Elisabeth is gone. Maria. Yes.

Sabine. Chanting *eternity eternity eternity eternity eternity eternity eternity*

He listens carefully, intensely, repeats the words after her. As long as he hears the voices he will survive the night.

Eyes watch him through the slot.

In the hall outside the cell the guard shakes his head and walks away. Back in the tiny room which holds four chairs and table with hot plate and coffeepot, he interrupts a card game.

"One cigarette says he's screaming before the night's done."

The card players take him on without looking up. He loses the bet and his next-to-last smoke.

DAY 1. Late in the day the prisoner is moved to a regular cell, Number 92 on the third floor. Here his cot holds a thin mattress and thinner, but relatively clean, blanket. He has a wooden bench and a stool. The slop bucket stinks but is empty. Soon enough, he supposes, the odor will be his own and he will be able to stomach it, perhaps even be comforted by it, like a dog which has marked its territory.

The new room is smaller than the holding cell, perhaps because it is only meant for one. One large step takes him across it, and he stands for a long time with his chest pressed against the plaster wall. He turns. Two and a half strides take him the length of the cell. There is a small barred window above his head. If he stands on his cot he will be able to see out, but he resists the temptation. He will save the window for last. Something to look forward to.

He turns back toward the door. A slot like the one in the holding cell is set in the wood. Only this one is larger, to accommodate a tray of food. He remembers how hungry he is, and sinks slowly onto the edge of the cot. It tips slightly and he sits farther back to steady himself, then stretches full-length on his back, testing the feel of the mattress. It is lumpy, but adequate. When he turns his head he can smell the musty canvas cover. Then he notices the words on the wall opposite, scratched carefully in a small, patient script.

In 100 years it will all be over

He closes his eyes. Tears escape at the corners and he brushes them away with his knuckle, like a child. He does not know how long he cries, and when he has worn himself out, he sleeps.

DAY 2. When he wakes the cell is filled with morning light.

He decides to allow himself the treat of the window. Then he hesitates, frozen by fear. Suppose there is nothing to see, only a view of the rest of the prison, a guard tower perhaps, or worst of all, a wall?

But he is high up, near the roof. Above the wall surely. And the prison itself stands on a rise of ground north of the city. There must be something to see. He holds his breath and steps up onto the stool with his eyes shut.

He waits. The window is open and he feels a breeze on his face. He opens his eyes.

Berlin sprawls before him, a great beast, its back humped and gabled like a tyrannosaurus. The locomotive works of Borsig are closest, a warren of foundries and roundhouses, brick and stone, beveled windows laced with grimy pig iron, tracks running between the leviathan buildings like black spiderwebs. Beyond Borsig, domes, blocks, and the spikes of churches above the tunnel of greening fog that stretches the length of the Spree, roofs flaunting their red tile in the spring sun, the spires their filigree. The streets are mysterious twisting caverns. As the sky lightens the buildings seem to stand up and walk around. He grips the bars with both of his large hands and leans forward as far as he can. Nearly lost among the smoke-stacks of Borsig he notices a nearby tower topped by a green copper dome in the Bavarian style. A Roman Catholic church. He imagines the singing of its choir, airy and weightless, a Gregorian chant. He hears the words *sursam corda*.

The city grows even larger and enters his cell.

At midday, his first meal. A crust of bread with a thin edge of mold. A bowl of brown soup. When he moves his spoon through the bowl a few bits of carrot and a fatty piece of meat swirl to the top. He has also been given a small, rather dry roasted potato.

He eats hungrily. The soup is possible if he doesn't stop to smell it.

But before he eats he goes to the slot in the door, which has opened to allow the tray of food to be shoved through, then closed at once. He longs to see the guard—a human being—and he has discovered he can open the slot from the inside. He puts his eyes to the rectangular hole. All that is visible is the wall across the way. He can hear slots opening and closing to his left, and the squeaking wheels of a trolley. He starts to call out, but a feeling of foolishness keeps his mouth shut. What, after all, would he say to the man?

He goes back to the cot where the tray of food waits. He scrapes carefully at the mold with a dirty fingernail.

DAY 6. He has glimpsed the guard twice. A man with the peaked and fanned ears of a bat.

Otherwise he has seen no one. Spoken to no one. He hears distant screams. Wails. Nothing close by.

He considers suicide. No great step, for he has begun to think himself already dead. And he fears torture, knows he will not be able to stand up under the pain and will tell everything he knows. Which is a world too much.

He is best dead. But how to do it? They have taken his shoelaces and there is no sheet on the cot. There is the spoon which arrives with his soup, but if he tries to keep it, it will be missed. Besides, what can he do with a spoon? He has nothing with which to file it to sharpness. He lacks the nerve to stab or cut himself.

He lies on his back on the cot and stares at the ceiling. Now and then he holds his breath but gasps and gives up after a few seconds. He thinks he might lie on the floor and jam the cot leg into his head but knows he will only injure himself.

He cannot think of a way to die.

DAY 10. No one talks. There is no music. No sound. Now and then a footstep, a door opens. The air is heavy. The air thrums.

The accumulation of despair makes the cell's air intolerably heavy. He has read, perhaps Karl-Friedrich has told him, that when events of great intensity occur, the air becomes freighted with electricity so that a person who comes empty to that space will be touched or even burned.

In 100 years it will all be over

He recalls the countless memorials to the dead of countless wars he has seen in Germany and England.

their memory shall remain forever green

But nothing is green. Those who knew the war dead are themselves dead or will be. He himself will die, and so will all who know him. No matter what happens next. One hundred years is oblivion.

He feels the weight of the air pressing against his chest, threatening to smother him. How would Karl-Friedrich explain this? The air holds time? Something to do with Einstein? The capacity—

He cannot think, cannot hold a thought, not at all. He shakes his head to clear it. He speaks out loud.

Hello, he says to the wall.

That helps.

Hello

It is Dietrich talking. He recognizes the voice and remembers his name.

Blessed is he who comes in the name of the Lord, he says aloud.

He says *Father forgive them for they know not what they do*.

Anything that comes into his mind, he says, or sings. *Onward Christian Soldiers, marching as to war Lloyd George knew my father Father knew Lloyd George*

If it is in his mind he must release it, relieve the air of its burden, decorate the cell with words.

There are more things in heaven and earth Horatio than are dreamt of in your philosophy

He sings loudly *In München ist ein Hofbrauhaus, ein zwei*—

The bat-eared guard bangs on his door and yells, "Shut up, you bastard!"

Dietrich is on his feet at once. "Talk to me!" he cries.

There is no answer except retreating footsteps.

DAY 14/GOOD FRIDAY. He has come to expect forty days and forty nights.

He hears footsteps outside his cell and stands in anticipation. It is the bat-eared guard, whose tread he knows now as surely as a dog knows its master's. (He has detected a slight dragging of the foot in the guard's gait. A former soldier most likely, furloughed to the prison after a leg wound.) But followed by another, slower and measured step. The panel in the door slides open and the eyes study him, then a key in the lock, a rasping turn, and the door swings open.

The guard looms in the open door as though ready to pounce, hand on truncheon. Behind him a voice says, "At ease, Linke. This one isn't dangerous."

Linke stands aside, hand still on truncheon, to reveal a small balding man, grayskinned in a rumpled gray uniform.

The man says, "Bonhoeffer."

To hear his name spoken aloud after fourteen days is like a sharp blow. Dietrich sways, puts a hand to the wall to steady himself.

"I am Maetz, the commandant here at Tegel. You are informed that your term of solitary confinement is hereby ended. You will now be allowed to join the other prisoners in the exercise yard once a day. You may write a letter to your family every ten days and you may receive letters from them as well as packages, once they have been inspected, of course."

Dietrich blinks. Maetz is holding out a parcel wrapped in brown paper. "Your father brought this after your arrest. You may receive it now."

Dietrich takes the parcel, presses it to his chest. He cannot speak. Maetz studies him for a moment, then says, "You may thank your uncle for this. General Rüdiger Graf von der Goltz is one of the most powerful and respected men in Berlin. And married to your mother's sister, I believe?"

"Uncle Rudi."

"Yes." Maetz nods. "He'll not plead special favors for you, of course, but he has persuaded Judge Advocate Bauer to stop making a special case of you. It's not as though you're considered a great danger to the Reich."

He turns to leave, but Dietrich says, "And Judge Advocate Bauer? When shall I be able to speak with him?"

"In his own time, I'm sure. The judge advocate is known to be a most thorough and careful investigator."

"Please, can you ask him if I might have books and writing paper? It would be a great comfort to me."

The commandant looks irritated for a moment, then seems to recall Uncle Rudi, who is in fact his superior officer and a man whose good regard is not to be cast away. "I shall pass on your request," Maetz agrees, "but I can't promise results," and takes his leave.

The guard Linke glances back at Dietrich as he pulls the cell door to. Dietrich nods in what he hopes is a friendly manner, and Linke hesitates, then nods in return, his eyes narrowed thoughtfully and his bat's ears at attention.

Linke has provided his first favor—a pencil stolen from the guardroom in return for a packet of malt extract included by Dr. Karl Bonhoeffer in the parcel sent from the Marienburger Allee. (An item of no conceivable use to Dietrich except as a bribe. He marvels at his father's shrewdness.)

He arranges the rest of his bounty, item by item, on the cot. A small loaf of pumpernickel and a tin of pork fat. Four cigarettes carefully wrapped in a handkerchief (there were six, but he has smoked one and given the other to Linke in return for some matches). A wool sweater and a blanket. A volume of Fontane. And best of all, the pencil and the wrapping paper, large and blank.

Dietrich sprawls on the cot chewing a heel of the bread torn from the loaf and dipped in pork fat—he has no knife for spreading—and considers what to write. A letter to his parents, and perhaps a short note to Maria, even though he will not be allowed to post it. Perhaps he shall keep a journal. Perhaps write poetry, or a novel, something he has always wanted to do but never had time for. (He will not be able to work on his volume of *Ethics* in prison—part of the manuscript has been confiscated by Bauer and part is buried in a strongbox in the garden of the Marienburger Allee. He doesn't want to work on his *Ethics* in prison anyway, because he has lately been bargaining with God. The *Ethics* will be the crowning achievement of his life's work and must be completed. Therefore, Dietrich must be released from Tegel.)

At last he picks up the book—the pattern is set, this putting off of that most longed for until last, a way of redeeming time—and opens it to the flyleaf, where his name has been written and underlined: <u>Dietrich Bon-hoeffer</u>. It is the signal they have agreed upon ahead of time when a secret message is included. He flips to the back of the book. Every ten pages from the end, a letter is faintly underlined in pencil. He turns pages slowly and silently mouths the words:

UNCLE RUDI WELL. KEEP AWAY FROM HIM AS PLANNED. HANS IN PLÖTZENSEE. CHRISTEL ALSO ARRESTED. LOVE.

DAY 27. He now has his Bible and hymnal and writing paper. He has slippers, matches, shaving cream and razor, needle and thread. Plus a pipe and a small store of tobacco and cigarettes. He has received the good news that the authorities have found no reason to hold Christel and have released her to her family.

And there is a letter from Hans von Dohnanyi, written on Easter Sunday, lamenting that he has somehow been the cause of Dietrich's imprisonment. A noble and probably useless attempt to put distance between them, Dietrich thinks. He would rather be linked; it is less lonely. For he gathers from the letter that Dohnanyi is already being interrogated by Judge Advocate Bauer. They will consider Dietrich less important and will save him for later, hoping he will help them catch Dohnanyi out in some lie. Dietrich spends hours lying on his back, going over and over the story he and Hans agreed on months earlier.

He is also allowed newspapers. Linke the guard even brings him back issues. On Good Friday the *Deutsche Allgemeine Zeitung* carried a reproduction of Dürer's *Apocalypse*, which Dietrich sees a few days later.

The lines are fuzzy because of wartime newsprint and ink, but the contorted visages of the horsemen are no less ghastly. Dietrich studies the print for signs—the mounted rampage of Famine, Pestilence, War, and skeletal

Death upon a rib-caved horse surrounded by bug-eyed monsters and howling sufferers. A grotesque face grows from the blouse of a harried man, and,
hovering above all, an angel of the Lord. Seeming to approve? Dietrich
shudders and hopes, Surely not.

　　He tears the newsprint and carefully folds back the edges to make a neat
square. A dab of breakfast porridge at each corner provides a remarkable

glue. He stands on the cot and covers *In 100 years it all will be over* with the Four Horsemen of the Apocalypse.

Linke comes for the slop bucket. On the way out he looks up. He stops and studies the print.

"Is that supposed to be better?" He looks at Dietrich.

Dietrich laughs, for the first time since he entered Tegel. Linke smiles back. Then he says, to Dietrich's surprise, "I think I know you. From before."

"Before?"

Linke tosses his head. "You know."

Dietrich searches his memory. "I don't see how—"

But Linke says, "That play in Charlottenburg, at the youth club. That terrible play that the SS raided. I was in it, and so were you. We had a scene together at the beginning. You were friends with the fellow who directed it. I remember. You're the only rich guys I ever met until I went into the army."

The play. Falk Harnack and his Georg Kaiser. Dietrich narrows his eyes, trying to remember. "Which character were you?"

"The Bank Manager, remember? I had to borrow a suit for that one." It is a memory he clearly relishes, a high point of his life. "And I was the Policeman at the end." Leans close and whispers, "Thought I was a dead man when the SS came in. Never ran so fast in my life. Christ, those were some days."

Dietrich nods at his leg. "You've been wounded?"

"Early on," Linke agrees with the good nature of a man who has had time to come to terms with an infirmity. "On the way into Belgium. My own mate shot me in the kneecap while we were fooling around with our pistols. Everyone was green, you see." He steps closer. "But we had to cover it up," he says with a wink. "Back then you could be court-martialed for fooling around. So we found a dead Belgian and said he did it. I got a medal, instead of doing time in here with you lot."

"Perhaps you shouldn't talk about it so openly."

Linke waves his hand. "Nobody would bother about it now. Got more on their plate than they can eat, don't they?"

Day 38. It is the first of many conversations with Linke, who latches onto Dietrich as a long-lost souvenir from happier times. Dietrich hears the story of Linke's life, how he worked at Borsig through the thirties. ("Half of Wedding worked at Borsig. Pulled the Reich's trains on our bloody backs, we did. Where'd Adolf be without us, eh?") How he married a woman in 1935 who promptly gained eighty pounds and does nothing but complain. ("A good cook, though, and raises a garden. Even with this wartime crap they give us, I eat well." Dietrich, listening and observing the bribes pass back and forth, decides Linke's position at the prison has something to do with this as well. Linke likes Dietrich because he reminds him of his youth but also because Dietrich will receive interesting parcels from home.) How he has three children, all girls thank God, for the war looks like never ending, not a time for sons.

When Linke takes the prisoners to the exercise yard he often walks beside Dietrich, chattering away about something that has happened on his rounds. In this way Dietrich learns about the prison and the men forced to live in it. Most of those kept in Tegel are military men serving time after court-martial. Some were apprehended after going AWOL or were charged with sabotage—many of them awaiting execution—but there is also an assortment of screw-ups, petty thieves, brawlers. Some are junior officers or enlisted men charged with insubordination, much of it justified according to Linke, who regales Dietrich with stories of absurd orders issued from on high. He also hints, though only vaguely, that some of Tegel's inmates might have tried to undermine actions against Jews and civilians in the East. When Dietrich asks once, point-blank, Linke looks furtively round and shakes his head. "Not many," he says, and runs his fingertip across his throat. But Dietrich in fact meets a Wehrmacht officer, Oberleutnant Pfifer, who is awaiting trial for refusing to order his squadron to execute a village of Polish Jews. Pfifer shrugs as he tells his story, smoking the cigarette Dietrich offers him. "I knew another fellow," Pfifer says, "who also disobeyed. He was transferred, nothing more as far as I know. I think I refused in a little too colorful language for my commanding officer, shall we say, and the man had it in for me anyway because I stood up to him at other times. Anyway, they weren't so threatened by refusing such duty. Most officers went along with no problem."

"Why didn't you?" Dietrich asks as they stroll around the exercise yard.

Pfifer shrugs. "Maybe I was just sick of putting up with this commanding officer of mine. I thought if it had to be done, it was a job for the SS. They're the ones who enjoy that sort of thing. Gives them hard-ons, you know what I mean?" He shrugs again as if to say *It doesn't matter*.

"I would have hoped," Dietrich says, "you might have been motivated by some concern for the Jews to the executed."

Pfifer studies him a moment, then says, in a voice that sounds casual, "Why are you in civvies?"

Dietrich tries to think what excuse to give but Pfifer is ahead of him.

"Who do you work for? The Abwehr?" When Dietrich doesn't answer, Pfifer's face goes blank. "Intelligence," he says. He drops his cigarette butt and grinds it beneath his boot. "Why are you here?"

"A mistake," Dietrich says. "I don't expect to be held long." He tries to keep a friendly expression on his face. "Actually I am a pastor."

But Pfifer is moving away, disengaging. He will most certainly be passing the word that one must be careful around the quiet man in the tweed jacket. Dietrich feels like weeping. The exercise yard is the place to meet the other prisoners, to enjoy a small amount of human contact. Dietrich has come to think of his time in prison as a stay in a monastery, with a discipline of silence, and the exercise yard is like the common meal where one is finally allowed to speak. There is no meal to share in the exercise yard, but cigarettes are sometimes passed around, and the more generous of the prisoners from time to time give out food sent from home, biscuits, perhaps, or bits of dried fruit. Dietrich is one of the sharers, partly because he knows his family's circumstances will mean he has more than most. But it is also necessary to share if the prison is to be what it must be in order for him to keep his sanity—his pastoral charge.

So he spends the hour before exercise on his knees beside his cot, praying for all the inmates and guards. When Linke opens his cell door and leads him among them, he greets them with a smile, a question about their health or news from home. He keeps an eye out for those who walk more slowly and painfully than usual as the result of a battering by their SS inquisitors, so that he might offer them comfort. (At quiet times the distant screams can be heard from the ground-floor cellblock used for interrogations. "What have these poor little souls to divulge?" Dietrich asks Linke. Linke shakes his head. "They pick on the weak ones," he says, "and learn what they can. Who knows what it will be? Just keep your head down.")

They all keep their heads down as they trudge around the exercise yard in three circles. This lasts half an hour, followed by another half hour when they are allowed to talk and barter, to wander on their own and inspect their surroundings. Dietrich is the only prisoner in civilian garb except for four Italians, former aides to Mussolini being held as scapegoats in the collapse of the Italian government. Many of the prisoners wear uniforms with light bare patches on the shoulders where insignia have been torn off— the ghosts of former rank. After two weeks in the exercise yard, Dietrich knows most by name. But after the conversation with Pfifer, he finds himself isolated. When he approaches, men who once greeted him as Pastor Bonhoeffer now nod coolly and move away, pretending to be engaged in conversation elsewhere. They gossip about him. Some of the guards have told them Bonhoeffer is a nephew of one of the top military brass in Berlin and therefore receives special treatment—better food, more packages from outside. It is as though he is once more in solitary. Only Otto Linke will talk to him.

DAY 46. While strolling around the prison yard Dietrich has discovered a tomtit's nest wedged in a crack of the masonry. By standing on tiptoe he can just see over the edge, though he is careful not to approach when the mother is in the nest. First the eggs—ten tiny speckled ovals. Then after several weeks the fuzzy heads and perpetually open mouths of the hatchlings. Dietrich no longer approaches the nest. From a careful distance he watches mother and father tomtit tend their young, and tries to guess when the nestlings will be ready to fly away.

Back in his cell he stretches out full-length on his cot—sometimes reading, sometimes napping—for the rest of the afternoon. It is the way he deals with the early-summer heat. Formal though he is, he strips to his underwear. Once Linke arrives with a package from home and finds him thus in dishabille. The guard is surprised at Dietrich's obvious embarrassment.

"All the fellows on this floor take off their clothes in summer," Linke says. "After all, you're at the top of the building and it's a tin roof. Just wait until August. You'll sweat off twenty pounds, like one of those Finnish saunas."

And he leaves Dietrich alone to contemplate this miserable scenario. "Perhaps I shall be out by then," Dietrich says to the wall.

The next morning as he is preparing to go out to the exercise yard, Commandant Maetz pays a visit.

"I understand you've been suffering from the heat," Maetz says. As though to express his sympathy, he takes a handkerchief from his pocket and wipes his own face.

"It is very warm," Dietrich agrees, "but I must learn to live with it."

"It's cooler on the ground floor," Maetz says. "I can put you down there."

Dietrich smiles his gratitude and starts to thank the commandant when a thought stops him. "What about the others on this floor?" he asks.

"I can't move everyone," Maetz says.

"And this cell? Will someone downstairs be put here?"

"Of course. There are only so many ground-floor cells."

"Then I can't move. It wouldn't be right."

Maetz looks surprised. "But I promised your uncle—"

"You can tell Uncle Rudi," Dietrich interrupts, "that I appreciate his concern. But I can rest far better in the heat than in the knowledge I am passing on my problems to another prisoner."

When Maetz is gone he kneels by the cot to pray, then walks to the exercise yard with a feeling of joy. He has not betrayed this his pastoral charge despite grave temptation. He looks around him at the three circles of trudging men, wondering which he has saved from the third-floor heat. He wants to love them all and wants them to love him. None of them knows this. None of them speaks to him.

DAY 54. In the exercise yard, they are done with their circles. Dietrich strolls, hands in pockets, toward the tomtit nest, then stops short and stares. The nest has been torn apart. The smashed bodies of the ten baby tomtits are scattered across the hard ground amid bits of twig and feathers. As though someone has ground them beneath the heel of a boot like cigarette butts.

He feels ill. Imagines the distress cries of the parent birds, who are nowhere about. When he looks away he sees many of the men are watching him. He turns back, takes out his handkerchief, and, one by one, gathers up the bodies of the baby birds. Behind him he hears laughter. *Look, the pastor is going to have a funeral.* He ignores this and stuffs the handkerchief into his pocket, not caring how eccentric his actions appear. On the way back to their cells they pass by the kitchen. Dietrich bends quickly and drops the tiny carcasses behind an overflowing garbage pail. He knows the prison rats will visit and make a meal. Death for life, he thinks bitterly.

In the emptiness of his cell, thoughts of Maria grow stronger. When after a month in prison he at last was allowed a letter from her, he had been ecstatic for days, had read and reread, folded and unfolded the letter until the flimsy wartime paper was coming apart. Then came a second letter, and a third. He was in an agony because he was allowed to write to no one except his parents and so could not tell her how much he loved her.

Maria's letters were much the same as they had been before his imprisonment—chatty, full of energy and youth and simplicity and ardent expressions of her affection. She was riding her beloved horse through the fields around Pätzig, she was helping her mother bake a cake, in her room at night she was making lists of furniture and linens she would like to have in their house once they were married, was even picking the music for the wedding service. He fell in love all over again, this time with the Maria of letter and memory and daydream, who always smiled except when she remembered her father and brother and needed comforting by Dietrich, who in the daydream kissed her and held her close.

In fact he had never kissed or held her. He had never been alone with her.

But in his mind, in his mind their house existed, complete with the furnishings Maria had described to him in her letters. In his mind they had done much, much more than kiss. For though he did not possess the imagination of a novelist, isolation and longing fed his dreams so that the Maria of his mind became the greatest pleasure of his bare existence. And when he had done talking with this Maria, they made love, their amorous exploits passing before his eyes like a motion picture projected against the blank wall of his cell.

Today he has nothing from Maria, but a letter has arrived from her mother, Frau von Wedemeyer. It is short but not unfriendly, kind even, as if her Christian duty to write to the prisoner has overcome her dislike of him. She wishes him good health and hopes and prays they will see him at Pätzig before the leaves turn, "so that you may share in the good fruits of the earth which summer bestows upon us here in the country."

He closes his eyes and tastes the produce of Pätzig—the plums and apples and blackberries, the bread baked with fresh-ground flour, the beets and carrots and peas and potatoes swimming in butter. When his own meager supper of turnips and potatoes arrives it is all he can do to eat it, and afterward he weeps like a child.

DAY 55. Through Commandant Maetz he sends a message to his Uncle Rudi, with whom he has not communicated in years. *If I may ask one favor only, it is that my fiancée Maria von Wedemeyer be allowed to visit me, and that I be allowed to write to her. I promise to bother you with no other requests.*

DAY 61. At last a black Mercedes carries Dietrich, handcuffed between two guards, to the War Court Building in the Witzlebenstraße. It is a painful journey. Since his imprisonment, the buds on the trees have exploded in bursts of limegreen. Dietrich stares out the car window like a country boy seeing the city for the first time, at the lindens some still in their ranks, others strewn about and broken by bomb damage, the shops with boarded facades, the masses of people passing on foot and bicycle with their disheveled clothes and subdued faces. Berlin has never looked more beautiful.

At the War Court he is hustled up a flight of stairs to a bare room with dark oak floors and woodwork. A bookcase, desk, and two chairs are the only furnishings, a picture of the Führer the only decoration. Not anyone's office, he decides, only a place to conduct interrogations, and a mercifully civilized-looking place. He has heard horror stories about the Gestapo interrogation cells in the Prinz-Albrecht-Straße—of tubs where heads are held underwater, boards of electrical wires hooked to genitals, concrete floors streaked with the blood and excrement of beating victims. This place could have witnessed nothing like that—it is too clean and simple, the floor too polished. Dietrich sinks gingerly onto the chair across from the desk. His heart, which has been beating rapidly, slows, his breathing becomes more even.

Then he is aware of the low murmur of voices behind the double oak doors on his right. The voices rise and fall, and one is familiar. The doors open suddenly by some invisible hand and he sees Hans von Dohnanyi, seated in an office that is the twin of the other. Dohnanyi's back is straight and he glances sideways at Dietrich, his eyes quick behind his glasses. He appears to be unmarked and, though thinner and with an air of weariness, in decent shape. An SS officer seated across from Dohnanyi rises and comes through the doors. Dietrich—surprised by the suddenness of his isolation's end—staggers to his feet and salutes, his *Heil Hitler* bouncing insincerely along the bare wood floors. He strains to keep Dohnanyi in his line of vision.

Judge Advocate Bauer says *Heil Hitler* quietly, and pulls the doors shut behind him.

"Pastor Bonhoeffer," he says. "We meet again."

Dietrich wonders if Bauer is referring to his arrest or if he recalls their earlier encounters. Bauer comes so close Dietrich could put his hand on the other man's shoulder if he wanted. They are of a height, though Bauer is more slender, and younger in appearance because he has not lost much of his light brown hair. Unlike Dietrich, he does not wear spectacles, but he keeps a monocle on the end of a string in his breast pocket for reading fine print. He regards Dietrich in a not unfriendly manner.

"Your brother-in-law does well," he says. "He seems to cooperate." A slight emphasis on *seems*.

"May I speak with him?"

"No," Bauer replies, as pleasantly as if he'd said yes. He goes to the desk and sits down, opens a folder lying on the polished surface and studies a few documents, monocle held between thumb and index finger. Without looking up he says, "I would ordinarily have gone to the prison to conduct this interview, but I thought you might enjoy an outing."

"Thank you," Dietrich says, feeling like a small child being handed a sweet.

Bauer nods genially. "I expect in return your cooperation."

"I shall do my best."

"Good." Bauer looks up with a pleased expression. "Because of course, Pastor Bonhoeffer, you are concerned for the welfare of your parents, are you not? And especially fond of your fiancée, Maria von Wedemeyer?"

Bauer waits a moment, until the fear registers clearly in Dietrich's face. And no doubt, it was the mention of the fiancée which elicited it. "Not that Fräulein von Wedemeyer is in any danger. After all, she's done nothing wrong. Has she? Though if one looked closely, one might find something irregular. Women can be so careless with their ration books, and then they have such loose tongues, terribly indiscreet sometimes. Anyway, I assume I shall have your full attention and cooperation during these little discussions of ours."

"Of course." Dietrich's right leg is trembling, and he shifts from one foot to the other to hide it.

The smile leaves Bauer's face and he is suddenly brisk, businesslike. "Good." He pretends to notice for the first time that Dietrich is still standing, and motions for him to sit, then goes back to his papers for a good five minutes. From the next room Dietrich can hear the scrape of a chair, footsteps and a door opening and closing, more footsteps out in the hall. Dohnanyi has been taken away.

"Why were you not called up when the war began?"

Bauer's question is so sharply posed that Dietrich gives a start. He takes a deep breath to settle himself.

"Because of my service in the Abwehr, I am not required—"

"I am well aware," Bauer interrupts, "that your position with the Abwehr counts as your military service. That is not my question. Why did you not join thousands of pastors—even pastors from the Confessing movement— and volunteer to serve in a front-line chaplaincy?"

"I serve the Führer best with my mind. I assure you, Judge Advocate, I would make an incompetent soldier. I would do more harm than good at the front, out of sheer clumsiness."

Bauer is shaking his head. "A chaplain need not be a good soldier. He only need be willing to live alongside the men in his charge, to offer them comfort and to die with them if necessary. Why are you not sharing the hardships of our fighting men, Pastor Bonhoeffer? Could it be you are a coward?"

He feels as though he were once more facing Elisabeth Hildebrandt who is demanding *why? why aren't you doing more?*

Bauer waits patiently, his eyes never leaving Dietrich's face. After a time he says softly, "Some would judge the avoidance of military service in wartime to be as despicable as treason."

"I have not avoided serving my country and I have taken some risks myself," Dietrich protests. "Not nearly so many risks as a front-line chaplain, of course. But the journeys abroad I have undertaken are more dangerous in wartime than in peacetime."

"Not that dangerous," Bauer scoffs.

Dietrich blushes at the absurdity of his own assertion and bumbles on. "I am more useful where I am. If I had joined the Abwehr as an enlisted man, I would not have been trusted by my contacts abroad. Few men in Germany have such international connections, and because of my background I have gained a certain amount of trust among these foreigners. I have been able to plant false information abroad and to learn things which have proved valuable to the Reich."

"Rubbish. You are a coward."

Dietrich sits up straighter. "You are my age," he says. "You are not on a front line. Also perhaps for good reas—"

He stops, for the judge advocate has left his chair like a shot and come around the desk.

"You are standing upon a bridge, Pastor Bonhoeffer. The bridge between the War Court and—" Bauer leans forward and speaks more softly—"the Gestapo. I am that bridge, Pastor Bonhoeffer. One word from me will fling you across to the far side. Where I doubt you wish to be?"

"No," Dietrich manages to say.

"I didn't think so. Now I shall repeat my earlier statement. You are a coward. Do you deny it?"

Dietrich recalls what a Catholic friend once told him, that the sins of a priest do not mar the efficacy of a sacrament. So, he is in a confessional with a most unholy confessor.

"Yes, I am a coward. A front-line position would terrify me. If I found myself in such a position, I would pray and do my best, but I am just as glad not to have to face it and to serve in other ways."

"Is this honesty supposed to impress me?"

"I have tried to offer the Reich what meager gifts I possess, in the belief that this is what the present situation requires. If it should come to pass, and I pray that it does not, that our military situation worsens to the point where even one such as I should be needed in the field, then I would without hesitation fight to the death to protect the Fatherland."

Bauer laughs and pats Dietrich on the shoulder. He goes back to his chair, scribbles something on a piece of paper, and sits tapping his pencil on the desktop. He asks, "This supposedly important position you hold with the Abwehr. Did it require you to take the oath of loyalty to the Führer?"

"No."

"How convenient. Once again you did not have to learn the limits of your courage."

"You believe I would have refused to take the oath?"

"It does cross my mind," Bauer says. "But I doubt you would have had the courage to refuse."

"The question is irrelevant," Dietrich protests. "I am a patriot."

"Then you would have taken the oath?"

"Of course."

"Would take it tomorrow if I required it of you?"

Dietrich has known, ever since he agreed to help kill Hitler, that he has also agreed to risk the destruction of his own soul. The oath would be one thing more, only one thing more. He says, "I would take the oath if it were required of me."

"Even though as I recall from an earlier encounter you have been an outspoken opponent of the Führer and his policies? I am speaking of the ecumenical conference in Denmark when you spoke and worked against our government in the most public and critical way possible."

"That was before the war."

"Are you telling me your opinions have changed so drastically? You were one of the most intractable and outspoken leaders of the Confessing Church movement."

"Before the war, yes," Dietrich admitted, "I did criticize our government. But only as one would criticize a beloved relative. That is the way of families, sometimes to quarrel out of concern for the common good. But when the Fatherland is under attack, all its true children rush to the defense. If I despised my Fatherland as you seem to suggest, why would I take it upon myself to become engaged to a young woman from a military family which has lost a father and son in this war? This Abwehr service of mine has been a welcome opportunity to prove my love for Germany."

Bauer rests his chin on his fist and smiles. "Most touching."

Dietrich waits uneasily for the interrogation to continue, but Bauer continues to watch him with an expression that says *You are the most interesting and amusing person I've come across in quite some time and I don't believe a word that's come out of your mouth.*

Dietrich thinks, *You* are very good at what you do, and finds to his surprise that he has said this out loud.

Bauer laughs delightedly. He says, "You were acquainted with the Harnacks, Arvid and Mildred."

No mention, Dietrich realizes with relief, of Falk.

"Acquainted, though not closely. I knew Arvid's uncle much better. My most respected theology professor at the university. He lived next door to my family in Grunewald."

"The Harnacks," Bauer says, and strokes his own chin as though he were petting a cat. "My work."

Dietrich sits with his head down. "Yes," he says, "I know."

"You followed the case in the Abwehr?"

"Yes."

"Good," Bauer says. He stands and gathers his papers into a neat stack, shoves them into a briefcase. At the door he turns.

"Next time, Pastor Bonhoeffer, I shall see you at Tegel. Enjoy your ride back to the prison."

DAY 62. He spends the next twenty-four hours in solitary confinement. No explanation is given. But he imagines it is a message from Bauer. Influential uncle or no, remember who is in charge here.

He spends hours pacing. It is boring but necessary. Sitting too long in such a tiny space causes his muscles to cramp, his bones to ache. Three long strides the length of the cell. Back and forth back and forth. Two steps across the cell. Back and forth. He bangs into the wall with his palms out, pushes off, back to the other side, pushes off. All around him others are doing the same. Pacing. Feet pounding the stone floor, hands slapping the walls. In Tegel it is a perpetual rhythm barely noticed by guards or inmates, a pleasant heartbeat of a sound to nap by.

Between pacing sessions Dietrich tries to write. Until now, his efforts to put words on paper have been frustrated by an inability to concentrate. The novel he began, a *roman à clef* based on his childhood, languishes with only half a chapter complete. A play about a distinguished Berlin family much like his own has progressed no more than two scenes. A modest stack of paper, all he has to show for these aborted attempts, lies forlornly in a corner of the cell. Paper is not easy to come by and he wishes he had these sheets back, clean and open to possibility once more. But he is still uncertain what he would say. The words only come when he writes to his parents. Or to Maria, though he is still not allowed to post the letters.

A parcel arrives. "Your sister brought it," Linke says.

"My sister?" Suse, he guesses. The war has turned Suse into a great cyclist, though he wonders if she would have come all the way from Dahlem on her bicycle. But he doubts it was Christel. Christel is not well, the secret messages in his books tell him. Not physically ill, exactly, but struck down by a depression which makes it difficult for her to get out of bed.

The new parcel contains a volume of Luther's sermons. Dietrich's name is underlined on the flyleaf. He turns to the back and looks for the letters underlined in pencil.

MESSAGE FROM HANS HE IS WELL THEY STILL DON'T KNOW ABOUT UNCLE RUDI CONTINUE TO DO ANYTHING YOU MUST TO KEEP AWAY

He realizes that Dohnanyi was barely mentioned by Bauer during the interrogation. A good sign or bad? What exactly is Bauer after? What does he expect to find? One could go crazy simply asking these questions.

And yet Bauer does not know about Uncle Rudi. If Dietrich can only hold out, lead Bauer down some other path until Uncle Rudi can act once and for all

everything will be all right.

DAY 69. In the exercise yard Dietrich has found an anthill. An entire world complete and self-contained, existing within the wall of Tegel Prison, its inhabitants as oblivious of what lies beyond their tunnels and patch of earth as— Dietrich knits his brow and imagines the earth as anthill. He is staring at the ground, mind wandering, when Linke comes for him.

"Pastor Bonhoeffer. The judge advocate is on his way to question you. I am to take you to the interrogation room."

Linke leads him around the corner and through a tunnel to a small red-brick building near the front gate of the prison. A guard with a rifle watches their approach, another stands outside the door, which Linke unlocks and pushes open. It is a plain room with high barred windows, whitewashed walls, and a rough plank floor. A battered table and two chairs are the only furnishing. Linke motions to a chair and Dietrich sits.

"His office said to expect him at half-past eleven," Linke says apologetically. "I expect he'll hold you through mealtime, but I'll slip a tray into your cell. I'm afraid it will be cold."

Dietrich shrugs. He has some cheese and ham and an apple—presents in the latest parcel from home—set by for just such a time. "Thank you, Linke," he says.

Linke nods and glances around. "Don't worry. They don't talk to the hardest cases here."

He touches his cap and leaves, closing the door behind him.

Dietrich sits still and tries to pray. A car draws up outside, its engine idling for a moment and then shutting off. A door opens and slams, then another, and another still. Three people. Dietrich watches the door curiously. When it opens, Bauer steps through, accompanied by an SS guard.

Dietrich stands and salutes. "Heil Hitler!"

"Heil Hitler!" Bauer answers. "You may sit, please."

Dietrich sinks back to his chair with a strange feeling of pleasure. He knows how he must have appeared just now. An obedient and enthusiastic servant of the Führer. One who belongs, even though in prison. One who shares this in common with his interrogator, who is removing files from his briefcase and arranging them on the table. When Bauer looks up, it is with an expression of interest, as though he is longing to renew their acquaintance. Dietrich responds with a smile.

"You look well," Bauer says. "Any problems?"

A doctor visiting his patient.

"None except that I seem to be developing some stiffness in my joints. Rheumatism perhaps. The heat and humidity affect me that way sometimes."

"Then you should go to the infirmary," Bauer says casually. He jots down a note on a piece of paper, signs it, and hands it to Dietrich. "Give this to Maetz."

Dietrich glances at the paper, sees it gives permission for the infirmary doctor to examine him for rheumatism. He folds it and puts it in his pocket. "Thank you."

Bauer waves his hand. "Don't worry. We want you healthy. After all, I've brought you a visitor."

"A visitor?"

Bauer nods to the SS guard, who opens the door and says, "Come in."

Maria von Wedemeyer enters the room.

"God," Dietrich says, coming to his feet.

She stops, pale and trembling. He is shocked at how young and frightened she looks. He steps to her side and takes her hand. He dares do no more, for Judge Advocate Bauer is watching.

"A charming girl," Bauer says. "We had a most interesting visit on the way here."

Dietrich squeezes Maria's hand and she looks at him. "She is a fine girl," he says. "And brave."

She manages a small smile.

Bauer says, "She tells me your engagement has not been announced publicly. Why is that, may I ask?"

"Her mother has some doubts about the matter," Dietrich says, and squeezes her hand again. Maria nods. "As you can see, the age difference is very great, and that concerns Frau von Wedemeyer."

"Nothing to do with your being in prison?"

"No. Maria's mother knows I've done nothing wrong." Dietrich is watching Maria's face carefully, trying to judge if he is saying the right thing. Again she nods and her eyes seem to warm. "In fact, we have decided to go ahead with the wedding as soon as I obtain my release."

"Marvelous," Bauer says dryly. "I assume I shall have an invitation."

Maria surprises Dietrich by turning to Bauer and saying, "Of course you must come, Judge Advocate. By the time you have finished interviewing my Dietrich, I am sure you will count him a great friend."

Bauer laughs heartily. "This one will make a faithful wife!" he says. "Tell me, Fräulein, is your fiancé as loyal to the Reich as you are to him?"

"Of course," Maria says.

"Then tell me, Pastor Bonhoeffer, why you helped a party of Jews to leave Germany in the middle of the war. Perhaps you knew of this, Fräulein?"

"I know nothing of Dietrich's work," Maria says.

Her fingernails bite into the flesh of Dietrich's palm.

"Surely, Judge Advocate, your questions are for me?" Dietrich says.

Bauer folds his arms. "Then answer them. By the way, Fräulein, did you know one of the Jews in question was an old girlfriend of your fiancé's? Elisabeth Fliess, née Hildebrandt?"

Dietrich raises Maria's hand and kisses it, turns to Bauer. "Maria never met Elisabeth. That was all over years ago."

"Then you don't deny your involvement with the Jewess?"

"We had a liaison, yes. It ended before the start of the war, and Elisabeth married someone else."

"A Jew."

"I believe so."

"And still you helped her escape Germany."

Beside him, Maria shifts uneasily.

"Please, Judge Advocate, may I offer my fiancée this chair?"

Bauer nods, and Dietrich takes the chair and places it near the door, away from the desk. As Maria sits he catches a glimpse of her face and sees she is near tears. He forces himself to look away and goes to stand in front of the desk.

"I did not help Jews escape," he says. "The Abwehr thought they might be useful as agents in Switzerland. As I am sure you know. None of this was done in secret."

"And Frau Fliess, née Hildebrandt, was so useful in Switzerland that upon giving birth to a child, she fled to London, where she now resides."

"I understood she might try to go to Britain," Dietrich replies. "Her father is there, so she had a good excuse, and there is certainly a great deal of intelligence work to be done there."

"And what exactly is the nature of the work Frau Fliess was to perform for you?"

"I was not told what her specific assignment would be. It was thought the fewer who had such information, the better."

Bauer says, "Of course, her personal connection to you had nothing to do with her leaving Germany."

"Only in that I could vouch for her reliability," Dietrich replies.

"The reliability of a Jew! How could a Jew be trusted to perform any service for the Reich?"

"I would remind you, since I am certain you have checked her background, that Elisabeth did not consider herself Jewish. She came from a family of baptized Christians. Although our racial purity laws define her as Jewish, she never saw herself as such, but continued to care deeply for the Fatherland. At the outbreak of the war she saw an opportunity to observe the Jewish population for signs of unrest. She was very helpful in keeping the Abwehr informed about unrest among the Jews until the beginning of the deportations. This led us to believe she and the others we chose were trustworthy."

Bauer is sitting with his hand over his eyes as though trying to sleep. But he is listening carefully, not only to Dietrich's answers but to the nervous creaking of the chair near the door. He says, "My dear Fräulein von Wedemeyer, your fiancé seems to know this Jewess very well."

Dietrich turns to look at Maria, who is trying to hide the evidence of her tears.

"Dietrich is older than I," she says, "and I am sure he is much more experienced."

"But he hadn't told you anything of this old girlfriend? Pastor Bonhoeffer! You have such fences to mend with this young lady. I can assure you, in matters of the heart, honesty is much to be desired. And speaking of honesty, your brother-in-law Hans von Dohnanyi is being investigated for fraudulently obtaining foreign currency to finance this Jewish scheme. Do you know anything about this?"

"I know nothing of the details. I only know he was arranging financial support for these agents, and that he was trying to do it in a way that complied with government regulations. If there was misconduct I assume some other party was responsible."

Bauer stares at Dietrich a moment, then says to the guard, "Take the girl back to the car."

Maria casts a last frightened glance at Dietrich and is gone.

Bauer gathers his papers, shuts his briefcase, talks as he works. "I will continue to allow her to write to you, and you may now write to her every four days. I shall also allow her to visit you once a month for one hour."

Dietrich begins to stammer his thanks, but Bauer interrupts.

"It's on her account, not yours. She told me on the way here about losing her father and brother on the Russian front. A patriotic family, the von Wedemeyers. And a wise choice, Pastor Bonhoeffer. Your connection to them makes you look very good indeed. As you so carefully reminded me last time we spoke."

He pats Dietrich on the shoulder.

"Good day, Pastor Bonhoeffer. And Heil Hitler."

Doppelgänger

SS JUDGE ADVOCATE Alois Bauer is chain-smoking in his office in the War Court. The desktop is covered with file folders and loose papers. Bauer sifts through one stack of papers, shifts another, moves folders like a sleight-of-hand artist running a shell game. It is the way he thinks when he is stumped.

At the end of the day he is joined by Franz Sonderegger of the Gestapo. Sonderegger pulls up a chair without asking, turns it around back to the desk, and straddles it. Bauer barely notices. Sonderegger smokes and watches him.

Finally Bauer leans back and sighs. "You see, I have been over it and over it. Nothing beyond the currency violation, that I can find. And their stories match. I haven't been able to catch them out except for a couple of conflicting dates which Bonhoeffer later corrected."

"Well then."

"But there is a smell, Franz, a distinct odor. Unfortunately I can't track it down. And to be honest, I don't know if it's worth pursuing. The way the war is going lately, we have larger fish to fry. Frankly I'm more concerned about the Communists."

"So what will you do?"

"They've never been formally arrested."

"No," Sonderegger agrees.

"If we hold them any longer, we at least have to come up with an arrest warrant. What do you think? Is it worth it?"

Sonderegger shrugs. "Why not? It doesn't hurt to keep them close a while longer. Set a trial date for this winter."

"I don't have time for a trial, not over something petty."

"Well, then, if you don't have anything by the time the trial comes up, let them go."

Bauer chews the end of a pencil. In his mind he sees the broad, open face of Pastor Bonhoeffer washed by successive waves of fear, anger, dread.

"Yes," Bauer says. "Let's hold them awhile longer. I rather enjoyed talking to the pastor anyway. I'm interested to see how he'll hold up."

"What charge for Bonhoeffer? After all, he wasn't directly involved in the currency irregularities."

Bauer thinks some more, then says, "How about 'Undermining the Morale of the Armed Forces'?"

And the warrants are duly issued for the arrests of Dietrich Bonhoeffer and Hans von Dohnanyi, to be served at the prisons where they already reside.

DAY 130. One night Linke comes to Dietrich's cell, opens the slot in the door, and whispers, "Pastor Bonhoeffer? Are you awake?"

Dietrich sits up and rubs his eyes. "What is it, Linke?"

"There's a new lad in the holding cell. Lots of them are frightened half to death when they first get here. But this one's hysterical, trying to bang his head against the wall. We thought being a pastor, you might be able to calm him down, talk to him."

Dietrich pulls on his trousers and follows the beam of Linke's electric torch along the black corridor and down the stairs, emerges blinking his eyes into the light of the ground-floor holding area. The boy's screams—loud even in the stairwell—carom off the stone walls. Dietrich enters the cell to find the prisoner on his knees in one corner, arms flailing as two guards seek to restrain him. Blood runs down the boy's face from a cut in his scalp; he flings his head from side to side as though still seeking to butt the wall with it. Dietrich goes down on his knees in front of the boy, who ignores him.

"What is his name?" Dietrich yells above the din.

Linke looks at a clipboard hanging outside the door.

"Schmidt," he says. "Carl Schmidt."

"Carl!" Dietrich says. He tries to look the boy in the face, but Carl is fixed on something no one else can see. "Carl!"

"Karin!" the boy screams. "Karin Karin Karin!"

Dietrich takes the boy's head in his own hands and forces him to stop his wild rocking back and forth. Schmidt goes rigid, his eyes locked and upturned as though they might roll back in his head.

"Carl!" Dietrich says again. "Who is Karin?"

"Karin," the boy repeats, more quietly this time. His voice has a broken edge to it, a mournful edge.

"Who is Karin?"

For the first time Schmidt meets Dietrich eyes.

"My girlfriend," he says, his voice sinking to a whisper.

"Your girlfriend," Dietrich repeats. "And where is Karin?"

Schmidt's body goes rigid once more and he strains against the guards. In the doorway Linke reads from the chart. "Schmidt was arrested for going AWOL. His girlfriend was wounded in a bombing attack and he decided to leave his post in Italy and come see her."

Dietrich strokes Schmidt's temples with his thumbs. "Carl," he says softly, "have you seen Karin?"

Schmidt stares at Dietrich. His eyes fill with tears. He nods his head.

"What has happened to Karin?" Dietrich coaxes.

"She's dead," Schmidt says. Then he goes limp and begins to sob. Dietrich wraps his arms around Schmidt's chest, lets the boy's head rest on his shoulder. He nods at the guards to leave. Linke follows them out, closing the door shut behind him.

In the early hours of the morning, after he has spent several hours holding Carl Schmidt, speaking to him, praying to him, even singing to him as one would to a small child, Dietrich tries to snatch a few more hours of sleep on his cot. He dreams, and in his dream he wrestles once more with the frantic Carl, but when he holds the boy's face between his hands, it is his own face that stares back at him, a face tormented with longing for a girl who doesn't exist.

After the episode with Schmidt, Pastor Bonhoeffer becomes well known throughout Tegel, a sort of trustee. When an inmate begins screaming in his cell, Linke and the other guards bring Dietrich, large and calm and quiet, to reason with him. On the eve before a condemned man is put to death, Dietrich sits all night with him if requested. He also becomes a familiar sight in the prison sick ward. This new responsibility is an improbable result of his bouts with rheumatism and lumbago. For weeks he suffered without complaint a growing stiffness and ache in his joints. Then one day in July, Linke came to his cell with the midday meal and found Dietrich hunched over on the edge of his bench where he had bent to tie his shoes, unable to straighten up. He was taken at once to the sick bay and hooked up to a brown diathermy machine that shot electrical current in relaxing warm waves through his muscles. The bed was softer as well, the ground-floor infirmary large and airy, almost luxurious with a high roof, a gently swirling ceiling fan, and whitewashed walls. He ate bowls of warm semolina and white bread, soaked his feet in pans of hot water, and swallowed a regular supply of aspirin. His worried parents sent a precious liver sausage (part of which he shared, the rest hoarded in his own cell) and ripe tomatoes from the garden.

He made himself useful in the sick bay, helping the orderlies, listening to the men's stories of home and family, joining in games of skat, sharing cigarettes, playing the out-of-tune piano which stood in one corner or finding the best music on the radio that occupied a table beside the door. When it was clear the treatments were helping his rheumatism and he expected to be sent back to his room day and night, Maetz called him to his office and informed him he should continue to visit the sick ward on a daily basis to prevent a recurrence of his symptoms, that the orderlies and doctors spoke highly of him and he was good for morale. Dietrich nodded and sipped the glass of champagne the commandant had given him.

"Your Uncle Rudi has been here," Maetz had added.

"I hope I am not receiving special favors simply because of my uncle."

"Not at all," Maetz had said. "Though he did bring me four bottles of that very fine champagne you are drinking. Quite a gift. I told him you're a help to me, and just between us, you will probably be more useful in the months to come. I don't wish to alarm anyone—" lowering his voice with a nod to the guard whose elbow was visible just beyond the open door— "but your uncle says we should expect some very rough treatment from the Allied bombers soon. Something on the order of Hamburg and Munich. I don't need to tell you that men in a prison are sitting ducks. There are no underground shelters here."

"No air-raid shelters? Not even for your staff?"

"Not even for me." Maetz shook his head glumly. "Even though we aren't in the city center, we're very close to the locomotive works. If this district is hit as hard as we expect, there'll be men killed and wounded in their cells, and the sick bay will be very busy. I'm going to instruct Linke to leave your cell open at night. I know you won't try to escape—there's no need for you to try, since your case isn't a serious one. As soon as the bombing begins you can go to the sick bay—the orderlies tell me you're a great help there."

"Assuming I survive the bombing."

"Yes, well, who of us can tell that? Anyway, listen for the sirens and keep an eye out your window. High up as you are, you may even see the bombers coming. When they're close, go on downstairs."

That evening, back in Dietrich's cell, a knife and fork appeared with his dinner for the first time since his arrival in Tegel. He stared at them as though he had forgotten what they were. Then he began to laugh.

On this night in late August he hears the distant wail of sirens and goes to look out his window. Berlin is a black pool, as devoid of light as if it remained the unsettled and impenetrable forest of ancient times. The sirens fall silent, the silence marred only briefly by a faint echo. Then there is the faint rapping of flak, and the sky to the southeast is streaked with infusions of orange and yellow. The pounding of exploding shells and answering artillery is a low pulse.

A key rattles in Dietrich's door and Linke enters.

"Close by?" he asks anxiously. He is thinking of his wife and daughters cowering in a basement in Wedding.

Dietrich moves to the end of his cot so Linke can stand on the stool. "It looks as though they're only hitting Neukölln and Rudow," he says. Most of Berlin's factories are in those districts.

"Better them than us, poor bastards," Linke says.

The two men stand side by side, faces pressed against the bars, until the light fades in the south.

DAY 133. Maria von Wedemeyer arrives at Tegel with a hamper of food for the prisoner Dietrich Bonhoeffer. The guard who lifts the yellow gingham cloth for inspection gives a sniff of appreciation at the aniseed biscuits, strawberry jam, and cheese. Maria takes out a box of a half-dozen fresh country eggs and hands it to the guard. A gesture recommended by Dietrich not only because it wins goodwill but because he knows from talking to the guards that many of their families are short.

In the room where prisoners receive their visitors Dietrich and Maria sit across from each other, a table between them, the guard at the door. It is difficult for them to talk. In truth even if there were no guard and no table and no prison, they would struggle to speak, for they have grown more uncomfortable with each other. Dietrich does not possess a natural gift for intimate conversation, and Maria, while gay and chatty with her school friends, is afraid of saying anything that will depress Dietrich or seem trivial to him. So they sit and search for words.

Maria, of course, asks after Dietrich's health. He has said just enough in his letters to cause her concern about his rheumatism. He assures her that he is much better, that the packages he receives do him great good and her letters cheer him.

"And how is Mother von Wedemeyer?"

"Her health is good. And this time of year she's very busy about the estate. They'll soon be bringing in the rye. She sends her love."

In fact Frau von Wedemeyer has sent only her regards, but Maria thinks this a permissible exaggeration.

"Are you still reading?" Dietrich asks. "You know it is important to me that you not allow your mind to stagnate until you are able to take up your studies again."

"I've tried Dostoevsky. *The Brothers Karamazov*."

He waits.

"It's very slow going," she says reluctantly. "I'm afraid I've never taken to the Russian novelists."

She slides her hand across the table and places it shyly in his own. He presses it distractedly, pats it, and lets it go.

"Keep trying," he says. "The more you read, the more comfortable you'll become. I do long for you to read some of these books I'm recommending to you. It would be a great joy to discuss them in our letters to each other."

"I suppose," she says. "It's just that sometimes it's difficult to concentrate just now, what with—" She breaks off, unwilling to let him see how difficult things are for her.

She nods and her eyes catch and hold his for a moment, then drop. When she returns to Pätzig and writes to him, she is more forthright, tells him she loathes Russian novels because they are overwritten and practically wallow in the most distasteful subjects. She defends her beloved Rilke, whom Dietrich despises as soft and sentimental. It is easier to write this way because she is not faced with Dietrich across the table, with his clothes that smell less than fresh, his tired and ill-shaven and—to her eighteen-year-old eyes, yes, she must admit it—his old face.

At home at Pätzig, at night, she writes in her diary. *Dear Dietrich, I placed my hand in yours and you did not hold it. Oh my darling, don't you like to be romantic?*

DAY 140. Influenza has run through the prison and the sick bay has been full for days, but is finally clearing. Most of the patients have returned to their cells, allowing the orderly on duty to wander off into the prison yard for a smoke and a bask in the early-autumn sunshine. Dietrich and four others—among them Oberleutnant Pfifer and the boy Carl Schmidt—are left to lounge on the beds and listen to the radio. The RRG is playing a recording of a concert held in honor of the Führer's birthday. A concert drenched, of course, in Wagner, with a large dollop of Nazi marching songs played by an SS band. The grand conclusion is a chorus of Berlin schoolchildren singing the "Horst Wessel Song" with pure lilting voices. It is the third time the concert has been broadcast in as many days. Dietrich listens to the children, pictures them standing upon the stage in their Hitler Youth uniforms, little ones of nine and ten, happy and proud to be singing in front of their parents and the nation and the Führer, who will be to them a god.

It is more than Dietrich can bear. He jumps up from his bed, goes to the radio, and twists the knob. The others look up from their games of solitaire, open their eyes from their naps, and watch him with surprise. The radio whines and pops and sounds clatter about the room like beads from a broken necklace. Then a voice clear as a bell says in English *The invasion has been underway since fourteen hundred hours. Anglo-American troops under the command of General Mark Clark have established a beachhead at Salerno and along a front extending from Amalfi to Agropoli. This follows the successful incursion four days ago into Calabria by British forces under Field Marshal Montgomery. Casualties around Salerno are reported to be heavy as expected but*

Dietrich takes his hand from the dial.

"My God!" Pfifer says. "It's the BBC!" He throws off his covers and sits up. "What are you trying to do, get us all shot?"

He gets out of bed and totters toward the radio as though he means to shut if off, but Dietrich is in the way.

"Don't touch it," Dietrich says. "I'll take responsibility. If necessary." He looks around the room as he speaks. He has gotten to know all the men present. Knows there is not a rabid Nazi among them, though there are no rebels either.

Schmidt says, "They're talking about Italy, aren't they? I was in Italy."

Dietrich begins to translate. Even Pfifer stands transfixed when he understands what the announcer is saying. "It is the beginning of the end," he says wonderingly. He is scheduled to go to trial in December and expects to receive a twenty-year sentence, a possibility that has precipitated his present illness. "The beginning of the end," he says again. He hides his smile by holding his sleeve to his face and pretending to cough, because he has caught the distraught look on the face of young Schmidt, a good patriot like most of his fellows.

"We'll hold them yet," Schmidt is saying to a friend in the other bed. "I was in Italy. The boys there are tough."

When the orderly, Kranz, returns he finds Dietrich seated beside the radio with his hand on the knob. He looks up, but doesn't move. The newscast is over and the BBC is featuring swing music, Benny Goodman and his orchestra playing "Jumpin' at the Woodside."

Kranz freezes. "*Verboten,*" he whispers. He glances nervously over his shoulder.

"Linke and Knobloch are on duty," Dietrich says. "They won't report it even if they hear it."

"I don't know," Kranz says.

"Do you know how to dance to this?" Dietrich asks.

"It's Negro music," Schmidt says, half suspicious, half curious. "And Jew music."

Dietrich feels like weeping for this boy and all he does not know, all he has never known. He takes a cigarette from his pocket and lights it, hands it to Schmidt. "Yes," he says. "Enjoy it."

He goes to Maetz at once, because he has frightened himself with this burst of audacity and decides it best to deal with it as quickly as possible. For who knows whether anyone will report him.

He gives Maetz one of Dr. Karl Bonhoeffer's cigars.

"I want you to know," he says, "I have broken a rule in the sick bay. Broken the law, to be precise. I have accidentally listened to the BBC. While trying to clear some interference on the radio. The infraction was mine alone."

Maetz looks startled but says nothing.

"I wanted to say," Dietrich continues, "that I think it does the men good. Not that they care for the BBC news broadcasts, which are of course pure propaganda. But there is music as well—it is quite lively although it is forbidden. I was thinking—"

He pauses.

"Yes?" Maetz says. He is still so surprised he hasn't decided how to respond. The face of the eminent General Rüdiger Graf van der Goltz is floating before him.

"I was thinking," Dietrich continues, "as the bombing comes closer. And it does. As the bombing comes closer and we sustain casualties and the sick bay fills, it might help."

Dietrich ends with a shrug and looks around as though his mind is elsewhere. Maetz is also studying the ceiling. "If anyone learns of this, I know nothing of it," he says at last.

"Of course," Dietrich says. "You will hear nothing more about it."

"I expect you to use good judgment."

"Yes."

Dietrich lets himself out of the office and Linke returns him to his cell.

AUTUMN. He remains appalled at his own rashness, since he is supposed to be circumspect, to avoid calling attention to himself. And yet he is relieved to learn that in Tegel things can be taken farther even than in the so-called freedom outside. Men in extremities are granted a few mistakes, a few risks. The very bars of his cell foster moments of extraordinary grace. Such as the day Linke enters and offers to smuggle Dietrich's letters out of the prison.

It is not unusual for Linke to pause in his duties to pass the time of day. He finds Dietrich always ready to ask after his family and enjoys talking about them. He has begun to notice that when he arrives Dietrich is usually writing.

"You must have a large family to write to," he says one day, for Dietrich has said little about his personal life.

"Parents, a brother and sisters, a fiancée. But I'm not just writing letters, Otto."

He tells Linke about his failed attempts to write fiction and drama. "But I have done some poems I'm pleased with. And then there's—" He starts to explain that he has once again been writing theology, especially a reflection on time based in part on his reading of Heidegger and his own renewed sense—thanks to his growing interaction with the other prisoners—that his stint in captivity is not time lost. But he can see the guard's attention begin to wander, so he only says, "I also try to do my work here—I write philosophy and theology, you see, though it is difficult because I am only allowed a few books at a time. And I actually don't send out many letters. One never knows what the censors will make of what I write, and I don't like to waste precious paper on trivialities."

Linke nods and thinks. On his next visit he asks, "Where do your parents live?"

"Just off the Heerstraße in the Marienburger Allee. North of the Grunewald."

"Not so far."

And again nothing more is said. But that night he talks to his wife. A risk, of course, but he will also be in contact with the Bonhoeffer parents, who are obviously better off than most. "You should see the packages he gets, Marta, cheese and sausage and even eggs. The father is a doctor and they know people in the country."

Marta agrees, and the next night when Linke wheels his bicycle into the gathering gloom of a Berlin evening he has a letter from Bonhoeffer to his parents tucked inside his waistband. A letter in which, because the censors will not touch it, Dietrich can ask freely about Hans, and Uncle Rudi, and can at last share his thoughts about the ordeal he is undergoing.

He writes not only to his parents but to his former students now serving as chaplains at the front. Writes to Elisabeth, though the letters won't be posted until war's end. In these letters he feels he is once again *doing* theology. His real work. A useless pursuit, his fellow prisoners would think, quibbling about abstractions while the world comes apart. And yet it is in the midst of such a crumbling world that he is able once again to write. There is some essence of God he longs to get at, which can only be approached at a slow pace with shoes in hand and eyes cast down. In the past, he thinks, this has not been his way. He has always possessed too much pride in his own intellect. This will no longer work, perhaps has never worked. The more one makes such a search for God the more everything dissolves, like an Impressionist painting approached slowly and reverently and too closely.

He scribbles, runs out of paper, lies on his cot and burns.

Day 211. Cold, end of November. Dietrich longing for Advent. Maria has sent a wreath, which he has propped upon the bench.

Outside the city waits. Waits not for the Christ child but for bombs. Waits for the familiar ritual of siren, silence, flak, explosion, whistling and howling of flame, weeping.

He sees it all from his window. Watches as Berlin is lit, quarter by quarter, like a diorama in a museum. Then disappears in fire and gray smoke. Closer and closer. Kreuzberg. Wilmersdorf. Charlottenburg. Moabit.

Linke comes to his cell, unlocks it. His face is haggard. Parts of Wedding are in flames. Two buildings in his block have been hit.

Linke says, "Your sister Suse came today on her bicycle. She brought a package—" hands over the parcel—"and a letter she says is very important." He pulls his shirttail above his pants and removes the letter from his waistband.

Dietrich nods his thanks. He unwraps the parcel while Linke sets a bowl of soup on the bench. He gives the guard a wedge of cheese. Linke goes out, leaving the door unlocked behind him. By the waning light of the window Dietrich unfolds the paper, which has no envelope because of the paper shortages. The cell is cold and Dietrich holds the letter in gloved hands.

He reads, *Dearest Dietrich, Hans has been seriously injured. His cellblock was hit during the last incendiary attack, and he was struck in the head by shrapnel. He is paralyzed on one side and cannot speak, but the doctors hold out some hope that he will at least partially recover. He has been taken under guard from the prison to the Charité for treatment. Try not to worry. He is in pain but is alert, and he will at last have comfortable quarters and decent food. He has been quite ill, you know, one thing after another. Perhaps if he recovers some good may come of this, for there is now no question of pursuing his case in the immediate future. This means your time in prison will be extended, but if you can hold out until the day we all await— Well, we must pray for this. Your loving Mother and Father.*

Dietrich reads the letter twice, then lights it with a match, careful to keep the flame away from the curtainless window. When the paper is nearly burned, he drops it to the floor and grinds the ashes beneath his heel.

DAY 213. The planes come in such numbers he can hear their deep-throated engines through the silence after the sirens. The barking of flak. Antiaircraft guns open fire from the Grunewald.

The explosions begin in the heart of the city. The Tiergarten, he thinks. The zoo. Orange blossoms open and close in the blackness.

Something is different. There is no pause between blasts, no seconds of held breath and still air. The flares of light move in a line, like an advancing orange tidal wave. Engulfing everything. Closer and closer. Dietrich grips the bars of his window, unable to look away as the molten wall leaps the hill toward Tegel.

He is on the floor. Unsure how he got there. His forehead throbs and his arm is stiff.

Screaming. The cell trembles. His ears hurt. He is up and limping, running along the corridor. Arms clutch at him through the door slots. The floor rolls, air whips back and forth.

Through the smoke he finds the stairway and hurtles down it, reaches the sick bay in time to see the first bodies carried in from the east wing, which has taken a direct hit.

DAY 214. The boy Schmidt dies of a crushed chest. Dietrich sits with him until the end, wipes away the bubbles of blood which well at the corners of his mouth. Tries to offer comfort, but Schmidt is out of his head and knows nothing of it.

Pfifer occupies a palette on the floor, since the beds are all taken. One thing after another for Pfifer. His leg was shattered during the raid when a portion of the wall fell on it. He lies on his back and talks to the ceiling.

They are listening to the BBC. It is what everyone wants now, guards and orderlies and prisoners, for it is the only way to learn what is going on outside. Because they listen to the BBC they know how to name what has happened to them. Carpet bombing. Saturation bombing. Something new.

Berlin, anyone knows without listening to the BBC, is a smoldering ruin.

In the Tiergarten, a bomb has landed in the zoo aquarium, killing all the amphibians and fish. Many of the animals are dead, others wounded or dying. The cages are damaged and soldiers are dispatched to kill the survivors, lest they escape into what is left of the city. Thuringian farm boys armed with machine guns mow down polar bears and lions and the last zebra amid smoldering piles of concrete. The crocodiles have managed to escape the reptile house and slither their way to the Spree, but they are caught at the riverbank and shot, thrown up white bellies first in the cold brown water.

DAY 253. CHRISTMAS EVE. Maria arrives first, bringing with her a small Christmas tree from Pätzig for Dietrich's cell. He is pleased to see her but upset. The air raids have continued sporadically, and he is frightened for her safety. But she promises him she will stay at Sacrow, at the Dohnanyi home on the lake, where his parents have also gone. It is too far from the city center, too sparsely populated, to be a target except by accident.

She tells him all this seated across from him at the table in the visitors' room, clutching the top of the tree with one hand to hold it upright even though Dietrich tries to persuade her to lay it on its side. No, she says, she has fashioned homemade ornaments out of various objects—pine cones and thistles and eggshells—and tied them to the branches so they won't come off easily. She is afraid they will be damaged if she lays the tree down. So Dietrich takes it from her, to spare her arm, and talks with her while one arm cradles the tree as tenderly as if it were Maria.

She gives him his present, wrapped in a handkerchief since paper is so dear, and watches with tearing eyes as he opens it. It is her father's wristwatch, which he was wearing when he was killed. A thin crack mars the glass face but the watch still keeps time.

"It's the only thing of his we got back," she says. "Mother didn't even receive his wedding ring. But she agreed I could give this to you. Because I begged her so very hard."

She does not tell him what a scene her request caused, how her mother wept and accused Maria of dishonoring her father's memory before giving in at last. Dietrich slips the gold band over his wrist.

"A perfect fit," he says, and hands her the handkerchief.

"Of course." She dabs at her eyes. "You're just like him. Aren't you?"

"A great deal," he says, and of all his deceptions this one causes him the greatest pang of guilt.

Then to the sick bay, where those who are able to leave their beds draw their chairs close to the piano. Dietrich is playing on request, wincing inwardly when the more banal popular songs are suggested, refusing to play blatantly Nazi anthems by claiming not to know them, relaxing when he can volunteer some work by Bach or Gerhard. There are no regular religious services in Tegel, only a chaplain who sticks his head in now and then. Dietrich has not pushed for anything more. He knows he will be expected to be in charge, and if he leads the men in worship he will have to pray aloud for the Führer and the successful prosecution of the war. This he hopes to avoid if at all possible. Besides, he has been surprised by how little he misses attending church. But as the hymn-singing progresses, he finds himself longing to pray in communion with others of like mind. He recalls the days when he ran the seminary in Pomerania, the time spent at the monastery in Ettal. Perhaps in a different world he would have chosen to be a monk. Perhaps in the world he inhabits he has become a subversive one.

The singing is interrupted by a summons from the office of Commandant Maetz. When he arrives he finds to his surprise that SS Judge Advocate Bauer is there, feet propped on the desk, enjoying a glass of Uncle Rudi's champagne.

Bauer doesn't rise but motions Dietrich to a chair.

"I heard you playing the piano," he says, raising his glass. "I stood in the sick-bay door for a time. Bach, it was. You're very good." He calls for another glass and offers it to Dietrich. "Tell me, Pastor Bonhoeffer, do you play Mozart?"

"Of course," Dietrich says. "But Bach is my favorite."

"Perhaps," Bauer says, "I can change your mind."

Dietrich is so taken aback by the tenor of the conversation that he doesn't know what to say. He nods and sips the champagne.

"I am not in Berlin so often," Bauer says. "The air raids have made it necessary to move many administrative offices out of Berlin. Impossible to carry on business as usual when buildings are coming down. In fact—" he coughs discreetly—"the War Court has taken a direct hit. Despite our precautions, thousands of folders, including the one holding the particulars of your own case, have been destroyed."

Dietrich waits, uncertain if this news is good or bad.

"The Gestapo is furious," Bauer continues. "I must tell you, Pastor Bonhoeffer, they want to go after you. Or I should say they're storming the walls of the Abwehr and they think you are a tiny chink in the masonry. I myself am inclined to think it as big a waste of time as your own so-called service to the Reich. But I'm not inclined to release you until my colleagues in the Prinz-Albrecht-Straße are satisfied. I'm sure this delay must distress you."

"Yes," Dietrich says. "I am most disappointed. I had hoped to be home soon, and to set a wedding date. Thank you, by the way, for allowing my fiancée's visits."

"A very young fiancée," Bauer observes, raising his glass. "When you are released, do you really expect this wedding to take place? Or is it simply an engagement of convenience? To impress me perhaps?"

"Of course we shall marry!" Dietrich says warmly. "We love each other very much!"

Bauer rubs his chin. "Funny, I would have thought not. Something in her eyes that day."

Dietrich goes rigid with anger. "The poor child was frightened to death."

"Yes." Bauer smiles. "It was fear, no doubt. The poor child." He shoves his empty glass over to Maetz, who has been listening with his usual obtuse expression on his face. "One more for the road, Herr Commandant. I am on my way to spend Christmas at my new quarters in the Thüringer Wald."

"Ah, the forest. As pleasant a corner of the Reich as one can find in such times," Maetz says as he pours the champagne.

"Yes," Bauer agrees, "and I have a valued personal possession stored in the area. So though I miss Berlin, I can't complain. By the way, Maetz, we have returned a verdict this morning against one of the men you're holding, an Oberleutnant Pfifer. He's been sentenced to death."

"Death?" Maetz says. "I don't think he expected that."

"Perhaps not. But his superior officer claims Pfifer not only disobeyed orders but also tried to kill him, and the tribunal believed it. Well, he'll be back in his cell by now. You should arrange a firing squad the day after Christmas." Bauer glances at Dietrich as though he has nearly forgotten him. "You may return to your piano playing, Pastor Bonhoeffer. Heil Hitler and Merry Christmas."

Maria. Judge Advocate Bauer. And finally the bombs. A veritable Bethlehem of visitors, Dietrich thinks bitterly as he stares up at the night sky. The flares dropped by the lead airplanes are descending directly above the prison. "Christmas trees," Berliners call them, because of their brightness and conical shape. As they drift down like holiday decorations Dietrich drops to his knees and prays. The nearness of the flares means the target will be Borsig, and the prison is once again in the way.

The guards are ready. Knobloch arrives to take him to the sick bay as the bombs begin to fall. (Linke is not on duty—he is one of the lucky ones who has Christmas off.) Just as they step into the hall the lights flicker and go out. A nearby explosion sends a shudder through the building, and up and down the row men begin to cry out. Dietrich and Knobloch feel their way slowly along the wall, hands splayed against the stone, searching for the door to the stairs. A blast knocks them to their feet, a door at the end of the hall bursts open, and bits of stone and shrapnel fly through the air. The screams rise and unite in a single shriek.

"Jesus, that one will be done for," Knobloch says.

They make their way toward the damaged cell. Knobloch enters and drags a body by the leg into the hall. The flare from an explosion near Borsig shows the head is missing. Dietrich retches and turns away, and Knobloch drops the leg. Someone will tend later to the dead.

Two doors down a man screams that he is wounded. Pfifer. Dietrich starts forward, but Knobloch grabs his arm.

"Careful, he might be faking. He's for it anyway."

Dietrich stops. "He was near the blast," he yells in Knobloch's ear. "He sounds in great pain."

"All right," Knobloch yells back. "But let me go first."

He fumbles with the key in the dark, misses the lock at first, but at last pulls the door open, and Pfifer lunges, stool held high, and brings it down hard. Knobloch just has time to raise his arm, which takes the brunt of the blow. Then Pfifer is on the hall floor crawling because of his shattered leg, trying to get up and crashing into Dietrich. They fall in a heap, and Pfifer struggles up. Dietrich has his arms around Pfifer's waist, but he cannot bear to impede the escape of a doomed man. Instead in the dark he pushes himself up and drags Pfifer along with him, offering one last blessed second of hope, so entangled with the other that by the time Knobloch recovers and reaches them he cannot tell that Dietrich is aiding an escape. The guard ignores the pain in his arm and pries the condemned man away from Pastor Bonhoeffer, hits him over the head with a truncheon, and carries him half senseless back to his cell. Dietrich remains huddled on the floor sobbing for breath and grief.

In the sick bay they work in the dark with candles, tending the wounded. The lights flicker on—an emergency generator thrown into service? Dietrich scarcely has time to wonder. Then his ears pop and his head slams against something hard. It takes him some time to realize he is sprawled on the floor. His ears ring and it hurts to lift his head, but he does so slowly and opens his eyes. Everything is black. His hand is lying in a pool of something wet. He thinks it is blood but smells his fingers. Alcohol. It soaks his shirt sleeve, and the acrid burn of it clears his head. He sits up. Beyond him matches flare, candles. A cold blast hits his face and curtains flap like limp birds. The windows have been blown out.

Dietrich stands and wobbles toward the candle. An arm holds the candle, an arm attached to the body of Kranz, the medical orderly, who turns his head, says, "Nothing we can do now." The circle of candlelight moves around the room. Each cabinet has toppled over and spilled its contents—pills and bandages and scissors and sutures and shards of broken glass caught in sticky pools of medicine.

"Maintain the blackout! Maintain the blackout!" a guard calls from the doorway.

Kranz says, "How?"

The blackout curtains are in shreds. The orderlies look around in the dark for something else but soon give it up. "It doesn't matter," someone says, perhaps Dietrich. "The electricity is out again anyway." This time for good, though they don't know it.

In the dark they tie bandages around the wounded, try to staunch their bleeding. No way to stitch up wounds until daylight, and then only if the supplies are salvageable. Someone goes in search of extra blankets, for the December air has rolled in and settled like a weight.

Kranz mutters as he works. "Beasts. They're beasts, the English. This on Christmas Eve. Monsters."

(In England, Dietrich's nieces, Sabine's daughters, pass a bucket each day in their school with a poster that reads "Ten Shillings for a Bomb on Berlin." The girls, who now speak English with no trace of a German accent and are desperate to appear well to their friends, sometimes drop a spare penny into the bucket, though they don't tell their mother and father.)

"We've done the same to them," Dietrich says without looking up from bandaging a head wound. "Done it first."

Kranz is unconvinced, continues to complain as if Dietrich has not even spoken. Kranz does not care what has been done first to the English. And even Dietrich, who cares very much, believes it indeed to be a monstrous thing for anyone to bomb a city on Christmas Eve, whoever bears the original blame. But also monstrous to say so if one is German and burning Jews every day of the year. There is no place to escape the hideousness of humanity, he thinks as he works, unless one is God, who seems to have managed the feat quite well.

Every window on the south side of the building has been blown out. Dietrich sits on his stool wearing his wool jacket, coat, shawl, hat, gloves. A fringe of snow decorates the windowsill in the cold Christmas dawn.

A stamping of boots in the corridor. The military escort has come to take Pfifer to the firing squad. Dietrich remains in his cell, for Pfifer has refused to see anyone. He hears the condemned man sob, hears his bad leg drag along the stone floor as he is taken out.

"It's all a lie!" Pfifer is crying. "You're treating me like a fucking Jew! Like a goddamn fucking Jew!"

Dietrich wants to pray for Pfifer, but the only word that will form in his mind is *Please*. Addressed to no one. He stares at the Advent wreath from Maria, which hangs on the wall. Beside it he has posted a reproduction of the Madonna and Child depicted in the Chichester roundel—an old present from George and Hettie Bell—which arrived in a package from home on his request. The happy mother and child. He takes it down and puts it beneath the cot.

He says, God is absent.

Silence.

The ancient Israelites never uttered the name of God.

He says,   is absent.

The light in the window is white with promised snow. He shivers, pounds his hands together, and analyzes the tingling of his fingertips. The movement of blood, he surmises, can be mistaken for the presence of God.

He stands beneath the window and listens for the crack of the rifles.

DAY 265. EVE OF THE EPIPHANY. A new year. 1944. *This year cannot be worse than the one previous*, Dietrich writes on a scrap of paper. Then he rolls a pinch of stale pipe tobacco in the paper and smokes it. He thinks of this as his burnt offering. (During an air raid the previous night he lay on the floor of the sick bay and listened to a fellow plead over and over *O God O God O God* without himself feeling the slightest emotion.)

Maria is visiting. She sits with her back to the guard, a boy of seventeen who is playing solitaire with studied indifference, pretending not to listen but listening very carefully indeed. Because it is obvious Maria is close to tears as soon as she enters the visitors' room.

"Has something happened?" Dietrich asks.

She shakes her head. She doesn't want to tell him it has been the worst Christmas of her life.

"Nothing," she manages to say. "Nothing new. It's just that I'm so—" she looks up with a face full of despair. "It's just that I'm so tired of it all."

Dietrich waits.

"Tired of everything. The war. Death. Coming here to see you."

She claps her hand over her mouth and stares at him.

"I don't mean—" she says. Then, "I mean seeing you *here*. Not seeing *you*."

"I understand. It's a long journey and a depressing end to it. If only we could be alone."

"Yes!" She leans forward. "Would they not allow it?"

He shakes his head. "I've asked. Not even Uncle Rudi can arrange it. Bauer's orders."

"I hate him," Maria says.

"You must be patient. Hating him does no good, and it isn't becoming."

She can almost hate Dietrich as well when he takes such a tone with her, but she won't say that, will hardly allow herself to admit it before turning away to some other thought.

Instead she says, "It's hard because in some ways I've felt I know you well and then when I come here I realize I know you so little."

"It takes time," he says.

"Or rather," she continues, "I know three of you. There is the Letter Dietrich I write to. That Dietrich I try to console so that you may be strong and brave and withstand your suffering. There is my Diary Dietrich. I tell that Dietrich everything. And then there is Visit Dietrich. Prison Dietrich."

She stops.

"A very different Dietrich indeed," he says, his voice hopeless because he has glimpsed something of the future.

"No. Yes. Just that I dread to visit you because I never know how it will go."

"It's my fault," he says. "I am so much alone now, and have been all these months. It is difficult for me to be around people, it tires me so, and as for sharing intimately with you—"

He takes her hand and squeezes it, not in the caressing romantic way she longs for but like a man caught in a swift current and in danger of being borne away.

"But I talk to you every day on my walks," she says. "Then I can tell you anything. In all my life only father has been like that. If only you could be there in the woods with me. Then we would be intimate."

He presses her hand to his mouth. After a moment she takes it away.

"I have something to tell you," she says, and looks away. "Mother says I must confess it. I danced."

"Danced?" he repeats, puzzled.

"Danced. With someone. There was a New Year's party at the von Kleists. Friedrich-Wilhelm von Diest was there on leave, you've never met him, he's a nephew of Frau von Kleist's and he's been in North Africa. You know how bad the fighting has been there. He looked very sad, and I danced with him. I didn't think it was anything bad, but Mother says it is because I am engaged. She says if I take on a burden I must bear it." She hesitates, wonders if her choice of words has once again been unfortunate but is too upset to consider the matter clearly. "So Mother says I must confess to you what I have done. I hope you aren't angry?"

In his mind he sees the tight assured smile of Frau von Wedemeyer. "I'm not angry," he says. "It was a natural and kind gesture on your part. I am the one in prison, Maria, not you."

"Oh," she says, and smiles for the first time. "Oh, I am so relieved to hear you say it. It has worried me ever since. And the night Mother and I argued about it I went outside for a late walk about the grounds because I could not sleep and it was such a clear cold night I could hear the Berlin guns. All the way to Pätzig, can you imagine? Of course, I thought of you at once and felt ever so terrible."

He is glad for the cold clear night, glad she heard the guns and thought of him. It is the first word of comfort he has received on this visit, and the last, for the time allowed visitors is soon up. When the guard says, "One minute," they stand.

Dietrich says, "A safe trip home, dear Maria."

Maria says, "I'm not going back to Pätzig. One of the teachers at my old boarding school in Altenburg has had an emergency appendectomy. They need someone for the next six weeks, and I have accepted the post. Mother wasn't pleased, but I insisted. I need to get away from her for a while. Except it's so much farther from Berlin."

"Not impossibly far," he says.

"It may be harder to get away," she says.

"Time," says the guard.

"Please," he says. "Please come. You don't know how I look forward to it."

"Time," the guard says again and opens the door. Maria goes to it, turns back with a puzzled look on her face as though she has one more question to ask, then disappears.

DAY 324. The letters from Maria do not arrive so often.

She has finished her teaching stint at the boarding school in Altenburg. But instead of returning to Pätzig, Maria has gone to stay with her father's niece, Hedwig von Truchsess, who is raising her children alone in the family manor near Bamberg while her husband serves as an officer in France. Cousin Hesi, as she is known in the family, is worn down by her duties in the neighborhood—the "old family" in the castle must ever be a source of strength and support for the people of the surrounding district—and by her brood of overactive children. In letters to Uncle von Wedemeyer's widow she has complained of her weariness, and received in return letters of despair over loss of husband and son, and over the future of Maria, who is throwing herself away on an older man, and one in prison no less. Cousin Hesi, secretly pleased to learn of someone with troubles greater than her own, in turn has written copious letters of comfort which moved Frau von Wedemeyer to tears. It was not long before it was agreed that a prolonged stay at the castle in Bundorf might be just the solution to both their problems. At first Maria resisted. She knew the von Truchsess children to be a handful, and she was homesick for Pätzig. She decided to try Bundorf for a few weeks, then persuade her mother to allow her to come home. But then she stepped from the train onto the station platform of a fairy-tale valley, carrying her large black suitcase, to be met by a servant and pony cart from the castle. Like the heroine of a Johanna Spyri novel. The servant pointed out the castle well before they reached it, a fantasy of stone towers and battlements perched upon a cliff wall. In the leisurely halfhour it took to navigate the twisting road up the hill, the castle vanished and reappeared like a sorcerer's tempting vision.

Maria has since had plenty of time to explore the castle, her family's ancestral home. She climbs staircases that spiral inside stone towers, walks beneath rows of ancient paintings and timbered ceilings, opens heavy oak doors onto oddly shaped rooms, discovers hidden nooks and crannies and passageways. Her own room is high in the west tower with a bay window that faces the sunset. (Faces away from Berlin, she realizes, then quickly forgets.)

At Bundorf she hears story after story of her father's childhood, and, when she writes to Dietrich, adds to these her own nostalgic memories of Hans von Wedemeyer and his simple piety. Simplicity indeed, Dietrich recalls as he unsuccessfully tries to recall one conversation of substance he had with Hans von Wedemeyer. But of course he could never say this to

Maria, can only reflect on it grumpily as he waits for her ever less frequent letters.

Because she brings up the subject again, he repeats his dislike of Rilke's poetry.

She writes back that under Cousin Hesi's influence she has also fallen in love with the poems of Bergengruen ("I know you will not approve").

He scoffs that Bergengruen is too explicit, not a writer who will last.

She replies she likes explicit poetry.

He recommends Kierkegaard and Cervantes.

She is trying to read his own book, *Discipleship*. But it is hard going, she is mostly lost in it. She confesses this.

She writes, *Theology seems to me an intellectual approach to what should be a matter of faith.*

He admires her forthrightness even as he wonders about the thoroughness of her education. That is where he puts the blame, it must be the fault of her parents and of the boarding school at Altenburg, not of Maria herself. If only he were out of prison and able to spend time with her, he could remedy the situation.

He longs for a letter like the ones she used to write, filled with dreams of their life together after prison—a house in Pomerania or the Grunewald, filled with French sofas, Dutch porcelain, English silver services, oak bookcases.

But Maria seldom thinks of the imaginary house. Cousin Hesi has introduced her to an officer who is staying in the neighborhood while recuperating from a leg wound. Hauptmann Weisbach has come to the castle for dinner, and afterward, when Maria asks him shyly, "Do you like Rilke, Hauptmann Weisbach?" he says at once, "My God, I adore Rilke!"

DAY 325. Berlin suffers through its first daylight air raid. Dietrich waits it out in the sick bay, whose windows have been fitted with makeshift shutters in place of glass. "It is the end of us," moans Kranz the orderly. "If they no longer need the night for protection then even God cannot save us."

They huddle in darkness because the shutters have been closed to keep out as much cold as possible, and are only opened when the orderlies make their rounds.

"Look at us," Kranz says again. "We hide in the dark like rats and the enemy flies in sunlight."

"Shut up," someone says. "What is worse, their bombs or your mouth?"

Someone else says, "Maybe they will pass over us. Maybe they're on their way to Stettin. It's Stettin's turn, isn't it?"

And another says, "Pray for us, Pastor Bonhoeffer."

In the darkness Dietrich sighs. He is glad no one can see his face. "Oh

God be our rock and fortress," he says aloud, and tries to invest his voice
with conviction. While with each inhaled breath he silently prays

> Forgive us our sin
> our most obvious and original sin
> as we all
> myself included
> long for the planes to bomb Stettin instead of us

DAY 349. Linke is in tears. He sits on the edge of his cot with his face
buried in his hands. His house has been destroyed in the bombing. Fortunately Marta and the girls are safe—they were hiding in the basement
shelter and neighbors managed to dig them out. Only a few cuts and bruises.
But the house is a ruin. The family will move in with Linke's brother in
Moabit.

Dietrich says nothing. He has learned in prison that words of comfort
are little more than gibberish. A hand on the shoulder is better.

Linke gives over the letter which was his excuse for visiting Dietrich's
cell. It is from Frau von Wedemeyer. Dietrich opens it as if it might go off
in his hand.

Maria is unhappy, writes her mother, *very very unhappy. I can't help but
believe it has to do with her most recent visit to the prison.*

He stops reading. Maria has been to see him within the week. And in
truth she was unhappy, as she has been lately, though she denied it and
would not tell him what was the matter.

He takes off his glasses and wipes them on his sleeve, replaces them on
his nose and continues.

*And not just the most recent visit, for each one seems to upset her more and
more. Frankly, I think it is a great strain on her. Put yourself in her place, a
young girl visiting a man in prison, a man she has hardly had a chance to become
acquainted with under normal circumstances. I know this is not your fault. And
I have been corresponding with your mother and your brother, Karl-Friedrich.
You are a member of a remarkable family and I have no doubt of your suitability
for Maria, once the war is over. As we all pray it will be soon. In the meantime
I do wonder if it is generous of you to insist on Maria's loyalty.*

Dietrich and Linke sit side by side until it is time for the guard to fetch
the dinner trays.

DAY 378. She tries not to cry, sitting across the table from him with the
guard looking on. Linke this time, who has managed to trade duties because
Dietrich wants him there, because he can say things in the presence of sensible, comfortable Linke that he could not with another. But Maria does
not know Linke and she does not want to break down in front of him.

She is desperately afraid she *will* break down. Not because she is in love with Hauptmann Weisbach, the wounded officer, though she thought she was for a week or so. But beyond their love of Rilke, they had nothing in common. Hauptmann Weisbach was a connoisseur of women and food and art, of a cynical nature, an atheist. His politics were the politics of convenience: whoever ruled, he would cheerfully follow. Even Father, political naif that he was, would have been appalled.

Father. There was the sore point, and after her failed attempt to distract Maria with Hauptmann Weisbach, Cousin Hesi was quick to find it. Her next dinner guest had been Pastor Stählin, who had long ago confirmed Maria's father in the village church at Bundorf.

The meal had not been extravagant except by wartime standards. Venison stew, fried eggs, a spice cake. Maria sat happily beside Pastor Stählin and listened as he described his preparations for Palm Sunday, when children would be distributing fronds sent specially by a parishioner serving in North Africa, "an astonishingly thoughtful act of piety, wouldn't you say, given the circumstances?" He leaned closer to Maria. "Though perhaps I shouldn't bring it up in front of you, my child. Stories of patriotism coupled with piety must be painful for you. You feel a great conflict, I'm sure, to be forced to choose between your father and his great sacrifice on the one hand, and your fiancé on the other."

Maria put down her fork. "I hadn't thought of it that way," she said in a halting voice. "Surely Father and Dietrich were friends and—"

"I meant," said Pastor Stählin, "that it must be difficult to be engaged to a man who is under such a cloud of suspicion."

"Dietrich hasn't done anything wrong," she said, and looked around for help.

"Nothing of which we are aware," Cousin Hesi said mildly.

"Nor did I mean to accuse," said Pastor Stählin. "I only wish to hold up the sterling reputation of my dear departed friend Hans von Wedemeyer. God rest his soul."

And he had raised his glass in a toast.

But Maria is a loyal girl, and more stubborn than Cousin Hesi realizes. She forces herself to think again of her fiancé, suffering in prison, and finds her passion growing, once again, for Letter Dietrich and Diary Dietrich.

But Visit Dietrich is more difficult. He is the one who smells bad, who looks older and more weary each time she comes to Tegel. She knows he is not eating well, that the already meager prison rations have been reduced, that he is allowed a bath and change of clothes only twice a month, that there is no hot water in the prison, that he has survived countless bombing raids unprotected. What a horrible person all this makes her, what an unfaithful lover, for she cannot summon up an ounce of romantic passion for Visit Dietrich despite his sufferings. Where once she hated the prison rules which kept him from holding her in his arms, now she is glad of them.

There is something she wants to tell him, but she doubts her strength today. She can only sit and listen and wait for moments when her eyes are somewhat dry and her features somewhat composed so she can at least raise her face to his.

Anyway, he is doing all the talking. He is as close as he has ever been to losing control of his own emotions.

"You're so young," he is saying. "And yet so much more mature than I ever was at your age. When I was twenty, all I thought of was books. Reading books, writing books. But who did I help? Who did I make glad? Maria, I missed so much of life. That's why you're so important to me. You are so alive! When you visit, it is an infusion of energy, like turning on an electric switch."

He pauses to rub his scalp, which often itches. Scaling red blotches show through his thinning hair.

"Maybe it's hard for us to believe we love each other because we know each other so little," he says. It is the most he will allow himself to admit. He says so aloud. "For myself, I don't doubt that I love you. And when I start to doubt that you love me, I just don't think about it."

Now is the time. Now. But not now.

"I do love you," she says at last, in a voice barely audible. "It's just that I get depressed. Because of the war. And because I miss you. Mother was wrong to say anything to you. You don't need another burden just now."

(She does not tell him what she told her mother in a letter, what compelled Frau von Wedemeyer to write in the first place. At Altenburg Maria ran into an old school chum who had been courted by a soldier. The girl in question did not love the soldier and told him so. A month later the soldier was killed in action. Remorse drove the girl to attempt suicide, and a white bracelet of scars around her wrist proved the story. When Maria wrote this to her mother, her tone was frantic, and what mother could not but imagine her own distraught girl wielding the razor blade?)

"Sometimes I think that except for finishing my *Ethics*, my life is over," Dietrich is saying. "I don't want it to be like that. I want to have children, raise a family."

Now she cannot hold back the tears.

"Please tell me that it is love and not pity that brings you here," he says.

"It is love," she sobs, not at all sure of anything except the kindness of falsehood.

He says, "Then tell me what I must do."

"Allow me to be sad. I can't explain and I can't make it go away."

"But we two are still in this together?"

"Yes," she says, at the end of her strength. She half-turns to Linke as though imploring him to call time.

Dietrich is nearly ill with relief. "Maria," he says, "I have an idea that may make things easier. Suppose you leave Bundorf and come live with my parents. They're at Sacrow now with Christel and the children, away from the bombs. You could visit me much more often."

And Linke, watching her face, is reminded of his girls when they hear the air-raid sirens.

"No," Maria says. "Hesi can't spare me. No. Not yet."

DAY 427. It is June, a warm day, and the shutters of the sick bay are flung open. The planes have not come for days. Now everyone knows why.

The RRG has issued a terse announcement. Allied troops have landed in Normandy.

On a cot in the corner, a man who is one of the more fervent Nazis breaks down in tears. Others curse or talk quietly among themselves.

Kranz the orderly goes by with a bedpan in each hand. "We're done for now," he says.

A man at the chessboard replies, "Not yet." He stares intently at the pieces, his finger resting tentatively on a rook. "They've still got to get across Europe, and no one fights like a German defending the Fatherland."

The weeping man wipes his face with the back of his hand. "At least we've still got time to square things with the Jews for what they've done to us," he says. "If God preserves our Führer long enough." He turns to Dietrich. "Will you pray for us, Pastor Bonhoeffer?"

Dietrich, who has been lounging near the doorway, goes rigid as though he has been struck. "I'll not pray for you, you whining piece of shit," he says. And leaves them in astonished silence.

After supper Linke comes to his cell.

"You're the talk of the sick bay," he says. "Not what they'd expect from a pastor, they're saying, your response to Schütze Riefenstahl, and unchristian as well."

Dietrich is mending a tear in his trousers. He doesn't look up. "Nothing says a Christian must listen to such whining without giving it a deserved response," he says.

"To refuse prayer—"

"Selfish prayers! Hateful prayers! 'Save me, O God! Be with me, O God! And by the way, let's kill all the Jews!' Such prayers are blasphemy."

"It is natural," Linke insists stubbornly. "People want to live. That's all."

"Oh yes. But no one needs prayer to live. Not anymore. No one needs

God to live. It's power that ensures survival, my friend. Raw power. And that is why I must deny that power."

Linke sits on the cot and crosses his arms to keep off the cold. "I pray," he says. "My family prays. To keep us safe."

Dietrich starts to answer and swallows his words. He does not want to hurt Linke, who has continued to smuggle Dietrich's letters outside, carrying them out of the prison tucked in his waistband. At what cost to Linke if he is caught?

"Linke," Dietrich says, "it is the only time people ask for God."

"What?" Linke says.

"To keep us safe," Dietrich repeats. "Or to destroy those we call our enemies. Otherwise people don't need God. They've outgrown God. People can't be religious anymore. Oh, there are plenty of people who call themselves religious. All the good people who still fill the pews of Germany's parishes each Sunday, no matter if the swastika hangs above the altar. All the narrow-minded pietists out saving souls while the world goes up in flames. The good Christians who despise Jews. They all claim they are religious. But they don't live as though they are." He shakes his head. "No, Linke, religion is dead. And a good thing too."

Linke blinks. He knows what is wrong with Pastor Bonhoeffer. Too long in prison. "You'll feel better in the morning," he says. "Get some sleep." Then he remembers why he has come to the cell. He places a package on the cot.

"Apparently your sister has been here," he says. He goes to the door and hesitates. Hopes Pastor Bonhoeffer will send him out with some word of comfort. When none is forthcoming, he goes out shaking his head.

In the clear white light of that June evening Dietrich opens the single book from the package. Luther's commentary on Romans. He flips the pages slowly.

WORD FROM HANS

He knows Dohnanyi has been sending messages from his own prison cell by the same means, letters underlined in books, and that Christel has in turn corresponded with General Oster, who has been forced into retirement but is still free and in touch with the resistance. As the message comes clear, Dietrich stands and begins to pace back and forth back and forth

UNCLE RUDI ARRIVES 20 JULY HOLD FAST

DAY 471. 20 JULY 1944. He has kept more and more to his cell. In anticipation. He sits on his stool beneath the window in a square of sunlight. Listens to the sounds of prison ritual. The tramping of feet in the exercise yard. (He has asked Linke if he might stay inside. His back hurts, he claims.) The footsteps of a passing guard. A clattering sound from an open door of the building across the way where the midday meal is being prepared.

The square of sunlight moves. Dietrich follows it for a time, then gives up and remains in shade.

From the city, sirens. Not the too familiar wail of air-raid sirens, but the urgent claxon of emergency vehicles. A rumble of engines. Tanks and trucks? Does he hear shouts? Gunshots? Are Wehrmacht units loyal to the resistance moving into place, preparing to take over government installations? He strains to listen. From time to time he gets up and looks out the window. Berlin is a maze of piled sunlit brick etched in shadow. Intact buildings stand alone like stumps. He sees movement, or perhaps only the shadows of passing clouds.

In the late afternoon Dietrich hears clamor outside his window. A group of guards, Linke among them, are talking excitedly among themselves, gesturing. He hears the words *Hitler* and *assassins*. "Who would believe it?" someone says. The rest is lost to him, words erased by a soft summer breeze. The guards disperse.

He waits.

Before long Linke has come to his cell, closes the door behind him, sits on the edge of the cot.

"Have you heard? Someone has tried to kill Hitler!"

He hears *tried* and understands he is a dead man.

"My God," he manages to say.

"Yes, it's true!" Linke continues. His face is flushed, neither from joy nor disappointment, but from being the first to impart great news. "The Führer has just been on the radio. And Goering and Dönitz along with him. It was Wehrmacht officers who tried it, can you believe?"

Dietrich shakes his head no.

"A bomb. In a briefcase they think. It was placed under a conference table where Hitler and the officers were meeting to discuss the Eastern Front. Several of them were killed but the Führer was spared. They're naming an Oberst von Stauffenberg as the culprit, it seems he left just before the bomb went off, very suspicious, they're looking for him now. I'd not like to be in his shoes. And they think there are others. 'A small clique of traitors in the officer corps,' Hitler said." Linke stops to consider the implications of this. "Knobloch has heard of Stauffenberg, the fellow's a decorated hero, Knobloch says. Why would someone like that try to kill the Führer? And the other officers? Unless they think the war is lost and it's the only way to save their hides?"

"Perhaps," Dietrich says, "they did it because it was the right thing to do. Because Hitler deserves to die for what he has done to Germany and especially for what he has done to the Jews and to Europe."

Linke crosses his legs, folds his arms. "They would kill you if they heard you talking like that," he says.

Dietrich nods. He feels light-headed.

"Of course I'm not going to tell," Linke says. He leans closer. "Do you think we'll lose the war?"

"I hope so," Dietrich says, testing his new freedom. "It's what we deserve."

If Linke is shocked he doesn't say so. He slumps on the cot deep in thought. Then he says, "I just hope the British and the Americans get here before the Russians do. And I hope someone gets here before Marta and my sister-in-law drive each other crazy. They can't stand each other's cooking, and Eva is always yelling at our girls. And you should hear them arguing over which radio program to listen to. It's hell, eleven people living in three rooms."

Yawns and stretches and goes out. Dietrich cannot move. Listening to Linke's last banalities he has realized with a shock that the world will go on without him. That the world goes on without God.

Maria and Suse

COUSIN HESI had been observing Maria with great concern for weeks, and writing faithfully to keep Frau von Wedemeyer apprised of the girl's condition. When Maria returned in mid-July, exhausted, from a long trip to Berlin to see Dietrich, Hesi put the girl to bed in the tower room and went at once to her writing desk. Maria spent the next two days in bed, claiming she was too tired to get up. Hesi wrote to Pätzig again.

Frau von Wedemeyer wrote back, *I really must put my foot down.*

And Hesi wrote a third time. *Patience. I believe she may come to a decision herself.* She did not say that she was writing at the breakfast table while a pale Maria sipped a cup of hot cider and nibbled a biscuit, the first solid food she had attempted. Did not say that the girl had fainted twice the previous day and been put to bed once more.

Cousin Hesi finished her letter, sealed it, and laid it on a tray for a servant to take away.

"Do you have something for Dietrich?" she asked Maria.

Maria shook her head. "Not yet."

"I don't recall your going so long between letters."

"I can't write him. I don't know what to say. Nothing that will help him, anyway."

Hesi placed her hand on top of Maria's thin one. "Perhaps," she said, "the truth would be best."

"The truth?" Maria stared at her, then burst into tears.

"The truth," Hesi persisted. "That you don't love him as a woman should love a man she would marry. That you have been kind for his sake because of his unfortunate circumstances but the burden is becoming too great for you to bear."

When Maria continued to sob, Hesi added gently, "Am I right?"

Maria threw down her napkin and ran from the room with her hand pressed to her mouth.

Maria was hunched in a chair by her window, reading, when the children burst in with news of the attempt on Hitler's life. She was shocked, uncertain whether to feel frightened or relieved, assumed the war must be going very badly indeed and might end soon one way or another. She wondered if Dietrich had heard and what he might be thinking. Had she known any more, she could not have written the letter.

She spent two days composing it, writing paragraphs and crossing them out, filling the margins with her revisions in a cramped hand to save precious paper.

I have tried so hard to put off writing this to you. More than anyone I am aware of the difficulty of your situation, for I have seen you more than anyone. I don't want to hurt you, because you see, I do care about you very much. But I'm afraid it is unavoidable. It is because of me, my fault, my lack of strength. Please believe me, dearest Dietrich, it is me, not anything you have done.

The truth is I have come to doubt whether I love you in the way a wife should a husband. Not, as I said, because I have ceased to care about you. Only I realize something I did not last year, when I was so distraught over the deaths of my father and my brother. The love I bear you is not a romantic love, there is no passion in it, no fire or desire. I believe I am capable of these feelings, Dietrich, but I do not connect them with my love for you. Do you understand? Please tell me I have not hurt you very much.

You so often seem reserved and formal when we visit. Perhaps you feel as I do and have not known how to tell me?

(This last she wrote several times and crossed out, put it back in the final draft. Wishful thinking, perhaps, but she convinced herself it might be true.)

I am reading again a letter you sent me some months back. In it you wrote how important it is, because of our separation, to feel free to tell each other everything. To not hold back. That is what I am trying to do, to be honest with you. It is not fair to you if I am not honest.

You mustn't think there is someone else. There is not. It's just that I can't say what I feel for you. There are many ways to love someone and you are dearer to me than any man, almost as dear as my father was to me. I doubt I shall know anything more for certain until you are released and we can meet freely, face to face and alone. Then I shall know, and if I still feel as I do, you will not be so upset because you will have your old life back once again. Please let me know this letter has not upset you too much.

I must tell you, and Cousin Hesi will confirm this if you wish to write to her, that I have not been well. There are days when I fear I can't go on, because of the strain. The trips to Berlin have been more and more difficult for me. Cousin Hesi and Mother both think, and I'm afraid I've finally come to agree with them, that it would be best if I not come to Berlin for a while. I pray you will understand.

She found his reply waiting for her when she returned from a trip to Bamberg with Hesi, fresh from a hike from the train station because the day was so lovely they had not called for the pony cart. Without a word to Cousin Hesi, who was taking off her hat and hanging it on the hall tree, she took the envelope to her room.

Two hours later she came downstairs. Hesi was on the veranda, knitting socks to send her husband, who was part of the German force falling back before the Allied advance on Paris. Maria laid the letter on the table beside her.

"He hasn't understood a word I wrote," she said. "He won't let himself understand."

"May I?" Hesi unfolded the letter and read

> *My most dear, most beloved Maria,*
>
> *Your letter has not made me sad at all. On the contrary I am not surprised by it. I am always amazed that you can love me at all. To be told that your love is not a love of frenzied desire is not upsetting. I am older than you, I have known such desires, and I know they are not all there is to love, or even the strongest kind of love. It is just as well you feel as you do. If you were wild with desire for me, how much more tormenting our separation would be for you. So our love is warm and not burning hot. I am quite content with such warmth.*
>
> *If you are beginning to doubt your love for me then know that I don't want anything from you, just you as you are. That should suffice. You fear you can't go on. But can you go on without me? I can't go on without you. If that is so, how can you go on without me? We belong together and I won't let go of you. When you are older you will come to understand this better.*
>
> *Of course if the trips to Berlin are too tiring for you, you must not come. But what is more important right now than seeing each other? Don't you know I only am happy when you are sitting beside me in the visitors' room? Each visit may be our last time together in this world. How can you stay away? Frau Niemöller, the wife of my friend Pastor Martin Niemöller, has visited her husband in the camp at Dachau twice a month since 1937.*
>
> *If you are ill, you must go to a doctor, by all means. Perhaps you are working too hard. You have told me those children you tend can be very taxing. Perhaps that is what is wrong. It really isn't fair of your cousin to*

ask you to do so much. Of course, if you went to Sacrow to stay with
Father and Mother and Christel, you would have much more quiet and
rest, and not so far to come for a visit at all.

    Please don't think I'm being selfish. I believe it is best for both of us and
for our future marriage if we come through this difficult time together.

    Your ever faithful

    Dietrich

"It's absolutely appalling!" Hesi cried. "I've never read anything so insen-
sitive in my life! You mustn't write back, Maria, and you certainly mustn't
visit. The man is totally unreasonable."

Late that night Maria wrote one more letter by candlelight, to the only
person she could think of who might reason with Dietrich—his sister Suse.

When Suse wheels her bicycle into Tegel Prison for the first time since the
coup attempt she does not know if she will be allowed to leave her package, does not know if Dietrich is still an inmate. Though his name has not
so far been mentioned in the daily news reports which revile those taken
away and executed. She fights to control her panic as she waits her turn in
the parcel reception room. When her turn comes she shoves the package
across the counter and waits for the guard's reaction. He runs his pencil
down the list.

"Bonhoeffer, D.," he says, and makes a mark beside the name. He opens
the package and examines the contents. Suse thrusts her hands into the
pockets of her skirt to stop them from shaking.

Outside she walks her bike slowly along the gravel path. The exercise
yard lies between the two buildings to her right, and she can see the prisoners taking their turns around the enclosure beyond the chain-link fence.
In fact she has timed her visit to coincide with the exercise period, has
risen at four in the morning and left Dahlem at five in order to arrive in
time. As the family rebel in a strict household, Suse learned young how to
get away with as much as possible, how to bluff her way out of tough scrapes
when the need arose. Now she leaves the path and meanders toward the
fence, pretending to have trouble holding the bike to a straight line. She
stops thirty feet from the yard, in full view of inmates and guards and an
armed sentry in a corner tower who has turned to stare at her. She bends
over and pretends to examine her front tire, then puts down the kickstand
and removes her pump from its brackets on the frame. She unscrews the
tire's valve cover and inserts the pump head incorrectly so that air hisses
from the tire. All the while she keeps her back to the guard tower and her
eyes on the exercise yard where she has seen her brother's familiar form

pace, stop, and turn toward a guard. She presses down on the bike's frame, her hair falling across her face until the tire is nearly flat. When she glances up again, Dietrich and a guard are strolling toward the fence. The guard waves at the sentry in the tower and motions her to approach. She goes slowly forward with the gimpy bike until she reaches the fence.

"Your tire is flat," the guard says with a toothy grin.

Suse is silent, waiting for Dietrich to speak.

"Suse," Dietrich says, "this is Linke. You can say anything in front of him."

Linke gives a brief nod. "I hear and I don't hear," he says. "But if you have something especially delicate, now is the time. Because if you'll wait a moment I'll come around and help you with your tire."

He strolls away toward a gate in the corner of the yard. Once again Suse is grateful for her strict upbringing, for the rigid discipline of her father, which not only gave her a target to rebel against but taught her to manage her emotions. Else neither Dietrich nor I would be able to say a word, she thinks.

"You are still here," she says.

He nods. "For the time being. I doubt it will last. They'll be ransacking the country for evidence of who else was involved. Eventually they'll find something."

Despite his assurances about Linke she glances toward the guard. He is slowly opening and closing the gate, just out of hearing distance.

"He knows," Dietrich says. "Or at least, he guesses. But he won't say anything, whether for liking me or because I give him food, I don't know."

"How are you keeping?"

He shrugs. "How do I look?"

"Under a great strain. But that is to be expected. Your health is holding up?"

"My rheumatism plagues me off and on, and I had the flu last month. Otherwise I'm all right."

"Perhaps they won't find anything," she says.

He shakes his head. "Let's not fool ourselves. It isn't likely I'll survive the war, Suse."

Linke has reached Suse and, kneeling, begins to fiddle with the tire.

"Oddly enough," Dietrich continues, "I can better face that possibility if I accept it, not if I try to avoid it. It's a new sensation, the acceptance of impending death. Somehow because it's my own situation I'm contemplating, death doesn't seem such an alien thing. More natural, actually, not so fearful if it's expected."

"You mustn't give up!"

"That's not the question," he says. "It's out of my hands. That's terribly freeing, you know. Though I admit I have my moments when I think it would be better for all concerned if I did take matters in my own hands."

She leans into the fence, gripping the metal so tightly it cuts into the flesh of her fingers. "You mustn't think like that."

"Why not? I don't believe suicide is necessarily a great sin, you know. In some circumstances it may be the most faithful act. But don't worry, whenever I think about it, it doesn't seem the right thing for me. And there is Maria to consider. She might blame herself. Things are hard enough for her as it is."

"Tell me about Maria," Suse coaxes. And hopes he does not notice the new edge to her voice. "Do you hear from her?"

He shakes his head. "I've had no letter in weeks, and she hasn't come to visit. It's such a long way from Bundorf to Berlin, especially with the bombings disrupting train service. And she hasn't been well. Her cousin is working her too hard. I know that's what it is. Maybe her cousin isn't even allowing her letters to be posted. And that mother of hers will make her feel guilty if she leaves her position there." He rubs his scalp, which is turning red in the August sun. "But I know she loves me. It's all hard for her because she's so young, but I know she loves me. That keeps me going."

Linke has taken the wheel off the bike frame. While he replaces it and pumps air back into the tire, Suse and Dietrich continue to talk, Dietrich asking after each member of the family, Suse answering and at the same time trying not to let on that she has learned what she came for. Then the prisoners are being called inside from their exercise, and the bicycle has been needlessly repaired. Dietrich says, "Remember, Suse, when we were children, you and Sabine and I. Remember how we would rap on the bedroom walls and think of God. Let's do that tonight." Linke tips his cap and goes back into the exercise yard. Dietrich walks backward as long as he can, eyes on Suse, then turns abruptly and disappears through a doorway.

Even before the war only one train a day served the small valley at Bundorf. Now a small engine and single car called from Bamberg on Tuesdays and Fridays. Bundorf did not possess a station house, and the platform, a wooden rectangle with two benches, was like a stage set for a performance at the edge of a field of rye. Maria sat alone on a bench, waiting, the pony and cart tethered at the foot of the steps. She heard the train before she saw it, and turned away from the sound back toward the distant castle dreaming on its limestone outcrop. It was a phantasm, and she could imagine the gate had been forever sealed behind her. Or would be sealed for want of a magic password she did not possess. Or the entire castle would vanish before her eyes, or she would herself be placed under a spell and fall asleep and never wake again. Or would wake in some gray distant city like Berlin.

The train glided alongside the platform, barely pausing for Suse, the only passenger, to jump from the last step before picking up speed again. Suse had no luggage, carried only a large handbag on a shoulder strap. She wore a dress of faded blue cotton and a wide-brimmed straw hat, which she removed so she could kiss Maria on both cheeks.

"I want to talk to you here," Suse said.

"On—on the platform?" Maria stammered.

"Yes, or we could go for a walk, since the sun is so bright here. But I'm not going to the castle." She opened her bag. "Look, I've brought sandwiches."

"But Cousin Hesi is expecting you for lunch."

"The train will be back through in two hours. That's time enough to say what I have to say, and to eat with you here. I'm staying tonight at the Bellevue in Bamberg and returning to Berlin first thing in the morning. I've taken a room with two beds."

Maria turned away. "Because you expect me to go back with you. Cousin Hesi said that's why you've come."

"Oh, yes, Cousin Hesi knows all right. That's why I've nothing to say to her. Only to you." Suse plopped onto a bench and began to fan herself with her hat. She motioned to Maria, who sat reluctantly beside her. "I'll get right to the point, Maria. There's a very good chance Dietrich won't survive the war. And he knows it. If he won't hear what you're trying to tell him, it's because he can't. He's hanging on by his fingertips."

A bee sailed past Maria's ear. She felt faint. "I think I should go back to the castle," she said. "I've been in the sun too long already." But found she could not move. As if Suse had cast a spell that held her fast.

"Maria," Suse said. And she pulled Maria close so the girl's head rested upon her shoulder. The clean scent of Suse's fresh-scrubbed neck caused Maria to close her eyes. "May I tell you about my sister Christel and her husband? Hans and Dietrich were arrested at the same time. Dietrich doesn't know it, but one reason their trials have been delayed is that Hans wanted it that way. He thought if they could just ride out the war in prison without coming to trial, they might survive. For if they did come to trial, the plot might be discovered, and their part in it."

"The plot?" Maria said.

"The plot to kill the Führer."

"Dietrich knew about that?"

"Has known about that and earlier failed attempts for years. And would be upset to know I told you, because the less you know the safer for you. But to my mind there's no help for it."

Maria, eyes still shut, saw her father, her dear father, resplendent in his

Wehrmacht uniform, going off to fight the Russians. A loyal German, a patriot. She recalled how much he had disliked Hitler, how he had made jokes about him when no one of consequence was around. But to kill the Führer?

Suse seemed to read her mind.

"Maria, the army officers involved in the plot were men like your father. Patriotic Germans who couldn't bear to see what has been done in the name of such patriotism. But Dietrich believes even they waited too late. He could not live with what he has known and could not refuse to act as he has done. Your father was a courageous man, but Dietrich's is a better sort of courage. If you cannot accept that, then of course you must turn away from Dietrich. But think, Maria, of what has been done in the name of Germany and with the help of brave soldiers like your father. Do you know how many Jews we have murdered, Maria? Do you? It must be in the millions by now."

"Even if it is true, how dare you blame it on Papa! He'd never agree to such a terrible thing!"

"I'm blaming all of us, Maria. You and me and your father. Yes, and Dietrich, for he'd say so himself."

"It's all exaggerated, I'm sure, what you're saying about the Jews."

"It isn't. And you know it. You remember the deportations, you've heard the talk, we all have. Only no one wants to think about it, so we pretend it's only a murmur that runs through our sleep, some nightmare—" Suse's voice trailed off.

"They must have done something to—"

"Maria! Think what you're saying!"

Maria took a handkerchief from her pocket, dabbed at her eyes, twisted the thin white cloth in her hands.

Suse said, "When Hans decided to delay his and Dietrich's trials, do you know how he did it? He asked Christel to obtain a culture of diphtheria bacilli from our father's hospital. She did as he asked, and she smuggled the culture into the prison in a batch of sweets. Hans ate this and became very ill. So the trial was postponed until he was well enough to attend it. Unfortunately the delay was all for naught, since the Führer has survived. But do you see, Maria? In such times as these a wife is called on to do strange things for her husband. Is it so odd then that I would ask you to stay in a relationship you might otherwise leave? Can you not hold out a few months more? If Dietrich should by some miracle survive, time enough then to call off your engagement."

When she saw Maria was unable to speak, Suse stood and pulled the girl to her feet. "I think," she said, "there is no need for me to say anything else. Go back to the castle for your things, and as you go, think about what I have said. I shall wait here. When I catch the return train at two o'clock, I pray you will be on it with me."

Maria ran down the steps and climbed into the cart, so blinded by tears she let the pony have its head to get them back to the castle. The gate stood open. Hesi was in the great hall, though so transparent that Maria ran past her and up the stairs to her room. She could not understand what Hesi was saying from the doorway, as if her cousin were speaking underwater, and was insensible to Hesi's leaving her, unaware that her cousin rode on horseback to the train platform, where she angrily confronted an unnaturally calm Suse. When at last Hesi rode back toward the castle, she met Maria on the road, suitcase in hand.

Hesi drew her horse up, blocking the way. Maria stopped, her face white and pinched.

"Your mother will be furious," Hesi said.

"I don't care."

"I won't allow you to go."

"You can't stop me."

"But you've said to me and even to him that you don't love him."

Then the color returned to Maria's cheeks and she said fiercely, "I don't want to sleep with him. I may never want to sleep with him. But I do love him, more than anyone living. He's part of my family and I'm going to be with him."

She plunged into the field beside the road and had outflanked Hesi before she could turn her horse. And as she fled, an invisible gate slammed shut barring Hesi from following, barring Maria from going back.

Sanctus
Dominus Deus Sabaoth!
Pleni sunt caeli et terra
gloria tua
Osanna in excelsis

Holy, holy, holy
Lord God of hosts!
Heaven and earth are full of thy glory
Hosanna in the highest.

(Double chorus with eight parts;
double fugue)

Doppelgänger
September 24, 1944

DIETRICH BONHOEFFER sat in the prison interrogation room, waiting. He heard the Mercedes pull up outside. Car doors slammed. SS Judge Advocate Alois Bauer entered the room with a stamp of boots, a crisp salute, and loud "Heil Hitler!"

Dietrich stood but did not return the salute. He said, "Hello."

And there was a flicker across Bauer's eyes like a flight of bats.

"Well." He set his briefcase on the table with a thump. "I have you now."

Dietrich nodded. "I don't doubt it."

The judge advocate allowed himself a brief smile, sat down and opened the briefcase, rifled through some papers. Without waiting for permission, Dietrich sat in the chair opposite.

Bauer looked up, disconcerted, but quickly regained his composure. "Ah, yes," he said. "Some men are undone by impending doom, and some are emboldened by it. I see you are one of the latter type, Pastor Bonhoeffer. At least for the moment." He held up a folder. "Two days ago we found your brother-in-law's secret cache of documents stashed in a safe at Zossen. There is even a canister of film which purports to show atrocities being committed against Jews in Poland. Did you know where this material was being kept?"

"No," Dietrich admitted. He remembered the last time he had seen the documents, Christel hunched over a typewriter while Hans dictated the X Report. Dohnanyi had removed the papers from the house soon afterward for fear of implicating his family. "But I knew it existed and that you would find it sooner or later."

Bauer took out his monocle and scrunched it into the socket of his right eye. He studied the papers in his hand. "The great dilemma one faces when trying to bring down a regime," he mused. "You want to document everything you condemn, so you can justify yourself once you carry out an overthrow. But alas, there is no way to document without leaving a trail of paper somewhere." He looked up. "Is there?"

"No," Dietrich said.

"And I am sad to say, Pastor Bonhoeffer, that your name appears through-out these papers." He sifted the sheets one by one. "Repeated trips to Switzerland, where you shared sensitive information with church represen-tatives from enemy or occupied nations. Trips also to the Vatican, where again sensitive information harmful to the war effort was passed on. The removal of Jews to Switzerland for purposes shown here to have nothing to do with espionage on behalf of the Reich. Contact in a neutral country between yourself and an English bishop, at which time you passed on to the enemy knowledge of a coup attempt. Detailed prior knowledge of a variety of attempts to assassinate the Führer."

Bauer looked up. The monocle dropped and dangled on the end of its string, flinging a wedge of dancing light across the tabletop.

"You'll hang," he said.

Dietrich had thought himself prepared to face what might come, but found he could not answer. He gripped the edge of his chair to steady him-self.

Bauer reached into his pocket, tossed a cigarette across the table. Die-trich stared at it in surprise. "What do you want?" he asked. "You have me, and you have come here personally to tell me so? There must be more. Is it names you want? I'll not give them to you unless you break me under tor-ture."

Bauer waved his hand and offered a lighted match, which Dietrich leaned forward to accept. The judge advocate settled back in his chair and blew smoke at the ceiling.

"We have plenty of names. Or at least, I doubt you were privy to any more information than those we have already interrogated. By the way, do you know what's happened to the others? Stauffenberg was shot on the very first evening. A quick end as befits a German military hero, even one who places a bomb at the feet of his Führer. Our most distinguished but guilty generals have been allowed to shoot themselves. Easier on the families, for it saves face, and on the nation, which is spared a great blow to its morale. But let me tell you about the civilian traitors. They're the reason I'm back in Berlin, actually. I've been overseeing the interrogations before their executions. A bother, since I've come to enjoy living in Thuringia. But I'll be going back there tomorrow. I've learned as much as Himmler needs to know, and the executions have been carried out. The Führer requested the same treatment the Harnacks received. Hanging with cord, slow cutting strangulation. Only this time he wanted it filmed. My superiors tell me he's watched this movie twice now. It seems to give him ease."

Dietrich twisted in his chair.

"Does that surprise you?" Bauer asked.

"Nothing surprises me. I was only thinking how pleased I am to be counted this man's enemy."

Bauer looked as though he would like to reply, but he turned away suddenly and stubbed out his cigarette. "You'll be happy to know," he said, "that your brother-in-law Hans von Dohnanyi was not among those executed."

And when Dietrich was able to meet Bauer's eyes, he was shocked to see in them what he took for compassion. Or was it only interest?

"And why not?" he asked. "And why not me?"

"Dohnanyi has been very ill, a severe case of diphtheria. He's too weak to withstand interrogation, so we're waiting. As for you? Well. When it comes down to it, Pastor Bonhoeffer, your involvement in these matters was quite enough to earn you a likely death sentence, but not nearly enough, perhaps, to assuage your pride. You may be Hitler's enemy, but not a very important one." Though Bauer was lighting another cigarette, he did not miss Dietrich's wince. "Besides," he added, "my boss Himmler has not yet recommended a final disposition of your case. He thinks you might still be useful."

"I told you I won't divulge—"

"And I have told you names won't be necessary," Bauer interrupted. "There are other uses."

"Such as?"

The judge advocate hesitated, then said, "These foreign contacts of yours. Are any of them connected to American or British intelligence?" He glanced at the folder. "George Bell? Willem Visser't Hooft? This assortment of priests in the Vatican?"

"No," Dietrich said wonderingly. "Not that I'm aware of. Though I wouldn't tell you if it were otherwise."

"Ah. A pity." Bauer moved the glowing tip of his cigarette farther away from his thumb. "Still."

"Why?" Dietrich asked, suddenly afraid he had given something away, though he couldn't imagine what it might be.

Bauer shook his head. "It's nothing to do with you or your situation, so you mustn't expect to get out of this mess you're in. Unless, of course, your God swoops down to the rescue and delivers you from your enemies. Hitler believes God intervened to save him from the assassin's bomb. And the church—your church, Pastor Bonhoeffer—has declared that to be the case. Tell me, do you pray for such deliverance?"

"No," Dietrich said. "That would be not only self-serving, but useless."

"Self-serving?"

"When so many have died, what right have I to ask?"

"And useless? Has prison weakened your faith?"

"No. Though I will say it has altered it. But my faith does not depend upon God's delivering me. In fact, I don't believe that God is in the delivery business."

Bauer's eyes narrowed. "A useless God, eh? Perhaps I agree with you. I used to pray for things that never came to pass. When I was a child, I prayed for my dog to be saved. You may think that frivolous, but the dog meant more to me than anything in the world, more even than my mother and father. Anyway, it didn't work. So I came to realize that God was a fraud."

Dietrich shrugged. "You are, of course, the final arbiter of that question," he said.

Bauer said in an agitated voice, "Of course it's true. Look at the Jews. They are foolish enough to believe God delivered them out of Egypt. Fat lot of good it's done them now!" He sat back in his chair.

"Not a lot of good," Dietrich agreed. "How many has God failed to deliver? How many have we killed so far, Alois?"

Bauer froze. "I have not given you permission to address me by my Christian name."

"How many, Alois? And what do you think the British and Americans will have to say about it when they get here?"

He waited for Bauer to call the guards, to consign him to the torture cell and the rope. Just to shut him up, to punish his insolence. But to his surprise his interrogator did not move. Then Dietrich realized with a shock what he had been seeing in the face of Judge Advocate Alois Bauer. Not compassion or a spectator's sadistic interest, but fear. Pure fear.

For a time they were still together while the room filled with an orange midday sun. Then Bauer gave a small sigh. He said, "Sometimes I feel like a boy who has been kidnapped by pirates."

Dietrich asked softly, "Did you kill Jews in Poland, Alois?"

"Of course. Everyone did. They had to be got out of the way, we were told. They would have strangled the Reich."

"That was before you were made judge advocate? Before you were given the Harnack case?"

"I begged for the Harnack case. I had to get out of Poland. For my own sake."

"Your own sake?"

Bauer seemed to shrink in his chair.

"I was drinking way too much. Everyone was. That's how we handled such work. Day after day, watching them dig the trenches, watching them strip. Ordering the shootings. All those women and children. That was hard. Don't let anyone tell you it's easy. It's not disloyal to admit as much. Everyone said it. That's why they made sure we had plenty of booze. And that's why I had to get out." Bauer ran a hand through his hair, which was suddenly damp with sweat. "My God, if I'd stayed in Poland I'd be a confirmed drunkard by now."

Dietrich fought back the impulse to reach across the table and strike the other man. "The worst possible thing that could happen," he said savagely.

"Yes," said an oblivious Bauer. "My father was a drunkard. I've always been determined not to be like him."

"Better a drunkard than a murderer," Dietrich persisted, determined not to let Bauer off.

"We were doing what we had to do."

"Oh, yes!" Dietrich scoffed.

Yet there was something disarming about Bauer, something irresistible, the way he reeked of evil and still was possessed of such yearning. He was leaning forward, elbows on the table and chin resting on the heel of his hand, asking, "If it was so wrong, why did God let it happen?"

"How was God supposed to stop it? You're a free man, Alois. There are no invisible strings connecting you to God, directing your every move."

"But if God is all-powerful, God could intervene. God could find a way."

"And because God didn't intervene, it was all right."

"Yes."

"Too bad you don't believe in God, then. You've lost your excuse."

Bauer blinked. He looked away. "Perhaps I do believe in God," he said.

"Oh yes," Dietrich said. "God makes a convenient scapegoat. Or people always think God is absent when things are going bad for *them*. Things go better and God is back. Well, I want to live in the world as if there were no God. That is the only way God can truly be with any of us. You, on the other hand, want a God you can blame for everything you've done. Oh yes, you will believe anything you must to exonerate yourself."

"You're not one to talk," Bauer lashed back. "If you're so holy, how many Jews did you save, eh? Not so many that I can see, an old girlfriend and a handful of others. And what about me? My squad used to come upon groups of Jews hiding in the Katyn forest trying to pass for Poles. Usually we lined them up and shot them. Those were our orders. But twice I pretended to believe the Jews. I let them go. People I didn't even know, yet I even gave them safe-conduct passes in case another squad should find them out."

"Why?"

Bauer shrugged. "In those two cases I liked the looks of them. Something about the eyes, and the way they carried themselves. In those two cases." He stood and began to pace. "Let me think how many." And counted silently on his fingers. "At least fifteen in the first group, and the second was a bit larger. Thirty-five or forty perhaps." He stopped and faced

Dietrich. "So you see, Pastor Bonhoeffer, I've saved more Jews than you have. Tell me, whom does God love more? You or me?"

He waited with arms folded.

Dietrich shut his eyes. "No doubt," he said at last, "God pities us both."

"That is no answer."

"No."

"I suppose God is not in the answering business either."

"No. Only now and then in a still small voice."

Bauer threw up his hands. "You're an odd sort of pastor. How could you comfort anyone? With you, there is nothing final, nothing certain." He snapped his briefcase shut and turned to go.

"Wait," Dietrich said. "I have somewhat of an answer for you. I do not know which of us God loves best. But I hope it is you. However, I warn you, the love of God burns like fire. You will not be able to stand in the face of it."

Bauer's face tightened. "I have tolerated your impudence throughout this interrogation," he said, "because it amuses me. Intrigues me even. But let me tell you, Pastor Bonhoeffer, I will not be mocked."

"I am not mocking you, Alois. I am telling you, you cannot escape the love of God. That is a warning."

Bauer stepped closer. "And this also is a warning. Whatever happens to you from now on for good or ill depends upon me. Your fate, your destiny—" he came so close Dietrich could feel Bauer's breath on his cheek— "in my hands."

"Then you must fight God for possession of me," Dietrich said.

The two men stared at each other as though a gauntlet had been thrown down between them. Then Bauer turned and went out without looking back.

White Tunnel

THE TEGEL WEHRMACHT INTERROGATION PRISON stood on its height like a medieval citadel presiding over a warren of stone hovels. The battered redbrick cellblocks were nearly empty, for army discipline had become a luxury. Anyone willing to fight, be he thirteen or threescore, was handed a makeshift weapon; prisoners were sent back to their units; anyone who flouted orders or deserted was either shot or vanished without facing charges.

But somewhere, someone maintained a list of names. Names crossed off as the executions continued. Dietrich Bonhoeffer was on the list. But he remained in Tegel and was not sent to the gallows.

He assumed Bauer was his angel, guardian and avenging. Or perhaps it was Hitler. The Führer was obsessed with those traitors who yet remained alive; harbored dreams of interrogating them personally so that he might dissect their hatred of the Fatherland beneath a microscope. But there was no time just now. The Reich was beset by enemies on all sides.

Dietrich learned something of the outside world from Linke, who had become a regular visitor at the Bonhoeffer home in the Marienburger Allee. The old people were often at Sacrow to escape the bombs and to tend to Christel, who had taken to her bed. Maria was with them as well, having come up from Franconia to take care of them. But since the discovery of the Zossen documents Dietrich's visiting privileges had been revoked and he had not seen her.

Karl and Paula Bonhoeffer insisted on spending Mondays and Fridays in their own house, which had so far escaped the bombardments with minor damage, and that was where Linke often saw them.

"They should stay in Sacrow," Dietrich said. "Not just because of the bombs. The Marienburger Allee is just off the Heerstraße, and that is a major east-west boulevard. Any army which conquers the city will come right through there."

"They go there in part because they hope you may turn up," Linke said once. And Dietrich shook his head. A vain hope.

But he listened not long after the visit of Judge Advocate Bauer when Linke came to his cell late at night and sat cross-legged on the floor like a Red Indian.

"You know I have Knobloch's uniform," Linke said.

Knobloch was dead. His wife had left their shelter during an air raid to call in the family dog. Seconds later a bomb struck the shelter, killing everyone inside, including Knobloch and his five children. The wife now talked to the dog as though he were Knobloch, and had surrendered the uniform without question.

"You know I have Knobloch's uniform," Linke repeated. "You know Maetz is always absent or drunk. You know the guards here are only marking time and praying the British reach Tegel before the Russians do."

Dietrich lay on his cot wrapped in a musty tweed jacket long past the help of cleaning. A cold early-autumn wind whistled between the bars of a window without glass.

"I can get you out of here. Very easy. Put you in Knobloch's uniform. Anyone who recognizes you will say nothing. Everyone who sees will be blind."

Dietrich said, "Bauer will see."

"He's not even in the city."

No matter, Dietrich thought. He imagined the judge advocate in a cave high in the mountains of the Thüringer Wald, hovering over a crystal ball.

"He'll notice too late," Linke said. "I'll take you from here to the Grunewald and dress you in the clothes of a tramp. I'll give you Knobloch's papers, which his widow was kind enough to surrender also. You can go on foot. Everyone is on foot now. Look at all the languages you speak. You can go to France, to Switzerland. Or find the Americans and tell them you lived in New York."

"What of you?" Dietrich asked.

"Nothing will happen. It's all broken down here. Your parents give me food and I use it. Everyone is beholden to me."

Dietrich closed his eyes and saw it all. He said, *"And he was with the wild beasts; and the angels waited on him."*

"What?" Linke said.

"Nothing. Let me think about it."

And he asked himself, Who do you think you are, Jesus Christ?

He sleeps and dreams.

He is in Manhattan. Stares out the window down a street filled with fog.

Wakes and remembers Hans von Dohnanyi. Who, according to the letters Linke smuggles in, has purposely infected himself with diphtheria bacilli sent him by his wife, Christel, so that he might not be forced to reveal any sensitive information. Who as a result suffers from paralysis of his limbs and weakness of the heart and is only semiconscious.

And who will surely be killed if Dietrich Bonhoeffer turns up missing.

Linke comes at night with a raw turnip, the only food available, since the kitchen is no longer in operation. Dietrich eats, the turnip chafing his teeth and gums.

He pauses once to say, "No. I will not escape."

He cannot sleep. The inside of the cell is coated with October frost. He huddles in a corner wrapped in his jacket and a foul-smelling blanket. The black sky outside the window is studded with white stars.

He prays, "Deliver me God."

Realizes what he has said, recalls the conversation with Bauer, and takes it back.

Does not want to pray.

Not the way everyone always prays, he says. *Not a religious prayer.*

He does not pray for God's help.

Instead he says over and over *come bauer come bauer come bauer*

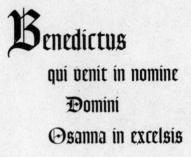

Benedictus
qui venit in nomine
Domini
Osanna in excelsis

Blessed is he who comes in the name
of the Lord
Hosanna in the highest

THE GESTAPO burrow like rats in the cellars of the Prinz-Albrecht-Straße. While others have fled the capital they remain behind to keep what is left of order. They now live entirely underground and their prisoners with them.

Suse and Maria have trouble finding the jail, though the address has been infamous in Berlin for thirteen years. They stand in a field of rubble, turning this way and that. Trying to decide which of the solitary hulks, jagged like rotted teeth, houses Gestapo headquarters. They believe Dietrich is being held there because of what Linke has told them, standing in the middle of the drawing room in the Marienburger Allee and twisting his cap in his hands. He felt terrible, he told the family, because he was not able to persuade Dietrich to escape. And now the Gestapo has come and taken him away to the Prinz-Albrecht-Straße. Dietrich was calm, he tells them, "and said goodbye to me, wished me well, as though nothing was happening. But his eyes were quite unnatural. I had to turn away."

So Suse and Maria stand in the middle of a rubblefield carrying a large hamper between them—which holds a wool sweater and scarf, because it is very cold and it is Christmas, and as much food as the family has been able to spare from its dwindling store. They hope to be allowed to see Dietrich, hope as well for some news of Hans von Dohnanyi, who has not been heard from for over a month.

"There."

Maria points to a solitary building whose upper floors are exposed at one end like a child's dollhouse with walls cut away to allow for the movement of furniture. A shattered scrap of wall backs a twisted stairwell. Just beyond the wall the helmeted head of a soldier is visible. The women go slowly forward, making plenty of noise so that they do not take the man unawares. He turns his head to watch them come, and as they approach he steps from behind the wall with his right hand resting lightly on the strap of the rifle slung across his shoulder.

"Halt," he says.

They stop, teetering on top of a loose pile of bricks.

"You must go back," he calls across the stone field.

"We are looking for the Gestapo prison," Suse calls back, brash as ever. "We believe my brother is being held there and we have brought some things for him."

"If he is here," the guard says, "it makes no difference. Prisoners here receive neither parcels nor visitors. Go back, please."

They hesitate, and the hand tightens on the rifle strap. So they turn and make their way back, slipping now and then on patches of frozen snow. In the brief time they stood there, they noticed the square hole near the guard's feet. The iron stairs disappearing into the earth.

Maria begins to weep, and Suse blinks back tears of her own.

"God help him now," she says.

The cellar interrogation room has a concrete floor with round metal drains set at intervals. At the end of each day a hose is turned on to wash away blood, urine, and excrement. The whitewashed brick walls are hosed down as well, but some dark stains remain. In one corner are the metal tubes with spikes inside which are placed around legs and slowly tightened. Two square tile tubs stand in another corner. For forcing heads beneath icy water.

A double row of cells runs between the interrogation room and the steps which lead down to the steel-reinforced bomb shelter. When the sirens sound the warders go along the rows opening doors with heavy keys that dangle on rings from their belts. The prisoners exit the cells with their hands on top of the heads, a position they must hold as they are hustled along the corridor and down the steps. Only when they are herded into the holding cell in the shelter and the door is shut behind them are they allowed to relax. They sink into weary heaps, close together to keep off the winter cold, and try to sleep.

They go down to the air-raid shelter almost every night, because the planes come almost every night. And the thunder of guns is louder in the East.

Dietrich sits on a cot in the tiny cell. Here he has no books, no writing paper or pen. He meditates with eyes shut. He holds imaginary conversations in his head with George Bell, Elisabeth Hildebrandt, Fred Bishop. He dreams of Maria. He imagines his life as it might have been. If he had stayed in New York. If he had never gone to New York in the first place. If he had stayed in England. If he had gone to Gandhi in India.

He prays. Not for deliverance, but for strength.

A key rattles the lock and two men—one in the uniform of the Gestapo, another in trench coat—enter the cell. They sit on the bench opposite him and study him, hands resting on their knees, like children at a zoo.

He stares back warily.

The Gestapo officer he knows by name—Sonderegger, in charge of interrogations. The other is a stranger. Dietrich does not think he wants to know his name.

But he asks anyway.

The man looks startled, then says, "I am SS Hauptsturmführer Huppenkothen. I have been assisting Judge Advocate Bauer in his investigation."

"And is the judge advocate well?"

"He is," Huppenkothen says. He turns to Sonderegger. "This is the one the judge advocate says not to touch."

Sonderegger nods. "It is. Though I think it a mistake myself." He moves to sit on the cot, lights a cigarette, and holds the glowing tip close to Dietrich's neck. Dietrich stares straight ahead, the muscles of his face taut. The heat of the cigarette is like scalding water. His eyes grow wet.

"See," Sonderegger says. "He'd break quickly."

"Bauer says he's a waste of time," Huppenkothen says in a bored voice.

"Then he's taking up space and eating valuable food," says Sonderegger.

"Is that so?" Huppenkothen leans close, and his coat falls open to reveal a pistol in a shoulder holster. "Then why not just shoot him now and have done with it?"

"Why not?" says Sonderegger, watching Dietrich carefully to gauge his reaction. "Except for the judge advocate's orders."

"Which, I suppose, must be followed." Huppenkothen never takes his eyes from Dietrich's face. "Though we could say he was trying to escape."

"We could," agrees Sonderegger.

Dietrich has difficulty breathing. Neither man moves. They seem to enjoy his discomfort. After a time Huppenkothen says, "Your brother-in-law, Pastor Bonhoeffer. Tell us anything you know of his involvement in this conspiracy. It will help your own case, believe me. The Führer will be grateful. He will remember you when sentences are passed down."

"I know nothing of a conspiracy," Dietrich says. "My own actions have been a personal Christian witness. No one else was involved."

"Not even your brother-in-law Hans von Dohnanyi?"

"Not even Hans."

"I don't believe you," Huppenkothen says.

Dietrich shrugs.

Huppenkothen leans forward and slaps Dietrich, whose eyeglasses fall into his lap, one earpiece bent at an angle.

The men leave.

Huppenkothen returns the next day but does not enter the cell. He stands outside and looks through the barred door. As though simply to remind Dietrich he is still there.

Dietrich says, "Where is your family?"

Huppenkothen looks surprised, seems to calculate whether there is any harm in answering. "They're in Dresden."

"Your home is there?"

"No. We're from Danzig. But with the Russians—" He stopped himself, then said, "My wife has a cousin in Dresden."

"You have children?"

"A boy and two girls. The boy is with the Wehrmacht in Breslau."

He does not have to say how things are in Breslau. The Russians are closing in fast.

"How old is the boy?"

"Eighteen," Huppenkothen says. "But he's an old hand. He's been in the army a year now."

"I shall pray for his safety," Dietrich says. He thinks how Bauer would laugh if he heard this. Expects Huppenkothen to scoff as well, but instead the SS officer seems lost in a reverie. He nods his head and doesn't reply. Then he reaches into his pocket and takes out a cigarette and lights it, then removes it from his mouth and thrusts it through the bars. Dietrich accepts the cigarette and puts it, still moist from Huppenkothen's mouth, to his lips.

"Thank you, Pastor Bonhoeffer," Huppenkothen says.

Despite the close quarters and the strict, often brutal attentions of the guards, the prisoners manage now and then to communicate with one another. And in the underground bunker they sometimes whisper, though it is *verboten* and punishment if caught is a severe beating. One of Dietrich's fellow prisoners is Josef Müller of the Munich Abwehr office, who with Dohnanyi served as the plotters' liaison to the Vatican. From Müller Dietrich learns that Dohnanyi is also being held in the Gestapo cellar.

"Hans? Here?" Dietrich whispers, his mouth next to Müller's ear as they huddle close together in the holding cell. "But I haven't laid eyes on him!"

"That's because he's very ill. He can't walk, so when the bombs come they leave him in his cell to take his chances. Though I notice they do open his cell door. It's the third from the end on the same side as yours."

When the guards return them to their cells, Dietrich slips out of line and into the third cell. In the gray morning light a small figure huddles on the cot, wrapped in a blanket. Were it not for the profile, the familiar sharp nose, Dietrich would not recognize his brother-in-law. Hans is thin, his

skin gray with raw peeling blotches, his scalp bald in odd places. He senses
Dietrich's presence and tries to raise his head.

Dietrich kneels beside the cot, puts his hand on Dohnanyi's arm. "Hans,"
he whispers. "My God, Hans. It's Dietrich."

"Dietrich?" Dohnanyi says in a raspy voice. "You've told them nothing?"

"Nothing."

"Nor I. I know they found the documents. But they'll learn nothing
more. Though they put me in the leg vise. But I've fooled them." A rattling
laugh. "I've no sensation at all in my legs. So I screamed for their benefit
but I didn't feel a thing."

Dietrich lifts the blanket, cannot look for long at the bloodied mess that
is Dohnanyi's right leg. He lowers the blanket quickly.

"I never quite got over the injury I had last year in the air raid," Dohnanyi is saying, "and on top of it, diphtheria."

"I can't stay," Dietrich whispers hurriedly. "They'll miss me." He leans
over Dohnanyi, slips his arm around the other man's bony shoulders. "God
bless, Hans."

"I'll see you by and by," Dohnanyi says.

And Dietrich is out of the cell in time to join the end of the line of prisoners. In the gloom of the cellar as the guards busily work their keys in the
locks like women at their knitting, he is not noticed.

Time means little in the cellars of Prinz-Albrecht-Straße. There is a time
of grayness and a time of darkness. A time of screams from the interrogation room and a time of silence. Time in the cells and time in the bomb
shelter.

It is always cold, except in the guardroom, where there is a small coal
stove.

A bomb would be almost welcome.

When it comes they are down below as they are supposed to be. Even
Dohnanyi, since Dietrich has asked Huppenkothen to allow it. They have
long speculated—in their prisoners' whispers, mouth to ear—how the
Gestapo building could have survived so long when everything around it
has been brought down. Like Hitler himself, who has seemed shielded from
attack by some divine providence.

But on this night—which night it is no one knows—the explosions are
close and the concrete floor vibrates. Then a deafening roar that lasts for
ages and the entire shelter pitches and rocks, as Müller says later, like a ship
in a storm. But holds.

Like the others Dietrich is on his feet, eyes upturned. Waiting for the
ceiling to come down. When it does not, he rolls his head from side to side

to loosen the muscles of his neck. Squares his shoulders. Looks around and says in a normal speaking voice, "Well then. That's the end of it."

AND SO EVEN THE GESTAPO must abandon Berlin. Their headquarters have been destroyed. Dresden has been firebombed. The Russians have overrun Poland and are closing in to the east, the Americans and British have crossed the Rhine in the west. And the prisoners in the Gestapo cellars, their fate still to be decided by a Führer harried on all sides, are called from their cells and placed in handcuffs.

"Is this necessary?" Dietrich protests.

"They are taking us to our deaths," Josef Müller says. "Let us go to God peacefully."

Stung by this reproach, Dietrich falls silent. Outside the cellar he is placed in line to board a truck, and watches anxiously as Dohnanyi is brought out on a stretcher and loaded onto another. In the weak March sun, Dohnanyi already seems white and bloodless as a corpse.

"Where is that truck going?" Dietrich asks the guard who is trying to pull him up into the canvas-covered bed.

"That one's for Sachsenhausen," the man said.

"And this one?"

"You're going south. Buchenwald."

Dietrich pulls his arms away. "I want to be put on the other truck."

"Not possible," the guard says, and hauls Dietrich up like a potato sack.

The place where an abandoned God has come to suffer with abandoned people. That is what he sees at Buchenwald. Only briefly, for they are taken straight from the trucks to the camp prison with its windowless cells. But the canvas flaps that cover the truck bed can easily be lifted so that the prisoners can see something of the camp as they pass by. The fences topped with barbed wire, the guard towers. Not a tree in sight in this place with a sylvan name. Rows of flimsy wooden barracks. Smoke from scattered bonfires and the crematorium stains a blue sky. Piles of naked skeletal bodies, and other skeletons in tattered striped uniforms leaning on shovels or dragging themselves across the blasted earth. Everywhere mud and shit and cinders and rotting flesh. The prisoners cover their faces against the stench as they climb down from the truck.

In the camp prison they find more than Germans present. Prisoners from all across the Reich have been brought to the interior, as far from the front as possible. As though the Nazis think there is something to salvage, Müller scoffs. Dietrich says nothing. He and Müller are sharing a cell. The doors of the cells are arranged at alternating intervals so that prisoners across the way can be heard but not seen. In Buchenwald the guards seem to have given up imposing some of the harsher rules. There is no longer any punishment for talking. So the two men across the way make themselves known by their voices. An Englishman named Payne Best who has been a prisoner since the beginning of the war when he was charged with espionage. And Vassiliev Kokorin, a captured Russian air force officer who might ordinarily have died in a forced labor camp but has been treated more tenderly because he is the nephew of Molotov, the Soviet foreign minister. Kokorin speaks little German but has some English, so Dietrich translates their conversations for Müller.

They are six weeks in Buchenwald. So Payne Best tells them, for he has retained what Dietrich sees as a very English quality of being practical in the midst of disaster and has kept track of the days by marking the wall. They hear bits and pieces of news. The Russians have overrun Pomerania and are closing on Berlin. (Pätzig, Dietrich thinks. Poor Maria. And wonders if Frau von Wedemeyer got out before the arrival of the advancing Soviet troops.) The Americans and British are racing for Berlin as well, their erstwhile Russian allies suddenly become rivals for pieces of German earth. South-central Germany is for the moment a backwater. Then the guards cease to receive any news themselves and nothing more is known about any place save their own.

"Surely we'll get of this," Müller says when they lie on their cots at night. "Surely Hitler has forgotten us. Can even such a man as he think of vengeance when he is himself facing the end?"

Dietrich says nothing.

Dietrich has quickly learned that Payne Best does not know Bishop Bell of Chichester, has never even heard of him, since he has no interest in the church and has not been in his own country since 1939. In fact he finds Best a bit tedious, a stupid sort of man given to petty complaints and little inclined to analyze their situation. Except to make his marks upon the wall. Kokorin, on the other hand, is genial, a young man of about twenty-five, and quite bright. He can talk of Dostoevsky and Tolstoy and Gogol. Can talk theology as well, for though he is a good Communist and therefore an atheist, he has the atheist's fascination with the wrongheadedness of believers.

"Look around," the voice of the still invisible Kokorin is saying in heavily accented English. "How can God allow this to happen?"

And once again, as with Bauer, Dietrich is defending God. Against the same charges, he realizes. Of failure to act. "And what more can God do," he asks, "than to take on flesh and suffer every humiliation and every fear and every pain that humanity suffers? What more without destroying human freedom?"

"Is freedom so important?" Kokorin says. "Ask any man who is hungry or who watches his children starve. Ask any woman who sees her children die or who lives in constant fear. Do they want freedom? No, no, no. Humanity does not care for freedom. Humanity wants to be delivered from suffering."

Müller, who has been listening carefully as Dietrich translates Kokorin's words, says, "The flight from freedom is a consequence of original sin."

"Ah, original sin," says Kokorin. "So we have a good Catholic here, a child of Saint Augustine."

Dietrich translates.

"What do you know of Augustine?" Müller says, surprised.

"I have read him, of course. Do you think I have no education because I am a Communist? But what does Pastor Bonhoeffer say? Give us the Protestant position, Pastor Bonhoeffer."

Payne Best is asleep, snoring lightly. Dietrich, who is weary to death of defending God, says nothing.

They receive a slice of bread for breakfast. A large bowl of soup at midday. More bread and marmalade in the evening. Sometimes butter or lard on the bread.

In the old days—that is how they refer to before prison—in the old days this would have seemed paltry, but now they feel as though they are feasting. The soup is actually edible, it has chunks of potato and carrots and now and then a piece of sausage. Beads of fat float in the broth.

"It's because of the POWs," Müller says. Müller has become quite talkative as time has passed and no harm has come to them. "They're treating the POWs well. The Allies are the new gods, and the Nazis are trying to buy their way into heaven."

Müller is whispering out his cell door to the prisoner on his right. Then he comes to Dietrich, who has been dozing on his cot, and shakes him awake.

"Guess who they brought in this morning," he says. "General Oster."

Oster. Dohnanyi's boss in the Abwehr. So the circle is closed, Dietrich thinks, and they will have everything and everyone they want.

"I wonder," he says as he sits up, "I wonder why my brother-in-law is not here."

In fact, everyone has lost patience with Hans von Dohnanyi. Interrogation has yielded nothing, and besides that the prisoner is often out of his head. Nothing he says can be trusted anyway. There is no one to properly tend a seriously ill man, and his guards at Sachsenhausen complain because he is too weak to walk to the latrine or use a slop bucket.

So a word from Hitler, who still keeps a close eye on the world, yes, even knows when a prisoner is shitting his bed.

A word from Himmler, who still listens to the Führer when it suits him.

A man too weak to walk to the latrine cannot be expected to make his way to a gallows. The guards haul him out on his stretcher. He passes in and out of lucidity, sees the rope being knotted into a noose at one end and slung over a wooden beam at the other, then stands on the deck of his sailboat which skims the blue surface of the Havel.

They hoist him up and the rope burns the raw skin of his neck and then he is thrown from the deck into cold clear water.

APRIL 1, 1945. EASTER SUNDAY. They can hear the guns in the west. The Americans, the guards say. They tell the prisoners to be ready to move. That night the men whisper back and forth along the row of cells. We must be ready to make a break. No, the Americans will be here soon and set us free. No, you heard the guards they are taking us out of here they mean to shoot us in the woods no they'll run with us until they can go no farther and then barter us no they'll surrender anyway.

That afternoon they are led outside at gunpoint and loaded onto a canvas-covered truck. It is a monstrous vehicle with a strange wood-burning engine of a type used more and more in the end days. The prisoners get their first looks at one another. Everyone is shocked at how terrible the others look, but no one says anything. Payne Best proves to be a tall ungainly man. Thin. Kokorin is short, with peaked cheekbones. Also thin. Everyone is thin. They climb into the truck, which travels south at the speed of a bicycle. Bonhoeffer, Müller, Payne Best, Oster, and Kokorin are crammed so tightly in one corner that it finally becomes more comfortable to take turns sitting on one another's lap.

"Why are they moving us?" Best wonders. "Surely they're short on petrol, food, time. Especially time. Why bother with this?"

Oster says, "It must be an order from Berlin. Otherwise we'd have been shot back there. That's what the contingency plans I've seen called for. But who can say what's going on? Who can tell what Hitler is thinking?"

"I believe," says Kokorin, "it will come clear when we arrive at our destination, and not before." He shrugs and smiles with the insouciant air of a Frenchman at a sidewalk café. And the braveness of the gesture moves Dietrich, who reaches inside his coat for a small treasure he has been hoarding ever since Tegel—a grimy handkerchief wrapped around half a dozen cigarettes. He passes them around to cries of appreciation. But of

course others in the truck have turned to look, and so the six cigarettes are
passed from one to another until thirty men have shared.

They travel through the night, sleep sitting up. Before dawn the truck pulls
to the side of the berm at a crossroads. A lone soldier stands watch outside
while the driver naps in the cab. The guard is himself tempted to sleep
where he stands, leaning against the truck's rear bumper. But he is jolted
into wakefulness by the sound of approaching engines. He stands to attention and squints into the gray dawn, one hand on his rifle and the other
clutching a white handkerchief in his pocket, just in case.

But the car which emerges from the fog is a Daimler, and behind it a
truck like the one he is guarding. He stuffs the handkerchief back into his
pocket and salutes the man in SS uniform who climbs from behind the
wheel of the car.

"Heil Hitler!" The guard's boyish voice—for he is only eighteen—rings
off the thick wall of trees beside the road.

"Stand down," the SS officer says quietly. He nods at the truck. "Prisoners? Order them to get out."

The boy does as he is told, and the prisoners rouse themselves, climb
gingerly from the back of the truck, testing their legs. Oster slips on the
bumper, which is wet with dew, and falls to the ground. Dietrich helps him
to his feet, then straightens to find himself face to face with Alois Bauer.
Bauer gives no sign of recognition and looks away.

He says, as though addressing the trees, "I have come with a truck bound
for KZ Flossenburg. The following men will get on board please."

A low murmur has begun. The concentration camp at Flossenburg does
not have a good reputation among the POWs, indeed has been known as a
deathtrap for years, especially among the Russians. Kokorin shudders with
fear. So does Dietrich; he has his own foreboding about what sort of destination Flossenburg will be. It is the most isolated of the camps, high in the
Fichtelgebirge mountains near what was once the Czech border.

Bauer has taken a sheet of paper from his coat pocket. A list, which he
scans for a moment. Then he begins to read names. Looks up now and then
to make sure that each time a name is read, a man leaves the group and
trudges slowly to the waiting truck, whose idling engine gives off puffs of
steam.

"Hans Oster," Bauer says.

Oster walks away with a gray face and disappears into the back of the
truck.

"Josef Müller."

Müller takes a deep breath, turns to shake hands with Best and Kokorin.
He does not shake Dietrich's hand, for he expects to see him momentarily.

It is clear that the German prisoners are being separated from the POWs.

Bauer is studying the list. He hesitates. Looks up. Locks eyes with Dietrich. Then says, "That's all. The rest of you back up on the truck." He waves his arms and points so it is clear to those who do not speak German what he expects them to do.

Dietrich cannot move. Bauer stands beside him.

"Did you hear what I said? Back on that truck or I'll shoot you where you stand."

Dietrich glances at the truck bound for Flossenburg, which is already backing up, preparing to take the left fork in the road.

"Go on," Bauer says.

Kokorin is stretching out a helping hand to pull Dietrich up. And after he scrambles on board, Dietrich is surprised to see that Bauer has returned to his car and is stripping off his SS uniform—hat, coat, pants. He stands for a moment in his underwear, then opens a satchel and removes a pair of corduroy pants, and a blue shirt and tweed jacket. Puts them on. The uniform goes in the satchel, which is stowed in the boot of the car. Then Bauer walks to the truck carrying a small suitcase. He has not bothered to lower the back flap to hide what he has done. When he sees Dietrich watching, he gives a small wave and climbs into the cab. The engine, which the driver has been stoking with wood chips, shudders and starts, and the truck heads south once more.

FOR THE VILLAGERS OF SCHÖNBERG in the Bavarian Forest, the arrival of the truck was first a cause for fear. But as soon as it became known that the truck held Allied prisoners of war, people grew calm. Their corner of the Reich had seen little fighting; at the same time, everyone knew the war was lost. If the POWs had been sent to Schönberg to wait out the last days, then the people were safe. The Allies would not hurt their own. Nor, it was hoped, would they harm those who had been kind to them.

So it was that the prisoners found themselves lodged in the infirmary of a school. A large sunny room with white walls. After a time women from the village arrived with offerings of bread and cheese and potato soup. The infirmary beds had real mattresses with white sheets, and the filthy men were careful to shower before they touched them, though they had to put their dirty clothes back on. At last they stretched out and slept. The last thing Dietrich heard before falling asleep was Kokorin saying, "Heaven."

They sit side by side on a sunny April morning on a large flat rock overlooking a Bavarian meadow sharing slices of apple and cheese.

Bauer is waving his arms expansively. "So you see, I have saved you. Set you apart, called you out from your fellow heroes and given you back to the people. But perhaps you don't consider that salvation?" He looks slyly at Dietrich. "Perhaps you'd rather be a saint, and I've taken the chance away from you."

Dietrich chews slowly. He says, "I once had a friend when I was student in New York. A Frenchman. He told me then he wanted to be a saint. And it's likely, given what I knew of him, that living in France during these last years, he became one. But as for me, I've found that I'm unable to make anything of myself. Not saint, not a good man, or a bad man for that matter. I've failed in most everything I've tried to do."

"A useless man to go with your useless God." Bauer cocks his arm and throws an apple core down the hillside. He takes out a penknife and peels another apple. "On the other hand, look at what the Führer has done! The Führer is mortally wounded and still he casts the length and breadth of Germany for his enemies. The Führer delivers and the Führer destroys. And what of me?"

A coil of apple peel drops to the ground.

"I have brought you here," Bauer continues. "I have prepared a place for you in the presence of thine enemies. Have I not?"

"What then?" Dietrich says. "Am I to bow down and worship you?"

Bauer laughs and hands Dietrich the skinned fruit.

"No thank you," Dietrich says. "I like the toughness of the skin." He picks up another apple and bites into it. He says, "Who are you meeting here, Alois, the Americans or the British?"

Bauer laughs again.

"Because I know what you expect," Dietrich says. "You expect them to find you with me, and you expect me to vouch for you. To tell them how you saved me, an enemy of Hitler. And then I'm to reminisce about the wonderful time I spent in New York. Or will it be London? And we'll all laugh and shake hands and they'll let you go. But it won't happen that way. I'm not going to give you a character reference."

Bauer shakes his head and continues to smile. "That isn't what I expect at all," he says. "And that isn't why I took you off that transport. You're way behind me, good Pastor Bonhoeffer. I've no need for an introduction to the Americans. I've already met them. On several occasions."

At the look on Dietrich's face, Bauer laughs delightedly and so hard that he topples over on his back.

"In fact," he says, and wipes his mouth with the back of his hand as he squints at the sun, "they do know I'm here. This meeting has been arranged in advance. I've been to Switzerland, you see. Met with the chief OSS officer there. Officially known only as 110, though my own sources tell me his name is Dulles. We've friends in common, by the way. The Abwehr's man in Switzerland, Gisevius, is a double agent working for the Americans."

Gisevius. The German consul in Zurich who had considered Dietrich too much of an amateur to be operating in Switzerland. "You know Gisevius?"

"Oh yes," Bauer says. "Have for years. Never quite trusted him, and with good reason, it turns out, but now we appear to be on the same side, so all that's water under the bridge."

"And what have you to offer the Americans?"

"Oh, I've already done quite a bit. Arranged the recent surrender of German troops in Italy, for one thing. The whole thing was planned over lunch with Dulles on the shore of Lake Maggiore. The Americans wanted Italy out of the way, you see, so they can concentrate on taking as much of Germany as they can before the Red Army arrives. A good idea for Germany too, don't you agree? Himmler thinks so." Bauer sits up and scans the valley as though expecting sight of American troops at any moment. "But they've other plans for me as well. Through some personal research of mine, I've become well acquainted with certain caverns in southern Germany where works of art have been stored for safekeeping. The Americans think once the art has been removed, these caverns will make excellent storage places for caches of weapons. In case the Russians overrun central Europe, you see, so that the weapons will be available for anti-Communist partisans. I'm to help the Americans carry out this project. And if all goes well,—" He turns toward Dietrich and beams. "Well, Dulles knows my record. He thinks they can continue to use me."

"You!"

"Why not? The Americans are very concerned about the Communists, and they know the British are too beat up to be of much use now. And who has more experience at ferreting out Communists and other subversives than—" Bauer stands, spreads his arms wide, and takes a mocking bow.

Dietrich feels dizzy. He lies on his back in the sun with his eyes shut and perceives the movement of the earth in its orbit, feels the ground pitch and reel beneath him.

"And what has this to do with me?" he asks at last.

"Nothing," Bauer says. "I just decided to save you. So, you will soon be at home with your family. Oh, but there is a favor I'd like to ask." He sees Dietrich's expression and hastens to add, "Believe me, nothing to which you can object. In fact, it will be a treat for you. Come back to the village with me."

As they stroll back down the hill, Bauer puts his arm around Dietrich's shoulders. "You know," he says, "we have much in common, you and I. Even the failed attempt to betray our country. Do you know, at the very same time you were meeting the British in Sweden, I was in Switzerland trying to do the same thing. Contingent upon the SS overthrowing Hitler, of course. Himmler sent me. He knew even then Germany would lose the war, and thought it would be best if we cut our losses. But he got cold feet. He couldn't bring himself to do away with the Führer, couldn't break the oath of loyalty he'd taken."

"Something you'd have had no trouble with," Dietrich manages to say.

"I wish we'd done it," Bauer says. "See? Just like you, my friend!"

The school they are lodged in has a small auditorium with a polished floor and a baby grand piano. Dietrich has already been playing. The piano is slightly out of tune, and three keys, including middle C, are missing their ivory, but all in all a better sound than the poor battered instrument at Tegel. Dietrich waits on the bench while Bauer goes off to his room and returns with a cardboard folder.

"Here," he says. He locks the door behind him. "So the others won't come in."

"Why shouldn't they?"

"No one must know about this," Bauer says. "I've no way to safeguard it until the Americans give me a place to live."

Slowly he opens the folder to reveal a sheaf of brittle papers, gets down on his knees, and spreads them sheet by sheet across the floor. Dietrich, bending over them, sees page after ancient page of musical notations in a faded spidery hand.

"Have you any idea what it is?" Bauer whispers reverently. He still holds a single sheet in his hand. Now he lays it down alongside the others. Dietrich reads

Große Meße c-moll KV 427
W. A. Mozart

"My God," he says. "Is this the original?"

Bauer nods, unable to speak. It is the first time he has shared his treasure.

"Where on earth did you get it?" Dietrich says. "You shouldn't have this."

Bauer looks up with the pained expression of a hurt child. "Why shouldn't I? No one loves it as I do."

"But it belongs—" Dietrich casts about for the sort of argument Bauer might understand. "It belongs to the people."

"Well," says Bauer, "I am the people." He turns back to the manuscript, takes up the next page. "I heard you play at Tegel. You're very good. I want you to play this for me."

He hands the page to Dietrich, who sees it is the Kyrie.

"Have you played it before?" Bauer asks.

Dietrich nods yes, he has. "Long ago," he adds. "But that was a piano arrangement. This is the original, written for an orchestra. See here, the different lines for different instruments. In order to play this I'd have to improvise as I go, pick out the melody but add my own accompaniment."

Bauer waves his hand. "It doesn't matter, I don't expect some polished performance. But I don't read music, you see. I want to hear the melody, at least, from the master's hand directly to an instrument. As Mozart himself might have played it, as undiluted as possible."

He gathers up all the pages which encompass the Kyrie and hands them to Dietrich, who starts to refuse, but something in Bauer's face, something of a lost soul, causes him to change his mind. "Only if the others can hear it as well," he says. "I'll need time to practice anyway if I'm to make heads or tails of this."

"I told you, no one must know I have it."

"They needn't be told the manuscript is original," Dietrich says. "They'd never dream that."

Bauer considers. He likes the idea of others listening with pleasure while only he, Alois, possesses the sacred knowledge of the true nature of the object before them. Alois and his priest, Pastor Bonhoeffer.

"All right," he says. "Can any of them sing?"

Dietrich has admired the voice of Kokorin, who has been teaching them Russian folk songs. "The Russian," he says.

Bauer nods his agreement.

They decide to wait until evening. It is Saturday night, April 7. Dietrich sits on the piano bench and arranges the manuscript while Bauer lights candles for him to play by. Kokorin stands at Dietrich's shoulder. He has noticed the age of the manuscript, noticed what sort of arrangement it is, and the cramped style of the handwriting. But when he has raised his eyebrows Dietrich has said, "Don't ask."

The prisoners sit on folding chairs. Some villagers have come as well, crowding into the auditorium as they have always done for school recitals, a row of old men standing along the back wall and shifting uneasily from one foot to the other. Bauer goes to take a seat in the front row. He sits with his legs crossed and his hands clasped tightly and resting upon his knee.

Dietrich sets his hands to the keyboard. For a moment he is a boy again at the Berlin Conservatory, hears the scraps of voices—*no lust no passion*—then he begins to play. There is no choir, only Kokorin, no orchestra, only Dietrich. Because of the difficulty of following the manuscript he keeps the accompaniment simple. Kokorin sings in a pure tenor *kyrie eleison christe eleison kyrie eleison*

Behind them Bauer weeps openly. He has been half afraid that something will be wrong, that the scratches on the old parchment will not be the Mass at all but something else, something hideous. But it is true, the music and words are true and familiar and the most beautiful in all the world.

Dietrich hears Bauer sob, and his own eyes fill. Kokorin squeezes Dietrich's shoulder and reaches over to turn a page.

The next morning, Sunday, a delegation of prisoners approaches Dietrich at breakfast and says, "Pastor Bonhoeffer, we'd like you to hold a service for us this morning."

He is filled with sudden joy, and a longing to lead them in prayer, to preach to them and sing with them and share with them the bread and wine. Then he hesitates. "Kokorin," he says. "Kokorin is an atheist and I would not wish to offend him."

Kokorin, hearing this, says at once, "No no no, you must by all means have this service. And I should like to share in it if I may."

Dietrich smiles and nods. Then he remembers Bauer, who eats by himself in a room off the entrance hall. "Gruber," he says, using the name that Bauer has given himself in front of the POWs.

"Ask him."

And why should he mind asking permission of Bauer when he did not with Kokorin? He swallows his distaste and asks anyway, standing in the door of what was once the headmistress's office. Bauer considers as though he has been told a mildly amusing joke.

"By all means," he agrees. "As long as you don't expect me to attend."

"Of course not."

"Fine. Then hold your service, as thanks for the wonderful gift of last night."

"Thank you."

Bauer sits hunched over his plate. He waves his hand. "You would hold the service anyway, would you not? I have no power here anymore. Not, at least, until the Americans arrive."

"It is common courtesy that causes me to ask," Dietrich says.

"Ah." Bauer wipes his mouth on his shirtsleeve. "Tell me, Pastor Bonhoeffer. I have been thinking long and hard about the Sanctus and Benedictus of our Mass, which have been missing for quite some time. Since the mid-nineteenth century, to be exact. Where do you think they might have got to? And how do we know that the Sanctus and Benedictus we hear today are as Mozart intended?"

Dietrich says, "The Sanctus and Benedictus of that particular work are magnificent. If they are not what Mozart intended, they suffice."

"Yes," Bauer says, somewhat mollified. "They suffice. But I cannot help but wish I had them safe and sound in my folder."

They are Protestant and Catholic and atheist, but none of that matters after what they have been through. Dietrich is painfully aware that no Jews are present. He reads from an English Bible, a present from Bishop Bell, a gift he has carried with him throughout his ordeal, standing near the grand piano in the auditorium while the men huddle in the patches of white sun that spatter the wood floor. *Who hath believed our report? And to whom is the arm of the Lord revealed? He is despised and rejected of men; a man of sorrows, and acquainted with grief, and we hid as it were our faces from him; he was despised and we esteemed him not. Surely he hath borne our griefs, and carried our sorrows; yet we did esteem him stricken, smitten of God, and afflicted. But he was wounded for our transgressions, he was bruised for our iniquities; the chastisement of our peace was upon him; and with his stripes we are healed. All we like sheep have gone astray: we have turned every one to his own way, and the Lord hath laid on him the iniquity of us all.*

Dietrich begins to speak in a quiet voice. "Everyone here will attest to the blessing of the last few days," he says. "Yet as we have witnessed a renewal of hope and joy we must never forget those who have died."

The window is open and green curtains move on the spring breeze. A distant thickness of air resolves itself into the whine of an engine. Dietrich continues to speak.

"We have all of us seen the horrors of this war, the depravity of the regime which has ruled this country and wrecked this continent. In these last few days as people of many countries come together under the most brutal circumstances, we have—"

He has lost his train of thought. He stares as the window. A small truck pulls up outside the door. The others turn to look. Kokorin guesses first. "No no," he says. He stands and goes toward Dietrich as if to shield him. Dietrich waves him away.

"Go back to your quarters," he says.

There is a banging on the front door, then it is thrown open. Boots sound in the hall and then Sonderegger enters the room. His eyes light on Dietrich.

"Bonhoeffer," he says. "We've been looking for you. You will come with me."

Dietrich looks around wildly, trying to think of one last thing to say, to do. He sees Payne Best standing near the window. "For God's sake," Dietrich calls, "when you get to England, look up the Bishop of Chichester and tell him what has happened. Tell him." Sonderegger takes Dietrich's arm, and Dietrich shakes him off. "Tell him, 'For me it is the beginning.' Can you remember that?"

"'For me it is the beginning,'" Best repeats.

Dietrich looks around the room once more and goes out. He does not see Bauer when he leaves, for the former judge advocate is hiding in a closet.

ON THE ROAD they pass a caravan of Jews being driven on foot from Auschwitz and Treblinka to the Reich. Dietrich watches through a crack between the slats of the truck's wooden sides as the scarecrow men, women, and children make their painful way, driven by armed guards like draft horses ready to die in the traces. The passing truck forces them from the road, and they do not look at it but stand with heads bowed taking what rest they can as they wait to be forced on.

"The absent ones," Dietrich says.

And thinks he is better off on the road with them.

On the road the truck stops at Weiden to take on fuel and then begins a painful twelve-mile climb into the mountains to KZ Flossenburg. They pass through a series of villages, then a wild rough terrain. The engine wheezes and protests. With each lurch Dietrich feels the muscles of his throat tighten. When it seems they can go no farther without climbing off the face of the earth, the truck passes between two granite pillars and drops down a narrow dirt road into a ravine. Trees abruptly disappear and a moonscape opens up of mud and hovels like Buchenwald only smaller and tucked in a bowl between two hills.

The truck draws to a halt outside a concrete cellblock. Sonderegger helps Dietrich out of the back. "Bonhoeffer, Bonhoeffer," he says, shaking his head. "You've caused us quite a bit of trouble. Do you think we don't keep lists? Did you think the Führer would not find you?"

Oster is present, and Josef Müller, and the former head of the Abwehr, Admiral Canaris, along with several others of the conspirators who are not familiar to Dietrich. They stand before a judge, Otto Thorbeck, who has been brought from Nuremberg especially for their trial. Charges are read, guilt is pronounced, sentence passed, all within moments. All are to die except for Josef Müller, who has inexplicably been given life in prison. Canaris, who is old and frail, moans, then falls silent. The prisoners are returned to their cells.

Dietrich lies on his cot and remembers people. His mother and father. Suse and Christel and Karl-Friedrich. George and Hettie Bell. Elisabeth Hildebrandt. Maria von Wedemeyer. Sabine. Sabine, his twin, whom he has not seen in so many years. He tries to conjure her, but when he reaches out for her, she is not there. So Sabine, he says, I must fly on alone.

He cannot bear to keep his thoughts in his head. Cannot bear silence. He speaks softly to the wall. *Of all those I have most loved,* he says, *only Fred Bishop has gone on ahead. So I shall look forward to seeing Fred. I shall tell Fred everything that has happened here. If Fred has faced this so can I.*

He lies still and tries to recall Fred's voice. He can't hear it. But sometime between black night and gray dawn he is riding in the back of a truck upon a bed of corpses and Fred is tracing a cross on Dietrich's forehead with a dusty fingertip. *Go on in,* Fred says. *Go on in.*

At dawn they are taken outside.

The bowl of Flossenburg is filled with cold white fog.

They are ordered to strip.

Dietrich unbuttons his shirt and removes it, drops his trousers and steps out of them, thinks, This is one of the last things I shall feel on this earth, the tickle of cloth against cold flesh, and so it must be treasured.

The chill causes him to suck in his stomach. His genitals shrivel and draw up in search of warmth. He wraps his arms around his chest and bows his head until someone comes and ties his hands behind his back.

Tries to pray but can only whisper O God O God.

He is the last to go. Does not watch the others, tries to block out the sound. They are being hung from a metal spike that protrudes from the concrete wall. Are hauled up from the ground for lack of a scaffold.

On his turn he walks forward without stumbling. It is already difficult to breathe. The rope is thicker than he had imagined, and so coarse it cuts his flesh as Sonderegger slides the knot down. Dietrich squints along the length of the cellblock that falls away into white fog but the upward tug forces his eyes shut white and red streaks his head is bursting *eternity eternity eternity eternity eternity*

Postscript

THE BODIES of Dietrich Bonhoeffer and those executed with him were stacked near the cellblock and burned. Josef Müller sat alone in his cell as flakes of gray ash floated through his open window.

At war's end, Maria von Wedemeyer went to Buchenwald in search of Dietrich but could learn nothing of his fate. None of his family knew what had become of him until Payne Best was able to make his way to England and inform Bishop Bell. On July 27, 1945, two and a half months later, a memorial service was held at Holy Trinity Church, Brompton, London. The service was broadcast by the BBC.

In Berlin, Karl and Paula Bonhoeffer turned on their radio in the middle of an Anglican hymn, "For All the Saints." They listened with half an ear, Karl, whose health was failing, beginning to doze, when they heard Dietrich's name. Then the voice of Bishop Bell—a voice which would have been at once recognized by their son—*He was quite clear in his convictions, and for all that he was so young and unassuming, he saw the truth and spoke it out with absolute freedom and without fear. When he came to me all unexpectedly in 1942 at Stockholm as the emissary of the resistance to Hitler, he was, as always, absolutely open and quite untroubled about his own person, his safety. His death is a death for Germany, indeed, for all Europe . . .*

They listened without speaking, Paula Bonhoeffer weeping silently. When the last hymn was done and a staid British voice announced a program of light classical music to follow, Dr. Karl Bonhoeffer switched off the radio.

Afterword

IN A WORK OF FICTION whose characters are based on people who actually lived, the reader will naturally wonder, "What really happened?" The novelist comes to the task of writing with the full understanding that a collection of facts does not make an engaging story, and that fact and truth are not necessarily synonymous. Furthermore, the question "What really happened?" is impossible to answer, despite the claims to objectivity of some journalists and historians. This novel is a work of the imagination, first and foremost, and yet I hope it is also true. Some "facts" have been altered because of the demands of the story.

However, Dietrich Bonhoeffer was a real person and his character is based on extensive research, always, of course, filtered through the mind of the novelist. Likewise Dietrich's parents and his fiancée Maria von Wedemeyer and her family, and such figures as Reinhold Niebuhr, Myles Horton, Jean Lasserre, Martin Niemöller, Frank Buchman, T. S. Eliot, the von Harnacks, the Scholls, Bishop George Bell, and even Earl Harvey.

Other characters are either fictional versions of actual people in Bonhoeffer's life, composites, or outright inventions. These include Alois Bauer, Fred Bishop, Elisabeth Hildebrandt, and Dietrich's many siblings and in-laws, who have been reduced to a few for the sake of manageability (an important instance being the merging of Dietrich's courageous brother Klaus and brother-in-law Rüdiger Schleicher with his brother-in-law Hans von Dohnanyi. Klaus Bonhoeffer and Rüdiger Schleicher were also killed by the Nazis for their resistance activities and their memories should be honored.)

I have also taken the liberty here and there of combining several historical personages into one, and rearranging dates to streamline the story and keep reader confusion at a minimum. For example, the first official bookburning in Unter den Linden occurred on May 10, 1933, and not immediately upon Hitler's accession. T. S. Eliot began writing *Murder in the Cathedral* a few months later than he does here. The World Council of Churches was before and during World War II known as the World

Alliance of Churches, but I have used the more familiar name throughout. Another military officer, not Oster, tried to recruit General Brauchitsch to overthrow Hitler. And I have combined details of Bonhoeffer's journey to meet Bishop Bell in Sweden with a visit to Norway a few weeks earlier in the company of another resister, Helmut von Moltke.

Perhaps the greatest departure from "fact" has been to leave Bonhoeffer's great friend and biographer Eberhard Bethge out of this work. This is especially notable because many of the central missives in Bonhoeffer's classic *Letters and Papers from Prison* were addressed to Bethge. I was privileged to meet Bethge personally a few years ago, and perhaps this encounter with the flesh-and-blood man made it more difficult to recreate him as a fictional character. In addition, Bethge entered Bonhoeffer's life fairly late in the narrative, and I found it awkward to simply insert him into the story, as it were, at that point. I can only hope that the friendships of the fictional Bonhoeffer with Fred Bishop, Elisabeth Hildebrandt, and George Bell have captured some of the special nature of this relationship.

For those wishing a "factual" account of the life of Dietrich Bonhoeffer, several excellent biographies are available, as well as Bonhoeffer's own writings. And of course there are numerous histories of the Third Reich and the German resistance to draw upon as well.

I am especially grateful for the work of Robert Jay Lifton, *The Nazi Doctors*; Claudia Koonz, *Mothers in the Fatherland*; Lynn Nicholas, *The Rape of Europa*; William L. Shirer, *The Rise and Fall of the Third Reich, Berlin Diaries*, and *The Nightmare Years*; Eberhard Bethge, *Dietrich Bonhoeffer*; Edwin Robertson, *The Shame and the Sacrifice*; Renate Wind, *Dietrich Bonhoeffer*; Geffrey B. Kelly and F. Burton Nelson, *A Testament to Freedom*; Anton Gill, *An Honorable Defeat: A History of German Resistance to Hitler, 1933–1945*; Richard Hanser, *A Noble Treason*; Inge Scholl, *The White Rose*; Annette E. Dumbach and Jud Newborn, *Shattering the German Night*; and Martin Cherniack, *The Hawk's Nest Incident: America's Worst Industrial Disaster*.

This work was made possible with the financial support of West Virginia State College, the West Virginia Graduate College, Appalshop, the Kentucky Arts Council, and the National Endowment for the Arts.

For help with my research I would like to thank the archivists at the *Charleston* (W.V.) *Gazette*, the reference librarians at the Kanawha County (W.V.) Public Library, Steve Fesenmeier and the West Virginia Film Commission, and Taylor Books in Charleston, W.V. For advice and encouragement I would also like to thank the Rev. Arthur Holmes, the Rev. Bill Kirkland, the Rev. Karl Ruttan, the Rev. Claire Lofgren, Dr. Hazo Carter, Dr. Barbara Oden, Susan Harpold, Gordon Simmons, Topper and Katja

Sherwood, Martin Japtok, Ann Saville, David Wohl, Sky Kershner, Bernice Hosey, Gigi Janeshek, Lavinia Carney, Ann Bird, Sue Harpold, Roy and Rosie Pfeiffer, Colleen Anderson, Arla Ralston, Tim Alderman, Arline Thorn, Ancella Bickley, and Kate Long. For a wonderful travel companion and translator in Germany, thanks to Kristin Layng Szakos. Also thanks to David Roberts and the Bonhoeffer House in Berlin; my Mississippi friends and theologians Chuck Lewis, Dave Bell, and Francis King; Barbara Towers and the Rev. Stephen Masters in Chichester, England; Leon Howell of the regrettably defunct *Christianity and Crisis;* Larry Rasmussen and the Union Theological Seminary; and the International Bonhoeffer Society. For inspiration, special gratitude goes to Frank Pisano, Rob Bennett, Pete Swartz, and the rest of the cast and crew of *Murder in the Cathedral* performed at St. John's Episcopal Church, Charleston, W.V., in June 1995.

And to the Rev. Jim Lewis, who introduced me to *Letters and Papers from Prison.*

Finally, thanks to Gerald Howard, Jane Gelfman, and Mary Cunnane for unwavering patience, advice, and friendship.

Saints and Villains

DENISE GIARDINA

A Reader's Guide

A Conversation with Denise Giardina

Q: **How did you come to choose Dietrich Bonhoeffer as the subject of this novel?**

DG: I think my subjects choose me. I tend to write about things that obsess me since they are with me for so long in the writing process. I first read Bonhoeffer's classic text *Letters and Papers from Prison* in the mid-70s and he has been with me ever since. I have always been intrigued by World War II and the rise of the Nazis and I have long wanted to write on these topics. For a long time, I thought I would write about the students resisters of the White Rose League with Bonhoeffer as a minor character. But, in part, since I had gotten older by the time I came to write this, I found myself less interested in the college students. I began by researching the White Rose League, but Bonhoeffer's voice and the images from his story took over.

Q: **How did you go about researching his life and times?**

DG: I read everything I could get my hands on by and about Bonhoeffer. There are a few biographies about Bonhoeffer though we could still use a good, popular biography on him. There is a lot of material both in and out of print and I tracked down everything I could find. I also immersed myself in the time period in general, reading biographies and histories on topics such as the Weimar Republic and the rise of the Nazis; books on the period like those of William Shirer were enormously helpful. I also listened to the music of the period to try and soak up a sense of life as it was lived then. I found myself listening to Nazi drinking songs on the tape deck in my car. I also listened to the music as I wrote, especially German classical music. I attended conferences devoted to Bonhoeffer, including one held at the Union Theological Seminary, and Bonhoeffer's good friend and biographer Eberhardt Bedke was there. Bedke has written the most important biography on Bonhoeffer. I was able to ask him some questions and speak to people who knew Bonhoeffer and who have studied him. Also, visiting Union Theological Seminary helped me to imagine Bonhoeffer's experiences there. I traveled to England and Germany and visited the houses Bonhoeffer lived in. The Bonhoeffer family's two residences in Germany are still standing. One is a private residence so I could not go inside, but the other has been turned into a Bonhoeffer museum. I was able to stand at the window in his room where he watched as the Gestapo came for him which was very evocative. I just immersed myself in this history for a year and a half before I ever began writing.

Q: **What aspects of the research and writing of this novel presented the greatest challenges?**

DG: While there is a great deal of material on his professional and political life, including his own writings, there was very little personal information available to me. His family was very private, there was very much an upper-class German reticence about them which meant they did not publicly discuss their private lives or feelings—a very "stiff upper lip" kind of attitude. I knew a few details of his personal life, but these things were not widely talked about.

For example, I knew he had a girlfriend and while they might not have been officially engaged, they had an "understanding" though they eventually broke off their relationship. It seems that she later married another theologian who knew Bonhoeffer and, for whatever reasons, perhaps to maintain her privacy, she decided not to publicly reveal her relationship with Bonhoeffer. While his family, friends, and colleagues knew her identity, they did not reveal it either. I did not find out her name until I was halfway through my book. I was at a Bonhoeffer conference and many of the participants were discussing the fact that her name had finally been released to the general public. I discovered her first name was Elisabeth, the same name I had already chosen for the fictional character of his girlfriend, Elisabeth Hildebrandt.

Q: **All of your work is very rooted in historical events and characters. What draws you to work within the genre of historical fiction?**

DG: I have always been drawn to history and particular time periods. For this book and my first book, *Good King Harry*, a historical novel about Henry V of England, I chose to fictionalize the lives of real historical characters while in *Storming Heaven* and

The Unquiet Earth, I chose to create fictional characters based on actual historical events. As a child, I often fantasized about traveling in a time machine. As an adult, I continue to be fascinated with imagining life in other eras and immersing myself in the past.

Q: **How do you balance the demands of crafting a good story with the demands of the historical record?**

DG: What is most difficult for me is approaching the work like any piece of fiction and giving myself permission to make changes and to use my imagination. For me, the story comes first, but there are lines you cannot cross. Violating the spirit and truth (if I can use this word) of the subject matter is a line I will not cross. To write a novel in which the Nazis were portrayed as good guys who didn't kill Jews and many others would be vile. However, if it is a question of rearranging the chronology to make events more comprehensible, while remaining true to the spirit and significance of these events, I think this is totally reasonable. One exercise I do with my students is have them think about how they might have to compress or rearrange things in order to tell someone a compelling story about a particular event in their own lives. The shape of real life is very rarely the shape of a good story that speaks to people and draws them in.

While we don't know for sure if T. S. Eliot and Bonhoeffer actually met, we do know that Bishop Bell was Eliot's patron and Bonhoeffer's friend. We also know that Eliot was with Bell at the Swedish conference that Bonhoeffer attended. I think it is very legitimate to ask the "what if" question. What if Bonhoeffer and Eliot met? What kind of influence might they have had on each other? How might meeting someone like Bonhoeffer have influenced Eliot's writing of *Murder in the Cathedral* which is the story of a famous religious martyr? Fiction gives us a chance to raise these important "what if" questions and explore the complexity of the human condition.

Q: **What are some of the advantages and disadvantages in building a novel around a real person?**

DG: I had to go through a whole lot of soul-searching to decide what I could change and what I would have to leave out. Writing a historical novel about a real person requires a different kind of discipline than with other forms of fiction because I am bound, to some extent, by the historical record. I know he was born on this day, went to school here, got married on this day, and died on that day. The historical reality takes away some of the writer's creative freedom and restricts the imagination on some levels. With fictional characters, the characters can dictate to me what happens and I can choose when they are born, if they marry, and if they die, but those were not choices with Bonhoeffer. On the other hand, having the facts of a person's life provides a ready-made narrative framework and allows me to focus my energy elsewhere—addressing the larger questions and creating complex, human characters.

Q: Given the tremendous scope of this novel, how did you decide what to use and what to leave out?

DG: It was very difficult. This was one reason it took me six years to write this book. There was so much information. I would compare the process to that of a sculptor faced with a big block of stone that must be chipped away at to leave behind a sculpture. I could not have written this novel first. I needed experience as a writer before I could take on this subject and be able to "follow my nose" as a storyteller through the immense amount of material. Early on, I was working on some scenes of Bonhoeffer working with the youth group in Berlin, but the scenes felt forced and weren't working. Though this was an important part of his life, it was a path I decided not to follow in as much detail as I originally intended. He also spent a year in Barcelona prior to going to New York City, but I decided to focus instead on his time spent in New York City. Every step of the way, I had to make decisions like this. Of course, some aspects of the story were always there and offered very strong visual and literary imagery.

Q: How does the writing process work for you?

DG: I don't start writing until I feel comfortable with my characters and have fully immersed myself in their lives. I just jot down scenes and sentences as they come to me, recording odds and ends. I spend a great deal of time getting know my characters and savoring their stories. I enjoy this "marinating" process which can last one or two or even three years. While I admire writers who are very prolific and can write a book a year, that is not for me.

When I sit down to write the first draft, I try to tell the story and let it flow without getting bogged down by details. For example, if I use a word I am unsure of, I simply underline it and come back to it later. I write a section one day and then go back the next day and rewrite and try to keep pushing forward this way. When I finish the first draft, I go back and do another rewrite and then send it off for input and so forth.

The process has changed for me over the years as I have become computerized. For my first book, I wrote everything in longhand and then typed up the final draft. For my next two books, I began to work on a computer and these books were a mixture of working in longhand and on the computer. This book marked the first time I worked exclusively on the computer from beginning to end.

Q: How do your own experiences impact upon your work in terms of subject matter and themes?

DG: Like anyone, I write about the things I am interested in: how people make ethical decisions, how people determine right from wrong, and what people draw sustenance from. I know in my own life I have developed a growing sense of how complex human existence is. There is a tendency in our society to make clear distinctions between right and wrong which are not always so easy to make. The overly simplistic way in which we often raise children and impart values does not always allow for the complexity of the human condition and the difficult decisions we must all confront in our lives.

I use my own experiences to add detail; my perspective as a writer from West Virginia is part of the mix of research and character development that goes into all my stories. My work is shaped by who I am and where I come from. For me, as I think is true for many writers, all of my characters contain bits and pieces of me, expressing many of the different aspects of my personality. I also draw on people I've known. I am, in fact, drawn to people who I think would make good, complex characters and I try to analyze them and use them in my work. I am very interested in history and theology and political activism, and these interests are reflected in my work.

Q: What themes do you find yourself returning to again and again?

DG: Sin and redemption, moral choices, the nature of good and evil. I try to explore the human side of evil and the flawed aspects of good and see moral complexity.

Q: In the afterword, you mention that some of the characters are your inventions and composites to varying degrees, including Alois Bauer, Fred Bishop, and Elisabeth Hildebrandt. How and why did you create them?

DG: It varies from character to character. I created composites because of the enormous number of people in Bonhoeffer's life—to retain all of them would have made the narrative unwieldy and difficult for the reader to follow. Also, combining a number of individuals helped to create richer, more complex characters in the novel. The character of Alois Bauer was a composite of several Nazis who interrogated Bonhoeffer. Especially near the end of the novel, when Bonhoeffer is imprisoned as things began to break down in Nazi Germany, a whole series of Nazis interrogated him, but that offered no continuity for the reader. To use a series of interrogators would have meant creating a large number of characters the reader could not really get to know in any depth. The character of Bauer offers an opportunity to explore the human side of evil, to try to understand why he did what he did. As I was researching this novel, I learned of the disappearance of Mozart's Mass in C Minor from the Prussian State Library during World War II and I began to wonder who stole it. What kind of person would have done this? From here the character of Bauer began to develop.

As for Elisabeth, she was also a composite character drawn from many sources. Bonhoeffer's sister Suse had a Jewish friend who was involved in a youth group with the Bonhoeffers though she fled Germany before Hitler came to power. Bonhoeffer also had a friend named Franz Hildebrandt, a fellow minister of Jewish heritage, who helped him confront Nazi policies and decide where he stood on these issues—a role that the character of Elisabeth plays in my novel. Also, I knew from my research that one female member of the group of Jews that Bonhoeffer and his fellow resisters rescued included a personal friend of Bonhoeffer's.

Fred Bishop was based on Frank Fisher, a friend Bonhoeffer made at Union Theological Seminary. Fisher was from Georgia and returned South after his time at Union, so I used this person to create a character who would bring Bonhoeffer to West Virginia.

Q: **Was it difficult to make the heroic and martyred Bonhoeffer a multi-dimensional, flawed, and complex human being?**

DG: No, because I don't believe in such things as paragons of virtue or evil monsters. I never saw him as a paragon of virtue; I am predisposed to see complexity. I saw the flaws and was more interested in the complexities and layers that made him a real human being. As you begin to read about and get to know someone, you find the strange, quirky stuff that makes them distinct and interesting as individuals. Whether your subject is St. Francis of Assisi or Martin Luther or Dietrich Bonhoeffer, you don't have to dig too deep to find the flaws, those are the things that interest readers and make people tick. Reading about a man such as Bonhoeffer being depressed and having trouble sleeping are details that make him human and interest me as a reader and writer.

Q: **Is the Gauley Mountain industrial disaster which claimed the lives of Fred Bishop and countless workers based on a real incident?**

DG: Yes. It is based on the Hawks Nest industrial disaster, an incident that was well-known in the 1930s. The reason we have worker safety laws and federal regulatory agencies such as OSHA grew out of the scandal surrounding Hawks Nest. It helped to illustrate why we need to regulate industry and led to major reforms and laws to protect workers that are still in place.

Q: **Why was Bonhoeffer's confrontation with racism in the United States so important to his intellectual and political development?**

DG: Bonhoeffer first came to the United States before Hitler came to power and his letters home reveal how appalled he was at racism in the United States. In his letters, he commented on lynching and segregation and discussed how blacks were not welcome in white churches. He reflected on his own experience of being kicked out of a New York City restaurant because his black friend was not welcome. He also traveled in the South. He did not know what was coming in Germany when he wrote those letters. Then he returned home and Hitler came to power. The first anti-Jewish laws passed were basically segregation laws—no intermarriage and so forth. In fact, the Nazis modeled their initial policies after the treatment of blacks in the United States. Bonhoeffer recognized that the Germans were treating Jews as Americans treated blacks in the United States—he saw the connections. Of course, the end result would be very different in Germany as the Nazis opted for total annihilation, but the beginnings were very similar. Bonhoeffer's experiences in the United States made him very conscious of the dangers in Nazi Germany from the outset.

Q: **How are Bonhoeffer and other members of the German resistance remembered in Germany today?**

DG: Certainly, they are held up as examples that not all Germans did nothing. There is a street named after him in Berlin and, as I mentioned earlier, his family's home has been turned into a museum dedicated to his memory and his work. Yet, it was only a few years ago, in 1994 or so, that Bonhoeffer was officially cleared of the charges of treason. Despite the rather hurried nature of his sentencing and death, the charges remained legal and binding until just a few years ago. What is interesting is that he is treated mainly as a political opponent of Hitler, not as a religious opponent. When a plaque was erected in his name in Germany, the local bishop did not attend because in the church's opinion he was a political rather than a religious martyr. I think he is both.

Q: Did his family actually find out about his death over the radio as you describe?

DG: Yes. Communications were so bad at the end of the war that while family members tried for several months to find out what happened to him, including going to the concentration camp in which he was held, they couldn't find out anything. They just happened to be listening to the BBC one evening and that is how they learned of his death.

Q: What do you imagine was Alois Bauer's ultimate fate?

DG: I imagine that the O.S.S. (which would later become the C.I.A.) took him up on his offer of assistance and employed him as part of the Cold War apparatus. As an employee of the C.I.A., he would have been able to live out the rest of the life in relative peace and quiet.

Q: What is next for you? What will your next project be?

DG: After taking a bit of a break from writing, I have been doing some reading and researching and writing on a new project. I have written a chapter of a new novel which will be a fantasy. While it will have a historical aspect since time travel will be involved, I want to cut loose from the strictures of history and write something that is more humorous and playful this time around.

Reading Group Questions
and Topics for Discussion

1. This story raises important questions about personal responsibility in the face of inhumane behavior. What led Dietrich Bonhoeffer, a painfully shy and introspective man, to join the German resistance?

2. Why does Bonhoeffer refuse to conduct the funeral service for his sister's father-in-law? Discuss the impact this choice has on his life.

3. This story illustrates how some people found the courage to challenge a corrupt and brutal regime. What did you know of the German resistance prior to reading this book? What factors do you think led some people to resist in the face of almost insurmountable odds?

4. Bonhoeffer made great sacrifices yet he was always battling his fears and demons. As one reviewer has said: "Giardina makes [Bonhoeffer] the reportedly stiff, bespectacled intellectual . . . into a hero to whom any reader can relate." What does the face of courage look like in this book? How do you define courage and heroism?

5. "He who believes does not flee." Bonhoeffer has opportunities to escape Nazi Germany yet he chooses to remain and fight. Why do you think is this so? In his place, what would you have done?

6. As a religious leader, Bonhoeffer struggled to reconcile his faith with his eventual decision to join what was, in part, a conspiracy to murder. Did he rest easy with this decision? Under what circumstances, if any, is murder is justifiable?

7. Discuss the impact of Bonhoeffer's experiences in the United States on his later understanding of the plight of Jews in Nazi Germany. How is Bonhoeffer changed by his time abroad? How do his experiences in Harlem and on Gauley Mountain affect his actions upon his return to Nazi Germany?

8. This story recounts the Allied rejection of overtures by the German resistance. Why do you think the German resistance

failed to get foreign assistance? What if the German resistance had received aid in time? Do you think the outcome might have been different?

9. Why do Elisabeth Hildebrandt and Bonhoeffer separate? What forces drive them apart?

10. Why do you think Alois Bauer ultimately tries to save Bonhoeffer? What might account for the very different paths these two men have chosen?

11. There are no simple villains in this story. How do you understand the very patriotic German couple that sent their son off to fight for Hitler, yet also befriended Elisabeth in her time of need?

12. As this story illustrates, the rise to power of Hitler and Nazi Germany was facilitated by compromise and accommodation in the international community. Why do you think this was so? Why did a dissenting voice such as Bonhoeffer's get lost or shouted down?

13. Many people would wonder what kind of God would allow something like the Holocaust to happen and would lose their religious faith in the wake of the Holocaust. How does Bonhoeffer address these issues and maintain his faith? How does the nature of his faith change over the course of his lifetime?

14. The tremendous scope of death and destruction in the Holocaust can be difficult to comprehend. How did this man's story help you to process such acts of unimaginable evil?

15. Bonhoeffer once said, "We must live as if God does not exist." What was this minister and theologian trying to tell us with this statement?

16. In this story, Mozart's Mass in C Minor (the original manuscript of which was lost during the war) plays a pivotal role. Recently there has been much news coverage of renewed attempts to retrieve art and money lost during World War II. How do we assess blame in such situations? Who should be held accountable for such losses?

17. Which characters, besides Bonhoeffer, did you find to be the most compelling and why?

18. Why did your group choose to read this particular work? How does this novel compare with other works your group has read?

KATHLEEN FEELEY, author of this reading group guide, is a doctoral candidate in U.S. history at the City University Graduate Center and assistant editor of *Reviews in American History*. In her spare time, she is also a founding member of her Park Slope, Brooklyn, reading group.

Excerpts from reviews of Denise Giardina's
Saints and Villains

"Giardina . . . surpasses herself with this powerful re-creation of the life and martyrdom of German pastor and theologian Dietrich Bonhoeffer . . . A big novel in every sense of the word, and a triumphant portrayal of one of the century's authentic heroes."

—*Kirkus Reviews*

"The story—compelling in and of itself—is engrossingly narrated, with an eye for significant detail, a strong sense of life's bitter ironies, and a powerful feeling of immediacy. The characters, especially Bonhoeffer himself, are lifelike and complex. Giardina also does a fine job of evoking the temper of the times she portrays."

—*Newsday*

"Giardina's strength lies in her ability to show how historical particulars craft individuality."

—*Washington Post Book World*

"In a series of telling scenes brought to life with unerring choice of detail . . . Giardina exerts an admirable grip on her panoramic story."

—*Publishers Weekly*

"Giardina creates a fictional account of Bonhoeffer that transcends the usual 'historical novel' as it becomes a dramatic meditation on the meaning of his life. Giardina breathes new life into Bonhoeffer. He is no longer the pristine icon of his worshipful admirers. Giardina makes him again a credible, though exceptional, person."

—*Herald-Leader* (Lexington, KY)

"Bonhoeffer becomes a nervous, sympathetic everyman who, when faced with inhumanity rises to greatness. Giardina makes the reportedly stiff, bespectacled intellectual . . . into a hero to whom any reader can relate."

—*The Boston Globe*

"[A] novel whose message of moral internationalism deserves to be read throughout the world . . . the images of Dietrich Bonhoeffer evoked in the pages of *Saints and Villains* are so vivid that the word that comes to mind is resurrection."

—*Oregonian* (Portland, OR)

"Denise Giardina displays a thorough knowledge of the historical and theological record."

—*New York Times Book Review*

"The story is an important one. The Bonhoeffer drawn by Giardina is a complex character."

—*Republic* (Phoenix, AZ)

"Giardina . . . succeeds in fleshing out Bonhoeffer's factual biographies with fine and detailed human touches—the more 'believable' because they are based on diligent research."

—*Philadelphia Inquirer*

"*Saints and Villains* depicts a mental and physical adventure of one man. It is a treatise on man's inhumanity to man and one person's courage in rising above such horrors to find his own faith strengthened in the process."

—*The Chattanooga Times*

© James L. Mairs

ABOUT THE AUTHOR

Denise Giardina is the author of *Good King Harry*, *Storming Heaven*, and *The Unquiet Earth*. *The Unquiet Earth* won Berea College's Weatherford Award for outstanding writing about Appalachia as well as the American Book Award and the Lillian Smith Award for the year's best Southern fiction. She was born in Bluefield, West Virginia, and grew up in a coal camp. A graduate of West Virginia Wesleyan College and Virginia Theological Seminary, Giardina teaches English and literature at West Virginia State College in Charleston, West Virginia. She is a licensed lay preacher in the Episcopal Church.